William Ward

A View of the History, Literature, and Religion of The Hindoos

Including a minute description of their manners and customs, and translations from their principal works

SALZWASSER VERLAG

William Ward

A View of the History, Literature, and Religion of The Hindoos

Including a minute description of their manners and customs, and translations from their principal works

Reprint of the original, first published in 1863.

1st Edition 2022 | ISBN: 978-3-37500-773-7

Verlag (Publisher): Salzwasser Verlag GmbH, Zeilweg 44, 60439 Frankfurt, Deutschland
Vertretungsberechtigt (Authorized to represent): E. Roepke, Zeilweg 44, 60439 Frankfurt, Deutschland
Druck (Print): Books on Demand GmbH, In de Tarpen 42, 22848 Norderstedt, Deutschland

A

VIEW

OF THE

HISTORY, LITERATURE, AND RELIGION

OF

THE HINDOOS:

INCLUDING

A MINUTE DESCRIPTION OF

THEIR MANNERS AND CUSTOMS,

AND

TRANSLATIONS FROM THEIR PRINCIPAL WORKS.

BY THE REV. W. WARD,

ONE OF THE BAPTIST MISSIONARIES AT SERAMPORE, BENGAL.

THE FIFTH EDITION,

CAREFULLY ABRIDGED AND GREATLY IMPROVED;

WITH A BIOGRAPHICAL SKETCH OF THE AUTHOR, AND AN AMPLE INDEX

1863.

GŬNÉSHŬ.

COMMONLY KNOWN IN MADRAS AS

PULIAR OR BELLY-GOD.

for description vide page 35

PRONUNCIATION OF HINDOO NAMES.

In endeavouring to give the sounds of Sŭngskritŭ words, the author has adopted a method, which he hopes unites correctness with simplicity, and avoids much of that confusion which has been so much complained of on this subject. If the reader will only retain in his memory, that the short ŭ is to be sounded as the short o in son, or the u in Burton; the French é, as a in plate; and the ēē as in sweet; he may go through the whole work with a pronunciation so correct, that a Hindoo would understand him. At the beginning and end of a word, the inherent vowel (ŭ) has the soft sound of au.

CONTENTS.

INTRODUCTORY REMARKS.

* In this Introduction, the author has gone over the whole of the Hindoo Pantheon, that he might supply a number of omissions in the body of the work; and hence it forms an epitome of the whole.

BOOK I.

OBJECTS OF WORSHIP.

CHAP. I.

OF GOD.

CHAP. II.

OF THE GODS.

CHAP. III.

OF THE GODDESSES.

CHAP. IV.

INFERIOR CELESTIAL BEINGS OBJECTS OF WORSHIP.

CHAP. V.

OF THE TERRESTRIAL GODS.

* This goddess is honoured as she who protects from serpents: but the author is assured, that, in the upper provinces, the serpent itself is worshipped, and that the image is formed into a circle, the head and tail of the serpent being joined. The legend respecting this serpent-god is, that the earth rests on his thousand heads.

CHAP. VI.

TERRESTRIAL GODDESSES.

CHAP. VII.

DEITIES WORSHIPPED BY THE LOWER ORDERS ONLY.

CHAP. VIII.

WORSHIP OF BEINGS IN STRANGE SHAPES.

CHAP. IX.

WORSHIP OF HUMAN BEINGS.

SECT. PAGE.

CHAP. X.

WORSHIP OF BEASTS.

CHAP XI.

THE WORSHIP OF BIRDS.

CHAP. XII.

THE WORSHIP OF TREES.

CHAP. XIII.

THE WORSHIP OF RIVERS.

CHAP. XIV.

CHAP. XV.

PAGE.

CHAP. XVI.

THE WORSHIP OF STONES.

CHAP. XVII.

A LOG OF WOOD WORSHIPPED.

BOOK II.

OF THE TEMPLES, IMAGES, PRIESTS, AND TEMPLE WORSHIP OF THE HINDOOS.

CHAP. I.

OF THE TEMPLES.

CHAP. II.

OF THE IMAGES.

CHAP. III.

OF THE PRIESTS.

CHAP. IV.

OF THE WORSHIP IN THE TEMPLES.

* One of these stones, by a fall, being split asunder, was lately shewn to the author. The internal appearance of this strongly indicates, that these stones are not, as has been supposed, (see Asiatic Researches, vol vii. p. 240.) perforated stones, but petrified shells: the shell in the inside of this was the Argonauta Argo.—May 8, 1815.

BOOK III.

OF THE STATED PERIODS OF WORSHIP, AND VARIOUS DUTIES AND CEREMONIES.

CHAP. I.

OF THE TIMES OF WORSHIP.

CHAP. II.

APPOINTED RITES AND CEREMONIES.

* These are not penances for sin: the yogee is not a penitent, but a proud ascetic.

PAGE.

BOOK IV.

DOCTRINES OF THE HINDOO RELIGION.

CHAP. I.

OF THE TRANSMIGRATION OF SOULS.

CHAP. II.

CHAP. III.

OF FUTURE HAPPINESS.

CHAP. IV.

OF FUTURE PUNISHMENTS.

BOOK V.

HINDOO SAINTS, OR MENDICANTS.

BOOK VI.

HINDOO RELIGIOUS SECTS.

CHAP. I.

ACCOUNT OF THE REGULAR HINDOO SECTS.

PAGE.

CHAP. II.

ACCOUNT OF THE BOUDDHUS.

CHAP. III.

ACCOUNT OF THE JOINUS.

CHAP. IV.

ACCOUNT OF THE SHIKHS.

CHAP V.

ACCOUNT OF THE FOLLOWERS OF CHOITUNYU.

CHAP. VI.

CONCLUDING REMARKS.

BIOGRAPHICAL INTRODUCTION.

THERE is a propriety, I think, in prefacing the following work by some account of the author; for upon our knowledge of his career and capabilities depends the amount of credibility and confidence which we award to his book. After a careful perusal of the Lives we have of him,* I have been led to conclude that we do not yet know all we ought to know of the Reverend William Ward of Serampore:—a man who, though not endowed with genius, was possessed of great capacity for mental toil and physical endurance, just such a man as the world wants and romance avoids:—a Missionary, expert and diligent in many varieties of toil;—a Christian, whose piety retained its freshness during a long and arduous career, breathed itself out in the last efforts of his pen†, and shed a quiet beauty over his end. Scant justice can be done to him in a sketch so brief as this; yet as far as space will admit, I will place before the reader the chief events of his life.

William Ward was born of middle-class parents, in Derby, on the 20th of October 1769. Soon after his birth, his mother, a good and pious woman, was left a widow. Up to her prayers, conversation and example, Ward traced his religious history. The first human hand that went to form his career and character was a mother's: so should it ever be. His school life was not spent under favourable auspices, and gave him an education plain and common enough. But the lad was studious, retired, self-forming, with high aims, which now and then peeped out and startled his more common place companions. So came it, that he saw after his own education when his masters had done with him, and by such ways and means as a determined young man will always find out, he acquired a knowledge of the literature and science of his country. He became a printer by trade, and

* Memoirs of the Life of the Rev. William Ward, by Samuel Stennett. London, 1825.

Life and Times of Carey, Marshman and Ward by John Clark Marshman. In two volumes. Longmans, London, 1859.

† "Reflections for every day in the year" Published in 1822. The work was highly prized by his Christian friends and brought into daily use in many families.

spent some ten years, first in putting up type for newspapers, and then in writing for them, in Derby, Stafford, and Hull; and he acquired more than ordinary influence as an Editor. But the power which fixed his future course lay not in these external circumstances, but in that inner life of piety, to the beginnings of which I have already adverted. In his case, the influence of maternal example and youthful associations did not supersede the exercise of individual decision. After much thought, it appeared to him that the opinions held by the Baptists were most in accordance with the word of God and, by public baptism, he became a member of that denomination, in 1794 or 1795, being about twenty-five years of age. Prior to that event, he passed through many troubles of heart,—"storms," "miry clay," "fierce volcano fires not to be quenched by a mere sprinkling of words"—such are his own phrases: but that rite spoke truly of a heart then resting quietly and lovingly in discipleship to Jesus. Prompted by his own earnest feelings, and drawn by the necessities of his neighbourhood, Ward occasionally presided at religious assemblies and gave "a word of exhortation" at cottage meetings: not without notice, for in 1797 he was selected as a man of promise for the future, and sent to Ewood Hall, near Halifax, where Dr. Fawcett, the tutor of Foster, trained a few young men for the ministry. There study, not wide, yet careful and regular, became a habit, bearing fruit afterwards in the translation work of the Serampore press and the uniform diligence of Serampore life. Yet then and there the missionary spirit of the man found a sphere for itself. He was often out preaching in the villages, amongst a rough people; men and women such as the Brontés describe, and among whom they also lived, listened to him and loved him. He had a cottage church all his own; rough handed, good hearted, long headed, plain spoken laborers crowding in to hear their lecturer as, "elevated on a three-legged stool with his little Bible in his hand, he preached with fervor and affection the unsearchable riches of Christ." There seemed every probability of his settling down to the pulpit and pastoral work of the home ministry, when a circumstance occurred which reversed every calculation, and led to his becoming one of India's pioneer missionaries, for which, after all, God had been fitting him by this twofold training of printing and preaching. So at least thought a member of the Baptist Missionary Committee, who went down casually to Halifax and saw Ward, and spoke to him of Brother Carey working alone on the banks of the Hoogly. Ward was now thirty years of age, a time of life when men generally allow their emotions to freeze a little, and act on something stronger than impulse. Add to this, that he had had fifteen years of practical life, forming him to prosaic steady work, and that at that time there was a future before him more hopeful than generally falls to the lot of ministerial novitiates. We need not then wonder at the absence of sentimentality in his decision to become a missionary. We feel the man will do his work well, when a sense of duty sends him to it. Speaking on the occasion of his ordination, of what is technically termed a "call," he said, "I have received no new revelation on the subject: I did not expect any. Our Redeemer has said 'Go ye into all the world and preach the Gospel unto every creature and lo, I am with you always even unto the end of the world.' This command I consider is still binding. In His strength, therefore I will go forth, borne up by your prayers, hoping that two or three stones at least may be laid of Christ's Kingdom in India, nothing doubting but that the fabric will rise from age to age, till time shall be no more." Thus much for his public confession; as to his heart preparation, we have the following sentence in a letter to a friend. "Every day's experience convinces me that 'tis safety, 'tis life, 'tis heaven to rest in the bosom of our God and no where else, but there. I am afraid lest my heart should deceive me, but I feel at present a resignation to the divine will, which I never felt before. With such views the voyage to India, seems but like crossing the Humber. A few more respirations, and the lungs shall cease to play, the pulse to beat, the tongue to move, and then

> 'What boots it where the high reward is given,
> Or whence the soul triumphant wings to heaven.'"

He embarked on the 24th of May 1799 with three companions, one of whom was Dr. Marshman.

There are few circumstances of note in the next nineteen years of Ward's life. Not that he lost his individuality; no, he gave it up to the steady carrying out of a system unique in the love, self denial and energy of the men who devised and worked it. His history henceforth, is one with that of the Serampore Mission. Calcutta was closed against him and his companions; so they moved up to that Danish Settlement, which their labors brought into celebrity; there Dr. Carey and his comrades joined them. Death speedily thinned their ranks, and Carey, Marshman and Ward, a memorable trio, were left to work alone.

It is evident from his letters, that Ward, from the beginning, cultivated a habit of constant observation, and enhanced its value by the admirable practice of taking accurate notes. In this lay the foundation of the Work, now re-printed more than fifty years after its materials were first gathered. Mission life was then for the most part what it is now; a daily diligence in unobtrusive labors; its motives, methods and effects being scarcely known to the outside public, save when some event more distinctive than usual attracts notice and awakens criticism. The language came but gradually, but work came at once. Ward did that which lay nearest to him, he preached and taught in English, and superintended the Mission Press; and God blessed him in these first labors.

When he could speak Bengali (and he spoke it fluently and well), bazaar preaching and touring formed his only relaxation from the toils of the printing office. Soon after his arrival, the first convert was baptized; in 1800, two thousand copies of the Bengali New Testament issued from the press,—2,000 Missionaries, he called them—and in 1803, the first native Minister preached his first sermon. New successes followed extending labors, and fresh crises of progress were gained almost yearly. In 1809 amidst all the opposition of Government, the missionaries "had succeeded in settling four stations in Bengal; they had sent a Missionary to Patna, and planted stations on the borders of Orissa and Bootan, and in Burmah; the number of members in church fellowship exceeded two hundred; they had obtained a footing in Calcutta, where a chapel had been erected at a cost of more than £3000, and a large church and congregation collected; the Scriptures had been printed in whole or in part, in six languages, and translations had been commenced in six others."* His prayer was fulfilled ere half his course was run; he saw laid the foundation stones of Christ's kingdom in Hindustan. One circumstance alone threatened Ward's peculiar work. In 1812 the printing offices were burnt down, and a loss of £10,000 was inflicted on the Mission. The public evinced their confidence in the Missionaries by ready and ample liberality, and before the close of the following year, he writes "ten presses are going, and nearly two hundred people are employed about the printing office." He knew the value of the press, and the spirit in which he wrought, would have dignified the meanest toil. When about to commence his career, he wrote thus in his diary, "but to me, who am less than the least of all Saints, is this grace given that I should" *print* "among the heathen, the unsearchable riches of Christ." Now again he writes; "what multitudes of Christian works will be wanted! We have not been able to print one argumentative work against idolatry; not one elaborate defence of Christianity. We have let off nothing but squibs. The Hindu Pundits have not yet felt in their learned languages the weight of Christian artillery; except in one or two parts of the Bible. We have not yet had the honor of an attack from one Hindu scholar. These times are all to come; they are coming. The struggle will be a tough one." What he anticipated, we realize, and it will be well with us, if we can use his weapon, the press, wisely and effectively.

Though this notice chiefly concerns the public career of Ward, it would scarcely be just to close this period without a reference to his domestic life, and that of the Missionaries with whom he was associated. He married the widow of his deceased colleague, Mr. Fountain, and the ceremony so far characterized the man and his fellows, as to warrant the extract in which it is narrated.

* Carey, Marshman and Ward. i. 421.

"1802 May 10th. This evening sister Fountain and I were married at our house in the presence of our Bengali friends and others. This connection was intended for sometime, but circumstances prevented. Brother Carey introduced the business by a few words and read the marriage agreement. I then took sister Fountain by the hand and walked up to the table, saying 'we sign this our solemn covenant to each other.' We then signed it, and about a dozen friends, European and Bengali added their signatures. Brother Carey then delivered a very appropriate address to the parties on the duties of husband and wife, and made a pleasing allusion to our family situation, in which all personal interests are swallowed up in the interest of the whole. A short prayer concluded the service. I gave some fruit and a few things of native manufacture amongst the native friends, and thus the marriage was celebrated."*

Let us now take a glance at "the situation" of Ward and his companions. These men who by their labors brought in £50,000 in eighteen years to defray the expenses of the Mission, practised the sternest economy in their household and personal expenditure. They all dined together at four long tables, Missionaries, wives, children and scholars, and this arrangement continued until the enlargement of the mission circle by the arrival of new missionaries rendered it no longer desirable or practicable.†

Including a child of his wife's, by her first husband, Ward had five children, two of whom died young; the remainder he trained, with anxious solicitude for their best interests. In 1815 Mrs. Ward was compelled to visit England for her health, and returned to find her husband so broken down in constitution as to be under medical orders for home. Leaving his family behind, he embarked in 1818, after nineteen years of almost unrelieved toil; yet he carried Serampore with him, and marked out for himself Serampore work to be done in England. His scheme was to obtain the help and sympathy of British Christians for the establishment of a Training College for native agents. His visit was paid at a time unseasonable for the accomplishment of his object, but seasonable enough for the general welfare of the Mission. He found the public mind disturbed by many calumnies as to the Serampore brethren and their work. He took joyfully upon himself the responsibility of their defence, and in a great measure succeeded in restoring confidence, and in placing the Mission in a less exceptional position than it had hitherto occupied. He travelled all over England, and visited Holland and America; pleading first for the Society with which he was connected, and then for the College, realizing for the latter, about £3,000.

* Life of Ward. 111.

† Carey, Marshman and Ward. i. 152.

"During the voyage from America, Mr. Ward employed his time in writing "Farewell Letters" to his friends in England and America. He was subsequently induced to publish them, and the work speedily went through three Editions. They are valuable as the effusion of those fervent and affectionate feelings which endeared him to all with whom he was associated. They also breathe the genuine spirit of Christian benevolence, expanded by the magnitude of the sphere in which he had laboured. In successive letters he presents a vivid picture of the superstitions of the natives, the impurity and cruelty to which they gave birth, and the moral and religious degradation they entailed."*

He embarked for India in 1821; as the event proved, he returned but to die. After his arrival at Serampore the Training School occupied his time along with the press. He was at work when his Master called him. "On Wednesday the 5th of March (1823) he preached the evening lecture, apparently in excellent health and spirits. The next morning he joined his brethren at their weekly breakfast, though suffering from what he considered a simple diarrhœa which he attributed to a cold caught during the night. After breakfast he proceeded as usual to his labours, and began a letter to the Rotterdam Bible Society. At noon he was obliged to leave the letter unfinished, and retired to his room which he never left. At three in the afternoon he was seized with cramps; and it then became evident that the disease from which he was suffering was cholera of a virulent type. Two medical gentlemen were immediately called in, and under their treatment the dangerous symptoms appeared to abate. His friends never left his couch the whole of that night. He was placed in a warm bath, and fell into a sound sleep, which gave hopes of his recovery, and induced Dr. Carey to go down to his collegiate duties at Calcutta. But at eleven in the forenoon of Friday his pulse began to sink, and at five in the afternoon he was a corpse. The scene of distress was heart rending. The three old men had lived and laboured together for twenty three years as if one soul animated them, and it was difficult to realize the fact that one of them was gone. Dr. Marshman had been afflicted for some days with deafness which the present distress served to aggravate, and for a time he was altogether deprived of the power of hearing. He paced the room in silent dismay, watching with intense anguish the gradual dissolution of his beloved colleague; yet unable to receive any communication. Thus at the age of fifty-three died the first of the men at Serampore."† Ward was no genius; no *dilettante* missionary, but a conscientious worker, who amidst his labour kept alive a spiritual mind, and graced it with an amiable disposition, and herein he is a model of what the Mission field requires in all its laborers, in all spheres and at all times.

* Carey, Marshman and Ward. ii. 245.

† Carey, Marshman and Ward. ii. 278.

A word or two is now required about that work which keeps alive the name of Ward, and a new edition of which is here presented to the reader. The idea of such a composition appears to have suggested itself to the author soon after his arrival in India, and he forthwith began to collect materials for it. It was first printed at Calcutta in 1806, in two volumes quarto,* and was well received. In 1815 a second edition was published in one volume, and in the list of subscribers were found the names of more than two hundred and fifty individuals of high position in the service of the East India Company. It was re-printed in England soon after its appearance in Calcutta, and whilst the Author was sojourning there in 1820, he carried a new edition through the press, the preface to which is dated at sea, June 1st 1821. We have here then the result of a process of observation, research, and correction, which extended over twenty years of the Author's life.

The present re-print is from the edition published in London in 1817, by order "of the Committee of the Baptist Missionary Society," said in the title page "to be carefully abridged and greatly improved." The edition of 1821 was on the other hand, "arranged according to the order of the original work printed at Serampore." There being no preface to the edition of 1817, we are left to surmise by whom and upon what principle the abridgment was effected. As the dedication however bears date at "Serampore, June 1815," I am inclined to think that the Author himself revised the work, and it is not difficult by a comparison of the two editions to discover the principle upon which he acted. He appears to have regarded those parts of the first edition which referred to the historical traditions and literature of India as foreign to the purpose of the new issue, and these he left to the antiquarian and the scholar. There was wanted *for general use* a book that should, in a popular way, treat of the belief, institutions, and practices of the Hindus, and this he found to his hand in the remaining portions of the original work. This we have in the edition of 1817. Subsequent circumstances have proved that such a selection has preserved to us the truly valuable parts of Ward's work. Oriental scholars, too numerous to name, have superseded the productions of Ward's pen upon subjects so abstruse as the history and philosophy of India, so wide as its ancient literature. But no one has followed him, much less surpassed him in his own sphere, in the subjects brought before us in this volume. At first sight, one might regret the absence of one chapter of the first edition; I mean that which treats of some features of social life in India, not directly religious. But more detailed accounts of these matters are found in the work of Abbé Dubois and to *us*, the Abbé's narrations have this additional value, that they specifically refer to the Hindus of South India.

* Life of Ward, it is said in 1806:—Carey, Marshman and Ward, 1810.

On the whole, the publisher appears to have done wisely and well for the public, in selecting for publication the edition of 1817, rather than the bulky volumes of 1821. From the latter however he has taken the glossary, in which the several terms used in the work are explained.

"In the introduction, the author has gone over the whole of the Hindu Pantheon, that he might supply a number of omissions in the body of the work and hence it forms an epitome of the whole." Coming to the work itself, after a few sentences upon the views of philosophers as to the Deity he introduces us (Book 1.). to the whole assemblage of Hindu Deities. No name of note in that long muster roll is omitted from these descriptions. Gods and goddesses, powers celestial and powers terrestrial, avatárs and symbols, devils and monsters, birds and beasts, trees and stones, have each assigned to them their modicum of divinity, their quantum of reverence. The machinery of worship is next described; the shrine, the idol and the priest. (Book ii.). We attend the Hindu in his lunar fasts and annual ceremonies; we follow him to his ablutions and stand by his sacrificial fire; we listen to the mystic ejaculations of his prayers and the intoned music of his hymns; we share his weary pilgrimages, watch the kindling of his funereal fires, and are spectators of the repeated and sacred hospitalities that give repose to his soul. (Book iii.). Betaking ourselves to the "lotus feet" of the Guru, we learn the laws that guide the wanderings of the soul in future births, the nature of perfect bliss, and the modes of future retribution. (Book iv.). We are introduced to the Brotherhood of Holy Mendicants and made familiar with the tricks and trappings of religious beggary. (Book v.). Lastly we become acquainted with the orthodox sections of the Hindu community; and then with heretics and schismatics, Buddhists, Jainas, Sikhs and Bháktas (Book vi.).

The Author gathered the materials for his work by personal observation, by information derived from others, and by translations from standard native works. For the acquisition of information on reliable authority, few men have ever had so favorable an opportunity; for the extensive translations carried on by the Serampore press gathered round the Missionaries a large body of Pundits from all parts of India, whilst their philological acquirements and official position associated them, not only with learned natives unconnected with themselves, but with a circle of Oriental scholars, amongst whom may be mentioned the names of Colebrooke and Leyden. Ward taxed all the stores thus placed within his reach for the production of this work. He is generally however careful to cite his authority, so that the reader may be fairly warned as to the degree of confidence to be placed in the several statements. It is no slight voucher both for the facts and opinions of the book, that it should have received the sanction of eminent scholars, and that it should have gone through so many editions during the very period (1803-1821) when Hindu matters were discussed with the greatest interest, when the bitterest hostility was manifested towards the Missionaries both as to their evangelistic and literary enterprises. I may be permitted to quote one illustration of the style of criticism with which the book was received. It is taken from an article in the Asiatic Journal for 1817,* written it should be observed, when the work had reached its third edition and after a good deal of adverse criticism had been exercised upon it. "As a *general survey* of whatever is connected with Hindustan, we mean the most essential concern of morals and religion, the singular book which we are now about to review will be found the most luminous and comprehensive of any ever published in this country, speaking to facts and to facts only, upon the evidence of the senses:—the scrutinising eye and the attentive ear whose accuracy could not be deceived. The distinguishing, the sterling merit of this publication is that direct translations from the original Sanscrit accompany all the assertions, however apparently incredible, made in the course of it. To the versions already published by Mr. Colebrooke, Mr. Patterson and other members of the Asiatic Society, are added those made by the Missionaries, assisted by learned brahmans, from the Vedas and the sastras, illustrative of each object discussed; so that the authenticity of the facts narrated can admit of no doubt, however revolting may be the enormities displayed to the mind of refined sentiment."

About 100 pages of Professor H. H. Wilson's Essay on the Religious Sects of the Hindus,† coincide with part of the following work and I find many references to this work, cited as substantiations of the text, a proof that that great oriental scholar considered Ward a reliable authority, and made him the companion of his own researches.

As I have before hinted, this work is specially adapted for popular use. It gives an answer to the casual observer on points about which he is most curious, the temples that meet the eye in every street; the festivals with which every Hindu home is busy, the worship which attracts his notice by the banks of lake or river, the books by which the youth of India is still instructed and upon which its manhood feeds. This book is a *sine qua non* to every one who has not the leisure or liking for deep research, yet wishes to have some key to the ongoings of Hindu life and the elements of Hindu faith. In this respect it is as welcome to-

* Asiatic Journal, iii, 1817, 34, 35.

† Works of H. H. Wilson, Vol. I. 1862. Trubner and Co., 152, 168, 171, 181, 196, 253, 258, 262, 277.

day as when first issued. We have little books without end that nibble at Indian life and manners; but Ward remains yet unrivalled as a repertory of detailed information, and an indispensable book of reference. The present publisher has recognised this, as the worth of the work, and greatly aided it by the portable form of the present volume, and by the devices of modern typography; I refer to the detailed table of contents, the page headings, the ample Index, and the beautiful colored plates, doing for us by the eye what can scarcely be done by the pen;—helping us to shape a correct idea of those "holy forms" of the principal deities before which, painted, carved, moulded or graven, millions of Hindus daily bend in reverence.

One fault however has been charged upon this work with considerable uniformity. It is said that the views contained in it upon Hindu morals, manners and worship, are prudish and condemnatory beyond reasonable limits. Nor can the book be altogether acquitted; yet some considerations should be taken into account which may modify censure. One is suggested by a phenomenon of our own times. Let any one refer to the papers, speeches, and pamphlets of modern Hindu reformers, from the days of Rammohun Roy to our own, and he will find young Bengal, or young Madras dealing in opinions and terms as to the creed and practices of his grand-father much more in accordance with the pages of this work than the oily apologies of a Twining or a Scott Waring. Only the other day I observed in the public prints the following expressions used by a brahman, a graduate of the Madras University, in the course of a very able address on female education. "In one point of view, a forgetful course is advisable for some of our females. For some of the Hindu works, be they Sanscrit, Telugu or Tamil, which our *families* use, are interspersed with delineations and pictures that we males cannot read without a blush; and we altogether abstain from reading such portions, if females chance to be near us. Just imagine the effects that may flow from our females reading such books! When a girl quits her school, her parents in general put into her hands books like the Neishadam, Camba-Ramayanam, Arichendra-Vilâsam, Sakunthalie-Vilâsam and Mathana-Kkâma-râja-Kathei. These are dangerous instruments, especially in the hands of young inexperienced persons"—and so on. The very sensible conclusion of the whole address may be put thus; "if we educate our children, especially our girls, we must have a new literature."—Such evidence is surely of some weight.

Another consideration, which, I suggest, should qualify our censure, arises from the state of public feeling when the book made its several appearances before the public. At that time an influential section of Indian politicians, who could both write and speak well, ventured boldly to assert and defend opinions of a character very opposite to those of Ward; according to them the

Hindus were almost immaculate in morals, the possessors of a literature and religion singularly perfect. For instance, a Mr. Charles Marsh, a quondam Madras barrister, had a seat in the House of Commons, during the Indian Debate of 1813, and delivered a very effective speech against the opening of India to the labors of Missionaries, whom he spoke of as "crawling from the holes and caverns of their original destinations; apostates from the loom and the anvil, renegades from the lowest handicraft employments." In that speech occurs this paragraph. "When I turn to her philosophers, lawyers and moralists, who have left oracles of political and ethical wisdom to restrain the passions and awe the vices which disturb the commonwealth:—when I look at the peaceful and harmonious alliances of families guarded and secured by the household virtues;—when I see among a cheerful and well ordered society, the benignant and softening influences of religion and morality, a system of manners founded on a system of mild and polished obeisance, and preserving the surface of social life, smooth and unruffled, I cannot hear without surprise, mingled with horror, of sending Baptists and Ana-Baptists to civilize or convert such a people at the hazard of disturbing or deforming institutions which appear hitherto to have been the means ordained by Providence for making them virtuous and happy."* By the way, one cannot help the question, was there any work for lawyers in a land where the surface of social life was so smooth and unruffled? Had this barrister ever a brief? Views, such as those stated above, were spawned multitudinously from the public press, and uttered eloquently in public addresses by Anglo-Indians, the very men apparently most fitted to write and speak on such subjects. If a voice was to be raised in qualification of these high flown eulogies, it must come from India, and it could not come better than from those who had unwillingly been made the scape-goats of the controversy, the Serampore Missionaries. Intimate acquaintance with popular literature—that literature which is both the index of popular morality, and the power that fashions it—and personal observation, gave Ward a right to speak, and speak he did, and for the most part gave chapter and verse for his utterances. We cannot be surprised if, under the circumstances, he did not care to smooth the roughness of his sentences, or stay to count the grains of his indignation. Deduct something for the heat of controversy, and the Missionary's views escape censure. Certainly the sober opinion of our own day leans rather to the plain spoken printer of Serampore, than the polished apologists of the senate. The biographer of Carey, Marshman and Ward says significantly enough: "But all these suspicions of exaggeration have been at once and for ever dispelled by recent events. While these pages are passing through the press, the mutiny of a hundred thousand of our native soldiery has been announced

* Carey, Marshman and Ward. ii. 36.

and Mr. Ward's view of the genuine character of Hinduism has been lamentably verified by the wanton and unparralléled atrocities committed on unoffending women and helpless babes, by the mild and humane Hindus, when released from all restraint, and at liberty to indulge their passions."*

Whether these views were narrowly accurate or not, they were the author's own, and no subsequent publisher has a right to omit, or modify them. They therefore stand in the present edition in the very terms in which the author originally expressed them.

W. O. SIMPSON.

ROYAPETTAH, *November* 12, 1863.

* Carey, Marshman and Ward. i. 444.

INTRODUCTORY REMARKS

ON THE

HINDOO RELIGION.

The whole system of Hindoo theology is founded upon the doctrine that the Divine Spirit, as the soul of the universe, becomes, in all animate beings, united to matter; that spirit is insulated or individuated by particular portions of matter, which it is continually quitting, and joining itself to new portions of matter;[a] that the human soul is, in other words, God himself; that the knowledge of this, leading men to seek complete deliverance from the degrading and polluting influence of material objects, is the only means of being re-united to the divine nature; that this deliverance from matter may be obtained in the present state by separation from human intercourse, the practice of bodily austerities, and entire abstraction of mind; and that, if not obtained in one birth, it is to be sought through every future transmigration till obtained.

[a] There are two opinions among the Hindoos on this subject; some philosophers maintaining, that it is one soul which is united to sentient creatures; while others support a contrary opinion, and affirm, that human souls must be emanations from the Great Spirit, otherwise, when one person obtained absorption into the divine nature, all would obtain it at the same moment. The védantŭ philosophers teach, 'that God exists in millions of forms, from the ant to Brŭmha, the grandfather of the gods, as one moon is seen at once in twenty different pans of water.'

The agreement betwixt these opinions and those of the Greek philosophers is very remarkable:—'Almost all ancient philosophers agreed in admitting two principles in nature, one active and the other passive; but they differed in the manner in which they conceived these principles to subsist. Some held God and Matter to be two principles, which are eternally opposite; not only differing in their essence, but having no common principle by which they can be united. This was the doctrine taught by Anaxagoras, and after him by Plato, and the whole Old Academy. This system, for the sake of perspicuity, we will call the Dualistic system. Others were convinced, that nature consists of these two principles; but finding themselves perplexed by the difficulty with which they saw the Dualistic system to be encumbered, that of supposing two independent and opposite principles, they supposed both these to be comprehended in one universe, and conceived them to be united by a necessary and essential bond. To effect this, two different hypothesis were proposed: some thought God to have been eternally united to matter in one whole, which they called Chaos, whence it was sent forth, and at a certain time brought into form, by the energy of the divine inhabiting mind. This was the System of Emanation, commonly embraced by the ancient barbaric philosophers, and afterwards admitted into the early theogonies of the Greeks. Others attempted to explain the subject more philosophically, and, to avoid the absurdity which they conceived to attend both the former systems, asserted that God, the rational and efficient principle, is as intimately connected with the universe, as the human mind with the body, and is a forming power, so originally and necessarily inherent in matter, that it is to be conceived as a natural part of the original chaos,

This doctrine is taught in many parts of the Hindoo writings, especially in the Dŭrshŭnŭs ; which works, though almost wholly speculative, make known a method of abstraction, to assist ascetics in obtaining deliverance from mortal birth.

Udwŭyanŭndŭ, a sŭnyasēē, and the compiler of 'the Essence of the Védantŭ,' says, 'Brŭmhŭ and life are one : that which, pervading all the members of the body, gives to them life and motion, is called jēēvŭ, life ; that which, pervading the whole universe, gives life and motion to all, is Brŭmhŭ ; therefore these two are one. Every kind of matter is without life ; that which is created cannot possess life : therefore all life is the creator, or Brŭmhŭ ; God is the soul of the world. This is the substance of the Védantŭ philosophy.

Not only is God thus declared to be the soul of the world, but the writer of the above work affirms, that the world itself is God—God expanding himself in an infinite variety of forms : 'All things past, present, and to come ; all that is in the earth, sky, &c. of every class and description ; all this is Brŭmhŭ, who is the cause of all things, and the things themselves.' Yet this writer, in another part of this work, seems to affirm, that the universe is the *work* of God :—'The principle of life is Brŭmhŭ ; that which is animated is the work of Brŭmhŭ,[b] who directs every thing, as the charioteer directs the chariot. Brŭmhŭ is everlasting and unchangeable ; the world, which is his work, is changeable.'

This work represents Brŭmhŭ, in his state of repose, as destitute of ideas or intelligence, and entirely separated from all intelligences. It describes this repose by comparing it to whatever may communicate the idea of undisturbed tranquillity ; to the bosom of the unruffled ocean ; or to the rest enjoyed in a deep sleep, in which there is an entire cessation even of the faculties of the mind.

The Védantŭ writers add, that at certain revolutions of time, 'Brŭmhŭ awaking from this repose, unites to himself his own energy, and creates the universe ;[c] that as soon as souls are united to matter, they become impressed,

This system seems not only to have been received by the Ionic philosophers, Thales and Anaximander ; but by the Pythagoreans, the followers of Heraclitus, and others. Zeno, determining to innovate upon the doctrine of the Academy, and neither choosing to adopt the Dualistic nor the Emanative System, embraced the third hypothesis, which, though not originally his own, we shall distinguish by the name of the Stoical System. Unwilling to admit, on the one hand, two opposite principles, both primary and independent, and both absolute and infinite ; or on the other, to suppose matter, which is in its nature diametrically opposite to that of God, the active efficient cause, to have been derived by emanation from him ; yet finding himself wholly unable to derive these two principles from any common source, he confounded their essence, and maintained that they were so essentially united, that their nature was one and the same.' *Enfield*, p. 329, 330.

[b] Or, as some writers explain it, exists as an effect, as heat is an effect of fire.

[c] 'When Brŭmhŭ withdraws his energy, the destruction of the world succeeds ; when he employs it, creation springs to birth.' *The Védantŭ-sarŭ.*

according to their destiny, with more or less of three qualities[d] :—as 1st, with that which gives rise to excellence of character;—2ndly, with that which excites to anger, restlessness, worldly desire, &c.—and 3dly, that which leads to inactivity, ignorance, and such-like errors. The character is formed, and the future destiny regulated, by the preponderance of any one of these qualities. Krishnŭ is represented in the Shrēē-Bhagŭvŭtŭ-Gēētŭ as teaching Urjoonŭ, that, 'the man who is born with divine destiny is endued with certain qualities, [here follow a number of excellent qualities;] that those who come into life under the influence of the evil destiny, are distinguished by hypocrisy, pride, presumption, harshness of speech, and ignorance; that divine destiny is for eternal absorption into the divine nature; and that the evil destiny confineth the soul to mortal birth.'[e]

The soul then, by these writers, is considered as separated from the source of happiness when it takes mortal birth, and as remaining a miserable wanderer in various births and states, till it regains its place in the divine essence. A devotee, sighing for absorption, is described as uttering his feelings in words to this purport: 'When shall I be delivered from this world, and obtain God!'

In consonance with these ideas, a system of devotion has been formed, to enable men to emancipate themselves from the influence of material objects, and thus to prepare them for absorption. In the first place, the devotee is to acquire the right knowledge of Brŭmhŭ, namely, that God and matter are the same; that Brŭmhŭ is the soul of the world. 'That error[f] which excites earthly desires, and impels to worldly exertions, is destroyed,' says the writer of the work already quoted, 'by the knowledge of Brŭmhŭ.' The person possessed of these ideas of God is called 'the wise man.' *Brŭmhŭ gnanee*; and he who is destitute of this knowledge is considered as in a state of pitiable ignorance, like an insect incrusted with matter.

Further to enable him to subdue his passions, and renounce all natural desires, he is directed to retire from the world; to counteract all his natural propensities; and to confine himself to intense meditation on Brŭmhŭ, till he has thoroughly established in his mind this principle, that, 'seeing every thing proceeded from Brŭmhŭ, and that, at the end of the four yoogŭs, when the universe shall be dissolved, every thing will be absorbed into him again, therefore Brŭmhŭ is every thing.'

The Védantŭ-sarŭ says, 'There are four ways by which the knowledge of

d The possession of more or less of any one of these qualities is owing to the balance of merit or demerit in the preceding birth. Many Hindoo philosophers, however, have no idea of accountability as the cause of reward or suffering: they suppose that all actions, good and bad, produce certain natural effects, which ripen in a future birth; as poverty, disease, and wickedness, or riches, health, and works of merit.

e See Wilkins's translation of this work.

f Error here refers to the false idea, that a man's self and spirit are different, as that *I* is any thing different from spirit. This idea of the separate existence of *I* leads to the idea of *mine*, and thus to every worldly desire.

Brŭmhŭ is perfected :—1st, By that reflection, in which the person decides upon what is changeable and what is unchangeable in the world;—2dly, By cultivating a distaste of all sensual pleasures, and even of the happiness enjoyed by the gods;—3dly, By the following qualities, an unruffled mind, the subjugation of the passions, unrepenting generosity, contempt of the world, the rejection of whatever obstructs the acquisition of the knowledge of Brŭmhŭ;—and 4thly, By unwavering faith in the shastrŭs, added to the desire of absorption.'

Krishnŭ, in his conversation with Urjoonŭ, makes the perfection of religion to consist in subduing the passions, in perfect abstraction from all objects of the senses, and in fixing the whole mind on Brŭmhŭ: I extract a few paragraphs from Wilkins.—'A man is said to be confirmed in wisdom, when he forsaketh every desire which entereth into his heart, and of himself is happy and contented in himself. His mind is undisturbed in adversity, he is happy and contented in prosperity, and he is a stranger to anxiety, fear, and anger. Such a wise man is called a sage. The wisdom of that man is established, who, in all things, is without affection, and having received good or evil, neither rejoiceth at the one, nor is cast down by the other. His wisdom is confirmed, when, like the tortoise, he can draw in all his members, and restrain them from their wonted purpose.' 'The wise neither grieve for the dead nor for the living.' 'The wise man, to whom pain and pleasure are the same, is formed for immortality.' 'The heart, which followeth the dictates of the moving passions, carrieth away the reason, as the storm the bark in the raging ocean.' 'The man whose passions enter his heart as waters run into the unswelling placid ocean, obtaineth happiness :[s] Even at the hour of death, should he attain it, he shall mix with the incorporeal nature of Brŭmhŭ.' 'The man who may be self-delighted and self-satisfied, and who may be happy in his own soul, hath no interest either in that which is done, or that which is not done.' 'The learned behold Brŭmhŭ alike in the reverend bramhŭn perfected in knowledge, in the ox, and in the elephant; in the dog, and in him who eateth of the flesh of dogs.' 'Those whose minds are fixed on this equality, gain eternity even in this world. They put their trust in Brŭmhŭ, the eternal, because he is every where alike free from fault.' The enjoyments which proceed from the feelings, are as the wombs of future pain.' 'To the yogēē, gold, iron, and stones, are the same.' 'The yogēē constantly exerciseth the spirit in private. He is recluse, of a subdued mind and spirit; free from hope, and free from perception. He planteth his own seat firmly on a spot that is undefiled, neither too high nor too low, and sitteth upon the sacred grass which is called kooshŭ, covered with a skin and a cloth. There he, whose business is the restraining of his passions, should sit, with his mind fixed on one object alone, in the exercise of his devotion for the purification of his soul; keeping his head, neck, and body steady without motion, his eyes fixed on the point of his nose, looking at no other place around.' 'The man whose mind is endued with this devotion, and looketh on all things alike, beholdeth

[s] This is strange doctrine in the mouth of Krishnŭ, who spent his youth in licentious amours; and afterwards cohabited with Radha, the wife of Ayanŭ-ghoshŭ, while he retained 1,600 mistresses.

the supreme soul in all things, and all things in the supreme soul.' 'He who having closed up all the doors of his faculties, locked up his mind in his own breast, and fixed his spirit in his head, standing firm in the exercise of devotion, repeateth in silence Om! the mystic sign of Brŭmhŭ, shall, on his quitting this mortal frame, calling upon me, without doubt go the journey of supreme happiness.' 'He my servant is dear unto me, who is unexpecting, just, and pure, impartial, free from distraction of mind, and who hath forsaken every enterprize. He is worthy of my love, who neither requireth, nor findeth fault; who neither lamenteth, nor coveteth; and being my servant, hath forsaken both good and evil fortune; who is the same in friendship and in hatred, in honor and dishonor, in cold and in heat, in pain and in pleasure; who is unsolicitous about the events of things; to whom praise and blame are as one; who is of little spirit, and pleased with whatever cometh to pass; who owneth no particular home, and who is of a steady mind.' 'Wisdom is exemption from attachments and affection for children, wife, and home; a constant evenness of temper upon the arrival of every event, whether longed for or not; a constant and invariable worship paid to me alone; worshipping in a private place; and a dislike to the society of man.'

A most singular ceremony, called yogŭ, is said to have been formerly practised by ascetics to prepare them for absorption. I give an account of this ceremony from the first part of the Patŭnjŭlŭ Dŭrshŭnŭ, and the Gorŭkshŭsŭnghita:—

The yogēē must in the first place, by medicines (here described) reduce the appetites of the body, and increase its strength; he must then learn the proper posture for the ceremony; this posture may be various, but a particular one is here enjoined—the yogēe is to put his legs across in a sitting posture, and to hold his feet with his hands crossed behind him. The next act of austerity is that of learning to inhale and discharge his breath; in doing which, he is to take a piece of cloth fifteen cubits long and four fingers in breadth, and swallow it repeatedly, drawing it up and taking it down his throat, drinking water at intervals. He must next choose a seat on some sacred spot, at the bottom of a vŭtu tree, at some place frequented by pilgrims, near an image of an uncreated lingŭ, or in any place peculiarly pleasant to a yogēē; but it must be a secret one.—That on which he must sit may be either kooshŭ grass, or the skin of a tiger or a deer, or a blanket; he must not sit on wood, nor on the earth, nor on cloth; his back, neck, and head must be exactly erect; and he must remain motionless, keeping his eyes fixed on his nose. The act of yogŭ consists of several parts: the devotee must first with his thumbs and fingers prevent the air from issuing through his eyes, ears, nostrils, and mouth, and with his feet bind up the two other avenues of respiration. This he is to practise by degrees till he is able to exist without inspiration and respiration. He who is thus far perfected will be able to subdue his passions, and to disrelish all the pleaures of the senses. Should the mind, at any time, be again entangled in worldly attachments, the devotee must study the essential virtue of things, as, that the world is a dream; that God is the all in all; and, thus bring back the mind to abstraction. He is next to meditate on his guardian deity according to the rules of the shastrŭ. After thus annihilating, as it were, the body and the world, he is then to fix in his mind that he and Brŭmhŭ are one, and so to settle this point as never to lose sight of it, nor return to earthly attachments. From this state of mind arises complete pleasure; he becomes dead to food and to every other bodily want.

The yogēē who has attained this state of perfection becomes emancipated in the following manner:—while he sits confining the air within his body, and closing his eyes, by the power of wisdom all his members become dead to action; he unites the energy which is lodged in the body to the soul, and they both ascend by means of the veins and arteries to the skull, from which the soul escapes, by the *basilar suture*: and the body being thus shaken off, he is reunited to the supreme soul.[m]

The Védantŭ-saru also pronounces in favour of an opinion of the philosopher Shŭnkŭrŭ, that the practice of ceremonies is to be renounced by the person seeking absorption, in whom all desires respecting himself are to be annihilated.

From the preceding sketch, the reader will be able to form some idea of this system of Hindoo theology, which is doubtless very ancient. No yogēēs, however, now exist, who perform these bodily austerities to the extent laid down in the shastrŭs. A number of mendicants may be seen, who profess to aim at abstraction of mind, and contempt of the world; but they are in general the greatest sensualists in the country.

Amongst the learned, a few are to be found, who consider the attainment of divine wisdom, as the only means of securing future beatitude: these persons either renounce all wordly connections and become pilgrims, or they remain in a secular state, and ground their expectations (if they have any) of future happiness, on their speculative opinions being less gross than those of the vulgar. As an apology for not practising severe austerities, and for continuing in a secular state, they quote a sentence of Jŭnŭkŭ: 'A man does not become a a hermit by residing in a forest; but he is a hermit, who even in his own house subdues his passions.' Some of those persons despise the popular superstition.

The absurdity and impiety of the opinions upon which the practices of these yogēēs are founded, need not be exposed: the doctrine which destroys all accountability to the Creator, and removes all that is criminal in immorality, must be condemned by every good man; and the absurdity of rejecting those rational enjoyments which at once prove the beneficence of the Creator, and contribute to the refinement of our nature, is so flagrant, that the slightest notice of it may surely be considered as more than necessary to the discharge of our duty to the interests of Christian morals.

The author may however remark, that he has had many opportunities of witnessing the pernicious effects of the belief, that it is God in man who

[m] For further remarks on absorption, and on those mendicants who practise austerities leading to it, the reader is referred to pages 285, 286, 298—301.

is the author of every volition, and that evil and good actions are both to be referred to him. A Hindoo, perverted by these ideas, does not perceive the evil of ascribing every villainous action to God; though when the dreadful and unavoidable result of this doctrine has been pointed out, many revolt from the conclusion. Under the influence of this doctrine, that the human soul is God, the crimes of a malefactor lose their turpitude, and he is bewailed as a person who has acted under unfortunate influence, or as one born with evil destiny. It is also easy to perceive, that where such a belief prevails, all efforts to fly from evil, and to attain moral perfection, are out of the question:—'God does every thing;' 'My evil destiny follows me every where, as a shadow the body,' is the method by which the Hindoo accounts for all his evil propensities and unjust actions.

Another class of Hindoos place a greater reliance on DEVOTION than on divine knowlege. They derive their opinions from different parts of the Hindoo writings, and from favourite books of their own, as the Madhyŭ-bhashyŭ, Bhŭktee-rŭsamritŭ-sindhoo, &c. One of the sentiments of this sect is thus given in the Shrēē-bhagŭvŭtŭ:—'He who, renouncing the service of God, enters the path of wisdom, (practises religious austerities,) works hard at bruising the straw, but obtains only chaff.' Another of their poets has a verse to this purport:—'He who dies at Kashēē obtains absorption: true; but the cause of his emancipation is his devotion.' Vŭrahŭ, a poet belonging to the court of Vikrŭm-adityŭ, says, personifying a person of this sect, 'O God! I ask not for the merit of works; nor for riches; nor for fame; I leave all this to fate; nor do I refuse to endure the fruit of my actions:—but this I ask, that, through every transmigration, I may be thy devoted servant.'—Vilwŭ-mŭngŭlŭ, another poet of this sect, says, addressing himself to Vishnoo, 'O God! I desire not absorption. I ask for a distinct existence, and to be always near thee, as my lord and master.' Some of these persons express attachment to their guardian deity in the most familiar acts of devotion—as his friends, or servants; in songs or prayers; by bowing or making offerings to his image, by washing its feet, by repeating his name, or listening to his praise, or meditating on his qualities. These persons are mostly found among the followers of Krishnŭ and Choitŭnyŭ.

Such a worshipper presents himself before the image of Krishnŭ, and says, 'Oh, t'hakoorŭ! thou art God, the maker of the world, the saviour, the friend of the friendless: I am destitute; I am thy servant; save me!' Others, more fervent in their attachment, omitting the usual purifications and ablutions before morning worship, hasten, as soon as they rise, to pay all those marks of respect and attention to the image which belong to the character under which they worship it. For instance, one man's image is that of the infant Krishnŭ: he imagines it necessary, that the god should be honoured as a child, and he therefore makes an offering of sweetmeats to him early in the morning; he is very careful too that the image should be laid down to rest, and raised up again, only at the appointed hours; he bathes, anoints it, and adorns it with the utmost fondness. Songs in praise of Krishnŭ are very common amongst this sect; and sometimes an enthusiast falls to the ground while singing, and exhibits all the symptoms of superstitious frenzy. These persons reject many of the Hindoo ceremonies; but they repeat the name of Krishnŭ, worship the common images of this god, and observe the national festivals to his honor. Some individuals are directed in their religious duties by the Hindoo writings: but the great body are enthusiasts, following the impulse of feelings enkindled by their own impure imaginations. Some of them wander from village to village, proclaiming the name and reciting the praises of Krishnŭ.

Those who reverence the philosophical doctrine, and those who thus adhere to devotion, form however but a very small part of the Hindoo population. The great majority of the community are attached to the popular ceremonies, considering them as at least *leading to* the knowledge of God, or as laying in a stock of merit which will influence their condition in this or a future birth.

The other branch of Hindoo theology enjoins RELIGIOUS DUTIES, as preparing a person for that state which leads to absorption. Krishnŭ, in his address to Urjoonŭ, thus holds up the value of religious practice:—'Perform thy duty, and make the event equal whether it terminate in good or evil. The miserable are so on account of the event of things. Wise men, who have abandoned all thought of the fruit of their actions, are freed from the chains of birth, and go to the regions of eternal happiness.[i] Jŭnŭkŭ and others have attained perfection even by works. Wise men call him a pŭndit, whose every undertaking is free from the idea of desire. He abandoneth a desire of a reward of his actions; he is always contented and independent, and although he may be engaged in a work, he as it were doth nothing. God is to be obtained by him who maketh God alone the object of his works. The speculative and the practical doctrines are but one, for both obtain the self-same end, and the place which is gained by the followers of the one is gained by the followers of the other. The man who, performing the duties of life, and quitting all interest in them, placeth them upon Brŭmhŭ the supreme, is not tainted by sin; but remaineth, like the leaf of the lotus, unaffected by the waters.—If thou shouldest be unable, at once, steadfastly to fix thy mind on me, endeavour to find me by means of constant practice. If after practice thou art still unable, follow me in my works supreme, for by performing works for me thou shalt obtain perfection.'

This brings us to the popular superstition of the Hindoos, of which I shall now endeavour to give a summary account, beginning with their mythology.

It is very difficut, perhaps, to speak decisively on the precise origin of any of the *Ancient Systems of Idolatry*; but not so difficult to trace idolatry itself to certain natural causes, and to prove, that the heathen deities owe their origin to the common darkness and depravity of men; who, rejecting

[i] Mr. Wilkins has thus translated this part of the Bhagŭvŭtŭ; but the fact is, that there is no *distinct* happiness in the Hindoo absorption, because there is no remaining individuality. The spirit being liberated from every thing which is not spirit, and absorbed in the ocean of universal spirit, or deity, there can be no such thing as individnal enjoyment. The Hindoos illustrate their idea on this subject, by comparing the soul to air confined in a vessel, which, when the vessel breaks, is immediately lost in the vast body of air which composes the atmosphere.

the doctrine of the divine unity, and considering God as too great or too spiritual to be the object of human worship, chose such images as their darkness or their passions suggested. Hence idolatry has arisen out of circumstances common to all heathen nations; which fact, and another hereafter mentioned, will account for many coincidences in the mythology of nations the most remote, while differences in manners and customs, and in the degrees of civilization, may account for most of the diversities found in the images and worship of different idolatrous nations.

It is not to be supposed that any of the images invented by the heathen were intended to be representations of the One God, according to the ideas given of this adorable Being in the sacred Scriptures; they are images of beings formed by the fancies of men, who 'by wisdom knew not God.' It is probable, indeed, that no heathen nation ever made a single idol in honour of 'the one living and true God;' and that direct worship to Him was never offered by any heathens.

Nor does it appear, from the various systems of idolatry, that the heathen regarded the gods as intercessors with the Supreme Being. It is certain that no such idea exists among the Hindoos, who never worship the One God, either directly or through the intercessions of others. The gods are regarded as the only divine beings from whom evil is to be dreaded, or good to be expected. It is true, I have heard the bramhŭns often speak of the worship of the gods as introducing the worshipper to a great approximation to final beatitude, but this has nothing to do with the Christian doctrine of mediation.

Writers on heathen mythology have frequently supposed, that the extraordinary bodily organs of the gods were intended to represent the *perfections of Deity*. Such writers, in elucidating the Hindoo system, would have said, 'Indrŭ is represented as full of eyes,[k] to exhibit the divine omniscience; Brŭmha with four faces, to display the perfect wisdom of God; and Doorga with ten hands, to teach that God is almighty.' It is a fact, however, that the Hindoos are never thus instructed by the forms of their idols. When the author once interrogated a learned bramhŭn on this subject, he rejected this Christian explanation of the forms of his idols, and referred him to the image of Ravŭnŭ, the cannibal, who is painted with a hundred arms, and ten heads.[l]

It has been common too to represent the idols as personifications of the *virtues*, and as teaching, by hieroglyphics, a theory of morals. As it respects

k The Hindoo fable on this subject is so insufferably gross, that it cannot be printed.

l Thus Briareus, one of the monsters brought forth by the earth, is said to have had a hundred arms, with which he threw up to heaven the rocks from the sea shore against Jupiter.

the Hindoos, however, the fact is, that they have still, for popular use, a system of morals to seek : some of their idols are actually personifications of *vice ;* and the formularies used before the images, so far from conveying any moral sentiment, have the greatest possible tendency to corrupt the mind with the love of riches and pleasure.[m]

To the author it seems equally improbable, that the original framers of idols designed to teach by them a system of *natural science.* The distance of time betwixt the formation of different images, militates strongly against such an idea : men of science, also, have generally held idolatrous rites in contempt; but before a man would sit down to frame an image, to teach the sciences, his mind must have been enthusiastically attached to idolatry. Nor does it appear probable, that the Hindoo poets were the first who set up idol worship; though we admit, that many ideas on this subject were borrowed from their extravagant descriptions, and ethereal visions. The introduction of new idols seems, in most instances, to have been the work of kings, who sought the *gratification* of the populace, rather than their instruction; and the exhibition of popular sentiments, rather than the teaching of profound mysteries, or the principles of science. It appears from the Brŭmhŭ-voivŭrttŭ pooranŭ, that king Soorŭt'hŭ first set up the image of Doorga; king Mŭngŭlŭ, that of Lŭkshmēē; Ushwŭpŭtee, that of Savitrēē, the wife of Brŭmha; king Sooyŭgnŭ, that of Radha, the mistress of Krishnŭ; Rŭmyŭ-rŭt'hŭ, king of Oojjŭnyinēē, that of Kartikéyŭ; king Shivŭ, that of Sōōryŭ; and the sage Boudhayŭnŭ, that of Gŭnéshŭ.

The author imagines, that the disclosure of real facts respecting the Mythology of the Hindoos, would greatly tend to elucidate the origin of that of ALL THE EASTERN NATIONS: and he here offers to the consideration of his readers a conjecture or two, the fruit of his own enquiries. The philosophers of all these nations conceived, that the Great Spirit remains for ever unknown, that he neither comes within the thoughts nor the speech of men. In the Chandogyŭ oopŭnishŭd of the Rig védŭ, we have a discourse on this subject, in which Shwétŭ-kétoo enquired of Boudhayŭnŭ respecting Brŭmhŭ: the sage answered him by an impressive silence: on being called upon for the reason of this silence, he answered, '*Brŭmhŭ is undescribable*: he who says, "I know Brŭmhŭ," knows him not; he who says, "I know him not," has obtained this knowledge.' The védŭ declares, that 'he is that which has never been seen nor known.' In other words, he is the Athenian 'unknown God.' The One God is never worshipped by the Hindoos as a mere spiritual being, but always as united to matter, and before some image.

[m] See Mr. Colebrooke's translation of many of these formularies, in his excellent Essays on the Religious Ceremonies of the Hindoos, in the fifth and seventh volumes of the Asiatic Researches.

When Brŭmhŭ resolved to create, according to the pooranŭs,[n] he looked upon[o] that which is denominated by the Hindoo philosophers delusion, or inanimate energy,[p] and became subject to the three qualities (goonŭs) of which it is composed—that which leads to truth, and is called sŭttŭ; that which excites desires, (rŭjŭ;) and that which leads to sensuality, (tŭmŭ.) He now created time, nature, and future consequences; the primary elements; the organs of sense, of action, and of intellect: he next became the first form, or pattern, or the aggregate, of life, and individuated himself into separate portions of animal life; and then, under the name of Vishnoo, he created the universe from the waters, and entered it as the soul of the world.

While Vishnoo lay asleep on the waters, a lotus ascended from his navel, from which sprung Brŭmha, the creator. Shivŭ, Vishnoo, and Brŭmha, are considered as the representations of the three goonŭs: Vishnoo of the sŭttŭ goonŭ, Brŭmha of the rŭjŭ, and Shivŭ of the tŭmŭ. We have no regular account of the creation of Vishnoo and Shivŭ. Almost all the other Hindoo deities are found to be derived from the three principal gods:—Indrŭ, Kamŭ-dévŭ, Doorga, Sōōryŭ, Ugnee, Pŭvŭnŭ, Vŭroonŭ, Gŭroorŭ, Vishwŭ-kŭrma, Sŭrŭswŭtēē, Yŭmŭ, &c. are the descendants of *Brŭmha*;—Gŭnéshŭ, Jŭgŭnnat'hŭ, Bŭlŭramŭ, Ramŭ, Krishnŭ, Gopalŭ, Gopēē-nat'hŭ, Valŭ-Gopalŭ, Choitŭnyŭ, Sŭtyŭ-Narayŭnŭ, Lŭkshmēē, &c. are forms of *Vishnoo*;—Karti-kéyŭ, Pŭnchanŭnŭ, Roodrŭ, Kalŭ-Bhoirŭvŭ, &c. are forms of *Shivŭ*. 'Thus' as Sir W. Jones has observed, 'we must not be surprised at finding, on a close examination, that the characters of all the Pagan deities, male and female, melt into each other, and at last into one or two.'

But the enquiry returns, 'What is the object of worship among the Hindoos?' It is not the ONE GOD, but this compound being, the soul of the world enclosed in matter, the primeval energy, the prolific and vivifying principle dwelling in all animated existences[q] or in other words the personification of

[n] The Shrēē-Bhagŭvŭtŭ, &c. The Noiyayikŭs declare, that the universe was created from atoms; while the Mēēmangsŭkŭs, equally wise, affirm, that the consequences of actions were the only things united to birth.

[o] 'Or,' as the word is explained by some Hindoo scholars,' the first inclination of the Godhead to diversify *himself*, by creating worlds. *Sir W. Jones.*

[p] It is called delusion, or appearance, to shew, that it is something assumed for an occasion, and which, when that occasion is served, will be destroyed: hence they say, that matter is from everlasting, but is subject to destruction. It is called inanimate energy, as it supplies the forms of things, though the vivifying principle is God.

[q] When the following lines of Pope were read to Gopalŭ-tŭrkalŭnkarŭ, a learned bramhŭn, he started from his seat, begged for a copy of them, and declared that the author must have been a Hindoo:—

'All are but parts of one stupendous whole,
Whose body Nature is, and God the soul;—
Warms in the sun, refreshes in the breeze,
Glows in the stars, and blossoms in the trees;
Lives through all life, extends through all extent,
Spreads undivided, operates unspent.'

whatever the disordered imaginations of the Hindoos have attributed to this God encompassing himself with delusion.[r] This energy is said to have created the universe; and therefore this, as displayed in the grandest of the forms it assumes,[s] is the object of worship. Hence the gods, the heavens collectively, the sun and moon, as well as the stars, the sea, mighty rivers, and extraordinary appearances in nature, receive the adorations of the Hindoos.[t] This energy itself has been personified and worshipped, not only in the form of Bhŭgŭvŭtēē,[u] but, as it is manifested equally in creation, in the government of the world, and in the work of destruction, in Brŭmha, Vishnoo, and Shivŭ. The universe being full of the divine majesty, a deity has been consecrated as the regent of every element; and, to complete this mass of folly, the bramhŭn and the devout mendicant, as sharing more largely of the indwelling deity, have received the adoration of the multitude.

If we recur to the bodily powers of the different images worshipped by the Hindoos, we see the same principle exhibited: hence Unŭntŭ has a thousand heads; Brŭmha has four faces; Indrŭ is full of eyes; Doorga has ten, and even Ravŭnŭ, the giant, has an hundred arms:—the formidable weapons[x] of the gods too, have evidently the same allusion, as well as their symbols and vehicles, among which we find the eagle,[y] the serpent, the lion,

[r] The Tŭntrŭs teach, that after Brŭmhŭ had entered the world, he divided himself into male and female.

[s] 'It seems a well-founded opinion, that the whole crowd of gods and goddesses in ancient Rome, and modern Vánáres, mean only the powers of nature, and principally those of the Sun, expressed in a variety of ways, and by a multitude of fanciful names.' *Sir W. Jones.*—'Nature herself, and its plastic powers, originating solely in the sovereign energies of the supreme creative source of all being, they (the Asiatics) absurdly dignified by the majestic denomination of God. This supreme creative energy, diffused through nature, they distinguished by various names: sometimes it was Osiris, the fountain of LIGHT, the SUN, the prolific principle by which that was invigorated; sometimes it was the life-generating FIRE, the divine offspring of the solar deity; and it was sometimes called by an appellation consonant to the SOUL OF THE WORLD. The FIRST VIVIFIC PRINCIPLE, emanating from the primeval source of being, is visibly of Chaldaic origin; and thence, through the medium of the Egyptians, the Stoic philosophers doubtless had their doctrine of 'the fiery soul of the world,' by which they supposed all things to be created, animated, and governed.' *Maurice.*

[t] They (the pagans) called the elementary fire Pitha, Vulcan, Ugnee; the solar light they denominated Osiris, Mithra, Sooryŭ, Apollo, and the pervading air, or spirit; Cneph, Narayŭnŭ, Zeus, or Jupiter.' *Maurice.*

[u] Many Hindoos are denominated shaktŭs, as devoted to the worship of this shŭktee, or energy. It is remarkable, also, that all the goddesses are called the energies of their lords, as well as matrees, or mothers.

[x] Indrŭ's thunder-bolt; the Brŭmhastrŭ, a weapon wielded by the gods, which infallibly destroys an enemy. 'Vishnoo's chŭkra, a weapon in the form of a circle, continually vomiting flames.'—*Maurice.*

[y] 'Vishnoo riding upon his Gŭroorŭ, or eagle,' says Maurice, 'puts us in mind of the thunder-bearing eagle of the Grecian Jupiter.'

the tiger, the elephant, the bull, the buffalo, &c. The abominable lingŭ worship too, (the last state of degradation to which human nature can be driven,) no doubt took its rise from the same doctrine.

Under the influence of this doctrine, the philosophic mind chose, as the objects of its adoration, the forms in which this energy displays itself with the greatest magnificence, and almost confined its worship to the primary elements, the heavenly bodies, and aërial beings;—the great body of the community became attached to this energy in its forms of preservation:—persons of gloomyhabits, as ascetics and yogēēs, adored it in the work of destruction, as connected with emancipation and with return to ineffable repose in the divine essence. The first class chose the retirement of forests as the scene of their contemplations; the second, the public streets, to adore the prolific power; and the last retired to gloomy caverns,[1] for the celebration of those horrid rites, which took their rise in the common error, that the energetic principle is the chief object of worship.

Thus the indwelling principle is adored in whatever form it is supposed to display itself: in the cow, as a form of Bhŭgŭvŭtēē; in the boar, as an incarnation of Vishnoo; and in an ascetic, who has passed through religious austerities supposed to be too dreadful to be borne without support from the divine inhabiting energy. Exactly conformable to the Hindoo idea was the declaration respecting Simon Magus, 'This man is the great power of God.'

The object of adoration being thus simple power, or energy, wherever this is supposed to reside, the impiety of the possessor forms no obstacle to his becoming an object of worship: it is sufficient that he be a god or a bramhŭn. 'The learned,' says Krishnŭ, 'behold Brŭmhŭ alike in the reverend bramhŭn, perfected in knowledge, in the ox and the elephant; in the dog, and in him who eateth of the flesh of dogs.' Upon the same principle the Hindoo, when he sees the force with which the flood-tide comes into the Ganges or any other similar phenomena of nature, recognizes it as God, or the energy of God. The blessing which he supposes a yogēē obtains, as the fruit of his religious austerities, he confines to power—power to heal or to kill others, to ride in the air on the back of a tiger, to foretel future events, &c. Benevolent dispositions and actions procure for a man praise, but not reverence. *Howard* would have obtained the encomiums of this people, and would have been complimented on the exaltation he was likely to have in the next birth, but nobody would have worshipped him; this honour is always reserved for men of pretended supernatural powers.

If these conjectures be just, they may perhaps afford a solution of the

[1] The Scythians, the Druids, and other ancient nations, it is well known, worshipped this energy in its destructive forms in gloomy recesses, and there offered human and other victims. In the caverns of Salsette and Elephanta, too, the same horrid rites were practised by gloomy ascetics.

difficulties attending the worship of the Egyptians,[a] the Scythians, the Greeks, the Persians, and other idolaters; some of them adoring, by sanguinary rites, this principle in its destructive forms, and others in its prolific forms, fire, and the solar orb.[b] It is the same energetic principle that is also worshipped in the wonderful motions of the heavenly bodies, and in the conflicting gods and the giants, shaking to its centre the solid world; in the warring elements;[c] and even in all the forms of brute matter in which it appears.

These ideas the author offers to the examination of men of greater leisure and erudition, not without the hope, that they may tend to elucidate a subject exceedingly complicated, and upon which a great variety of opinions have been held. As the same ideas respecting the divine energy were held in common by almost all the ancient philosophers, it is not wonderful that the same objects of worship should be seen among all nations, subject to those variations and additions which might be expected when man had abandoned the doctrine of the divine unity, and had resolved to worship every form and appearance of this energy.

The Hindoo mythology, in its present mixed state, presents us with gods of every possible shape, and for every possible purpose, (*even to cure the itch!*) but most of them appear to refer to the doctrine of the periodical creation and destruction of the world,[d] —the appearances of nature,[e] —the heavenly bodies,[f] —the history of deified heroes,[g] —the poetical wars of the giants with the gods,[h] —or to the real or imagined wants of mankind.[i]

[a] 'Taut, or Thoth, was the true Anubis of the Egyptians, one of their eight greater gods. Thoth considers the cosmogony of Phœnicia as founded on the doctrine which maintains two principles in nature, matter or darkness, and spirit or intelligence. By the former, he would understand the chaos, obscure and turbid; by the latter, the agitative wind or spirit, which put that chaos in motion, and ranged in order the various parts of the universe.' *Maurice.*

[b] In this island of Albion, the image of the sun was placed upon an high pillar, as half a man, with a face full of rays of light, and a flaming wheel on his breast. He was worshipped in the same manner as Mithra in Persia, and the divinities of the East. The Persian Magi preserved a continual fire upon an altar in honour of the sun and the lights in the firmament, as the Romans did their holy fire dedicated to Vesta. The Jewish writers affirm, that this was the god Abraham refused to worship in Ur of the Chaldees.' *Galtruchius.*—'The sun became the deity adored by the Sabian idolaters.' *Maurice.*

[c] 'Sees God in clouds, and hears him in the wind.'

[d] As Brŭmha and Shivŭ.

[e] The deified elements, as Pŭvŭnŭ, Vŭroonŭ, &c.

[f] Sōōryŭ, Chŭndrŭ, &c.

[g] Ramŭ, who, in reference to his forest residence, is painted green, and carries a bow and arrow.

[h] Doorga, who has a giant at her feet, and the head of another in her hand. The author will not presume to decide, whether these wars of the gods have reference to human contests, and as such are to be regarded as real history disguised in fable; or whether images of this class have been borrowed merely from the reveries of the poets.

[i] Sŭrŭswŭtēē, the goddess of learning; Unnŭ-pōōrnŭ, the goddess of plenty, &c.

It cannot be doubted, from what has been published of the védŭs, said to be the most ancient of the Hindoo writings, that the PRIMARY ELEMENTS, fire, air, water, earth, and space, with the HEAVENLY BODIES, and AERIAL BEINGS, were the first objects of worship among this people.

The worship of the *primary elements* possibly originated in the doctrine of the védŭs respecting the eternity of matter; for we find in these writings the elements deified, and called by appropriate names, as in the modern mythology of the Hindoos.

The worship of the *heavenly bodies* may probably be attributed to the astronomical notions of the Hindoos: and, as the worship of heathens has always been dictated by their fears and hopes rather than by their reason, it is not a matter of surprise that they should have worshipped the host of heaven, while they believed the stars to have such a mighty and immediate influence on their destiny here and hereafter. In the prayers of the védŭs, the name of Indrŭ is found, who was probably considered as a personification of the heavens: his name, Indrŭ, signifies the glorious; and his body, covered with stars, might easily be supposed to resemble 'the spangled heavens.'

The worship of *aërial beings*, under the general name of spirits, is easily accounted for from the proneness of mankind to superstitious fears respecting invisible existences, and from the notion found in the Hindoo writings, that every form of animated existence has its tutelar divinity presiding over it.[k]

These appear to have been the first gods worshipped in India, though such a system of mythology could in no way account for the existence and government of the universe; which exhibited a process for which this system made no provision. This might therefore induce later Hindoo theologians to add three new gods, under the characters of the CREATOR, the PRESERVER, and the DESTROYER,—Brumha, Vishnoo, and Shivŭ; and the pooranŭs exhibit each of these gods at his post, committing faults and absurdities that would disgrace beings destitute of every spark of divinity, and even of reason.

A philosophical doctrine found in the Tŭntrŭs, having reference to the supposed union of spirit and matter in the formation of the world,[l] has introduced an order of FEMALE deities among this people, at the head of which stands Bhŭgŭvŭtēē, or Doorga. Of this goddess, many forms are worshipped among the Hindoos; and indeed almost all the goddesses are only different forms of Bhŭgŭvŭtēē, as the image of Prŭkritee, or nature.

Jŭgŭnnat'hŭ, the lord of the world; Koovérŭ, the god of riches; Kamŭdévŭ, the god of love; Kartikéyŭ, the god of war; Yŭmŭ, the regent of death;

k Diseases also, and divisions of time, as well as places, have their tutelar deities. The god Bhŭgŭ, who is blind of both eyes, presides over the members of the body.

l Mr. Paterson thinks, that the mixed image of Hŭrŭ-Gourēē, in which Shivŭ and Doorga are united in one image, is intended to represent this union.

and Vishwŭ-kŭrmŭ, the architect of the gods; seem to have originated in the fables of the Hindoos, and in the imagined necessities of a people destitute of just ideas respecting Divine Providence.

Krishnŭ, Ramŭ, and other terrestrial gods, are evidently deified HEROES.

These general remarks may probably account for the whole system of Hindoo idolatry, without the absolute necessity of admitting that this people borrowed their gods from their neighbours. That they borrowed some, or the features of some, many striking coincidences hereafter mentioned seem to indicate; but, these coincidences excepted, we have found no further evidence of this fact.[m]

I shall now give some account of the gods found in the HINDOO PANTHÉON,[n] as a very brief notice of what the reader has to expect in this volume.

It may be necessary, however, to premise, that the Hindoos profess to have 330,000,000 of gods: not that they have even the names of such a number; but they say, that God performs all his works by the instrumentality of the gods, and that all human actions, as well as all the elements, have their tutelar deities.

Images have been chosen to fix the mind of the worshipper, and attributes of power and splendour, and various fables, having been added in the forms of devotion and the addresses to the gods, all these attributes are recognized, and the contents of these fables rehearsed, to raise in the mind of the worshipper the highest thoughts of the power of the idol.

He who approaches an idol, seeking the happiness of a future state, is required to fix in his mind only one idea, that the god can save him . and in this respect all the gods, however various their images, are equal. But when a Hindoo is anxious to obtain any peculiar favour, he applies to the god whose province it is to bestow it: thus, he who prays to Brŭmha, entreats that he may be like him, in order to absorption; but he who is anxious that his members may continue perfect, and that he may enjoy the pleasures of the senses, worships Indrŭ; he who desires children, prays to the progenitors of mankind; he who seeks worldly prosperity, worships Lŭkshmēē; he who prays for a shining body, supplicates Ugnee; the person who is anxious for strength, applies to Roodrŭ; the glutton prays to Uditee; he who pants for a crown, applies to Vishwŭdévŭ or Swayŭmbhoovŭ; a king intreats Sadhyŭ, that his kingdom may be free from sedition; he who prays for long life, addresses him-

[m] Should the reader, however, be inclined to pursue this subject, he will find much ingenious conjecture, and many apparent resemblances betwixt the Egyptian, Greek, and Roman mythology and that of the Hindoos, in Mr. Paterson's essay already alluded to.

[n] The Hindoos have no temple like the Pantheon at Rome; but the palaces of some Hindoo rajas contain courts filled with idols, each of which has an establishment of priests, who daily perform the ceremonies of worship.

self to Ushwinēē-koomarŭ; he who desires corpulence, addresses Prit'hivēē; he who prays that he may preserve his homestead, petitions Prit'hivēē and the regents of space; he who seeks beauty, prays to the Gŭndhŭrvŭs; he who prays for a good wife, calls on Oorvŭsēē, a celestial courtezan; he who seeks honour, prays to Yŭgnŭ: he who is anxious for store-houses full of wealth; calls on Prŭchéta; the seeker of wisdom, solicits the favour of Shivŭ; he or she who seeks union and happiness in the marriage state, addresses Doorga; he who wishes to destroy his enemy, supplicates Noiritŭ; he who is anxious for strength of body, prays to Vayoo; he who prays to be preserved from obstruction in his affairs, calls on Koovérŭ; he who prays for the merit of works, applies to the regent of verse; he who prays for pleasure in the enjoyment of earthly things, addresses Chŭndrŭ; he who desires freedom from worldly passions, he who asks for the completion of all his desires, he who prays for absorption, and the person free from all desire, worship Brŭmha. Hence it appears, that all the Hindoo gods, except Brŭmha, are considered as bestowing only temporal favours; and it has been already observed, that this god has been abandoned, and left without either temples or images. Thus the whole system excites in the mind of the worshipper only cupidity and the love of pleasure; and to this agrees what I have repeatedly heard from sensible bramhŭns, that few if any persons now attend the public festivals with a direct view to a future state.

It is common for the Hindoos to speak of some of their gods as benevolent, and to treat others as malignant beings[o]: Shivŭ, as well as other gods, unites both these qualities; in one hand he holds a dreadful weapon, and with two others he blesses a worshipper, and invites him to approach. Not one of these images, however, conveys the least idea of the moral attributes of God.

1. *Brŭmha.* This god may be properly noticed first, as he is called the *creator*, and the grandfather of gods and men; in the latter designation he resembles Jupiter, as well as in the lasciviousness of his conduct, having betrayed a criminal passion towards his own daughter. Brŭmha's image is never worshipped, nor even made; but the Chŭndēē describes it as that of a red man with four faces.[p] He is red, as a mark of his being full of the rŭjŭ goonŭ; he has four faces, to remind the worshipper that the védŭs proceeded from his four mouths. In one hand he has a string of beads, to shew that his power as creator was derived from his devotion. The pan of water in his left hand points out, that all things sprang from water. It has excited much surprise, that this deity, supre-eminent, should be entirely destitute of a temple and of

o Hindoo women, and the lower orders, regard Pŭnchanŭnŭ, Dŭkshinŭrayŭ, Mŭnŭsa, Shēētŭla, Shŭsht'hēē, as malignant demons, and worship them through fear, still praying to them for protection. The superior deities, though arrayed with attributes of terror, are considered as using their power only in favour of the worshipper.

p Brŭmha had five heads, but Shivŭ deprived him of one, as a punishment for his lust.

worshippers. Mr. Paterson supposes, that, in some remote age, the worshippers of Shivŭ carried on a contest with the followers of Brŭmha, and wholly suppressed the worship of this god. This conjecture opens a wide field of enquiry; but this gentleman does not adduce any historical evidence of the fact. The story of Shivŭ's cutting off one of the heads of Brŭmha, and the existence of violent contentions betwixt different sects of Hindoos at the present day, can scarcely be considered as establishing it, though the conjecture appears not altogether improbable. These contentions for superiority are annually renewed at Hŭrēē-dwarŭ, Uyodhya, &c. betwixt the Voishnŭvŭs (Ramatŭs) and the followers of Shivŭ, in which quarrels many perish.[q]

2. *Vishnoo.* This is the image of a black man, with four arms, sitting on Gŭroorŭ, a creature half-bird, half-man, and holding in his hands the sacred shell, the chŭkrŭ, the lotus, and a club. His colour (black) is that of the destroyer, which is intended to show, that Shivŭ and he are one; he has four hands, as the representative of the male and female powers; the shell (blown on days of rejoicing) implies that Vishnoo is a friendly deity; the chŭkrŭ is to teach that he is wise to protect; the lotus is to remind the worshipper of the nature of final emancipation, that, as this flower is raised from the muddy soil, and after rising by degrees from immersion in the waters, expands itself above the surface to the admiration of all, so man is emancipated from the chains of human birth; the club shews that he chastises the wicked. Gŭroorŭ is a portion of Shivŭ; his body represents the védŭ. Vishnoo is distinguished as being the source of most of the Hindoo incarnations; in which forms he commands the worship of the greatest division of the Hindoo population. I know of no temples nor festivals in honour of Vishnoo. He is called the *Preserver*, but the actions ascribed to him under this character are referred to other forms and names. The shalgramŭ, a stone, is a form of Vishnoo. During four months of the year, all the forms of this god are laid to sleep. From the agreement of this fact with what is said of Horus, Mr. Paterson gathers a resemblance betwixt Vishnoo and Horus, and supposes that the Hindoos derived their system from the Egyptian: he conjectures, also, that the fable of Vishnoo's lying down to sleep, turning to one side, and rising, refer to the increase, the greatest rise, and the retiring of the waters of the Ganges, the Indian Nile. The state of the river in these four months agrees with this supposition, though the bramhŭns I consulted were not aware that this ceremony had any connection with the Ganges. Vishnoo is sometimes called the household god.

3. *Shivŭ* is a white man with five faces and four arms, riding on a bull. In one hand he holds an axe, as the destroyer of the wicked; in another a deer,

[q] Raja-Ramŭ, a learned Shikh, employed as a translator in the Serampore printing-office, says, that about forty years ago, not less than 10,000 persons, and, about twenty years ago, 4 or 5,000 perished in these contests at Hŭree-dwarŭ. Another proof, added to that respecting the Bouddhŭs, that the Hindoo is not free from the fiercest spirit of persecution.

alluding to a sacrifice, when the deer, fleeing from the sacrificial knife, took refuge with Shivŭ; with another hand he is bestowing a blessing, and with the last forbidding fear. Four of his faces are designed to point out the sixty-four tŭntrŭs, and the other a different tŭntrŭ. The bull is a form of Vishnoo, as the personification of religion; its four feet are, religious austerities, purity, compassion, and truth. In some particulars, this god strongly reminds us of Vulcan and Bacchus. The few Hindoos in Bengal who adopt Shivŭ as their guardian deity, are called soivyŭs. Except those of the lingŭ and Pŭnchanŭnŭ, very few temples exist in honour of any other form of Shivŭ: and none of his form riding on a bull. Before the lingŭ, Shivŭ is however daily worshipped under eight separate names, answering to the sun, moon, wind, fire, water, earth, air, and an officiating priest at a sacrifice. Mr. Paterson thinks, that there were once fierce contentions amongst the four principal sects, and that as the Soivyŭs first prevailed against the worshippers of Brŭmha, so, in its turn, this sect was subdued by the followers of Vishnoo and of the female deities. The filthy appearance of Shivŭ as a mendicant covered with ashes, and his quarrels with Doorga, his wife, have given rise to several ludicrous stories found in the pooranŭs. This marriage excited the same surprise as that betwixt Venus and Vulcan, and seems an unaccountable event, unless it was intended to illustrate the gross idea of the Tŭntrŭ writers respecting the origin of the universe Shivŭ has three eyes like Jupiter, wears a tiger's skin like Bacchus, and like him wandered about when on earth as a bloated mendicant, accompanied by satyrs. Bacchus wore a deer's skin; and Shivŭ is represented as holding a deer in his hand. The worship of the lingŭ, also, strongly resembles the worship of the Phallus in honour of Bacchus. The sŭnyasēē festival in honour of Shivŭ (see p. 12-16) appears to resemble much the orgies of Bacchus, especially in the behaviour of the devotees,[r] who are said to have run up and down the streets with their hair disheveled, and with lighted torches in their hands. In the months Voishakhŭ and Kartikŭ, the lingŭ is worshipped daily in the numerous temples dedicated to this abomination throughout Bengal. It is difficult to restrain one's indignation at the shocking violation of every thing decent in this image; nor can it be ground of wonder, that a chaste woman, faithful to her husband, is scarcely to be found among all the millions of Hindoos, when their very temples are polluted with filthy images, and their acts of worship tend to inflame the mind with licentious ideas.[s] Another form of Shivŭ is that of *Kalŭ-Bhoirŭvŭ*, in which form he

[r] A most singular coincidence appears to exist here betwixt the Hindoo and the Roman ceremonies.—These sŭnyasēēs, though taken from the lowest order, wear the poita as bramhŭns during this festival. Kennett, in his Roman Antiquities, book v. p. 305, says, respecting the shows after a funeral, 'Though the exhibitors of these shows were private persons, yet during the time of the celebration, they were considered as of the highest rank and quality, having the honour to wear the Prætexta.'

[s] I am credibly informed, that a Hindoo, once on a visit at a temple near Serampore, asked the officiating bramhŭn to give him a proof that the idol was able to con-

cut off Brŭmha's head, which is seen in one of his hands. A sect of mendicants, called yogŭbhogŭ-vadēēs, who wear a large stone inserted through an incision in each ear, live at the temples of this god, and are sometimes seen, with a prostitute in one hand, a pan of hot coals in the other, with each of which (the representatives of pleasure and pain) they profess to be equally pleased. Another form of this god is that of *Mŭha-Kalŭ*, in which he appears as the *destroyer*. 'Mŭha-kalŭ, as represented in the caverns of Elephanta,' says Mr. Paterson, 'has eight arms; in one hand he holds a human figure; in another, a sword or sacrificial axe; in a third, a basin of blood; and with a fourth he rings over it the sacrificial bell: two other arms are broken off, but with the two remaining he is drawing behind him a veil, which extinguishes the sun, and involves the whole universe in one undistinguished ruin. In the hieroglyphic of the Mŭha Prŭlŭyŭ, (or grand consummation of all things,) Shivŭ is represented as trodden under foot by Mŭha Kalēē,[t] or Eternity. He is there deprived of his crescent, trident, and necklaces, to show that his dominion and powers are no more; and is blowing the tremendous horn, which announces the annihilation of all created things.'

4. *Indrŭ*. This is the king of heaven, and the infamous violator of the wife of his religious guide: he is painted as a yellow man, sitting on an elephant, with a thunder-bolt in one hand, and a club in the other; and, like Argus, is full of eyes. All the attributes of his image are only the signs of his office as a king. He has one annual festival, and is very famous in the pooranŭs for the number of wars and intrigues in which he has been engaged. His throne changes masters at the end of seventy-one yoogŭs of the gods. Jupiter was called the king of heaven, and the Fulminator: Indrŭ's names, Divŭs-pŭtee and Vŭjrēē, are significant of similar offices.

5. *Yŭmŭ*, the Indian Pluto, is a dark-green man, clothed in red, with inflamed eyes; he sits on a buffalo, has a crown on his head, and holds in his right hand a club with which he drives out the soul from the body, and punishes the wicked. This is his form of terror, as king of the souls of the dead; but he is also worshipped in a form less terrific, which he is said to assume when he passes a sentence of happiness on the meritorious. Beside his annual festival, he is worshipped on other occasions; and receives the homage of the Hindoos in their daily ablutions. There are several remarkable coincidences between Yŭmŭ and Pluto, as will be seen by comparing the fables respecting the latter and those in page 48 of this work: the images of

verse with him. The bramhŭn entered the temple, shutting the door after him, and the visitor, astonished at immediately hearing voices, interrogated the priest respecting it, who solemnly affirmed from within, that it was Jŭgŭnnat'hŭ who was speaking; —but the visitor, determined to ascertain so interesting a fact, forced open the temple door, and—whom should he see, inquisitive reader, but the mistress of the officiating bramhŭn?

[t] This is the famous image worshipped at Kalēē-Ghatŭ, near Calcutta.

both 'Grin horribly a ghastly smile.' Pluto had a rod in his hand; Yŭmŭ is called Dŭndŭ-dhŭrŭ, because he holds in his hand the rod of punishment. Yŭmŭ is the shraddhŭ dévŭ, or the regent of funeral rites; and the institution of funeral obsequies is ascribed to Pluto. The dead, in going to Yŭmŭ's judgment-hall, cross Voitŭrŭnēē, the Indian styx;[a] the waters of which, like those of Phlegethon, the fourth river of hell which the dead were obliged to cross, are said to be boiling hot. Yŭmŭ has several assistants, like Minos, who keep a register of human actions. There is something in the story inserted in page 51, which seems to coincide with Pluto's being obliged to steal his wife Proserpine, because he could obtain no other goddess, his visage being so horrible and his habitation so gloomy. The Hindoos consider hell as situated at the southern extremity of the earth; the Greeks and Romans thought it was a large subterraneous spot in the earth.

6. *Gŭnéshŭ.* A fat short red man, with four arms and an elephant's head, sitting on a rat. His corpulency is a type of Brŭmha, as the aggregate of all things. In one hand he holds a bell, which is the pattern of a temple, and also points out that this god banishes fear; in another he holds a serpent-weapon, to show that he throws impediments in the way of the wicked; another grasps the hook by which elephants are guided, which points out that he guides the mind; and with the other he forbids fear. His elephant's head is a sign of the mystical sound *Om*, and the trunk is the type of the instrument with which clarified butter is poured on the fire at a sacrifice. The author of the Roodrŭ-yamŭlŭ, from whom this is extracted, assigns no reason for Gŭnéshŭ's riding on a rat. Though he has been compared to Janus, I find but two instances of coincidence betwixt them: every act of worship (pōōja) is preceded by an invocation to Gŭnéshŭ;[x] and men in business paint his image over the doors of their shops, or suspend it amongst their merchandize, to insure prosperity. Gŭnéshŭ has been complimented as the god of wisdom; but the Hindoo deity presiding over knowledge, or wisdom, is Sŭrŭswŭtēē, a goddess. Gŭnéshŭ receives many honours from the Hindoos, and is considered as bountiful in bestowing wisdom and other favours, though there are no temples erected to his honour in Bengal. Those who adopt him as their guardian deity, are called Ganŭpŭtyŭs.

7. *Kartikéyŭ* is the Indian Mars, or commander-in-chief to the gods. He has in some images one, and in others six faces; is of a yellow colour; and rides on the peacock, an incarnation of Indrŭ. In one hand he holds a bow, and in the other an arrow. He is worshipped as the giver of bodily strength.

8. *Sōōryŭ*, (the sun.) I do not find the least resemblance betwixt this Hindoo deity and Sol, either in their images or history. The Hindoos, in

[a] This river encircled the infernal regions nine times: Voitŭrŭnēē encircles this hall six times.

[x] 'In the Roman sacrifices, the priest always mentioned first the name of Janus.' *Kennett*, p. 85.

a most indelicate fable respecting this god, have described the twelve signs of the zodiac. Yŭmŭ, the regent of death, is his son; and Chaya, *a shadow*, the name of one of his wives.[y] The image of Sōōryŭ is that of a dark-red man, from whose body issue a thousand streams of light: he has three eyes, and four arms; in each of two of his hands he holds a water-lily, with another he is bestowing a blessing, and with the last forbidding fear. He sits on a red lotus, in a chariot drawn by seven horses. He is painted red, to show that his glory is like flame; his three eyes represent the day, evening, and night; and his four arms indicate, that in him are united prŭkritee and poorooshŭ, or matter and spirit. One lotus explains the nature of emancipation, *(see Vishnoo;)* and the other, upon which the rays of Sōōryŭ are reflected, is a type of sound, which some Hindoo philosophers believe to be eternal. The red lotus represents the earth; his chariot, the measures of time; and the seven horses, the seven poetical measures of the védŭs. The image of this god is never made, but the sun itself is worshipped daily; the shalgramŭ is also his constant representative in the bramhinical worship. The disciples of this god are called Sourŭs.

9. *Ugnee*, the regent of fire, is represented as a corpulent man, riding on a goat, with copper-coloured eye-brows, beard, hair, aud eyes; his belly is the colour of the dawn; he holds a spear in his right hand, and a bead-roll in his left; from his body issue a thousand streams of glory, and he has seven flaming tongues. His corpulency points out, that he grants the desires of his worshippers; the colour of his eye-brows, &c. represents the flame of the burnt-offering when it ascends of a copper-colour, at which time he who desires secular blessings offers his clarified butter; but he who desires emancipation, pours his offering on the fire when its colour is like that of the dawn. The goat teaches, that Ugnee devours all things; his spear, that he is almighty; and his bead-roll, that he is propitious. The rays of glory are to encourage the worshipper to expect that he shall obtain the greatest blessings from this god. Ugnee has neither temples nor images consecrated to him, but has a service in the daily ceremonies of the bramhŭns; and one class of his worshippers, called sagnikŭ bramhŭns preserve a perpetual fire like the vestal virgins.[z] He presides over sacrifices, and is called the mouth of the gods.

10. *Pŭvŭnŭ*, the god of the winds, and the messenger of the gods, is represented as a white man, sitting on a deer, holding in his right hand the hook used by the driver of an elephant. He is painted white, to shew that he

[y] The pooranŭs contain a fable respecting Sōōryŭ and his wife, which almost literally corresponds with the filthy story of Neptune and Ceres, when the latter turned herself into a mare.

[z] There seems to be no order of females among the Hindoos resembling these virgins; but many Hindoo women, at the total wane of the moon, to fulfil a vow, watch for twenty-four hours over a lamp made with clarified butter, and prevent its being extinguished till the time for the appearance of the new moon.

preserves life. The deer represents the swiftness of his flight; the elephant driver's hook explains his power over the body. He is worshipped daily, but has neither separate festival, image, nor temple. I can find little or no resemblance betwixt this god and Mercury.

11. *Vŭroonŭ*, the Indian Neptune, is a white man, sitting on a sea animal, having a serpent-weapon in his right hand. He is painted white, to shew that he satisfies the living; and he wields a terrific weapon, to point out, that he is approached with fear by the worshipper. His name is repeated in the daily worship of the bramhŭns, but he has neither public festival nor temple.

12. *Sŭmoodrŭ*, the sea, is worshipped by the Hindoos when they visit the sea, as well as at the different festivals, and on the sixth day after the birth of a child.

13. *Prit'hivēē*, the earth, is worshipped daily by the Hindoos. She is a form of Bhŭgŭvŭtēē, and may be called the Indian Ceres. The Hindoos have divided the earth into ten parts, and assigned a deity to each. These are, Indrŭ, Ugnee, Yŭmŭ, Noiritŭ, Vŭroonŭ, Vayoo, Koovérŭ, Eeshŭ, Brŭmha, and Unŭntŭ.

14. *The heavenly bodies.* It is a remarkable fact, that almost all heathen nations have fallen into the worship of the heavenly bodies. Perhaps the evident influence which the sun and moon have over the seasons and the vegetable kingdom, might, in the primeval ages, lead men to make them objects of worship: after the introduction of judicial astrology, this species of idolatry becomes less surprising. Whatever may be the antiquity of the védŭs, it is very plain, that the worship of the sun, moon, and other planets is there inculcated: many of the forms of praise and petition in those books, are addressed to the heavenly bodies; and to this day the worship of all the planets in one service, and of different planets on separate occasions, has place among the Hindoos.

Rŭvee,[a] *the sun.* See the article Sōōryu. *Somŭ,*[b] *the moon.* We do not perceive the least agreement betwixt this god and Diana. The Hindoo feasts are regulated by the revolutions of the moon, but Somŭ is not greatly honoured in the Hindoo mythology, being esteemed a malignant planet, as is also *Mŭngŭlŭ,*[c] *or Mars.* *Booddhŭ,*[d] *or Mercury,* is a fortunate planet; and so is *Vrihŭspŭtee,*[e] *or Jupiter,* who is the preceptor of the gods. *Shookrŭ,*[f] *or Venus,* preceptor to the giants, is also a fortunate planet. This god is represented as blind of one eye. *Shŭnee,*[g] *or Saturn,* the son of Sōōryŭ, an evil planet. *Rahoo* and *Kétoo, the ascending and descending nodes.* The

[a] From this god the first day of the week is named Rŭvee-varŭ, as Sunday derives its name from the Sun: day and varŭ are synonymous.

[b] Hence Somŭ-varŭ, Monday.

[c] Mŭngŭlŭ-varŭ, Tuesday.

[d] Booddh-varŭ, Wednesday.

[e] Vrihŭspŭtee-varŭ, Thursday.

[f] Shookrŭ-varŭ, Friday.

[g] Shŭnee-varŭ, Saturday.

planets are not honoured with temples, images, or festivals in Bengal. When hope or fear, respecting their benign or malignant influence, is excited in the mind of a Hindoo, he is drawn or driven to worship them.

15. *Doorga*. The image of this goddess and that of Minerva, in one or two instances, exhibit a pretty strong resemblance: both are described as fond of arms; and it is remarkable, that Doorga derives her name from the giant Doorgŭ, whom she slew, as Pallas (Minerva) obtained hers from the giant Pallas, whom she destroyed. She resembles Minerva also as a goddess difficult of access, which is one signification of the name Doorga. Sir W. Jones says, 'As the mountain-born goddess, or Parvŭtēē, she has many properties of the Olympian Juno: her majestic deportment, high spirit, and general attributes are the same; and we find her both on Mount Koilasŭ, and at the banquets of the deities, uniformly the companion of her husband. One circumstance in the parallel is extremely singular: she is usually attended by her son Kartikéyu, who rides on a peacock; and in some drawings, his own robe seems to be spangled with eyes: to which must be added that, in some of her temples, a peacock, without a rider, stands near her image.' The image of Doorga is that of a yellow female with ten arms, sitting on a lion. The weapons she wields, the trident, the scimitar, the discus, the arrow, the spear, the club, the bow, the serpent-weapon, the hook for guiding an elephant, and the axe, are to point out, that with these ten arms and weapons she protects the ten points. She has one foot on Mŭhéshŭ, a giant, to shew that she subdues the enemies of her worshippers; and she sits on a lion, a form of Vishnoo, as the giver of success to her worshippers, and as exciting fear in their enemies. The quarrels of this goddess with Shivu, her husband, strongly remind us of those betwixt Jupiter and Juno, arising from the jealousy of the latter. The festivals in honour of Doorga and of Krishnŭ draw the whole Hindoo population to the temples, while those in honour of other gods are comparatively neglected. Before the temples of this goddess, thousands of victims are annually slaughtered, and offered to her image. She is not merely honoured as Doorga, but, under other names, distinct temples, images, festivals, and ceremonies have been instituted. Doorga, as has been already observed, is also the representative of matter in the creation of the universe, and in this character she is called Prŭkritee.[h] Her wars with the giants also add to her fame, and make her extremely popular among the Hindoos: she is adopted by many, who take the name of *shaktŭs*,[i] as their guardian deity. In Bengal, the greater number of bramhuns are shaktŭs: in the western and southern provinces this sect tis less numerous.

16. *Kalee*, the Indian Diana Taurica. Though this is another form of Doorga, her fame is so great, that it seems necessary to devote a few lines exclusive to her. The dark image of this goddess is a truly horrid figure: her hair is disheveled; her tongue hangs out; she holds in one hand a scimitar, in another a giant's scull, with another she forbids fear, and with the last is

[h] Literally, the chief, or nature. [i] Shaktŭ, means energy.

bestowing a blessing. Her colour is that by which time is designated, and she stands upon her husband, the destroyer, to keep him in subjection till the time of the universal conflagration, when, with the eye in the centre of his forehead, he will burn the universe. Her four arms represent the four védŭs ; the two inspiring terror point out those portions of the védŭ which relate to the destruction of enemies and the government of the world, and the other two allude to those parts of the védŭ which belong to devotion. Her disheveled hair represents the clouds, and intimates too that time has neither beginning nor end. Her tongue is the representative of lightning. She exhibits altogether the appearance of a drunken frantic fury. Yet this is the goddess whom thousands adore, on whose altars thousands of victims annually bleed, and whose temple at Kalēē-ghatŭ, near Calcutta, is the resort of Hindoos from all parts of India. This temple, it is said, frequently receives presents from persons of the highest rank, and not unfrequently from persons called Christians. There are two things respecting Kalēē which remind us of Laverna . she is the protectress of thieves, and her image at Kalēē-ghatŭ is a head without a body. Another form of this goddess, under the name of Siddhéshwŭrēē, is to be seen in clay temples all over Bengal. Human victims, it is said, have often been immolated on the altars of Kalēē and Siddhéshwŭrēē.

17. *Lŭkshmēē*, the goddess of fortune, is the wife of Vishnoo : she is said to have been produced at the churning of the sea, as Venus was said to be born of the froth of the sea. At her birth, all the gods were enamoured of her. She is painted yellow, with a water-lily in her right hand ; (in which form she is worshipped frequently by Hindoo women ;) but no bloody sacrifices are offered to her. The Hindoos avoid all payments of money on the Thursday, (Lŭkshmēē-varŭ,) from the fear of offending this goddess.

18. *Sŭrŭswŭtēē*, the goddess of learning, another wife of Vishnoo. She is painted white, and stands on the water lily. In some images she is seen holding a lute ; and in others as possessed of three eyes, with a fan in one hand and a book in the other. Her colour is to point out, that she is the source of wisdom ; the lute reminds the worshipper that she is the author of melody ; her three eyes represent the three védŭs ; the book and pen obviously belong to her character as the goddess of learning. I find no goddess in the Roman or Grecian pantheon who resembles her. She has an annual festival, when clay images are set up, and worshipped all over Bengal. Some of her worshippers, on the last day of the festival, dance naked before the procession of the image through the streets. Even prostitutes, at this festival, make an image of this goddess, and set it up near their houses, to draw the spectators to their brothels. On this day students, merchants, and others, refuse to touch a pen ; for the Hindoos ascribe their ability to read, write, and even to speak, to the favour of Sŭrŭswŭtēē.

19. *Shēētŭla*, the goddess who cools the body when afflicted with the small-pox, receives many honours from the lower orders of Hindoos, among

whom the ravages of the small-pox are often dreadful. This goddess is also worshipped to procure the removal of cutaneous diseases.

20. *Mŭnŭsa*, the queen of the snakes, or she who protects men from their fatal bite. The lower orders crowd to the three annual festivals held in honour of this goddess.

21. *Susht'hēē*, the goddess of fecundity. She is honoured with six annual festivals, celebrated chiefly by females. Her image is that of a yellow woman, sitting on a cat, and nursing a child; though, in general, a rough stone, painted on the top, and placed under a tree, is the object worshipped.

These may be considered as the *celestial deities* worshipped by the Hindoos. The *terrestrial goddesses* are, Sēēta, the wife of Ramŭ;[k] Radha, the mistress of Krishnŭ; Rookminēē and Sŭtyŭ-bhama, the wives of Krishnŭ; and Soobhŭdra, the sister of Jŭgŭnnat'hŭ.[l] The *terrestrial gods* are the following:—

1. *Krishnŭ* resembles Appollo in his licentious intrigues; in his being a herdsman,[m] and an archer; in his destroying a dreadful serpent; in his love of music; and in the celebrity to which he attained. Krishnŭ's image is that of a black man, with a flute in his hand. His colour points out, that he fills the mind with sensual desires, and the flute designates him as the author of musical sounds. Apollo had in one hand a harp, and in the other a shield of arrows. The history of Krishnŭ is chiefly found in the Shree-Bhagŭvŭtŭ; the outline of which will be seen in p. 119, &c. Several festivals in honour of this god are held annually, at which times the greatest licentiousness prevails among all ranks. A great proportion of the Hindoo population in Bengal are devoted to Krishnŭ.[n] His intrigues with the milk maids, and especially with Radha, his favourite mistress, are familiar to every Hindoo, being incorporated into their popular songs, and the image of Radha being placed by that of Krishnŭ in many of the temples. Under several other names Krishnŭ is worshipped, to which forms separate temples have been erected; among the rest to Gopalŭ, the herdsman; to Valŭ-gopalŭ, the

[k] This goddess, it is said, was dug out of the ground by king Jŭnŭkŭ, when he was ploughing his field. A boy who was ploughed up out of the ground among the Tuscans, gave rise to the order of Roman priests, whose business it was to divine from appearances in the annual sacrifice.

[l] It does not appear that Jŭgŭnnat'hŭ was ever married.

[m] The pooranŭs contain a story of this god much resembling that of Mercury's stealing a cow from Apollo. In the Hindoo fable, Brŭmha is the thief.

[n] Sometimes Hindoos are seen licking up the very dust of the place where the crowd are celebrating the praises of Krishnŭ; and others are said to faint with joy on these occasions. In memory of Krishnŭ's lewd conduct with the milk-maids in the forest of Vrindavŭnŭ, persons of property sometimes spend a day in the fields, and entertain their friends.

infant Gopalŭ, to Gopēē-nat'hŭ, the lord of the milk-maids. Krishnŭ is one of the ten incarnations of Vishnoo. The Rev. Mr. Maurice calls him 'the amiable Krishnŭ!'

2. *Jŭgŭnnat'hŭ*, another deified hero, complimented with the title of lord of the world, a form of Vishnoo. He is honoured with several annual festivals, but the car festival is the most popular. Imitations of his ponderous car abound in many of the large towns in Bengal[o]: that in Orissa, connected with the ancient temple erected in honour of this god, has crushed to death hundreds of victims, perhaps thousands, and immolates a number every year. This god receives the homage of pilgrims from all parts of India, for whose accommodation roads have been cut, and lodging-houses erected. Such, however, is the great mortality among the pilgrims, that a Hindoo of property always makes his will before he sets out on this journey, and takes a most affecting farewell of his disconsolate relations. Southey's description,[p] 'in his Curse of Kehama,' though not literally correct, conveys to the mind much of the horror which a Christian spectator of the procession of the car cannot but feel. Mr. Paterson finds in the images of this god, and his brother and sister, which are worshipped together, an hieroglyphic of the mystical word *Om*.

[o] Krishnŭ-vŭsoo gave to the temple of Jŭgŭnnat'hŭ, near Serampore, an immense car, which could not cost less than four or five thousand rupees. He also added an allowance of six rupees a day for the expenses of the worship of this idol. Gourŭ-mŭlikŭ, a goldsmith of Calcutta, who gave the interest of his mother's weight in gold to different temples, added six rupees more to the daily offerings at this temple; but these two benefactors, perceiving that the bramhŭns of the temple, instead of expending these sums in offerings to the god, and in alms to strangers, applied the greater part to their private use, reduced the six rupees to one rupee four annas a day. To extort more money from the donors, the bramhŭns of this temple, at two succeeding festivals, prevented the car from proceeding to an adjoining temple in which the donors were interested, pretending that the god was angry with them for their parsimony and would not go

[p] 'A thousand pilgrims strain,
Arm, shoulder, breast, and thigh, and might and main,
To drag that sacred wain,
And scarce can draw along the enormous load.
Prone fall the frantic votaries in its road,
And, calling on the god,
Their self-devoted bodies there they lay
To pave his chariot way;
On Jŭgŭnnat'h they call,
The ponderous car rolls on, and crushes all.
Through blood and bones it ploughs its dreadful path;
Groans rise unheard; the dying cry,
And death and agony
Are trodden under foot by yon mad throng,
Who follow close, and thrust the deadly wheels along.'

3. *Ramŭ*, a deified monarch, and the hero of the Ramayŭnŭ, comes in for a considerable share of the wretched devotion of the Hindoos, especially in the western provinces. His history, found in Valmēēkee's epic poem, is partly before the public. He is adored as the seventh Hindoo incarnation; has an annual festival, and is daily worshipped in the temples dedicated to him, his brother, and his friend Hŭnoomanŭ; in which temples he appears as a green man, with a bow and arrows in his hands, sitting on a throne, having Sēēta on his left: his brother Lukshmŭnŭ holds a white umbrella over his head, and Hŭnoomanŭ stands before him as his servant with joined hands. He is considered as a beneficent deity. Some think that Ramŭ was deified on account of a successful attack on Ceylon, when he was king of Mut'hoora.

4. *Choitŭnyŭ*, i. e. the wise, a form of Krishnŭ; the god of a sect of voiragēēs, whose leader was a religious mendicant. His most famous temple in Bengal is at Ugrŭ-dwēēpŭ, where an annual festival is held, and to which crowds resort from all parts of Bengal. The bramhŭns despise this sect.

5. *Vishwŭ-kŭrmŭ*, the son of Brŭmha, as architect of the gods, may be regarded as the Hindoo Vulcan. He is worshipped at an annual festival, the implements of each artificer being the representative of the god. He employs no Cyclops with one eye, but has a workman named Mayŭ, a giant, who is capable of exhibiting all manner of illusive edifices.

6. *Kamŭdevŭ*, the Indian Cupid. This god is also said to be the sun of Brŭmha: he is painted as a beautiful youth, carrying a bow and arrow of flowers. He has an annual festival, but his image is not made; nor does this festival command much celebrity. Petitions are addressed to him by the bride and bride-groom anxious for offspring.

7. *Sŭtyŭ Narayŭnŭ*. I have not discovered the origin of this idol: the name implies that he is the true Vishnoo. He is worshipped frequently in the houses of the rich, from the desire of insuring prosperity.

8. *Pŭnchanŭnŭ*, a form of Shivŭ, worshipped by the lower orders, who consider him as the destroyer of children. The image used as his representative is a mis-shapen stone, anointed, painted, and placed under the vŭtŭ and other trees.

9. *Dhŭrmŭ-t'hakoorŭ*, another form of Shivŭ, held in much the same estimation as Pŭnchanŭnŭ.

10. *Kaloo-rayŭ*, the god of forests, another form of Shivŭ. He is painted as sitting on a tiger, and carrying a bow and arrows: is worshipped by the wood-cutters in the forests, to insure protection from wild beasts.

11. *Deified Beings in strange shapes.—Urdhŭ-narēēshwŭrŭ.* This compound deity is Shivŭ and Doorga united in one body. The fable respecting this singular transformation will be found in p. 147. Religious worship is paid to this idol.—*Krishnŭ-Kalēē.* In this image of Krishnŭ and Kalēē united in one body, vice itself is personified and worshipped. See p.

148.—*Huree-Huru.* Another compound deity, Vishnoo and Shivŭ. The worship paid to these idols appears to owe its origin to stories in the pooranŭs; but the original idea, meant to be conveyed by two of them, no doubt, was, that the Great Spirit and matter are one.

12. *The worship of Human Beings.* The Hindoos worship their spiritual guides; also bramhŭns, and their wives and daughters: and, among the vamacharēēs, women of the lowest caste, and even prostitutes, are worshipped with rites too abominable to be recorded. See p. 152.

13. *The worship of Beasts.* The *cow*, as a form of Bhŭgŭvŭtēē, is an object of worship, and receives the homage of the Hindoos at an annual festival:[q] (see p. 154.) *Hŭnoomanŭ*, the *monkey*, has also been placed among the gods, as a form of Shivŭ. Temples to this god are to be seen, and in some places his image is worshipped, daily; he is even chosen by many as their guardian deity. Hŭnoomanŭ bears some resemblance to Pan, and like him owes his birth to the god of the winds. The dog, the *jackal*, and a number of other animals, have also places among the Hindoo deities, though they are not greatly honoured.

14. *Worship of Birds.* Gŭroorŭ, the carrier of Vishnoo, half a bird and half a man, has received deification, as well as his brother Uroonŭ, the charioteer of Vishnoo. Jŭtayoo, another bird, the friend of Ramŭ, receives divine honours; as do the eagle of Coromandel, (said to be an incarnation of Doorga,) the wag-tail, the peacock, the goose, and the owl; but the honours they receive are not of the highest kind.

15. *Worship of Trees.* The Hindoos do not seem ever to have consecrated groves, but several trees they esteem sacred. Toolŭsēē, a female raised to deity by Vishnoo, was cursed by Lŭkshmēē, his wife, in a fit of jealousy, and turned into the tree of this name; which the Hindoos preserve with great care near their houses, erect pillars to its honour,[r] esteem its leaves and wood sacred, and with the latter make the beads with which they repeat the names of their guardian deities. Several other trees receive almost an equal homage: (see p. 162.) It is considered as a great sin among the Hindoos for any member of a family to cut down trees planted by an ancestor, and the misfortunes of many a family have been ascribed to such an act of indiscretion.

[q] The very dung of the cow is eaten as an atonement for sin, and, with its urine, is used in worship. A Hindoo does not carry any thing out of his house in the morning, till he has rubbed his door-way with cow-dung. Notwithstanding this reverence, the bullocks employed in carrying burdens and at the plough, are used more cruelly by the Hindoos than any other animals. 'The Athenians and almost all other nations thought it a very great crime to kill the ox, insomuch that the offender was thought to deserve death.' *Potter's Antiquities of Greece*, vol. i. p. 217.

[r] The heads of these pillars, which commonly open like a cup, are filled with earth, and the plant is placed in them. 'The Romans and Grecians,' says Potter 'consecrated certain trees to their gods.'

16. *River worship.* The Hindoos not only reverence their rivers, but actually worship them, dividing them into male and female deities. But Gŭnga, (the Ganges,) both in their poems, their pooranŭs, and in the superstitious customs of the natives, appears to rank highest among the river deities. She is declared to have descended from Vishnoo's heaven, the anniversary of which event is celebrated by particular festivities. The most extravagant things are related in the pooranŭs respecting the purifying nature of these waters; and several works have been written to extol the saving properties of the Ganges.[s] Its waters are carried to immense distances; every thing they touch becomes purified; crowds of Hindoos perform their worship on the banks of the river daily, after purifying themselves in its stream; the sick are laid on its banks, expecting recovery from the mere sight of this goddess; and it is reckoned a great calamity not to die within view of Gŭnga. Many other rivers receive the honours of divine worship, as will be seen in page 171.

17. *Worship of Fish.* Even the finny tribes are honoured by the Hindoos, though the worship paid to them is of an inferior nature.

18. *The worship of Books* is very common among this people. The lower orders have such a profound respect for a book, that they think every thing in such a form must be divine. On several occasions a book is converted into an image, and worshipped with all the forms used before the most popular idol.

19. *Worship of Stones.* The shalŭgramŭ, as a form of Vishnoo, is more frequently worshipped than any other idol in India,[t] not excepting the lingŭ itself; which perhaps ought to be placed next, and which is also a stone. The representatives of Pŭnchanŭnŭ and other gods are shapeless stones. Many images of idols sold in the markets are made of stone, and worshipped.

20. *A log of wood.* The pedal with which rice is cleansed from the husk has also been raised to godship by the Hindoos. See p. 176.

Such are the objects adored by the Hindoos. Such is the deplorable state into which the mind continues to sink, after it has once renounced the doctrine of the UNITY OF GOD. Divine Worship is confessedly the highest act of reverence and homage of which man is capable. How shocking then, how

[s] The Gŭnga-vakya-vŭlēē, &c.

[t] 'The shalŭgramŭs are black stones, found in a part of the Gŭndŭkēē river, within the limits of Nepal. They are mostly round, and are commonly perforated in one or more places by worms, or, as the Hindoos believe, by Vishnoo in the shape of a reptile. According to the number of perforations, and of spiral curves in each, the stone is supposed to contain Vishnoo in various characters. For example, such a stone perforated in one place only, with four spiral curves in the perforation, and with marks resembling a cow's foot, and a long wreath of flowers, contains Lŭkshmēē-Narayŭnŭ. In like manner stones are found in the Nŭrmŭda, which are considered as types of Shivŭ, and are called Vanŭ-Lingŭ. The shalŭgramŭ is found, upon trial, not to be calcareous: it strikes fire with steel, and scarcely at all effervesces with acids.' *Asiatic Researches*, vol vii. p. 240.

afflicting to a philanthropic mind, to see man prostrated before a beast, or a log of wood! How greatly is the horror increased, when this prostration of intellect respects many millions!

I have repeatedly conversed with learned Hindoos on the use of idols in worship: the best account I have ever received may amount to this.—God is every where; this is allowed, but his spirituality perplexes the mind. To collect and fix the ideas on the object of adoration, therefore, an image is chosen; into which image, by the power of incantations, the deity is imagined to be drawn. Hence, in dedicating an image, they call upon the god to come and dwell in it. I have urged in reply, that if this were the whole end to be answered, any image might do,[u] but that I saw amongst them many sorts of idols. To this the bramhŭn says, 'God has made himself known in these forms, and directed these various images to be made, that men may be fascinated and drawn to the love of worship; that none of these images are intended to exhibit the natural perfections of God, but his actions when incarnate; and that images are only necessary while men continue in a rude state, and may be laid aside by those who can attain to devotion by means of rational speculation.' This is the best apology I have obtained for the worship of idols. Yet, surely, instead of elevating the mind, and carrying it to a Being so glorious as God, images debase a subject so sublime, and destroy all reverence for Him, who is 'glorious in holiness, fearful in praises, doing wonders.' Images of God are therefore highly offensive, and their makers and worshippers justly expose themselves to the cutting reproof of Isaiah: 'To whom then will ye liken God? or what likeness will ye compare to him? Behold, the nations are as drop of a bucket, and are counted as the small dust of the balance: all nations before him are as nothing, and are counted to him less than nothing, and vanity.' But that idols are not necessary, even to the rude and ignorant, let the experience of every protestant country bear witness. Where shall we find piety more elevated, or morals more correct, even among individual in the lowest orders of society, than in our own land?

But what shall we say, when many of these idols are monstrous personifications of vice; and when it is a fact, that not a single virtuous idea is ever communicated by any of them? The image of Kalēē exhibits a female with inflamed eyes, standing on the body of her husband, her hair disheveled, slavering the blood of her enemies down her bosom, her tongue hanging from her mouth, wearing a necklace of skulls, and holding a skull in the left hand, and a sword in the right. Another image, that of Krishnŭ Kalēē, exhibits Krishnŭ and Radha, his mistress, united in one body, to conceal Radha's infidelity from her husband. Another image is the lingŭ! Another that of a monkey, an incarnation of 'the great god' Shivŭ; the offspring of the god of the winds by a female monkey![x] The image of Doorga is that of a female warrior: and

[u] They admit this: a pan of water is indeed often substituted for an idol.

[x] Pan is said to have been the son of Mercury.

one form of this goddess is that of a female so athirst for blood, that she is represented as cutting off her own head; and the severed head, with the mouth distended, is seen devouring the blood streaming from the trunk. This goddess stands upon two other deities in an attitude so abominably indecent that it cannot be described: the common form of Kalēē, standing on her husband Shivŭ, has secret meaning, well known to a Hindoo, but which is so indelicate that even they, licentious as they are, dare not make it according to the genuine meaning of the fable to which it belongs.[y] Some of the formulas used at the festival in honour of this goddess, called the Shyama-pōōja, relate to things which can never become the subject of description; but perhaps in this concealed state they are more pernicious than if painted, and exhibited to the open gaze of the mob. To this it may be added, that amidst all the numerous idols worshipped by the Hindoos, there is not one to represent any of the *Virtues*. In this respect, the Hindoo mythology sinks far below the European; for the Greeks and Romans adored Virtue, Truth, Piety, Chastity, Clemency, Mercy, Justice, Faith, Hope and Liberty, and consecrated images and temples to these deities. Among the Hindoos, the most innocent part of the system, and that which existed in the purest ages, was the worship of the primary elements, the adoration of inanimate matter!

The manifest effect of idolatry in this country, as held up to thousands of Christian spectators, is an immersion into the grossest moral darkness, and a universal corruption of manners. The Hindoo is taught, that the image is really God, and the heaviest judgments are denounced against him, if he dare to suspect that the image is nothing more than the elements of which it is composed. The Tŭntră-sarŭ declares, that such an unbeliever will sink into the regions of torment. In the apprehensions of the people in general, therefore, the idols are real deities; they occupy the place of God, and receive all the homage, all the fear, all the service, and all the honours which HE so justly claims. The government of God is subverted, and all the moral effects arising from the knowledge of his perfections, and his claims upon his rational creatures, are completely lost.

It is a fact too, that the festivals in honour of the gods have the most pernicious effects on the minds of the people. During the ceremonies of worship before the image, the spectators are very few, and these feel no interest whatever in the mummery going forward; and were it not for those who come to pay a visit of ceremony to the image, and to bring their offerings, the temple would be as little crowded on festival, as on common days: but as soon as the well-known sound of the drum is heard, calling the people to the midnight orgies, the dance and the song, whole multitudes assemble, and almost tread one upon another; and their joy keeps pace with the number of loose women present, and the broad obscenity of the songs. Gopalŭ-Tŭrkkalŭnkarŭ, a pŭndit employed in the Serampore printing office, and a very respectable man

[y] Hindoos of the baser sort may be seen whispering to each other before this image, and dilating on that which is too filthy for *them* to utter in an audible voice.

among the Hindoos, avowed to a friend of mine, that the only attractives on these occasions were the women of ill-fame, and filthy songs and dances; that these songs were so abominable, that a man of character, even amongst them, was ashamed of being present; that if ever he (Gopalŭ) remained, he concealed himself in a corner of the temple. He added, that a song was scarcely tolerated which did not contain the most marked allusions to unchastity; while those which were so abominable that no person could repeat them out of the temple, received the loudest plaudits.[z] All this is done in the very face of the idol; nor does the thought, 'Thou God seest me,' ever produce the slightest pause in these midnight revels. In open day, and in the most public streets of a large town, I have seen men entirely naked, dancing with unblushing effrontery before the idol, as it was carried in triumphant procession, encouraged by the smiles and eager gaze of the bramhŭns. Yet sights even worse than these, and such as can never be described by the pen of a Christian writer, are exhibited on the rivers and in the public roads, to thousands of spectators, at the Doorga festival,[a] the most popular and most crowded of all the Hindoo festivals in Bengal; and which closes with libations to the gods so powerful, as to produce general intoxication. What must be the state of morals in a country, when its religious institutions and public shows, at which the whole population is present, thus sanctify vice, and carry the multitude into the very gulph of depravity and ruin!

There is another feature in this system of idolatry, which increases its pernicious effects on the public manners:—The history of these gods is a highly coloured representation of their wars, quarrels, and licentious intrigues; which are held up in the images, recitations, songs, and dances at the public festivals. At the separate recitations, which are accompanied with something of our pantomime, these incredible and most indecent fables are made still more familiar to the people; so familiar indeed, that allusions to them are to be perceived in the most common forms of speech. Many works of a pernicious tendency in the European languages are not very hurtful, because they are too scarce and expensive to be read by the poor; but the authors of the Hindoo mythology have taken care, that the quarrels and revels of the gods and goddesses shall be held up to the imitation of the whole community.

In some of these histories and pantomimes, Shivŭ is represented as declaring to Lŭkshmēē, that he would part with all the merit of his works for the gratification of a criminal passion; Brŭmha as burning with lust towards his own daughter; Krishnŭ as living with the wife of another, murdering a

[z] Sometimes the Hindoos open a subscription to defray the expense of a grand act of worship in honour of some idol. If 400 rupees be subscribed on such an occasion, I am assured, that 300 will be spent on the songs and dancing-girls.

[a] The author has more than once been filled with alarm, as this idolatrous procession has passed his house, lest his children should go to the windows, and see the gross obscenity exhibited by the dancers.

washerman and stealing his clothes, and sending his friend Yoodhist'hirŭ to the regions of torment by causing him to utter a falsehood; Indrŭ and Chŭndrŭ are seen as the paramours of the wives of their spiritual guides.—But these stories are so numerous in the pooranŭs, that it seems unnecessary to drag more of them to light. The thing to be deplored is, that the Hindoo objects of worship were themselves monsters of vice.

Painful as this is, it is not all: there is a numerous and growing sect among the Hindoos in Bengal, and perhaps in other provinces, who, in conformity with the rules prescribed in the works called Tŭntrŭ, practise the most abominable rites. The proselytes to this sect are chiefly bramhŭns, and are called vamacharēēs. I have given some account of them in p. 152, and p. 232, and should have declined blotting these pages with any further allusion to these unutterable abominations, had I not omitted in those accounts an article which I had prepared, and which throws much additional light on the practices of a sect so singularly corrupt.

The rules of this sect are to be found more or less in most of the Tŭntrŭs; but particularly in the Nēēlŭ, Roodrŭ-yamŭlŭ, Yonee, and Unnŭda-kŭlpŭ. In these works the writers have arranged a number of Hindoo sects as follows:—Védacharēēs, Voishnŭvacharēēs, Shoivacharēēs, Dŭkshinacharēēs, Vamacharēēs, Siddhantacharēēs, and Koulacharēēs; each rising in succession, till the most perfect sect is the Koulacharŭ. When a Hindoo wishes to enter into this sect, he sends for a person who has been already initiated, and who is well acquainted with the forms of initiation; and presenting to him garments, ornaments, &c. begs him to become his religious guide. The teacher then places this disciple near him for three days, and instructs him in the ceremonies of the sect: at the close of which period, the disciple spreads some loose soil on the floor of the house in which the ceremonies of initiation are to be performed; and sows a small quantity of barley, and two kinds of peas, in this soil, sprinkling water upon it. He next proceeds to perform some parts of the ten ceremonies practised by the regular Hindoos from the time of birth to that of marriage: after which he makes a declaration, that he has from that period renounced all the ceremonies of the old religion, and is delivered from their yoke; and as a token of joy celebrates what is called the Vriddhee shraddhŭ. All these ceremonies are to be performed in the day; what follows is to be done in darkness: and therefore, choosing the darkest part of the night, the seed sown in the house having sprung up, the disciple and his spiritual (it would not be too harsh to say infernal) guide enter the house, with eight men, (vamacharēēs,) and eight females, (a dancing-girl, a weaver's daughter, a woman of ill-fame, a washerwoman, a barber's wife or daughter, a bramhŭnēē, the dauhghter of a land-owner, and a milkmaid.) Each of the vamacharēēs is to place by his side one of the females, and the teacher and his disciple are to sit close to each other. The teacher now informs his disciple, that from henceforward he is not to indulge shame, nor dislike to any thing, nor prefer one plan to another, nor regard ceremonial cleanness, or uncleanness nor caste ; and that, though he may freely enjoy all the pleasures of sense, the mind must be fixed on his guardian deity : that is, he is neither to be an epicure nor an ascetic, but to blend both in his character ; and to make the pleasures of sense, that is, wine and women, the medium of obtaining absorption into Brŭmha ; since women are the representatives of the wife of Cupid, and wine prevents the senses from going astray. A pan of spirits, or of water mixed with spirits, is placed near each man and woman ; and in the centre another pan of spirits, different kinds of flesh, (of which that of the cow makes a part,) rice, fruits, &c. and upon each of the eight pans different branches of trees, and garlands of red flowers are placed ; the pans also are to be marked with red paint : all these are surrounded with eighty pounds of flour formed into different colours. A pan of intoxicating beverage, called siddhee, is next consecrated ; of which each partakes : after which they chew the panŭ leaf. Next, before all the things placed in the centre of the room, the spiritual guide rehearses the common ceremonies of worship, addressing them to any one of the female deities who happens to be the guardian deity of this disciple. The vessels from which the company are to drink, and the offerings, are next consecrated : these vessels may be formed of earth, copper, brass, silver, gold, or stone, the cocoanut, or a human skull ; but the latter is to be preferred. The spiritual guide then gives as much as a wine glass of spirits to each female, as the representative of the divine energy ; and the men drink what they leave. At this time the spiritual guide declares, that in the sŭtyŭ yoogŭ the people were directed in their religious duties by the védŭs, in the trétŭ by the writings of the learned, in the dwapŭrŭ by the different pooranŭs, and, in the kŭlee yoogŭ, the tŭntrŭs are the only proper guides to duty. As if well pleased with this sentiment, each one of the company now drinks two more glasses of the spirits. The disciple next worships each male and female separately, applying to them the names of Bhoirŭvŭ and Bhoirŭvēē, titles given to Shivŭ and Doorga, and presents to each of them spirits, meat-offerings, garments, ornaments, &c. ; after which the spiritual guide offers a burnt-sacrifice, with the flesh and other meat-offerings, pouring on them, as they burn, clarified butter : the disciple also repeats the same ceremony. The eight females now anoint the disciple by sprinkling upon him, with the branches which were placed on the pan, spirits and water ; and after mixing together the whole of the spirits, or spirits and water, from all the pans, the spiritual guide, with all the branches, again sprinkles the disciple : to whom he declares that he has now, for the good of his soul, instructed him, according to the commandment of the great god Shivŭ, in all the ceremonies belonging to the profession of a vamacharēē ; urging him, in practising these ceremonies, to keep his mind on Shivŭ, and that he will be happy after death : at the close, he causes him to drink the liquor thus mixed, repeating separate incantations. During his initiation he is not to drink so as to appear intoxicated, or to cause his mind to wander ; but having habituated himself to a small quantity, he may take more, till he falls down in a state of intoxication; still however so as to rise again after a short interval: after which he may continue drinking the nectar, till he falls down completely overcome, and remains in this state of joy, thinking upon his guardian deity. He is now known as an Uvŭdhootŭ, that is, as one who has renounced all secular affairs; and receives a new name, perhaps Anŭndŭ-nat'hŭ, or the joyous. He is to drink spirits with all of the same profession; to sleep constantly in a house of ill-fame; and to eat of every thing he pleases, and with all castes indiscriminately. The next thing is to offer a burnt-sacrifice; after which the spiritual guide and the guests are dismissed with presents, and the new disciple spends the night with an infamous female. These vamacharēēs adore the sex, and carefully avoid offending a woman. They also practise the most debasing rites, using the heads of persons who have been guilty of suicide, also when sitting on a dead body, and while naked and in the presence of a naked female.—It might seem impossible to trace ceremonies gross as these to any principle except that of moral depravity; but the authors of this system attempt to reconcile it with the pursuit of future happiness. The reader is aware that the regular Hindoo theologians attribute all the vices to the passions, and consider their subjugation, or annihilation, as essential to final beatitude; they therefore aim at the accomplishment of this object by means of severe bodily austerities. The vamacharēēs profess to seek the same object, not by avoiding temptation, and starving the body, but by blunting the edge of the passions with excessive indulgence. They profess to triumph over the regular Hindoos, reminding them that *their* ascetics are safe only in forests, and while keeping a perpetual fast; but that *they* subdue their passions in the very presence of temptation.

Thus, that which to the Hindoo should be divine worship, is the great source of impiety and corruption of manners: and, instead of returning from his temple, or from religious services, improved in knowledge, grieved for his moral deficiences, and anxious to cultivate a greater regard to the interests of morality and religion, his passions are inflamed, and his mind polluted to such a degree, that he carries the pernicious lessons of the temple, or the festival, into all the walks of private life. His very religion becomes his greatest bane, and where he should have drank of the water of life, he swallows the poison that infallibly destroys him.

In conversation with a learned bramhŭn, in the year 1813, he acknowledged to the author, that, at present, reverence for the gods made no part of the attractions to the public festivals. One man celebrates a festival to preserve himself from disgrace, another to procure the applause of his countrymen, and a third for the sake of the songs, dances, &c. This bramhŭn instanced cases of images being made without any reference to the rules of the shastrŭ. At one place, a Hindoo, having prepared an image, at an expense which he could not meet, permitted it to be broken, and its head, arms, and legs to be trodden upon in the streets;—another, who had been thus disappointed, threw the image into the water;—and a third, having made an enormous image, had fastened it to a cart, but on the first motion of the vehicle, the head of the idol had fallen off, and the rest of the image was permitted to lie in the street as a dead carcase. I give these instances, to confirm what I have already said, that it is not devotion that leads the Hindoo to the temple, but a licentious appetite; and to afford another proof, that idolatry always tends to sink, but never to raise its votaries. In the account of Kalēē, (p. 94,) the reader will find a fact respecting the execution of two Hindoos, who, when under sentence of death, became Roman Catholics, in pure revenge upon Kalēē; who did not, as she was believed to have done in many other cases, protect them in the act of robbery. One of the pŭndits who assisted me in this work begged, if I mentioned this fact, that I would assure the English reader, that although this goddess assisted public robbers, she always informed them that they must suffer hereafter for their crimes, though she did assist them in their perpetration.

The Reverend Mr. Maurice seems astonished that a people so mild, so benevolent, so benignant as the Hindoos, 'who (quoting Mr. Orme) *shudder at the very sight of blood,*' should have adopted so many bloody rites. But are these Hindoos indeed so humane?—these men, and women too, who drag their dying relations to the banks of the river at all seasons, day and night, and expose them to the heat and cold in the last agonies of death, without remorse;—who assist men to commit self-murder, encouraging them to swing with hooks in their backs, to pierce their tongues and sides, to cast themselves on naked knives, to bury themselves alive,[b] throw themselves into rivers,[c] from precipices,[d] and under the cars of their idols;—who murder their own children,

[b] 'Instances are not unfrequent, where persons afflicted with loathsome and incurable diseases, have caused themselves to be buried alive.' *Asiatic Researches,* p. 257.

[c] Mr. W. Carey, of Cutwa, in a letter to the author, dated the 4th of November, 1814, says, 'Two or three days ago I witnessed a scene more shocking than any I ever saw in this place:—A poor weaver was brought here, and cast into the water, with a pan of water tied round his waist to make him sink; but providentially the river was shallow, and he was taken out, after being in the water a day and a night. Hearing of the circumstance, I went to see him, and found the poor man only affected with rheumatic pains. I had him brought to my house, but could not prevail on the unfeeling natives to carry him up till I procured an order from an officer of the police. I hope he will be restored to health in a fortnight, when he will return home, with some knowledge of the gospel. What adds to the horror of this narration, is, that the perpetrators of this intended murder were the mother and brother of this unfortunate Hindoo.'

[d] 'A very singular practice prevails among the lowest tribes of the inhabitants of Berar and Gondwŭnŭ. Suicide is not unfrequently vowed by such persons in return for boons solicited from idols; and to fulfil his vow, the successful votary throws himself from a precipice named Kalŭ-Bhoirŭvŭ, situated in the mountains between the Taptee and Nŭrmŭda rivers. The annual fair, held near that spot at the beginning of spring, usually witnesses eight or ten victims of this superstition.' *Asiatic Researches,* vol. vii. p. 257.

by burying them alive, throwing them to the alligators, or hanging them up alive in trees for the ants and crows before their own doors,[e] or by sacrificing them to the Ganges;—who burn alive, amidst savage shouts, the heart-broken widow, by the hands of her own son, and with the corpse of a deceased father[f];—who every year butcher thousands of animals, at the call of superstition, covering themselves with their blood, consigning their carcases to the dogs, and carrying their heads, in triumph through the streets?—Are these the 'benignant Hindoos'?—a people who have never erected a charity-school, an alms'-house, nor an hospital; who suffer their fellow-creatures to perish for want before their very doors, refusing to administer to their wants while living, or to inter their bodies, to prevent their being devoured by vultures and jackals, when dead; who, when the power of the sword was in their hands, impaled alive, cut off the noses, the legs, and arms of culprits; and inflicted punishments exceeded only by those of the followers of the mild, amiable, and benevolent Booddhŭ in the Burman empire[g]!

[e] I fancy this is done when the child is born with bad omens, or is supposed to be afflicted by some evil spirit.

[f] At Benares and near Buxar numerous brick monuments have been erected to perpetuate the memory of women who have been burnt alive with the bodies of their deceased husbands.

[g] It is well known, that the Burmans are the followers of Booddhŭ, whose principal aim was to excite in mankind a horror of shedding blood, and of destroying animal life. The following facts will show how much humanity there is among a people far exceeding the Hindoos in their care not to injure whatever contains life. Mr. F. Carey thus writes to his friends in Bengal:—'I will now relate what has taken place in this single town of Rangoon since my residence in this country, which does not exceed four years. Some of the criminals I saw executed with my own eyes; the rest I saw immediately after execution. One man had melted lead poured down his throat, which immediately burst out from the neck, and various parts of the body. Four or five persons, after being nailed through their hands and feet to a scaffold, had first their tongues cut out, then their mouths slit open from ear to ear, then their ears cut off, and finally their bellies ripped open. Six people were crucified in the following manner: their hands and feet were nailed to a scaffold; their eyes were then extracted with a blunt hook; and in this condition they were left to expire: two died in the course of four days; the rest were liberated, but died of mortification on the sixth or seventh day. Four persons were crucified, viz. not nailed, but tied with their hands and feet stretched out at full length, in an erect posture, in which they were to remain till death; every thing they wished to eat was ordered them, with a view to prolong their lives and misery. In cases like this, the legs and feet of the criminals begin to swell and mortify at the expiration of three or four days; some are said to live in this state for a fortnight, and expire at last from fatigue and mortification. Those which I saw were liberated at the end of three or four days. Another man had a large bamboo run through his belly, which put an immediate end to his existence. Two persons had their bellies ripped up, just sufficient to admit of the protrusion of a small part of the intestines; and after being secured by the hands and feet at full stretch with cords, were placed in an erect posture upon bamboo rafters, and set adrift in the river, to float up and down with the tide for public view. The number of those who have been be-

and who very often, in their acts of pillage, murder the plundered, cutting off their limbs with the most cold-blooded apathy, turning the house of the murdered into a disgusting shambles !—Some of these cruelties, no doubt, arise out of the religion of the Hindoos, and are the poisoned fruits of superstition, rather than the effects of natural disposition . but this is equally true respecting the virtues which have been so lavishly bestowed on this people. At the call of the shastru, the Hindoo gives water to the weary traveller during the month Voishakhu ; but he may perish at his door without pity or relief from the first of the following month, no reward being attached to such an act after these thirty days have expired. He will make roads, pools of water, and build lodging-houses for pilgrims and travellers ; but he considers himself as making a good bargain with the gods in all these transactions. It is a fact, that there is not a road in the country made by Hindoos except a few which lead to holy places ; and had there been no future rewards held out for such acts of merit, even these would not have existed. Before the kŭlee-yoogŭ it was lawful to sacrifice cows ; but the man who does it now, is guilty of a crime as heinous as that of killing a bramhŭn ; he may kill a buffalo, however, and Doorga will reward him with heaven for it. A Hindoo, by any direct act, should not destroy an insect, for he is taught that God inhabits even a fly : but it is no great crime if he should permit even his cow to perish with hunger ; and he beats it without mercy, though it be an incarnation of Bhŭgŭvŭtēē—it is enough, that he does not really deprive it of life ; for the indwelling Brŭmhŭ feels no stroke but that of death. The Hindoo will utter falsehoods that would knock down an ox, and will commit perjuries so atrocious and disgusting, as to fill with horror those who visit the courts of justice ; but he will not violate his shastrŭ by swearing on the waters of the Ganges.

Idolatry is often also the exciting cause of the most abominable frauds. Several instances are given in this work : one will be found in page 75, and another respecting an image found under ground by the raja of Nŭdēēya, in p. 125.[h]

Indeed keeping gods is even a trade among the Hindoos : the only difficulty to be overcome, is that of exciting attention to the image. To do this,

headed I do not exactly recollect ; but they must be somewhere between twenty and thirty. One man was sawn to death, by applying the saw to the shoulder bone, and sawing right down until the bowels gushed out. One woman was beat to death with a large cudgel.—These are most of the punishments I have seen and heard of during my stay in this place ; but many other instances happened during my absence, which I have not related. As for the crimes for which these punishments were inflicted, I shall only add, the crimes of some deserved death, some were of a trivial nature, and some of the victims were quite innocent.'

[h] Plutarch says, that Romulus, when he instituted the Ludi Consuales, to surprise the Sabine virgins, gave out, that he had discovered the altar of the god Consus hid under ground ; which discovery attracted great multitudes to the sacrifice.

the owner of the image frequently goes from village to village, to call the attention of the neighbourhood: he also persuades some one to proclaim, that he has been warned in a dream to perform vows to this image; or he repeats to all he sees, that such and such cures have been performed by it. In the years 1807 and 1808, almost all the sick and imaginary sick Hindoos in the south of Bengal presented their offerings to an image called Tarŭk-éshwŭrŭ, at a place bearing this name. The bramhŭns owning this image became rich. This excited the attention of some bramhŭns near Nŭdēēya, who proclaimed another image of Shivŭ, in their possession, to be 'the brother of Tarŭk-eshwŭrŭ;' and the people of those parts flocked to this image as others had done to the original one.

The author has devoted a volume (Book I.) of this work to the gods. The next article (Book II.) relates to the Hindoo temples, none of which appear to be distinguished for the elegance of their architecture: they are not the work of a people sunk in barbarism; neither will they bear any comparison with the temples of the Greeks or Romans.[i] They are not constructed so as to hold a crowd of worshippers, who are always accommodated in an area opposite the temple. The room in which the idol is placed is considered sufficiently spacious if it hold the officiating priest, the utensils for worship, and the offerings.

These temples answer none of the ends of a lecture room, nor of a Christian temple. Here the passions are never raised to heaven by sacred music, nor by the voices of a large and devout congregation celebrating the praises of the Deity in the strains of sacred poetry; here no devout feelings are awakened by the voice of prayer and confession, nor are the great truths of religion explained, or enforced upon the mind of an attentive crowd by the eloquence of a public speaker: the daily worship at the temple is performed by the solitary priest with all the dulness, carelessness, and insipidity necessarily connected with a service always the same, repeated before an idol made of a cold stone, and in which the priest has no interest whatever; and when the crowd do assemble before the temple, it is to enter upon orgies which destroy every vestige of moral feeling, and excite to every outrage upon virtue.

The dedication of a temple is a work of great ceremony,[k] if the building belong to a man of wealth; the expense incurred in presents to the bramhŭns and others is also very great. The person who employs his

[i] We learn from the Ain Akbŭree, however, that the entire revenues of Orissa, for twelve years, were expended on erecting a temple to the sun.—*Maurice's Indian Antiquities.*

[k] Circumambulating a temple is an act of merit, raising the person to a place in the heaven of the god or goddess whose temple he thus walks round. At Benares the devout do it daily. If the circumambulator be a learned man, he repeats the praise of the god as he is walking, and bows to the image every time he arrives at the door of the temple. The ignorant merely walk round, and make the bow. The right hand is always kept towards the object circumambulated.

wealth in this manner is considerably raised in the estimation of his countrymen: he frequently also endows the temple, as well as raises it; which is generally done by grants of land. The annual produce of the land thus bestowed, is expended in wages to the officiating priest, in the daily offerings to the idol, and in lighting and repairing the temple. Many temples, however, do not depend entirely on their endowments: they receive considerable sums from occasional offerings, and from what is presented at festivals.[1] Some temples are supported at an expense so trifling as to astonish a reader not acquainted with the forms of idolatry: many individuals who officiate at temples obtain only the offerings, the value of which does not amount, in many instances, to more than twenty shillings a year. Some few temples are however, splendidly endowed, and many families receive their maintenance from them. Where an idol has become very famous, and the offerings have amounted to a large sum, even kings have been anxious to lay hold of such a source of revenue.

The images of the gods may be made of almost all the metals, as well as of wood, stone, clay, &c. Most of the permanent images are made of wood or stone; those which are destroyed at the close of a festival, are made of clay. Small images of brass, silver, and gold, are not uncommon. The sculpture of the stone images resembles that of the Popish images of the 12th century; those cast in brass, &c. exhibit a similar progress of the arts. The consecration of an image is accompanied with a number of ceremonies, the most singular of which is that of conveying sight and life to the image, for which there are appropriate formulas, with prayers, inviting the deity to come and dwell in it. After this ceremony, the image becomes sacred, and is carefully guarded from every offensive approach. The shastrŭs contain directions for making idols, and the forms of meditation used in worship contain a description of each idol. but in many instances these forms are disregarded, and the proprietor, though compelled to preserve the identity of the image, indulges his own fancy. Some images are very diminutive, especially those made of the precious metals; but others, if for temporary use, are very large: a stone image of the lingŭ is to seen at Benares, which six men with joined hands can hardly grasp. At the festival of Kartikéyŭ, the god of war, an image is sometimes made thirty cubits high. Whatever may have been the case in other countries, idolatry in this has certainly not contributed to carry the arts of painting or sculpture to any perfection.

Any bramhŭn, properly qualified by rank and knowledge, may officiate in a temple, and perform the general work of a priest. There is no order of bramhŭns to whom the priesthood is confined:[m] many bramhŭns employ others

[1] In the year 1809, at the temple of Jŭgŭnnat'hŭ, near Serampore, at the car festival, about 570 rupees were presented to the idol, in vegetables, fruits, sweetmeats, garments, and money. About 150 bramhŭns, 50 females, and 150 shōōdrŭs, were entertained daily; and, at the close of the festival, the priests of the temple received 420 rupees.

[m] I insert a short extract from Bryce's 'Sketch of the State of British India,' in order to assure the author, that, as it respects Bengal, it is wholly without foundation.

as priests; a shōōdrŭ must employ a bramhŭn, but he has his own choice of the individual; he cannot repeat a single formula of the védŭs himself without being guilty of the highest offence. There are different offices in which priests are employed; but any bramhŭn, properly qualified, may perform the ceremonies attached to them all: (see p. 186.) In general, a family, able to bear the expense, employs a priest on a regular allowance: some priests are retained by many families of the same caste; such a person is called the joiners' priest, or the weavers' priest, &c. The bramhŭns employed as priests to the shōōdrus are not in high estimation among their brethren, who never fail to degrade the shōōdrŭ in every stage and state of life. The fees of the priest are in general very small: on some occasions, at the dedication of a temple, at the ceremonies for the dead when performed for a rich man, at the great festivals, &c., the priest receives very liberal presents. Female priests are almost unknown to the Hindoos; one or two instances are recorded in pp. 143, 145.

The ceremonies at the temples are in most cases performed daily, morning, noon, and evening, at which times food is presented to the idol: the services are short, consisting of a few forms of petition and praise; during the presentation of flowers, leaves and (except to Shivŭ) a few articles of food, the priest is commonly the only person present. The doors of the lingŭ temples are generally open all day; multitudes of these temples are never honoured with worship, though they contain an idol: this is accounted for by there being several of these temples erected in one spot belonging to the same individual. Hindoos in general bow to the image as they pass the temple, whether the doors be open or shut. Where the deity is honoured by bloody sacrifices, a post is erected in front of the temple, for the slaughter of animals. No assemblies can be formed in these edifices; but on particular occasions the people are collected before the door, and sit or stand under an awning. The idols in honour of Vishnoo are laid down to sleep in the day, if the image be not too large;—a poor compliment to a god, that he wants rest. The utensils employed in the ceremonies at the temples are, several dishes to hold the offerings, a hand bell, a lamp, jugs for holding water, an incense dish, a copper cup to receive drink-offerings for deceased ancestors and the gods, another smaller one to pour from, a seat of kooshŭ grass for the priest, a large metal plate used as a bell, and a conch or shell. All these articles do not cost more than twenty shillings, unless the owner wish them to be costly.

Daily, weekly, monthly, and annual ceremonies abound among this people, to whom may truly be applied the remark of Paul to the Athenians, (Acts xvii. 22;) the festivals are noted in the Hindoo almanacs, and are generally held at the full or total wane of the moon. In the month of February, they have one festival in honour of the goddess of learning, Sŭrŭswŭtēē, which continues one day. In March three, in honour of Shivŭ, Krishnŭ, and Gŭnga. In April

'The laws have always confined a certain proportion of bramhŭns to the service of the pagodas, to the education of youth, and to study.' p. 57. 'No pains are spared in rendering accomplished those females, who, as the fascinating instruments of superstition, are employed in the service of their temples.' p. 54.

two; one on the anniversary of the birth of Ramŭ, and the other the horrid swinging festival. In June two; one in the honour of Gŭnga, and the other Jŭgŭnnat'hŭ's car festival; the latter is again revived in July, when the car returns to the temple. In August the cow is worshipped, and the birth of Krishnŭ celebrated. In September the memory of deceased ancestors is commemorated, and the Doorga festival held. In October one, in honour of the goddess Rŭtŭntēē; and in November another, in honour of Kartikēyŭ, the god of war. On all these occasions the public offices are closed; but many other holidays are kept by the Hindoos, which are not honoured as public festivals.

The reader will find, in p. 193, an account of the daily duties of a bramhŭn; by which it appears, that if he strictly conform to the rules of his religion, he must spend almost his whole time in religious ceremonies. The present race of bramhŭns curtail these ceremonies, especially those engaged in secular affairs, who spend perhaps ten or twenty minutes in the morning, after their ablutions, in repeating the usual formulas before the lingŭ, or the stone called the shalŭgramŭ, or a pan of water. Many, however, content themselves with bathing, and repeating the name of their guardian deity.

The form of initiation into the service of a person's guardian deity consists in giving him the name of this deity, and exhorting him to repeat it continually. The ceremony of initiation is given in p. 199. From this time, the initiated becomes entitled to all the privileges of the Hindoo religion, is placed under the protection of the gods, and receives the benediction of his spiritual guide. The Hindoos are careful to conceal the words of initiation, and do not wish to declare to strangers what god they have chosen for their guardian deity.

The spiritual guide, who is chosen by the person himself, receives the highest reverence from the disciple, and is sometimes worshipped by him as a god. Disobedience to this guide is one of the highest offences a Hindoo can commit, and his anger is dreaded more than that of the gods. When the disciple approaches him, he prostrates himself at his feet, and the priest places his foot on his head. To such a state of degradation does the Hindoo superstition reduce the people! These priests are notorious for covetousness and impurity: some of them plunder the disciple of their all, and others violate the chastity of their wives. They are not distinguished by any particular dress, nor do they perform any offices of worship for their disciples.

Bathing in the Ganges, or in some other sacred river, or pool, is one of the most constant and necessary duties enjoined upon the Hindoos; the bramhŭns, after bathing, frequently complete their devotions on the banks of the river; others go home, and repeat the requisite forms before the shalŭgramŭ, or a pan of water. The people are taught that bathing is a religious ceremony, by which they become purified from sin[n]! They are never directed to

[n] And yet so far are the Hindoos from having any moral feelings, even in their acts of *purification*, that few men bathe in a retired situation; the majority choose those places to which the female bathers resort, and on their account remain in the water long beyond the time necessary for their ablutions. Many an infamous assignment is

bathe to promote bodily health. In the act of bathing, they pour out drink-offerings to deceased ancestors.—To be convinced how entirely the present race of Hindoos are influenced by the promises of salvation held out in their sacred books on this subject, it is only necessary for a person to attend to what is passing around him, viz., to the crowds bathing at the landing-places of the Ganges; to the persons bearing the sacred water into distant countries, in vessels suspended from their shoulders; to the shraddhŭs and other religious ceremonies performed on its banks; to the number of temples on both sides of the river; to so great a part of the Bengal population having erected their habitations near the river; to the number of brick landing-places, built as acts of holiness, to assist the people in obtaining the favour of Gŭnga; to the houses erected for the sick by the sides of the river; to the people bringing their sick relations, and laying them on bedsteads, or on the ground, by the side of the Ganges, waiting to burn them there, and to throw their ashes into the river; to the immense crowds on the banks, waiting for a junction of the planets, at which moment they plunge into the stream with the greatest eagerness; to the people committing the images of their gods to the sacred stream, at the close of their festivals; and, finally, to the boats crowded with passengers going to Sagŭr island (Gŭnga-sagŭrŭ) every year[o].

The forms of worship (pōōja[p]) before the idol are particularly laid down in p. 215. The priest who officiates has the common dress of a bramhŭn; it must, however, be clean: he has occasionally one or two bramhŭns to assist him in presenting the offerings.

made by looks, &c. while they are thus washing away their sins. A number of bramhŭns engage as cooks to opulent families, to facilitate their licentious intrigues: this is become so common, that the bramhŭns, proverbially known by the name of cooking bramhŭns, are treated with the greatest suspicion by those who care for the chastity of their wives. *Multitudes of bramhŭns likewise are employed as priests to prostitutes,* and actually perform the offices of religion in houses of ill-fame;—so completely absent is the moral principle from the religion of the Hindoos!

o Till lately, eople used to throw themselves, or their children, to the alligators at this place, under the idea that dying at Gŭnga-sagŭrŭ, in the jaws of an alligator, was the happiest of deaths. This is now prevented by a guard of sepoys sent by Government.

p The Ain Akbŭree says, the Hindoos 'divide pōōja into *sixteen* ceremonies. After the devotee has performed his usual and indispensable ablutions, with the sŭndhya and homŭ, he sists down, looking towards the east or the north, with his legs drawn up in front. Then, taking in his hand a little water and rice, he sprinkles the idol, and conceives this act to be a proper preface to the commencement of his adoration. Next follows the worship of the idol's flagon. Then succeeds the worship of the conch-shell. Last in order, a ceremony which consists in plastering the bell with ashes of sandal-wood. When he has finished, he throws down a little rice, and wishes that his god may be manifested. These various duties are all comprised in the first of the sixteen ceeemonies.—In the second, he prepares and places a table of metal, either gold, silver, or copper, as a seat or throne for a deity.—In the third, he throws water into a vessel to wash his feet; for in Hindoost'hanŭ it is the custom, that, when a superior enters the house of an inferior, he washes his feet.—In the fourth, he sprinkles water thrice. to represent the idol rincing his mouth. since it is

Short forms of praise and prayer to the gods[q] are continually used, and are supposed to promote very highly a person's spiritual interests. The following is an example of praise addressed to Gŭnga :—' O goddess, the owl that lodges in the hollow of a tree on thy banks, is exalted beyond measure; while the emperor, whose palace is far from thee, though he may possess a million of stately elephants, and may have the wives of a million of conquered enemies to serve him, is nothing.' Example of prayer:—' O god! I am the greatest sinner in the world; but thou, among the gods, art the greatest saviour: I leave my cause in thy hands.' Praise is considered as more prevalent with the gods than prayer, as the gods are mightily pleased with flattery. Some unite vows to their supplications, and promise to present to the god a handsome offering if he be propitious.

Another act of Hindoo devotion is meditation on the form of an idol. Mr. Hastings, in his prefatory letter to the Gēēta, says, the Rev. Mr. Maurice describes the bramhŭns as devoting a certain period of time to the contemplation of the deity, his attributes, and the moral duties of life. The truth is, that in this Hindoo act of devotion there is not a vestige of reference to

also the custom for an inferior to bring to a superior water to rince his mouth with before meals.—In the fifth, sandal, flowers, betel, and rice are offered to the idol.—In the sixth, the idol and his throne are carried to another spot: then the worshipper takes in his right hand a white conch-shell full of water, which he throws over the idol, and with his left hand rings the bell.—In the seventh, he wipes the idol dry with a cloth, replaces it upon its throne, and adorns it with vestments of silk or gold stuff.—In the eighth, he puts the zennar upon the idol.—In the ninth, he makes the tilŭk upon the idol in twelve places.—In the tenth, he throws over the idol flowers or green leaves.—In the eleventh, he fumigates it with perfumes.—In the twelfth, he lights a lamps with ghēē.—In the thirteenth, he places before the idol trays of food, according to his ability; which are distributed among the by-standers, as the holy relics of the idol's banquet.—In the fourteenth, he stretches himself at full length with his face towards the ground, and disposes his body in such a manner, as that his eight members touch the ground, namely, the two knees, two hands, forehead, nose, and cheeks. These kinds of prostration are also performed to great men in Hindoost'hanŭ.—In the fifteenth, he makes a circuit around the idol several times.—In the sixteenth, he stands in the posture of a slave, with his hands uplifted, and asks permission to depart.'—At some of the great festivals, boys in play make an image, paint it, and beg from house to house for the offerings, as rice, fruits, &c. When all things are ready, some one becomes the priest, and performs the ceremonies. Thus early are the Hindoo children initiated into their idolatrous rites. If, however, the parents of these children discover what is going on, they forbid it, and warn the children, that the god will be displeased. If it be an image of Kalēē, or any ferocious deity, they endeavour to terrify the children, by telling them that the goddess is a fury, and will certainly devour them. If any elderly boy be concerned, and the image made be a good one, the parents will sometimes, rather than destroy it, call a bramhŭn, and have the ceremonies performed in a regular way.

[q] Instead of hymns in honour of the gods, the Hindoos, at present, as has been already noticed, introduce before the idol little beside filthy songs. Some bramhŭns acknowledge, that not a single Hindoo seeks in his religion any thing of a moral nature. A real Christian, when he approaches God, prays, 'Create in me a clean heart, and renew a right spirit within me.' 'Lead me not into temptation, but deliver me from evil.' 'Give me neither poverty nor riches.' 'Guide me with thy

the divine attributes, nor to moral duty. The Hindoo rehearses in his mind the form of the god, his colour, the number of his heads, eyes, hands, &c. and nothing more.

Repeating the names of the gods, particularly of a person's guardian deity, is one of the most common, and is considered as one of the most efficacious acts of devotion prescribed in the shastrŭs. The oftener the name is repeated, the greater the merit. Persons may be seen in the streets repeating these names either alone, or at work, or to a parrot; others, as they walk along, count the repetitions by the beads of their necklace, which they then hold in the hand.

A great number of prescribed ceremonies, called vrŭtŭs, exist among the Hindoos, which are practised with the hope of obtaining some blessing: females chiefly attend to these ceremonies.

Fasting is another act of religious merit among the Hindoos. Some fasts are extremely severe, and a Hindoo who is very religious must often abstain from food. It is commended, not as an act of preparation for some duty, calling for great attention of mind, but as an instance of self-denial in honour of the gods, which is very pleasing to them. One man may fast for another, and the merit of the action is then transferred to the person paying and employing another in this work.

Gifts to bramhŭns are highly meritorious, as might be expected in a system exclusively formed for their exaltation: the more costly the gift, the more valuable the promissory note, drawn on heaven, and presented to the giver. Giving entertainments to bramhŭns is also another action which procures heaven.

Hospitality to travellers is placed among the duties of the Hindoos, and is practised to a considerable extent, though the distinctions of caste destroy the feelings which should give efficacy to this excellent law. So completely do these distinctions destroy every generous and benevolent feeling, that many unfortunate creatures perish in the sight of those who are well able to relieve them, but who exonerate themselves from this duty, by urging, that they are of another caste: a bramhŭn finds friends every where, but the caste has sunk

counsel, and afterwards receive me to glory.' A Hindoo, when he supplicates his god, prays for riches, or for recovery from sickness, or for a son, or for revenge upon his enemy. Sometimes the worshipper places himself before the image in a sitting posture, and, closing his eyes, prays, 'Oh, god! give me beauty, let me be praised, give me prosperity, give me a son, give me riches, give me long life, or, give me health, &c.' The eldest female of the house, throwing her garment over her shoulder, and sitting on her hams, joining her hands, in the same manner, prays, 'O god! preserve these my childen, and my son's wife; do not suffer us to have sorrow again in our family, (referring to some death in the preceding year,) and then I will present offerings to thee every year:' saying this, she prostrates herself before the image. Sometimes a woman, after bathing, stretches her arms towards the sun, and says, 'O god of day! such a one has ill-treated me; do thou afflict her. See! I supplicate thee without having touched or tasted food.' A poor man, in the presence of an image, sometimes prays, 'O god! fill me every day with food. I ask no more.'

the afflicted shōōdrŭ to the level of the beasts[r]: when a bramhŭn is relieved, however, he is not indebted to the benevolence of his countrymen, so much as to the dread which they feel lest neglect of a bramhŭn should bring upon them the wrath of the gods.

Digging pools, planting trees for fruit or shade, making roads for pilgrims, &c. are other duties commanded by the shastrŭ, and practised by the modern Hindoos.

Reading and rehearsing the pooranŭs are prescribed to the Hindoos as religious duties, and many attend to them at times in a very expensive manner.

Other ceremonies contrary to every principle of benevolence exist among this people, one of which is to repeat certain formulas, for the sake of injuring, removing, or destroying enemies. Here superstition is made an auxiliary to the most diabolical passions.

But what shall we say of the murder of widows on the funeral pile?—this too is an act of great piety. The priest assists the poor wretch, in her last moments, before she falls on the pile, with the formulas given by the Hindoo legislators: and, to complete this most horrible of all religious customs, the son of this wretched victim kindles the fire in the very face of the mother who gave him birth. Can there possibly be a greater outrage on human nature? Is there any thing like it in all the records of the most wild and savage nations? The North American Indian proceeds with the utmost coolness, it is true, in the work of scalping and murder, but the victim is his enemy, taken in battle; here the victim is an innocent woman—a mother—a widow, her heart fresh bleeding under the loss of the companion of her youth—the murderer, her own child—dragged to the work by the *mild* bramhŭn, who dances, and shouts, and drowns the cries of the family and the victim in the horrid sounds of the drum. Such is the balm which is here poured into the broken heart of the widow. Nor are these unheard of, unparallcled murders, perpetrated in the night, in some impenetrable forest; but in the presence of the whole population of India, in open day:—and oh! horrible! most horrible! not less than *five thousand* of these unfortunate women, it is supposed, are immolated every twelve months. I have heard that the son sometimes manifests a great reluctance to the deed[r] and that some of these human sacrifices are almost dead before they are touched by the flames.[s] It is certain, that in many cases the family do much to prevent the female from being thus drawn into the flaming gulph; but such are the effects of superstition, and the influence of long established customs,

[r] The shastrŭ prescribes, that he should do it with his head turned from the pile. Kennett, describing the Roman funeral, says, 'The next of blood performed the ceremony of lighting the pile, which they did with a torch, turning their face all the while the other way, as if it was done out of necessity and not willingly.'

[s] These barbarous murderers say, that when a woman is thus frightened to death, the gods, charmed with her devotion, have taken her before she entered upon this holy act.

joined to the disgrace and terrors of a state of widowhood, that, in the first moments of grief and distraction for the loss of her husband, reason is overpowered, and the widow perishes on the funeral pile, the victim of grief, superstition, and dread. Many widows are buried alive with the corpses of their husbands.[t]

Voluntary suicide is not only practised to a dreadful extent among the Hindoos, but the shastrŭs positively recommend the crime, and promise heaven to the self-murderer, provided he die in the Ganges! Nay, the bramhŭns, as well as persons of other castes, assist those who design thus to end life, of which the reader will find instances recorded in pp. 245, 246, 248. In some places of the Ganges, deemed peculiarly sacred and efficacious, infatuated devotees very frequently drown themselves. A respectable bramhŭn assured the author, that in a stay of only two months

[t] The following circumstance took place at Gondŭl-para, about 20 miles N. of Calcutta, on the 18th of March, 1813, and was communicated to the author by Captain Kemp, an eye-witness. The description is nearly in his own words:—'On Thursday last, at nine in the morning, Vishwŭnat'hŭ, one of our best workmen, who had been sick but a short time, was brought down to the river side to expire: he was placed, as is customary, on the bank, and a consultation held respecting the time he would die; the astrologer predicted, that his dissolution was near at hand. This sick man was then immersed up to the middle in the river, and there kept for sometime; but death not being so near as was predicted, he was again placed on the beach, extended at full length, and exposed to a hot sun, where he continued the whole of the day, excepting at those intervals, when it was supposed he was dying, when he was again immersed in the sacred stream. I visited him in the evening; he was sensible, but had not the power of utterance; he however was able to make signs with his hand, that he did not wish to drink the river water, which they kept almost continually pouring into his mouth by means of a small shell. He remained in this situation during the night: in the morning the immersions commenced, and were continued at intervals till about five in the evening, when he expired, or was literally murdered. His wife, a young woman about sixteen years of age, hearing of his death, came to the desperate resolution of being buried alive with the corpse. She was accompanied by her friends down to the beach where the body lay, where a small branch of the Mango tree was presented to her, which (as I understood) was setting a seal to her determination; from which, after having accepted the branch, she could not retreat. I went to her, and questioned her with respect to the horrid act she was about to perform, whether it was voluntary or from persuasion: nothing of the latter appeared; it was entirely her own desire. I spoke to her relations on the heinousness of the crime they were guilty of, in allowing the young creature thus to precipitate herself into the presence of her Creator uncalled for. Mrs. K. spoke both to the mother and the daughter a good deal, but all to no purpose. The mother declared, that it was her daughter's choice, who added, that she was determined to "go the road her husband had gone." There was not the least appearance of regret observable in the mother's countenance, or conduct. A woman, then, can "forget her sucking child, and forsake the child of her womb:" the prophet seemed to think it only possible that there might exist such a monster, but here it was realized; here was a monster of a mother, that could resign her child, the gift of a gracious Providence, and designed to be the comfort and support of her old age;—could, without the least apparent emotion, consign this child alive to the tomb, and herself continue an unmoved spectator of the horrid deed. At eight P. M. the corpse, accompanied by this self-devoted victim, was conveyed to a place a little below our grounds, where I repaired, to behold the prepetration of a crime which I could scarcely believe possible to be committed by any human being.

at Allahabad, he saw about *thirty* persons drown themselves! Lepers are sometimes burnt alive with their own consent, to purify themselves from disease in the next birth. Others throw themselves under the wheels of Jŭgŭnnat'hŭs ponderous car, and perish instantly. Thousands perish annually by disease and want on idolatrous pilgrimages; and notwithstanding the benevolent efforts of Mr. Duncan, it is pretty certain, that infanticide is still practised to a great extent in various parts of Hindoost'hanŭ, (see p. 251.) I have, in p. 254, ventured to offer a calculation respecting the probable number of persons who perish annually, the victims of the bramhinical superstition, and find, that it cannot be less than *Ten Thousand Five Hundred.*

Another very popular act of Hindoo devotion is that of visiting sacred places.[u] There are few Hindoos grown up to mature age, who have not visited one or more of these places, the resort of pilgrims: many spend their whole lives in passing repeatedly from one end of Hindoost'hanŭ to the other as pilgrims: nor are these pilgrimages confined to the lower orders, householders and

The corpse was laid on the earth by the river till a circular grave of about fifteen feet in circumference and five or six feet deep was prepared; and was then (after some formulas had been read) placed at the bottom of the grave in a sitting posture, with the face to the N., the nearest relation applying a lighted wisp of straw to the top of the head. The young widow now came forward, and having circumambulated the grave seven times, calling out Hŭree Bŭl! Hŭree Bŭl! in which she was joined by the surrounding crowd, descended into it. I then approached within a foot of the grave, to observe if any reluctance appeared in her countenance, or sorrow in that of her relations: in hers no alteration was perceptible; in theirs, there was the appearance of exultation. She placed herself in a sitting posture, with her face to the back of her husband, embracing the corpse with her left arm, and reclining her head on his shoulders; the other hand she placed over her own head, with her forefinger erect, which she moved in a circular direction. The earth was then deliberately put round them, two men being in the grave for the purpose of stamping it round the living and the dead, which they did as a gardener does around a plant newly transplanted, till the earth rose to a level with the surface, or two or three feet above the heads of the entombed. As her head was covered some time before the finger of her right hand, I had an opportunity of observing whether any regret was manifested; but the finger moved round in the same manner as at first, till the earth closed the scene. Not a parting tear was observed to be shed by any of her relations, till the crowd began to disperse, when the usual lamentations and howling commenced, without sorrow.'

[u] A journey to Benares, &c. and the performance of religious ceremonies there, are actions in the highest repute, for religious merit amongst the Hindoos. Many sirkars in Calcutta indulge the hope, that they shall remove all the sins they commit in the servise of Europeans (which every one knows are neither few nor small) by a journey to Benares, before they die. The Hindoo pŭndits declare, that even Europeans, dying at Benares, though they may have lived all their days upon cow's flesh, will certainly obtain absorption into Brŭmhŭ. On this subject, they quote a couplet, in which Benares is compared to a loose female, who receives all, and destroys their desire of sin, by quenching their appetites. The Hindoo learned men also admit, that Englishmen may partake of the blessings of their religion in two other instances, viz., if they become firm believers in Gŭnga, or die at Jŭgŭnnat'hŭ-kshétrŭ. In all other respects, the Hindoo heavens are all shut against eaters of cow's flesh.

learned bramhŭns are equally infatuated, and think it necessary to visit one or more of these spots for the purification of the soul before death. In some instances, a river; in others, a phenomenon in nature; and in others, a famous idol, attracts the Hindoos. Large sums are expended by the rich, and by the poor their little all, in these journies, in the fees to the bramhŭns, and in expenses at the sacred place. I have given an account of the ceremonies preparatory to the pilgrimage, as well as of those which are performed when the pilgrims arrive at the consecrated place; to which are also added particulars of the most frequented of these haunts of superstition.

For the expiation of sin, many different methods of atonement are prescribed in the Hindoo writings; many of which, however, have fallen into disuse.

Lest the observance of all these acts of religious homage should fail to secure happiness in a future state, the Hindoos are taught to repeat the names of the gods in their last hours; and are also enjoined to make presents to the bramhŭns, especially to their spiritual guides: their relations also immerse the body of a diseased person up to the middle in the Ganges, and pour copiously of this sacred water into the dying man.

To procure relief for the wandering spirit after death, they make to it offerings of rice, &c., in a religious ceremony, almost universally attended to, called the shraddhŭ, and on which very frequently a rich man expends not less than 3 or 400,000 rupees. To make this offering at Gŭya, is supposed to be attended with the certain deliverance of the deceased from all sorrow.[1]

The pooranŭs teach, that after death the soul becomes united to an aërial body, and passes to the seat of judgment, where it is tried by Yŭmŭ, the Indian Pluto, who decides upon its future destiny. It, however, remains in this aërial vehicle, till the last shraddhŭ is performed, twelve months after death; when it passes into happiness or misery, according to the sentence of Yŭmŭ.

The same works teach, that there are many places of happiness for the devout, as well as of misery for the wicked; that God begins to reward in this life those who have performed works of merit, and punishes the wicked here by various afflictions; that indeed all present events, prosperous or adverse, are the rewards or punishments inevitably connected with merit or demerit, either in a preceding birth, or in the present life; that where merit preponderates, the person, after expiating sin by death and by sufferings in hell, rises to a higher birth, or ascends to the heaven of his guardian deity.

[1] 'Ah!' said a Hindoo one day, in the hearing of the author, lamenting the catastrophe, 'it is not every one, even of those who set out for Gŭya, who reaches the place.' Another Hindoo, in the presence of the author, reproving a young bramhŭn, who refused to afford pecuniary help to his aged infirm parent, asked him, if this was not the grand reason why a person entered into the marriage state, that he might have a son, who, by offerings at Gŭya, might procure for him happiness after death?

The joys of the Hindoo heavens are represented as wholly sensual, and the miseries of the wicked as consisting in corporal punishment: the descriptions of the former digust a chaste mind by their grossness, and those given of the latter offend the feelings by their brutal literality.

Anxious to obtain the CONFESSION of FAITH of a BRAMHUN, from his own pen, I solicited this of a man of superior understanding, and I here give a translation of this article:—

'God is invisible, independent, ever-living, glorious, uncorrupt, all-wise, the ever-blessed, the almighty; his perfections are indescribable, and past finding out; he rules over all, supports all, destroys all, and remains after the destruction of all; there is none like him; he is silence; he is free from passion, from birth, &c., from increase and decrease, from fatigue, the need of refreshment, &c. He possesses the power of infinite diminution, and lightness, and is the soul of all.

'He created, and then entered into, all things, in which he exists in two ways, untouched by matter, and receiving the fruits of practice.[y] He now assumes visible forms, for the sake of engaging the minds of mankind. The different gods are parts of God, though his essence remains undiminished, as rays of light leave the sun his undiminished splendour. He created the gods to perform those things in the government of the world of which man was incapable. Some gods are parts of other gods, and there are deities of still inferior powers. If it be asked, why God himself does not govern the world, the answer is, that it might subject him to exposure, and he chooses to be concealed: he therefore governs by the gods, who are emanations from the one God, possessing a portion of his power: he who worships the gods as the one God, substantially worships God. The gods are helpful to men in all human affairs, but they are not friendly to those who seek final absorption; being jealous lest, instead of attaining absorption, they should become gods, and rival them.

'Religious ceremonies procure a fund of merit to the performer, which raises him in every future birth, and at length advances him to heaven, (where he enjoys happiness for a limited period,) or carries him towards final absorption.

'Happiness in actual enjoyment is the fruit of the meritorious works of preceding births; but very splendid acts of merit procure exaltation even in the birth in which they are performed. So, the misery which a person is now enduring, is the fruit of crimes in a former birth: enormous crimes however meet with punishment in the life in which they are committed. The miseries

y Here an objection presses hard on the bramhŭn, that it is God, or Spirit, then, in matter, that suffers, since matter cannot suffer. To this he answers, that the heart, though it be inanimate, and, in consequence, unconscious matter, by its nearness to spirit, becomes capable of joy and sorrow, and that this is the sufferer.

of a future state arise out of sins unremoved by former sufferings: an inanimate state, and that of reptiles, are also called states of suffering. Absorption can be obtained only by qualifications acquired on earth; and to obtain this, even an inhabitant of heaven must be born on earth. A person may sink to earth again by crimes committed in heaven. The joys of heaven arise only from the gratification of the senses. A person raised to heaven is considered as a god.

'Every ceremony of the Hindoo religion is either accompanied by a general prayer for some good, or is done from pure devotion, without hope of reward; or from a principle of obedience to the shastrŭ, which has promised certain blessings on the performance of such and such religious actions.

'Various sacrifices are commanded, but the most common one at present is the burnt-offering with clarified butter, &c. It is performed to procure heaven.—The worship of the gods is, speaking generally, followed by benefits in a future state, as the prayers, praise, and offerings, please the gods.—Repeating the names of the gods procures heaven, for the name of god is like fire, which devours every combustible.—Bathing is the means of purification before religious services, and when attended to in sacred places, merits heaven.—Gifts to the poor, and to persons of merit, and losing life to save another, are actions highly meritorious, and procure for the person future happiness.—Fasting is an act of merit, as the person refuses food in devotion to the gods.—Vows to the gods procure heaven.—Praise offered to the gods in songs, is efficacious in procuring future happiness.—Visiting holy places, a spiritual guide, a father or a mother, destroys all sin.—Compassion, forbearance, tenderness, (regarding the shedding of blood,) speaking truth, entertaining strangers, becoming the refuge of the oppressed, planting trees, cutting pools of water, making flights of steps to holy rivers, and roads to holy places, giving water to the thirsty, building temples and lodging-houses for travellers, hearing the praise of the gods or a sacred book, &c. are actions which merit heaven.—Religious austerities are useful to subdue the passions, and raise the mind to a pure state. These austerities are rewarded either by heaven or absorption.'

Thus far this bramhinical Confession of Faith. Its author has scarcely noticed the amazing efficacy ascribed to religious abstraction, and the austerities practised by anchorites, though the doctrine of the védŭs evidently favours an ascetic life. Indeed, retirement from the world and abstraction of mind, assisted by bodily austerities, is considered as the direct way to final beatitude; yet it is not denied, but that a person who continues in a secular state, may, by performing the duties of his religion, accelerate his approach, either in this or some future birth, to divine destiny. The yogēē being thus exalted in the Hindoo system of theology, and in consequence honoured by his countrymen, it has become very common to embrace the life of a religious mendicant; to do which, indeed, among an idle, effeminate, and dissolute people, there are many inducements very different from those of a religious nature: disappointments in life, disagreeable domestic occurrences, wandering propensities, illicit connections, and very often a wish to procure impunity in the commission of flagrant crimes,[z] induce many to embrace such a life. Perhaps there is not a single instance at present known, of a person's becoming an ascetic from the pure desire of absorption. In cases where there is the greatest appearance of such a desire, the hermit possesses a motive no higher than that of exemption from the troubles of mortal existence. I have given in this work an account of nearly twenty orders of mendicants, (p. 294, &c.) the followers of different deities: these are the scourge of the country, though the legitimate offspring of this baneful superstition. Nor need we now expect to see realized the description of a yogēē as laid down in the shastrŭ: this description never was realized; those who have received the highest fame as yogēēs, were as corrupt, perhaps, as the present wretched imitators of these austerities. Many actions are attributed to them which put human nature to the blush.

The sum of the Hindoo doctrine, then, is this:—spirit dwelling in bodies, and partaking of the passions incident to residence in matter, is purified by austerities and numerous transmigrations, and at length re-obtains absorption into the divine nature. Religious practice leads to better destiny, and divine destiny draws the person to abstraction and religious austerities.

Such is the Hindoo religion; let us examine how far it is practised at present. The ceremonies most popular are—the daily ablutions, repeating the names of the gods, the daily worship of some idol, and visiting holy places. The works of merit in greatest estimation are, entertaining bramhŭns, building temples, cutting pools, erecting landing-places to the Ganges, and expensive offerings to deceased ancestors.

The strict bramhŭns are distinguished by a scrupulous regard to bathing, the daily worship of their guardian deity, and a proud contempt of the lower orders. The voishnŭvŭs are more sociable, and converse much among each other on their favourite Krishnŭ, and the accidents connected with religious pilgrimages.

'At present,' says the bramhŭn whose confession of faith has been given in the preceding pages, '*nine parts in ten of the whole Hindoo population have abandoned all conscientious regard to the forms of their religion.* They rise in the morning without repeating the name of god, and perform no religious ceremony whatever till the time of bathing at noon, when, for fear of being reproached by their neighbours, they go and bathe: a few labour through the usual ceremonies, which occupy about fifteen minutes; the rest either merely bathe, or hypocritically make a few of the signs used in worship, and then re-

[z] I have noticed in p. 293 the fact, that many hordes of mendicants are armed, and live by public plunder; but perhaps there are quite as many secret robbers to be found in the garb of religious mendicants. Since this fact has become more generally known, many have suffered the punishment of their crimes.

turn home, and eat. This constitutes the whole of their daily practice. Among these nine parts, moreover, there are many who spend the time of bathing in conversation with others, or in gazing at the women; and some are to be found who ridicule those who employ a greater portion of time in religious ceremonies: "What! you have taken an ass's load of religion." "Faith! you are become very religious—a very holy man. Rise, and go to your proper work." Three-fourths of the single tenth part attend to the daily duties of their religion in the following manner:—when they rise, they repeat the name of their guardian deity, make a reverential motion with the head and hands in remembrance of their absent spiritual guide, then wash themselves in the house, and pursue their business till noon. Should the wife or child have neglected to prepare the flowers, &c. for worship, the master of the family scolds his wife in some such words as these:—"Why do I labour to maintain you? It is not because you can answer for me, or preserve me from punishment at death; but that you may assist me in these things, that I may repeat the name of God, and perpare for a future state." If the son is to be reproved for such a neglect, the father asks him, if he is not ashamed to spend so much time in play, careless how much fatigue he undergoes to please himself, while he is unwilling to do the smallest trifle to please the gods. He declares himself ashamed of such a family, and desires to see their faces no more. He then gathers the flowers himself, and going to the river side, takes some clay, examines whether it be free from every impurity, lays it down, taking a morsel with him into the water, immersse himself once, and then rubs himself with the clay, repeating this prayer, "O earth! thou bearest the weight of the sins of all: take my sins upon thee, and grant me deliverance." He then invites to him the river goddesses Yúmoona, Godavŭrēē, Sŭrŭswŭtēē, Nŭrmŭda, Sindhoo, and Kavérēē, that he may, in Gŭnga, have the merit of bathing in them all at once, and again immerses himself, after repeating, "On such a day of the month, on such a day of the moon, &c. I (such a one) bathe in the southwards-flowing Gŭnga." He then offers up a prayer for himself in some such words as these;—"Ubbŭyŭ-chŭrŭnŭ praying for final happiness for ten millions of his family, bathes in Gŭnga:" and then immerses again. Next, he repeats the day of the month, of the moon, &c., and immerses himself, while he utters, "Let my guardian deity be propitious;" and then ascends the bank, wiping his hair, and repeating the praises of Gŭnga, as, "O Gŭnga, thou art the door of heaven, thou art the watery image of religion, thou art the garland round the head of Shivŭ: the very craw-fish in thee are happy, while a king at a distance from thee is miserable." He then sits down, and repeats certain prayers to the sun for the removal of his sins, among which is the celebrated gayŭtrēē, "*Let us meditate on the adorable light of the divine Ruler,* (Savitrēē:) *may it guide our intellects.*" He next pours out drink-offerings to Yŭmŭ, to Brumha, Vishnoo, Roodrŭ, the eight progenitors of mankind, to all the gods, and all living things in the three worlds, to certain sages, and at length to his forefathers, praying that they may hereby be satisfied. Now he forms, with the clay he had prepared, an image of the lingŭ, and worships it; which act includes praise to one of the gods, prayers for preservation, meditation on the form of the idol, hymns on the virtues of some deity, and repetitions of the names of the gods. He then returns home, and repeats, if he has leisure, certain portions of one of the shastrŭs. Before he begins to eat, he offers up his food to his guardian deity saying, "I offer this food to such a god;" and after sitting, with his eyes closed, as long as would be requisite to milk a cow, he takes the food and eats it. In the evening, just before sun-set, if he have a temple belonging to him, he presents some fruits, &c. to the image, repeats parts of the ceremonies of the forenoon, and the name of some deity at considerable length. When he retires to rest, he repeats the word Pŭdmŭ-nabhŭ, a name of Vishnoo. Perhaps one person in ten thousand carries these ceremonies a little farther than this.'

As a person passes along the streets and roads he is continually reminded of one or other of these ceremonies :—here sits a man in his shop, repeating the name of his guardian deity, or teaching it to his parrot[b] —there go half a dozen voiragēēs, or other persons, making their journey to some holy place—here passes a person, carrying a basket on his head, containing rice, sweetmeats, fruits, flowers, &c. an offering to his guardian deity—here comes a man with a chaplet of red flowers round his head, and the head of a goat in his hand, having left the blood and carcase before the image of Kalēē—there sits a group of Hindoos, listening to three or four persons rehearsing and chanting poetical versions of the pooranŭs —here sits a man in the front of his house reading one of the pooranŭs[c] moving his body like the trunk of a tree in a high wind—and (early in the morning) here comes a group of jaded wretches, who have spent the night in boisterously signing filthy songs, and dancing in an indecent manner, before the image of Doorga—add to this, the villagers, men and women, coming dripping from the banks of the Ganges—and the reader has a tolerable view of the Hindoo idolatry, as it stalks every day, along the streets and roads, and as it may be recognized by any carelesss observer.

The reader will perceive, that in all these religious ceremonies not a particle is found to interest or amend the heart; no family bible, 'profitable

[b] This ceremony is supposed to bring great blessings both on the teacher and the scholar : the parrot obtains heaven, and so does its master. Numbers of Hindoos, particularly in a morning and evening, may be seen in the streets walking about with parrots in their hands, and repeating aloud to them, 'Radha-Krishnŭ, Radha-Krishnŭ, Krishnŭ, Krishnŭ, Radha, Radha,' or 'Shivŭ-Doorga,' or 'Kalēē-tŭraŭ. Some are thus embloyed six months, others twelve or eighteen, before the parrot has learnt his lesson. The merit consists in having repeated the name of a god so great a number of times.

[c] Reading a book, or having it read at a person's house, even though the person himself should not understand it, is a most meritorious action. The love of learning for its own sake is unknown in Bengal : a Hindoo, if he applies to learning, always does it to obtain rupees—or heaven. When he opens one of the shastrŭs, or even an account book, he makes a bow to the book. A shopkeeper, when he is about to balance his books, uncertain how the balance will fall, makes a vow to some god, that if by his favour he should not find himself in debt, he will present to him some offerings.

for doctrine, for reproof, for instruction in righteousness, that men may be thoroughly furnished unto all good works;' no domestic worship;[d] no pious assembly where the village preacher 'attempts each art, reproves each dull delay, allures to brighter worlds, and leads the way.' No standard of morals to repress the vicious; no moral education in which the principles of virtue and religion may be implanted in the youthful mind. Here every thing that assumes the appearance of religion, ends (if you could forget its impurity) in an unmeaning ceremony, and leaves the heart cold as death to every moral principle. Hence the great bulk of the people have abandoned every from and vestige of religious ceremony. The bramhŭn who communicated this information, attributed this general disregard of their religion to the kŭlee-yoogŭ; and consoled himself with the idea, that this deplorable state of things was an exact fulfilment of certain prophecies in the pooranŭs.

Some persons may plead, the doctrine of a state of future rewards and punishments has always been supposed to have a strong influence on public morals: the Hindoos not only have this doctrine in their writings, but are taught to consider every disease and misfortune of life as an undoubted symptom of moral disease and the terrific appearances of its close-pursuing punishment—can this fail to produce a dread of vice, and a desire to merit the favour of the Deity? I will still further assist the objector, and inform him, that the Hindoo writings declare, that till every immoral taint is removed, every sin atoned for, and the mind has obtained perfect abstraction from material objects, it is impossible to be re-united to the Great Spirit; and that, to obtain this perfection, the sinner must linger in many hells, and transmigrate through almost every form of matter. Great as these terrors are, there is nothing more palpable than that, with most of the Hindoos, they do not weigh the weight of a feather, compared with the loss of a rupee. The reason is obvious: every Hindoo considers all his actions as the effect of his destiny; he laments perhaps his miserable fate, but he resigns himself to it without a struggle, like the malefactor in a condemned cell. To this may be added, what must have forced itself on the observation of every thoughtful observer, that, in the absence of the religious principle, no outward terrors, especially those which are invisible and future, not even bodily sufferings, are sufficient to make men virtuous.—Painful experience proves, that even in a Christian country, if the religious principle does not exist, the excellency and the rewards of virtue, and the dishonour and misery attending vice, may be held up to men for ever, without making a single convert.

But let us now advert to the pernicious errors inculcated in the Hindoo writings, and to the vices and miseries engendered by the popular superstition:—

The Bhŭgŭvŭt-Gēēta contains the following most extraordinary description of God:—'*Sŭnjŭyŭ.* The mighty compound and divine being Hŭree, having, O raja, thus spoken, made evident and to Urjoonŭ his supreme and

[d] The women and children take no share in the worship performed by the master of the family. It is not supposed to belong to them. See p. 198.

heavenly form; of many a mouth and eye; many a heavenly ornament; many an upraised weapon; adorned with celestial robes and chaplets; anointed with heavenly essence; covered with every marvellous thing; the eternal God, whose countenance is turned on every side! The glory and amazing splendour of this mighty being may be likened to the sun rising at once into the heavens, with a thousand times more than usual brightness. The son of Pandoo then beheld within the body of the god of gods, standing together, the whole universe divided into its vast variety. He was overwhelmed with wonder, and every hair was raised an end. He bowed down his head before the god, and thus addressed him with joined hands:—*Urjoonŭ.* I behold, O god! within thy breast, the dévŭs assembled, and every specific tribe of beings. I see Brŭmha, that diety sitting on his lotus-throne; all the rishees and heavenly oorŭgŭs: I see thyself, on all sides, of infinite shape, formed with abundant arms, and bellies, and mouths, and eyes; but I can neither discover thy beginning, thy middle, nor again thy end. O universal lord, form of the universe! I see thee with a crown, and armed with club and chŭkrŭ, a mass of glory, darting refulgent beams around. I see thee, difficult to be seen, shining on all sides with light immeasurable, like the ardent fire, or glorious sun. I see thee of valour infinite; the sun and moon thy eyes; thy mouth a flaming fire; and the whole world shining with reflected glory! The space between the heavens and the earth is possessed by thee alone, and every point around; the three regions of the universe, O mighty spirit! behold the wonders of thy awful countenance with troubled minds. Of the celestial bands, some I see fly to thee for refuge; whilst some, afraid, with joined hands sing forth thy praise. The mŭhŭrshees, holy bands, hail thee, and glorify thy name with adoring praises. The roodrŭs, the adityŭs, the vŭsoos, and all those beings the world esteemeth good; ŭshwinŭ, and koomarŭ, the mŭroots and the ooshmŭpas, the gŭndhŭrvŭs and yŭkshŭs, with the holy tribes of ŭsoorŭs; all stand gazing on thee, and all alike amazed! The worlds, alike with me, are terrified to behold thy wondrous form gigantic; with many mouths and eyes; with many arms, and legs, and breasts; with many bellies, and with rows of dreadful teeth! Thus as I see thee, touching the heavens, and shining with such glory; of such various hues; with widely-opened mouths, and bright expanded eyes; I am disturbed within me; my resolution faileth me, O Vishnoo! and I find no rest! Having beholden thy dreadful teeth, and gazed on thy countenance, emblem of time's last fire, I know not which way I turn! I find no peace! Have mercy then, O god of gods! thou mansion of the universe! The sons of Dhritŭrashtrŭ, now, with all those rulers of the land, Bhēēshmŭ, Dronŭ, the son of Sōōtŭ, and even the fronts of our army, seem to be precipitating themselves hastily into thy mouths, discovering such frightful rows of teeth! whilst some appear to stick between thy teeth with their bodies sorely mangled.'[e] —It should be observed, that this frightful description of the Hindoo Supreme Being does not relate to the ferocious Kalēē,

[e] Wilkins's translation of the Bhŭgŭvŭtŭ Gēēta.

drinking the blood of the giants; but it is the playful Krishnŭ who thus shews his dreadful teeth, with the mangled bodies of the family of Dhritŭrashtrŭ sticking between them.

No question occurs so frequently in the Hindoo shastrŭs as this—'What is God?' To know whether he exists or not, page upon page has been written; and this question has been agitated in every period of Hindoo history, wherever two or three pŭndits happened to meet, with a solicitude, but, at the same time, with an uncertainty, which carries us at once to the apostolic declaration, 'The world by wisdom knew not God.' Some pŭndits call him the invisible and ever-blessed; others conceive of him as possessing form. others have the idea that he exists like an inconceivably small atom; sometimes he is male; at other times female; sometimes both male and female, producing a world by conjugal union; sometimes the elements assume his place, and at other times he is a deified hero. Thus in 330,000,000 of forms, or names, this nation, in the emphatical language of St. Paul, has been, from age to age, 'feeling after' the Supreme Being, like men groping 'in the region and shadow of death;' and, after so many centuries, the question is as much undetermined as ever—What is God?

One day, in conversation with the Sŭngskritŭ head-pŭndit of the College of Fort William, on the subject of God, this man, who is truly learned in his own shastrŭs, gave the author, from one of their books, the following parable: —In a certain country there existed a village of blind men, who had heard of an amazing animal called the elephant, of the shape of which, however, they could procure no idea. One day an elephant passed through the place: the villagers crowded to the spot where the animal was standing; and one of them seized his trunk, another his ear, another his tail, another one of his legs. After thus endeavouring to gratify their curiosity, they returned into the village, and sitting down together, began to communicate their ideas on the shape of the elephant to the villagers: the man who had seized his trunk said, he thought this animal must be like the body of the plantain tree; he who had touched his ear was of opinion, that he was like the winnowing fan; the man who had laid hold of his tail said, he thought he must resemble a snake; and he who had caught his leg declared, he must be like a pillar. An old blind man of some judgment was present, who, though greatly perplexed in attempting to reconcile these jarring notions, at length said—'You have all been to examine this animal, and what you report, therefore, cannot be false: I suppose, then, that the part resembling the plantain tree must be his trunk; what you thought similar to a fan must be his ear; the part like a snake must be the tail; and that like a pillar must be his leg.' In this way the old man, uniting all their conjectures, made out something of the form of the elephant.—'Respecting God,' added the pŭndit, 'we are all blind; none of us have seen him; those who wrote the shastrŭs, like the old blind man, have collected all the reasonings and conjectures of mankind together, and have endeavoured to form some idea of the nature of the divine

Being.'[e] It is an irresistible argument in favour of the majesty, simplicity, and truth of the Holy Scriptures, that nothing of this uncertainty has been left on the mind of the most illiterate Christian. However mysterious the subject, we never hear such a question started in Christian countries—What is God?

The doctrine of a plurality of gods, with their consequent intrigues, criminal amours, quarrels, and stratagems to counteract each other, has produced the most fatal effects on the minds of men. Can we expect a people to be better than their gods? Brŭmha was inflamed with evil desires towards his own daughter.[f] —Vishnoo, when incarnate as Bamŭnŭ, deceived king Bŭlee, and deprived him of his kingdom.[g] —Shivŭ's wife was constantly jealous on account of his amours, and charged him with associating with the women of a low caste at Cooch-Behar. The story of Shivŭ and Mohinēē, a female form of Vishnoo, is shockingly indelicate.[h] —Vrihŭspŭtee, the spiritual guide of the gods, committed a rape on his eldest brother's wife.[i] —Indrŭ was guilty of dishonouring the wife of his spiritual guide.[k] —Sōōryŭ ravished a virgin named Koontee.[l] —Yŭmŭ, in a passion, kicked his own mother, who cursed him, and afflicted him with a swelled leg, which to this day the worms are constantly devouring.[m]—Ugnee was inflamed with evil desires towards six virgins, the daughters of as many sages; but was overawed by the presence of his wife[n]—Bŭlŭramŭ was a great drunkard[o].—Vayoo was cursed by Dŭkshŭ, for making his daughters crooked when they refused his embraces. He is also charged with a scandalous connection with a female monkey.[p] —When Vŭroonŭ was walking in his own heaven, he was so smitten with the charms of Oorvŭshēē, a courtezan, that, after a long contest, she was scarcely able to extricate herself from him.[q]—Krishnŭ's thefts, wars, and adulteries are so numerous, that his whole history seems to be one uninterrupted series of crimes.[r] —In the images of Kalēē, she is represented as treading on the breast of her husband.[s] —Lŭkshmee and Sŭrŭswŭtēē, the wives of Vishnoo, were continually quarrelling.[t] —It is worthy of enquiry, how the world is governed by these gods more wicked than men, that we may be able to judge how far they can be the objects of faith, hope, and affection. Let us open the Hindu sacred writings: here we see the Creator and the Preserver perpetually counteracting each other. Sometimes the Preserver is destroying, and at other times the Destroyer is preserving. On a certain occasion,[u] Shivŭ granted to the great enemy of the gods, Ravŭnŭ, a blessing which set all their heavens in an uproar, and drove the 330,000,000 of gods into a state of desperation. Brŭmha created Koombhŭ-kŭrnŭ, a monster larger than the whole island of Lŭnka; but was obliged to doom him to an almost perpetual sleep, to prevent his producing an universal famine. This

[e] Acts xvii. 27. [f] See Kalika pooranŭ. [g] See Mŭhabharŭtŭ.
[h] Ibid. [i] Ibid. [k] Ibid. [l] Ibid.
[m] See Mŭhabharŭtŭ. [n] Ibid. [o] Ibid. [p] See Ramayŭnŭ. [q] Ibid.
[r] See the Shrēē-bhagŭvŭtŭ. [s] See the Markŭndēyŭ pooranŭ. [t] See the Vrihŭddhŭrmŭ pooranŭ. [u] See the Ramyŭnŭ.

god is often represented as bestowing a blessing, to remove the effects of which Vishnoo is obliged to become incarnate: nay, these effects have not in some cases been removed till all the gods have been dispossessed of their thrones, and obliged to go a begging; till all human affairs have been thrown into confusion, and all the elements seized and turned against the Creator, the Preserver, and the Reproducer. When some giant, blessed by Brŭmha, has destroyed the creation, Vishnoo and Shivŭ have been applied to; but they have confessed that they could do nothing for the tottering universe.

Reverence for the gods, especially among the poor, as might be expected, does not exceed their merits; yet it is a shocking fact, that language like the following should be used respecting what the Hindoos suppose to be the Providence which governs the world:—when it thunders awfully, respectable Hindoos say, 'Oh! the gods are giving us a bad day;' the lower orders say, 'The rascally gods are dying.' During a heavy rain, a woman of respectable caste frequently says, 'Let the gods perish! my clothes are all wet.' A man of low caste says, 'These rascally gods are sending more rain.'

In witnessing such a state of gross ignorance, on a subject of infinite moment to men, how forcibly do we feel the truth and the wisdom of the declaration of the Divine Author of the Christian religion, 'This is life eternal, to know thee the only true God!' A correct knowledge of the Divine perfections, in the mind of a sincere Christian, is a treasure which transcends in value all the riches of the earth: for instance, how much does the doctrine of the Divine Unity tend to fix the hope and joy of the Christian! but the poor Hindoo knows not, amongst so many gods, upon whom to call, or in whom to trust. In the spirituality of the Divine Nature, united to omniscience and omnipresence, the Christian finds a large field for the purest and most sublime contemplations; but the degraded idolater, walking round his pantheon, sees beings that fill him only with shame or terror: he retires from the image of Kalēē overwhelmed with horror, and from those of Radha-Krishnŭ with confusion and contempt—or else inflamed with concupiscence. How effectual to awaken the fears and excite the salutary apprehensions of those who neglect their best interests, is the scripture doctrine of the Divine Purity and Justice; but the wretched Hindoo has the examples of the most corrupt beings, even in his gods, to lead him to perdition. How necessary to the happiness of a good man, are just ideas of the wisdom, and equity, and beneficenee, of providential dispensations:—the reader has seen how impossible it is for a Hindoo to derive the smallest consolation in adversity from the doctrine of the shastrŭs respecting the government of the world. How consoling to a person, sensible of many failings, is the doctrine of the Divine Mercy:—but these heathens have nothing held out to encourage the hopes of the penitent; nothing short of perfect abstraction, and the extinction of every desire, qualify for deliverance from matter.—The sincere Christian, with his knowledge of God, 'casteth all his care on his Father, who is in heaven;' and the language of his mind, invigorated by the living waters flowing from the fountain of eternal truth, is, 'Thou shalt guide me with thy counsel;' 'Though I walk through the valley and even the shadow of death, I will fear no evil, for thou art with me; thy rod and thy staff they comfort me.'

The Hindoo writings farther teach, that it is the Great Spirit which is diffused through every form of animated matter; that actions *of every kind* are his; that he is the charioteer, and the body the chariot;[x] that it is the highest attainment of human wisdom to realize the fact, that the human soul and Brŭmhŭ are one and the same. By this doctrine all accountability is destroyed, and liability to punishment rendered preposterous. How often has the author heard it urged by the most sensible Hindoos, that the moving cause of every action, however flagitious, is God; that man is an instrument upon which God plays what tune he pleases. Another modification of this doctrine is that of fate, or unchangeable destiny, embraced, without a dissentient voice, by all the Hindoos. Thus the Deity on his throne is insulted as the author of all crimes, and men are emboldened to rush forward in the swiftest career of iniquity.

The sacred writings of the Hindoos encourage the bramhŭns to despise the great body of the people, and teach them, that the very sight and touch of a shōōdrŭ renders them unclean. To be contented in ignorance is the duty of a shōōdrŭ, as well as to drink with reverence and hope the water in which the bramhŭn has dipped his foot. The services too and the hopes held forth by this religion, are almost exclusively confined to the bramhŭns. The shōōdrŭ is supposed to be born to evil destiny; and the only hope he can indulge is, that after a long succession of transmigrations he may probably be born a bramhŭn.

The subjugation of the passions, so much insisted upon in the Hindoo shastrŭs, applies to all virtuous as well as vicious desires. The person who is divested of all desire, even that of obtaining God, is described as having arrived at the summit of perfection. The love of parents, of children, &c. is an imperfection, according to the Hindoo code: hence says Krishnŭ, 'Wisdom is exemption from attachment and affection for children, wife, and home[y].'

[x] See the Vedantŭ-sarŭ.

[y] At the time a learned native was assisting the Rev. Mr. Carey in the translation of the New Testament into the Sŭngskritŭ, when such passages as these were translating, 'Henceforth know I no man after the flesh;' 'We are dead, and our life is hid,' &c. 'I am crucified to the world;' 'We are fools for Christ;' 'We are made a spectacle,' &c. he exclaimed, 'This is pure voirageēism: Paul was a true Purumhungsee.' Yet the divine principles upon which Paul trampled upon the world, and devoted himself supremely to God, have no existence in the shatrŭs. The Hindoo principle is mere stoicism; its origin is either selfishness, or infatuated ambition: but the principle of the apostle, was the love of Christ, who died on a cross for his enemies—as he himself says, 'The love of Christ, like an irresistible torrent, bears us away;' 'If we are beside ourselves, it is for your sakes.'

These shastrŭs also teach, that sin may be removed by the slightest ceremony; and thus, instead of reforming, they promise impunity in transgression. See different stories in pp. 51, 168, 170.

The ŭt'hŭryvŭ vedŭ contains many prayers for the destruction of enemies; and gives a list of offerings proper to be presented to Bhŭgŭvŭtēē, that she may be induced to assist in the gratification of revengeful passions: among the rest, the worshipper is to make a paste image of a man, cut off its head, and offer this head to the goddess, with a burnt-sacrifice, &c. Is it not reasonable to suppose, that human sacrifices preceded the cutting off the head of this man of paste; and that one man was sacrificed and offered to the gods to induce them to destroy another?

In the Institutes of Mŭnoo a man is allowed to commit adultery, if the female consent; to steal, for the sake of performing a religious ceremony; and to perjure himself, from benevolent motives: they also allow of lying, to preserve the life of a bramhŭn, to appease an angry wife, or to please a mistress. [z] What is still worse, in this code a bramhŭn, in case of want, is permitted to steal, not from the rich merely, but—from his slave! It is a common sentiment among this people, that in secular transactions lying is absolutely necessary; and perjury is so common, that it is impossible to rely upon the testimony of Hindoo witnesses. The natives ridicule the idea of administering justice by oral testimony.

I have given in p. 282, a few examples of persons raised to heaven by their own works, to shew that these works have nothing to do with real morality. But how shall we describe the unutterable abominations connected with the popular superstition? The author has witnessed scenes which can be clothed in no language, and has heard of other abominations practised in the midst of religious rites, and in the presence of the gods, which, if they could be described, would fill the whole Christian world with disgust and horror. Let impenetrable darkness cover them till 'the judgment of the great day.'

Men are sufficiently corrupt by nature, without any outward excitements to evil in the public festivals; nor have civil nor spiritual terrors, the frowns of God and governors united, been found sufficient to keep within restraint the

[z] If a man, by the impulse of lust, tell lies to a woman, or if his own life would otherwise be lost, or all the goods of his house spoiled, or if it is for the benefit of a bramhŭn, in such affairs falsehood is allowable.' *Halhed's Code of Gentoo Laws.*—How can we wonder that the Hindoos should be so addicted to falsehood, when even in the rig-védŭ, approached with profound reverence by so many Christian infidels, we find monstrous exaggerations like the following?—'Bhŭrŭtŭ distributed in Mŭshnarŭ a hundred and seven thousand millions of black elephants with white tusks, and decked with gold.' 'A sacred fire was lighted for Bhŭrŭtŭ, son of Dooshŭntŭ, in Sachigoonŭ, at which a thousand bramhŭns shared a thousand millions of cows a piece.' *See Mr. Colebrooke's Essay.*

overflowings of iniquity :—but what must be the moral state of that country, where the sacred festivals, and the very forms of religion, lead men to every species of vice! These festivals and public exhibitions excite universal attention, and absorb, for weeks together, almost the whole of the public conversation: and such is the enthusiasm with which they are hailed, that the whole country seems to be thown into a ferment: health, property, time, business, every thing is sacrificed to them. In this manner are the people prepared to receive impressions from their national institutions. If these institutions were favourable to virtue, the effects would be most happy; but as, in addition to their fascination, they are exceedingly calculated to corrupt the mind, the most dreadful consequences follow, and vice, like a mighty torrent, flows through the plains of Bengal, with the force of the flood-tide of the Ganges, carrying along with it young and old, the learned and the ignorant, rich and poor, all castes and descriptions of people—into an awful eternity!

In short, the characters of the gods, and the licentiousness which prevails at their festivals, and abounds in their popular works, with the enervating nature of the climate, have made the Hindoos the most effeminate and corrupt people on earth. I have, in the course of this work, exhibited so many proofs of this fact, that I will not again disgust the reader by going into the subject. Suffice it to say, that fidelity to marriage vows is almost unknown among the Hindoos; the intercourse of the sexes approaches very near to that of the irrational animals. The husband almost invariably lives in criminal intercourse during the pupilage of his infant wife; and she, if she becomes a widow, cannot marry, and in consequence, being destitute of a protector and of every moral principle, becomes a willing prey to the lascivious.

Add to all this, the almost incredible number of human victims which annually fall in this Aceldama. I have ventured on an estimate of the number of Hindoos who annually perish, the victims of the bramhinical religion; (p. 254,) and have supposed, that they cannot amount to less than 10,500! Every additional information I obtain, and the opinions of the best informed persons with whom I am acquainted, confirm me in the opinion, that this estimate is too low, that the havoc is far greater, however difficult it may be to bring the mind to contemplate a scene of horror which out-does all that has ever been perpetrated in the name of religion by all the savage nations put together. These cruelties, together with the contempt which the Hindoos feel for the body as a mere temporary shell, cast off at pleasure, and the disorganizing effects of the caste, render them exceedingly unfeeling and cruel: of which their want of every national provision for the destitute; their leaving multitudes to perish before their own doors, unpitied and even unnoticed; the inhuman manner in which they burn the bodies of their deceased relations, and their savage triumph when spectators of a widow burning in the flames of the funeral pile, are awful examples.

But to know the Hindoo idolatry, AS IT IS, a person must wade through the filth of the thirty-six pooranŭs and other popular books—he must read and hear the modern popular poems and songs—he must follow the bramhŭn through his midnight orgies, before the image of Kalēē, and other goddesses; or he must accompany him to the nightly revels, the jatras, and listen to the filthy dialogues which are rehearsed respecting Krishnŭ and the daughters of the milkmen; or he must watch him, at midnight, choking, with the mud and waters of the Ganges, a wealthy rich relation, while in the delirium of a fever; or, at the same hour, while murdering an unfaithful wife, or a supposed domestic enemy; burning the body before it is cold, and washing the blood from his hands in the sacred stream of the Ganges; or he must look at the bramhŭn, hurrying the trembling half-dead widow round the funeral pile, and throwing her, like a long of wood by the side of the dead body of her husband, tying her, and then holding her down with bamboo levers till the fire has deprived her of the power of rising and running away.—After he has followed the bramhŭn through all these horrors, he will only have approached the threshold of this temple of Moloch, and he will begin to be convinced, that to know the Hindoo idolatry, AS IT IS, a man must become a Hindoo—rather, he must become a bramhŭn; for a poor shōōdrŭ, by the very circumstances of his degradation, is restrained from many abominations which bramhŭns alone are privileged to commit. And when he has done this, let him meditate on this system in its effects on the mind of the afflicted or dying Hindoo, as described in pp. 277, 278, and 285; on reading which description he will perceive, that in distress the Hindoo utters the loudest murmurs against the gods, and dies in the greatest perplexity and agitation of mind.

The state of things serves to explain the mysterious dispensations of Providence, in permitting the Hindoos to remain so long in darkness, and in causing them to suffer so much formerly under their Mahometan oppressors. The murder of so many myriads of victims has armed heaven against them. Let us hope that now, in the midst of judgment, a gracious Providence has remembered mercy, and placed them under the fostering care of the British government, that they may enjoy a happiness to which they have been hitherto strangers.

If then this system of heathenism communicates no purifying knowledge of the divine perfections, supplies no one motive to holiness while living, no comfort to the afflicted, no hope to the dying; but on the contrary excites to every vice, and hardens its followers in the most flagrant crimes; how are we to account for the conduct of its apologists, except in the recollection, that the sceptical part of mankind have always been partial to heathenism. Voltaire, Gibbon, Hume, &c. have been often charged with a strong partiality for the Grecian and Roman idolatries; and many Europeans in India are suspected of having made large strides towards heathenism. Even Sir Wm. Jones, whose recommendation of the Holy Scriptures (found in his Bible after his death) has been so often and so deservedly quoted, it is said, to please his pŭndit, was accustomed to study the shastrŭs with the image of a Hindoo god placed on his table:—his fine metrical translations of idolatrous hymns are known to every lover of verse.[d] In the same spirit, we observe, that figures and allusions to the ancient idolatries are retained in almost all modern poetical compositions, and even in some Christian writings.

However wonderful this partiality of professed Christians to heathenism may be, it is not more extraordinary than the extravagant lengths into which some learned men have gone in their expectations from the antiquity of the Hindoo writings. Mr. Halhed seems to prefer Hindooism to Christianity purely on account of its boasted antiquity[e]. Dr. Stiles, president of Yale College, in North America, formed such an enthusiastic expectation from the amazing antiquity of the Hindoo writings, that he actually wrote to Sir William Jones, to request him to search among the Hindoos for the Adamic books. Had not this gentleman been a zealous Christian, it is likely his extravagant expectations might have led him to ask Sir William to translate and send him a book two or three millions of years old, written in some kúlpŭ amidst the endless succession of worlds.

For sometime, a very unjust and unhappy impression appeared to have been made on the public mind, by the encomiums passed on the Hindoo writings. In the first place, they were thus elevated in their antiquity beyond the Christian Scriptures, the writings of Moses having been called the productions of yesterday, compared with those of the bramhŭns. The contents of these books also were treated with the greatest reverence; the primitive religion of the Hindoos, it was said, revealed the most sublime doctrines, and inculcated a pure morality. We were taught to make the greatest distinction between the ancient and modern religion of the Hindoos; for the apologists for Hindooism did not approve of its being judged of by present appearances. Some persons endeavoured to persuade us, that the Hindoos were not idolaters, because they maintained the unity of God; though they worshipped the works of their own hands as God, and though the number of their gods was 330,000,000. It is

d 'I could not help feeling a degree of regret, in reading lately the Memoirs of the admirable and estimable Sir William Jones. Some of his researches in Asia have no doubt incidentally served the cause of religion; but did he think the last possible direct service had been rendered to Christianity, that his accomplished mind was left at leisure for hymns to the Hindoo gods? Was not this a violation even of the neutrality, and an offence, not only against the gospel, but against theism itself? I know what may be said about personification, license of poetry, and so on: but should not a worshipper of God hold himself under a solemn obligation to adjure all tolerance of even poetical figures that can seriously seem, in any way whatever, to recognize the pagan divinities, or abominations, as the prophets of Jehovah would have called them? What would Elijah have said to such an employment of talents? It would have availed little to have told him, that these divinities were only personifications (with their appropriate representative idols) of objects in nature, of elements, or of abstractions. He would have sternly replied—And was not Baal, whose prophets I destroyed, the same?' *See Foster's incomparable Essays.*

e Is Mr. Halhed an example of the amazing credulity of unbelievers in every case, wherein the *Holy Bible* is not concerned? When he wrote his 'Code of Gentoo Laws,'

very probable, that the unity of God has been a sentiment amongst the philosophers of every age; and that they wished it to be understood, that they worshipped the One God, whether they bowed before the image of Moloch, Jupiter, or Kalēē: yet mankind have generally concluded, that he who worships an image is an idolater; and I suppose they will continue to think so, unless, in this age of reason, common sense should be turned out of doors.

Now, however, the world has had some opportunity of deciding upon the claims of the Hindoo writings, both as it respects their antiquity, and the value of their contents. Mr. Colebrooke's essay on the védŭs, and his other important translations; the Bhŭgŭvŭt-Gēēta, translated by Mr. Wilkins; the translation of the Ramayŭnŭ, several volumes of which have been printed; some valuable papers in the Asiatic Researches; with other translations by different Sŭngskritŭ scholars; have thrown a great body of light on this subject:—and this light is daily increasing.

Many an object appears beautiful when seen at a distance, and through a mist; but when the fog has dispersed, and the person has approached it, he smiles at the deception. Such is the exact case with these books, and this system of idolatry. Because the public, for want of being more familiar with the subject, could not ascertain the point of time when the Hindoo shastrŭs were written, they therefore at once believed the assertions of the bramhŭns and their friends, that their antiquity was unfathomable.

The Reverend Mr. Maurice has attempted to describe the Hindoo ceremonies, which he never saw, in the most captivating terms, and has painted these 'abominable idolatries' in the most florid colours. It might have been expected, (idolatry being in itself an act so degrading to man, and so dishonourable to God,) that a Christian divine would have been shocked while writing in this manner. If Mr. Maurice think there is something in Hindooism to excite the most sublime ideas, let him come and join in the dance before the idol;—or assist the bramhŭns in crying *Hŭree bul! Hŭree bul*[f] *!* while the

he hesitated to believe the Bible, because it was out done in chronology by the histories of the Chinese and Hindoos. With sacred reverence he exclaims, at the close of his account of the four yoogŭs, 'To such antiquity the Mosaic creation is but as yesterday; and to such ages the life of Methuselah is no more than a span!' He says, in another page, 'The conscientious scruples of Brydone will always be of some weight in the scale of philosophy.' If the age or reign of Brŭmha, viz., 55,987,200,000,000 years, excited such sacred awe in the mind of this gentleman, what would have been his sensations, and how strong his faith in 'holy writ' of the Hindoos, if he had happened to read in the Ramayŭnŭ the account of Ramu's army; which, this 'holy writ' says, amounted to 1,000,000,000,000,000,000,000 soldiers, or rather monkies? Again, two thousand times the four yoogŭs, or 8,640,000,000 years, is the age of the sage Markŭndéŭ! What, in the name of Mr. Halhed, is the life of Methuselah to this?—This unbeliever in Moses became at last, it is said, a firm believer in *Richard Brothers!*

[f] Sounds of triumph, which the bramhŭns use when the fire of the funeral pile begins to burn, and when they are choking a dying person with the water of the Ganges. These words literally mean, 'call upon Hŭree,' or repeat the name of Hŭree, viz., Krishnŭ. In their popular use, they are like the English phrase, *huzza! huzza!*

fire is seizing the limbs of the young and unfortunate Hindoo widow;—or let him attend at the sacrificing of animals before the images of Kalēē and Doorga;—or come and join in the dance, stark naked, in the public street, in open day, before the image of Doorga, in the presence of thousands of spectators, young and old, male and female. He will find, that the sight will never make these holy bramhŭns, these mild and innocent Hindoos, blush for a moment.—Seriously, should sights like these raise the ardour of enthusiasm, or chill the blood of a Christian minister? Say, ye who blush for human nature sunk in shame. As a clergyman, Mr. Maurice should have known, that antiquity sanctifies nothing:—'The sinner, being an hundred years old, shall be accursed.'

What will a sober Christian say to the two following paragraphs, inserted in the fifth volume of the Indian Antiquities?[g] 'Mr. Forbes, of Stanmore-hill, in his elegant museum of Indian rarities, numbers two of the bells that have been used in devotion by the bramhŭns. They are great curiosities, and one of them in particular appears to be of very high antiquity, in form very much resembling the cup of the lotos; and the tune of it is uncommonly soft and melodious. I could not avoid being deeply affected with the sound of an instrument which had been actually employed to kindle the flame of that superstition, which I have attempted so extensively to unfold. My transported thoughts travelled back to the remote period, when the bramhŭn religion blazed forth in all its splendour in the caverns of elephanta: I was, for a moment, entranced, and caught the ardour of enthusiasm. A tribe of venerable priests, arrayed in flowing stoles, and decorated with high tiaras, seemed assembled around me; the mystic song of initiation vibrated in my ear; I breathed an air fragrant with the richest perfumes, and contemplated the Deity in the fire that symbolized him.' In another place:—'She [the Hindoo religion] wears the similitude of a beautiful and radiant CHERUB from HEAVEN, bearing on his persuasive lips the accents of pardon and peace, and on his silken wings benefaction and blessing.'

The sacred scriptures, of which this writer professes to be a teacher, in every part, mark idolatry as THE ABOMINABLE THING WHICH GOD HATETH. Mr. Maurice calls it, 'a beautiful and radiant cherub from heaven.' How this Christian minister will reconcile his ideas of idolatry with those of his GREAT MASTER in the great day of final account, I must leave; but I recommend to him, and to all Europeans who think there is not much harm in Hindooism, the perusal of the following passages from the word of the TRUE and LIVING GOD:—

'If thy brother, the son of thy mother, or thy son, or thy daughter, or the wife of thy bosom, or thy friend, which is as thine own soul, entice thee secretly, saying, Let us go and serve other gods, which thou hast not known,

[g] While the author cannot but withhold his assent from Mr. Maurice's application of the Hindoo triad, and the whole of his attempt to illustrate Scripture doctrines from the ancient systems of idolatry, he embraces this opportunity of expressing his admiration of the great merit of this singular and masterly work.

thou, nor thy fathers; (namely, of the gods of the people which are round about you, nigh unto thee, or far off from thee, from the one end of the earth even unto the other end of the earth;) thou shalt not consent unto him, nor hearken unto him; neither shall thine eye pity him, neither shalt thou spare, neither shalt thou conceal him: but thou shall surely kill him; thine hand shall be first upon him to put him to death, and afterwards the hand of all the people. And thou shalt stone him with stones, that he die; because he hath sought to thrust thee away from the Lord thy God, which brought thee out of the land of Egypt, from the house of bondage. And all Israel shall hear and fear, and shall do no more any such wickedness as this is among you.' *Deut.* xiii. 6, 7, 8, 9, 10, 11.—I quote this remarkable passage, not because I think the Christian dispensation allows of punishing idolaters with death, but to shew how marked is the divine abhorrence of this sin.

'And I will destroy your high places, and cut down your images, and cast your carcases upon the carcases of your idols, and my soul shall abhor you.' *Leviticus* xxvi. 30.—'Cursed be the man that maketh any *graven image*, any *graven* or *molten image*, an abomination unto the Lord, the work of the hands of the craftsmen, and putteth it in a secret place. And all the people shall answer and say, Amen.' *Deut.* xxvii. 15.—'Thus saith the Lord of Hosts, the God of Israel, Ye have seen all the evil that I have brought upon Jerusalem, and upon all the cities of Judah; and, behold, this day they are a desolation, and no man dwelleth therein. Because of their wickedness which they have committed to provoke me to anger, in that they went to burn incense, and to serve *other gods*, whom they knew not, neither they, ye, nor your fathers. Howbeit, I sent unto you all my servants the prophets, rising early and sending them, saying, O DO NOT THIS ABOMINABLE THING THAT I HATE. But they hearkened not, nor inclined their ear to turn from their wickedness, to burn no incense unto *other gods*. Wherefore my fury and mine anger was poured forth, and was kindled in the cities of Judah, and in the streets of Jerusalem; and they are wasted and desolate, as at this day.' *Jeremiah* xliv. 2, 3, 4, 5, 6. —'And what agreement hath the temple of God with *idols?*' 2 *Cor.* vi. 16.—'For the time past of our life may suffice us to have wrought the will of the Gentiles, when we walked in lasciviousness, lusts, excess of wine, revellings, banquetings, and *abominable idolatries*.' 1*st Peter* iv. 3.—'But the fearful, and unbelieving, and the abominable, and murderers, and whore-mongers, and sorcerers, and *idolaters*, and all liars, shall have their part in the lake which burneth with fire and brimstone: which is the second death.' *Rev.* xxi. 3.

Let every conscientious Christian fairly weigh these portions of the divine word, and then say, whether there be not, according to the spirit of these passages, a great degree of criminality attached to the person who in any way countenances idolatry. I am not ashamed to confess, that I fear more for the continuance of the British power in India, from the encouragement which Englishmen have given to the idolatry of the Hindoos, than from any other quarter whatever. The Governor of the world said to the Israelites, in particular reference to idolatry, 'If ye walk contrary to me, I will walk contrary to you.' Moses, in the name of Jehovah, thus threatens the Jews, if they countenance idolatry:—'I call heaven and earth to witness against you this day, that ye shall soon utterly perish from off the land whereunto ye go over Jordan to possess it: ye shall not prolong your days upon it, but shall utterly be destroyed.' It cannot be doubted, that in every case in which either a person, or a nation, begins to think favourably of idolatry, it is a mark of departure in heart and practice from the living God: it was always so considered among the Jews. There is scarcely any thing in Hindooism, when truly known, in which a learned man can delight, or of which a benevolent man can approve; and I am fully persuaded, that there will soon be but one opinion on the subject, and that this opinion will be, that the Hindoo system is less ancient than the Egyptian, and that it is the most PUERILE, IMPURE, AND BLOODY OF ANY SYSTEM OF IDOLATRY THAT WAS EVER ESTABLISHED ON EARTH.

To this description of the Hindoo Mythology, the author has added accounts of the principal Hindoo Seceders, including the sects founded by Booddhŭ, Rishŭbhŭ-dévŭ, Nanŭkŭ, and Choitŭnyŭ.

All the founders of these sects appear to have been religious mendicants, who, animated by excessive enthusiasm, have attempted to carry certain points of the Hindoo system farther than the regular Hindoos, particularly those which respect severe mortifications. Nanŭkŭ and Choitŭnyŭ were less rigid, and do not seem to have pressed the importance of religious austerities. Booddhŭ and Rishŭdhŭ-dévŭ evidently adhered to the systems of those Hindoo philosophers who were atheists.[h]

Both these systems are comprised in two or three doctrines:—the world is eternal, and possesses in itself the energy which gives rise to what we call creation, preservation, and resuscitation; religion (Dhŭrmŭ) regulates all states, and is in fact what Christians call providence, connected with absolute predestination; the person who acquires the greatest portion of dhŭrmŭ becomes a personification of religion, procures happiness for himself, and deserves the worship of others. Amongst all excellent qualities, compassion is the cardinal virtue, especially as manifested in a rigid care not to hurt or destroy sentient beings.

Without abating an atom of our abhorrence and contempt of a scheme of religion which excludes a God, it is a singular feature of this system of atheism, that it has placed the sceptre of universal government in an imagined being under the name of Religion; or, to speak more correctly, in the hands of two beings, Religion and Irreligion, who have the power of rewarding and punishing the virtuous and the vicious. In short, these heresiarchs have not promulgated a system of atheism, without making some provision for the interests of morality in their way; and if the idea of punishment alone would make men virtuous, a Bouddhŭ and a Joinŭ might attain a place in the niche of fame not much below thousands who believe in a First Cause.

h The Shēē-bhagŭvŭtŭ mentions Booddhŭ as the son of Unjŭnŭ, of Kēēkŭtŭ; and that Charvvakŭ, a celebrated atheist, embraced and published the real opinions of Booddhŭ. See Shrēē-bhagŭvŭtŭ, chap. i. sect. 3.

As men are born under a certain destiny and as every action produces its destined fruit, little is left to human exertion, and in consequence religious ceremonies have little place in these systems. The only object of worship is a deceased or living perfect ascetic: the former has temples erected to his memory, which contain his image, and before which a few ceremonies are performed similar to those before the Hindoo idols; and the living mendicant is worshipped by the devout, wherever he happens to rest from his peregrinations.

These men have almost entirely excluded from their system a social life; and at present those Joinŭs, who find the rules of their guides too strict, are obliged to solicit the forms of marriage at the hands of some Hindoo priest. In the translation of the Témee Jatŭ, a Bouddhŭ work, (see p. 312,) the reader will perceive, that a monarch and all his subjects abandoned a civil life at the call of the monarch's son, an ascetic, and sought in a forest that abstraction from secular concerns which they considered as an essential preparation for re-union to the divine essence.

The ceremonies of these two sects are all comprised in the worshipping of their saints, rehearsing their praises, listening to their sayings or written works, and a rigid care to avoid the destruction of animal life, even in its most diminutive forms. The Booddhŭs and Joinŭs have not excluded, it is true, every thing pleasant from their religion, for a number of festivals are celebrated among them monthly or annually: but there is reason to suppose, that these are no parts of the original system, but the additions of mendicants less rigid in their principles and less austere in their manners.

The Joinŭs speak of the Bouddhŭs with a degree of contempt, as being very loose in their practice, praticularly as it regards the destruction of animal life. From this circumstance, and from the Joinŭs being still found in Hindoost'-hanŭ, as well as from the fact that they trace their religion up to a very early Hindoo monarch, it may be conjectured, that they are the oldest of the two sects, and are the scattered remnants of those persecuted under the name of atheists, after the destruction of the Goutŭmŭ dynasty, or, as they were then called, Bouddhŭs.

Nanŭkŭ, the Shikh leader, does not appear to have had any connection with the atheists; he disapproved of the excessive polytheism of the Hindoos, and wished to draw them to the worship of the one God, whom, however, he called by the names usually adopted by the Hindoos: Brŭmhŭ, Pŭrŭm-eshwŭrŭ, Unadee, Nirakarŭ, &c. He did not publicly reprobate those parts of the Hindoo system to which he was most averse, but contented himself with observing, that while he left them indifferent, the practice of them would not be accompanied with the benefits held out by the Hindoo writers. He formed, from the bramhinical system, a new one, having little polytheism in it, but borrowing all its principal doctrines from the Hindoo writings; and he and his successors incorporated the whole in two volumes. The principal tenets of this seceder are: There is one invisible God, who is to be worshipped or honoured in holy men; his name is to be repeated; that spiritual guide is to be reverenced; all evil avoided: if images be adopted, they should be those of eminent ascetics.

Future happiness, consisting in union to the divine nature, is secured to those Shikhs who observe the rules laid down by their sacred books.

Choitŭnyŭ, the last of the seceders, departed still less from regular Hindooism: his principal opposition was aimed at the rising sect of the shaktŭs, or those who worship the female deities with bloody sacrifices: he testified his abhorrence of the destruction of animal life in sacrifices, and professed to be a rigid Voishnŭvŭ, adopting Krishnŭ, or Hŭree, as his favourite deity. He did not proscribe the other gods, but set up Vishnoo as uniting all in himself; nor did he explode any tenet of Hindooism beside that relating to bloody sacrifices. A devout attachment to Krishnŭ; a strict union among all his followers; reverence for religious mendicants; visiting holy places; repeating the name of Hŭree, and entertaining mendicant Voishnŭvŭs, compose the prime articles in the creed of this sect.

Such are the systems established by these Hindoo heresiarchs, each of which, though different in many essential points, is distinguished by one remarkable feature, reverence for mendicant saints, especially those who seem to have carried abstraction of mind, seclusion from the world, and religious austerities to the greatest lengths. Among the atheistical sects, these mendicants are regarded as personifications of religion; and among the two last, as partial incarnations, or persons approaching the state of re-union to the Great Spirit.

Respecting the priority of the atheistical or the bramhinical systems, the author has not been able entirely to satisfy his own mind. Some persons conjecture, that they see a coincidence betwixt the doctrines of the védŭs, and of the atheistical sects, respecting the origin of things, and the worship of the elements. It may be safely added, that to these systems succeeded the pouranic mythology, and after that the worship of the female deities with bloody sacrifices. The whole of these systems, however, when more generally known, will, no doubt, exceedingly endear the 'WORD of TRUTH' to every sincere Christian, and more and more prove, how deep and important a stake he has in the *glorious gospel* of the BLESSED GOD.

THE
HINDOO MYTHOLOGY.

BOOK I.

OBJECTS OF WORSHIP.

CHAPTER I.

OF GOD.

It is a painful reflection to every benevolent mind, that not a single Hindoo temple, dedicated to the One God, is to be found in all Hindoost'han ; nor is any act of worship, in any form, addressed by this people to God. The doctrines respecting the Divine Nature are considered as mere philosophical speculations, totally unconnected with religious services.

It is true, indeed, that the Hindoos believe in the unity of God. 'One Brŭmhŭ, without a second,' is a phrase very commonly used by them when conversing on subjects which relate to the nature of God. They believe also that God is almighty, allwise, omnipresent, omniscient, &c., and they frequently speak of him as embracing in his government the happiness of the good, and the subjection or punishment of the bad : yet they have no idea of God's performing any act, either of creation or providence, except through the gods ; and thus are prevented all the beneficial effects which might have arisen out of their notions of the divine perfections : for in the whole of the reigning superstition the gods alone are seen ; and these gods bear no more resemblance to the one true God, than darkness to light, than vice to virtue.

Perceiving, therefore, that the speculations of the Hindoo philosophers on the divine nature have no place whatever in the religion of the country, I have placed these dogmas in the preceding volume*

* See Introduction.

CHAPTER II.

OF THE GODS.

THE deities in the Hindoo pantheon amount to 330,000,000. Yet all these gods and goddesses may be resolved into the three principal ones, Vishnoo, Shivŭ, and Brŭmha; the elements; and the three females, Doorga Lŭkshmēē, and Sŭrŭswŭtēē. The following pages will contain accounts of all those at present worshipped by the Hindoos, particularly in the provinces of India under the English government.

SECT. I.—*Vishnoo.*

THIS god is represented in the form of a black man, with four arms; in one of which he holds a club, in another a shell, in the third a chŭkrŭ[a], and in the fourth a water-lily. He rides on Gŭroorŭ, an animal half-bird and half-man, and wears yellow garments.

The Hindoo shastrŭs give accounts of ten appearances or incarnations of Vishnoo, in the character of the Preserver; nine of which are said to be past.

The first is called the Mŭtsyŭ incarnation. Brŭmhŭ[b], the one God, when he resolves to recreate the universe after a periodical destruction, first gives birth to Brŭmha, Vishnoo, and Shivŭ, to preside over the work of creation, preservation, and destruction. After a periodical dissolution of the universe, the four védŭs remained in the waters. In order to enter upon the work of creation, it was necessary to obtain these books, for the instruction of Brŭmha. Vishnoo was therefore appointed to bring up the védŭs from the deep; who, taking the form of a fish, (some say one kind and some another,) descended into the waters, and brought up these sacred books.

In the Kŭchyŭpŭ incarnation, Vishnoo assumed the form of a tortoise, and took the newly created earth upon his back, to render it stable. The Hindoos believe that to this hour the earth is supported on the back of this tortoise.

The Vŭrahŭ incarnation happened at one of the periodical destructions of the world, when the earth sunk into the waters. Vishnoo, the preserver, appearing in the form of a bŏar (vŭrahŭ), descended into the waters, and with his tusks drew up the earth.

[a] An iron instrument of destruction like a wheel.

[b] The reader will please to keep in mind that Brŭmhŭ means the one God, and that Brŭmha means the idol of that name.

VISHNOO.

What contemptible ideas on such a subject! The earth, with all its mountains, &c. &c. made fast on the back of a turtle, or drawn up from the deep by the tusks of a hog!

The fourth incarnation is called Nŭrŭsinghŭ[c]. Among other descendants of Dŭkshŭ, (the first man that Brŭmha created,) was Kŭshyŭpŭ, a moonee, and his four wives, Ditee, Ŭditee, Vinŭta, and Kŭdroo. From Ditee, sprang the giants; from Ŭditee, the gods; from Vinŭta, Gŭroorŭ; and from Kŭdroo, the hydras. The giants possessed amazing strength, and amongst them two arose of terrific powers, named Hirŭnyakshŭ and Hirŭnyŭ-kŭshipoo, both of whom performed religious austerities many thousand years to obtain immortality. Brŭmha at length gave them a blessing apparently equivalent to that which they desired. He promised, that no common being should destroy them; that they should not die either in the day or in the night, in earth or in heaven, by fire, by water, or by the sword. After this these giants conquered all the kingdoms of the earth, and even dethroned Indrŭ, the king of heaven. Indrŭ, collecting all the gods, went to Brŭmha, and intreated him to provide some way of deliverance, as the universe which he had created was destroyed. Brŭmha asked the gods, how he could destroy those who had obtained his blessing? and advised them to go to Vishnoo. They obeyed, and informed this god of the miseries brought upon the universe by these giants, whom Brŭmha had blessed. Narayŭnŭ promised to destroy them, which he did in the following manner: Hirŭnyŭ-kŭshipoo's son Prŭlhadŭ was constantly absent from home performing religious austerities, at which his father became angry, and, tying a stone to his body, threw him into the water; but Vishnoo descended, and liberated him. His father next threw him under the feet of an elephant; but the elephant took him up, and put him on its back. He then built a house of sealing wax, put his son into it, and set it on fire; the wax melted, and fell upon Prŭlhadŭ, but he received no injury. The father next gave him poison, but without effect. At length, wearied of trying to kill him, he said, 'Where does your preserver Vishnoo dwell?' 'He is every where,' says Prŭlhadŭ. 'Is he then in this pillar?' 'Yes,' said the son. 'Then,' said Hirŭnyŭ-kŭshipoo, 'I will kill him,' and gave the pillar a blow with his stick—when Vishnoo, in the form of half-lion, half-man, burst from the pillar; laid hold of Hirŭnyŭ-kŭshipoo by the thighs with his teeth, and tore him up the middle. This was in the evening, so that it was neither in the day nor in the night; it was done under the droppings of the thatch, about which the Hindoos have a proverb, that this place is out of the earth; he was not killed by a man, but by a being half-man, half-lion: so that the promise of Brŭmha to him was not broken. Vishnoo next destroyed Hirŭnyakshŭ. After the death of his father, Prŭlhadŭ began to worship Vishnoo under

[c] From nŭrŭ, a man; and singhŭ, a lion.

the form which he had assumed, and with tears. enquired into the future fate of his father. Vishnoo assured him, that as he had died by his hands, he would surely ascend to heaven. Vishnoo was so pleased with the praises which Prŭlhadŭ bestowed on him, that he began to dance, hanging the entrails of Hirŭnyŭ-kŭshipoo round his neck. By Vishnoo's dancing, the earth began to move out of its place, so that Brŭmha and all the gods were frightened, but durst not go near him. However, at the entreaties of Prŭlhadŭ, Vishnoo gave over dancing; the earth became fixed, and Vishnoo gave Prŭlhadŭ this promise, that by his hands none of his race should die.

The fifth is the Vamŭnŭ incarnation. Prŭlhadŭ's grandson Bŭlee followed the steps of his great-grandfather, and committed every kind of violence. In contempt of the gods, he made offerings in his own name. He performed the ŭshwŭmédhŭ sacrifice one hundred times, by which he was entitled to become the king of the gods; but as the time of the then reigning Indrŭ was not expired, the latter applied for relief to Vishnoo, who promised to destroy this giant: to accomplish which he caused himself to be born of Uditee, the wife of Kŭshyŭpŭ, the moonee. Being exceedingly small in his person, he obtained the name of Vamŭnŭ, i. e., the dwarf. At a certain period king Bŭlee was making a great sacrifice, and Vamŭnŭ's parents being very poor, sent him to ask a gift of the king. It is customary, at a festival, to present gifts to bramhŭns. Vamŭnŭ was so small, that in his journey to the place of sacrifice, when he got to the side of a hole made by a cow's foot, and which was filled with water, he thought it was a river, and entreated another bramhŭn to help him over it. On his arrival, he went to ask a gift of Bŭlee. The king was so pleased with him, on account of his diminutive form, that he promised to give him whatever he should ask. He petitioned only for as much land as he could measure by three steps. Bŭlee pressed him to ask for more, intimating that such a quantity was nothing; but Vamŭnŭ persisted, and the king, ordered his priest to read the usual formulas in making such a present. The priest warned the king, declaring he would repent of making this gift; for the little bramhŭn was no other than Vishnoo himself, who would deprive him of all he had. The king, however, was determined to fulfil his promise, and the grant was made. Vamŭnŭ then placed one foot on Indrŭ's heaven, and the other on the earth, when, lo! a third leg suddenly projected from his belly, and he asked for a place upon which he might rest this third foot. Bŭlee, having nothing left, and being unable to fulfil his promise, was full of anxiety. His wife, having heard what was going forward, came to the spot, and, seeing the king's perplexity, advised him to give his head for Vamŭnŭ to set his foot upon. He did so; but Vamŭnŭ then asked for what is called dŭkshinŭ, a small present which accompanies a gift, and without which the gift itself produces no fruit to the giver. Bŭlee knew not what to do for dŭkshinŭ: his all was gone. His wife advised him to give his life to Vamŭnŭ as dŭkshinŭ. He did this also; but the latter told him, that as he had promised Prŭlhadŭ not to destroy any of his race, he would not take his life. He therefore gave him his choice either of ascending to heaven, taking with him five ignorant persons; or of descending to patŭlŭ, the world of the hydras, with five wise men[d]. Bŭlee chose the latter, but said that as he had done much mischief on earth, he was afraid of going to patŭlŭ, lest he should there be punished for his crimes. Vamŭnŭ told him not to fear, as he would, in the form of Vishnoo, become his protector. At the close, this god, having restored every thing on earth to a state of order and prosperity, returned to heaven.

The sixth is the Pŭrŭshoo-ramŭ incarnation. Pŭrŭshoo is the name of an instrument of war. The occasion of this appearance of Vishnoo is thus related:—The kshŭtriyŭs, from the king to the lowest person of this caste, were become very corrupt. Every one did as he pleased, the king was without authority, all order was destroyed, and the earth was in the greatest confusion. In these circumstances the goddess Prit'hivēē[e] went to Vishnoo, and prayed for relief. Her petition was heard, and one part of Vishnoo was incarnate as the son of Jŭmŭdgŭnee, a descendant of Bhrigoo the sage. After twenty-one different defeats the kshŭtriyŭs were exterminated by Pŭrŭshoo-ramŭ; but after a lapse of years they again became numerous: Ŭrjoonŭ, a kshŭtriyŭ king with a thousand arms, overcame the greatest monarchs, and made dreadful havock in the world: he beat Ravŭnŭ, and tied him to the heels of a horse; but Brŭmha delivered him, and reconciled them again. One evening in the rainy season, Ŭrjoonŭ, being in the forest, took refuge in the hut of Jŭmŭdŭgnee, the learned ascetic. He had with him 900,000 people; yet Jŭmŭdŭgnee, entertained them all. Ŭrjoonŭ, astonished, enquired of his people how the sage, living in the forest, was able to entertain so many people? They could not tell; they saw nothing except a cow which Brŭmha had given him; but it was by her means perhaps that he was able to entertain so many guests: its name was Kamŭ-dhénoo.[f] In fact, when Ŭrjoonŭ was to be entertained at the sage's house, this cow in a miraculous manner gave him all kinds of food, clothes, &c. The king on his departure asked for the cow; but the sage refused it to him, though he offered for it his whole kingdom. At length, Ŭrjoonŭ made war on Jŭmŭdŭgnee; and though the cow gave an army to her master, he was unable to cope with Ŭrjoonŭ, who destroyed both him and his army. After the victory, however, Ŭr-

[d] It is a proverb among the Hindoos, that there is no pleasure in the company of the ignorant in any place or circumstances; and that a bad place, in the company of the wise, is better than a good one in that of the ignorant.

[e] The earth personified.

[f] That is, the cow which yields every thing desired.

joonŭ could not find the cow, but went home disappointed. Pŭrŭshoo-ramŭ, hearing of the defeat and death of his father Jŭmŭdŭgnee, went to complain to Shivŭ, on the mountain Koilasŭ; but could not get access to him till he had knocked down the gods Gŭnéshŭ and Kartikŭ, Shivŭ's door-keepers. Shivŭ gave Pŭrŭshoo-ramŭ the instrument pŭrŭshoo, and promised him the victory. On his return Pŭrŭshoo-ramŭ met his mother, who was about to throw herself on the funeral pile of her husband. After attending upon this ceremony, Pŭrŭshoo-ramŭ went to the residence of Urjoonŭ, and killed him[g].

These six incarnations are said to have taken place in the sŭtyŭ yoogŭ[h]. There are no images respecting them made for worship.

The seventh incarnation is that of Ramŭ to destroy the giant Ravŭnŭ; for the history of which, see the Translation of the Table of Contents of the Ramayŭnŭ, toward the close of this volume.—The eighth incarnation is that of Bŭlŭramŭ, to destroy Prŭlŭmbŭ and other giants. This latter incarnation is said to have taken place in the dwapŭrŭ-yoogŭ.—The ninth is the Booddhŭ incarnation, in which Vishnoo appeared as Booddhŭ, to destroy the power of the giants. In order to effect this, Booddhŭ produced among mankind by his preaching, &c. a disposition to universal scepticism; that having no longer any faith in the gods, the giants might cease to apply to them for those powers by which they had become such dreadful scourges to mankind. In this appearance the object of Vishnoo, the preserver, was accomplished by art, without the necessity of war; though the dreadful alternative to which he was driven to accomplish his object, that of plunging mankind into a state of universal scepticism, affords another proof how wretchedly the world would be governed if every thing depended on the wisdom of man.—The tenth incarnation is still expected, under the name of the Kŭlkee Ŭvŭtarŭ. See translation from the Kŭlkee pooranŭ, in the second volume.

The appearance of Vishnoo, when he took the name of Krishnŭ to destroy the giant Kungshŭ, is called the descent of Vishnoo himself, and not an incarnation of this god. There are, however, beside the preceding ten incarnations, and this of Krishnŭ, many others mentioned in the pooranŭs, all having their source in Vishnoo.—The Shrēē-bhagŭvŭtŭ contains accounts of the following: Soo-yŭgnŭ created certain gods, and removed distress from the three worlds;—Kŭpilŭ taught his mother the knowledge of

[g] This story is told variously in the pooranŭs: according to the Ramayŭnŭ, Vŭshis'thŭ was the owner of this cow, and Vishwŭmitrŭ the person who fought with the moonee to obtain it.

[h] These ravages of tyranny, and bloody contests, form a sad specimen of the happiness of the Hindoo sŭtyŭ yoogŭ, could we believe that there ever had been such a period.

Brŭmhŭ, by which she obtained absorption ;—Dŭttatréyŭ delivered all his disciples, by means of the ceremony called yogŭ, from future birth, and obtained for them absorption ;—Koormarŭ declared the events that had happened in a former age; that his, previous to the dissolution of things which preceded his incarnation ;—Nŭrŭ-Narayŭnŭ was such a perfect ascetic that the courtezans, sent by the gods to allure him from his religious austerities, were unsuccessful ; Vishnoo himself created a female on purpose to divert him from his devotions, but her attempts were equally abortive ;—Prit'hoo opened the bowels of the earth, and brought forth its treasures ;—Rishŭvŭ was an incomparable yogēē, who was worshipped by the pŭrŭm-hŭngsŭs and other ascetics ;—Hŭyŭgrēēvŭ was so great a saint, that the words of the védŭ were uttered every time he breathed ;—Hŭree delivered his disciples from all their enemies, whether among men or the inferior animals ;—Hŭngsŭ taught his disciples the mysteries of yogŭ, and obtained absorption himself while performing the ceremonies of a yogēē ;—Mŭnoo's fame filled the three worlds, and ascended even as far as Sŭtyŭ-lokŭ ;—Dhŭnwŭntŭree delivered all diseased persons from their disorders on their mere remembrance of his name, and gave the water of immortality to the gods ;—Vyasŭ arranged the védŭs, was the author of the pooranŭs, &c.—Vibhoo was the spiritual guide of 80,000 disciples, whom he taught the knowledge of Brŭmhŭ, and the ceremonies of yogŭ ;—Sŭtyŭsénŭ cleared the earth of hypocrites and wicked persons ;—Voikoont'hŭ created the heaven of Vishnoo known by this name, and performed other wonders ;—Ŭjitŭ instructed the gods to churn the sea to obtain the water of immortality, and did other things which distinguished him as an incarnation ;—Mohŭnēē was incarnate, to prevent the giants from obtaining the water of immortality at the churning of the sea ; —Narŭdŭ revealed the work called Voishnŭvŭ Tŭntrŭ. The following incarnations are expected : Sarvŭbhoumŭ to dethrone the present Indrŭ, and instate Bŭlee in his stead ;—Vishwŭksénŭ as the friend of Shŭmbhoo, when he becomes the king of heaven ; —Dhŭrmŭ-sétoo to nourish the three worlds ;—Soodhama to assist Roodrŭ-savŭrnee, the twelfth of the fourteen mŭnoos ;—Yogéshwŭrŭ to place Divŭs-pŭtee on the throne of Indrŭ ;—Vrihudbhanoo to make known many new religious ceremonies.—The reader, however, is not to suppose that there are no other incarnations mentioned in these marvellous books : every hero, and every saint, is complimented by these writers as an incarnate deity.

I have not discovered any proof in the Hindoo writings, or in conversation with learned natives, that these incarnate persons are personifications of any of the divine attributes ; or that these stories have any other than a literal meaning. No doubt they were written as fables, which the ignorance of modern Hindoos has converted into facts ; or many of them may relate to common events here magnified into miracles.

Stone images of Vishnoo are made for sale, and worshipped in the houses of those who have chosen him for their guardian deity. There are no public festivals in honor of this god, yet he is worshipped at the offering of a burnt sacrifice; in the form of meditation used daily by the bramhŭns; at the times when 'the five gods' are worshipped, and also at the commencement of each shraddhŭ. No bloody sacrifices are offered to Vishnoo. The offerings presented to him consist of fruit, flowers, water, clarified butter, sweetmeats, cloth, ornaments, &c.

Many choose Vishnoo for their guardian deity. These persons are called Voishnŭvŭs. The distinctive mark of this sect of Hindoos consists of two lines, rather oval, drawn the whole length of the nose, and carried forward in two straight lines across the forehead. This mark is common to the worshippers of all the different forms of Vishnoo. It is generally made with the clay of the Ganges; sometimes with powder of saudel wood.

Vishnoo has a thousand names[i], among which are the following:—Vishnoo; that is, the being into whom, at the destruction of the world, all is absorbed.—Narayŭnŭ, or, he who dwelt in the waters[k], and he who dwells in the minds of the devout.—Voikoont'hŭ, or, the destroyer of sorrow.—Vishtŭrŭ-shrŭva, or, he who, in the form of Viratŭ, is all eye, all ear, &c.—Rhishēēkéshŭ, viz., the god of all the members, and of light.—Késhŭvŭ, or, he who gave being to himself, to Brŭmha and Shivŭ; or, he who has excellent hair.—Madhŭvŭ, or, the husband of Lŭkshmēē.—Mŭdhoosōōdhŭnŭ, the destroyer of Mŭdhoo, a giant.—Swŭmbhōō, or, the self-existent.—Doityaree, or, the enemy of the giants.—Poondŭrēēkakshŭ, or, he whose eyes are like the white lotus.—Govindŭ, or, the raiser of the earth.—Pitamvŭrŭ, or, he who wears yellow garments.—Uchyootŭ, or, the undecayable.—Sharŭngēē, or, he who possesses the horn bow.—Vishwŭkshénŭ, or, he whose soldiers fill all quarters of the world.—Jŭnarddŭnŭ, or, he who afflicts the wicked, and, he of whom emancipation is sought.—Pŭdmŭnabhŭ, or, he whose navel is like the water lily.—Vishwŭmvŭru, or, the protector of the world.—Koitŭbhŭjit, or, he who overcame the giant Koitŭbhŭ.

Vishnoo has two wives[l], Lukshmēē, the goddess of prosperity,

[i] The meaning of the principal names of some of the gods is to be found in the comment upon the Umŭrŭ-koshŭ, by Bhŭrŭtŭ-mŭllikŭ.

Jupiter had so many names, they could scarcely be numbered; some of them derived from the places where he lived and was worshipped, and others from the actions he performed.

[k] At the time of a prŭlŭyŭ, when every thing is reduced to the element of water, Vishnoo sits on the snake Unŭntŭ, which has 1,000 heads.

[l] One of the Hindoo poets, in answer to the question, Why has Vishnoo assumed a wooden shape? (alluding to the image of Jŭgŭnnat'hŭ,) says, 'The troubles in his family have turned Vishnoo into wood: in the first place, he has two wives, one of whom (the goddess of learning) is constantly talking, and the other (the goddess of

SHIVŬ.

WITH HIS WIFE PARVŬTTEE.

and Sŭrŭswŭtēē, the goddess of learning. The former was produced at the churning of the sea: Sŭrŭswŭtēē is the daughter of Brŭmha.

The following description of the heaven of Vishnoo is taken from the Mŭhabharŭtŭ. This heaven, called Voi-koont'hŭ[m], is entirely of gold, and is eighty thousand miles in circumference. All its edifices are composed of jewels. The pillars of this heaven, and all the ornaments of the buildings are of precious stones. The chrystal waters of the Ganges fall from the higher heavens on the heads of Droovŭ, and from thence into the bunches of hair on the heads of seven rishees in this heaven, and from thence they fall and form a river in Voi'koont'hŭ. Here are also fine pools of water, containing blue, red, and white water-lilies, the flowers of some of which contain one hundred petals, and others a thousand; gardens of nymphœas, &c. On a seat as glorious as the meridian sun, sitting on water-lilies, is Vishnoo, and on his right hand the goddess Lŭkshmēē. From the body of Lŭkshmēē the fragrance of the lotus extends 800 miles. This goddess shines like a continued blaze of lightning. The dévŭrshees, rajŭrshees, and sŭptŭrshees constantly celebrate the praise of Vishnoo and Lŭkshmēē, and meditate on their divine forms. The brŭmhŭrshēēs chant the védŭs. The glorified voishnŭvŭs approach Vishnoo, and constantly serve him. The gods[n] are also frequently employed in celebrating the praises of Vishnoo; and Gŭroorŭ, the bird-god, is the door-keeper.

SECT. II.—*Shivŭ.*

SHIVŬ, the detroyer, has the second place among the Hindoo deities, though in general, in allusion to their offices, these three gods are classed thus: Brŭmha, Vishnoo, Shivŭ.

This god is represented in various ways. In the form of meditation used daily by the bramhŭns, he is described as a silver coloured man, with five faces; an additional eye[o] and a half-moon grace each forehead[p]. He has four arms; in one hand he holds a

prosperity) never remains in one place: to increase his troubles, he sits on a snake; his dwelling is in the water, and he rides on a bird.' All the Hindoos acknowledge that it is a great misfortune for a man to have two wives; especially if both live in one house.

[m] The work called Kŭrmŭ-Vipakŭ says, that the heavens of Vishnoo, Brŭmha, and Shivŭ are upon three peaks of the mountain Sooméroo; and that at the bottom of these peaks are the heavens of twenty-one other gods.

[n] These gods are supposed to be visitors at Vishnoo's.

[o] One of the names of Shivŭ is Trilōchŭnŭ, viz., the three-eyed. One of the names of Jupiter was Trioculus, (Triophthalmos,) given him by the Greeks, because he had three eyes. An image of this kind was set up in Troy, which, beside the usual two eyes, had a third in the forehead.

[p] At the churning of the sea, Shivŭ obtained the moon for his share, and fixed it, with all its glory, in his forehead.

pŭrŭshoo; in the second a deer; with the third he is bestowing a blessing, and with the fourth he forbids fear: he sits on a lotus[q], and wears a tyger-skin garment.

At other times Shivŭ is represented with one head, three eyes, and two arms, riding on a bull, covered with ashes, naked, his eyes inflamed with intoxicating herbs[r], having in one hand a horn, and in the other a drum.

Another image of Shivŭ is the lingŭ, a smooth black stone almost in the form of a sugar-loaf, with a projection at the base like the mouth of a spoon.

There are several stories in the pooranŭs respecting the origin of the lingŭ worship, three of which I had translated, and actually inserted in this work, leaving out as much as possible of their offensive parts: but in correcting the proofs, they appeared too gross, even when refined as much as possible, to meet the public eye. It is true I have omitted them with some reluctance, because I wish that the apologists for idolatry should be left without excuse, and that the sincere Christian should know what those who wish to rob him of the Christian Religion mean to leave in its stead.

From these abominable stories, temples innumerable have arisen in India, and a Shivŭ lingŭ placed in each of them, and WORSHIPPED AS A GOD!! These temples, indeed, in Bengal and many parts of Hindoost'han, are far more numerous than those dedicated to any other idol; and the number of the daily worshippers of this scandalous image, (even among the Hindoo women,) who make the image with the clay of the Ganges every morning and evening, is beyond comparison far greater than the worshippers of all the other gods put together.

The account of the origin of the phalli of the Greeks bears a strong and unaccountable resemblance to some parts of the pouranic accounts of the lingŭ: Bacchus was angry with the Athenians, because they despised his solemnities, when they were first brought by Pegasus out of Bœotia into Attica; for which he afflicted them with a grievous disease, that could have no cure, till, by the advice of the oracles, they paid due reverence to the god, and erected phalli to his honour; whence the feasts and sacrifices called Phallica were yearly celebrated among the Athenians.—The story of Priapus is too indecent, and too well known to need recital.

[q] It appears that this plant was formerly venerated by the Egyptians as much as it is now by the Hindoos. The sacred images of the Tartars, Japanese, and other nations are also frequently represented as placed upon it.

[r] Bacchus, who appears to bear a pretty strong resemblance to Shivŭ, is said to have wandered about naked, or to have had no other covering than a tyger's skin, which is the common garment of Shivŭ, and of his followers, the sŭnyasēēs. The bloated image of Shivŭ corresponds with that of Bacchus; and though the Indian god did not intoxicate himself with wine, yet his image is evidently that of a drunkard. Shivŭ perpetually smoked intoxicating herbs.

Should the reader wish for farther information on this subject, he is referred to an extract from Diodorus Siculus, as given in the Reverend Mr. Maurice's second volume of Indian Antiquities. The perusal of this extract may help further to convince the reader that the old idolatry, and that of the present race of Hindoos, at least in their abominable nature, and in some of their prominent features, are ONE.

Beside the clay image of the lingŭ, there are two kinds of black stone lingŭs : these are set up in the Hindoo temples[s]. The first is called swŭyŭmbōō, (the self-existent,) or ŭnadee[t], that which has no beginning. The second they call vanŭ-lingŭ, because Vanŭ, a king, first instituted the worship of this image. These stones are brought from the neighbourhood of the river Gŭnd-kŭhēē, which falls into the Ganges near Patna. The images are made by Hindoo and Mŭsŭlman stone-cutters.

There is another form in which Shivŭ is worshipped, called Mŭha-kalŭ. This is the image of a smoke-coloured boy with three eyes, clothed in red garments. His hair stands erect ; his teeth are very large ; he wears a necklace of human skulls, and a large turban of his own hair ; in one hand he holds a stick, and in the other the foot of a bed-stead ; he has a large belly, and makes a very terrific appearance. Shivŭ is called Mŭha-kalŭ, because he destroys all ; by which the Hindoos mean, that all is absorbed in him at last, in order to be reproduced[u].

Images of this form of Shivŭ are not made in Bengal ; but a pan of water, or an ŭnadee-lingŭ, is substituted, before which bloody sacrifices are offered, and other ceremonies performed, in the month Choitrŭ, at the new moon. Only a few persons perform this worship. Except before this image, bloody sacrifices are never offered to Shivŭ, who is himself called a voishnŭvŭ, i. e., a worshipper of Vishnoo, before whose image no animals are slain, and whose disciples profess never to eat animal food.

Under different names other images of Shivŭ are described in the shastrŭs ; but none of these images are made at present, nor is any public worship offered to them.

Those who receive the name of Shivŭ from their spiritual guides, are called Soivyŭs. The mark on the forehead which

[s] It is remarkable, that a stone image, consecrated to Venus, bore a strong resemblance to the lingŭ. Of this stone it is said, that it was "from the top to the bottom of an orbicular figure, a little broad beneath ; the circumference was small, and sharpening towards the top like a sugar loaf. The reason unknown."

[t] At the time of a great drought, the Hindoos, after performing its worship, throw very large quantities of water upon this ŭnadee-lingŭ, in order to induce Shivŭ to give them rain.

[u] Some say Saturn received his name, because he was satisfied with the years he devoured. Saturn was also represented as devouring his children, and vomiting them up again.

these persons wear, is composed of three curved lines like a half-moon, to which is added a round dot on the nose. It is made either with the clay of the Ganges, or with sandal wood, or the ashes of cow-dung.

Worship is performed daily at the temples of the lingŭ; when offerings of various kinds are presented to this image. If the temple belong to a shōōdrŭ, a bramhŭn is employed, who receives a small annual gratuity, and the daily offerings[x]. These ceremonies occupy a few minutes, or half an hour, at the pleasure of the worshipper. Many persons living in Bengal employ bramhŭns at Benares to perform the worship of the lingŭ in temples which they have built there.

Every year, in the month Phalgoonŭ, the Hindoos make the image of Shivŭ, and worship it for one day, throwing the image the next day into the water. This worship is performed in the night, and is accompanied with singing, dancing, music, feasting, &c. The image worshipped is either that of Shivŭ with five faces, or that with one face. In the month Maghŭ also a festival in honour of Shivŭ is held for one day, when the image of this god sitting on a bull, with Parvŭtēē on his knee, is worshipped. This form of Shivŭ is called Hŭru-Gourēē[y].

In the month Choitrŭ an abominable festival in honour of of this god is celebrated; when many Hindoos, assuming the name of sŭnyasēēs, inflict on themselves the greatest cruelties. Some of the chief sŭnyasēēs purify themselves for a month previously to these ceremonies, by going to some celebrated temple or image of Shivŭ, and there eating only once a day, abstaining from certain gratifications, repeating the name of Shivŭ, dancing before his image, &c. Other sŭnyasēēs perform these preparatory ceremonies for fifteen, and others for only ten days; during which time parties of men and boys dance in the streets, having their bodies covered with ashes, &c. and a long piece of false hair mixed with mud wrapped round the head like a turban. A large drum accompanies each party, making a horrid din.

On the first day of the festival, these sŭnyasēēs cast themselves from a bamboo stage with three resting places, the highest about twenty feet from the ground. From this height these persons cast themselves on iron spikes stuck in bags of straw. These spikes are laid in a reclining posture, and when the person falls they almost constantly fall down instead of entering his body. There are instances however of persons being killed, and others wounded;

[x] The shastrŭs prohibit the bramhŭns from receiving the offerings presented to Shivŭ: the reason I have not discovered. The bramhŭns, however, contrive to explain the words of the shastrŭ in such a manner, as to secure the greater part of the things presented to this idol.

[y] Hŭrŭ is the name of Shivŭ, and Gourēē that of Doorga.

but they are very rare. A few years ago, a person at Kidŭrpoorŭ, near Calcutta, cast himself on a knife used in cleaning fish, which entered his side, and was the cause of his death. He threw himself from the stage twice on the same day; the second time, (which was fatal,) to gratify a prostitute with whom he lived.—In some villages, several of these stages are erected, and as many as two or three hundred people cast themselves on these spikes in one day, in the presence of great crowds of people. The worshippers of Shivŭ make a great boast of the power of their god in preserving his followers in circumstances of such danger.

The next day is spent in idleness, the sŭnyasēēs lying about Shivŭ's temple, and wandering about like persons half drunk, or jaded with revelling. On the following day, a large fire is kindled opposite Shivŭ's temple; and when the burnt wood has been formed into a great heap, one of the chief sŭnyasēēs, with a bunch of canes in his hand, flattens the heap a little, and walks over it with his feet bare. After him, the other sŭnyasēēs spread the fire about, walk acorss it, dance upon it, and then cast the embers into the air and at each other.

The next morning early the work of piercing the tongues and sides commences. In the year 1806 I went to Kalēēghatŭ, in company with two or three friends, to witness these practices; at which place we arrived about five o'clock in the morning. We overtook numerous companies who were proceeding thither, having with them drums and other instruments of music; also spits, canes, and different articles to pierce their tongues and sides. Some with tinkling rings on their ancles were dancing and exhibiting indecent gestures as they passed along, while others rent the air with the sounds of their filthy songs. As we entered the village where the temple of this great goddess is situated, the crowds were so great that we could with difficulty get our vehicles along, and at last were completely blocked up. We then alighted, and went amongst the crowd. But who can describe a scene like this?—Here, men of all ages, who intended to have their tongues pierced, or their sides bored, were buying garlands of flowers to hang round their necks, or tie round their heads;—there, others were carrying their offerings to the goddess:—above the heads of the crowd were seen nothing but the feathers belonging to the great drums, and the instruments of torture which each victim was carrying in his hand. These wretched slaves of superstition were distinguished from others by the quantity of oil rubbed on their bodies, and by streaks and dots of mud all over them: some of the chief men belonging to each company were covered with ashes, or dressed in a most fantastic manner, like the fool among mountebanks. For the sake of low sport, some were dressed as English women; and others had on a hat, to excite the crowd to laugh at Europeans. As soon as we could force our way, we proceeded to the temple of Kalēē, where the crowd, inflamed to madness, almost trampled upon one another, to obtain a sight of the idol. We went up to the door-way, when a bramhŭn, who was one of the owners of the idol, addressed one of my companions in broken English: "Money—money—for black mother." My friend, not much liking the looks of his black mother, declared he should give her nothing. From this spot we went into the temple-yard, where two or three blacksmiths had begun the work of piercing the tongues and boring the sides of these infatuated disciples of Shivŭ. The first man seemed reluctant to hold out his tongue; but the blacksmith, rubbing it with something like flour, and having a piece of cloth betwixt his fingers, laid firm hold, dragged it out, and, placing his lancet under it in the middle, pierced it through, and let the fellow go. The next person, whose tongue we saw cut, directed the blacksmith to cut it on a contrary side, as it had been already cut twice. This man seemed to go through the business of having his tongue slit with perfect *sang froid*. The company of natives were entirely unmoved, and the blacksmith, pocketing the trifling fee given by each for whom he did this favour, laughed at the sport. I could not help asking, whether they were not punishing these men for lying.—After seeing the operation performed on one or two more, we went to another group, where they were boring the sides. The first we saw undergoing this operation was a boy, who might be twelve or thirteen years old, and who had been brought thither by his elder brother to submit to this cruelty. A thread rubbed with clarified butter was drawn through the skin on each side, with a kind of lancet having an eye like a needle. He did not flinch, but hung by his hands over the shoulders of his brother. I asked a man who had just had his sides bored, why he did this? He said, he had made a vow to Kalēē at a time of dangerous illness, and was now performing this vow: a bye-stander added, it was an act of holiness, or merit. Passing from this group, we saw a man dancing backwards and forwards with two canes run through his side as thick as a man's little finger. In returning to Calcutta we saw many with things of different thicknesses thrust through their sides and tongues, and several with the pointed handles of iron shovels, containing fire, sticking in their sides. Into this fire every now and then they threw Indian pitch, which for the moment blazed very high. I saw one man whose singular mode of self-torture struck me much: his breast, arms, and other parts of his body, were entirely covered with pins, as thick as nails or packing needles. This is called vanŭ-phōra[t]. The person had made a vow to Shivŭ thus to pierce his body, praying the god to remove some evil from him.

Some sŭnyasēēs at this festival put swords through the holes in their tongues; others spears; others thick pieces of round iron which they call arrows. Many, as a bravado, put other things

[t] Piercing with arrows.

through their tongues, as living snakes, bamboos, ramrods, &c. Others, to excite the attention of the crowd still more, procure images of houses, gods, temples, &c. and placing them on a single bamboo, hold them up in their hands, and put the bamboo through their tongues. In 1805, at Calcutta, a few base fellows made a bamboo stage, placed a prostitute upon it, and carried her through the streets, her paramour accompanying them, having one of her ancle ornaments in the slit of his tongue. Another year a man put his finger through the tongue of another person, and they went along dancing and making indecent gestures together. Others put bamboos, ropes, canes, the stalk of a climbing plant, the long tube of the hooka, &c. through their sides, and rubbing these things with oil, while two persons go before and two behind to hold the ends of the things which have been passed through the sides, they dance backwards and forwards, making indecent gestures. These people pass through the streets with these marks of self-torture upon them, followed by crowds of idle people. They are paid by the towns or villages where these acts are performed, and a levy is made on the inhabitants to defray the expense. On the evening of this day some sŭnyasēēs pierce the skin of their foreheads, and place a rod of iron in it as a socket, and on this rod fasten a lamp, which is kept burning all night. The persons bearing these lamps sit all night in or near Shivŭ's temple, occasionally calling upon this god by different names. On the same evening, different parties of sŭnyasēēs hold conversations respecting Shivŭ in verse.

On the following day, in the afternoon, the ceremony called Chŭrŭkŭ, or the swinging by hooks fastened in the back is performed. The posts are erected in some open place in the town or suburbs: they are generally fifteen, twenty, or twenty-five cubits high. In some places a kind of worship is paid at the foot of the tree to Shivŭ, when two pigeons are let loose, or slain. In other parts, i. e., in the neighbourhood of Calcutta, the worship of Shivŭ is performed at his temple; after which the crowd proceed to the swinging posts, and commence the horrid work of torture. The man who is to swing prostrates himself before the tree, and a person, with his dusty fingers, makes a mark where the hooks are to be put. Another person immediately gives him a smart slap on the back, and pinches up the skin hard with his thumb and fingers; while another thrusts the hook through, taking hold of about an inch of the skin: the other hook is then in like manner put through the skin of the other side of the back, and the man gets up on his feet. As he is rising, some water is thrown in his face. He then mounts on a man's back, or is elevated in some other way; and the strings which are attached to the hooks in his back are tied to the rope at one end of the horizontal bamboo, and the rope at the other end is held by several men, who, drawing it down, raise up the end on which the man swings, and by their running round with the rope the machine is turned. In swinging, the man describes a circle of about thirty feet diameter. Some swing only a few minutes, others half an hour or more: I have heard of men who continued swinging for hours. In the southern parts of Bengal, a piece of cloth is wrapt round the body underneath the hooks, lest the flesh should tear, and the wretch fall, and be dashed to pieces; but the whole weight of the body rests on the hooks. Some of these persons take the wooden pipe, and smoak while swinging, as though insensible of the least pain. Others take up fruit in their hands, and either eat it or throw it among the crowd. I have heard of a person's having a monkey's collar run into his hinder parts[a], in which state the man and the monkey whirled round together. On one occasion, in the north of Bengal, a man took a large piece of wood in his mouth, and swung for a considerable time without any cloth round his body to preserve him, should the flesh of his back tear. On some occasions these sŭnyasēēs have hooks run through their thighs as well as backs. About the year 1800 five *women* swung in this manner, with hooks through their backs and thighs, at Kidŭrpoorŭ near Calcutta. It is not very uncommon for the flesh to tear, and the person to fall: instances are related of such persons perishing on the spot. A few years ago a man fell from the post at Kidŭrpoorŭ, while whirling round with great rapidity; and, falling on a poor woman who was selling parched rice, killed her on the spot: the man died the next day. At a village near Bŭjbŭj, some years since, the swing fell, and broke a man's leg. The man who was upon it, as soon as he was loosed, ran to another tree, was drawn up, and whirled round again, as though nothing had happened. I have heard of one man's swinging three times in one day on different trees; and a bramhŭn assured me, that he had seen four men swing on one tree; while swinging, this tree was carried round the field by the crowd.

On the day of swinging, in some places, a sŭnyasēē is laid before the temple of Shivŭ as dead, and is afterwards carried to the place where they burn the dead. Here they read many incantations and perform certain ceremonies, after which the (supposed) dead sŭnyasēē arises, when they dance around him, proclaiming the name of Shivŭ.

The next morning the sŭnyasēēs go to Shivŭ's temple, and perform worship to him, when they take off the poita which they had worn during the festival. On this day, they beg, or take from their houses, a quantity of rice, and other things, which they make into a kind of frumenty, in the place where they burn the dead. These things they offer, with some burnt fish, to departed ghosts.

Each day of the festival the sŭnyasēēs worship the sun, pouring

[a] At Kidŭrpoorŭ.

water, flowers, &c. on a clay image of the alligator, repeating mŭntrŭs.

These horrid ceremonies are said to derive their origin from a king named Vanŭ, whose history is related in the Mŭhabharŭtŭ. This work says, that Vanŭ, in the month Choitrŭ, instituted these rites, and inflicted a number of the cruelties here detailed on his own body, viz., he mounted the swing, pierced his tongue and sides, danced on fire, threw himself on spikes, &c. At length he obtained an interview with Shivŭ, who surrounded his palace with a wall of fire, and promised to appear whenever he should stand in need of his assistance. Those who perform these ceremonies at present, expect that Shivŭ will bestow upon them some blessing either in this life or in the next.

Doorga is the wife of Shivŭ. This goddess is known under other names, as Bhŭgŭvŭtēē, Sŭtēē, Parvŭtēē, &c. In one age Shivŭ was married to Sŭtēē, the daughter of king Dŭkshŭ, and in another to the same goddess under the name of Parvŭtēē, the daughter of the mountain Himalŭyŭ: hence she is the mountain-goddess.

When Doorga was performing religious austerities to obtain Shivŭ in marriage, the latter was so moved that he appeared to her, and enquired why she was thus employed? She was ashamed to assign the reason, but her attendants replied for her. He, in jest, reproved her, observing that people performed religious austerities to obtain something valuable; in the article of marriage they desired a person of a good family, but he (Shivŭ) had neither father nor mother;—or a rich person, but he had not a garment to wear;—or a handsome person, but he had three eyes.

When Shivŭ was about to be married to Parvŭtēē, her mother and the neighbours treated the god in a very scurrilous manner: the neighbours cried out, "Ah! ah! ah! This image of gold, this most beautiful damsel, the greatest beauty in the three worlds, to be given in marriage to such a fellow—an old fellow with three eyes; without teeth; clothed in a tiger's skin; covered with ashes; incircled with snakes; wearing a necklace of human bones; with a human skull in his hand; with a filthy jŭta (viz., a bunch of hair like a turban) twisted round his head; who chews intoxicating drugs; has inflamed eyes; rides naked on a bull, and wanders about like a madman. Ah! they have thrown this beautiful daughter into the river[b]!"—In this manner the neighbours

[b] In allusion to the throwing of dead bodies into the river. This resembles the surprise said to have been excited by the marriage of Venus to the filthy and deformed Vulcan. Another very singular coincidence betwixt the European idolatry and that of the Hindoos is furnished by the story of Vulcan and Minerva, and that respecting Shivŭ and Mohinēē as given in the Markŭndēyŭ pooranŭ; but which I have suppressed on account of its offensive nature.

exclaimed against the marriage, till Narŭdŭ, who had excited the disturbance, interfered, and the wedding was concluded.

A number of stories are related in some of the Hindoo books of an inferior order, respecting the quarrels of Shivŭ and Parvŭtēe, occasioned by the revels of the former, and the jealousy of the latter. These quarrels resemble those of Jupiter and Juno. Other stories are told of Shivu's descending to the earth in the form of a mendicant, for the preservation of some one in distress; to perform religious austerities, &c.

Shivŭ is said, in the pooranŭs, to have destroyed Kŭndŭrpu (Cupid), for interrupting him in his devotions, previous to his union with Doorga. We find, however, the god of love restored to existence, after a lapse of ages, under the name of Prŭdyoomŭ, when he again obtained his wife Rŭtee. After his marriage with the mountain-goddess, Shivŭ on a certain occasion offended his father-in-law, king Dŭkshŭ, by refusing to bow to him as he entered the circle in which the king was sitting. To be revenged, Dŭkshŭ refused to invite Shivŭ to a sacrifice which he was about to perform. Sŭtēē, the king's daughter, however, was resolved to go, though uninvited and forbidden by her husband. On her arrival Dŭkshŭ poured a torrent of abuse on Shivŭ, which affected Sŭtēē so much that she died[c]. When Shivŭ heard of the loss of his beloved wife, he created a monstrous giant, whom he commanded to go and destroy Dŭkshŭ, and put an end to his sacrifice. He speedily accomplished this work, by cutting off the head of the king, and dispersing all the guests. The gods, in compassion to Dŭkshŭ, placed on his decapitated body the head of a goat, and restored him to his family and kingdom.

This god has a thousand names, among which are the following: Shivŭ, or, the benefactor. Mŭhéshwŭrŭ, the great god[d]. Eeshwŭrŭ, the glorious god. Chŭndrŭshékŭrŭ, he whose forehead is adorned with a half-moon. Bhōōtéshŭ, he who is lord of the bhōōtŭs[e]. Mrirŭ, he who purifies. Mrityoonjŭyŭ, he who conquers death. Krittivasa, he who wears a skin. Oogrŭ, the furious. Shrēēkŭntŭ, he whose throat is beautiful[f]. Kŭpalŭbhrit, he whose alms' dish is

[c] In reference to this mark of strong attachment, a Hindoo widow burning with her husband on the funeral pile is called Sŭtēē.

[d] The pŭndits give proofs from the shastrŭs, in which Shivŭ is acknowledged to be the greatest of the gods, or Mŭha-dévŭ: from mŭha, great, and dévŭ, god.

[e] Bhōōtŭs are beings partly in human shape, though some of them have the faces of horses, others of camels, others of monkeys, &c. Some have the bodies of horses, and he faces of men. Some have one leg, and some two. Some have only one ear, and thers only one eye. Shivŭ is attended by a number of these bhōōtŭs, as Bacchus had body of guards consisting of drunken satyrs, demons, nymphs, &c.

[f] After Shivŭ, to preserve the earth from destruction, had drank the person which arose out of the sea, when the gods churned it to obtain the water of immortality, he fell into a swoon, and appeared to be at the point of death. All the gods were exceedingly alarmed; the ŭsoorŭs were filled with triumph, under the expectation that

a skull[g]. Smŭrŭ-hŭrŭ, the destroyer of the god of love. Tripoorantŭkŭ, he who destroyed Tripoorŭ, an ŭsoorŭ. Gŭnga-dhŭrŭ, he who caught the goddess Gŭnga in his hair[h]. Vrishŭ-dwŭjŭ, he whose standard is a bull[i]. Shōōlēē, he who wields the trident[k]. St'hanoo, the everlasting. Shŭrvŭ, he who is every thing. Girēēshŭ, lord of the hills, he who dwells on the hills.

The following account of the heaven of Shivŭ is translated from the work called Krityŭ-tŭtwŭ. This heaven, which is situated on mount Koilasŭ, and called Shivŭpoorŭ, is ornamented with many kinds of gems and precious things, as pearls, coral, gold, silver, &c.—Here reside gods, danŭvŭs[l], gŭndhŭrvŭs[m], ŭpsŭrŭs[n], siddhŭs[o], charŭnŭs[p], brŭmhŭrshees[q], dévŭrshees[r], and mŭhŭrshees[s]; also other sages, as Sŭnatŭnŭ, Sŭnŭtkoomarŭ, Sŭnŭndŭ, Ŭgŭstyŭ, Ŭngira, Poolŭstyŭ, Poolŭhŭ, Chitrŭ, Angirŭsŭ, Goutŭmŭ, Bhrigoo, Pŭrashŭrŭ, Bhŭrŭdwajŭ, Mrikŭndŭ, Markŭndéyŭ, Shoonŭshéphŭ, Ŭshtavŭkrŭ, Dhoumyŭ, Valmēēkee, Vŭshisht'hŭ, Doorvasa, &c. These persons constantly perform the worship of Shivŭ and Doorga, and the ŭpsŭrŭs are continually employed in singing, dancing, and other festivities.—The flowers of every season are always in bloom here: among which are, the yōōthēē[t], jatēē[u], mŭllika[x], malŭtēē[y], dorŭ[z], tŭgŭrŭ[a], kŭrŭvēērŭ[b], kŭlharŭ[c], kŭrnikarŭ[d], késhŭrŭ[e], poonnagŭ[d], drona[e], gŭndhŭrajŭ[f], shéphalika[g], chŭmpŭkŭ[h], bhōōmee-chŭmpŭkŭ[i], nagŭ-késhŭrŭ[k], moochŭkoondŭ[l], kanchŭnŭ[m], pioolee[n], jhintēē[o], nēēlŭ-jhintēē[p], rŭktŭ-jhintēē[q], kŭdŭmbŭ[r], rŭjŭnēēgŭndhŭ[s], tŭrku[t], tŭroolŭta[u], parijatŭ[x], &c. &c. Cool, odoriferous, and gentle winds always blow on these flowers, and diffuse their fragrance all

one of the gods (even Shivŭ himself) was about to expire. The gods addressed Doorga, who took Shivŭ in her arm, and began to repeat certain incantations to destroy the effects of the poison: Shivŭ revived. This was the first time incantations were used to destroy the power of poison. Though the poison did not destroy Shivŭ, it left a blue mark on his throat; and hence one of his names is Nēēlŭ-kŭntŭ, the blue-throated.

g This is Brŭmha's skull. Shivŭ in a quarrel cut off one of Brŭmha's five heads, and made an alms' dish of it. Brŭmha and other gods, in the character of mendicants, are represented with an earthen pot in the hand which contains their food. This pot is called a kŭmŭn dŭloo.

h In Gŭnga's descent from heaven, Shivŭ caught her in the bunch of hair tied at the back of his head.

i Shivŭ's conduct, on the day of his marriage with Parvŭtēē, puts us in mind of Priapus. The Indian god rode through Kamŭ-rōōpŭ on a bull, naked, with the bride on his knee.

k Here Shivŭ appears with Neptune's sceptre, though I cannot find that he resembles the watery god in any thing else.

l A particular kind of giants. m The heavenly choristers. n Dancers and courtezans. o p Gods who act as servants to some of the other gods. q Sacred sages. r Divine sages. s Great sages. t Jasminum auriculatum. u J. grandiflorum. x J. zambae. y Gætnera racemosa. z Unknown. a Tabernæmontana coronaria. b Nerium odorum. c Nymphæa cyanea. d Pterospermum accrifolium. e Mimusops elengi. d Rottlera tinctoria. e Phlomis zeylanica. f Gardenia florida. g Nyctanthes arbor tristis. h Michelia champaca. i Kempferia rotunda. k Mesua ferrea. l Pterospermum suberifolia. m Bauhinia (several species). n Linum trigynum. o Barleria cristata. p Barleria cœrulea. q Barleria ciliata. r Nauclea orientalis. s The tuberose. t Æschynomene sesban. u Ipomea quamoclit. x Phœnix paludosa.

over the mountain. The shade produced by the parijatŭ tree is very cooling. This mountain also produces the following trees and fruits: shala[y], talŭ[z], tŭmalŭ[a], hintalŭ[b], kŭrjōōrŭ[c], amrŭ[d], jŭmvēērŭ[e], goovakŭ[f], pŭnŭsŭ[g], shrēēphŭlŭ[h], draksha[i], ingoodēē[k], vŭtŭ[l], ŭshwŭt'hŭ[m], kŭpitt'hŭ[n], &c. A variety of birds are constantly singing here, and repeating the names of Doorga and Shivŭ, viz., the kakŭ[o], shookŭ[p], paravŭtŭ[q], tittiree[r], chatŭkŭ[s], chasŭ[t], bhasŭ[u], kōkilŭ[x], sarasŭ[y], datyōōhŭ[z], chŭkrŭvakŭ[a], &c. &c. The waters of the heavenly Ganges (Mŭndakinēē) glide along in purling streams. The six seasons are uninterruptedly enjoyed on this mountain, viz., vŭsŭntu (spring), grēēshmŭ (summer), vŭrsha (rainy), shŭrŭt (sultry), shishirŭ (dewy), and shēētŭ (cold). On a golden throne, adorned with jewels, sit Shivŭ and Doorga, engaged in conversation.

The Shrēē-bhagŭvŭtŭ contains another description of the heaven of Shivŭ:—Sixteen thousand miles from the earth, on mount Koilasŭ[t], resides this god, in a palace of gold, adorned with jewels of all kinds. This palace is surrounded with forests, gardens, canals, trees laden with all kinds of fruit, flowers of every fragrance. The kŭlpŭ tree also grows here, from which a person may obtain every kind of food and all other things he may desire. In the centre of a roodrakshŭ[u] forest, under a tree, Shivŭ frequently sits with his wife Parvŭtēē. The fragrance of the parijatŭ flowers extends 200 miles in all directions; and all the seasons are here enjoyed at the same time. The winds blow softly, filled with the most refreshing odours. At the extremities of this heaven southwards and northwards Shivŭ has fixed two gates, one of which is kept by Nŭndēē, the other by Mŭha-kalŭ. A number of gods and other celestial beings constantly reside here, among whom are Kartikéyŭ and Gŭnéshŭ, the sons of Shivŭ; also the female servants of Doorga, Jŭya, and Vijŭyar, eight nayikas, and sixty-four yoginēēs, with bhōōtŭs, pishachŭs, Shivŭ's bull, and those disciples of Shivŭ (shaktŭs) who have obtained beatitude. The time is spent here in the festivities and abominations of the other heavens.

[y] Phœnix sylvestris. [z] Erythrina fulgens. [a] Shorea robusta. [b] Borassus flabelliformis. [c] Diospyrus cordifolia. [d] Mangifera Indica. [e] The citron or lime tree. [f] Areca catechu. [g] Artocarpus integrifolia. [h] Ægle marmelos. [i] The grape vine. [k] Unknown. [l] Ficus Indica. [m] Ficus religiosa. [n] Feronia elephantium. [o] The crow. [p] The parrot. [q] The pigeon. [r] The partridge. [s] The sparrow. [t] Coracias Indica. [u] Unknown. [x] The Indian cuckow. [y] The Siberian crane, [z] The gallinule. [a] Anas casarca.

[t] Sonini, "during his travels in Greece and Turkey, made a journey into ancient Macedonia, and paid a visit to mount Olympus, the abode of the gods. It was the middle of July when this excursion was made, and although the heat was extreme towards the base of the mountain, as well as in the plain, vast masses of snow rendered the summit inaccessible. "It is not astonishing," says Sonini, "that the Greeks have placed the abode of the gods on an eminence which mortals cannot reach." The monks of the convent, "who have succeeded them in this great elevation," confirmed what has been sometimes disputed, the perpetual permanence of ice and snow on the top of the mountain. With the exception of chamois and a few bears, there are hardly any quadrupeds to be seen beyond the half of the height of Olympus. Birds also scarcely pass this limit.

[u] Eleocarpus ganitrus.

BRŬMHA.

SECT. III.—*Brŭmha.*

As has been already mentioned, Brŭmha, Vishnoo, and Shivŭ derived their existence from the one Brŭmhŭ. The Hindoo pŭndits do not admit these to be creatures, but contend that they are emanations from, or parts of, the one Brŭmhŭ.

Brŭmha first produced the waters, then the earth; next, from his own mind, he caused a number of sages and four females to be born: among the sages was Kŭshyŭpŭ, the father of the gods, giants, and men. From Ŭditee were born the gods; from Ditee the giants; from Kŭdroo the hydras; and from Vinŭta, Gŭroorŭ and Ŭroonŭ. After creating these sages, who were of course bramhŭns, Brŭmha caused a kshŭtriyŭ to spring from his arms, a voishyŭ from his thighs, and a shōōdrŭ from his feet. In this order, according to the pooranŭs, the whole creation arose. The Hindoo shastrŭs, however, contain a variety of different accounts on the subject of creation. I have thought it necessary to give this brief statement, as it seems connected with the history of this god.

Brŭmha is represented as a man with four faces, of a gold colour; dressed in white garments; riding on a goose. In one hand he holds a stick, and in the other a kŭmŭndŭloo, or alms' dish. He is called the grandfather (pitamŭhŭ) of gods and men[g]. He is not much regarded in the reigning superstition; nor does any one adopt him as his guardian deity.

The bramhŭns, in their morning and evening worship, repeat an incantation, containing a description of the image of Brŭmha; at noon they perform an act of worship in honour of this god, presenting to him sometimes a single flower: at the time of a burnt offering, clarified butter is presented to Brŭmha. In the month Maghŭ, at the full moon, an earthen image of this god is worshipped, with that of Shivŭ on his right hand, and that of Vishnoo on his left. This festival lasts only one day, and the three gods are, the next day, thrown into the river. This worship is accompanied with songs, dances, music, &c. as at all other festivals; but the worship of Brŭmha is most frequently celebrated by a number of young men of the baser sort, who defray the expences by a subscription.—Bloody sacrifices are never offered to Brŭmha.

Brŭmha, notwithstanding the venerable name of grandfather, seems to be as lewd as any of the gods. At the time that intoxicating spirits were first made, all the gods, giants, gundhŭrvŭs, yŭkshŭs, kinnŭrŭs, &c. were accustomed to drink spirits, and no blame was then attached to drunkenness: but one day Brŭmha, in a state of intoxication, made an attempt on the virtue of his own daughter,

[g] Jupiter was called the father and king of gods and men.

by which he incurred the wrath of the gods. Sometime afterwards, Brŭmha boasted in company, that he was as great a god as Shivŭ. Hearing what Brŭmha had been saying, the latter, inflamed with anger, was about to cut off one of Brŭmha's heads, but was prevented by the intercessions of the assembled gods. Brŭmha complained to Doorga, who appeased him by saying, that Shivŭ did not attempt to cut off his head because he aspired to be greater than he, but because he (Brŭmha) had been guilty of a great crime in endeavouring to seduce his daughter. Brŭmha was satisfied with this answer, but pronounced a curse on whatever god, gŭndhurvŭ, or ŭpsŭra should hereafter drink spirits.

The above is the substance of the story as related in the Mŭhabharŭtŭ. The Kashēē-khŭndŭ of the Skŭnda pooranŭ says, that Brŭmha lost one of his heads in the following manner:—this god was one day asked by certain sages, in the presence of Krŭtoo, a form of Vishnoo, who was greatest, Brŭmha, Vishnoo, or Shivŭ? Brŭmha affirmed that he was entitled to this distinction. Krŭtoo, as a form of Vishnoo, insisted that the superiority belonged to himself. An appeal was made to the védus; but those books declared in favour of Shivŭ. On hearing this verdict, Brŭmha was filled with rage, and made many insulting remarks upon Shivŭ; who, assuming the terrific form of Kalu-Bhoirŭvŭ, appeared before Brŭmha and Krŭtoo, and, receiving farther insults from Brŭmha, with his nails tore off one of Brŭmha's five heads. Brŭmha was now thoroughly humbled, and with joined hands acknowledged that he was inferior to Shivŭ. Thus this quarrel betwixt the three gods was adjusted; and Shivŭ, the naked mendicant, was acknowledged as Mŭha-dévŭ, the great god.

Brŭmha is also charged with stealing several calves from the herd which Krishnŭ was feeding.

This god, assuming the appearance of a religious mendicant, is said to have appeared many times on earth for different purposes. Stories to this effect are to be found in several of the pooranŭs.

The Mŭhabharŭtŭ contains the following description of the heaven of Brŭmha:—this heaven is 800 miles long, 400 broad, and 40 high. Narŭdŭ, when attempting to describe this heaven, declared himself utterly incompetent to the task; that he could not do it in two hundred years; that it contained in a superior degree all that was in the other heavens; and that whatever existed in the creation of Brŭmha on earth, from the smallest insect to the largest animal, was to be found here.

A scene in the heaven of Brŭmha:—Vrihŭspŭtee, the spiritual guide of the gods, on a particular occasion went to the place of his elder brother Ootŭt'hyŭ, and became enamoured of his pregnant wife. The child in the womb reproved him. Vrihŭspŭtee cursed the child ; on which account it was born blind, and called Dēērghŭ-tŭma[c]. When grown up, Dēērghŭ-tŭma followed the steps of his uncle, and from his criminal amours Goutŭmŭ and other Hindoo saints were born. Dēērghŭ-tŭma was delivered from the curse of Vrihŭspŭtee by Yoodhist'hirŭ.

This god has many names, among which are the following : Brŭmha, or, he who multiplies [mankind]. Atmŭbōō, the self-existent. Pŭrŭmést'hēē, the chief sacrificer[d]. Pitamŭhŭ, the grand-father. Hirŭnyŭ-gurbhŭ, he who is pregnant with gold. Lokéshŭ, the god of mankind, the creator. Chŭtoor-anŭnŭ, the four-faced. Dhata, the creator. Ubjŭ-yonee, he who is born from the water-lily. Droohinŭ, he who subdues the giants. Prŭjapŭtee, the lord of all creatures. Savitrēē-pŭtee, the husband of Savitrēē.

SECT. IV.—*Indrŭ*

INDRŬ is called the king of heaven, and his reign is said to continue 100 years of the gods ; after which another person, from among the gods, the giants, or men, by his own merit, raises himself to this eminence. The sacrifice of a horse[e] one hundred times raises a person to the rank of Indrŭ.

The Shrēē-bhagŭvŭtŭ gives the following list of the persons who have been or will be raised to the rank of king of the gods during the present kŭlpŭ : Hŭree, Rochŭnŭ, Sŭtyŭ-jit Trishikhŭ, Vibhoo, Mŭntrŭ-droomŭ, and Poorŭndŭrŭ, the present Indrŭ. To him will succeed Bŭlee, Shrootŭ, Shŭmbhoo, Voidhritŭ, Gŭndhŭ-dhama, Divŭspŭtee, and Shoochee.

Indrŭ is represented as a white man, sitting on an elephant called Oiravŭtŭ, with a thunderbolt in his right hand, and a bow in his left. He has 1,000 eyes.

The worship of Indrŭ is celebrated annually, in the day time, on the 14th of the lunar month Bhadrŭ. The usual ceremonies of worship are accompanied with singing, music, dancing, &c. In Bengal the greater number of those who keep this festival are women ; in whose names the ceremonies are performed by officiating bramhŭns. It lasts one day, after which the image is thrown into the river. This festival, which is accompanied by the greatest festivities, is celebrated all over Bengal ; each one repeating it annually during fourteen years. On the day of worship, a few blades of dōōrva grass are tied round the right arm of a man, and

[c] From dēērghŭ, long ; tŭma, darkness.

[d] That is, as the first bramhŭn, he performed all the great sacrifices of the Hindoo law. To every sacrifice a bramhŭn is necessary.

[e] The horse, on account of his usefulness in war, was sacrificed to Mars.

the left of a woman. Some persons wear this string, which contains fourteen knots, for a month after the festival is over. Fourteen kinds of fruits, fourteen cakes, &c. must be presented to the image. This worship is performed for the purpose of procuring riches, or a house, or a son, or pleasure, or a residence after death in Indrŭ's heaven.

Indrŭ is supposed to preside over the elements, so that in times of drought prayers are addressed to him as the giver of rain.

He is also one of the ten guardian deities of the earth, and is said to preside in the east. To render the worship of any other god acceptable, it is necessary that the worship of these deities be previously performed, viz., of Indrŭ, Ŭgnee, Yŭmŭ, Noiritŭ, Vŭroonŭ, Pŭvŭnŭ, Eeshŭ, Ŭnŭntŭ, Koovérŭ, and Brŭmha; also that of 'the five deities', viz., Sōōryŭ, Gŭnéshŭ, Shivŭ, Doorga, and Vishnoo; and of the nine planets, viz., Rŭvee, Somŭ, Mŭngŭlŭ, Boodhŭ, Vrihŭspŭtee, Shookrŭ, Shŭnee, Rahoo, and Kétoo. In consequence of this rule, a few ceremonies of worship are performed to Indrŭ at the commencement of every festival.

The pooranŭs and other writings contain a number of stories respecting this king of the gods, who is represented as particularly jealous lest any persons should, by the performance of sacred austerities, out-do him in religious merit, and thus obtain his kingdom. To present these devotees from succeeding in their object, he generally sends a captivating female from his own residence to draw away their minds, and thus throw them down from the ladder of religious merit, and send them back again to a life of gratification among the delusive forms of earth. But that which entails the greatest infamy on the character of this god is, his seducing the wife of his spiritual guide Goutŭmŭ. This story is related in the Ramayŭnŭ as follows: 'After receiving the highest honours from Prŭmŭtee, the two descendants of Rŭghoo, having passed the night there, went towards Mit'hila. When the sages beheld at a distance the beautiful city of Jŭnŭkŭ, they joyfully exclaimed, 'Excellent! excellent!' Raghŭva, seeing a hermitage in a grove of Mit'hila, asked the chief of sages, 'What solitary wilderness is this, O divine one? I desire to hear whose hermitage this is, beautiful, of impenetrable shade, and inhabited by sages.' Vishwamitru,, hearing these words, in pleasing accents thus answered the lotus-eyed Ramŭ: 'Attend, I will inform thee whose is this hermitage, and in what manner it became solitary, cursed by the great one in his wrath. This was the sacred hermitage of the great Goutŭmŭ, adorned with trees, flowers, and fruits. For many thousand years, O son of Rŭghoo, did the sage remain here with Ŭhŭlya, performing sacred austerities. One day, O Ramŭ, the sage being gone far distant the king of heaven, acquainted with the opportunity, and sick with impure desire, assuming the habit of a sage[f], thus addres-

[f] That is, the habit of Goutŭmŭ. This resembles Jupiter's seducing Alcmena, the wife of Amphytrion, in her husband's absence, in the likeness of Amphytrion.

sed Ŭhŭlya, 'The menstrual season deserves regard[g], O thou........

....

This depraved woman, O afflicter of enemies, knowing Shŭkrŭ[d] in the disguise of a sage, through wantonness consented, he being king of the gods. The chief of the gods having perpetrated his crime, she thus addressed him: 'O chief of gods, thou hast accomplished thy design, speedily depart unobserved. O sovereign of the gods, effectually preserve thyself and me from Goutŭmŭ.' Indrŭ smiling replied to Ŭhŭlya, 'O beautiful one, I am fully pleased; I will depart; forgive my transgression.' After this, he, O Ramŭ, with much caution left the hermitage, dreading the wrath of Goutŭmŭ. At that instant he saw Goutŭmŭ enter, resplendent with energy, and, through the power of sacred austerities, invincible even to the gods[e]; wet with the waters of the sacred tēēr'-thŭ[f], as the fire moistened with clarified butter[g], he saw him coming to the hermitage, laden with sacrificial wood, and the sacred kooshŭ. Perceiving him, Shŭkrŭ was overwhelmed with sadness. The sage clothed in virtue, beholding the profligate lord of the gods in the disguise of a sage, in dreadful anger thus addressed him: 'O profligate wretch, assuming my form thou hast perpetrated this crime: therefore become an eunuch.' At the word of the magnanimous and angry Goutŭmŭ, the thousand-eyed god instantly became an eunuch. Deprived of manly energy, and rendered an eunuch by the anger of the devout sage, he, full of agonizing pain, was overcome with sorrow[h]. The great sage, having cursed him, pronounced a curse upon his own wife: 'Innumerable series of years, O sinful wretch, of depraved heart, thou, enduring excessive pain, abandoned, lying constantly in ashes, invisible to all creatures, shalt remain in this forest. When Ramŭ, the son of Dŭshŭrut'hŭ, shall enter this dreadful forest, thou, beholding him, shalt be cleansed from thy sin. Having, O stupid wretch, entertained him without selfish views, thou, filled with joy, shalt again approach me without fear.' Having thus addressed this wicked woman, the illustrious Goutŭmŭ, the

g 'According to the shastrŭs, sixteen days from the appearance of the menses is reckoned the menstrual season. All connubial intercourse is forbidden during the first three of these days. The guilt incurred by a violation of this rule, on the first day is equal to that of a criminal connection with a female chŭndalŭ, on the second day equal to the same act with a washerwoman, and on the third to the same act with a female shōōdrŭ.'

d A name of Indrŭ, signifying strength.

e The Hindoos believe that the merit of works is such as to be sufficient to raise a person higher than the gods themselves.

f Tēērt'hŭs are certain places esteemed peculiarly sacred by the Hindoos. Bathing in these places is reckoned highly meritorious.

g That is, the fire of the burnt offering.

h Other accounts say, that Goutŭmŭ imprinted a thousand female marks upon him as proofs of his crime, and that Indrŭ was so ashamed, that he petitioned Goutŭmŭ to deliver him from his disgrace. The sage, therefore, changed these marks into eyes, and hence Indrŭ became the thousand-eyed god.

great ascetic, abandoned this hermitage, and performed austerities on the pleasant top of Himŭvŭt, frequented by the siddhŭs and charŭnŭs[c].

Indrŭ was also guilty of stealing a horse consecrated by king Sŭgŭrŭ, who was about to perform, for the hundredth time, the sacrifice of this animal.

Indrŭ, though king of the gods, has been frequently overcome in war: Méghŭ-nadŭ[d], the son of Ravŭnŭ, the giant, once overcame him, and tied him to the feet of his horse. On condition of releasing the king of the gods, Brŭmha conferred on Méghŭ-nadŭ the name Indrŭ-jit, that is, the conqueror of Indrŭ. He was called Méghŭ-nadŭ because he fought behind a cloud,(méghŭ;) and this enabled him to overcome Indrŭ, who, in the engagement, was unable to see him, though he had a thousand eyes.

Kŭshyŭpŭ, the sage, once performed a great sacrifice, to which all the gods were invited. Indrŭ, on his way to the feast, saw 60,000 dwarf bramhŭns trying in vain to cross a cow's footstep which was filled with water, and had the misfortune to laugh at these pigmies; at which they were so incensed, that they resolved to make a new Indrŭ, who should conquer him, and take away his kingdom. Indrŭ was so frightened at these 60,000 pigmy bramhŭns, who could not get over a cow's footstep, that he entreated Brŭmha to interfere; who saved him from their wrath, and continued him on his throne.

Description of Umŭravŭtēe, the residence of Indrŭ, from the Mŭhabharŭtŭ:—This heaven was made by Vishwŭ-kŭrma, the architect of the gods. It is 800 miles in circumference, and 40 miles high; its pillars are composed of diamonds; all its elevated seats, beds, &c. are of gold; its palaces are also of gold. It is so ornamented with all kinds of precious stones, jasper, chrysolite, sapphire, emeralds, &c. &c., that it exceeds in splendour the brightness of twelve suns united. It is surrounded with gardens and forests, containing among other trees the parijatŭ, the fragrance of the flowers of which extends 800 miles, that is, fills the whole heaven[e]. In the pleasure grounds are pools of water, warm in winter and cold in summer, abounding with fish, water-fowl, water-lilies, &c. the landing places of which are of gold. All kinds of trees and flowering shrubs abound in these gardens. The winds are most refreshing, never boisterous; and the heat of the sun is never oppressive. Gods, sages, ŭpsŭras, kinnŭrŭs, siddhŭs, saddhyŭs, dévŭrshees, brŭmhŭrshees, rajŭrshees, Vrihŭspŭtee, Shookrŭ, Shŭnee, Boodhŭ, the winds, clouds, Oiravŭtŭ, (Indrŭ's elephant,) and other celes-

[c] Carey and Marshman's Translation of the Ramayŭnŭ, vol. i., page 433.
[d] This word signifies thunder.

[e] It is a curious fact, that though this flower is so celebrated in the pooranŭs for its fragrance, it has no scent at all.

tial beings, dwell in this heaven. The inhabitants are continually entertained with songs, dances, music, and every species of mirth. Neither sickness, sorrow, nor sudden death, are found in these regions, nor are its inhabitants affected with hunger or thirst.—When the god Narŭdŭ was sitting in an assembly of princes at king Yoodhist'hirŭ's, the latter asked him whether he had ever seen so grand a scene before. Narŭdŭ, after some hesitation, declared he had beheld a scene far more splendid in Indrŭ's heaven, of which he then gave the above account; but confessed that the place exceeded all his powers of description.

A scene in Indrŭ's heaven:—On a certain occasion an assembly of the gods was held in this place, at which, beside the gods, Narŭdŭ and the rishees, the gŭnŭs, dŭkshŭs, gundhŭrvŭs, &c. were present. While the courtezans were dancing, and the kinnŭrŭs singing, the whole assembly was filled with the highest pleasure. To crown their joys, the gods caused a shower of flowers to fall on the assembly. The king of the gods, being the most distinguished personage present, first took up a flower, and, after holding it to his nose, gave it to a bramhŭn. The assembled gods laughing at the brumhŭn for receiving what Indrŭ had used, he went home in disgrace; but cursed Indrŭ, and doomed him to become a cat in the house of a person of the lowest cast. Suddenly, and unknown to all, he fell from heaven, and became a cat in the house of a hunter. After he had been absent eight or ten days, Shŭchēē, his wife, became very anxious, and sent messengers every where to enquire for her husband. The gods also said among themselves, 'What is become of Indrŭ?—A total silence reigns in his palace, nor are we invited to the dance and the usual festivities! What can be the meaning of this?'—All search was in vain; and the gods assembled to enquire where he was. They found Shŭchēē in a state of distraction, of whom Brŭmha enquired respecting the lost god. At length Brŭmha closed his eyes, and by the power of meditation discovered that Indrŭ, having offended a bramhŭn, had become a cat. Shŭchēē, full of alarm, asked Brŭmha what she was to do. He told her to go to the house of the bramhŭn, and obtain his favour; upon which her husband would be restored to her. Shŭchēē obeyed the directions of Brŭmha, and went to the house of the bramhŭn; who was at length pleased with her attentions, and ordered her to descend to the earth, and go to the house of the hunter, whose wife would tell her what to do that her husband might be restored to his throne in heaven. Assuming a human form, she went to the house of the hunter, and, looking at the cat, sat weeping. The wife of the hunter, struck with the divine form of Shŭchēē, enquired with surprise who she was. Shŭchēē hesitated, and expressed her doubts whether the hunter's wife would believe her if she declared her real name. At length she confessed who she was, and, pointing to the cat, declared that that was her husband, Indrŭ, the king of heaven. The hunter's wife, petrified with astonishment, stood speechless. Shŭchēē, after some farther discourse, said, she had been informed that she (the hunter's wife) alone could assist her in obtaining the deliverance of her husband. After some moments of reflection, this woman directed Shŭchēē to perform the Kalika-vrŭtŭ. She obeyed; and poor Indrŭ, quitting the form of the cat, ascended to heaven, and resumed his place among the gods. No doubt he took care in future not to offend a bramhŭn.

Another scene in the heaven of Indrŭ, from the Shrēē-bhagŭvŭtŭ.—On a certain occasion, the heavenly courtezans and others were dancing before the gods, when Indrŭ was so charmed with the dancing and the person of Oorvŭshēē, one of the courtezans, that he did not perceive when his spiritual guide Vrihŭsputee entered the assembly, and neglected to pay him the usual honours. Vrihŭspŭtee was so incensed at this, that he arose and left the assembly. The gods, perceiving the cause, in the utmost consternation[f] went to Indrŭ, and made him acquainted with what had passed. The latter intreated the gods to join him in seeking for the enraged Vrihŭspŭtee; but the spiritual guide had, by the power of yogŭ, rendered himself invisible. At last they found the angry gooroo in his own house; and the gods, joining their petitions to those of Indrŭ, entreated that the offence might be forgiven. Vrihŭspŭtee declared that he had for ever rejected Indrŭ, and that his resolution would not be changed. Indrŭ, offended that for so small an offence he should be so harshly treated, declared that he would make no farther concessions, but seek another religious guide. The gods approved of his resolution, and advised him to choose Vishwŭ-rōōpŭ, a giant with three heads. In process of time, at the suggestion of his mother, Vishwŭrōōpŭ began a sacrifice to procure the increase of the power of the giants, the natural enemies of the gods. Indrŭ heard of this, and, hurling his thunders on the head of the faithless priest, destroyed him in an instant. The father of Vishwŭrōōpŭ heard of his son's death, and, by the merit of a sacrifice, gave birth to a giant, at the sight of whom Indrŭ fled to Brŭmha; who informed the king of the gods that this giant could not be destroyed by all his thunders, unless he could persuade Dŭdhēēchee, a sage, to renounce life, and give him one of his bones. The sage consented, and by the power of yogŭ renounced life; when Vishwŭ-kŭrma made this bone into a thunder-bolt, and the giant was destroyed. But immediately on his death, a terrific monster arose from the body, to punish Indrŭ for his bramhŭnicide Wherever the king of the gods fled, this monster followed him with his mouth open, ready to swallow him up, till Indrŭ took refuge in a place where the monster could not approach him; however he sat down, and watched the trembling culprit. After some time the gods began to be alarmed: there

[f] A Hindoo considers the anger of his spiritual guide as the greatest possible misfortune.

was no king in heaven, and every thing was falling into complete disorder. After consultation, they raised to the throne of heaven, in his bodily state, Nŭhooshŭ, who had performed the sacrifice of a horse one hundred times. When Nŭhooshŭ enquired for Shŭchēē, the queen of heaven, he found she was in the parijatŭ forest. He sent for her; but she declared she would not come, as he had a human and not a divine body. The messengers remonstrated with her, but she fled to Brŭmha; who advised her to send word to the new Indrŭ, that she would live with him, if he would come and fetch her with an equipage superior to whatever had been seen before in heaven. This message was conveyed to the new Indrŭ; who received it with much joy, but took several days to consider in what way he should go to fetch home the queen. At last, he resolved to be carried to her in the arms of some of the principal sages. As the procession was moving along, the king, in his excessive anxiety to arrive at the parijatŭ forest, kicked the sacred lock of hair on the head of Ŭgŭstyŭ; who became filled with rage, and, pronouncing a dreadful curse on the new Indrŭ, threw him down, and he fell, in the form of a snake, upon a mountain on the earth.—Vishnoo, perceiving that one Indrŭ was kept a prisoner, and that another had been cursed and sent down to the earth, resolved to find a remedy for this evil, and, cursing the monster who had imprisoned the former king of the gods, restored him to his throne and kingdom.

Another scene in Indrŭs heaven, from the Mŭhabharŭtŭ.—Narŭdŭ one day called at Krishnŭ's, having with him a parijatŭ flower from the heaven of Indrŭ. The fragrance of this flower filled the whole place with its odours. Narŭdŭ first called on Rookminēē, one of Krishnŭ's wives, and offered the flower to her. She recommended him to give it to Krishnŭ, that he might dispose of it as he chose. He next went to Krishnŭ, who received him with great respect: 'Well, Narŭdŭ, you are come after a long absence: what flower is that?' 'Can't you tell by its fragrance?' said Narŭdŭ, 'it is the parijatŭ. I brought it from Indrŭ's garden, and I now present it to you.' Krishnŭ received it with pleasure, and, after some further conversation, Narŭdŭ retired into another part of the house and watched Krishnŭ, to see to which of his wives he would give this flower; that he might excite a quarrel in Krishnŭ's family, and ultimately a war betwixt Krishnŭ and Indrŭ. Krishnŭ, after Narŭdŭ had retired, went to Rookminēē, and gave the flower to her, warning her to keep it secret, lest Sŭtyŭ-bhama (another of Krishnŭ's wives) should hear of it. As soon as Narŭdŭ saw to whom Krishnŭ had given the flower, he paid a visit to Sŭtyŭ-bhama, who received him with great attention. After the first compliments were over, Narŭdŭ fetched a deep sigh, which Sŭtyŭ-bhama noticing, enquired the cause. He seemed to answer with reluctance, which made Sŭtyŭ-bhama still more inquisitive. He then acknowledged that his sorrow was on her account. Her anxiety was now inflamed to the highest degree, and she begged him to tell her without delay what he meant. 'I have always considered you,' says Narŭdŭ, 'as the most beloved wife of Krishnŭ; the fame of your happiness has reached heaven itself: but from what I have seen to-day, I suspect that this is all mistake.' 'Why? Why?' asked Sŭtyŭ-bhama most anxiously. Narŭdŭ then unfolded to her, in the most cautious manner, the story of the flower: 'I brought from heaven,' says he, 'a parijatŭ flower, (a flower which is not to be obtained on earth,) and gave it to Krishnŭ. I made no doubt but he would present it to you—to whom else should he present it? But instead of that he went secretly to the apartments of Rookminēē, and gave the flower to her. Where then is his love to you?'—Sŭtyŭ-bhama asked what kind of flower this was. Narŭdŭ declared that it was not in his power to describe it. 'Do you not perceive,' said he, 'its odours?' 'I perceived,' said Sŭtyŭ-bhama, 'the most delightful fragrance, but I thought it was from your body.' Narŭdŭ declared that his body was offensive, and that it was the parijatŭ that diffused its odours all around. 'But,' says he, 'when you see Krishnŭ, ask him to let you look at it.' 'And do you think then,' said Sŭtyŭ-bhama, 'that I shall speak to Krishnŭ, or see his face any more!'—'You are right,' said Narŭdŭ: 'he did not even let you see so precious a jewel; but secretly gave it to another.'—The enraged Sŭtyŭ-bhama made the most solemn protestations that she had done with Krishnŭ for ever. Narŭdŭ praised her for her resolution, but hinted, that if she ever did make up the matter with Krishnŭ, she should insist upon his fetching one of the trees from heaven, and giving it to her. Narŭdŭ, having thus laid the foundation of a dreadful quarrel betwixt Krishnŭ and his wife, and of a war with Indrŭ, withdrew, and Sŭtyŭ-bhama retired to the house of anger[g].—Some days after this, Krishnŭ went to see Sŭtyŭ-bhama, but could not find her: on asking the servants, they told him that she had on some account retired to the house of anger. Not being able to discover the cause, he went to her, and made use of every soothing expression; but in vain. At last he threw himself at her feet, when, after many entreaties, she consented to be reconciled, on condition that he should fetch one of the trees from heaven, and plant it in her garden. This he engaged to do, and sent Gŭroorŭ to Indrŭ with his respects: but commissioned Gŭroorŭ in case of refusal to threaten him with war; and if this did not avail, to add, that Krishnŭ would come and trample on the body of his queen, overturn his throne, and take the tree from him by force. Neither the entreaties nor threats of Krishnŭ moved Indrŭ; who, on the contrary, sent him a defiance. Krishnŭ, on the return of Gŭroorŭ, collected his forces, and invaded heaven. Dreadful havock was made on both sides. All the heavens were in a state of frightful

[g] A house set apart for an angry wife, where she retires till her husband reconciles himself to her.

uproar; and the gods, full of alarm, advised Indrŭ to submit, as he would certainly be overcome. At length Krishnŭ let fly a weapon called Soodŭrshŭnŭ, which pursued the foe wherever he went. The gods again exhorted Indrŭ to sue for peace, to prevent his immediate destruction: he at length took this advice, and submitted to the enraged Krishnŭ, who carried off the tree in triumph, and appeased his jealous wife Sŭtyŭ-bhama.

The following are some of the names of this god: Indrŭ, or, the glorious.—Mŭrootwan, he who is surounded by the winds. —Pakŭshasŭnŭ, he who governs the gods with justice. Pooroohōōtŭ, he who is invited to a sacrifice performed by king Pooroo.—Poorŭndŭrŭ, he who destroys the dwellings of his enemies.—Jishnoo, the conqueror.—Shŭkrŭ, he who is equal to every thing. —Shŭtŭmŭnyoo, he who performed a hundred sacrifices.—Divŭspŭtee, the god of the heavens.—Gotrŭbhid, he who clipt the wings of the mountains[i].—Bŭjree, he who wields the thunder-bolt[k].—Vritrŭha, he who destroyed the giant Vritrŭ.—Vrisha, the holy.—Soorŭ-pŭtee, the king of the gods.—Bŭlaratee, the destroyer of Bŭlŭ, a giant.—Hŭrihŭyŭ, he who is drawn by yellow horses. —Nŭmoochisoodŭnŭ, the destroyer of Nŭmoochee, a giant.—Sŭnkrŭndŭnŭ, he who causes the wives of his enemies to weep. —Toorashat, he who is able to bear all things.—Méghŭ-vahŭnŭ, he who rides on the clouds.—Sŭhŭsrakshŭ, he who has a thousand eyes.[l].

SECT. V.—*Sōōryŭ*[m].

THIS god is said to be the son of Kŭshyŭpŭ, the progenitor of gods and men. He is represented as a dark-red man, with three eyes, and four arms; in two hands he holds the water-lily; with another, he is bestowing a blessing, and with the other forbidding fear. He sits on a red water-lily, and rays of glory issue from his body.

The bramhŭns consider Sōōryŭ as one of the greatest of the gods, because in glory he resembles the one Brŭmhŭ, who is called téjomŭyŭ, or the glorious. In the védŭs also this god is much noticed: the celebrated incantation called the gayŭtrēē, and many of the forms of meditation, prayer, and praise, used in the daily ceremonies of the bramhŭns, are addressed to him. He is at present worshipped daily by the bramhŭns, when flowers, water, &c. are offered, accompanied with incantations.

i It is said, that formerly the mountains had wings, and that they flew into all parts of the earth, and crushed to atoms towns, cities, &c.

k In this Indrŭ resembles Jupiter Fulminator.

l Mr. Wilkins considers Indrŭ, with his thousand eyes, as a deification of the heavens.

m The Sun.

On a Sunday, at the rising of the sun, in any month, but especially in the month Maghŭ, a number of persons, chiefly women, perform the worship of Sōōryŭ: I shall give an account of this worship in the words of a respected friend.—'The sun is annually worshipped on the first Sunday in the month Maghŭ. The name of this worship is called Dhŭrmŭ-bhaoo, or Sōōryŭ-bhaoo. The ceremonies vary in different places, but in this district the women appear to be the principal actors; though none are excluded, and even Mŭsŭlmans are so far Hindooized as to join in the idolatry. I saw it once thus conducted:—at the dawn of the morning a great number of offerings were carried into the open field, and placed in a row. The offerings consisted of fruits, sweatmeats, pigeons and kids. A small pot was placed by each person's offering, containing about a pint and a half of water. A device made of a water-plant, a species of Millingtonia, intended to represent the sun, was placed on the edge of the pot, and a small twig of the mango-tree, with a few leaves on it, put into it, as people in England keep flowers. The pot with all its appendages represented the sun perhaps as the vivifier of nature. By each offering also was placed (what shall I call it?) an incense-altar, or censer called dhoonachee. It resembled a chafing-dish, made of copper, and stood upon a pedestal about a foot long. It contained coals of fire, and a kind of incense from time to time was thrown into it, principally the pitch of the salŭ-tree, called dhoona. Near each offering was placed a lamp, which was kept burning all day. The women also took their stations near the offerings. At sun-rise they walked four times round the whole row of offerings, with the right hand towards them, and the smoking dhoonachees placed on their heads; after which they resumed their stations again, where they continued in an erect posture, fasting the whole day, occasionally throwing a little incense into the dhoonachee. Towards evening, the bramhŭn who attended the ceremony, threw the pigeons up into the air; which, being young, could not fly far, and were scrambled for and carried away by the crowd. The officiating bramhŭn perforated the ears of the kids with a needle; after which they were seized by the first person who touched them. About sun-set, the offerers again took up the smoking dhoonachees, and made three circuits round the rows of offerings. After this, the offerings and lighted lamps were taken away by their respective owners, who threw the lamps into a pool of water.'

Women frequently make a vow to Sōōryŭ to worship him, on condition that he give—to one, a son; to another, riches; to another, health, &c. Some perform these ceremonies after bearing a son. This worship is sometimes attended to by one woman alone; at other times by five, six, or more in company.

Sōōryŭ and the other planets are frequently worshipped in order to procure health. This the Hindoos call a sacrifice to the nine planets, when flowers, rice, water, a burnt-sacrifice, &c. are offered to each of these planets separately. It is said, that two or three hundred years ago Mŭyōōrŭbhŭttŭ, a learned Hindoo, in order to obtain a cure for the leprosy, began to write a poem of one hundred Sŭngskritŭ verses in praise of Sōōryŭ; and that by the time he had finished the last verse, he was restored to health. These verses have been published under the title of Sōōryŭshŭtŭkŭ, the author at the close giving this account of his cure. Sometimes a sick person procures a bramhŭn to rehearse for him a number of verses in praise of Sōōryŭ, offering at the same time to this god rice, water, and jŭva[n] flowers. If the person be very ill, and a man of property, he employs two or three bramhŭns, who repeat as many as a thousand verses. This ceremony must be performed standing in the sun: when a thousand verses are rehearsed, the recitation occupies more than a day. The origin of this method of obtaining relief from sickness is ascribed to Shambŭ the son of Krishnŭ, one of the most beautiful youths in the three worlds, who was directed in a dream to repeat, twice a day, the twenty-one names of Sōōryŭ then revealed to him.

The persons who receive the name of Sōōryŭ, and adopt this god as their guardian deity, are called Sourŭs: they never eat till they have worshipped the sun, and when the sun is entirely covered with clouds they fast. On a Sunday, many Sourŭs, as well as Hindoos belonging to other sects, perform, in a more particular manner, the worship of this idol; and on this day some of them fast.

The Ramayŭnŭ contains the following story respecting Sōōryŭ, Hŭnoomanŭ, &c. In the war betwixt Ramŭ and Ravŭnŭ, an arrow discharged by Rŭvŭnŭ pierced the body of Lukshmŭnŭ: Ramŭ and all his friends were exceedingly alarmed for the life of Lŭkshmŭnŭ; the physicians tried all their efforts in vain. At last one physician declared that if four kinds of leaves could be brought from the mountain Gŭndhŭ-madhŭnŭ, and applied to the wound, Lŭkshmŭnŭ might probably be restored to health. The god who had given this arrow to Ravŭnŭ had declared, that whoever was wounded with it in the night should not recover, if a cure were not obtained before day-light. It was night when the wound was inflicted, but Hŭnoomanŭ engaged to bring the leaves before morning. To secure the fulfilment of his promise, he leaped into the air, and alighted on the mountain; but searched in vain for the medicinal leaves. While in his search, Ravŭnŭ, who had heard what was going forward, sent Sōōryŭ to arise on the mountain at midnight. Hŭnoomanŭ, in a rage, leaped up, and seizing Sōōryŭ's chariot wheels, placed the blazing god under his arm and the mountain on his head, and carried them to the camp of Ramŭ; where the friends of Lŭkshmŭnŭ searched out the plants, applied

[n] Hibiscus rosa Sinensis.

the leaves, and restored him to health : after which Hŭnoomanŭ permitted Sōōryŭ to depart.

Sōōryŭ has two wives, Sŭvŭrna and Chaya. The former is the daughter of Vishwŭkŭrma. After their marriage, Sŭvŭrna, unable to bear the power of his rays, made an image of herself; and, imparting life to it, called it Chaya[o], and left it with Sōōryŭ. She then returned to her father's house; but Vishwŭkŭrma reproved his daughter for leaving her husband, and refused her an asylum; but promised that if she would return, he would diminish the glory of Sōōryŭ's rays. Sŭvŭrna resolved not to return, and, assuming the form of a mare, fled into the forest of Dŭndŭkŭ. Chaya and Yŭmŭ, whom Sŭvŭrna had left with Sōōryŭ, could not agree; and Yŭmŭ one day beating Chaya, she cursed him, so that he ever since has had a swelled leg. Yŭmŭ, weeping, went to his father Sōōryŭ, shewed him his leg, and related what had happened; upon which Sōōryŭ began to suspect that this woman could not be Sŭvŭrna, for no mother ever cursed her own son; and if she did, the curse could not take effect. He immediately proceeded to the house of his father-in-law, who received him with great respect, but unperceived gave him a seat consisting of different sharp weapons, by which he became divided into twelve round parts. Sōōryŭ was enraged, and could not be pacified till his father-in-law informed him that his daughter, unable to bear the glory of his rays, had forsaken him. On enquiring where she was gone, the father said he had sent her back to him immediately on her arrival, but that where she now was he could not say. Sōōryŭ, by the power of dhyanŭ[p], perceived that Sŭvŭrna had become a mare, and was gone into some forest. The story here becomes too obscene for insertion.——Sōōryŭ and Sŭvŭrna, in the forms of a horse and a mare, had two children, to whom they gave the names of Ŭshwinēē and Koomarŭ[q]. When Sōōryŭ returned to his palace, he asked his wife who this woman (Chaya) was. She gave him her history, and presented her to him as a wife; and from that time Chaya was acknowledged as Sōōryŭ's second wife.

There are no temples dedicated to Sōōryŭ in Bengal. The heaven of this god is called Sōōryŭ-lokŭ. A race of Hindoo kings, distinguished as the descendants of the sun, once reigned in India; of which dynasty Ikshwakoo was the first king, and Ramŭ the sixty-sixth.

The following are the principal names of Sōōryŭ: Sōōrŭ, or, he who dries up the earth.—Sōōryŭ, he who travels, he who sends

[o] This word means a shadow.

[p] When the old Hindoo ascetics wished to ascertain a fact, they performed what is called dhyanŭ, viz., they shut their eyes, and began to meditate, when, it is said, the information they sought was revealed to them.

[q] That is, the sons of a mare: these are now physicians to the gods.

men to their work.—Dwadŭshatma, he who assumes twelve forms[r]. —Divakŭrŭ, the maker of the day.—Bhaskŭrŭ, the creator of the light.—Vivŭswŭt, the radiant.—Suptashwŭ, he who has seven horses in his chariot.—Vikŭrttŭnŭ, he who was made round by Vishwŭkŭrma in his lathe.—Ŭrkŭ, the maker of heat.—Mihirŭ, he who wets the earth[s].—Pōōshŭnŭ, he who cherishes all.—Dyoomŭnee, he who sparkles in the sky.—Tŭrŭnee, the saviour.—Mitrŭ, the friend of the water-lily[t].—Grŭhŭpŭtee, the lord of the stars.—Sŭhŭsrangshoo, the thousand-rayed.—Rŭvee, he who is to be praised.

SECT. VI.—*Gŭnéshŭ.*

THIS god is represented in the form of a fat short man, with a long belly, and an elephant's head[u]. He has four hands; holding in one a shell, in another, a chŭkrŭ, in another, a club, and in the fourth, a water-lily. He sits upon a rat. In an elephant's head are two projecting teeth, but in Gŭnéshŭ's only one, the other having been torn out by Vishnoo, when in the form of Pŭrŭsoo-ramŭ he wished to have an interview with Shivŭ. Gŭnéshŭ, who stood as door-keeper, denied him entrance, upon which a battle ensued, and Pŭrŭsoo-ramŭ, beating him, tore out one of his teeth.

The work called Gŭnéshŭ-khŭndŭ contains a most indecent story respecting the birth of this god; which, however necessary to the history, is so extremely indelicate that it cannot possibly be given. It is mentioned in this story, that Doorga cursed the gods; so that they have ever since been childless, except by criminal amours with females not their own wives.

When it was known that Doorga had given birth to a son, Shŭnēē and the rest of the gods went to see the child. Shŭnēē knew that if he looked upon the child it would be reduced to ashes; but Doorga took it as an insult that he should hang down his head, and refuse to look at her child. For some time he did not regard her reproofs; but at last, irritated, he looked upon

r Alluding to his progress through the twelve signs.

s The Sōōryŭ-shŭtŭkŭ says, the sun draws up the waters from the earth, and then lets them fall in showers again.

t At the rising of the sun this flower expands itself, and when the sun retires shuts up its leaves again.

u Sir W. Jones calls Gŭnéshŭ the god of wisdom, and refers, as a proof of it, to his having an elephant's head. I cannot find, however, that this god is considered by any of the Hindoos as properly the god of wisdom; for though he is said to give knowledge to those who worship him to obtain it, that is what is ascribed also to other gods. The Hindoos in general, I believe, consider the elephant as a stupid animal, and it is a biting reproof to be called as stupid as an elephant.

Gŭnéshŭ, and its head was instantly consumed[x] The goddess, seeing her child headless[y], was overwhelmed with grief, and would have destroyed Shŭnēē ; but Brŭmha prevented her, telling Shŭnēē to bring the head of the first animal he should find living with its head towards the north. He found an elephant in this situation, cut off its head, and fixed it upon Gŭnéshŭ, who then assumed the shape he at present wears. Doorga was but little soothed when she saw her son with an elephant's head : to pacify her, Brŭmha said, that amongst the worship of all the gods, that of Gŭnéshŭ should for ever bear the preference. In the beginning of every act of public worship therefore, certain ceremonies are constantly performed in honour of Gŭnéshŭ[z]. Not only is Gŭnéshŭ thus honoured in religious ceremonies, but in almost all civil concerns he is particularly regarded : as, when a person is leaving his house to go a journey, he says, 'Oh ! thou work perfecting Gŭnéshŭ, grant me success in my journey ! Gŭnéshŭ ! Gŭnéshŭ ! Gŭnéshŭ !'—At the head of every letter, a salutation is made to Gŭnéshŭ[a]. When a person begins to read a book, he salutes Gŭnéshŭ ; and shop-keepers and others paint the name or image of this god over the doors of their shops or houses, expecting from his favour protection and success.

No public festivals in honour of Gŭnéshŭ are held in Bengal. Many persons however choose him as their guardian deity, and are hence called Ganŭpŭtyŭs.

At the full moon in the month Maghŭ, some persons make or buy a clay image, and perform the worship of Gŭnéshŭ ; when the officiating bramhŭn performs the ceremonies common in the Hindoo worship, presenting offerings to the idol. This god is also worshipped at considerable length at the commencement of a wedding, as well as when the bride is presented to the bridegroom. Great numbers, especially from the western and southern provinces, celebrate the worship of Gŭnéshŭ on the 4th of the new moon in

[x] This property is ascribed to Shŭnēē, (Saturn,) to point out, no doubt, the supposed baneful influence of this planet. This resembles the fable of Saturn's devouring all his male children. The Ramayŭnŭ contains a story respecting Dŭshŭrŭt'hŭ and Shŭnēē, in which it is said, that Dŭshŭrŭt'hŭ was once angry with this god for preventing the fall of rain in his kingdom : he ascended his chariot to make war with him, when Shŭnēē, by a single glance of his eyes, set the king's chariot on fire, and Dŭshŭrŭt'hŭ, in the most dreadful state of alarm, fell from the skies.

[y] One cause of this misfortune is said to be this : Doorga had laid her child to sleep with its head to the north, which is forbidden by the shastrŭ. The Anhikŭtŭtwŭ declares, that if a person sleep with his head to the east, he will be rich ; if to the south, he will have long life ; if to the north, he will die ; and if to the west, (except when on a journey,) he will have misfortunes.

[z] It will occur to the reader, that in all sacrifices among the Romans, prayers were first offered to Janus.

[a] Gŭnéshŭ is famed as writing in a beautiful manner : so that when a person writes a fine hand, people say, 'Ah ! he writes like Gŭnéshŭ.' This god is said to have first written the Mŭhabharŭtŭ from the mouth of Vyasŭdévŭ.

Bhadrŭ, when several individuals in each place subscribe and defray the expence. Many persons keep in their houses a small metal image of Gŭnéshŭ, place it by the side of the shalgramŭ, and worship it daily. At other times, a burnt-offering of clarified butter is presented to this idol Stone images of Gŭnéshŭ are worshipped daily in the temples by the sides of the Ganges at Benares; but I cannot find that there are any temples dedicated to him in Bengal.

Gŭnéshŭ is also called Hŭridra-Gŭnéshŭ. This name seems to have arisen out of the following story:—When Doorga was once preparing herself for bathing, she wiped off the turmerick, &c. with oil, and formed a kind of cake in her fingers[b]. This she rolled together, and made into the image of a child; with which she was so much pleased, that she infused life into it, and called it Hŭridra-Gŭnéshŭ[c]. The image of this god is yellow, having the face of an elephant. He holds in one hand a rope; in another, the spike used by the elephant driver; in another, a round sweetmeat, and in another, a rod.

The principal names of Gŭnéshŭ are:—Gŭnéshŭ, or, the lord of the gŭnnŭ dévtas[d].—Dwoimatoorŭ, the two-mothered[e].—Ekŭdŭntŭ, the one-toothed.—Hérŭmbŭ, he who resides near to Shivŭ.—Lŭmbodŭrŭ, the long-bellied.—Gujanŭnŭ, the elephant-faced.

Sect. VII.—*Kartikéyŭ.*

This is the god of war. He is represented sometimes with one, and at other times with six faces; is of a yellow colour; rides on a peacock[f]; and holds in his right hand an arrow, and in his left, a bow.

The reason of the birth of Kartikéyŭ is thus told in the Koomaru-sŭmbhŭvŭ, one of the kavyŭs:—Tarŭkŭ, a giant, performed religious austerities till he obtained the blessing of Brŭmha, after which he oppressed both bramhŭns and gods. He commanded that the sun should shine only so far as was necessary to cause the water-lily to blossom; that the moon should shine in the day as well as in the night. He sent the god Yŭmŭ to cut grass for his horses; commanded Pŭvŭnŭ to prevent the wind from blowing any stronger than the puff of a fan; and in a similar manner tyrannized

b The Hindoos have a custom of cleaning their bodies by rubbing them all over with turmerick; and then, taking oil in their hands, wiping it off again, when it falls as a paste all round them.

c Hŭridra the name for turmerick.

d These are the companions of Shivŭ.

e One of Gŭnéshŭ's mothers was Doorga, and the other the female elephant whose head he wears.

f Juno's chariot was said to be drawn by peacocks.

over all the gods. At length Indrŭ called a council in heaven, when the gods applied to Brŭmha: but the latter declared he was unable to reverse the blessing he had bestowed on Tarŭkŭ; that their only hope was Kartikéyŭ, who should be the son of Shivŭ, and destroy the gaint.—After sometime, the gods assembled again to consult respecting the marriage of Shivŭ, whose mind was entirely absorbed in religious austerities. After long consultations, Kŭndŭrpŭ[g] was called, and all the gods began to flatter him in such a manner that he was filled with pride, and declared he could do every thing: he could conquer the mind even of the great god Shivŭ himself. That, 'says Indrŭ,' is the very thing we want you to do.' At this he appeared discouraged, but at length declared, that he would endeavour to fulfil his promise. He consulted his wife Rŭtēē; who reproved him for his temerity, but consented to accompany her husband. They set off, with Vŭsŭntŭ[h], to mount Himalŭyŭ, where they found Shivŭ sitting under a roodrakshŭ[i] tree, performing his devotions.

Previously to this, Himalŭyŭ[k] had been to Shivŭ, and proposed that Doorga, his daughter, should wait upon him, that he might uninterruptedly go on with his religious austerities; which offer Shivŭ accepted. One day, after the arrival of Kŭndŭrpŭ and his party, Doorga, with her two companions Jŭya and Vijŭya, carried some flowers and a necklace to Shivŭ. In the moment of opening his eyes from his meditation, to receive the offering, Kŭndŭrpŭ let fly his arrow; and Shivŭ, smitten with love, awoke as from a dream, and asked who had dared to interrupt his devotions.—Looking towards the south he saw Kŭndŭrpŭ, when fire proceeded from the third eye in the centre of his forehead, and burnt Kŭndŭrpŭ to ashes[l]. The enraged god left this place for another forest, and Doorga, seeing no prospect of being married to Shivŭ, returned home full of sorrow. She sought at last to obtain her object by the power of religious austerities[m], in which she persevered till Shivŭ was drawn from his devotions, when the marriage was consummated.

The Mŭhabharŭtŭ and Ramayŭnŭ contain accounts of the

[g] The god of love.

[h] The spring. The Hindoo poets always unite love and spring together.

[i] From the fruit of this tree necklaces are made, the wearing of which is a great act of merit among the Hindoos.

[k] The mountain of this name personified.

[l] Through the blessing of Shivŭ to Rŭtēē, Kŭndŭrpŭ was afterwards born in the family of Krishnŭ, and took the name of Kamŭ-dévŭ; after which Rŭtēē (then called Mayavŭtēē) was again married to him.

[m] When this goddess, says a kavyŭ shastrŭ, told her mother that she would perform austerities to obtain Shivŭ, her mother, alarmed, exclaimed—"Ooma! (Oh! mother!) how can you think of going into the forest to perform religious austerities? Stay and perform religious services at home, and you will obtain the god you desire. How can your tender form bear these severities? The flower bears the weight of the bee, but if a bird pitch upon it, it breaks directly."

birth of Kartikéyŭ, the fruit of this marriage; but they are so indelicate that the reader, I doubt not, will excuse their omission.

On the last evening in the month Kartikŭ, a clay image of this god is worshipped[n], and the next day thrown into the water. These ceremonies differ little from those at other festivals: but some images made on the occasion are not less than twenty-five cubits high; that is, a whole tree is put into the ground, and worshipped as a god. The height of the image obliges the worshippers to fasten the offerings to the end of a long bamboo, in order to raise them to the mouth of the god. This festival is distinguished by much singing, music, dancing, and other accompaniments of Hindoo worship.

The image of Kartikéyŭ is also made and set up by the side of his mother Doorga, at the great festival of this goddess in the month Ashwinŭ; and each day, at the close of the worship of Doorga, that of her son is performed at considerable length. In the month Choitrŭ also the worship of Kartikéyŭ accompanies that of his mother.—No bloody sacrifices are offered to this idol.

At the time when the above festival is held, some persons make [o] or purchase clay images, which they place in their houses, and before which the officiating bramhŭn performs the appointed ceremonies; preceding which a prayer is made for offspring. This is repeated sometimes on the anniversary of this day, for four years together. If the person, long disappointed, should, in these years, or soon after, happen to have a child, particularly a son, the whole is ascribed to Kartikéyŭ[p]. When persons have made a vow to Kartikéyŭ, they present offerings to this idol at the completion of the vow. These vows are sometimes made to obtain the health of a child, or a son; a woman, when she makes this vow, thus addresses the god: 'Oh! Kartikéyŭ t'hakoorŭ [q], give me a son, and I will present to thee [here she mentions a number of offerings, as sweetmeats, fruits, &c.]—I do not want a female child.' This vow may be made at any time, or place, without any previous

[n] Vast numbers of these images are made; in some towns as many as five hundred. It is supposed that in Calcutta more than five thousand are made and worshipped.

[o] He who makes an image for his own use is supposed to do an act of much greater merit than the person who purchases one.

[p] A part of the Mŭhabharŭtŭ is sometimes recited to obtain offspring. The part thus read is a list of the ancestors of Hŭree, (a name of Vishnoo.) When a person wishes to have this ceremony performed, he employs a learned native to recite these verses, and another to examine, by a separate copy, whether the verses be read without mistake: if they be read improperly, no benefit will arise from the ceremony. If the person who seeks offspring be unable to attend himself during the ceremony, he engages some friend to hear the words in his stead.—Some verses of praise, addressed to Shivŭ, are also occasionally read in the ears of a husband and wife who are anxious to obtain offspring.

[q] A term of respect, meaning excellent.

ceremony. When several women are sitting together, another woman perhaps comes amongst them, and, in the course of the conversation, asks the mistress of the house, 'Has your daughter-in-law any children yet?' She replies, in a plaintive manner, 'No, nothing but a girl.' Or she answers altogether in the negative, adding, 'I have again and again made vows to Kartikéyŭ, and even now I promise before you all, that if the god will give her a son, I will worship him in a most excellent manner, and my daughter-in-law will do it as long as she lives.'

There are no temples in Bengal dedicated to Kartikéyŭ, nor are any images of him kept in the houses of the Hindoos except during a festival.

The principal names of Kartikéyŭ, are: Kartikéyŭ, or, he who was cherished by six females of the name of Krittika[r].—Mŭha-sénŭ, he who commands multitudes.—Shŭranŭnŭ, the six-faced.—Skŭndŭ, he who afflicts the giants.—Ŭgnibhoo, he who arose from Ŭgnee.—Goohŭ, he who preserves his troops in war.—Tarŭkŭjit, he who conquered Tarŭkŭ.—Vishakhŭ, he who was born under the constellation of this name.—Shikhi-vahŭnŭ, he who rides on a peacock.—Shuktee-dhŭrŭ, he who wields the weapon called shŭktee.—Koomarŭ, he who is perpetually young[s].—Krounchŭ-darŭnŭ, he who destroyed the giant Krounchŭ.

It is said that Kartikéyŭ was never married, but that Indrŭ gave him a mistress named Dévŭséna. He has no separate heaven, nor has Gŭnéshŭ: they live with Shivŭ on mount Koilasŭ.

Sect. VIII.—*Ŭgnee.*

This god is represented as a red corpulent man, with eyes, eyebrows, beard, and hair, of a tawny-colour. He rides on a goat; wears a poita, and a necklace made with the fruits of eleocarpus ganitrus. From his body issue seven streams of glory, and in his right hand he holds a spear. He is the son of Kushyŭpŭ and Ŭditēē.

Ŭgnee has his forms of worship, meditation, &c. like other gods; but is especially worshipped, under different names, at the time of a burnt-offering, when clarified butter is presented to him. The gods are said to have two mouths, viz., that of the bramhŭn, and of fire (Ŭgnee).

[r] Six stars, (belonging to ursa major) said to be the wives of six of the seven rishees. These females are called Krittika. They cherished Kartikéyŭ as soon as he was born in the forest of writing-reeds, and hence his name is a regular patronymic of Krittika, because they were as his mothers.

[s] Under sixteen years of age.

At the full moon in the month Maghŭ, when danger from fire is considerable, some persons worship this god before the image of Brŭmha, with the accustomed ceremonies, for three days. When any particular work is to be done by the agency of fire, as when a kiln of bricks is to be burnt, this god is worshipped ; also when a trial by ordeal is to be performed.

Some bramhŭns are distinguished by the name sagnikŭ, because they use sacred fire in all the ceremonies in which this element is used, from the time of birth to the burning of the body after death. This fire is preserved in honour of the god Ŭgnee, and to make religious ceremonies more meritorious[t].

Ŭgnee, as one of the guardian deities of the earth, is worshipped at the commencement of every festival. He presides in the S. E.

Bhrigoo, a sagnikŭ bramhŭn and a great sage, once cursed his guardian deity Ŭgnee, because the latter had not delivered Bhrigoo's wife from the hands of a giant, who attempted to violate her chastity when she was in a state of pregnancy. The child, however, sprang from her womb, and reduced the giant to ashes. Bhrigoo doomed the god to eat every thing. Ŭgnee appealed to the assembled gods, and Brŭmha soothed him by promising, that whatever he ate should become pure. Ŭgnee was also once cursed by one of the seven rishees, who turned him into cinders.

Ŭrjoonŭ, the brother of Yoodhisthirŭ, at the entreaty of Ŭgnee, set fire to the forest Khŭndŭvŭ, in order to cure him of a surfeit contracted in the following manner:—Mŭrootŭ, a king, entered upon a sacrifice which occupied him twelve months, during the whole of which time clarified butter had been pouring on the fire, in a stream as thick as an elephant's trunk: at length Ŭgnee could digest no more, and he intreated Ŭrjoonŭ to burn this forest, that he might eat the medicinal plants, and obtain his appetite again.

Swaha, the daughter of Kŭshyŭpŭ, was married to Ŭgnee. Her name is repeated at the end of every incantation used at a burnt-offering, as well as in some other ceremonies. The reason of this honor is attributed to Ŭgnee's uxoriousness.

The heaven of this god is called Ŭgnee-lokŭ. His principal names are.—Vŭnhee, or, he who receives the clarified butter in the burnt-sacrifice (homŭ).—Vēētihotrŭ, he who purifies those who perform the homŭ.—Dhŭnŭnjŭyŭ, he who conquers (destroys) riches.—Kripēētŭyonee, he who is born from rubbing two sticks together.—Jwŭlŭnŭ, he who burns.—Ŭgnee, he to whom fuel is presented.

t There may be some resemblance in this to the custom of the Romans, in preserving a perpetual fire in the temple of Vesta.

SECT. IX.—*Pŭvŭnŭ.*

THIS is the god of the winds, and the messenger of the gods[u]. His mother Ŭditēē, it is said, prayed to her husband, that this son might be more powerful than Indrŭ: her request was granted; but Indrŭ, hearing of this, entered the womb of Ŭditēē, and cut the fœtus, first into seven parts, and then each part into seven others. Thus Pŭvŭnŭ assumed forty-nine forms[x]. He is meditated upon as a white man, sitting on a deer, with a white flag in his his right hand.

Pŭvŭnŭ has no separate public festival, neither image, nor temple. As one of the ten guardian deities of the earth, he is worshipped, with the rest, at the commencement of every festival. He is said to preside in the N. W. Water is also offered to him in the daily ceremonies of the bramhŭns; and, whenever a goat is offered to any deity, a service is paid to Vayoo, another form and name of Pŭvŭnŭ. In the work called Ŭdikŭrŭnŭ-mala, a burnt-sacrifice of the flesh of goats[y] is ordered to be offered to this god.

The following story is related of Pŭvŭnŭ in the Shrēē-bhagŭvŭtŭ:—On a certain occasion Narŭdŭ paid a visit to Sooméroo[z], and excited his pride in such a manner, that he protested the god Pŭvŭnŭ could not approach his summit. Narŭdŭ carried the news of Sooméroo's insolence to Pŭvŭnŭ, and advised him to go and break down the summit of Sooméroo; which, even to the depth of 800 miles below the surface, was of solid gold. Pŭvŭnŭ went, and produced such a tempest, that the earth trembled to its centre; and the mountain god, terribly alarmed, invoked Gŭroorŭ, who came to his relief, and, covering the mountain with his wings, secured it from the wrath of Pŭvŭnŭ. For twelve months, however, the storm raged so that the three worlds were hastening to destruction. The gods desired Narŭdŭ to prevail on Pŭvŭnu to compose the difference with Sooméroo: instead of complying with which the mischievous rishee went, and calling Pŭvŭnŭ a fool for exciting such a storm to no purpose, told him that as long as Gŭroorŭ protected the mountain with his wings, there was no hope; but that, if he would attack Sooméroo, when Gŭroorŭ was carrying Vishnoo out on a journey, he might easily be revenged. This opportunity soon occurred: all the gods

[u] I can find no agreement betwixt this god and either Mercury or Æolus.

[x] The forty-nine points. The Hindoos have 49 instead of 32 points; and the pooranŭs, which contain a story on every distinct feature of the Hindoo philosophy, have given this fable: and in the same manner all the elements are personified, and some remarkable story invented to account for their peculiar properties.

[y] The goat, it will be remembered, was slain in the sacrifices of Bacchus.

[z] The mountain of this name personified.

(330,000,000) were invited to Shivŭ's marriage with Parvŭtēē, among whom were the mountains Sooméroo, Trikōōtŭ, Oodŭyŭ[a], Ŭstŭ[b], Vindhyŭ, Malyŭvanŭ, Gŭndhŭma-dŭnŭ, Chitrŭkōōtŭ, Mŭlŭyŭ, Nilŭ, Moinakŭ[c], &c. Vishnoo, riding on Gŭroorŭ, also went to the marriage, and all the heavens were left empty. Seizing this opportunity, Pŭvŭnŭ flew to Sooméroo, and, breaking the summit of the mountain, hurled it into the sea[d].

Pŭvŭnŭ is charged with an adulterous intercourse with Ŭnjŭna, the wife of Késhŭrēē, a monkey. The fruit of this intercourse was Hŭnoomanŭ.

Pŭvŭnŭ was once inflamed with lust towards the hundred daughters of Kooshŭnabhŭ, a rajŭrshee; and because they refused his offers, he entered the body of each, and produced a curvature of the spine. They were made straight again by a king named Brŭmhŭ-dŭttŭ, to whom they were married.

The name of the heaven of this god is Vayoo-lokŭ. His principal names are:—Shwŭsŭnŭ, or, he who is the giver of breath.—Spŭrshŭnŭ, the toucher.—Vayoo, he who travels.—Matŭrishwa, he who gave his mother sorrow[e].—Prishŭdŭshwa, he who rides on the deer.—Gŭndhŭvŭhŭ, he who carries odours.—Ashoogŭ, he who goes swiftly.—Marootŭ, without whom people die.—Nŭbhŭswŭtŭ, he who moves in the air.—Puvŭnŭ, the purifier.—Prŭbhŭngjŭnŭ, the breaker.

SECT. X.—*Vŭroonŭ.*

THIS is the god of the waters. His image is painted white; he sits on a sea-animal called mŭkŭrŭ, with a rope[f] in his right hand.

Vŭroonŭ's name is repeated daily in the worship of the bramhŭns; but is image is never made for worship, nor has he any public festival or temple in Bengal. He is worshipped however as one

[a] Mountains over which the sun rises.

[b] Behind which the sun sets.

[c] Some of these belong to the snowy range north of India, and others to the tropical range dividing south from north India. These and other mountains are personified, and by the Hindoo poets are designated as the residence of the gods, and by poetical licence ranged among the inferior gods.

[d] Here it became the island of Ceylon, (Lŭnka.)

[e] When Indrŭ cut him into forty-nine pieces in the womb.

[f] This weapon is called pashŭ, and has this property, that whomsoever it catches, it binds so fast that he can never get loose. All the gods, giants, rakshŭsŭs, &c. learn the use of this weapon.

of the guardian deities of the earth; and also by those who farm the lakes in Bengal, before they go out a fishing: and in times of drought people repeat his name to obtain rain[g].

A story of this god is contained in the Pŭdmŭ pooranŭ to this purport:—Ravŭnŭ was once carrying an ŭnadee-lingŭ from Himalŭyŭ to Lŭnka[h], in order that he might accomplish all his ambitious schemes against the gods: for it was the property of this stone, also called kamŭ[i]-lingŭ, to grant the worshipper all his desires, whatever they might be. Shivŭ, however, when permitting Ravŭnŭ to remove this his image to Lŭnka, made him promise, that wherever he suffered it to touch the ground, there it should remain. When the gods saw that Ravŭnŭ was carrying this stone to Lŭnka, all the heavens were in a state of agitation: for the gods knew, that if Ravŭnŭ could be permitted to accomplish his wishes, neither Indrŭ nor any other god would continue on his throne. Council after council was held, and applications made to different gods in vain. It was at last resolved that Vŭroonŭ should enter the belly of Ravŭnŭ, who would thereby be compelled to set the stone down, while discharging his urine[k]. Vŭroonŭ accordingly entered the belly of Ravŭnŭ, as he was carrying the lingŭ on his head; and the latter soon began to feel the effects of his visit. His belly swelled prodigiously:—he proceeded however on his journey, till at last he could wait no longer. At this moment Indrŭ, in the form of an old bramhŭn, meeting him, Ravŭnŭ, after asking who he was, and where he was going, entreated him to hold the lingŭ for a short time, promising to bestow on him the greatest favours; to which the bramhŭn consented, agreeing to hold the stone an hour, but no longer. Ravŭnŭ told him he would not detain him half that time; and squatted on his hams to rid himself of Vŭroonŭ. After he had thus sat for four hours, the bramhŭn, complaining he could hold the stone no longer, threw it down—when the lower part sunk into the world of the hydras, and the top is said to be visible to this day at Voidyŭ-na'thŭ, a place in the zillah of Beerbhoom, where the river Khŭrsoo is believed te have arisen from the urine of this enemy of the gods[l]. Ravŭnŭ, when he arose, and saw what had taken place, went home full of

[g] At the time of a drought, it is common for bramhŭns to sit in crowds by the sides of the Ganges, or any other river, and address their prayers to this god. A bramhŭn once informed me, that he remembered when Krishnŭ-Chŭndrŭ, the rajá of Nŭvŭdwēēpŭ, gave presents to vast multitudes of bramhŭns thus employed; and that, in the midst of their prayers, Vŭroonŭ sent a plentiful supply of rain.

[h] Ceylon.

[i] Kamŭ means desire.

[k] Ravŭnŭ could not hold the lingŭ while in this act, as a person hereby becomes unclean until he has bathed. This is the strict rule of the shastrŭ: at present, however, should a person, in the midst of his worship, be compelled to discharge urine, he does not bathe, but only changes his clothes.

[l] The Hindoos do not drink the water of this river, but bathe in and drink the water of a pool there, which they have called Nŭvŭ-gŭnga, viz., the New Gŭnga.

rage and disappointment: some accounts add, that he went and fought with the gods in the most furious manner.

The heaven of this god, called Vŭroonŭ-lokŭ, is 800 miles in circumference, and was formed by Vishwŭkŭrma, the divine architect. In the centre is a grand canal of pure water. Vŭroonŭ, and his queen Varooneē, sit on a throne of diamonds; and around them the court, among whom are Sŭmoodrŭ, Gŭnga, and other river gods and goddesses[m]; the twelve Adityŭs, and other deities; the hydras; Oiravŭtŭ; the doityŭs; the danŭvŭs, &c. The pleasures of this heaven consist in the gratification of the senses, as in the heavens of Indrŭ and others. There does not seem to be a vestige of any thing here, but what would exactly meet the wishes of a libertine.

A scene in the heaven of Vŭroonŭ:—Nimee, a king, invited Vŭshisht'hŭ to preside as priest over the ceremonies at a sacrifice he was about to perform. Vŭshisht'hŭ, being engaged at that time as priest to perform a sacrifice for some other king, from whom he expected very large presents, excused himself for the present; when Nimee, after using entreaty in vain, employed another sage as priest. Vŭshisth'hŭ, having concluded the sacrifice in which he was engaged, proceeded to the palace of Nimee; but hearing that the king had employed another priest, was filled with rage, and pronounced a curse on the king, by which he was reduced to ashes. Before the curse took effect, however, the king cursed Vŭshisht'hŭ, and reduced his body also to ashes. The soul of Vŭshisht'hŭ ascended to Brŭmha, to enquire how he was to procure a body again. Brŭmha said, 'Go to the gods Vŭroonŭ and Sōōryŭ.' He went, and obtained his body in the following manner; Sōōryŭ, captivated with the sight of Oorvŭshēē, a courtezan, as she was dancing in Indrŭ's heaven, invited her to his house. As she was going, Vŭroonŭ met her, and became enamoured of her also. [Here the story becomes too filthy to be written.——] From the inflamed passions of these two gods, Ŭgŭstyŭ, an eminent ascetic, was born, and Vŭshisht'hŭ, one of the most exalted of the Hindoo saints, obtained a new body. The priests who had been employed by Nimee, fearing they should lose all employment hereafter if they suffered the king thus to perish, at the close of the sacrifice formed from the ashes a young man, to whom they gave the name of Jŭnŭkŭ; who became the father of Sēēta, the wife of Ramŭ.

The meaning of the name Vŭroonŭ is, he who surrounds.—This god is also called Prŭchéta, or the wise.—Pashēē, he who holds a rope.—Yadŭsang-pŭtee, the lord of the watery tribes.—Ŭppŭtee, the lord of waters.

m Among these deities are included gods of wells, pools, lakes, basins, whirlpools, &c.

Sect. XI.—*Yŭmŭ.*

This god is called the holy king, who judges the dead. His image is that of a green man, with red garments; inflamed eyes; having a crown on his head, and a flower stuck in his hair[n]; sitting on a buffaloe, with a club in his right hand. His dreadful teeth, grim aspect, and terrific shape, fill the inhabitants of the three worlds with terror.

An annual festival is held in honour of Yŭmŭ on the second day of the moon's increase in the month Kartikŭ, when an image of clay is made, and worshipped with the usual ceremonies for one day, and then thrown into the river. No bloody sacrifices are offered to this god.

Yŭmŭ is also worshipped at the commencement of other festivals, as one of the ten guardian deities of the earth. He presides in the south.

Every day the Hindoos offer water to Yŭmŭ, in the ceremony called tŭrpŭnŭ, as well as annually on the 14th of the month Ŭgrŭhayŭnŭ, when they repeat several of his names.

At the time of other festivals, the Hindoos sometimes make an image of the mother of Yŭmŭ[o], and worship it. At other times children in play make this image, and pretend to worship it.

On the first of the month Kartikŭ, a curious ceremony takes place in every part of Bengal:—the unmarried girls of each house engage a near relation to dig a small pit near the front of the house, at the four corners of which they sow rice, or barley, or wheat, and plant some stalks of the plantain or other tree: they also plant other branches in the midst of the pit. The place being thus prepared, every morning for a month these girls, after putting on clean apparel, and sprinkling their heads with the water of the Ganges to purify themselves, present flowers, &c. to Yŭmŭ by the side of this small pit, repeating an incantation. Each day they put a single kouree[p] in an earthen pot, and at the end of the ceremony present the thirty kourees to the person who dug the pit. They perform this ceremony to procure from Yŭmŭ either husbands, or sons, or happiness, and also that they may escape punishment after death.

[n] It is very common to see a flower, which has been presented to an image, stuck in the bunch of hair which the Hindoos tie behind the head. This is done under the idea that the flower has some virtue in it. Several shastrŭs prescribe this practice, and promise rewards to the person who places in his hair flowers which have been presented to his guardian deity, or to any other god.

[o] A very old woman, who is at the same time a great scold, is called by the Hindoos the mother of Yŭmŭ.

[p] Shells from the Maldive islands, which pass for money in Bengal. More than six thousand of these shells may be bought for a rupee.

I have heard of some Hindoos, who, rejecting the worship of other gods, worship only Yŭmŭ; alleging that their future state is to be determined only by Yŭmŭ, and that they have nothing therefore to hope or to fear from any beside him.

Yŭmŭ is judge of the dead. He is said to hold a court, in which he presides as judge, and has a person to assist him, called Chitrŭ-gooptŭ[q], who keeps an account of the actions of men. A number of officers are also attached to the court, who bring the dead to be judged. If the deceased persons have been wicked, Yŭmŭ sends them to their particular hell; or if good, to some place of happiness. The poor Hindoos, at the hour of death, sometimes fancy they see Yŭmŭ's officers, in a frightful shape, coming to fetch them away.

Yŭmŭ is said to reside at Yŭmalŭyŭ, on the south side of the earth[r]. All souls, wherever the persons die, are supposed to go to Yŭmŭ in four hours and forty minutes; and a dead body cannot be burnt till that time have elapsed.

The following account of Yŭmalŭyŭ, and of Voitŭrŭnēē, the river to be crossed after death, is taken from the Mŭhabharŭtŭ:—After Brŭmha had created the three worlds, viz., heaven, earth, and patŭlŭ, he recollected that a place for judgment, and for the punishment of the wicked, was wanting. He therefore called Vishwŭkŭrma, the architect of the gods, and gave him orders to prepare a very superb palace. Opposite the south door Vishwŭkŭrma made four pits for the punishment of the wicked. Three other doors were reserved for the entrance of the good, that they might not see the place of punishment when they went to be judged. Brŭmha, taking with him the gŭndhŭrvŭs, the giants, &c. went to see the place, and gave it the name of Sŭnjēē-vŭnēē. The gŭndhŭrvŭs asked Brŭmha to give them this beautiful palace. Brŭmha asked them if they were willing to inflict the punishments on the wicked: to which they replied in the negative. The giants were next about to seize the place by force; to prevent which Brŭmha ordered Vishwŭkŭrma to form a vast trench around, and to fill it with water, which became the river Voitŭrŭnēē. Brŭmha next ordered Ŭgnee to enter the river, and the waters became hot. Having thus surrounded the hall of judgment with a river of boiling water, the creator ordered, that after death each one should be obliged to swim across. This, however, subjected the good to punishment: to prevent which it was ordained, that the offering of a black cow to a bramhŭn should cool the river, and render the person's passage easy[s]. It was still necessary, that some one should occupy this place, and judge the dead; and Brŭmha assigned this work to Yŭmŭ.

[q] That is, he who paints in secret; or, he who writes the fates of men in secret.

[r] One Hindoo sometimes jokes with another, by asking him where he is going, as he seems to be proceeding southwards.

[s] I do not find that the Hindoos have any ferryman, like Charon, or boat to cross this river; though they talk of crossing it by laying hold of the tail of the black

The Ramayŭnŭ contains the following story about Yŭmŭ :—Soon after Gŭnga came down to the earth, Yŭmŭ was very angry with the gods, as she left him nothing to do in his office of judge; all the people, however sinful, through her power ascending to heaven. His officers, in a rage, were about to give up their places, and leave him. On applying to Indrŭ, he advised him not to place his messengers in any situation where the wind, passing over Gŭnga blew; for that all persons touched even by the wind of this sacred river had all their sins removed, and would go to heaven[t].

Many other stories are to be found in the pooranŭs, some of them supposed to be related by persons who have been at Yŭmalŭyŭ: the following are of this description.—In a certain village lived two persons of the same name; one of whom had lived out his whole time, the other had many years to live. Chitrŭ-gooptŭ, examining his register, sent Yŭmŭ's messengers to fetch the person whose appointed time was expired: the messengers went, but brought the wrong person. On re-examining his records, Chitrŭ-gooptŭ found out the mistake, and directed the officers to hasten back with the soul before the relations had burnt the body. While at Yŭmalŭyŭ, this person looked all around, and saw, in one place, the punishments inflicted on the wicked: Yŭmŭ's officers were chastising some, by casting them into pits of ordure; others, by throwing them into the arms of a red hot image of a woman[u]; others, by making their bellies immensely large, and their mouths as small as the eye of a needle; others, by feeding them with red hot balls; others, by throwing them into pits filled with devouring worms and insects, or with fire. In other places he saw those who had practised severe mortifications living in a state of the greatest magnificence; and women who had been burnt on the funeral pile, sitting with their husbands, enjoying the greatest delights. As he was coming away, he saw preparations making for the reception of some one in the highest style of grandeur, and asked the messengers who was to enjoy this. The messengers replied that it was for one of his neighbours, a very holy man, whose appointed time was nearly expired; and who, in fact, died soon afterwards.

A story very similar to this is often related of a person named Bŭlŭramŭ, of the voidyŭ cast, who lived some years ago at Choopēē, near Nŭdēēya. This man, to all appearance, died; and was lying by the side of the Ganges, while his relations were collecting the wood and other materials to burn the body. Before the fire was

cow which they offered in order to obtain a safe passage. It is very common in Bengal for a herdsman to cross a river by taking hold of a cow's tail.

[t] Whatever the Hindoos may think of Gŭnga's taking away their sins, it is acknowledged by all, that the inhabitants who live on the banks of the Ganges are the most corrupt and profligate of all the Hindoos.

[u] This instrument is used for the punishment of adulterers. When Ravŭnŭ was carrying off Sēēta by force, she reminded him, that for this crime he would have to go into the burning arms of this image after death.

lighted, however, the body began to move, and in a little while the dead man arose, and told his friends of his having been carried by mistake to Yŭmalŭyŭ, where he saw terrific sights of the punishments of the wicked. This man lived fifteen years after this journey to Yŭmŭ's palace.

The following story was invented, no doubt, in order to check excessive sorrow for deceased relations.—A rich bramhŭn had only one son, who grew up to manhood, and was loved almost to distraction by his parents[x]. This son, however, died in his youth, and his wife was burnt with him on the funeral pile. The father and mother were so overwhelmed with distress, that for years they refused all comfort. During this time an old servant, who had served the bramhŭn many years, and had eaten of his food[y], died, and, for his merit, was made one of Yŭmŭ's officers. This man was going one day to fetch the soul of some one from the village where he had once lived, and saw his former master weeping by the side of the road for the loss of his son. Assuming his old form, he raised up his master, and endeavoured to comfort him, but in vain. He then told him, that he was become one of Yŭmŭ's officers, on account of the merit he had obtained by serving him (the bramhŭn), and eating of his food; and that now, to remove his sorrow, he would take him and shew him his son. The old man got on his back, and the officer immediately carried him to the residence of Yŭmŭ, and shewed him his son and daughter-in-law in the greatest happiness, surrounded with every delight, playing at chess. But the son, having lost all affection for his parent, would not even look at him, though exhorted to it by his wife. He replied, that in numerous transmigrations, it was very likely that this old man might have been *his* son again and again. The old man was so incensed, to see that his daughter-in-law had more affection for him than his own son, for whom he was dying with grief, that he desired the constable to carry him back. The old bramhŭnēē would not believe that her son's affections were thus alienated from them: the constable, therefore, carried her also to see him; but she met with the same treatment. They both immediately renounced their grief for a son who had lost all his filial affection, and resolved to think no more about him.

Other stories abound in the pooranŭs respecting Yŭmŭ, some of which relate to disputes betwixt the messengers of this god and those of some other god, about the soul of a departed person, whether it shall be happy or miserable. I insert two of these stories :—

x The Hindoos in general carry their attachment to children, especially to sons, to the greatest excess.—They are amazed at the supposed want of affection in Europeans, who leave their parents in order to traverse foreign countries; some of them without the hope of ever seeing them again.

y It is a very meritorious action for a shōōdrŭ to eat the leavings of a bramhŭn. Hence a shōōdrŭ will serve a bramhŭn for rather less wages than another person.

7

When the sage Ŭnimandŭvyŭ was a child of five years old, he put a straw into the tail of a locust, and let it fly away. In advanced years, while once employed in performing religious austerities, he was seized as a thief by the officers of justice, and, as he gave no answer on his trial, the king took it for granted that he was guilty, and ordered him to be impaled. After he had been impaled four years, his body had undergone no change, and, though he appeared perfectly insensible to human objects, he was evidently alive. The king, being informed of this, was filled with astonishment, and declared that he was certainly some great ascetic, equal to one of the gods. He then immediately ordered him to be taken down; but in endeavouring to extract the wood upon which he had been impaled, it broke within his body. The sage was then suffered to depart, and, after sometime, his religious abstraction was interrupted; though his mind had been so set upon his god, that neither impaling him for four years, nor breaking the stake within his body, had disturbed his intense devotion. On awaking from this state he discovered what had been done to him, and that he had suffered all this from the hands of Yŭmŭ, for having pierced the locust when he was a child. He was exceedingly angry with Yŭmŭ for such unrighteous judgment. To punish a person for a sin committed at the age of five years, and for so small a crime to impale him for four years, was what he could not bear. He then cursed Yŭmŭ, and doomed him to be born on earth, and to take the name of Vidoorŭ, the son of a servant girl in the house of the mother of Védŭ-vyasŭ.—How the administration of justice in the other world was carried on after Yŭmŭ assumed human birth, this story does not relate.—What an excellent religion for a wicked man: the criminal can punish his judge!

Ŭjamilŭ had committed the most enormous crimes, having killed cows and bramhŭns, drank spirits, and lived in the practice of evil all his days. He had four sons; the name of one was Narayŭnŭ. In the hour of death Ŭjamilŭ was extremely thirsty, and thus called to his son: 'Narayŭnŭ, Narayŭnŭ, Narayŭnŭ, give me some water.' After his decease, the messengers of Yŭmŭ seized him, and were about to drag him to a place of punishment, when Vishnoo's messengers came to rescue him. A furious battle ensued, but Vishnoo's messengers were victorious, and carried off Ŭjamilŭ to Voikoontŭ, the heaven of Vishnoo. The messengers of Yŭmŭ, enraged, returned to their master, threw their clothes and staves at his feet, and declared that they would serve him no longer, as they got nothing but disgrace in all they did. Yŭmŭ ordered Chitrŭ-gooptŭ, the recorder, to examine his books. He did so, and reported that this Ŭjamilŭ had been a most notorious sinner, and that it was impossible for him to reckon up his sins, they were so numerous. Yŭmŭ hastened to Voikoontŭ, and demanded of Vishnoo an explanation of this affair. Vishnoo reminded him, that however wicked this man might have been, he had repeated the name Narayŭnŭ in his last moments; and that he (Yŭmŭ) ought to know, that if a man, either when laughing, or by accident, or in anger, or even in derision, repeated the name of Vishnoo, he would certainly go to heaven, though, like Ŭjamilŭ, covered with crimes, he had not a single meritorious deed to lay in the balance against them.—This is the doctrine that is universally maintained by the great body of the Hindoos: hence, when a person in a dying situation is brought down to the river side, he is never exhorted to repentance, but is urged in his last moments to repeat the names of certain gods, as his passport to heaven. A Hindoo shopkeeper one day declared to the author, that he should live in the practice of adultery, lying, &c. till death; and that then, repeating the name of Krishnŭ, he should, without difficulty, ascend to heaven. How shocking this sentiment! How dreadful this mistake!

Description of the heaven of Yŭmŭ, from the Mŭhabharŭtŭ. This heaven, formed by Vishwŭkŭrma, is 800 miles in circumference. From hence are excluded the fear of enemies, and sorrow both of body and mind; the climate is mild and salubrious; and each one is rewarded in kind, according to his works: thus he, who has given much away on earth, receives a far greater quantity of the same things in heaven; he who has not been liberal, will have other kinds of happiness, and will see food, houses, lands, &c. but will receive nothing. All kinds of excellent food are here heaped up into mountains[z]. To this heaven have been raised a great number of Hindoo kings, whose names are given in the Mŭhabharŭtŭ. The pleasures of this heaven are like those of Indrŭpoorŭ: the senses are satiated with gratifications as gross as the writer of this pooranŭ, the licentious Vyasŭ, could make them.

Yŭmŭ married Vijŭyŭ, the daughter of Vēērŭ, a bramhŭn. The Bhŭvishyŭt pooranŭ contains the following story respecting this marriage:—Yŭmŭ was so pleased with this female, on account of her having performed the Boodhashtŭmēē vrŭtŭ, that he appeared to her, and offered her marriage. She was alarmed at the sight of this stranger, and asked him who he was. When she found it was Yŭmŭ, the judge of the dead, who was thus paying his addresses to her, she was filled with terror. Yŭmŭ calmed her fears, and permitted her to acquaint her brother; as he would be full of distress after her departure, if he were left in ignorance. Her brother told her she was certainly mad:—'What, to be married to Yŭmŭ! A fine husband truly!' She however consented, and Yŭmŭ conveyed her to his palace, but charged her never to go to the southwards. She suspected that there Yŭmŭ had another favourite, and would not be satisfied till he had explained to her, that his reasons for forbidding her to go southwards were, that there the wicked were punished, and that she would not be able to bear so dreadful a sight. All these warnings, however, were given in vain: while

[z] This seems to be a heaven for gluttons!

Yŭmŭ was one day busy, she took another female or two, and went southwards, till the cries of the damned had nearly terrified her to distraction: to add to the horror of the scene, she saw her mother in torments. On her return, Yŭmŭ found her in a state of the greatest distress, and soon discovered the cause. She insisted on Yŭmŭ's delivering her mother that very day, or he should see her face no more. Yŭmŭ declared this to be impossible; that her own bad conduct had brought her there, and that she could only be delivered, according to the forms of the shastrŭ, after suffering the punishment due to her. Vijŭyŭ became impatient and clamorous; till Yŭmŭ told her, that if she could get the merit of the Boodhashtŭmēē vrŭtŭ, transferred to her by some one, she might deliver her mother. Yŭmŭ further informed her, that on earth a certain queen, who had performed the Boodhashtŭmēē vrŭtŭ, had been three days in the pains of child-birth; and that, if she would perform a certain ceremony, which he described to her, the queen would be delivered, and would in return transfer the merits of this vrŭtŭ to her mother, who would immediately be delivered from torments. Vijŭyŭ took this advice, and thus procured the deliverance of her mother from hell.

Yŭmŭ's principal names are: Dhŭrmŭ-rajŭ, or, the holy king.—Pitripŭtee, the lord of the ancients.—Sŭmŭvurttee, he who judges impartially.—Prétŭ-rat, the lord of the dead.—Kritantŭ, the destroyer.—Yŭmoona-bhrata, the brother of Yŭmoona[a].—Shŭmŭnŭ, he who levels all.—Yŭmŭ-rat, the chief of the fourteen Yŭmŭs[b].—Yŭmŭ, he who takes out of the world.—Kalŭ, time.—Dŭndudhŭrŭ, he who holds the rod of punishment.—Shraddhŭ-dévŭ, the god of the ceremonies paid to deceased ancestors; or, he who eats his share of the shraddhŭ.—Voivŭswŭtŭ, the son of Vivŭswŭt, or Sōōryŭ.—Ŭntŭkŭ, he who kills, or puts an end to life.

Sect. XII.—*The Worship of the "Host of Heaven"*

The Hindoos, like other idolatrous nations, have gone into the worship of the heavenly bodies. The planets, the constellations, the signs of the zodiac, the stars in general, the star Canopus[c], the star Kalŭ-pooroosbŭ, &c. have all been deified, and are worshipped with appropriate forms of petition, praise, &c. some of them at the festivals of other gods, and others at different times. The constellations are worshipped separately at the births of children, as well as at the anniversaries of these births till the time of death.

[a] The river Yŭmoona.

[b] Yŭmŭ has thirteen assistants, whose names are here given as different names of this judge of the dead.

[c] Called by the Hindoos Ugŭstyŭ, the sage.

Some persons suppose, that the worship of the elements was the primitive idolatry of the Hindoos, and that of heroes the invention of later times. It is plain, however, that the védus, supposed to be the most ancient of the Hindoo writings, countenance the worship of deified heroes. These books contain accounts of Brŭmha, Vishnoo, and Shivŭ, and most of the other deities. A paragraph in the Rig-védŭ speaks of the gods choosing Indrŭ to be their king, whom they placed on a throne fancifully constructed with texts of the védŭ: (amongst all the gods none are charged with greater crimes than Indrŭ, who seduced the wife of his spiritual guide :) indeed from a variety of facts it is highly probable, that to the védŭs we are to attribute the foundation of this whole fabric of superstition. These books contain prayers to procure the destruction of enemies, as well as encourage the burning of widows alive[d], which is surely a far greater crime than any thing done in the presence of the images of Ramŭ or Krishnŭ. The ancient idolatry, therefore, seems to have been as corrupt as any thing practised at present.—Is it not probable that the horrid worship of Moloch was really that of the element of fire?

I do not find, however, that the heavenly bodies are worshipped on the tops of houses, as appears to have been the case among those nations from whom the Jews learnt their idolatry. It is said of Manasseh, that 'he worshipped all the host of heaven, and served them.' Josiah, the son of Manasseh, put down all that burnt incense unto Baal, to the sun, and to the moon, and to the planets, and to all the host of heaven. By the prophet Jeremiah, God threatens, that the people shall bring out the bones of the king of Judah, of the princes, priests, prophets, and people; and adds, 'And they shall spread them before the sun, the moon, and all the host of heaven, whom they have served; they shall not be gathered nor be buried; they shall be for dung upon the face of the earth.' By the prophet Zephaniah, God threatens to cut off them 'that worship the host of heaven upon the house-tops.' Stephen, in rehearsing the history of the children of Israel before the Jewish council, declares, that God formerly gave up their forefathers to worship the host of heaven; and mentions among other objects of worship the star of the god Remphan.

This worship, which has been so general among heathen nations, seems to have originated in judicial astrology, and in the belief that the heavenly bodies have a great influence upon human events. Hindoos, whose birth under a supposed evil planet has been ascertained, are often filled with melancholy; some abandon themselves to despair, careless of what becomes of an existence

[d] 'O fire, let these women, with bodies anointed with ghee, eyes (coloured) with stibium and void of tears, enter the parent of water, that they may not be separated from their husbands, may be in union with excellent husbands, be sinless, and be jewels among women.' *Rig-védŭ.*

connected with such omens. The reader will perceive, in reading the account of Saturn, to what a degree the Hindoos dread the influence of this planet, especially at the time when it is in a certain sign. Against fears of this kind the prophet Jeremiah warned the Jews: 'Learn not the way of the heathen, and be not dismayed at the signs of heaven, for the heathen are dismayed at them.'

SECT. XIII.—*The Worship of the Nine Grŭhŭs*[e] *or Planets.*

AT the great festivals a small offering is presented to all the planets at once; but except on these occasions they are never worshipped together. They are, however, frequently worshipped separately by the sick or unfortunate, who suppose themselves to be under the baneful influence of some planet. At these times the nine planets are worshipped, one after the other, in regular succession. The ceremonies consist of the common forms of worship before other images, and close with a burnt-offering to each planet.

To Sōōryŭ are offered in the burnt-sacrifice small pieces of the shrub ŭrkŭ[f]; to Chŭndrŭ, those of the pŭlashŭ[g]; to Mars, those of the khŭdirŭ[h]; to Mercury, those of the ŭpamargŭ[i]; to Jupiter, those of the ŭshwŭtt'hŭ[k]; to Venus, those of the ooroombŭrŭ; to Saturn, those of the shŭmēē[l]; to Rahoo, blades of dōōrva grass; and to Kétoo, blades of kooshŭ grass.

In honour of Sōōryŭ boiled rice, mixed with molasses, is burnt; milk is to be mixed with the rice offered to Chŭndrŭ; with that to Mars, curds; with that to Mercury, clarified butter: to Jupiter is offered frumenty; to Venus, boiled rice alone; to Saturn, various kinds of food; to Rahoo, goat's flesh or fish; to Kétoo, blood from the ear of a goat, mixed with rice.

The image of Sōōryŭ is to be a round piece of mixed metal, twelve fingers in diameter; that of Chŭndrŭ is to be like a half moon, a cubit from end to end; that of Mars, a triangular piece of metal measured by the thickness of six fingers; that of Mercury, a golden bow measuring the thickness of two[e] fingers from one extremity to the other; that of Jupiter, like a flower of the water-lily; that of Venus, a four-square piece of silver; that of Saturn, an iron scymitar; that of Rahoo, an iron mŭkŭrŭ; and that of Kétoo, an iron snake.

[e] These stars are called grŭhŭs, because they make known to people good and evil.

[f] Asclepias gigantiæ.

[g] Butea frondosa.

[h] Mimosa catechu.

[i] Achyranthes aspera.

[k] Ficus religiosa.

[l] Mimosa albida.

The fees accompanying the worship of the different planets are various: at that of Sōōryŭ, a milch cow; of Chŭndrŭ, a shell; of Mars, a bull; of Mercury, a morsel of gold; of Jupiter, a piece of cloth; of Venus, a horse; of Saturn, a black cow; of Rahoo, a piece of iron; and of Kétoo, a goat.

When the officiating bramhŭn performs the worship of separate planets, he must put on vestments of divers colours, and offer different kinds of flowers.

SECT. XIV.—*Rŭvee*[m], *the Sun.*

THIS god, the son of Kŭshyŭpŭ, the sage, is painted red. He holds a water-lily in each hand, and rides in a chariot drawn by seven yellow[n] horses.

Rŭvee, as one of the planets, is worshipped only at the great festivals. The Jyotish-tŭtwŭ says, that if a person be born under the planet Rŭvee, he will possess an anxious mind, be subject to disease and other sufferings, be an exile, a prisoner, and endure much sorrow from the loss of his wife, children, and property.

This god has been already noticed under the name of Sōōryŭ: but in that account several particulars were omitted by mistake; and which I insert here, though they properly belong to another form of this idol.—While bathing, the Hindoos repeat certain incantations, in order to bring the waters of all the holy places in the heaven of this god into the spot where they are standing, and thus obtain the merit of bathing not only in Gŭnga, but in all the sacred rivers, &c. in the heaven of Sōōryŭ. After bathing too, the Hindoos make their obeisance to this god in a standing posture; the more devout draw up their joined hands to the forehead, gaze at the sun, make prostration to him, and then turn round seven times, repeating certain forms of petition and praise. On these occasions they hold up water in their joined hands, and then 'pour out a drink-offering' to the sun.

When the terrific being which sprung out of Shivŭ's bunch of hair went with all the bhōōtŭs, &c. to destroy Dŭkshŭ's sacrifice, all the gods being present, this monster seized on Sōōryŭ and knocked out his teeth: in consequence, at the time of worship, only soft things, as flour, &c. are now offered to this god, such as a toothless old man might eat.

Sōōryŭ is charged in the Mŭhabharŭtŭ with ravishing Koonte, a virgin, from whence Kŭrnnŭ, a gaint, was born.

m Hence Rŭvee-varŭ, or Sunday.

n Not green, as mentioned by Mr. Maurice.

SECT. XV.—*Somŭ*[o], *or Chŭndrŭ, the Moon.*

THE image of Somŭ is that of a white man, drawn by ten horses, or sitting on the water-lily. With his right hand he is giving a blessing, and in the other he holds a club.

In the work called Ŭdhikŭrŭnŭ-mala, a sacrifice is ordered to be performed to Somŭ, and the worshipper is promised a place in the heaven of this god.

All the Hindoo ceremonies are regulated by the rising or setting, the waxing or waning of the moon. The Jyotishtŭtwŭ says, 'If a person be born under the planet Somŭ, he will have many friends; will possess elephants, horses, and palanqueens; be honourable and powerful; will live upon excellent food, rest on superb couches, &c.'

A race of Hindoo kings are said to have descended from Somŭ by Rohinēē[p], and are called the children of the moon. The first of these was Boodhŭ, and the forty-sixth Yoodhist'hirŭ.

This god on a certain occasion was forcibly carried away by Gŭroorŭ, the bird on which Vishnoo rides, and delivered up to the giants. The giants, anxious to become immortal as well as the gods, promised Gŭroorŭ that if he would bring the moon by force, so that they might drink the nectar supposed to exist in the bright parts of that planet, they would deliver his mother from the curse pronounced against her by her son Ŭroonŭ, by which she had been doomed to become the slave of her sister. Gŭroorŭ soon seized the god, and placed him trembling among the assembled giants; but while the latter were gone to bathe, and prepare for partaking of the waters of immortality, Indrŭ arrived and delivered the captive, and thus disappointed these implacable enemies of the gods.

Somŭ is charged with seducing the wife of Vrihŭspŭtee, his preceptor.—See p. 57.

The chief names of this god are: Somŭ, or, he from whom the water of immortality springs.—Himangshoo, he whose beams are cooling.—Chŭndrŭ, he at whose rising people rejoice.—Indoo, the great.—Koomoodŭ-bandŭvŭ, the friend of the flower Koomoodŭ[q].—Vidhoo, he who causes the gods to drink the water of life.—Soodhangshoo, he whose rays are as the water of life.—Oshŭdhēēshŭ, the lord of medicinal plants.—Nishapŭtee, the lord of night.—Ŭbjŭ, he who was born from the waters.—Joivatrikŭ, the preserver of men.—Glou, he who decreases.—Mrigrankŭ, he on whose

[o] Hence Somŭ-varŭ, or Monday.   [p] The Hyades.

[q] Nymphœa lotus. After the rising of the moon this flower is said by the Hindoos to expand.

lap sits a deer[r].—Kulanidhee, he with whom are the kŭlas[s].—Dwijŭrajŭ, the chief of the bramhŭns.—Nŭkshŭtréshŭ, the lord of the planets.—Kshŭpakŭrŭ, he who illumines the night.

SECT. XVI.—*Mŭngŭlu*[t], *or Mars.*

THIS god is painted red; rides on a sheep; wears a red necklace, and garments of the same colour; and has four arms: in one hand he holds a weapon called shŭktee; with another he is giving a blessing; with another forbidding fear; and in the fourth he holds a club.

'If a person be born under the planet Mŭngŭlŭ, he will be full of anxious thoughts, be wounded with offensive weapons, be imprisoned, be oppressed with fear from robbers, fire, &c., and will lose his lands, trees, and good name.'—*Jyotish-tŭtwŭ.*

SECT. XVII.—*Boodhŭ*[u], *or Mercury.*

THIS god has four arms; in one hand he holds the discus, in another a club, in another a scymitar, and with the fourth is bestowing a blessing. He rides on a lion; is of a placid countenance; and wears yellow garments.

The following is an account of the birth of Boodhŭ:—On a certain occasion Vrihŭspŭtee, the spiritual guide of the gods, made a great feast, to which he invited all the gods. Chŭndrŭ was present among the rest; who, during the festival, fell in love with Tara, the wife of Vrihŭspŭtee. Not knowing how to accomplish his wishes, after his return home he invited Vrihŭspŭtee to a sacrifice, begging him to bring his wife with him. Vrihŭspŭtee and his wife proceeded to the palace of Chŭndrŭ, but saw no preparations for the sacrifice. The former expressing his surprise at this circumstance, Chŭndrŭ told him that the sacrifice was unavoidably delayed, and advised him to return for a short time to

[r] See a story of the birth of Boodhŭ in the following page.

[s] Kŭla is the one 16th part of the disk of the moon, viz., that quantity which it increases or decreases in one day.

[t] Mŭngŭlŭ-varŭ, or Tuesday. Mŭngŭlŭ is also called Ungarŭkŭ, or, he who travels; Koojŭ, the son of the earth; and Lohitangŭ, the blood-coloured.

[u] Boodhŭ-varŭ, or Wednesday. The meaning of Boodhŭ is, the wise. He is also called Rouhinéyŭ, the son of Rohinēē, and Soumyŭ, the son of Somŭ.

his devotions, leaving his wife at his house. Vrihŭspŭtee consented, and during his absence Chŭndrŭ dishonoured the wife of his spiritual guide; who on his return, finding his wife pregnant, cursed Chŭndrŭ, and hurled him into the sea, where he continued like a cinder, leaving the earth in darkness for two kŭlpŭs, or 864,000,000 years. Vrihŭspŭtee compelled his wife to deliver herself, and, on the birth of the child Boodhŭ, reduced her to ashes. Brŭmha afterwards raised her from her ashes, and, thus purified, Vrihŭspŭtee took her to his embraces again. Sŭmoodrŭ, (the sea,) incensed at his son for this horrid crime of dishonouring the wife of his divine teacher, disinherited him. Chŭndrŭ then applied to his sister Lŭkshmēē[x], the wife of Vishnoo, by whose power part of his sin was removed, and he became light like the moon when three days old. She also applied in his behalf to Parvŭtēē, who resolved to restore Chŭndrŭ to heaven, and for this purpose planted him in the forehead of her husband[y]; who went, thus ornamented, to a feast of the gods. Vrihŭspŭtee, on seeing Chŭndrŭ again in heaven, was greatly incensed, and could only be appeased by Brŭmha's ordaining, that the lascivious god should be excluded from heaven, and placed among the stars; and that the sin by which his glory had been obscured should remain for ever. Chŭndrŭ now asked Brŭmha to remove the vomiting of blood, with which he had been seized since his fall from heaven; who directed him, as a certain cure, to hold a deer on his knees.

'If a person be born under the planet Boodhŭ, he will be very fortunate, obtain an excellent wife, &c.'—*Jyotish-tŭtwŭ.*

SECT. XVIII.—*Vrihŭspŭtee*[z], *or Jupiter.*

THE image of this god, the son of the sage Ŭngira, is painted yellow. He sits on the water-lily; has four arms; in one hand he holds a roodrakshŭ bead-roll; in another, an alms' dish; in another, a club; and with the fourth, he is bestowing a blessing.

Vrihŭspŭtee is preceptor and priest to the gods; in whose palaces he explains the vēdŭs, and performs a number of religious ceremonies.

If a person be born under the planet Vrihŭspŭtee, he will be endowed with an amiable disposition; possess palaces, gardens, lands, and be rich in money, corn, &c.; obtaining the affections of all, his honours will increase; he will possess much religious merit;

[x] Lŭkshmēē was born, like Chŭndrŭ, at the churning of the sea by the gods.

[y] In Shivŭ's forehead is placed a half moon.

[z] Vrihuspŭti-varŭ, or Thursday.

and, in short, will have all his wishes gratified. Kshŭtriyŭs, Voishyŭs, and Shōōdrŭs, if born under this planet, will be prosperous and happy; but bramhŭns will not be so fortunate: the reason given is, that Vrihŭspŭtee is a bramhŭn, and therefore does not wish to exalt those of his own cast.—*Jyotish-tŭtwŭ.*

This god is charged in the Mŭhabharŭtŭ with deflowering the wife of his eldest brother Ootŭt'hyŭ.

Names.—Vrihŭspŭtee, or, preceptor to the gods.—Soorachargyŭ, the priest of the gods.—Gishpŭtee, the eloquent.—Gooroo, the preceptor.—Jēēvŭ, he who revives the gods[a].—Angirŭsŭ, the son of Ŭngira.—Vachŭspŭtee, the lord of words, viz., the eloquent.

SECT. XIX.—*Shookrŭ*[b], *or the Planet Venus.*

THIS god, the son of the sage Bhrigoo, is dressed in white; sits on the water-lily; has four hands: in one, he holds a roodrakshŭ bead-roll; in another, an alms' dish; in another, a club; and with the other is bestowing a blessing.

Shookrŭ is preceptor and officiating priest to the giants. He is represented as blind of one eye; the reason of which is thus related:—When Vamŭnŭ went to king Bŭlee, to solicit a present, Shookrŭ, being Bŭlee's preceptor, forbad his giving him any thing. The king disregarding his advice, the priest was obliged to read the necessary formulas, and to pour out the water from a vessel, to ratify the gift. Shookrŭ, still anxious to withhold the gift, which he foresaw would be the destruction of his master, entered the water in an invisible form, and by his magic power prevented it from falling; but Vamŭnŭ, aware of the device, put a straw into the bason of water, which entered Shookrŭ's eye, and gave him so much pain, that he leaped out of the bason: the water then fell, and the gift was offered.

'If a person be born under the planet Shookrŭ, he will have the faculty of knowing things past, present, and future; will have many wives; have a kingly umbrella, (the emblem of royalty;) and other kings will worship him; he will possess elephants, horses, palanqueens, footmen, &c.'—*Jyotish-tŭtwŭ.*

Shookrŭ's daughter, Dévŭjanēē, was deeply in love with one of her father's pupils, Kŭchŭ, the son of Vrihŭspŭtee. This youth

[a] That is, when the gods die in battle, Vrihŭspŭtee by incantations restores them to life.

[b] Shookrŭ-varŭ or Friday.

had been sent by his father to learn from Shookrŭ an incantation for raising the dead. One day Dévŭjanēē sent Kŭchŭ to bring some flowers to be used in worship[c] from a forest belonging to the giants. Previously to this, Kŭchŭ had been devoured several times by different giants; but Shookrŭ by the above incantation had restored him to life: when he tore open the bellies of these cannibals, and destroyed them. The giants now resolved to make Shookrŭ himself eat this boy; for which purpose they caught him in the forest, cut him into the smallest pieces, boiled him up in spirits, and invited Sookrŭ to the entertainment. Kŭchŭ not returning from the forest, Dévŭjanēē wept much, and told her father, that she would certainly kill herself[d] if he did not bring back her lover. Shookrŭ at length, by the power of meditation, discovered that he had eaten this youth, so beloved by his daughter; and he knew not how to bring him back to life, without the attempt being fatal to himself. At last, however, while the boy continued in his belly, he restored him to life, and taught him the incantation for raising the dead; after which Kŭchŭ, tearing open Shookrŭ's belly, came forth, and immediately restored his teacher to life. Kŭchŭ, having obtained the knowledge of revivifying the dead, took leave of his preceptor, and was about to return to his father Vrihŭspŭtee, when Dévŭjanēē insisted upon his marrying her. Kŭchŭ declined this honour, as she was the daughter of his preceptor; at which she was so incensed that she pronounced a curse upon him, by which he was doomed to reap no advantage from all his learning. In return Kŭchŭ cursed Dévŭjanēē, and doomed her to marry a kshŭtriyŭ; which curse after sometime took effect, and she was married to king Yŭjatee. After Dévŭjanēē had borne two children, she discovered that the king maintained an illicit connection with a princess of the name of Sŭmmisht'ha, by whom he had three sons. She appealed to her father Shookrŭ, who pronounced a curse on Yŭjatee; when his hair immediately became grey, his teeth fell from his head, and he was seized with complete decrepitude. Yŭjatee remonstrated with his father-in-law, and asked him who should live with his daughter, who was yet young, seeing that he had brought old age upon him. Shookrŭ replied, that if he could persuade any one to take upon him this curse, he might still enjoy connubial felicity. Yŭjatee returned home, and asked his eldest son by Dévŭjanēē to take this curse for a thousand years, and possess the kingdom; at the close of which time he should become young again, and continue in the kingdom: but this son, his brother, and the two eldest sons of Sŭmmisht'ha refused the kingdom on these conditions; which so enraged the father, that he cursed them all. The youngst son, however, by Sŭmmisht'ha accepted the conditions,

[c] Gathering flowers for the worship of the gods is often at present the employment of young persons.

[d] The Hindoo children often resort to this threat to extort some favour from their parents.

and instantly became weak and decrepid ; when the father assumed his former youth, and returned to the company of his wives.

Names.—Shookrŭ, or, he who sorrows at the destruction of the giants.—Doityŭ-gooroo, preceptor to the giants.—Kavyŭ, the poet.—Ooshŭna, the friend of the giants.—Bhargŭvŭ, the descendant of Bhrigoo.

SECT. XX.—*Shŭnee*[e], *or Saturn.*

THIS god is dressed in black ; rides on a vulture[f]; has four arms ; in one he holds an arrow ; in another, a javelin ; in another a bow ; and with the other is giving a blessing. He is said to be the son of Sōōryŭ by Chaya.

All the Hindoos exceedingly dread the supposed baneful influence of this god, and perform a number of ceremonies to appease him. Many stories of him are to be found in the writings of the Hindoos, such as that of his burning off the head of Gŭnéshŭ ; his burning Dŭshŭrŭt'hŭ's chariot in his descent from heaven ; his giving rise to bad harvests, ill fortune, &c.

'If a person be born under the planet Shŭnee,' says the Jyotish-tŭtwŭ, 'he will be slandered, his riches dissipated, his son, wife, and friends destroyed ; he will live at variance with others ; and endure many sufferings.' The Hindoos are under constant fear of bad fortune from this planet. Some persons, if absent from home at the time of his appearance, return through fear, and others forsake their business lest they should meet with misfortunes. If one person persecute another, the latter sometimes takes it patiently, supposing it to arise from the bad fortune which naturally springs from the influence of this star. The Hindoos believe that when Shŭnee is in the ninth stellar mansion, the most dreadful evils befal mankind : hence, when Ramŭ broke the bow of Shivŭ, which was the condition of obtaining Sēēta in marriage, and when the earth sunk, and the waters of the seven seas were united in one, Pŭrŭshoo-ramŭ, startled at the noise of the bow, exclaimed, 'Ah ! some one has laid hold of the hood of the snake, or fallen under the ninth of Shŭnee.' At present, when a person is obstinate, and

[e] Shŭnee-varŭ, or Saturday. One of the names of Shŭnee is Shŭnoish-chŭrŭ, viz., he who travels slowly.

[f] This god is represented as sitting on this bird, probably, to denote his destructive power. Saturn, in the Grecian system of idolatry, was represented as devouring his children. The vultures in Bengal are highly useful in devouring the dead bodies of men and beasts, many of which are left in the roads and on the banks of rivers. It is astonishing how swiftly these birds collect wherever a dead body falls, though one of them should not have been seen in the place for weeks or months before ; illustrating, in the most striking manner, the words of our Lord, "Wheresoever the carcase is, there will the eagles be gathered together."—*Matt.* xxiv. 28.

will not hearken to reason, a bye-stander says, 'I suppose he has fallen upon Shŭnee, or he has laid his hand upon the hood of the snake, viz., he is embracing his own destruction.' When Ramŭ found that some one had stolen Sēēta, in the midst of his rage he exclaimed, 'This person must have been born when Shŭnee was in the ninth mansion.'

Sect. XXI.—*Rahoo*[h].

This god, the son of Singhika, is painted black: he rides on a lion; has four arms, in three of which he holds a scymitar, a spear, and a shield, and with the other hand is bestowing a blessing.

'If a person be born under the planet Rahoo,' says the work already quoted, 'his wisdom, riches, and children will be destroyed; he will be exposed to many afflictions, and be subject to his enemies.'

Rahoo was originally a giant, but at the churning of the sea he took his present name and form; (that is, he became one of the heavenly bodies[i];) which transformation is thus described in the pooranŭs:—At the time when the gods churned the sea to obtain the water of life, Sōōryŭ (the sun) and Chŭndrŭ (the moon) were sitting together. When the nectar came up, these gods hinted to Vishnoo, that one of the company who had drank of the nectar was not a god, but one of the giants. Vishnoo immediately cut off his head; but after drinking the water of life, neither the head nor the trunk could perish. The head taking the name of Rahoo, and the trunk that of Kétoo, were placed in the heavens as the ascending and descending nodes; and leave was granted, by way of revenge on Sōōryŭ and Chŭndrŭ, that on certain occasions Rahoo should approach these gods, and make them unclean, so that their bodies should become thin and black. The popular opinion, however, is, that, at the time of an eclipse, Rahoo swallows the sun and moon, and vomits them up again[k].

[h] The ascending node.

[i] We are here reminded of Jupiter's deflowering Calisto, the daughter of Lycaon, king of Arcadia. It will be remembered, that when her disgrace became known, Juno turned her into a bear, which Jupiter afterwards advanced into heaven, and made it a constellation, now called Ursa major.

[k] It is a most unaccountable coincidence in the notions of remote nations, that the Chinese and the Greenlanders, as well as the Hindoos, should think that the sun or the moon is devoured at the time of an eclipse. "As soon as they (the Chinese) perceive that the sun or moon begins to be darkened, they throw themselves on their knees, and knock their foreheads against the earth. A noise of drums and cymbals is immediately heard throughout the whole city. This is the remains of an ancient opinion entertained in China, that by such a horrid din they assisted the suffering luminary, and prevented it from being devoured by the celestial dragon." Crantz in his History of Greenland asserts, that a similar custom exists among this people, who could certainly never have learnt it either from the Hindoos or the Chinese.

Many persons perform a number of ceremonies on these occasions, as, those to the manes; pouring out water to deceased ancestors; repeating the names of the gods; setting up gods; making offerings, &c. The Jyotish-tŭtwŭ declares, that performing these duties now is attended with benefits infinitely greater than at other times. Nobody must discharge the fæces or urine, or eat any food, until they have seen the sun or moon after the eclipse, though it be till their rising the next day. He who does not observe this law, will have a million of hells in one.

Names.—Tŭmŭ, the dark, or, he who is possessed of a great proportion of the quality of darkness.—Rahoo, he who swallows and afterwards vomits up the sun or moon.—Swŭrbhanoo, he who shines in the heavens.—Soinghikéyŭ, the son of Singhika.—Vidhoontoodŭ, he who afflicts the moon.

SECT. XXII.—*Kétoo*[1].

KETOO is the headless trunk of Rahoo, which became immortal at the churning of the sea. This god is painted of a light green colour. He rides on a vulture; in one hand holds a club, and with the other is bestowing a blessing.

THE preceding may be called the Hindoo CELESTIAL GODS. I dare not say, that I have given every deity of this order, as I have not found any book containing an exact list of them. I could easily have enlarged the number, by inserting accounts of other forms of these gods; but this would have swelled the work, without adding to its value.

[1] The descending node.

CHAP. III.

OF THE GODDESSES.

SECT. I.—*Doorga.*

In those parts of the Hindoo shastrŭs which treat of the production of the world, this goddess is spoken of as the female power, under the name of Prŭkritēē or Bhŭgŭvŭtēē. She was first born in the house of Dŭkshŭ, one of the progenitors of mankind, and called Sŭtēē; under which name she was married to Shivŭ, but renounced her life on hearing her father reproach her husband. On her second appearance, we recognize her under the name of Parvŭtēē, the daughter of Himalŭyŭ[a]; when she was again married to Shivŭ, by whom she had two children, Kartikéyŭ and Gŭnéshŭ.

Doorga has had many births to destroy the giants[b]. The reason of her being called Doorga is thus given in the Kashēē-khŭndŭ:—On a certain occasion Ŭgŭstyŭ, the sage, asked Kartikéyŭ, why Parvŭtēē, his mother, was called Doorga. Kartikéyŭ replied, that formerly a giant named Doorgŭ, the son of Rooroo, having performed religious austerities in honour of Brŭmha, obtained his blessing, and became a great oppressor: he conquered the three worlds, and dethroned Indrŭ, Vayoo, Chŭndrŭ, Yŭmŭ, Ŭgnee, Vŭroonŭ, Koovérŭ, Bŭlee, Eēshanŭ, Roodrŭ, Sōōryŭ, the eight Vŭsoos, &c. The wives of the rishees were compelled to celebrate his praises. He sent all the gods from their heavens to live in forests; and at his nod they came and worshipped him. He abolished all religious ceremonies; the bramhŭns, through fear of him, forsook the reading of the védŭs; the rivers changed their courses; fire lost its energy; and the terrified stars retired from sight: he assumed the forms of the clouds, and gave rain whenever he pleased; the earth through fear gave an abundant increase; and the trees yielded flowers and fruits out of season. The gods at length applied to Shivŭ. Indrŭ said, 'He has dethroned me;'—Sōōryŭ said, 'He has taken my kingdom:' and thus all the gods related their misfortunes. Shivŭ, pitying their case, desired Parvŭtēē to go and destroy the giant. She willingly accepting of the commission, calmed the fears of the gods, and first sent Kalŭ-ratree, a female whose beauty bewitched the inhabitants of the three worlds, to order the giant to restore things

[a] The mountain of this name.

[b] Sir W. Jones, not improperly, considers Doorga as bearing a pretty strong resemblance to Juno, as well as to Minerva.

to their ancient order. The latter, full of fury, sent some soldiers to lay hold of Kalŭ-ratree; but, by the breath of her mouth, she reduced them to ashes. Doorgŭ then sent 30,000 other giants, who were such monsters in size, that they covered the surface of the earth. Among them were the following: Doordhŭrŭ[c], Doormookhŭ[d], Khŭrŭ[e], Shirŭ-panee[f], Pashŭ-panee[g], Sooréndrŭ[h], Dŭmŭnŭ[i], Hŭnoo[k], Yŭguŭhanee[l], Khŭrgŭ-roma[m], Oograsyŭ[n], Dévŭkŭmpŭnŭ[o], &c. At the sight of these giants, Kalŭ-ratree fled through the air to Parvŭtēē, and the giants followed her. Doorgŭ, with 100,000,000 chariots, 200 ŭrvoodŭs (or 120,000,000,000) of elephants, 10,000,000 of swift-footed horses, and innumerable soldiers, went to fight with Parvŭtēē on the mountain Vindhŭ. As soon as the giant drew near, Parvŭtēē assumed 1,000 arms, and called to her assistance different kinds of beings, as jŭmbhŭ[p], mŭhajŭmbhŭ[q], vijŭmbhŭ[r], vikŭtanŭnŭ[s], pingakshŭ[t], mŭhishŭ[u], mŭhogrŭ[x], ŭtyoogrŭ[y], vigrŭhŭ[z], krōōrakshŭ[a], krodhŭnŭ[b], krŭndŭnŭ[c], sŭnkrŭndŭnŭ[d], mŭha-bhŭyŭ[e], jitantŭkŭ[f], mŭha-vahoo[g], mŭha-vŭktrŭ[h], mŭhēēdhŭrŭ[i], doondoobhŭ[k], doondoobhirŭvŭ[l], mŭha-doondoo-bhinasikŭ[m], oograsyŭ[n], dēērgŭ-dushŭnŭ[o], méghŭ-késhu[p], vrikanŭnŭ[q], singhasyŭ[r], shōōkurŭ-mookhŭ[s], shiva-rŭvŭ-mŭhotkŭtŭ[t], shookŭt-oondŭ[u], prŭchŭndasyŭ[x], bhēēmakshŭ[y], kshoodrŭ-manŭsŭ[z], oolōōkŭnétrŭ[a], kŭnŭkasyŭ[b], kakŭtoondŭ[c], khŭrŭnŭkhŭ[d], dēērgŭ-grēēvŭ[e], mŭhajŭnghŭ[f], shiroddhŭrŭ[g], rŭktŭ-vrindŭ-jŭvanétrŭ[h], vidyootjivhŭ[i], ŭgninétrŭkŭ[k], tapŭnŭ[l], dhōōmrakshŭ[m], dhoomŭnishwasŭ[n], shoorŭ-chŭndangshoo-tapŭnŭ[o], mŭhabhēēshŭnŭ-mookhŭ[p], &c. She also brought a number of weapons out of her body, as ŭsee[q], chŭkrŭ[r], bhooshoondēē[s], gŭda[t], moodgŭrŭ[u], tomŭrŭ[x], bhindipalŭ[y], pŭrighŭ[z], koontŭ[a], shŭlyŭ[b], shŭktee[c], ŭrdhŭ-chŭndrŭ[d], kshoorŭprŭ[e], narachŭ[f], shilēēmookhŭ[g], mŭhabhŭllŭ[h], pŭrŭshoo[i], bhidooru[k], and mŭrmŭbhédŭ[l]. The troops of the giant poured their arrows on Parvŭtēē, sitting on the mountain Vindhŭ, thick as the drops of rain in a storm; they even tore up the trees, the mountains, &c.

[c] Difficult to catch. [d] Foul-mouthed. [e] Cruel. [f] Holding a human skull in the hand. [g] Wielders of the pashŭ. [h] Sovereigns of the gods. [i] Bullies. [k] Of high cheek bones. [l] Sacrifice-destroyers. [m] They whose hair is like scymitars. [n] Of terrific countenance. [o] They who make the gods tremble. [p] Malicious. [q] Very malicious. [r] In various ways malicious. [s] Of fear-exciting countenance. [t] Of yellow eyes. [u] Like buffaloes. [x] Wrathful. [y] Exceedingly wrathful. [z] Warriors. [a] Cruel-eyed. [b] Wrathful. [c] Causers of crying. [d] Causing to cry excessively. [e] Fear exciting. [f] Death conquering. [g] Large-armed. [h] Large-faced. [i] Mountain-like. [k] Noisy like the doondoobhee. [l] Dittoo. [m] With noses like the doondoobhee. [n] With wrathful countenance. [o] Long toothed. [p] With hair like clouds. [q] Leopard-faced. [r] Lion-faced. [s] Pig-faced. [t] Exciting terrors by making sounds like the jackal. [u] With bills like a parrot. [x] Terrible-faced. [y] Terrific-eyed. [z] Little-minded. [a] Owl-eyed. [b] Gold-faced. [c] Crow-faced. [d] Sharp-nailed. [e] Long-necked. [f] Long-thighed. [g] Large-veined. [h] With eyes red like the yŭva flower. [i] With tongues like lightning. [k] Fiery-eyed. [l] Inflamers. [m] Smoke-eyed. [n] With breath like smoke. [o] Giving pain to the sun and moon. [p] Of horrid countenance. [q] A scymitar. [r] A discus. [s] A hatchet. [t] A bludgeon or club. [u] A hammer. [x] An iron crow [y] A short arrow. [z] A bludgeon.

[a] A bearded dart. [b] A javelin. [c] Another. [d] An arrow like a half-moon. [e] A weapon like a spade. [f] A small arrow. [g] A round arrow. [h] A very long spear. [i] A hatchet like a half-moon. [k] A thunderbolt full of spikes. [l] A bearded arrow.

and hurled at the goddess; who however threw a weapon which carried away many of the arms of the giant: when he, in return, hurled a flaming dart at the goddess; which she turning aside, he discharged another; but this also she resisted by a hundred arrows. He next let fly an arrow at Parvŭtēē's breast; but this too she repelled, as well as two other instruments, a club and a pike. At last Parvŭtēē seized Doorgŭ and set her left foot on his breast; but he disengaged himself, and renewed the fight. The beings (9,000,000) whom Parvŭtēē caused to issue from her body then destroyed all the soldiers of the giant; in return Doorgŭ caused a dreadful shower of hail to descend, the effect of which Parvŭtēē counteracted by an instrument called Shoshŭnŭ[m]. He next, breaking off the peak of a mountain, threw it at Parvŭtēē, who cut it into seven pieces by her arrows. The giant now assumed the shape of an elephant as large as a mountain, and approached the goddess; but she tied his legs, and with her nails, which were like scymitars, tore him to pieces. He then arose in the form of a buffalo, and with his horns, cast stones, trees, and mountains at the goddess, tearing up the trees by the breath of his nostrils. The goddess next pierced him with her trident, when he reeled to and fro, and, renouncing the form of the buffalo, assumed his original body as a giant, with a thousand arms, and weapons in each. Going up to Parvŭtēē, the goddess seized him by his thousand arms, and carried him into the air, from whence she threw him down with dreadful force. Perceiving however, that this had no effect, she pierced him in the breast with an arrow; when the blood issued in streams from his mouth, and he expired. The gods were now filled with joy: Sōōryŭ, Chŭndrŭ, Ŭgnee, &c. obtained their former splendour; and all the other deities, who had been dethroned by this giant, immediately re-ascended their thrones; the bramhŭns resumed the study of the vēdŭs; sacrifices were regularly performed, and every thing assumed its pristine state: the heavens rang with the praises of Parvŭtēē, and the gods, in return for so signal a deliverance, honoured her with the name of Doorga.

Mŭhishŭ, king of the giants, at a certain period overcame the gods in war, and reduced them to such a state of indigence, that they were seen wandering about the earth like common beggars. Indrŭ, after a time, collected them together, and they went in a body to Brŭmha, and afterwards to Shivŭ, but met with no redress. At last they applied to Vishnoo, who was so enraged at beholding their wretchedness, that streams of glory issued from his face, from which sprang a female named Mŭha-maya (Doorga). Streams of glory issued also from the faces of the other gods, and entering Mŭha-maya, she became a body of glory resembling a mountain on fire. The gods then gave their weapons to this female, and with a frightful scream, she ascended into the air.

[m] A weapon which dries up liquids.

[The work Chŭndēē, in this place, contains a long account of the dreadful contest betwixt Mŭha-maya and this giant, which ended in the destruction of the latter.]

After the victory, the gods chanted the praises of Mŭha-maya; and the goddess, pleased with their gratitude, promised to succour them whenever they were in distress, and then disappeared.

The Hindoos believe that the worship of Doorga has been performed through the four yoogŭs; but that Soorŭtŭ, a king, in the end of the dwapŭrŭ-yoogŭ, made known the present form of worshipping the goddess, and celebrated these orgies in the month Choitrŭ; (hence called the Vasŭntee, or spring festival.) Soorŭtŭ offered a very great number of goats, sheep, and buffaloes to Doorga; believing, according to the shastrŭ, that he should enjoy happiness in heaven as many years as there were hairs upon the different animals offered. After his death, however, his case excited much discussion in the court of Yŭmŭ; who at length decided, that though Soorŭtŭ had much merit, he had destroyed the lives of many animals, and that he must be born and suffer death from all these beasts assembled in one place, when he should immediately be advanced to heaven. Others interpret this passage of the shastrŭ as meaning, that the king was to assume in succession the forms of all these beasts, and be put to death in each form before he could ascend to heaven. In the trétŭ-yoogŭ Ramŭ is said to have performed the worship of Doorga in the month Ashwinŭ; and from him it is continued in this month, and called the Sharŭdēēya, or autumnal festival.

This festival, celebrated in the month Ashwinŭ, the most popular of all the annual festivals held in Bengal, I shall now attempt to describe. Immense sums are expended upon it[n]; all business throughout the country is laid aside for several days, and universal festivity and licentiousness prevail. A short time before the festival, the learned men and sirkars[o] employed in Calcutta almost universally return home; some of them enjoy a holiday of several weeks.

The image of Doorga has ten arms. In one of her right hands is a spear, with which she is piercing the giant Mŭhishŭ; with one of the left she holds the tail of a serpent, and the hair of the giant, whose breast the serpent is biting. Her other hands are all stretched behind her head, and filled with different instruments of war. Against her right leg leans a lion, and against her left the above

[n] In the city of Calcutta alone, it is supposed, upon a moderate calculation, that half a million sterling is expended annually on this festival. About fifty years ago, (1811) Kŭndŭrpŭ-goorŭ, a kaist'hŭ, expended in this worship 38,000 pounds, and spent 12,500 pounds annually as long as he lived in the same manner.

[o] Natives who direct the business of Europeans are commonly called sirkars. The proper name is Mootsŭddee, or Moohŭree.

giant.—The images of Lŭkshmēē, Sŭrŭswŭtēē, Kartikéyŭ, and Gŭnéshŭ, are very frequently made and placed by the side of this goddess.

On the 9th day of the decrease of the moon this festival begins, when the ceremony called sŭnkŭlpŭ is performed, by the officiating bramhŭn's taking into his joined hands a metal kosha, (which contains water, flowers, fruits, sesamum, rice, and a blade of kooshŭ grass,) reading an incantation, and promising that on the succeeding days such a person will perform the worship of Doorga. After this, Doorga is worshipped before a pan of water with the accustomed formularies.

On the 10th, 11th, 12th, 13th, 14th, and 15th days of the moon, the same ceremonies are performed before the pan of water; and, with some trifling variations in the offerings, continued on the 16th, 17th, 18th, 19th and 20th.

On the 21st day of the moon, at the close of the worship, what is called ŭdhivasŭ is performed. This also is a preliminary ceremony, and consists in taking rice, fruits, &c., and touching with them a pan of water, and afterwards the forehead of the image, at intervals repeating incantations.

On the 22d, early in the morning, the officiating bramhŭn consecrates the image, placing it on the spot prepared for it in the temple, and repeating the proper formulas. After this, the principal ceremonies before the image begin. First, the business of giving eyes and life to the images is performed; when they become objects of worship. In this curious ceremony, the officiating bramhŭn touches with the two fore-fingers of his right hand the breast, the two cheeks, the eyes, and the forehead of the image. When he touches these places, he says, 'Let the soul of Doorga long continue in happiness in this image.' After this, he takes a leaf of the vilwŭ tree, rubs it with clarified butter, and holds it over a burning lamp till it be covered with soot; of which he takes a little on the stalk of another vilwŭ leaf, and touches the eyes, filling up with the soot a small white place left in the pupil of the eye.

The worship of Gŭnéshŭ and other gods is now performed; then that of the demi-goddesses, the companions of Doorga in her wars, who are represented by the dots of paint on the canopy which covers the image of the goddess. The offerings presented to them consist of very small slices of plantains, on each of which are stuck two or three grains of rice, &c. Then follows the worship of the other images set up with that of Doorga; to which succeeds the principal worship, that of Doorga. First, the officiating barmhŭn perforus dhyanŭ; in which, sitting before the image, he closes his eyes, and repeats the proper formulas, meditating on the form of the goddess, and repeating to himself, 'I present to the goddess all these flowers, fruits, &c. [here he goes over all the offerings;] I slay all these animals,' &c. He then calls the goddess, saying, 'O goddess, come here, come here; stay here, stay here. Take up thine abode here, and receive my worship.' The priest next places before the image a small piece of square gold or silver, for the goddess to sit upon, and asks if she has arrived happily; adding the answer himself, 'Very happily.' After this, water for washing the feet is offered, by taking it with a spoon from one vessel, and pouring it out into another, while the incantation is repeated. Ten or fifteen blades of dōōrvŭ grass, a yŭva flower, sandal powder, rice, &c. are then offered with an incantation, and laid at the feet of Doorga. Next follows water to wash the mouth; curds, sugar, and a lighted lamp. Then water to wash the mouth, and to bathe; then cloth, or garments; then jewels, or ornaments for the feet, arms, fingers, nose, ears, &c., with sandal wood, and red or white lead; then flowers of different kinds, one at a time, with a separate incantation for each flower: also a vilwŭ leaf, with some powder of sandal wood put upon it. Then are offered thrice successively two handfuls of flowers of different kinds; afterwards incense, a lighted lamp, and meat offerings. At the close, the bramhŭn walks round the image seven times, repeating forms of petition and praise.

Now the bloody sacrifices are offered. If the animal be a sheep or a goat, as is always the case on the first day, the officiating bramhŭn, after bathing it either in the river or in the house, puts his left hand on its forehead, marks its horns and forehead with red lead, and reads an incantation, in which he offers it up to the goddess, thus: 'O goddess, I sacrifice this goat[p] to thee, that I may live in thy heaven to the end of ten years.' He then reads an incantation in its ear, and puts flowers, and sprinkles water on its head. The instrument with which the animal is killed is consecrated by placing upon it flowers, red lead, &c, and writing on it the incantation which is given to the disciples of Doorga. The officiating bramhŭn next puts the instrument of death on the neck of the animal, and, after presenting him with a flower as a blessing[q], then into the hand of the person appointed to slay the animal, who is generally the black-smith[r], but sometimes a brmhŭn. The assistants put the goat's neck into an upright post, excavated at the top so as to admit the neck betwixt its two sides; the body remaining on one side of the post, and the head on the other. An earthen vessel containing a plantain is placed upon a plantain leaf; after which the blacksmith cuts off the head at one blow,

p Only male animals are offered.

q It is common among the Hindoos for a superior to give a blessing while presenting a flower.

r The Hindoos covet the honour of cutting off the head of an animal dexterously at the time of these sacrifices. If it be not done at one blow, they drive the blacksmith away in disgrace. The shastrŭs have denounced vengeance on the person who shall fail to cut off the head at one blow: his son will die, or the goddess of fortune (Lŭkshmēē) will forsake him.

and another person holds up the body, and drains out the blood upon the plantain in the bason If the person who performs the sacrifice does not intend to offer the flesh to Doorga[s], the slayer cuts only a small morsel from the neck, and puts it on the plantain ; when some one carries it, and the head, and places them before the image, putting on the head a lighted lamp. After all the animals have been thus killed, and some of the flesh and the heads carried before the image, the officiating bramhŭn repeats certain prayers over these offerings, and persents them to the goddess, with the blood which fell on the plantains : then, taking the blood from the bason, he puts it on a plantain leaf, and cuts it into four parts, presenting it to the four goddesses who attend upon Doorga.

Offerings of rice, plantains, sugar, sweetmeats, sour milk, curds, pulse of different sorts, limes, fruits, &c. are next presented with prayers. Now the names of Doorga are repeated by the priest, who afterwards presents camphorated water to the goddess ; then betle-nut, limes, spices, &c., made into what is called panŭ[t]. After repeating a number of forms of praise, this part of the service closes with the prostration of the officiating bramhŭn before the idol. Next, food is presented with many prayers to the goddess ; which food consists of what is called khĕchŭrŭ[u], fried fruits, fried fish and flesh. &c. About four in the afternoon, large quantities of food are presented to the goddess ; amongst which are, prepared greens of three or four kinds ; prepared peas of three or four kinds ; fried fruits, sweet potatoes, &c ; fried fish, mixed with fruits of four or five different sorts ; the flesh of sheep and goats, stewed in two or three ways ; preparations of tamarinds, two or three sorts ; rice boiled in milk, two or three sorts ; fifteen or sixteen sorts of sweetmeats &c. ; all which are offered with separate prayers : after which water, betle, &c. are presented.

The bramhŭns are entertained either with sweetmeats, or prepared food, by the person at whose house the worship is performed : some of them are expressly invited, and others attend to see the ceremonies. The food which has been presented to the goddess, being considered almost as ambrosia, is given to the guests with a sparing hand ; some of whom (mothers) beg to take a morsel home to cure their children, or relatives, of diseases. Food is also sent to the neighbours, and persons of inferior cast carry away great quantities[x].

[s] This is rarely or never done at present. There are no parts of the animal, however, which may not be offered.

[t] Chewed by almost all the natives.

[u] A common dish in Bengal, made of rice, boiled up with turmeric, peas, spices, clarified butter, &c.

[x] In some places a family or several families of bramhŭns are supported by the revenues attached to a temple, and by the offerings presented to the idol. At the time of a festival, the heads of these families wait on those who come to make offerings to the idol, and present them with betle, sweetmeats, fruits, water, &c., according to their quality.

In the evening, the officiating bramhŭn waves a brass candlestick, or lamp with five lights, before the goddess, repeating incantations; afterwards a shell with water in it, and then a piece of cloth. At night the temple is lighted up, and, about eight o'clock, unleavened bread, butter, fruits, sweetmeats, curds, milk, &c., are presented to the goddess. At midnight some persons repeat the worship; but in this case the offerings are few, and there are no bloody sacrifices.

After the worship of the day, many rich men engage a number of prostitutes, richly dressed and almost covered with ornaments, to dance and sing before the idol. The songs are exceedingly obscene; the dances highly indecent; and the dress of the dancing women no less so: their clothing being so fine as scarcely to deserve the name of a covering. The tresses of some are thrown loose, hanging down to the waist. During the dances, the doors are shut to keep out the crowd, as well as Europeans, who are excluded. Six, seven, or eight women thus dance together, assisted by music, for about four hours. Rich spectators, when remarkably pleased with a part of the song, throw to the singer as much as four, eight, or sixteen rupees; beside which, those who engage these women make them presents of garments, and of considerable sums of money. The sons of the rich natives are highly pleased with these dances.

On the second day, the worship and sacrifices are much the same as on the first, except that the bathing of the goddess, called the great Snanŭ, is attended with more ceremonies. In this ceremony the priest first brings some earth said to have been thrown up by the teeth of a wild hog, and, mixing it with water, presents it with prayers to the goddess, to be used as soap. Then in succession earth from before the door of the king, or lord of the soil; from before that of a courtezan; from the side of the Ganges; earth raised by ants; and, lastly, earth from any river side, not the Ganges, is presented with the same ceremonies. After this, turmeric, fruits and spices; the water of the cocoa-nut, and of the water melon; the juice of the sugar cane; honey, clarified butter, sour milk, milk, cow's urine, cow-dung, sugar, treacle, and different sorts of oil, are presented in succession, with the necessary formulas. While the officiating bramhŭn is going through these ceremonies, he revolves in his mind that he is making these gifts to assist the goddess in bathing. At the close, he presents some water of the Ganges, and after this the water of four seas; or, if unable to obtain this, the water of the Ganges again, and then the water of some other river. The bathing ceremonies are closed by a present of cloth for the loins. In the evening, or else in the night, according to the conjunction of the stars, worship is again performed, in which only one bloody sacrifice is offered; and in some cases none. Widows fast on this day, particularly a widow with children; the latter deriving great benefits from the meritorious actions of the mother.

On the third day, the goddess is worshipped only once, but the offerings and sacrifices are many; buffaloes are offered only on this day. A respectable native once told me, he had seen one hundred and eight buffaloes sacrificed by one Hindoo at this festival: the number slain in the whole country must therefore be very great. Formerly, some of the Hindoo kings killed a thousand animals on these occasions[y]. The males only are sacrificed; and they are in general young and very tame, costing from five to sixteen rupees each. None of the Hindoos eat the sacrificed buffaloes, except the shoemakers[z]. Each animal is bathed before it is slain; after which the officiating bramhŭn puts red lead on its horns, and, with a red string, ties a piece of wool smeared with red lead on the forepart of the breast; he also puts a piece of cloth coloured over with turmeric on his back, and a necklace of vilwŭ leaves on his neck, repeating prayers during these actions. The ceremony of cutting off the heads of the buffaloes, and presenting them to the goddess, is similar to those already described respecting the sacrifice of goats and sheep.

After the beasts are all slain, the multitude, rich and poor, daub their bodies all over with the mud formed with the blood which has collected where the animals were slain, and dance like furies on the spot; after which they go into the street, dancing and singing indecent songs, and visit those houses where images of the goddess have been set up.

At the close of the whole, the officiating bramhŭn presents a burnt-offering, and gives to the goddess a sum of money, commonly about four rupees: some indeed give one hundred, and others as much as a thousand rupees; which at length return into the hands of the officiating bramhŭn.

In the year 1806, I was present at the worship of this goddess, as performed at the house of Raja Raj-Krishnŭ at Calcutta. The buildings where the festival was held were on four sides, leaving an area in the middle. The room to the east contained wine, English sweetmeats, &c. for the entertainment of English guests, with a native Portuguese or two to wait on the visitors. In the opposite room was placed the image, with

[y] The father of the present king of Nŭdēēya, at one of these festivals, offered a great number of goats and sheep to Doorga. He began with one, and, doubling the number each day, continued it for sixteen days. On the last day he killed 33,768, and in the whole he slaughtered 65,535 animals. He loaded boats with the bodies, and sent them to the neighbouring bramhŭns; but they could not devour them fast enough, and great numbers were thrown away.—Let no one, after this, tell us of the scruples of the bramhŭns about destroying animal life, and eating animal food.

[z] In some places, the tame hog is offered to Doorga by the lowest casts, who, among other offerings, present spirituous liquors to the goddess. At the end of the ceremonies, these persons cook and eat the flesh, drink the spirits, and then, in a state of intoxication, the men and women dance together, and commit the greatest indecencies. No bramhŭn, on pain of losing cast, can assist at these ceremonies; and indeed all bramhŭns, who perform ceremonies for persons of low cast, sink in society.

vast heaps of all kinds of offerings before it. In the two side rooms were the native guests, and in the area groups of Hindoo dancing women, finely dressed, singing, and dancing with sleepy steps, surrounded with Europeans who were sitting on chairs and couches. One or two groups of Mŭsŭlman men-singers entertained the company at intervals with Hindoost'hanee songs, and ludicrous tricks. Before two o'clock the place was cleared of the dancing girls, and of all the Europeans except ourselves ; and almost all the lights were extinguished, except in front of the goddess ; —when the doors of the area were thrown open, and a vast crowd of natives rushed in, almost treading one upon another ; among whom were the vocal singers, having on long caps like sugar loaves. The area might be about fifty cubits long and thirty wide. When the crowd had sat down, they were so wedged together as to present the appearance of a solid pavement of heads ; a small space only being left immediately before the image for the motions of the singers, who all stood up. Four sets of singers were present on this occasion, the first consisting of bramhŭns, the next of bankers, the next of voishnŭvŭs, and the last of weavers ;[a] who entertained their guests with filthy songs, and danced in indecent attitudes before the goddess, holding up their hands, turning round, putting forward their heads towards the image, every now and then bending their bodies, and almost tearing their throats with their vociferations. The whole scene produced on my mind sensations of the greatest horror. The dress of the singers—their indecent gestures—the abominable nature of the songs—the horrid din of their miserable drum—the lateness of the hour—the darkness of the place—with the reflection that I was standing in an idol temple, and that this immense multitude of rational and immortal creatures, capable of superior joys, were, in the very act of worship, perpetrating a crime of high treason against the God of heaven, while they themselves believed they were performing an act of merit—excited ideas and feelings in my mind which time can never obliterate.

I would have given, in this place, a specimen of the songs sung before the image, but found them so full of broad obscenity that I could not copy a single line. All those actions, which a sense of decency keeps out of the most indecent English songs, are here detailed, sung, and laughed at, without the least sense of shame. A poor ballad-singer in England would be sent to the house of correction, and flogged, for performing the *meritorious actions* of these wretched idolaters.[b] The singing is continued for three days, from about two o'clock in the morning till nine.

[a] Distinguished among the natives by the name of Hŭroo-t'hakoorŭ, Bhŭvanŭndŭ, Nitaee, and Lŭkshmee.

[b] The reader will recollect that the festivals of Bacchus and Cybele were equally noted for the indecencies practised by the worshippers, both in their words and actions.

The next morning, between eight and nine, a short time is spent in worship, but no bloody sacrifices are offered. Amongst other ceremonies at this time the officiating bramhŭn, in the presence of the family, dismisses the goddess, repeating these words: 'O goddess! I have, to the best of my ability, worshipped thee. Now go to thy residence, leaving this blessing, that thou wilt return the next year:' after which the priest immerses a looking-glass, the representative of the goddess, in a pan of water; and then takes some of this water, and sprinkles himself and the company with it. When the goddess is thus dismissed, the women set up a cry—some even shed tears In the afternoon, the mistress of the house and other women go to the image, put a rupee and some betle in its hand, strew some turmeric at its feet, and rub the dust of its feet on their own foreheads and those of their friends. On their retiring, the crowd assemble, with their bodies daubed with turmeric, oil, and sour milk; and, bringing out the image, place it on a stage, to which they fasten it with cords, and carry it on their shoulders to the water. It is here placed in the centre of two boats lashed together, and filled with people, among whom are dancers, musicians, singers, &c. At this time, in many instances, men dance stark naked on the boat before many thousands assembled, who only laugh at this gross indecency. Perhaps in one place on the river twenty or thirty images will be exhibited at once, while the banks are crowded with spectators rich and poor, old and young, all intoxicated with the scene.[c] The last ceremony is that of letting down the image, with all its tinsil and ornaments into the river.

The women of the house to which the temple belongs go to the room from whence the goddess has just been taken, and place a pan of water upon the spot where the image stood, and put upon the top of the pan a branch of the mango tree. After the goddess has been drowned, the crowd return to the temple; and the officiating bramhŭn, taking his place by the side of the pan of water, dips the branch of the mango tree into the water, and sprinkles all the people, repeating incantations; and thus blessing the people they are dismissed, when each one clasps his neighbour in his arms. Adjourning to their own houses, they partake of sweetmeats, and of an intoxicating beverage made with hemp leaves. In a vast

[c] In a memorandum of my own, dated Sept. 26, 1803, I find these remarks, made one evening in the course of a journey:—'About five in the afternoon, we came to Bŭlargŭr. The people of about twenty villages, more than 2,000 in number, including women and children, were assembled to throw their images into the river, this being the termination of the Doorga festival. I observed that one of the men standing before the idol in a boat, dancing and making indecent gestures, was naked. As the boat passed along, he was gazed at by the mob; nor could I perceive that this abominable action produced any thing beside laughter. Before other images, young men dressed in women's clothes, were dancing with other men, making indecent gestures. I cannot help thinking the most vulgar mob in England would have turned with disgust from these abominable scenes. I have seen the same abominations exhibited before our own house at Serampore.'

number of instances, this festival is thus closed with scenes of the most shameful intoxication : almost all the Hindoos in Bengal think it a duty to indulge to a certain degree in drinking this liquor at this festival.

Presents to the bramhŭns and their wives are made on each of the fifteen days of the festival by the person at whose house the image is set up, if he be very rich. If he be not rich enough to bear so great an expense, he gives presents on the nine or three last days of worship ; and if he be still poorer, on the last day. These presents consist of gold and silver female ornaments, silk and cloth garments, brass and other metal dishes, basons, &c. Some persons expend the greatest sums on the dances and other exhibitions, and others in feasting and giving presents to bramhŭns.

Some classes of Hindoos, especially those who are the disciples of Vishnoo, do not offer bloody sacrifices to Doorga, though they celebrate this festival with much shew. These persons, instead of slaying animals, cut pumkins in two, or some other substitute, and offer them to the goddess.

In the month Choitrŭ, a number of Hindoos hold a festival to this goddess, after the example of king Soorŭtŭ.

Many Hindoos are initiated into the rites by which this goddess becomes their guardian deity ; and as she is considered as the image of the divine energy, her disciples are called Shaktŭs, a word signifying energy.

Images of Doorga, made of gold, silver, brass, &c., are preserved by many, and worshipped daily.

In the year 1808, a bramhŭn of Calcutta, who had celebrated the worship of Doorga, pretended that he had seen the goddess in a dream ; who had declared that she would not descend into the river till he had sacrificed his eldest son to her : and that when the people went to convey the image to the river, it was found so heavy that it could not be lifted. Vast crowds of people flocked to see this new miracle, many of whom made offerings to this terror-inspiring goddess ; and others assisted the poor man, by their contributions, to pacify the goddess in some way consistent with the preservation of his son.

One of the Tŭntrŭs contains an account of an incarnation of Doorga in the form of a jackal, in order to carry the child Krishnŭ over the river Yŭmoono, when he was flying from king Kŭngsŭ. Some of the heterodox Hindoos, called vamacharēēs, feed the jackal daily, by placing the offerings in a corner of the house, or near their dwellings, and then calling the goddess (in the form of some one of these animals) to come and partake of them. As this is done at the hour when the jackals come out of their lurking places to seek for food, one of these animals sometimes comes and eats the offerings in the presence of the worshipper; and this is not wonderful, when he finds food in this place every day. Images of the jackal are made in some parts of Bengal, and worshipped, sometimes alone, and at others with the images of Doorga and Shmŭshanŭ-Kalēē. Some Hindoos bow to the jackal; if it pass by a person on his left, it is a fortunate omen.

The cow is regarded by the Hindoos as a form of Doorga, and called Bhŭgŭvŭtēē.

This goddess has a thousand names, among which are Katyayŭnēē, or, the daughter of the sage Katyŭ.—Gourēē, the yellow coloured.—Kalēē, the black.—Hoimŭvŭtēē, the daughter of Himalŭyŭ.—Eēshwŭrēē, the goddess.—Shiva, the giver of good.—Bhŭvanēē, the wife of Shivŭ—Sŭrvŭmŭngŭla, she who blesses all.—Ŭpŭrna, she who amidst religious austerities abstained from eating even leaves.—Parvŭtēē, the daughter of the mountain.—Doorga, she who destroyed the giant Doorgŭ; the inaccessible.—Chŭndika, the terrible.—Ŭmbika, the mother of the universe.

SECT. II.—*The ten Forms of Doorga.*

THIS goddess is said to have assumed ten different forms in order to destroy two giants, Shoombhŭ and Nishoombhŭ.

The following account of these wars is translated from the Markŭndéyŭ pooranŭ:—At the close of the tréta yoogŭ, these two giants performed religious austerities for 10,000 years; the merit of which actions brought Shivŭ from heaven,[e] who discovered that by these works of extraordinary devotion they sought to obtain the blessing of immortality. Shivŭ reasoned long with them, and endeavoured to persuade them, though in vain, to ask for any other blessing short of immortality. Being denied, they entered upon more severe austerities, which they continued for another thousand years; when Shivŭ again appeared, but refused to grant what they asked for. They now suspended themselves with their heads downwards over a slow fire, till the blood streamed from their heads; and continued thus for 800 years, till the gods began to tremble, lest, by performing such rigid acts of holiness, they should be supplanted on their thrones. The king of the gods assembled a council, and imparted to them his fears: the gods admitted that there was great ground for fear, but asked what remedy there was. Agreeably to the advice of Indrŭ, Kŭndŭrpŭ (Cupid), with Rŭmbha and Tilottŭma, the most beautiful of the celestial courtezans, were sent to fill the minds of these giants with sensual

[e] It is a maxim of the Hindoo religion, that by performing religious austerities the gods become subject to the wishes of men.

desires; and Kŭndŭrpŭ, letting fly his arrow, wounded them both: upon which, awaking from their absorption, and seeing two beautiful women, they were taken in the snare, and abandoned their devotions. With these women they lived 5,000 years, after which they began to think of the folly of thus renouncing their hopes of immortality for the sake of sensual gratifications. They suspected that this must have been a contrivance of Indrŭ's; and driving the courtezans back to heaven, renewed their devotions, cutting the flesh off their bones, and making burnt-offerings of it to Shivŭ; which they continued for another thousand years, till they became entire skeletons, when Shivŭ again appeared, and bestowed upon them this blessing—that in riches and strength they should excel the gods.

Being thus exalted above the gods, they soon began to make war with them. After various success on both sides, the giants were every where victorious; till Indrŭ and all the gods, reduced to the most deplorable state of wretchedness, solicited the interference of Brŭmha and Vishnoo; but they referred them to Shivŭ: who also declared that he could do nothing for them. When, however, they reminded him that through his blessing they had been ruined, he advised them to perform religious austerities to Doorga. They did so; and after sometime the goddess appeared, gave them her blessing, and immediately, disguised like a common female carrying a pitcher of water, passed the assembled gods. This female asked them whose praise they were chanting? While she uttered these words, she assumed her proper form, and replied, 'They are celebrating my praise.' The new goddess then disappeared, and ascended mount Himalŭyŭ, where Chŭndŭ and Mundŭ, two of Shoombhŭ and Nishoombhŭ's messengers, resided. As these messengers wandered on the mountain, they saw the goddess, and were exceedingly struck with her charms, which they described to their masters; and advised them to engage the affections of this female, even if they gave her all the glorious things which they had obtained in plundering the heavens of the gods. Shoombhŭ sent Shoogrēēvŭ, a messenger, to the goddess, to inform her that the riches of the three worlds were in his palace; that all the offerings which used to be presented to the gods were now offered to him; and that all these riches, offerings, &c. should be her's if she would come to him. The goddess replied, that this offer was very liberal; but she had resolved, that the person whom she married must first conquer her in war, and destroy her pride. Shoogrēēvŭ, unwilling to return unsuccessful, still pressed for a favourable answer; promising that he would engage to conquer her in war, and subdue her pride; and asked in an authoritative strain, 'Did she know his master, before whom none of the inhabitants of the three worlds had been able to stand, whether gods, hydras, or men? How then could she, a female, think of resisting his offers? If his master had ordered him, he would have compelled her to go into his presence immediately.' She said all this was very correct, but that she had taken her resolution, and exhorted him, therefore, to persuade his master to come and try his strength with her. The messenger went to his master, and related what he had heard from this female; on hearing which Shoombhŭ was filled with rage, and without making any reply, called for Dhōōmlochŭnŭ, his commander-in-chief, and gave him orders to go to Himalŭyŭ, and seize a certain goddess, (giving him particular directions,) and bring her to him; and if any attempted to rescue her, utterly to destroy them. The commander went to Himalŭyŭ, and acquainting the goddess with his master's orders, she, smiling, invited him to execute them; but, on the approach of this hero, she set up a dreadful roar, (as is usual among the Hindoo warriors when two combatants meet,) by which he was reduced to ashes; after which she destroyed the army of the giant, leaving only a few fugitives to communicate the tidings. Shoombhŭ and Nishoombhŭ, infuriated, sent Chŭndŭ and Mŭndŭ, who, on ascending the mountain, perceived a female sitting on an ass, laughing; but on seeing them she became full of rage, and drew to her ten, twenty, or thirty of their army at a time, devouring them like fruit. She next seized Mŭndŭ by the hair, cut off his head, and, holding it over her mouth, drank the blood. Chŭndŭ, on seeing the other commander destroyed in this manner, came to close quarters with the goddess; but she, mounted on a lion, sprang on him, and dispatching him as she had done Mŭndŭ, devoured part of his army, and drank the blood of the greater part of the rest. The two giants no sooner heard this alarming news, then they resolved to go themselves, and engage the furious goddess; for which purpose they collected all their forces, an infinite number of giants, and marched to Himalŭyŭ. The gods looked down with astonishment on this army of giants, and all the goddesses descended to help Muha-maya (Doorga), who however soon destroyed the giants. Rŭktŭvēējŭ, the principal commander under Shoombhŭ and Nishoombhŭ, seeing all his men destroyed, encountered the goddess in person; but though she filled him with wounds, from every drop of blood which fell to the ground arose a thousand giants equal in strength to Rŭktŭ-vēējŭ himself;[f] hence innumerable enemies surrounded Doorga, and the gods were filled with alarm at this amazing sight. At length Chŭndēē, a goddess who had assisted Kalēē in the engagement, promised that if she would open her mouth, and drink his blood before it fell on the ground, she (Chŭndēē) would engage the giant, and destroy the whole of his strangely-formed offspring. Kalēē consented, and this commander and his army were soon dispatched. Shoombhŭ and Nishoombhŭ, in a state of desperation, next engaged the goddess in single combat, Shoombhŭ making the first onset. The battle was dreadful, inconceivably dreadful, on both sides, till at

[f] This arose from a blessing given by Brŭmha.

last both the giants were killed, and Kalēē sat down to feed on the carnage she had made. The gods and goddesses then chanted the praises of the celestial heroine, and she in return bestowed a blessing on each.

After the destruction of these enemies of the gods, the sun (Sōōryŭ) shone resplendently forth ; the wind (Vayoo) blew salubriously ; the air became pure ; the gods ascended their thrones ; the hydras attended to the duties of their religion without fear ; the sages performed their devotions without interruption ; and the people at large were restored to happiness.

The Chŭndēē, a part of the Markŭndéyŭ pooranŭ, places these forms of Doorga in the following order : First, as Doorga, she received the messenger of the giants ; 2, as Dŭshŭbhooja,[g] she destroyed part of their army ; 3, as Singhŭ-vahinēē,[h] she fought with Rŭktŭ-vēējŭ ; 4, as Mŭhishŭ-mŭrdinēē,[i] she slew Shoombhŭ, in the form of a buffalo ; 5, as Jŭgŭddhatrēē,[k] she overcame the army of the giants ; 6, as Kalēē,[l] she destroyed Rŭktŭ-vēējŭ ; 7, as Mooktŭ-késhēē,[m] she again overcame the army of the giants ; 8, as Tara,[n] she killed Shoombhŭ ; 9, as Chinnŭmŭstŭka,[o] she killed Nishoombhŭ ; 10, as Jŭgŭdgourēē,[p] she was praised by all the gods.

Such of the above forms as are honoured by separate festivals, will be noticed hereafter under their different names.

SECT. III.—*Singhŭ-vahinēē.*[q]

THIS goddess with yellow garments is represented as sitting on a lion. She has four hands ; in one a sword ; in another a spear ; with a third is forbidding fear, and with the fourth bestowing a blessing.

Many people make this image, and worship it in the daytime, on the 9th of the increase of the moon, in whatever month they please, but in general in the month Ashwinŭ or Choitrŭ, for two or three days. The ceremonies, including bloody sacrifices, are almost entirely the same as those before the image of Doorga. Sometimes a rich man celebrates this worship at his own expense, and at other times several persons, who expect heaven as their reward, unite in it.

Some Hindoos keep in their houses images of all the following forms of Doorga, made of gold, silver, brass, copper, crystal, stone, or mixed metal, and worship them daily.

[g] Having ten arms. [h] Sitting on a lion. [i] Destroyer of the buffalo, [viz., of Shoombhŭ in this form.] [k] Mother of the world. [l] The black. [m] With flowing hair. [n] Saviour. [o] Headless. [p] The yellow. [q] She who sits upon a lion.

SECT. IV.—*Mŭhishŭ-mŭrdinēē.*[r]

THIS is the image of a yellow woman, sitting on a lion; having either six or ten arms. In her hands are seen a conch, a discus, a club, a water-lily, a shield, a large spear, and the tail of a snake.

Some persons make this image, and worship it with the accustomed ceremonies, including bloody sacrifices, on the 9th of the month Choitrŭ.

The Tŭntrŭ-saru declares, that those who worship this goddess will obtain present riches and future happiness.

Many of the regular Hindoos, as well as the heterodox sects, receive the initiatory rites of this goddess, and adopt her as their guardian deity.

SECT. V.—*Jŭgŭddhatrēē.*[s]

THIS is the image of a yellow woman, dressed in red, and sitting on a lion. In her four hands she holds a conch,[t] a discus, a club, and a water-lily.

A very popular festival in honour of this goddess is held in the month Kartikŭ, on the 7th, 8th and 9th of the increase of the moon, when bloody sacrifices are offered as at the Doorga festival: the formulas are necessarily different. Very large sums are frequently expended on these occasions, especially in the illuminations, dances, songs, entertaining of bramhŭns, &c., as many as one hundred and fifty persons being employed as singers and dancers, beside others who sing verses from the Chŭndēē, the Krishnŭmŭngŭlŭ, the Ramayŭnŭ, &c. A number of men like guards are also hired, and placed near the temple for the sake of shew. Much indecent mirth takes place, and numbers of men dance naked before the image, *and call this the way to heaven;* the venerable bramhŭns smiling with complacency on these works of *merit,* so acceptable to the gods. The benefits expected from this worship are, the fruit of meritorious actions, riches, the gratification of every desire, and future happiness. These four things are commonly mentioned in the Hindoo shastrŭs, as promised by the gods to their worshippers.

[r] She who destroyed Mŭhishŭ, a giant.

[s] The mother of the world.

[t] This shell is blown at the times of worship, and at other festivals.

SECT. VI.—*Mooktŭ-késhēē*[u].

THIS is the image of a naked woman, painted blue, standing on the breast of Shivŭ, and having four arms: the upper right arm is placed in the posture of bestowing a blessing; with the other she is forbidding fear, and in her left hand she holds a sword and a helmet.

The festival of this goddess is held on the 14th of the decrease of the moon in the month Maghŭ: the ceremonies are like those before the image of Kalēē, but the bloody sacrifices are very numerous. Spirituous liquors are privately presented to the goddess, at a late hour at night, or rather early in the morning. Some of the Hindoo shastrŭs allow of this practice, yet it is far from being honourable. I have been credibly informed, that numbers of bramhŭns, in different places, at the annual festival of this goddess, join in drinking the spirits which have been offered to her, and, in a state of intoxication, pass from the temples into the streets, preceded by lighted torches, dancing to the sound of music, and singing indecent songs. Some are hugging one another; others fall down quite intoxicated; others lose their way, and go along lifting up their hands, dancing and singing alone. The purer Hindoos stand gazing at a considerable distance, lest they should be dragged among this crowd of drunken bramhŭns.

The benefits promised to the worshippers of this goddess are riches now, and heaven hereafter.

Very many persons are initiated into the rites of this goddess as their guardian deity.

SECT. VII.—*Tara*[x].

THIS is the image of a black woman, with four arms, standing on the breast of Shivŭ: in one hand she holds a sword; in another a giant's head; with the others she is bestowing a blessing, and forbidding fear.

The worship of Tara is performed in the night, in different months, at the total wane of the moon, before the image of Siddhéshwŭrēē; when bloody sacrifices are offered, and it is reported, that even human beings were formerly immolated in secret to this ferocious deity; who is considered by the Hindoos as soon incensed, and not unfrequently inflicting on an importunate worshipper the most shocking diseases, as a vomiting of blood, or some other dreadful complaint which soon puts an end to his life.

[u] Of flowing hair. [x] The deliverer.

Almost all the disciples of this goddess are from among the heterodox: many of them, however are learned men, Tara being considered as the patroness of learning. Some Hindoos are supposed to have made great advances in knowledge through the favour of this goddess; and many a stupid boy, after reading some incantations containing the name of Tara, has become a learned man.

SECT. VIII.—*Chinnŭ-mŭstŭka*[y].

THIS is the image of a naked yellow woman, with her head half severed from her body[z], wearing a necklace of skulls, and standing on the body of Shivŭ. She is surrounded with dead bodies; has a scymitar in one hand; a giant's skull in another; and with two others is forbidding fear, and bestowing a blessing.

This image is not made at present, but the worship may be celebrated before the images of any other female deities. Those who receive the initiatory rites of this goddess worship her daily before the shalgramŭ, or water, or flowers, or an incantation written on a metal dish[a]. She promises her disciples riches, learning, or absorption[b], but principally riches. Some people are afraid of becoming her disciples, lest, in a fit of anger, she should bring upon them a violent death[c].

SECT. IX.—*Jŭgŭdgourēē*[d].

THIS is the whole length figure of a yellow woman, with four arms; holding in her hands a conch, a discus, a club, and a water-lily. She is mostly worshipped on the 7th, 8th, and 9th of the increase of the moon in Maghŭ. Very few persons learn the initiatory rites of this goddess.

[y] The headless.

[z] The Tŭntrŭs give the following explanation of this monstrous feature in the image of this goddess:—At a certain time, not being able to procure any of the giants for her prey, to satisfy her thirst of blood, Chinnŭ-mŭstŭka actually cut her own throat, that the blood issuing thence might spout up into her mouth. I have seen a picture of this image, agreeing with this description; and at Chachra, in Jessore, such an image may be seen at present, the half-severed head resting on the left hand of the goddess, and streams of blood falling into her mouth.

[a] Before any one of these things, the worship of any of the gods may be performed; but the shalgramŭ is mostly preferred.

[b] A person can receive only one blessing at a time from his god. The Hindoos, however, relate a story of a blind man, who put a trick on his guardian deity, by obtaining three blessings from him at once: he asked that he might see—his child eat from off a golden dish every day. He was then childless.

[c] The following story, current among the Hindoos, I give as a proof of the dread in which they live of some of their deities:—A bramhŭn who had received the initiating incantation of this goddess, to avoid dying an unnatural death, used to confine himself to his house; where, however, a hatchet, hung up for sacrificing animals, fell upon and killed him as he lay asleep.

[d] The yellow.

SECT. X.—*Vŭgŭlamookhēē*[e].

THE image of this deity is never made; though she is sometimes worshipped on the 7th, 8th, and 9th of the moon in Maghŭ, before a pan of water, or some other proper substitute. The officiating bramhŭn, in yellow garments, presents yellow flowers, flesh, fish, and spirituous liquors to her: the animals sacrificed are not numerous.

This goddess is frequently worshipped in the hope of procuring the removal, the injury, or the destruction of enemies, or whatever else the worshipper desires—which is sometimes *the wife of another.* He makes no doubt, if he can please the goddess by presents, or flattery, or by inflicting, for her sake, certain cruelties on his body, that she will be disposed to grant him even this last favour. If the ceremonies be not performed in strict conformity to the rules laid down in the shastrŭ, it is believed that the worshipper will be deprived of reason, or of speech, or that some other dreadful calamity will befal him.

In the burnt-sacrifice presented to this goddess, turmeric, oil, and salt, form the principal ingredients. The Hindoos believe that after performing the proper ceremonies for the destruction of an enemy, the goddess soon complies with the prayers of the worshipper. Shoodrŭs, of course, employ bramhŭns in thus attempting to accomplish their murderous wishes. Particular forms of praise and of petition, referring in many cases to the injury or destruction of enemies, addressed to this goddess, are contained in the Tŭntrŭsarŭ.

SECT. XI.—*Prŭtyŭngira*[f].

THE image of this idol is never made, but is worshipped in the night whenever a person chooses, which is, generally, when he wants to injure or destroy another. The officiating bramhŭn dressed in red, and wearing a roodrakshŭ necklace, offers, among other things, red flowers, spirituous liquors, and bloody sacrifices. The flesh of crows, or cats, or of some other animal, after having been dipped in spirituous liquors, sometimes makes a part of the burnt-offerings; the worshippers believing that the flesh of the enemy, for whose injury these ceremonies are performed, will swell on his body as the sacrificed flesh does on the fire. Particular forms of praise are also repeated before this image to accomplish the destruction of enemies. I here give a specimen: 'Oh! Prŭtyŭngira, mother! Destroy, destroy my enemies! Kill! kill! Reduce them to

[e] Of fear-exciting countenance.

[f] The well-proportioned.

ashes! Drive them away! Devour them! devour them! Cut them in two! Drink, drink their blood! Destroy them root and branch! With thy thunder-bolt, spear, scymitar, discus, or rope, destroy them.'

A story to the following purport is very current among the Hindoos:—Jafŭr-alee-kha, the nabob of Moorshŭdŭbad, was much attached to Ramŭ-khantŭ, his Hindoo treasurer; who was at enmity with Kalēē-shŭnkŭrŭ, a very learned Hindoo, and a great worshipper of the female deities. The latter, to effect the destruction of Ramŭ-kantŭ, began to worship the goddess Prŭtyŭngira. He had not performed the ceremonies long, before Ramŭ-kantŭ became sick, and it was made known to him and the nabob, that Kalēē-shŭnkŭrŭ was thus employed. The nabob, full of rage, ordered that Kalēē-shŭnkŭrŭ should be brought before him: but he fled before the messengers could seize him, and began to perform these ceremonies for the destruction of the nabob. A servant, mistaken for Kalēē-shŭnkŭrŭ, was, however, seized; but he bribed the messengers, that they might protract his journey as much as possible. They did so, and the day before they arrived at Moorshŭdŭbad the nabob died. I give this story to shew, what a strong possession the popular superstition has taken of the minds of the people; who, while smoaking together, listen to these stories with the utmost eagerness and surprise, as the villagers in England tell stories current amongst them while sitting round the winter's fire.

SECT. XII.—*Unnŭ-pōōrna*[g].

THIS image may be made standing, or sitting on the water-lily: in the right hand is a spoon, like that with which the Hindoos stir their boiling rice, and in the other a rice dish: Shivŭ, as a naked mendicant, is standing before the image asking relief.

The worship paid to this form of Doorga is performed on the 7th, 8th, and 9th days of the moon's increase in the month Choitrŭ: bloody sacrifices, fish, and spirituous liquors are among the offerings. Ŭnnŭ-pōōrna being the guardian deity of many of the Hindoos, (who have a proverb amongst them, that a sincere disciple of this goddess never wants rice,) very great festivities take place at this festival, accompanied with music, dancing, filthy songs, and every thing else calculated to deprave the heart.

A Hindoo rising in a morning, before his eyes are well open, repeats the name of this goddess—'Ŭnnŭ-pōōrna! Ŭnnŭ-pōōrna!' and hopes, that through her favour he shall be well fed that day.

g She who fills with food; from ŭnnŭ, food, and pōōrnŭ, full.

When one Hindoo wishes to compliment another on his riches or liberality, he says, 'Oh! Sir, your house is as full of riches as that of Ŭnnŭ-pōōrna:' or, if he speak of another when absent, he says, 'Such a one, in liberality, is like Ŭnnŭ-pōōrna.'

SECT. XIII.—*Gŭnéshŭ-jŭnŭnēē*[h].

THIS name Doorga assumed after the birth of Gŭnéshŭ: she is here represented as sitting on the water-lily, dressed in red, and supporting with one arm the infant Gŭnéshŭ at the breast, while the other hand rests on the knee of the infant.

A small festival in honour of this goddess is celebrated in the month Ŭgrŭhayŭnŭ or Phalgoonŭ, on the 7th, 8th and 9th of the increase of the moon. Some years ago, at Gooptee-para, a village about forty miles north of Calcutta, a great festival was held in honour of Gŭnéshŭ-jŭnŭnēē, when fifty thousand rupees or more were expended. The bramhŭns of the village collected money to defray the expenses; some gave one thousand, others two, and others five thousand rupees: and crowds came two or three days journey to be present. The dancing, singing, music, &c. began a month before the principal day of worship; all the visitors were entertained, and more than two thousand animals were slain.

SECT. XIV.—*Krishnŭ-krora*[i].

THIS is an image of Doorga giving suck to Krishnŭ, to destroy the poison which he had received in a quarrel with Kalēēyŭ, a hydra.

A festival in honour of this goddess is held on the 7th, 8th, and 9th of the increase of the moon, in the day, in the month Maghŭ.

The history of this idol is thus related:—In the west of Hindoost'han, a stone image was once found in a pool; and no information could be obtained to what it related, until a Brŭmhŭcharēē referred them to the following story in one of the Tŭntrŭs.—In the neighbourhood of Vrinda-vŭnŭ, by the river Yŭmoona, Soubhŭree, a sage, for a long time performed religious austerities. One day, while in the midst of his devotions, he saw a shŭkoolŭ and some other fish playing together; with which sight he was much pleased, till Gŭroorŭ, the king of the birds, descended into the water, and snatched up the shŭkoolŭ fish. The sage, unable to punish Gŭ-

h The mother of Gŭnéshŭ.

i She who holds Krishnŭ in her arms.

roorŭ, pronounced a curse upon this bird-god, or any other bird, who should hereafter come to destroy the fish in this spot; and this curse was afterwards the means of preserving the king of the hydras from the wrath of Gŭroorŭ in the following manner.—The mountain Hŭlŭyŭ was the resort of many serpents, who daily collected a number of frogs, &c. and presented them to Gŭroorŭ, to conciliate him, and to prevent his devouring them. At last Kalēēyŭ, the king of the hydras, commanded his subjects to give the frogs to him, promising to protect them from Gŭroorŭ: but the latter on his arrival, finding no food, attacked and overcame Kalēēyŭ; who, though defeated, amused Gŭroorŭ by rehearsing some verses which no one understood but himself[k], till he had made good his retreat into a deep place of the river, where Gŭroorŭ durst not follow him for fear of the curse of the sage. In consequence of the serpent's remaining in this spot, the poison proceeding from his body had destroyed all the trees, water, &c. for two miles round, and whoever drank of the water died. About this time Krishnŭ was born; who in his childhood, on a certain day, discovering that a dreadful mortality existed among the cows and the boys who kept them, asked the reason, and was informed that they had been poisoned by the waters of the Yŭmoona. Krishnŭ then jumped from a tree into the river; overcame the serpent, and drove him out of the place. Kalēēyŭ, full of fear, asked where he was to go, for that Gŭroorŭ would certainly kill him. Krishnu, putting his foot on his head, assured him that when Gŭroorŭ discovered the mark of his foot, he would not destroy him. The waters now became wholesome; the trees gained their verdure; and the boys and cows were restored to life: but the pain arising from the poison in the wounds which Kalēēyŭ had given to Krishnŭ was intolerable. He therefore prayed to Doorga, who made him suck the milk from her own breast, by which he was immediately restored to health.

SECT. XV.—*Vishalakshēē*[l].

A CLAY image of this goddess is set up at Shyénŭhatēē, a village in Burdwan, which is become a place of great resort for pilgrims. Vast multitudes of buffaloes, sheep, goats, &c. are offered at different times to this goddess, not unfrequently for the destruction of enemies: sheep and goats are offered every day, and it is said that formerly human sacrifices were offered to this goddess. Many persons, it is affirmed, have obtained the privilege of conversing with their guardian deities in consequence of worshipping this image with very shocking ceremonies, while others thus employed are said to have been driven mad; yet some persons receive the name of Vishalakshēē as their guardian deity.

[k] These verses, it is said, now compose one of the kavyŭs called Pingŭlŭ.

[l] Of large or beautiful eyes.

SECT. XVI.—*Chŭndēē*[m].

IMAGES of this form of Doorga are not made at present in Bengal; but this goddess is worshipped by many of the bramhŭns, &c., before a metal cup containing the water of the Ganges. This worship is celebrated daily, or at the time of the full or change of the moon, or when the sun enters a new sign, or on the 9th of the moon.

The Kalikŭ-pooranŭ directs that birds, tortoises, alligators, fish, buffaloes, bulls, he-goats, ichneumons, wild boars, rhinoceroses, antelopes, guanas, rein-deer, lions, tigers, men, and blood drawn from the offerer's own body, be offered to this goddess. The following horrid incantation is addressed to the goddess Chŭndēē, when offering an animal in order to effect the destruction of an enemy: 'O goddess, of horrid form, O Chŭndika! eat, devour such a one, my enemy, O consort of fire! Salutation to fire! This is the enemy who has done me mischief, now personated by an animal: destroy him, O Mŭhamarēē! Sphéng! sphéng! eat, devour.'

Women sometimes make a vow to Chŭndēē to engage her to restore their children to health, or to obtain some other favour. If a person recover in whose name such a vow has been made, his neighbours ascribe it to Chŭndēe.

The exploits of this goddess are celebrated in a poem written by the poet Kŭnkŭnŭ, and recited on various occasions, under the name of Chŭndēē-ganŭ, or Chŭndēē-yatra.

SECT. XVII.—*Other forms of Doorga.*

Kamakhya[n].—This goddess is worshipped daily by persons of property before a pan of water, or some other substitute; and also by many shaktŭs on the 8th of the moon in both quarters. Those who worship her monthly, generally present some particular request in favour of themselves or families. At the Doorga festival, this goddess is also worshipped with many ceremonies and at a great expense. A few persons receive the initiatory rites of this goddess, and worship her as their guardian deity.

Vindhyŭ-vasinēē[o].—This is the image of a yellow female, sitting on a lion, with either four or eight arms: she is worshipped in the month Voishakhŭ, on the 9th, or on the 7th, 8th, or 9th of

[m] The wrathful.

[n] She who is called desire.

[o] She who dwelt on mount Vindhyŭ.

the increase of the moon : at Benares she is worshipped daily. The destruction of several giants is ascribed to this goddess.

Mŭngŭlŭ-Chŭndika[p].—This is the image of a yellow female, sitting on three skulls, clothed in red ; having in her right hand a book, and in her left a roodrakshŭ bead-roll. She is mostly worshipped by females, or rather by bramhŭns employed by them, in consequence of some particular distress in their families ; when they make a vow to the goddess to worship her a certain number of times if she will deliver them. Even the wives of Mŭsŭlmans sometimes send offerings to the house of a bramhŭn, to be presented to her with prayers. In the month Poushŭ a small festival is held in honour of this goddess.

Kŭmŭlé-kaminēē[q].—This is the image of a female sitting on the water-lily, swallowing an elephant, while with the left hand she is pulling it out of her throat[r].—She is worshipped on the 8th of Voishakhŭ, with the usual ceremonies and festivities.

Rajŭ-rajéshwŭrēē[s].—This goddess is represented as sitting on a throne, the three feet of which rest on the heads of Brŭmha, Vishnoo, and Shivŭ. She is worshipped on the 7th, 8th, and 9th of Voishakhŭ, with the ceremonies common to all the female deities to whom bloody sacrifices are offered.

Yoogadya[t] is represented as sitting on a lion, having ten arms. —A festival in honour of this goddess is held on the last day of Voishakhŭ, at Kshēērŭ, a village in Burdwan, where many animals are slain, and large quantities of spirituous liquors offered : the goddess at the time of worship is taken out of a tank near the temple. It is supposed that not less than 100,000 people assemble at this place on this occasion. Human sacrifices, I am informed, were formerly offered to this goddess.—So numerous are the sacrifices, that the water of the pool, in which the dead bodies are thrown immediately after decapitation, becomes the colour of blood. These bodies are taken out of the pool again in a little time after the sacrifice. The disciples of this goddess are very numerous.

Kŭroonamŭyee[u].—In some places the image of this goddess is set up and worshipped daily. At the festivals of Doorga, Kalēē, &c. she is worshipped in a more splendid manner. Some persons make vows to this goddess in times of distress, and many receive the initiatory rites by which she becomes their guardian deity.

p The fervent benefactress.

q She who sits on the water-lily.

r This image is said to owe its rise to a vision at sea ascribed to Shrēēmŭntŭ, a merchant, the particulars of which are related in the Kŭvee-kŭnkŭnŭ.

s The goddess who governs Brŭmha, Vishnoo, and Shivŭ.

t She who existed before the yoogŭs.

u The compassionate.

KALĒĒ.

SECT. XVIII.—*Other Forms of Doorga.*

Tripoora[x],	Prŭchŭnda[i],	Jŭya[u],
Twŭrita[y],	Chŭndagra[k],	Dévŭ-séna[x],
Nitya[z],	Dhōōma-vŭtēē[l],	Swŭdha[y],
Prŭstabinēē[a],	Ŭbhŭya[m],	Swaha[z],
Jŭyŭ-doorga[b],	Sŭtēē[n],	Shantēē[a],
Shōōlinēē[c],	Gourēē[o],	Toostee[b],
Mŭha-lŭkshmēē[d],	Pŭdma[p],	Poostee[c],
Shrēē-vidya[e],	Shŭchēē[q],	Dhritee[d],
Tripoora-soondŭrēē[f],	Médha[r],	Atmŭ-dévta[e],
Vŭnŭ-dévēē[g],	Savitrēē[s],	Koolŭ-dévta[f],
Chŭndŭ-nayika[h],	Vijŭya[t],	&c. &c.

All these goddesses are worshipped at the festivals of Doorga, as well as at other times, before the proper representative of a god, as water, the shalgramŭ, &c., but their images are not now made in Bengal. Many persons receive the initiatory rites of these deities, and pay their devotions daily to the particular goddess whom they have chosen as their guardian deity. Bloody sacrifices, fish, and spirituous liquors, are presented to these goddesses. The last sixteen are worshipped when rice is first given to a child, at the investiture with the poita, at the time of marriage, and in general at all the ceremonies performed for a son before marriage. Jŭyŭ-doorga is worshipped to obtain deliverance from danger.

Beside the above forms of Doorga, there are many others, whose names end with the word Bhoirŭvēē, viz., the terrific; and temples consecrated to Bhoirŭvŭ and Bhoirŭvēē are erected at many of the holy places visited by the Hindoo pilgrims. When a person performs any of the ceremonies of Hindoo worship at these places, he must first, on pain of meeting with some misfortune, worship these two deities.

SECT. XIX.—*Kalēē.*

THIS goddess may also be considered as a form of Bhŭgŭvŭtēē, or Doorga. According to the Chŭndēē, the image of Kalēē, at present worshipped in Bengal, had its origin in the story of Rŭktŭvēējŭ, already inserted in page 78[r]. Kalēē was so overjoyed at the victory she had obtained over this giant, that she danced till the

[x] She who governs the three worlds, heaven, earth, and the world of the hydras. [y] She who speedily executes her will. [z] The everlasting. [a] The praise-worthy. [b] The destroyer of the giant Doorgŭ. [c] She who wields the weapon of this name. [d] The great goddess of fortune. [e] The learned. [f] The beauty of the three worlds. [g] The goddess of forests. [h] The destroyer of the giant Chŭndŭ. [i] The wrathful. [k] The furious. [l] She who is the colour of smoke. [m] She who removes fear. [n] The wife of Shivŭ. [o] The yellow. [p] She who sits on the water-lily. [q] She who tells the truth of all. [r] The wise. [s] The cause of all. [t] The victorious. [u] Ditto. [x] The celestial heroine. [y] She who presides over the manes. [z] Ditto. [a] The comforter. [b] Ditto. [c] The nourisher. [d] The patient. [e] The goddess of souls. [f] She who presides over the generations of men.

earth shook to its foundation; and Shivŭ, at the intercession of the gods, was compelled to go to the spot to persuade her to desist. He saw no other way, however, of prevailing, than by throwing himself among the dead bodies of the slain. When the goddess saw that she was dancing on her husband, she was so shocked, that to express her surprise she put out her tongue to a great length, and remained motionless; and she is represented in this posture in almost all the images now made in Bengal.

The Ŭdhyatmŭ Ramayŭnŭ[g] gives another story from which the image of Kalēē may have originated:—Ramŭ, when he returned home with Sēēta from the destruction of Ravŭnŭ, began to boast of his achievements before his wife; who smiled, and said, 'You rejoice because you have killed a Ravŭnŭ with ten heads; but what would you say to a Ravŭnŭ with 1,000 heads?' 'Destroy him,' said Ramŭ. Sēēta, again smiling, advised him to stay at home; but he, collecting all the monkies, the giants, and his own soldiers together, with Sēēta, Lŭkshmŭnŭ, Shŭtrŭghnŭ, and Bhŭrŭtŭ, immediately departed for Shŭtŭ-dwēēpŭ to meet this new Ravŭnŭ; sending Hŭnoomanŭ before to discover the residence of this thousand-headed monster, and bring a description of his person. Hŭnoomanŭ, after a little play with him, returned to Ramŭ, who soon after attacked the giant: but he, looking forward, beheld Ramŭ's army as so many children; and discharged three arrows, one of which sent all the monkies to Kishkindha, their place of residence; another sent all the giants to Lŭnka, (Ceylon;) and the third sent all the soldiers to Ŭyodhya, Ramŭ's capital. Ramŭ, thunderstruck at being thus left alone in a moment, and thinking that all his adherents had been at once annihilated, began to weep: when Sēēta, laughing at her husband, immediately assumed the terrific form of Kalēē, and furiously attacked this thousand-headed Ravŭnŭ. The conflict lasted ten years, but she at length killed the giant, drank his blood, and began to dance and toss about the limbs of his body. Her dancing shook the earth to its centre, so that all the gods, filled with alarm, applied to Shivŭ: but he declared that he almost despaired of calming her passions, for she was mad with joy; he promised, however, to do all that could be expected from a god in so desperate a case; but, pausing for some time, and seeing no other alternative, he, in the presence of the assembled gods, threw himself among the dead bodies under her feet. Brŭmha called to the goddess, and said, 'O goddess! what art thou doing? Dost thou not see that thou art trampling on thy husband?' She stooped, and saw Shivŭ under her feet; and was so ashamed, that she stood still, and threw out her tongue to an uncommon length[h].

[g] There are four Ramayŭnŭs, one written by Valmēēkee, another by Vyasŭ-dēvŭ, and two others, called the Ŭdbootŭ and the Udhyatmŭ Ramayŭnŭs; but the others are in little estimation compared with the work of Valmēēkee.

[h] When the Hindoo women are shocked or ashamed at any thing, they put out their tongues, as a mode of expressing their feelings.

By this means Shivŭ saved the universe ; and Sēēta, again assuming her proper form, went home with Ramŭ and his brothers.

In the images commonly worshipped, Kalēē is represented as a very black female, with four arms ; having in one hand a scymitar, and in another the head of a giant, which she holds by the hair ; another hand is spread open bestowing a blessing ; and with the other she is forbidding fear. She wears two dead bodies for ear-rings, and a necklace of skulls ; and her tongue hangs down to her chin. The hands of several giants are hung as a girdle round her loins, and her tresses fall down to her heels. Having drank the blood of the giants she has slain in combat, her eye-brows, are bloody, and the blood is falling in a stream down her breast ; her eyes are red like those of a drunkard. She stands with one leg on the breast of her husband Shivŭ, and rests the other on his thigh[i].

This deity is equal in ferocity to any of the preceding forms of Doorga. In the Kalika pooranŭ, MEN are pointed out, amongst other animals, as proper for sacrifice. It is here said that the blood of a tiger pleases the goddess for one hundred years, and the blood of a lion, a rein-deer, or a MAN, a thousand. But by the sacrifice of THREE MEN, she is pleased 100,000 years ! I insert two or three extracts from the sanguinary Chapter of the Kalika pooranŭ :—' Let a human victim be sacrificed at a place of holy worship, or at a cemetery where dead bodies are buried. Let the oblation be performed in the part of the cemetery called hérŭkŭ, or at a temple of Kamakshya, or on a mountain. Now attend to the mode : The human victim is to be immolated in the east division, which is sacred to Bhoirŭvŭ ; the head is to be presented in the south division, which is looked upon as the place of skulls sacred to Bhoirŭvŭ ; and the blood is to be presented in the west division, which is denominated hérŭkŭ. Having immolated a human victim, with all the requisite ceremonies at a cemetery, or holy place, let the sacrificer be cautious not to cast his eyes upon it. The victim must be a person of good appearance, and be prepared by ablutions, and requisite ceremonies, (such as eating consecrated food the day before, and by abstinence from flesh and venery,) and must be adorned with chaplets of flowers, and besmeared with sandal wood. Then causing the victim to face the north, let the sacrificer worship the several deities presiding over the different parts of the victim's body : let the worship be then paid to the victim himself by his name. Let him worship Brŭmha in the victim's rhŭndrŭ, i. e., cave of Brŭmha, cavity in the skull, under the spot where the *sutura coronalis* and *sagittalis* meet. Let him worship the earth in his nose, &c.—Worshipping

[i] The image of Minerva, it will be recollected, was that of a threatening goddess, exciting terror : on her shield she bore the head of a gorgon. Sir W. Jones considers Kalēē as the Proserpine of the Greeks.

the king of serpents, let him pronounce the following incantation: O best of men! O most auspicious! O thou who art an assemblage of all the deities, and most exquisite! bestow thy protection on me; save me, thy devoted; save my sons, my cattle, and kindred; preserve the state, the ministers belonging to it, and all friends; and as death is unavoidable, part with (thy organs or) life, doing an act of benevolence. Bestow upon me, O most auspicious! the bliss which is obtained by the most austere devotion, by acts of charity, and performance of religious ceremonies; and at the same time, O most excellent! attain supreme bliss thyself. May thy auspices, O most auspicious! keep me secure from rakshŭsŭs, pishachŭs, terrors, serpents, bad princes, enemies, and other evils; and, death being inevitable, charm Bhŭgŭvŭtēē in thy last moments by copious streams of blood spouting from the arteries of thy fleshly neck.'—When this has been done, O my children! the victim is even as as myself, and the guardian deities of the ten quarters take place in him; then Brŭmha and all the other deities assemble in the victim; and be he ever so great a sinner, he becomes pure from sin; and when pure, his blood changes to ambrosia, and he gains the love of Mŭhadévēē, the goddess of the yogŭ nidru, (i.e., the tranquil repose of the mind from an abstraction of ideas,) who is the goddess of the whole universe, the very universe itself. He does not return for a considerable length of time in the human form, but becomes a ruler of the gŭnŭ dévtas, and is much respected by me myself. The victim who is impure from sin, or ordure and urine, Kamakshya will not even hear named. The blind, the crippled, the aged, the sick, the afflicted with ulcers, the hermaphrodite, the imperfectly formed, the scarred, the timid, the leprous, the dwarfish, and the perpetrator of mŭha patŭkŭ, (heinous offences, such as slaying a bramhŭn, drinking spirits, stealing gold, or defiling a spiritual teacher's bed,) one under twelve years of age, one who is impure from the death of a kinsman, &c., one who is impure from the death of mŭha gooroo, (father and mother), which impurity lasts for one whole year—these severally are unfit subjects for immolation, even though rendered pure by sacred texts. Let not a bramhŭn or a chŭndalŭ be sacrificed; nor a prince, nor that which has been already presented to a bramhŭn, or a deity; nor the offspring of a prince; nor one who has conquered in battle; nor the offspring of a bramhŭn, or of a kshŭtriyŭ; nor a childless brother; nor a father; nor a learned person; nor one who is unwilling; nor the maternal uncle of the sacrificer. The day previous to a human sacrifice, let the victim be prepared by the text manŭshtŭkŭ and three dévēē gŭndhŭ shŭktŭs, and the texts wadrŭngŭ, and by touching his head with the axe, and besmearing the axe with sandal, &c. perfumes, and then taking some of the sandal, &c. from off the axe, and besmearing the victim's neck therewith. If the severed head of a human victim smile, it indicates increase of prosperity and long life to the sacrificer, without doubt; and if it speak, whatever it says will come to pass.'

This work further lays down directions for a person's drawing blood from himself, and offering it to the goddess, repeating the following incantation : 'Hail! supreme delusion! Hail! goddess of the universe! Hail! thou who fulfillest the desires of all. May I presume to offer thee the blood of my body ; and wilt thou deign to accept it, and be propitious towards me.'

A person's cutting off his own flesh, and presenting it to the goddess as a burnt-sacrifice, is another method of pleasing this infernal deity : 'Grant me, O goddess! bliss, in proportion to the fervency with which I present thee with my own flesh, invoking thee to be propitious to me. Salutation to thee again and again, under the mysterious syllables *ŭng, ŭng*.'

A person's burning his body, by applying the burning wick of a lamp to it, is also very acceptable to Kalēē, &c. On this occasion this incantation is used : 'Hail! goddess! Salutation to thee, under the syllables *ŭng, ŭng*. To thee I present this auspicious luminary, fed with the flesh of my body, enlightening all around, and exposing to light also the inward recesses of my soul.'[k]

It is observed in this work, that the head or the blood of an animal, in its simple state, forms a proper offering to a goddess, but that flesh must be presented as a burnt-offering. Other Tŭntrŭs observe, that the eating of the flesh of men, cows, and swine, and drinking spirits, after these things have been offered to an idol, must be done in secret ; or the person will commit a great crime, and sink into poverty. I am credibly informed, that very many bramhŭns in Bengal eat cow's flesh, and, after they have been offered to an idol, drink spirits, though none of them will publicly acknowledge it.

Thieves frequently pay their devotions to Kalēē, and to all the goddesses to whom bloody sacrifices are offered, under the hope of carrying on their villainous designs with security and success[l]. A gang of ten persons, perhaps, agree to plunder a house ; who meet together in a dark night, under a tree where an image of Siddéshwŭrēē is placed ; and bring to the spot spirituous liquors, fish, and other offerings. One of the company, a bramhŭn, goes through the ceremonies of worship : at the close of which a bloody sacrifice is offered, and the instrument worshipped which is to cut through the wall of the house ; at which time the following incantation from the Chorŭ-pŭnchashika is read: 'O! Sindhŭkatee! (the name of

[k] See Mr. Blaquiere's translation of the Sanguinary Chapter, Asiatic Researches, vol. v.——The author hopes Mr. Blaquiere will excuse the liberty he has taken of altering his spelling of Sŭngskritŭ words, as he has done it merely to preserve uniformity throughout the work.

[l] One of Jupiter's names, it is well known, was Prædator, because plunder was offered to him.

the instrument formed by the goddess Vishaī! Kalēē commanded thee to cut a passage into the house, to cut through stones, bones, bricks, wood, the earth, and mountains, and, through the blessing of Ŭnadya[m], to make a way by cutting the earth from the house of the Malinēē to that of Vidya[n], and that the soil brought out should be carried away by the wind. Haree-jhee[o] and Chamŭnda have given this blessing, and Kamakshya (Kalēē) has given the command.' After the reading of this incantation, the thieves sit down to eat and drink the things that have been offered; and when nearly intoxicated, they gird their garments firmly round their loins, rub their bodies well with oil, daub their eyes with lamp-black, and repeat an incantation to enable them to see in the dark; and thus proceed to the spot: when they cut a hole through the wall, plunder the house, and sometimes murder the inhabitants.

Sometime ago, two Hindoos were executed at Calcutta for robbery. Before they entered upon their work of plunder, they worshipped Kalēē, and offered prayers before her image, that they might be protected by the goddess in the act of thieving. It so happened, that the goddess left these disciples in the lurch; they were detected, tried, and sentenced to be hanged. While under sentence of death, a native Catholic, in the same place and circumstances, was visited by a Roman Catholic priest to prepare him for death. These Hindoos now reflected, that as Kalēē had not protected them, notwithstanding they had paid their devotions to her, there could be no hope that she would save them after death; they might as well, therefore renounce their caste: which resolution they communicated to their fellow-prisoner, who procured for them a prayer from the Catholic priest, translated into the Bengalee language. I saw a copy of this prayer in the hands of the native Catholic who gave me this account. These men at last, out of pure revenge upon Kalēē, died in the faith of the Virgin Mary: and the Catholics, after the execution, made a grand funeral for them; as these per-

[m] A name of Kalēē, which means, without beginning.

[n] Soondŭrŭ, the son of Goonŭ-sindhoo, raja of Kanchee-poorŭ, was overcome by the charms of Vidya, the daughter of Vēērŭ-singhŭ, the raja of Burdwan. For the purposes of courtship, he concealed himself at the house of a flower-seller (Malinēē) near the palace of Vēērŭ-singhŭ, and began to pay his devotions to the goddess Kalēē; who gave him this incantation, and the instrument Sindhŭkatee, that he might cut his way to his fair one. One night, however, Soondŭrŭ was caught in the palace, and seized as a thief. As he was led from prison to the place of execution, he composed fifty verses in praise of the raja's daughter, which verses have since received the name of Chorŭ-pŭnchashika. The Hindoos add, that when they were about to execute Soondŭrŭ, the cords by which he was bound miraculously burst asunder, and the executioners fell senseless to the ground; in consequence, the execution was postponed, and the next night Kalēē appeared to Vēērŭ-singhŭ in a dream, and directed him to marry his daughter to Soondŭrŭ; who was not a thief, but the son of the raja of Kanchee-poorŭ, a very proper person to become his son-in-law. The marriage was soon after celebrated in the most splendid manner.

[o] The Hindoos say, that a female of the Haree cast was once honoured with an interview by the goddess Kamakshya, who delivered to her a variety of incantations, now used by the lowest casts for the most ridiculous, as well as brutal and wicked purposes.

sons, they said, embraced the Catholic faith, and renounced their cast, *from conviction.*

Agŭm-vagēēshŭ, a learned Hindoo, about five hundred years ago, formed the image of Kalēē according to the preceding description, and worshipped it monthly, choosing for this purpose the darkest nights in the month ; he made and set up the image, worshipped it, and destroyed it, on the same night. At present the greater number of the worshippers of Kalēē hold a festival to her honour on the last night of the decrease of the moon in the month Kartikŭ, and call it the Shyama[p] festival.

A few persons celebrate the worship of Kalēē at the full moon in Kartikŭ ; the ceremonies of which are performed before a picture of this goddess, drawn on a stiff mat of reeds seven or eight feet long. This festival lasts three days, and on the fourth the picture is thrown into the river.

Some also worship Kalēē for one night on the 14th of the decrease of the moon, in the month Maghŭ ; and a few rich men do so monthly, on the last night of the moon : while others worship this goddess in the month Jyoisht'hŭ, when it is called the Phŭlŭ-hŭrēē festival, on account of the many mangoes, jack fruits. &c. offered to her.

A few years ago, I went to the house of Kalēē-shŭnkŭrŭ-ghoshŭ, at Calcutta, at the time of the Shyama festival, to see the animals sacrified to Kalēē. The buildings where the worship was performed were raised on four sides, with an area in the middle. The image was placed at the north end, with the face to the south ; and the two side rooms, and one of the end rooms opposite the image, were filled with spectators : in the area were the animals devoted to sacrifice, and also the executioner, with Kalēē-shŭnkŭrŭ, a few attendants, and about twenty persons to throw the animal down, and hold it in the post, while the head was cut off. The goats were sacrificed first, then the buffaloes, and last of all two or three rams. In order to secure the animals, ropes were fastened round their legs ; they were then thrown down, and the neck placed in a piece of wood fastened into the ground, and made open at the top like the space betwixt the prongs of a fork. After the animal's neck was fastened in the wood by a peg which passed over it, the men who held it pulled forcibly at the heels ; while the executioner, with a broad heavy axe, cut off the head at one blow : the heads were carried in an elevated posture by an attendant, (dancing as he went,) the blood running down him on all sides, into the presence of the goddess. Kalēē-shŭnkŭrŭ, at the close, went up to the executioner, took him in his arms, and gave him several presents of cloths, &c. The heads and blood of the animals, as well as different meat-offerings, are presented with

p A name of Kalēē, meaning black.

incantations as a feast to the goddess ; after which clarified butter is burnt on a prepared altar of sand. Never did I see men so eagerly enter into the shedding of blood, nor do I think any butchers could slaughter animals more expertly. The place literally swam with blood. The bleating of the animals, the numbers slain, and the ferocity of the people employed, actually made me unwell ; and I returned about midnight, filled with horror and indignation.

The gifts to bramhŭns and guests at this festival are numerous, and in some instances very expensive. The bramhŭns, and then the family and other guests, are entertained, when the spirituous liquors which have been presented to the goddess are drank privately by those who are in the secret. The festival closes with the dances and songs before the goddess.

The reader may form an idea how much idolatry prevailed at the time when the Hindoo monarchy flourished, from the following circumstance, which belongs to a modern period, when the Hindoo authority in Hindoost'hanŭ was almost extinct.—Raja Krishnŭ-chŭndrŭ-rayŭ, and his two immediate successors, in the month Kartikŭ, annually gave orders to all the people over whom they had a nominal authority to keep the Shyama festival, and threatened every offender with the severest penalties on non-compliance. In consequence of these orders, in more than ten thousand houses, in one night, in the zillah of Krishnŭ-nŭgŭrŭ, the worship of this goddess was celebrated. The number of animals destroyed could not be less than ten thousand. The officiating bramhŭns, especially those who perform religious ceremonies for shōōdrŭs, were greatly perplexed, as a single bramhŭn had to perform the ceremonies of worship at two hundred houses, situated in different villages, in one night. All the joiners, barbers, or blacksmiths, in fifteen or twenty villages, in many instances have but one officiating priest, the bramhŭns in general being unwilling to incur the disgrace which arises from performing religious services for shōōdrŭs.

Eeshanŭ-chŭndrŭ-rayŭ, the grandson of Krishnŭ-chŭndrŭ-rayŭ, in certain years, presented to Kalēē eighty thousand pounds weight of sweetmeats, the same quantity of sugar, a thousand women's cloth garments, the same number of women's China silk garments, a thousand offerings, including rice, plantains, peas, &c., and immolated a thousand buffaloes, a thousand goats, and the same number of sheep ; which altogether could not cost less than ten thousand rupees, while the other expenses amounted to scarcely less than twenty thousand. To defray these expenses, this rajah sold the greater part of his patrimony ; and in this and other idolatrous customs, he and other Hindoo rajahs have expended almost the whole of their estates.

Raja Ram-Krishnŭ also expended very large sums of money

upon the worship of Kalēē. He set up a stone image of this goddess at Vŭrahŭ-nŭgŭrŭ; on which occasion he is said to have spent a lack of rupees. He also endowed this image with such a large revenue, that at present five hundred persons are maintained there daily. In the service of this goddess he has nearly reduced himself to poverty, though formerly from the rents of the lands, &c., he used to pay fifty-two lakhs of rupees annually into the Company's treasury.

Kalēē is the guardian deity of very many of the Bengalees, especially of the bramhŭns.

At Kalēē-ghatŭ, near Calcutta, is a celebrated image of this goddess, 'whom (in the opinion of the Hindoos) all Asia, and 'the whole world worshippeth.' Having obtained an account of this tĕmple from a bramhŭn whom I sent to Kalēē-ghatŭ for the purpose, I here lay it before my readers :—

The temple consists of one room, with a large pavement around it. The image is a large black stone, to which a horrid face, partly cut and partly painted, has been given; there are neither arms nor legs, a cloth covering all the lower part which should be the body. In front of the temple is a very large building capable of seating two hundred people; in which, and on the pavement around the temple, many bramhŭns daily sit reading the Chŭndēē, a work on the wars of Kalēē: on some days, as many as a thousand bramhŭns may be seen thus employed. Beyond this building, in front of the image, the animals for sacrifice are slain. Not fewer than four thousand persons assemble on particular occasions at this temple, especially at the Shyama and Doorga festivals; and, twice a week, on the Chétŭla[q] market days, two thousand people or more visit this place, multitudes of whom (my informer says, not less than a thousand) present offerings. At these times it is common for a Hindoo to go up to the temple, and, presenting himself at the door with joined hands, to address himself thus to the idol: 'Oh! mother! I am going to the market for such and such a purpose. If thou grant me success, I will on the next market day present offerings to thee to the amount of.'— Or he says to another person standing near, 'See, brother, I have promised to mother so and so, if she will accomplish my wishes in the market.'[r]

About nine o'clock each day, the bramhŭn who in turn performs the duties at the temple, and who receives the offerings of the day, after cleaning and bathing the image, puts on it the garlands of flowers and other ornaments, sweeps the temple, and then throws open the doors, calling out, 'Victory to the great Kalēē!

[q] An adjoining village.

[r] It is said that formerly, especially in times of scarcity, numbers of men were sold at this market.

Victory to the great Kalēē!' These compliments on different mornings he changes at pleasure. After this, persons going to bathe, or coming from bathing, approach the door of the temple, and bow to the goddess: and now the daily worship is performed, which occupies about an hour; after which men and women are seen bringing their offerings to the idol, which continue to be presented during the greater part of the day. Some merely present them, without asking for any blessing: these persons take away a few flowers, or any other trifle of what they have offered, as something that will secure the good of the family; and friends on a visit at the house of such a person beg any thing of this kind, and eat it, or wear it in their hair. Other visitors to the temple leave part of the offerings there, and take away the other part to present to their friends. Others make a vow, while the offering is presented to the image, in some such words as these: 'Oh! goddess! mother Kalēē! If thou wilt deliver me out of such or such a trouble, or wilt bestow such or such a blessing, I will present to thee [here the petitioner repeats the names of all the offerings or bloody sacrifices.'] Disputes arise almost daily in the temple betwixt the worshippers and the priests respecting the offerings, and not unfrequently a violent scramble takes place for the meat-offerings in the presence of the goddess herself: the officiating bramhŭn says, 'Who is to have these offerings'? to which the worshipper replies, 'Oh! sir! our family priest always receives these things. I must carry them home for him.' Or a man bringing offerings procures a bramhŭn to go and tell a lie in the presence of the goddess, saying to him, 'Sir, the bramhŭns at the temple of Kalēē are such notorious cheats, that of all I give to the goddess, she will probably get nothing but a few flowers; and they are so rapacious that I shall never get these offerings out of their hands:' on which this bramhŭn carries the offerings to the temple, and declares, that they belong to the bramhŭns of such a temple, and must be returned to them. By these contrivances, the offerer obtains what he has given to the goddess; and, giving part to the bramhŭn who has extricated him from the rapacious hands of the proprietors of the temple, he takes the remainder home. About three o'clock in the afternoon, food is placed before the goddess, consisting of rice, greens, roots, fruits, milk, curds, clarified butter, flesh, spirituous liquors[s] (in a concealed form,) sweetmeats, &c. &c. Generally about 250 pounds of rice are cooked daily, but at particular time twice or thrice as much. After reserving as much as is necessary for his own family, the officiating bramhŭn sells the rest of the offerings to devout visitors or neighbours, and gives away what he cannot sell. When a bloody sacrifice is offered, the offerer either pays the priest for his trouble, or

[s] It is affirmed that the greater number of grown up persons in this village drink spirits. Bramhŭns may be seen in front of the temple, drinking spirits at noon-day; and religious mendicants walking about, naked, without the least sense of shame.

gives up the slaughtered animal. The slayer also receives a fee. Of this flesh, the officiating bramhŭn keeps what he pleases, and sells the rest to bramhŭns, shōōdrŭs, Portuguese, and persons from all parts of the neighbourhood.[t]

The daily offerings to this goddess are astonishingly numerous. On days when the weather is very unfavourable, not less than three hundred and twenty pounds of rice, twenty-four of sugar, forty of sweetmeats, twelve of clarified butter, ten of flour, ten quarts of milk, a peck of pease, eight hundred plantains, and other things, (the price of which may amount to about five shillings,) are offered, and eight or ten goats sacrificed. On common days, of all these things three times the quantity; and at great festivals, or when a rich man comes to worship, ten, twenty, or forty times this quantity; and as many as forty or fifty buffaloes and a thousand goats are slain.

Raja Nŭvŭ-Krishnŭ, of Calcutta, about fifty years ago, when on a visit to Kalēē-ghatŭ, expended, it is said, not less than 100,000 rupees on the worship of this goddess. Amongst the offerings was a gold necklace valued at 10,000 rupees, and, beside other ornaments, a rich bed, silver plates, dishes, and basons; sweetmeats, and other food sufficient for the entertainment of a thousand persons; and trifling presents of money to near two thousand of the poor.

About twenty years ago, Jŭyŭ-Narayŭnŭ-Ghoshalŭ, of Kiddŭr-poorŭ, near Calcutta, expended 25,000 rupees at this place: when he sacrificed twenty-five buffaloes, one hundred and eight goats, and five sheep; and presented to the goddess four silver arms, two gold eyes, and many gold and silver ornaments.

About ten years ago, a merchant from the east of Bengal expended 5,000 rupees on the worship of this goddess, beside the price of a thousand goats which were slaughtered.

In the year 1810, a bramhŭn from the east of Bengal expended on this idol about four thousand rupees, with part of which he bought a golden necklace, the beads of which were in the shape of giants' skulls.

In the year 1811, Gopēē-mohŭnŭ, a bramhŭn of Calcutta, expended ten thousand rupees in the worship of this goddess; but, being a voishnŭvŭ, he did not offer any bloody sacrifices.

The Hindoos, it seems, are not the only persons who worship

[t] The women belonging to the temple have become such good cooks, that it is not uncommon for persons to pay for a dinner from their hands, preferring it to any thing they could get elsewhere.

this black stone: I have received accounts several times of Europeans, or their native mistresses, going to this temple, and expending thousands of rupees in offerings. The bramhŭn with whom I wrote this account declares, that when he was a student at Vŭrisha, near Kalēē-ghatŭ, he several times saw the wives of Europeans come in palanqueens with offerings; though I suppose these ladies were born in India. But the proprietors of the temple positively assured this bramhŭn, (as he says,) that very frequently European men presented offerings, soliciting some favour at the hands[u] of the goddess; and that very lately a gentleman in the Hon. Company's service, who had gained a cause at law, presented thank-offerings to Kalēē which cost two or three thousand rupees[x]. I confess that I very reluctantly insert these accounts, because I should hope they mostly originate in wilful misrepresentation on the part of the bramhŭns of the temple, or in mistake. I suppose some Portuguese (who also go by the name Sahéb) may present offerings, and pray to this goddess—hence one source of misinformation; the mistresses of Europeans are supplied with money by their retainers, and hence the worship not unfrequently passes off, with many a triumph over degraded Christianity, as the worship of such a European; and many Europeans, who go for curiosity to see the temple and the image, inconsiderately or wantonly give presents to the clamorous and greedy bramhŭns, who proclaim it as an offering to their goddess. Actions the most innocent, (even going to view the image,) are construed by these ignorant idolaters into an approval of idolatry. A European who was lately there, says my informant, to make a drawing of the image, when he departed gave the officiating bramhŭn a gold mohŭr, and this present was probably enrolled among the gifts to the temple.

It is further affirmed, that many Mŭssŭlmans (four or five hundred) present offerings to Kalēē monthly—so strangely has the veneration for this image seized the minds of the natives! And it is added, that an equal number of prostitutes, from all parts of Bengal, pay their devotions at this temple: some pray for the health of their paramours, and others that great numbers may visit their houses of ill fame. It is not uncommon for a loose female to say to her paramour, after his recovery from sickness, 'I made vows to Kalēē, that if she would restore you to health, I would present her with such and such offerings: you are recovered; and I must now go and perform my vows.' Such a female sometimes thus prays for her paramour—'O mother Kalee! I pray for ——. If thou wilt increase his wealth, [or remove sickness from him—or make him successful in such a concern—or increase his attachment

[u] Silver *hands*, and gold *tongues* and *eyes* are among the presents made by rich men to this goddess. Such is the stupidity of idolaters.

[x] It is probable, that the real worshipper in this instance was a head-servant of this gentleman's; though the expense might be defrayed by the master. Without thinking of the guilt of such conduct, I have known frequent instances of Europeans making presents to their servants for the avowed purpose of idol worship.

to me, that he may always follow my advice] I will present to thee all these offerings [here she repeats the names of what she intends to give].' When she returns home, she takes off all her ornaments, laying them aside till her vow be either fulfilled or abandoned.

Merchants[y] and tradesmen present offerings to Kalēē once, twice, or thrice a year, to obtain success in their concerns;—many rich men (thirty or forty) place bramhŭns at this temple to worship the goddess, to walk round the temple, and read the Chŭndēē, daily in their names;—others place bramhŭns here for these purposes, for two or three months in the year;—sepoys from all parts of Hindoost'hanŭ resort to this temple as often as they can obtain leave of absence;—mothers present offerings, praying for the recovery of their children, and promising to bring the restored child in their arms when they come to fulfil their vows;[z] or, that it shall be invested with the poita,[a] or pass through some other ceremony at the temple;—servants in search of employment make vows to the goddess to present her with a month's wages, if she will raise them to such a situation;—in a word, the occasions of drawing people to this famous temple are as endless as the superstitious hopes and fears, the crimes and the wants of the worshippers.

Goats are devoted to Kalēē, and kept, in some cases, for a long time, till the owner be able to meet the other expenses attending the offerings and worship. These animals are called the goats of Kalēē.

The village of Kalēē-ghŭttŭ (or Kalēē-ghatŭ) owes the greater part of its present population to this temple; from which near two hundred persons derive their subsistence, exclusive of the proprietors, who amount to about thirty families. Some proprietors have a day in turn, others half a day, and others two or three hours; to whom all the offerings presented in the portion of time thus apportioned belong. All these families have become rich.

In the month Maghŭ, a festival is held in various places of Bengal in honour of Ghatoo, the god who presides over blotches on the skin; but the assembly at Kalēē-ghatŭ is very great. At the time of swinging in Choitrŭ also, the concourse of people at this place is also very large. See the account of Shivŭ.

[y] Hindoo merchants engaged in foreign commerce, after the successful voyage of a ship in which they had property, frequently present thank-offerings to this goddess.

[z] The hair of some children is not cut at all till the vow be fulfilled; others only separate a lock of the child's hair, tying it up in a bunch A large hillock of human hair, collected at the times of shaving when vows have been fulfilled, is formed near the temple.

[a] A bramhŭn once assured me, that he had seen not less than three hundred boys invested with the poita in one day at this place; on which occasion many bloody sacrifices were offered. The concourse of people was immense.

I here add a rough account of what is expended on this idol monthly :—

	Rs.	As.	P.
Buffaloes slain, (5)	30	0	0
Goats ditto, (1,000)	800	0	0
Sheep ditto, (30)...	40	0	0
Rice, (200 cwt.)	440	0	0
Salt, Spices, Pease, Fish, &c.	200	0	0
Clarified Butter, ...	7	0	0
Milk and Curds, ...	5	0	0
Sugar, (11 cwt.)	105	0	0
Sweetmeats, (22 cwt.)	360	0	0
Plantains, (25,000)	50	0	0
Evening offerings,...	60	0	0
Meat offerings,...	90	0	0
Dressed food, ...	80	0	0
Fees, ...	233	0	0
Travelling Expenses, ...	300	0	0
Alms given to the poor by visitors,...	200	0	0
Extraordinaries from rich men, and at festivals, ...	3,000	0	0
Sa. Rs.	6,000	0	0

Seventy-two Thousand Rupees annually, or Nine Thousand Pounds sterling.

Sect. XX.—*Other Forms of Kalēē, &c.*

Chamŭnda[b].—This image, which is similar to that of Kalēē, except that Chamŭnda is represented with two giants' heads in her hands, and as sitting on a dead body, is seldom or never made. The goddess is worshipped at the festival of Doorga, on three different days.

Shmŭshanŭ-Kulēē[c].—When this image is made, other figures are introduced, as those of the giants Shoombhŭ and Nishoombhŭ, of jackals, dead bodies, &c. These giants are represented as sitting on elephants, throwing arrows at the goddess ; while the latter is standing on her husband, and aiming blows at them with a sword. The ceremonies of worship are like those performed in honour of Kalēē : the worship begins at the total wane of the moon in Maghŭ, and continues for three nights. Revelling is carried to the greatest

[b] She who seized Chŭndŭ and Mŭndŭ, two giants.

[c] This name denotes, that Kalēē dwells in the place of burning the dead, and presides over cemeteries. Shmŭshanŭ means a cemetery.

pitch: some of the worshippers, and not unfrequently the sons of rich men, dance before the image naked, 'glorying in their shame.' A few Hindoos adopt this goddess as their guardian deity.

Manŭvŭ-Kalēē[d].—Another form of Kalēē, whose image it resembles except in the colour, which is blue. The worship is celebrated on the fifteenth night of the decrease of the moon in Maghŭ:—the present fruit, diversion;—and hereafter, heaven. Such are the ideas of the poor deluded Hindoos. A whole village sometimes joins to defray the expense, at other times a rich man bears it alone. Many bloody sacrifices are offered, and great shew made, especially with illuminations; to which are added dancing, singing, music, &c.

Phŭlŭ-hurēē.[e]—This form of Kalēē is that of a black female, with four arms, standing on the breast of Shivŭ. She is worship- at the total wane of the moon in the month Jyoisht'hŭ, or in any other month, at the pleasure of the worshipper. The offerings are numerous, especially of fruits: and buffaloes, goats, and sheep, are sacrificed. The day after the worship, the image is thrown into the river.

Bhŭdrŭ-Kalēē.[f]—An image similar to that of Kalēē; the worship also resembles that which is paid to that goddess. The image is in some places preserved, and worshipped daily.

Oogrŭ-chŭnda.[g] is worshipped at the total wane of the moon in the month Kartikŭ: in some places temples made of clay are erected in honour of this goddess, in which she is worshipped either daily or monthly.

Anŭndŭ-mŭyēē.[h]—A black female, with four arms, sitting on a throne; to whom a number of temples are dedicated, containing stone or clay images of the goddess. She is worshipped daily; also on fortunate days, at the pleasure of her numerous disciples; as well as at the great festivals of Doorga, Kalēē, &c. when bloody sacrifices are offered to her.

Nŭvŭ-pŭtrika.[i]—These nine goddesses are worshipped at the great festivals, but with the greatest shew as that of Doorga; when these assistants of Doorga in her wars are represented by nine branches of different trees: Rŭmbha, by a plantain;[k] Kŭchwēē-rōōpa, by a kŭchwēē;[l] Hŭridra, by a hŭridra;[m] Jŭyŭntēē by a jŭyŭntēē;[n] Vilwarōōpa, by a vilwŭ;[o] Darimēē, by a darimu;[p]

[d] Viz., in the form of man.

[e] She who receives much fruit. [f] The beneficent. [g] The furious. [h] The joyful.

[i] The nine goddesses. [k] Musa paradisaica. [l] Arum esculentum. [m] Curcuma longa. [n] Æschynomene seshan, [o] Ægle marmelos. [p] Punica granatum.

Ŭshoka, by a an ŭshokŭ;[q] Manŭka, by a manŭ;[r] and Dhanyŭ-rōōpa, by a dhanyŭ.[s]

Bhēēmŭ-chŭndēē.[t]—This image is made and worshipped at Benares: in Bengal also the goddess is worshipped, especially on a Tuesday, before another image, or a pan of water, or some appointed representative of an idol.

Upŭra-jita.[u]—There is no public festival in honour of this goddess, nor is her image set up for worship; but in times of sickness she is worshipped before the shalgramŭ, when forms of praise from the Tŭntrŭs are addressed to her.

Vimula.[x]—A stone image of this idol is worshipped in one of the temples erected in Orissa, near the famous temple of Jŭgŭn-nat'hŭ. Bloody sacrifices are offered to this goddess; but as this place is sacred to Vishnoo, these offerings are made in secret. Vimŭla is also worshipped in Bengal at the festivals of Doorga and Kalēē.

Siddhéshwŭrēē.[y]—In many villages in Bengal one, and in some large villages several of these images are set up. They are in general made of clay; but some are of stone. The image is commonly the property of one family, who worship her every day: others in the village worship her when they choose; but all the gifts and offerings come to the person who owns the image. If a child have a fever, the parents worship the goddess that it may recover, and promise to present various offerings to her if she be propitious. If a woman want a son, she procures a bramhŭn to worship the goddess in her name;—if another person be seeking employment, he prays the goddess to favour him;—if a koolinŭ bramhŭn wish his daughter to be married, he intercedes with the goddess, and promises to celebrate her worship if she be favourable. On all occasions of particular distress or want, the people resort to these images with their presents and vows. Thieves also worship Siddhéshwŭrēē, that they may be favoured with her smiles and be protected in thieving.[z] Honest and poor people also worship this image to obtain protection from thieves. An annual festival is held in honour of Siddhéshwŭrēē on the same day as the Shyama festival.

[q] Jonesia asoca. [r] Arum macrorhyzon. [s] Coriandrum sativum. [t] The terrific. [u] The unconquerable. [x] She who purifies. [y] She who fulfils the wishes of her worshippers.

[z] The goddess Laverna, it is well known, was the protectress of thieves, who, from her, were named Laverniones, and who worshipped her, that their designs and intrigues might be successful: her image was a head without a body.

SECT. XXI.—*Lŭkshmēē.*

Is called the goddess of prosperity: she is painted yellow, and sits on the water-lily, holding in her right hand the pashŭ, (a rope,) and in the left, a necklace.

Vishnoo is said to have obtained this goddess at the churning of the sea[a]; at which time all the gods were so charmed with her beauty that they desired to possess her, and Shivŭ was entirely overcome by his passion. The reader will remember something similar to this in the account of Venus, who is also said to have sprang from the froth of the sea; and whom, on being presented to the gods, they all desired to marry.

The worship of Lŭkshmēē is celebrated in five different months, viz. in Bhadrŭ, on the first Thursday of the increase of the moon, in the morning; in Ashwinŭ, at the full moon, in the evening; in Kartikŭ, on the last day of the decrease of the moon, in the night; on the last day in Poushŭ, in the morning; and in Choitrŭ, on the first Thursday of the increase of the moon, either in the day or night. The ceremonies are performed before a basket used as a corn-measure, painted red: the worshippers fill this measure with rice in the husk, and put round it a garland of flowers; then cover it with a white cloth; and, encircling it with a number of small shells, place before it a box containing red paint, a comb, &c. The officiating bramhŭn performs the usual ceremonies, varying but little from those at the worship of Vishnoo, in the name of the master or mistress of the house. No bloody sacrifices are offered. Bramhŭns are entertained rather liberally at this festival; but on the day of worship no alms must be given to the poor, (except cooked food,) nor any money lost; lest this goddess, who is supposed to preside over wealth, and to have taken up her abode at the worshipper's house, should be angry at her riches being wasted.

This worship is celebrated in almost every Hindoo family five times a year; the frequency of which is not to be wondered at, when it is considered that Lŭkshmēē is the goddess of prosperity. If a man be growing rich, the Hindoos say, 'Lŭkshmēē is gone to abide at his house;' if he be sinking into poverty, they say, 'Lŭkshmēē has forsaken him.' If they wish to abuse another, they call him Lŭkshmēē-chara.[b]

The morning after the festival, the women take up the corn-measure, and preserve it for some future time of worship: the rice is used in worship during the whole year. At the close of the festival, if a female of the family remember any stories respect-

[a] She is also called the daughter of Bhrigoo.

[b] In the provincial dialect it is Lŭkhēē-chara, that is, luckless; thus forming an extraordinary coincidence of sound and meaning in languages so extremely different.

ing Lŭkshmēē, she relates them ; and the rest of the family, joined by two or three neighbouring females, sit around and hear. In some places a number of persons subscribe towards the expense of making an image of Lŭkshmēē, and worship it on any of the days before-mentioned.

Names.—Lŭkshmēē, or, the goddess of fortunate signs ;—Pŭdmalŭya, she who dwells on the water-lily ;—Pŭdma, she who holds in her hand the water-lily ; Shrēē, she in whom all take refuge ;—Hŭree-priya, the wife of Hŭree.

SECT. XXII.—*Kojagŭrŭ-Lŭkshmēē.*[c]

THIS form of Lŭkshmēē is worshipped at the full moon in Ashwinŭ, in the evening, before a corn-measure, surrounded by four plantain trees; though some persons worship this goddess before an image of Lŭkshmēē. Bloody sacrifices are offered. The worshippers invariably drink the water of the cocoanut at this festival ; and numbers keep awake the whole night, listening to the filthy songs, and the horrid din of Hindoo music.

SECT. XXIII.—*Sŭrŭswŭtēē.*

THIS is the goddess of learning, the daughter of Brŭmha, and the wife of Vishnoo. She is represented as a white woman, standing on the water-lily, and playing on a lute.

On the 5th day of the increase of the moon, in Maghŭ, the worship of this goddess is performed before her image, or a pen, inkstand, and book ; the latter articles are supposed to form a proper substitute for the goddess, who is called Vagvadinēē, the eloquent. The image is placed on a table, either at the west or south side of the house. After the officiating bramhŭn has read the formulas and presented the offerings, each worshipper whose name has been read in the service takes flowers in his hands, and, repeating a prayer, presents them to the goddess; after which follow gifts to the bramhŭns, and a feast.

Every Hindoo who is able to read and write endeavours to celebrate the worship of this goddess : the raja of Bŭrdwan is said to expend 15,000 rupees annually at this festival. In every Hindoo college, the students keep the festival with great joy : many of them dance naked, and are guilty of every indecency.

[c] The shastrŭs have commanded that each Hindoo shall remain awake during the night of the full moon in Ashwinŭ, when a festival is held in honour of this goddess ; and from this circumstance this name is derived.

The day after the festival, the image is carried in procession through the town, and then thrown into the river. In passing through the streets of Serampore, at the time of this festival in the year 1806, I was exceedingly shocked at observing among the crowd, who were dancing, playing on music, bearing flags, &c. two or three young men quite naked, the mob triumphing in this shocking insult on public decency. To induce young men to resort to their houses, many prostitutes keep this feast, and connect with it all that low merriment which corrupts the mind and draws the attention of the crowd.[d]

On this day the Hindoos neither read nor write,[e] though they will do any other secular business. They eat only once during the day, and those who are accustomed to eat fish abstain from it on this day.

The Hindoos believe, that from this goddess they derive their learning and powers of eloquence,[f] as well as their ability to read and write. Some of those who can neither read nor write, insist upon it, that they ought to worship her, as they derive their powers of speech from her.[g] Others however complain, 'Sŭrŭswŭtēē has bestowed nothing on us—why should we perform her worship?'

The image of Sŭrŭswŭtēē is sometimes painted blue, and placed in temples; when she is called Nēēlŭ-Sŭrŭswŭtēē.

Names. Bramhēē, or, the daughter of Brŭmha;—Bharŭtēē, she who presides over words;—Bhasha, she who bestows the power of speech;—Sŭrŭswŭtēē, she who through the curse of a bramhŭn was turned into a river.

Sect. XXIV.—*Shēētŭla.*[h]

Is painted as a yellow woman sitting on the water-lily, dressed in red, and giving suck to an infant. Before this image, or a pan of water, the worship of this goddess is performed, in any part of the year; but in general on the 7th, 8th, and 9th of the increase

[d] In the year 1808, I saw a group of performers reciting the Ramayŭnŭ in the street; and on enquiry, I found it was before the door of some prostitutes, who had subscribed to bear the expense. The reason assigned was, that it would be an act of merit, helping them in another world; and would also draw men into whoredom. Offerings are sometimes brought home, and shared by a prostitute with her paramour; like the harlot, in the Book of Proverbs, who is represented as saying to the young man she met in the street, 'I have peace-offerings with me; this day have I payed my vows.'—*Prov.* vii. 14.

[e] The only reason I can find for this is, it is the command of the shastrŭ.

[f] Of an eloquent man, the Hindoos say, 'Sŭrŭswŭtēē sits on his tongue.'

[g] Of this fact they give the example of Ravŭnŭ, who, when Ramŭ was about to kill him, procured a reprieve by flattering his adversary; but the gods, afraid lest Ravŭnŭ should be spared, sent Sŭrŭswŭtēē into his throat, and caused him to say provoking things to Ramŭ.

[h] Or, she who cools the body at the time of the small-pox.

of the moon, in the day time. Bloody sacrifices are not offered. On the 10th, the image is thrown into the water.

This goddess is also worshipped to obtain preservation from the evil effects of the small-pox. In the months Choitrŭ and Voishakhŭ, the Hindoos inoculate those of their children who are two years old; on which occasion the inoculating bramhŭn[i] presents offerings and prayers to this goddess in the name of the child, promising for the parents, that if she be kind to the child, they will present to her certain offerings, &c. as soon as it is recovered. At the close of the ceremony, the bramhŭn places the flowers which have been offered in the hair of the child, telling the parents that the goddess will be favourable; and then performs the operation. When the child becomes affected with the disease, the family priest (if the parents be rich enough to pay for it) comes to the house every day, and repeats certain forms of prayer and praise to Shēētŭla; after recovery she is again worshipped. If the child become dangerously ill, it is carried to an image of Shēētŭla, and bathed in the water which has been offered to this goddess, some of which is given it to drink.

Beggars of different descriptions procure a stone, gild a small part of it, and carry it from place to place, singing the praises of Shēētŭla. These mendicants sometimes proclaim in a village, that Shēētŭla has appeared to one of them in a dream, and ordered, that in this village the mistress of each house shall beg at three, four, or more doors, and take whatever is given her, and eat it in some neighbouring garden or forest.[k] The most dreadful misfortunes being threatened in case of disobedience, the affrighted women beg from door to door, and fulfil the supposed commands of the goddess.

SECT. XXV.—*Mŭnŭsa*[l].

THIS goddess, the sister of Vasookee,[m] and the wife of Jŭrŭtkarŭ, a sage, is called the queen of the snakes, and is worshipped to obtain preservation from their bite. She is represented as sitting on the water-lily, clothed with snakes.

In the month Jyoist'hŭ, on the 10th of the increase of the moon; also on the 5th of the moon's increase and decrease in Ashwinŭ and Shravŭnŭ, as well as on the last day of Shravŭnŭ, this goddess is worshipped. On the three last occasions, the wor-

[i] The regular Hindoo doctors (voidyŭ) do not inoculate, but a lower order of bramhŭns called doivŭgnŭs, or astrologers.

[k] This is a trick to extort some part of the alms from these deluded women.

[l] Or Mŭnŭsa-dēvēē; the goddess who possesses pleasure in herself.

[m] The king of the serpents.

shippers plant branches of the Euphorbia before the house, and worship them. In Shravŭnŭ, the worship is celebrated with the greatest show; on which occasion an image, or some branches of the same tree, or a pan of water surrounded with snakes made of clay, is placed as the object of worship: in some places, twenty or thirty thousand people assemble; and amidst singing, dancing, music, &c. some persons play with snakes of different kinds, particularly the cobra capello, suffering them to bite them. This play, however, ends fatally when the venomous fangs have not been carefully extracted. The cast called Mal, who play with snakes for a livelihood, profess great regard for Mŭnŭsa. On the days of the festival, the Hindoos do not kindle a fire, alleging that one of the names of Mŭṇŭsa is Ŭrŭndhŭna, she who does not cook. A day or two before the festival, in some places, the women of the village (perhaps fifty or a hundred, or even two hundred) beg rice, either in their own or an adjoining village; which they offer, in a field in the neighbourhood, in the name of Mŭnŭsa, but without an image. After thus offering rice, milk, curds, sugar, &c. to the goddess, they eat them on the spot; and this act of holiness, they say, preserves their children from the bite of snakes, as well as assists the parents themselves on their way to heaven. A song founded upon the following story concludes the whole:—Chandŭ, a merchant, not only refused to worship the goddess, but professed the utmost contempt for her. In process of time, however, she caused his six youngest sons to be killed by the bite of snakes: to avoid the fate of whom, the eldest son, Lŭkindŭrŭ, made an iron house, and retired to it; yet Mŭnŭsa caused the snake Tŭkshŭkŭ to enter by a crevice, which destroyed Lŭkindŭrŭ on his wedding-day; his widow escaped, and went weeping into the presence of her mother-in-law. The neighbours again attempted to reason with Chandŭ; but he continued obstinate, declaring that Mŭnŭsa was no goddess. She appeared to people in dreams, and commanded them to persuade him to celebrate her worship; and, after much entreaty, to pacify the goddess, he was induced to comply: but declared he would present the offerings only with the left hand;[n] and, turning back his head, he threw a flower at her image with the left hand. Mŭnŭsa, however, was so pleased, that she restored his seven sons; and from this circumstance, the worship of this goddess has since been very much celebrated.

When the worship is performed before an image, sheep, goats, and buffaloes are offered to Mŭnŭsa, and even swine.[o]

When a Hindoo has been bitten by a snake, the persons who pretend to cure him read different incantations containing the

[n] The hand used in washing after stools.

[o] Among the Egyptians, swine, it is well known, were offered to Bacchus.

names of Mŭnŭsa. If one or two persons in a village have died by the bite of snakes, all the inhabitants become alarmed, and celebrate the worship of Mŭnŭsa.

SECT. XXVI.—*Shŭshtēē.*[p]

Is a yellow woman sitting on a cat, nursing a child. The Hindoos regard her as the protectress of their children.

Six annual festivals are held in honour of this goddess, viz., in Jyoisht'hŭ, Bhadrŭ, Ashwinŭ, Maghŭ, and two in Choitrŭ; on the 6th of the increase of the moon, and on the last day but one of the month.

The worship celebrated in Jyoisht'hŭ is performed by a bramhŭnēē, or an officiating bramhŭn, under the vŭtŭ tree,[q] or under a branch of this tree planted in the house. At the time of this worship, every woman of the village, dressed in her best clothes, with her face painted, her ornaments on, and her body anointed with oil, goes to the place of worship under the tree, taking in her hand an offering; over each of which the officiating bramhŭn performs the usual ceremonies. The offerings are sent to the house of the officiating bramhŭn, or distributed amongst the eager by-standers. Among others who are eager to obtain some of these offerings, are women who have not been blessed with children; each of whom sits down pensively among the crowd, and opens the end of her garment to receive what the assembled mothers are eager enough to bestow: when the giver says, 'May the blessing of Shŭshtēē be upon you, and next year may you bring offerings—with a child in your arms.' The receiver adds with eagerness, 'Ah! if she bestow this blessing, I will celebrate her worship; I will keep my vows, and bring offerings every year.' This festival is called Arŭnyŭ-shŭshtēē, because the worshippers are directed to walk in some forest on this day, with fans in their hands.

In those houses where the daughter is married, but has not left her parents, they send for the son-in-law; and at the close of the worship the girl's father sends to him, on a metal plate, a flower, some unhusked rice, a piece of string consecrated to the goddess, five or six blades of dōōrva grass, a garment, &c. The son-in-law, if a person of respectability, contents himself with sticking the flower in his hair. If a poor man, he puts on the garment, and raises all the other presents to his head. If the son-in-law neglect to stick the flower in his hair, the girl's father becomes very sorrowful; and all the spectators pronounce the former

[p] She is worshipped on the sixth lunar day.

[q] Ficus Indica.

a dead man, for throwing away a flower which has been offered to Shŭshtēē.

The worship in the month Bhadrŭ does not differ from the preceding, except in its being performed by the river side, or at a pool of water, before the stick which is whirled round in churning butter, upon which a fan is placed. In the midst of the worship the women make little paste images of children, and, placing them on leaves of the kŭntŭkēē tree,[r] present them to the goddess, and afterwards throw them into the river. This festival is called Chapŭra-shŭshtēē.[s]

The Ashwinŭ festival, distinguished by the name Doorga-shŭshtēē, is in almost every particular the same as the preceding.

At the Maghŭ festival, called Shēētŭla-shŭshtēē, the women, on the night preceding, boil a large quantity of rice and pulse for offerings; mixing with the latter, in boiling, a kind of kidney beans and varttakoos.[t] The next morning they bathe very early, and on their return go through the ceremonies of worship in the house, before the two stones with which they grind their spices; and upon which they throw a yellow cloth, smeared with red lead. The worship is finished before ten o'clock, and at noon they eat what the goddess has left, i. e. every thing they gave her.

The two festivals in Choitrŭ are held on the 6th, and on the last day but one of the month: on the 6th, in the morning, either before a branch of the vŭtŭ, the shalgramŭ, or some proper representative of an image; and at the close of the month, in the evening, before an image of Shivŭ. On the 6th the worshippers eat the bud of the Euphorbia inclosed in a plaintain; and at the latter festival they fast during the day, and after worship eat some fruit, and some barley flour mixed with curds or water. Rich persons eat sweetmeats. These festivals are called Ŭshokŭ-shŭshtēē and Nēēlŭ-shŭshtēē.

Another festival is held in honour of this goddess in some parts of Bengal, in the month Ŭgrŭhayŭnŭ, called Hŭree-shŭshtēē. The worship is celebrated before a clay pot, filled with water, having six spouts.

In addition to all these times of worship, females who have lost all their children by death, worship this goddess every month: beside which, after a child is six days old, every father, to preserve the child, performs the worship of the goddess, while the officiating bramhŭn reads the incantations; and on the 21st day of the child's age, the mother presents offerings to the goddess with her own hands, while the officiating bramhŭn reads the prayers. The

[r] Artecarpus integrifolia.

[s] In allusion to the making of these images.

[t] The fruit of solanum melongena.

first of these ceremonies takes place in the evening, before a branch of the vŭtŭ tree, fastened in the house floor; the two stones with which spices are ground being placed against the wall in the inside of the house, covered with a piece of cloth. The husband, at the close, asks the blessing of the goddess on the child, promising to present to her a number of offerings when the child shall be twenty-one days old. Before the door the family place the skull of a cow, rubbing some red lead on its forehead; and in three lumps of cow-dung, put on the forehead, they stick three cowries; upon which also they spread a yellow cloth. The head remains a month at the door of the house, as a kind of charm for the good of the children.

On the 21st day of the child's age, the mother invites ten or fifteen female neighbours, who, with the officiating bramhŭn, accompany her to a stone placed at the foot of the vŭtŭ tree, which is supposed to be the representative of thē goddess; around which they put a large necklace or garland of flowers, and go through the ceremonies of worship in the usual manner: at the close the mother promises, on condition that the goddess bless her child, that she will worship her every year. The mother distributes the sweetmeats, &c. that have been offered to the idol among the females present. This festival is called ékooshiya.[u]

Shŭshtēē has no temples in Bengal; her common representative, a rough stone, smeared with red paint, about as large as a man's head, is commonly placed at the root of the sacred vŭtŭ; to which passengers, especially women, pay a degree of reverence. In fulfilling particular vows to Shŭshtēē, some worshippers surround the vŭtŭ tree with garlands of flowers, and great numbers of artificial lamps made of clay: others fulfil their vows by building an earthen or brick seat around one of these trees. A female of property, as a thank-offering after child-birth, presents by the hands of a bramhŭn a child made of curds, which the bramhŭn never fails to devour.

Bloody sacrifices of bullocks, goats, sheep, and sometimes of tame hogs, are offered to Shŭshtēē. For receiving these latter offerings some persons call the goddess a cannibal.

At the close of the different festivals held in honour of Shŭshtēē, it is common for women to entertain the company with marvellous stories relating to this goddess. The wives of some of the lower castes beg for a share of the offerings at the doors of the bramhŭns.

Shŭshtēē rides on a cat: hence the Hindoos, especially mothers, avoid hurting this animal, lest the goddess should revenge herself on their children.

[u] From ékooshŭ, twenty-one.

CHAP. IV.

INFERIOR CELESTIAL BEINGS, OBJECTS OF WORSHIP.

THESE beings are either the enemies of the gods, as the ŭsoorŭs and rakshŭsŭs; or their companions: or those who are employed as dancers, singers, or musicians in the heavens of the gods. They are worshipped at the great festivals, but have no separate images.

SECT. I.—*The Usoorŭs, or Giants.*

THESE enemies of the gods, are the offspring of Kŭshyŭpŭ, the progenitor of gods, giants, men, serpents, and birds, by his different wives. They bear a resemblance to the titans or giants of the Grecian Mythology; and stories of their wars with the gods (some of which will be found in this work) abound in the pooranŭs. Indrŭ, Vishnoo, Kartikŭ, and Doorga, are distinguished among the Hindoo deities for their conflicts with these beings[a]. King Vŭlee, a giant, is worshipped by the Hindoos on their birth-days, with the same forms as are used in the worship of the gods.

Story of the churning of the sea by the gods and ŭsoorŭs.—The most rancorous hatred has always existed betwixt the ŭsoorŭs and the gods, although half-brothers; the former having been excluded by the gods from succeeding to the throne of heaven: and dreadful conflicts were carried on betwixt them with various success, till both parties sought to become immortal. The giants performed the most severe religious austerities, addressing their prayers alternately to Vishnoo, Shivŭ, and Brŭmha; but were always unsuccessful. The gods, however, at last obtained this blessing at the churning of the sea of milk; which story is related at length in the Mŭhabharŭtŭ and other works:—The gods first took mount Mŭndŭrŭ, placed it in the sea, and wrapping round it the serpent Vasookēē, began to whirl it round as the milk-men do the staff in making butter. The gods took hold of the head of the snake, and the giants of the tail; but being almost consumed by the poison from the mouth of the serpent, the gods privately entreated Vishnoo to prevail upon the giants to lay hold of the

[a] Jupiter was represented as aiming the thunder in his right hand against a giant under his feet: Doorga is aiming the spear in her right hand against an ŭsoorŭ under her feet.

head; upon which he thus addressed them: 'How is it' said Vishnoo, 'that you, giants as you are, have taken hold of Vasookēē's tail?' The gods and the giants then changed places; and the elephant Oiravŭtŭ first arose from the churned sea to reward their labours; afterward the gem Koustoobhŭ—the horse Oochoishrŭva—the tree Parijatu—many jewels—the goddess Lŭkshmēē—and then poison. Full of alarm at this sight, the gods applied to Mŭha-dévŭ (Shivŭ); who, to save the world from destruction, drank up the poison, and received no other injury than a blue mark on his throat.[b] Next came up the water of immortality; when the 330,000,000 gods, and the ŭsoorŭs without number, took their stand on each side, each claiming the mighty boon. Vishnoo proposed to divide it with his own hands: but while the ŭsoorŭs went to prepare themselves by bathing in the sacred stream, the gods drank up the greatest part of the nectar; and, to give them time to drink the whole, Vishnoo assumed the form of a most captivating female; with which the giants were so charmed, that they totally forgot the nectar. One of them, however, having changed his shape, mixed with the gods, and, drinking of the water of life, became immortal; but Vishnoo, being informed of this circumstance by Sōōryŭ and Chŭndrŭ, (the sun and moon,) cut off the head of the giant. The head and trunk, being thus immortalized, were made the ascending and descending nodes, under the names Rahoo and Kétoo.

SECT. II.—*The Rakshŭsŭs.*

MANY stories respecting the wars of the rakshŭsŭs, or cannibals, with the gods, are contained in the pooranŭs and other shastrŭs, and several will be found in different parts of this work. They are represented as assuming at pleasure the different shapes of horses, tigers, lions, buffaloes, &c.: some have a hundred heads, and others as many arms.[c] In the Hindoo writings Malēē, Soomalēē, Ravŭnŭ, Koombhŭ-kŭrnŭ, Vibhēēshŭnŭ, Indrŭ-jit, Ŭtikayŭ, and others, are distinguished as renowned rakshŭsŭs. As soon as born, these giants are said to arrive at maturity. They devour their enemies. All the rakshŭsŭs are bramhŭns, and are said to dwell in the S. W. corner of the earth.

Noiritŭ, a rakshŭsŭ, is one of the ten guardian deities of the earth, and presides in the S. W. In this character he is worshipped at all the great festivals. He is represented in the form of meditation used by the bramhŭns as a black man, having in his right hand a scimitar.

[b] Hence this god is called Neelŭ-kantŭ, the blue throated.

[c] Some of the giants of the Grecian Mythology, it will be remembered, had a hundred arms.

Story of Koombhŭ-kŭrnŭ.—Immediately after his birth, this cannibal stretched his arms, which were in proportion to his body, and gathered into his mouth every thing within his reach. At one time he seized five hundred courtezans belonging to Indrŭ; at another the wives of one hundred sages, and cows and bramhŭns without number. Brŭmha at length threatened to destroy him, unless he contented him with less, as he would presently eat up the earth. He now became more moderate, and began to perform the most severe austerities in honour of Brŭmha; which he continued for ten thousand years. The gods trembled on their thrones, lest Koombhŭ-kŭrnŭ, obtaining the blessing of Brŭmha, and especially the blessing of immortality, should swallow up every thing, gods and men. They appealed to Brŭmha, and persuaded Sŭrŭswŭtēē, the goddess of learning, to enter into Koombhŭ-kŭrnŭ, and excite him to ask this blessing, that he should continue to sleep day and night; which request Brŭmha granted, and sent the voracious rakshŭsŭ to enjoy his everlasting sleep. The friends of Koombhŭ-kŭrnŭ however persuaded Brŭmha to change his destiny: who now ordered that he should sleep uninterruptedly six months, but on the last day of the sixth should awake; during half of which day he should fight with and conquer Brŭmha, Vishnoo, and Shivŭ, and during the other half be permitted to devour as much as he chose. At one meal he devoured six thousand cows, ten thousand sheep, ten thousand goats, five hundred buffaloes, five thousand deer, and drank four thousand hogsheads of spirits, with other things in proportion. After all, he was angry with his brother Ravŭnŭ, for not giving him enough to satisfy nature. His house is declared to have been twenty or thirty thousand miles long, and his bed the whole length of the house. 'Lŭnka itself, says the Ramayŭnŭ, is eight hundred miles in circumference:—where then was the place for this bed?' I have heard this question put by a person to the bramhŭns, who, unable to find room for Koombŭ-kŭrnŭ's bed, were laughed at by the shōōdrŭs, their disciples.

The *Gŭndhŭrvŭs* and *Kinnŭrŭs* are celestial choiristers male and female. The latter have horses' heads!!![d]

The *Vidya-dhŭrŭs* are male and female dancers. The *Upsŭrŭs* are also female dancers, greatly celebrated for their beauty; they have been frequently sent down to earth to captivate the minds of religious devotees, and draw them from those works of merit which were likely to procure them the thrones of the gods. Eight of the ŭpsŭrŭs are mentioned as beyond all others beautiful: Oorvvŭshēē, Ménŭka, Rŭmbha, Pŭnchŭ-chōōra, Tilottŭma, Ghritachēē, Boodbooda, and Mishrŭ-késhēē. The five first of these are the mistresses of the gods, and keep houses of ill-fame in the

[d] Some idea may be formed of the taste of the early Hindoo poets, who here represent heavenly music as coming from beings with the mouths of horses!

heaven of Indrŭ. When any one of the gods visits the king of heaven, he generally spends some time with one or more of these courtezans.

Story respecting the son of Indrŭ and an Upsŭra.—On a certain occasion, many of the gods were invited to an entertainment at the palace of Indrŭ. In the midst of the dance Gŭndhŭrvŭ-senŭ, the son of Indrŭ, was fascinated with the charms of one of the ŭpsŭras; and behaved so indelicately, that his father commanded him to descend to the earth in the form of an ass. All the gods joined the son in endeavouring to appease the angry father; who ultimately directed that Gŭndhŭrvŭ-sénŭ should be an ass in the day, and a man in the night; he promised his son too, that when Dhara, the king, should burn him, he should recover his place in heaven. With this modification of the curse, Gŭndhŭrvŭ-sénu sunk to the earth, and alighted in the form of an ass near a pond at Dhara-nŭgŭrŭ. In the day the fallen son of Indrŭ remained in this form near the pond; and in the night, in that of a man, he wandered from place to place to appease his hunger. One day a bramhŭn came to this pond to bathe; when Gŭndhŭrvŭ-sénŭ told him that he was the son of Indrŭ, and requested him to speak to king Dharŭ, to give him his daughter in marriage. The bramhŭn consented; but on speaking to the king, the latter refused to believe that he was Indrŭ's son, unless he himself had some conversation with him. The next day the king went, with his counsellors and courtiers, and held a conversation with the ass; who related his history, and the cause of his degradation: but the king still refused assent, unless he performed some miracle. To this the ass consented; and in one night raised a fort of iron forty miles square and six high. The next day the king, seeing the fort finished, was obliged to consent, and to appoint the day of marriage. He invited bramhŭns, kings, and other guests without number, to the wedding; and, on the day appointed, with dancing, songs, and a most splendid shew, (the bride being adorned with jewels and the richest attire,) they marched to the iron fort to give the beautiful daughter of king Dharŭ in marriage to the ass. In that country weddings are celebrated in the day. When all was ready, they sent a bramhŭn to call Gŭndhŭrvŭ-sénŭ from the pond; who, elated in the highest degree, having bathed, accompanied the bramhŭn to the assembly. Hearing music and songs, Gŭndhŭrvŭ-sénŭ could not refrain from giving them an ass's tune: but the guests, hearing the braying of the ass, were filled with sorrow: some were afraid to speak their minds to the king; but they could not help whispering and laughing one amongst another, covering their mouths with their garments: others muttered to the king, 'O king, is this the son of Indrŭ? O great monarch! you have found an excellent bridegroom; you are peculiarly happy in having to give your daughter in marriage to the son of Indrŭ; don't delay the wedding; in doing good delay is improper; we never saw so glorious a wedding ; we have heard of a camel being married to an ass, when the ass, looking upon the camel, said, ' Bless me ! what a fine form !' and the camel, hearing the voice of the ass, said ' Bless me ! what a sweet voice !'—The bramhŭns continued : ' In that wedding, however, the bride and bridegroom were equal ; but in this marriage, that such a bride should have such a bridegroom is truly wonderful !' Other bramhŭns said, ' O king, at other weddings, as a sign of joy, the sacred shell is blown ; but thou hast no need of that,' (alluding to the braying of the ass.) The females cried out, ' O mother ! what is this ! at the time of marriage to have an ass ! What a miserable thing ! What ! will he give such an angelic female in marriage to an ass ?'—The king, ashamed, held down his head. At length Gŭndhŭrvŭ-sénŭ began to converse with the king in Sŭngskritŭ, and to urge him to the fulfilment of his promise ; reminding him, that ' there was no act more meritorious than speaking truth, (putting the king in mind of his promise ;) that the body was merely a garment, and that wise men never estimate the worth of a person by the clothes he wears : moreover, he was in this shape from the curse of his father, and during the night he should assume the body of a man. Of his being the son of Indrŭ there could be no doubt.' The minds of the guests were now changed, and they confessed, that though he had the outside of an ass, he was unquestionably the son of Indrŭ ; for it was never known that an ass could speak Sŭngskritŭ. The king, therefore, gave his daughter to him in marriage. By the time the guests were dismissed, night drew on, when Gŭndhŭrvŭ-sénŭ assumed the form of a handsome man, and, having dressed himself, respectfully went into the presence of the king. All the people, seeing so fine a man, and recollecting that in the morning he would become an ass, felt both pleased and sorrowful. The king brought the bride in great state to the palace, and the next day gave her servants, camels, jewels, &c. and dismissed the guests with many presents. Dhara, however, in the midst of his other cares, could not but feel anxious that Gŭndhŭrvŭ-sénŭ should throw off his ass's body. After a thousand contrivances, he said to himself, 'Gŭndhŭrvŭ-sénŭ is the son of Indrŭ ; therefore he can never die : at night he casts off his ass's body, and it lies like a dead body : I will therefore burn this body, and thus keep him constantly in the shape of a man.' Accordingly, one night, he caused the ass's body to be burnt,—when Gŭndhŭrvŭ-sènŭ appeared in his presence, told him that now the curse was removed, and that he should immediately ascend to heaven. After saying this he withdrew, and the king saw him no more.

Nayikas.—These are female companions of Doorga, and are worshipped at the festivals of this goddess. Eight of them have a pre-eminence over the rest. The Tŭntrŭ-shastrŭs declare, that these females visit the worshippers either as their wives, or as mothers ; and declare to them how they may obtain heaven: or, as sisters, bring to them any female they choose, and reveal whatever they desire to know of the present or future. He who wishes to obtain the company of a Nayika must worship her thrice a day, and repeat her name at night in a cemetery for seven, or fifteen, or thirty days. On the last night he must continue to repeat her name till she appears to him, and asks what he wishes for. She remains with him during the night, and departs the next morning, leaving with him presents to a large amount; which, however, he must expend the next day, or they will all evaporate. If the worshipper wishes to go to any place in the three worlds, the Nayika takes him thither in a moment. If after cohabiting with one of the Nayikas, he cohabit with any other female, the Nayika immediately destroys him. Anŭndŭ-chŭndrŭ, a bramhŭn of Soopoorŭ in Vēērŭ-bhōōmee, who died only a few years since, is said to have obtained the fruit of his worshipping the Nayikas.

The *Yŭkshŭs* are the servants of Koovérŭ, the god of riches, and fly through the world preserving the wealth of men. A number of stories, not worth detailing, principally referring to their wars or intrigues, are contained in the pooranŭs. In the form of meditation, Koovérŭ is described as a white man, having a hammer in his right hand. He is worshipped at the festival of the goddess Lŭkshmēē, and at all the other great festivals; but has no separate feast, image, nor temple. The Ramayŭnŭ relates that Koovérŭ, by prayer to Brŭmha, accompanied with religious austerities, obtained Lŭnka, (Ceylon;) the very mire of whose streets is gold. Here he reigned till Ravŭnŭ dispossessed him. Brŭmha also gave to this god the chariot Pooshpŭkŭ; which had the property of expansion, and, of going wherever the charioteer wished. From Lŭnka, Koovèrŭ went to mount Koilasŭ, where he is supposed to be at present.

Pishachŭs.—These messengers of the gods guard the sacred places, the resort of pilgrims. Sixty thousand are said to guard the streams of the Ganges from the approach of the profane.

The *Goodghŭkŭs*, the *Siddhŭs*, the *Bhōōtŭs*, and the *Charŭnŭs.*—These are beings of inferior orders, residing with the gods as servants.

There are several other orders of females, as the Yoginēēs, Dakinēēs, Kakinēēs, Shakhinēēs, Bhōōtinēēs, and Prétinēēs, who wait upon Doorga or Shivŭ, as their attendants. All these also are worshipped at the great festivals.

KRISHNŪ

Published by J. Higginbotham, Madras

CHAP. V.

OF THE TERRESTRIAL GODS.

THE Hindoo celestial goddesses, it will be seen, are very few. There are no more indeed than three which can be considered as really distinct, and as holding a distinguished place among this class of Hindoo deities: these are Doorga, Sŭrŭswŭtēē, and Lŭkshmēē. Many of the others are different forms of Doorga; and Mŭnŭsa, Shŭshtēē, and Shēētŭla, would have been placed among the terrestrial goddesses, but they do not seem to have had an earthly origin.—I now proceed to give an account of the terrestrial gods, some of whom are worshipped with more shew than any of the celestial deities.

SECT. I.—*Krishnŭ.*[e]

ACCORDING to the Shrēē-Bhagŭvŭtŭ, Mŭhabharŭtŭ, and other works, this god, a form of Vishnoo, was incarnate to destroy kings Shishoo-palŭ and Kŭngsŭ, and a number of giants.

Krishnŭ was born at Mŭt'hoora; his father's name was Vŭsoodévŭ, a kshŭtriyŭ, and his mother's Dévŭkēē; but Kŭngsŭ seeking to destroy him when an infant, his father fled to Vŭnda-vŭnŭ, and concealed him in the house of Nŭndŭ, a voishyŭ: hence he is sometimes called the son of Nŭndŭ.

Many stories are recorded of Krishnŭ in the pooranŭs: in his infancy he deprived a giant of her breath, who had poisoned her breasts before she gave him suck;[f]—soon after he destroyed a carriage against which he hurt his foot, when laid by his nurse at the door to sleep;[g]—Nŭndŭ's wife, when looking into his mouth one day, had a surprising view of the three worlds, with Brŭmha, Vishnoo, and Shivŭ sitting on their thrones;—at the age of eight years he took up mount Govŭrdhŭnŭ in his arms, and held it as an umbrella over the heads of the villagers and their cattle during a dreadful storm, with which the angry king of heaven was overwhelming them; he created a number of cattle, and also of boys and girls, to replace those which Brŭmha had *stolen* from Vrindavŭnŭ;—he destroyed a large hydra, which had poisoned the waters of the Yŭmoona;—he seduced the wife of Ayŭnŭ-ghoshŭ, a voishyŭ, and sported with 16,000 milk-maids in the wilderness

[e] The black.

[f] It is common for a Hindoo nurse to offer the breast to a neighbour's child when she happens to be on a visit.

[g] Mothers frequently lay their infants exposed to the rays of the sun to sleep, after rubbing their breasts with oil.

of Vrindŭ;—he next assumed four arms, destroyed Kŭngsŭ, and placed Kŭngsŭ's father on the throne; after this he was engaged in various quarrels, and had to combat with many formidable enemies; which induced him to build a fort at Dwarŭka, where he resided, and married two wives;—he next joined the family of Yoodhisht'hirŭ in their war with the race of Dooryodhŭnŭ;—and, lastly, destroyed Shishoo-palŭ. He closed his life with an act worthy of such a character, by destroying his whole progeny;[h] and was at length himself accidentally killed by an arrow, while sitting under a tree.

It is very possible, if any real Hindoo history could be discovered, that many of these facts would be found recorded in the life of a Hindoo king of this name; which facts have been embellished by the Asiatic poets till they have elevated the hero into a god. The images of this lascivious and blood-stained hero are now worshipped by the Hindoos with an enthusiasm, which transforms them into the very image of Krishnŭ himself.

This god is represented as a black man, holding a flute to his mouth with both hands: his mistress Radha stands on his left.

On the 8th of the moon's decrease in the month Bhadrŭ, an annual festival is held in the night, to celebrate the birth of this god. On this day all the worshippers fast[e]. The regular Hindoos, and the disciples of the Gosaees[f], sometimes differ a day or two in celebrating this feast. After the ceremonies of worship are concluded, the worshippers assemble before the temple near a hole cut in the ground, into which have been thrown water, oil, curds, turmeric, and earth; and seize first one person and then another, and throw them into this hole; and others jump into it. Music, dancing,

[h] The posterity of Krishnŭ, say several pooranŭs, were destroyed by the curse of a bramhŭn; but as all events are ascribed to Krishnŭ by his votaries, this of destroying his own family is referred to his agency. So infamous is the character of this god, even among those who hope for salvation through him, that Vilwŭ-mŭngŭlŭ, a blind poet, wrote the following verse, which certainly contains the severest possible censure of this profligate deity.

'Oh! Krishnŭ! thou who didst destroy thy own offspring;
Thou who didst renounce (Sēēta) the spotless daughter of Zŭnŭkŭ, in the wilderness;
Thou who didst cast down to hades Vŭlee, who had given thee his all;—
Who would think on thee, if thou wert not the deliverer from death?'

In exact agreement with this Sŭngskritŭ verse, was the declaration made before several persons in company in the year 1812, by Ram-nat'hŭ, the second Sŭngskritŭ pundit in the College of Fort-William; who, speaking of the universal profligacy of manners in Calcutta, declared, that 'every house contained a Krishnŭ.'

[e] In a Hindoo fast, the person abstains, for three days, from anointing himself with oil, from connubial intercourse, from fish, every thing fried, and eats only once a day. At the time of a Jewish fast, the person is said to have 'afflicted his soul:' but among the Hindoos fasting and merriment go together. The Jewish fast was connected with moral sentiment: the Hindoos fast as an act of mere ceremonial purity.

[f] The Gosaees are the religious leaders of a large portion of the worshippers of Krishnŭ. Gosaee is a term of respect equivalent to Sir.

singing obscene songs, &c. accompany these acts of rude merriment; at the close of which, dancing through the streets, the crowd go to some pool, or to the river, and wash themselves: and thus the festivity ends.

In the month Shravŭnŭ, another festival is held in honour of Krishnŭ, called Jhoolŭnŭ-yatra[g]. On the 11th night of the increase of the moon this festival begins; when a chair or throne, containing the image, being suspended from the ceiling of an adjoining room in the temple, the proprietor begins to swing the image, and other bramhŭn guests continue it at pleasure. At ten o'clock the god is taken to his usual place, when the different forms of worship are repeated, amidst the offering of flowers, incense, sweetmeats, fruits, and other acts of adoration. During the celebration of worship in the house, the crowd out of doors sing, dance, and make a horrid discord with barbarous instruments of music, connecting with the whole every kind of indecency. At twelve o'clock the owner of the image entertains a great multitude of bramhŭns. After eating and drinking, they literally 'rise up to play:' youths, dressed so as to represent Krishnŭ and his mistress Radha, dance together; and the festivities are thus continued till the crowd retire at day-light. Some keep this feast for five nights, beginning on the eleventh; and others for three nights, beginning on the thirteenth.

On the 15th of the increase of the moon in the month Kartikŭ, another festival is held during three nights, to celebrate the revels of this impure god with the milk-maids. It is called the Rasŭ. Each night, after the ceremonies in the temple are closed, the crowd carry the image out with much noise, music, singing, and dancing; and place it in a brick building in the street, which is open on all sides, and has one highly elevated sitting place. This building is annually gilt, ornamented, and grandly illuminated for this festival. Sixteen small images of Krishnŭ are necessary on this occasion; but a very small gold image, about the size of a breast-pin, is placed as the object of adoration, and afterwards given to the officiating bramhŭn. At the close of the festival, the clay images are thrown into the river.

Round the building in the street, booths are erected, filled with sweetmeats, playthings, and other articles, as at an English fair. Here fathers and mothers, leading their children by the hand, or carrying them on their hips,[h] come for *fairings*. Thieves

[g] The swinging festival.

[h] This is the way in which all Hindoos carry their children: a child is rarely seen in a person's arms, as in Europe. The same custom appears to have existed among the Jews: 'Ye shall be borne upon her sides, and be dandled upon her knees. *Isaiah* lxvi. 12.

and gamblers are very busy at these times[i]; and upon the whole it is amazing how much a European is here reminded of an English race-ground. At these times I have seen the grey-headed idolater and the mad youth dancing together; the old man lifting up his withered arms in the dance, and giving a kind of horror to the scene, which idolatry itself, united to the vivacity of youth, would scarcely be able to inspire[k]. In England the bait to corrupting amusements is merely a horse-race: but in Bengal the Hindoo is at once called to what he considers divine worship and to a licentious festival; no one imagining, but that worship and adultery may be performeed in the same hour. About four or five in the morning the crowd carry the god back to the temple; and then retire to cure their hoarseness and rest their wearied bodies.

On the fourth morning, having brought the god home, after the usual ceremonies, they sing songs in celebration of the actions of Krishnŭ; and continue them from ten till twelve or one o'clock in the day. Many come to hear, who present various offerings to the god; after which a grand feast is given to the bramhŭns. The expenses of this festival are defrayed either by rich natives, or from the revenues of the temples.

At the full moon in Phalgoonŭ, the Dolŭ,[l] another swinging festival is held.—Fifteen days before the full moon the holidays begin, from which time the Hindoos assemble in the night to sing and dance; and in the day they wander about the streets, throwing red powder[m] at the passengers, either with their hands or through a syringe. On the night before the full moon, the ceremonies of worship are performed; at the close of which, having besmeared themselves with red powder, they carry the god from his house to some distance, amidst the sounds of music, dancing, fireworks,

[i] In the year 1810, on account of the depredations of preceding years, the magistrate of Serampore forbad the erection of booths and all games at this festival: in consequence of which an expense of near four hundred rupees, incurred in performing the ceremonies of worship, fell upon the owner of the image of Krishnŭ, who would otherwise have received as much from the proprietors of the booths and gaming shops.

[k] Illuminations, fireworks, and the gilding of their temples, give a very shewy effect to Hindoo ceremonies, which are often performed at the time of the full moon, and at midnight. A moon-light night in India is highly pleasant. At the time of the Rasŭ festival, I have seen a scene so gaily illuminated and adorned, that the whole seemed enchantment; every native, as he approached the god, threw himself on the ground with the most profound reverence, and muttered his praise with rapture as he mingled in the delighted crowd. Could I have forgotten that these people were perpetrating a dreadful crime, and that these nightly festivals were connected with the greatest impurities, I should have been highly gratified.

[l] All these festivals are intended to represent the obscene acts or play of Krishnŭ. This is the play of swinging common to young folks in Europe. I am told that on this occasion, in various places in Hindoost'hanŭ, many families sit up all night, swinging by the light of the moon. They suspend a cord betwixt two trees, and while some are swinging, others are singing impure songs, and others dancing.

[m] This powder is made with the roots of wild ginger, coloured with sappan wood. Other ingredients are added to make superior kinds.

singing, &c. A bamboo, with a straw man tied to it, having been erected in some plain, they place the god here, and again worship him. After three hours have been spent in various sports, especially with fireworks, they set fire to the bamboo and straw, carrying back the image to the temple. Very early in the morning they bathe the god, set him on a chair, and then worship him, rocking him in this chair, and throwing upon him red powder. At twelve o'clock at noon these ceremonies are repeated with greater splendour; when many offerings are presented, and the bramhŭns entertained. About four the festival closes by another repetition of the same ceremonies. The god is then washed, anointed, clothed, and put into the temple; where food remains before him for some time, and is then given to the bramhŭns.

Besides these many other festivals less popular are held in the course of the year.

Many small black stones, having images of Krishnŭ cut in them, are to be found in the houses of the Hindoos; to which different names are given, but they are all forms of Krishnŭ. The temples dedicated to Krishnŭ are very numerous; and it is a scandalous fact that the image of Radha, his mistress, always accompanies that of Krishnŭ, and not those of his wives Rookminēē and Sŭtyŭ-bhama. Many persons may be heard in the streets, and when sitting in their shops, repeating to themselves and to parrots the names of Radha and Krishnŭ, as works of merit. Pantomimical entertainments are frequently represented, in which the lewd actions of this god are exhibited.

Six parts out of ten of the whole Hindoo population of Bengal are supposed to be the disciples of this god. The far greater part of these, however, are of the lower orders, and but few of them bramhŭns.[n] The mark on their foreheads consists of two straight lines from the tip of the nose to the back of the head.

A *story of Krishnŭ*.—The death of Shishoo-palŭ is thus related :—A quarrel arose at a sacrifice between Krishnŭ and this monarch, respecting the point of precedency, which Shishoo-palŭ would not resign to Krishnŭ: 'What!' says he, 'shall I be preceded by the son of a cowherd; one who has eaten with a cow-keeper, who has led cows to pasture, and has been guilty of all manner of abominations?' Krishnŭ restrained his rage for some time; but at length became exceedingly angry, and cut off his head at one blow. It was prophesied of Shishoo-palŭ, that as soon as he saw the person by whose hands he should die, two of his four arms would fall off; and this is said to have happened the moment he saw Krishnŭ at the meeting of the kings at this sacrifice.

[n] The greater part of the bramhŭns are disciples of the female deities, (Shaktus.)

Another Story.—On a certain occasion the lascivious Krishnŭ heard, that king Dŭndēē possessed a horse, which every night assumed the form of a beautiful female. Krishnŭ asked for this horse: but the king refused him, and fled to Bhēēmŭ, Krishnŭ's friend; who, rather than abandon a person who had claimed his protection, resolved to break the ties of friendship with Krishnŭ, and go to war with him. A war commenced, which continued to rage with the utmost fury, till the horse, assuming the shape of a kinnŭrēē, ascended to heaven, the period of the curse under which it lay being expired.

Krishnŭ ruining his friend by urging him to declare a deliberate falsehood.—In the war betwixt the family of Dooryodhŭnŭ and the Pandŭvŭs, Dronacharjyŭ was so mighty a warrior that the Pandŭvŭs had no hope of success, unless they could cut him off; to accomplish which, Krishnŭ contrived to throw Dronacharjyŭ off his guard, by causing it to be reported through the army, that his son Ushwŭtt'hama was killed. The father refused to believe the report, unless Yoodhist'hirŭ would say it was true. Krishnŭ pressed Yoodhist'hirŭ to tell this lie, as it would insure success to their affairs; and, in cases of extremity, the shastrŭ had declared it lawful to employ falsehood. Yoodhist'hirŭ at first positively refused, but was at length persuaded by the entreaties of Krishnŭ, Ŭrjoonŭ, and others; who told him the assertion would not be a lie, as an elephant of Dooryodhŭnŭ's, of the same name, had actually been killed in battle. Dronacharjyŭ was so overcome when he was thus brought to believe the news, that Ŭrjoonŭ soon dispatched him; which completely changed the face of the battle. On account of this falsehood, Yoodhist'hirŭ, in going to heaven, was terrified by a sight of the torments of hell.—Where did Krishnŭ, the father of this lie, go?

Theft and murder committed by Krishnŭ.—When Krishnŭ was going to Mŭt'hoora to destroy Kŭngsŭ, as he approached the city he felt ashamed of the meanness of his dress, which consisted only of some shreads of cloth, like ropes, tied round his loins; and said to his brother Bŭlŭ-ramŭ, 'All are going to this sacrifice elegantly dressed; we cannot go in this condition.' Krishnŭ then sent his brother to a washerman, who however would not part with the clothes in his possession, as they belonged to king Kŭngsŭ. A quarrel ensued, in the midst of which Krishnŭ killed the washerman, and carried off the clothes. These free-booters next went to a shop, and stole two necklaces; and afterwards seized some sandalwood, which a deformed woman was taking to the palace of Kŭngsŭ: but, to reward her, Krishnŭ pulled her straight, and made her more beautiful than the ŭpsŭras. The woman asked Krishnŭ, since he had made her so beautiful, who should marry her. Krishnŭ asked her, to whom she wished to be united. She said, to himself;—and from that time she became his mistress.

SECT. II.—*Gopalŭ.*[o]

THIS is an image of Krishnŭ in his childhood. He is resting on one knee, with his right hand extended, craving some sweet-meats from his mother.

This infant god is worshipped at the festivals in honour of Krishnŭ: the ceremonies are the same, though the formulas are different.

Those who preserve stone, or brass, or other images of this god in their houses, as many do, worship them every day, or whenever they choose. Many persons receive the initiating incantation of Gopalŭ as their guardian deity.

Girēēshŭ-chŭndrŭ, the rajà of Nŭdēēya, in the year 1807, had two dreams, in which the god Gopalŭ appeared to him, and told him, that in a certain place in Nŭdēēya, a beautiful image of him was buried deep in the ground. The raja paid no attention to his dreams, till the god appeared to him a third time, telling him the same thing: when he consulted his principal servants, who sent labourers to dig up the image; but none was found. A few nights after, Gopalŭ appeared again, and told the raja that he was to be found in such a place, describing the spot in a more particular manner. The raja again sent his servants, who found the image. The greatest rejoicings took place at Nŭdēēya on this occasion; learned bramhŭns were called; and a vast concourse of people collected from the surrounding country to behold this miraculously discovered god, and to witness his installation, at which four thousand rupees were expended: a temple was afterwards erected on the spot, and the god placed in it. This image is now become very famous: the offerings presented to it do not amount, it is said, to less than two hundred rupees monthly.

Another image of the infant Krishnŭ, called Balŭgopalŭ, made of stone or metal, is kept in the houses of many, and worshipped daily, as well as at the festivals in honour of Krishnŭ.

SECT. III.—*Gopēē-nat'hŭ.*[p]

THIS is another form of Krishnŭ. In some places the image is worshipped every day, as well as at the festivals in honour of Krishnŭ.

A celebrated image of this god is set up at Ŭgrŭ-dwēēpŭ where an annual festival is held, on the 11th and five following days of the decrease of the moon, in Choitrŭ. The origin of this image is so recent, that the story is known to every Hindoo:—

[o] The cowherd.

[p] The god of the milk-maids.

Two religious mendicants, since become famous among the followers of Krishnŭ, Choitŭnyŭ and Nityanŭndŭ, sent their disciple Ghoshŭ-t'hakoorŭ, who did not relish an austere life, to Ŭgrŭ-dwēēpŭ, and directed him to take a certain stone with him, and make an image of Gopēē-nat'hŭ, which he should set up there and worship. Ghoshŭ-t'hakoorŭ obeyed his spiritual guides; took the stone on his head; set it up as a god, the gift of Choitŭnyŭ and Nityanŭndu, and began to worship it in public daily. The god soon appeared to him in dreams, and revealed a number of secret things; so that by degrees Gopēē-nat'hŭ of Ŭgrŭ-dwēēpŭ became very famous. One night a stranger came to the temple at a very late hour, when no one was awake to give him refreshment. The god himself, however, in the form of Ghoshŭ-t'hakoorŭ, took an ornament from his ancle, and purchased some food for the stranger at an adjoining shop. In the morning there was a great noise in the town about this ornament, when the shopkeeper and the stranger declared these facts, so creditable to the benevolence of the god; and from this circumstance the fame of Gopēē-nat'hŭ spread still wider. After the death of Ghoshŭ-t'hakoorŭ, the god appeared to his successor, and directed him to perform the funeral rites; in the celebration of which it was contrived that the god himself should present the offering to the manes: for when the kooshŭ grass, the rice, and the water were put into the hands of the image, the god (a little more water than usual being poured into his hand) poured out the offering; when the crowd set up a great shout, declaring that the god himself had presented the offering to the manes. At present, it is said, this god brings in not less than 25,000 rupees annually to his owner.

At the above-mentioned festival, it is supposed that 100,000 people assemble each day at Ŭgrŭ-dwēēpŭ; among whom are great multitudes of lewd women, who accompany the religious mendicants. Filthy songs about Krishnŭ and his mistresses are sung by the crowd, and all manner of indecent diversions practised. Different castes eat together here.

After the death of Ghoshŭ-t'hakoorŭ, the image fell into the hands of the raja, or lord of the soil; who sent bramhŭns to perform the ceremonies before the image, and receive the offerings. Raja Nŭvŭ-krishnŭ, of Calcutta, once seized this image for a debt of three lacks of rupees, due to him from the owner, raja Krishnŭ-chŭndrŭ-rayŭ. The latter afterwards regained the image by a suit at law; but not till Nŭvŭ-krishnŭ had made another Gopēē-nat'hŭ exactly like it.

All this has arisen out of a stone given by two mendicants to one of their companions!—Who can avoid feeling a mingled sensation of disgust and pity, while he beholds such multitudes, the abject slaves of a superstition so degrading?

SECT. IV.—*Jŭgŭnnat'hŭ.*[q]

THE image of this god has no legs, and only stumps of arms:[r] the head and eyes are very large. At the festivals the bramhŭns adorn him with silver or golden hands.

Krishnŭ, in some period of Hindoo history, was accidentally killed by Ŭngŭdŭ, a hunter; who left the body to rot under the tree where it fell. Some pious person, however, collected the bones of Krishnŭ, and placed them in a box; where they remained till Indrŭ-dhoomnŭ, a king, who was performing religious austerities to obtain some favour of Vishnoo, was directed by the latter to form the image of Jŭgŭnnat'hŭ, and put into its belly these bones of Krishnŭ, by which means he should obtain the fruit of his religious austerities. Indrŭ-dhoomnŭ enquired who should make this image; and was commanded to pray to Vishwŭ-kŭrmŭ.[s] He did so, and obtained his request; but Vishwŭ-kŭrmŭ at the same time declared, that if any one disturbed him while preparing the image, he would leave it in an unfinished state. He then began, and in one night built a temple upon the blue mountain in Orissa, and proceeded to prepare the image in the temple: but the impatient king, after waiting fifteen days, went to the spot; on which Vishwŭ-kŭrmŭ desisted from the work, and left the god without hands or feet. The king was very much disconcerted; but on praying to Brŭmha, he promised to make the image famous in its present shape.

Indrŭ-dhoomnŭ now invited all the gods to be present at the setting up of this image: Brŭmha himself acted as high priest, and gave eyes and a soul to the god, which completely established the fame of Jŭgŭnnat'hŭ. This image is said to lie in a pool near the present temple, at Jŭgŭnnat'hŭ-kshétrŭ in Orissa, commonly known among the English by the name of Jŭgŭnnat'hŭ's pagoda. The particulars of this place will be found in the account of the Hindoo holy places, the resort of pilgrims.

Jŭgŭnnat'hŭ has many temples in Bengal, built by rich men as works of merit, and endowed either with lands, villages, or money. The worship of this god is performed in these temples every morning and evening; at which times people come to see the god, or prostrate themselves before him. During the intervals of worship, and after the god has partaken of the offerings, he is

[q] The lord of the world, from jŭgŭt, the world, and nat'hŭ, lord.

[r] The Athenians placed statues at their doors to drive away thieves, which they called Hermæ, from Mercury. These images had neither hands nor feet, and hence Mercury was called Cyllenius, and by contraction Cyllius, from Kullos, viz., without hands or feet.

[s] The architect of the gods.

laid down to sleep,[t] when the temple is shut up till the next hour of worship.

Bramhŭns may make offerings of boiled rice to this or to any other god, but shōōdrŭs cannot: they are permitted to offer only dried rice.[u] The food which is offered to Jŭgŭnnat'hŭ is either eaten by the bramhŭns and their families at the temples, or by passengers and others, who purchase it of those shopkeepers that have brought it of the bramhŭns; a little is given to the poor.

There are two annual festivals in Bengal in honour of this god; the Snanŭ-yatra, and the Rŭt'hŭ-yatra.

At the Snanŭ-yatra, in the month Jyoisht'hŭ, this lord of the world, wrapped in a cloth, is carried out and placed in a seat on a large terrace built in an open place near the temple. Here the bramhŭns, surrounded by an immense concourse of spectators, bathe the god by pouring water on his head, during the reading of incantations. The people at the close of the ceremony make obeisance, some by lifting their hands to their foreheads, and others by prostration, and then depart, assured by the shastrŭs that they shall be subject to no more births, but be admitted to heaven after the death of this body. The bramhŭns then wipe this creator of the world, and carry him back to the temple; after which the ceremonies of worship are performed before him with great shew. This snanŭ, however, is not confined to Jŭgŭnnat'hŭ; but at this time all the different images of Vishnoo, throughout the country, are bathed. It is the custom of the Hindoos to feed their children with rice for the first time when they are six, seven, or nine months old. On this day, before the ceremony of feeding the child, they bathe it, repeating incantations. Krishnŭ partook of his first rice at the full moon in Jyoist'hu; in commemoration of which, this snanŭ-yatra is performed annually by the worshippers of any separate form of Vishnoo.

About seventeen days after the snanŭ-yatra, on the second of the increase of the moon in Asharhŭ, the Rŭ'thŭ or car festival is held. Before the god is taken out of the temple to be placed on the car, the usual ceremonies of worship are performed. The car belonging to the image near Serampore is in the form of a tapering tower, between thirty and forty cubits high. It has sixteen wheels, two horses, and one coachman, all of wood. Jugŭnnat'hŭ, his brother Bŭlŭ-ramŭ, and their sister Soobhŭdra, are drawn up by ropes tied round the neck, and seated on benches in an elevated

[t] The images of the gods in all the Hindoo temples, at certain hours, are laid down to sleep; at least, all those that are small enough to be laid down and lifted up again.

[u] The bramhŭns do not eat the boiled rice of the shōōdrŭs. Sweetmeats, fruit, the water of the Ganges, &c. are things received from shōōdrŭs. Yet there are a few bramhŭns who refuse even sweetmeats and water from the hands of shōōdrŭs.

part of the carriage; when a servant on each side waves a tail of the cow of Tartary, called a chamŭrŭ.[x] The crowd draw the carriage by means of a hawser; their shouts, as the carriage proceeds, may be heard at the distance of a mile. Being arrived at the appointed spot, the bramhŭns take out the images, and carry them to the temple of some other god, or to a place prepared for them, where they remain eight days. At Serampore, Jŭgŭnnat'hŭ, and his brother and sister, visit the god Radhavŭllŭbhŭ;[y] and here the wives of bramhŭns, who are never seen at shews, and who seldom leave home, come to look at Jŭgŭnnat'hŭ. The car stands empty during this time, and the crowd flock to gaze at the indecent figures,[z] alluding to the abominations of the gods, which are painted all over it. Temporary shops are erected near the place where the car stands, like booths on a race-ground.[a] At the end of eight days, the god is again drawn up by the neck, placed in the car, and carried back to the place from whence he came; but the crowd is not quite so great as when the carriage is drawn out. Many recent instances might be collected of persons, diseased or in distress, casting themselves under the wheels of this ponderous car, and being crushed to death.

This festival is intended to celebrate the diversions of Krishnŭ and the milk-maids, with whom he used to ride out in his chariot.

SECT. V.—*Bŭlŭ-ramŭ.*[b]

THIS god was cotemporary with Krishnŭ. His image, painted white, almost always goes with that of Jŭgŭnnat'hŭ, though in a few temples it is set up alone. At the worship of Jŭgŭnnat'hŭ, and also at that of Krishnŭ, a short service is performed in the name of Bŭlŭ-ramŭ, whose image also sometimes accompanies that of Krishnŭ. Some place the image of Révŭtēē by the side of her husband. From the sŭtyŭ to the kŭlee-yoogŭ this female, the daughter of king Révŭtŭ, remained unmarried.[c] The king, at length, asked Brŭmha, to whom he should give his daughter in marriage: Brŭmha recommended Bŭlŭ-ramŭ, who saw her for the first time when ploughing. Notwithstanding her

[x] The chamŭrŭ is a necessary appendage to royalty among the Hindoos.

[y] Another form of Krishnŭ. The name intimates that this god is the paramour of Radha.

[z] Romans i. 27.

[a] The spirit of gambling is very prevalent at this festival. I have been credibly informed, that, a year or two ago, at Serampore, a man actually sold his wife for a slave, in order to supply himself with money for gaming.

[b] He who pursues pleasure, or bestows it, in his own strength.

[c] This old maid must have been 3,888,000 years old at the time of her marriage if we date her birth from the beginning of the sŭtyŭ-yoogŭ.

immense stature, (it is said her stature reached as high as a sound ascends in clapping the hands seven times.) Bŭlŭramŭ married her; and to bring down her monstrous height, he fastened a ploughshare to her shoulders.

SECT. VI.—*Ramŭ*[d].

THE following history of this god forms a brief table of contents of the Ramayŭnŭ,[e] an epic poem, much celebrated among the Hindoos.

At a certain period, king Dŭshŭ-rŭt'hŭ, having been cherished with great affection by his wife Kékoiyēē,[f] promised her whatever she should ask. She told him that she would avail herself of his promises on some future occasion; and when Ramŭ was called to the co-adjutorship by the voice of the people, and to which Dŭshŭ-rut'hŭ gladly assented, Kékoiyēē reminded the king of his promise; and at the instigation of a deformed and revengeful female slave, whom Ramŭ had formerly beaten, she petitioned that Ramŭ might be exiled to a distant forest to live as an ascetic, and that Bhŭrŭtŭ her son might be installed in his stead. The king reluctantly complied. Ramŭ however readily submitted, and went into the forest, taking with him Sēēta and his brother Lŭkshmŭnŭ. Dŭshŭ-rŭt'hŭ soon died of grief for Ramŭ; after which a shoe of Ramŭ's was placed on the throne, Bhŭrŭtŭ refusing the crown. When in the forest, Sōōrpŭ-nŭkha,[g] the sister of Ravŭnŭ, a giant who reigned at Lŭnka, (Ceylon,) proposed marriage to Ramŭ, who sent her to Lŭkshmŭnŭ; he sent her again to Ramŭ; Ramŭ sending her back to Lŭkshmŭnŭ, the latter cut off her nose: on this she fled to her brothers Khŭrŭ and Dōōshŭnŭ, who immediately made war upon Ramŭ; Ramŭ, however, destroyed them, as well as their army of 14,000 giants, (rakshŭsŭs.) Ravŭnŭ, on hearing of these events, requested Mŭrēēchŭ, another giant, to go to the residence of Ramŭ in the form of a beautiful deer, and tempt Ramŭ to pursue him, while he stole Sēēta. Marēēchŭ consented, and Ramŭ, at the urgent request of Sēēta, pursued the flying deer, leaving Lŭkshmŭnŭ to guard his family. When Marēēchŭ, in the form of the deer, was wounded, he set up a loud cry like the voice of Ramŭ; which greatly alarmed Sēēta, who prevailed on Lŭkshmŭnŭ to follow her beloved husband. While Sēēta was

[d] The happy, or he who makes happy.

[e] I have omitted the long table of contents of this work inserted in the first edition, thinking it unnecessary, as the Ramayŭnŭ with an English translation is issuing from the Serampore press. [The second edition is now published in England.—*Ed.*]

[f] Dŭshŭ-rŭt'hŭ had 250 wives.

[g] A name given to her on account of her having nails like a Hindoo fan for winnowing corn.

thus left alone, Ravŭnŭ carried her off in triumph. The poem then describes the grief of Ramŭ and his brother for the loss of Sēēta. Ravŭnŭ, in taking away Sēēta, was met by Jŭtayoo, a vulture, formerly the friend of Dŭshŭ-rŭt'hŭ. This bird endeavoured to deliver Sēēta by fighting with Ravŭnŭ; but being unsuccessful, Sēēta directed him to inform Ramŭ, that Ravŭnŭ was carrying her away. Ramŭ in his search for Sēēta met with this bird, which, as soon as it had delivered this account, died of the wounds it had received in fighting with Ravŭnŭ. Ramŭ and his brother now went forward in pursuit of Ravŭnŭ, and met with the giant Kŭbŭndhŭ, whom they destroyed. This giant immediately assumed another body, and informed Ramŭ, that he had formerly lived in the heaven of Indrŭ, but had been cursed, and sent down to take the body of a rakshŭsŭ. He further informed Ramŭ, that two brothers, (monkies,) Soogrēēvŭ and. Balēē, were in a state of warfare, Balēē having seduced his brother's wife; he therefore advised Ramŭ to destroy Balēē, and contract an alliance with Soogrēēvŭ, by whose means he should obtain Sēēta. Ramŭ took this advice, and having destroyed Balēē,[h] restored Soogrēēvŭ to his kingdom. To prove his gratitude to Ramŭ, Soogrēēvŭ collected his army of monkies, and sent them to seek for Sēēta. The monkies who went southward met Sŭmpatee, a vulture without wings, brother to Jŭtayoo, who informed them that he had seen Sēēta at Lŭnka, (Ceylon.) Hŭnooman, one of Soogrēēvŭ's generals, immediately leaped across the sea, (five hundred miles,)[i] to Lŭnka, where he found Sēēta in a garden belonging to Ravŭnŭ; to whom he gave a ring from Ramŭ, while she, in return, sent Ramŭ a jewel from her hair. Hŭnooman then began to destroy one of Ravŭnŭ's gardens; who sent people to kill Hŭnooman, but he destroyed those who were sent. Ravŭnŭ then sent his son Ŭksbŭyŭ against the mischievous monkey; but he also was destroyed. Ravŭnŭ next sent his eldest son Indrŭjit, who seized Hŭnooman, and bringing him before his father, the king ordered his attendants to set fire to his tail; when the enraged monkey, with his burning tail, leaped from house to house, and set all Lŭnka on fire: after finishing which he came to Sēēta, and complained that he could not extinguish the fire that had kindled on his tail; she directed him to spit upon it, and he, raising it to his face for this purpose, set his face on fire. He then complained, that when he arrived at home with such a black face, all the monkeys would laugh at him. Sēēta, to comfort him, assured him, that all the other monkeys should have black faces also; and when Hŭnooman came amongst his friends, he found that, according to the promise of Sēēta, they had all black faces as well as himself. After hearing the account

h Ramŭ, compared with Krishnŭ, is a pure character; yet we see him here, without provocation, destroy the rightful heir to a throne, and set up one who had seduced the wife of his brother.

i No one can doubt the propriety of making a spy of a monkey who can leap 500 miles at once.

brought by Hŭnooman, Ramŭ and Lŭkshmŭnŭ, with Soogrēēvŭ and his army of monkeys, proceeded to invade Lŭnka. They tore up the mountains, trees, and other large substances, and cast them into the sea to form a bridge;[k] which, however, Ravŭnŭ was constantly employed in breaking down. Vibhēēshŭnŭ, Ravŭnŭ's brother, perceiving that Ramŭ would make good his landing, recommended that Sēēta should be given up: but his brother, unable to bear this advice, quarrelled with Vibhēēshŭnŭ; who came over to Ramŭ, and advised him to throw into the sea a temple and image of Shivŭ, assuring him, that as Ravŭnŭ was a worshipper of Shivŭ, he would not destroy the temple and image of his god. Ramŭ followed this advice, soon made good his landing, and began the war with Ravŭnŭ. After many giants had been killed, Koombhŭkŭrnŭ, a monstrous giant, 2,400 cubits high, and 1,600 thick, brother to Ravŭnŭ, engaged Ramŭ and the monkeys. He began the combat by seizing and devouring his enemies. Some of them, as soon as they entered his mouth, came out at his nostrils and ears, and escaped. The terrified monkeys fled; but Ramŭ with his arrows first cut off his arms, then his legs. Still he waddled round, and endeavoured to devour all within his reach, till Ramŭ gave him a mortal wound in the neck. Next after Koombhŭkŭrnŭ, Indrŭjit engaged in the contest. He seized Ramŭ, and, by the power of enchantment, carried him down to patalŭ; where Hŭnooman went in search of him, and, while Mŭhēēravŭnŭ was there, instructing Indrŭjit how to prostrate himself before an image of the goddess Bhŭdrŭ-kalēē, Hŭnooman cut off his head, and rescued Ramŭ. At length Ravŭnŭ himself entered the combat; but after many conflicts, finding himself very weak, he resolved to restore Sēēta, and put an end to the war. To this Ramŭ consented; but while Ravŭnŭ was on the point of bringing Sēēta, he thought within himself, 'If I do this, every one will charge me with cowardice: shall I, a giant, refuse to fight?' The combat was again renewed, and Ravŭnŭ was slain.[l] Ramŭ then obtained his wife; but as a trial of her innocence while in the hands of Ravŭnŭ, he compelled her to pass through a fiery

[k] Ramŭ's bridge. See the map of Hindoost'han. Ramŭ was at a loss how to lead his army across the sea to Lŭnka. He fasted, and prayed to Sagŭrŭ for three days, and was angry with the god for not appearing to him. He therefore ordered Lŭkshmŭnŭ to fire an arrow, and carry away the god's umbrella. He did so, and the arrow, carrying away the umbrella, penetrated even as far as patalŭ. The god, aroused from his sleep, exclaimed, 'Is Ramŭ arrived by the sea side, and I have not known it?' He then directed Ramŭ to apply to king Nŭlŭ, to whom he had given a blessing, that whatever he threw into the sea should become buoyant. At the command of Nŭlŭ, the monkeys tore up the neighbouring mountains, and cast them into the sea. Hŭnooman brought three mountains on his head at once, each 64 miles in circumference; and one on each shoulder, equally large; together with one under each arm, one in each paw, and one on his tail. All these mountains being thrown into the sea, and becoming buoyant, a complete bridge was formed.

[l] The engagement betwixt Ramŭ and Ravŭnŭ lasted seven days: Ramŭ cut off the ten heads of Ravŭnŭ a hundred times, but they were always miraculously restored. Ramŭ then discharged an arrow which had these properties, that if it went into the air, it became a thousand; if it entered the body of an enemy, it became an innumer-

ordeal: which she did unhurt. He then returned to Ŭyodhya, and mounted the throne. After this, however, some person objected to Ramŭ, that it was not proper for him to receive Sēēta, after she had been in keeping of a giant. He therefore sent her into the forest to Valmēēkee, the writer of the Ramayŭnŭ, where she was delivered of two sons, Lŭvŭ and Kooshŭ; the latter of whom was afterwards stolen by the god Pŭnchanŭnŭ, when Valmēēkee, to comfort the mother, took a blade of kooshŭ grass, and secretly made a child so much like Kooshŭ, that Seeta did not know it from her own son. In a short time, however, Pŭnchanŭnŭ, not being able to destroy a child of Ramŭ's, restored Kooshŭ, and Valmēēkee caused the two boys to become one. Before his death Ramŭ performed the sacrifice of a horse;[m] and Sēēta and her two sons, Lŭvŭ and Kooshŭ, were restored to him: but Ramŭ wishing Sēēta again to pass through a fiery ordeal, she entered the fire; but the goddess Prŭt'hivee,[n] (Sēēta's mother,) opened her mouth, and received her into patalŭ. At length Kalŭpoorooshŭ, the angel of death, went to Ramŭ, expressing a wish for a secret conference. Ramŭ promised that while he was present no one should be admitted, and placed Lŭkshmŭnŭ at the door to keep out all intruders: but while Ramŭ and Kalŭ-poorooshŭ were closeted, Doorvasa, the sage, arrived, and demanded an interview with Ramŭ. This sage was so very passionate, that every one dreaded contradicting him; Lŭkshmŭnŭ, therefore, through fear, went in and announced his arrival. Ramŭ, for this offence, rejected his brother, who in a paroxysm of grief drowned himself in the sacred river Sŭrŭyoo, and went to heaven. Ramŭ afterwards put an end to his life in the same manner. Lŭvŭ and Kookshŭ succeeded him.[o]

able multitude. Ravŭnŭ at the sight of this arrow was filled with fear, and would have fled; but recollecting that Shivŭ had once given him an arrow that was to rescue him in a time of extreme peril, he discharged it, and destroyed Ramŭ's terrible arrow. Still however he was full of fear, for whichever way he turned, he saw Ramŭ; he shut his eyes, but still he saw him in his mind. At length, perceiving no way of escape, he began to flatter Ramŭ; who was so softened, that he declared he would never destroy Ravŭnŭ. The gods, alarmed lest Ravŭnŭ should be spared, excited him to reproach Ramŭ; who, indignant at such conduct, let fly an arrow which pierced Ravŭnŭ's body, proceeded through the earth into the regions below, and having there bathed, returned in the form of a goose, and again entered the quiver in its original shape. The gods were so much in fear of Ravŭnŭ, that they durst not begin to rejoice till they were sure he was dead: in whispers they asked each other, 'Is he dead?'—'Is he really dead?' &c. When it was known that he was certainly dead, the gods, Ramŭ, the monkeys, and the bears, all began to dance.—Mŭndodŭrēē, the chief wife of Ravŭnŭ, and mother of Indrŭjit, after the death of her husband, went to Ramŭ, weeping. Ramŭ, not knowing who she was, gave her this blessing, that she should never become a widow. Finding his mistake, (having just killed her husband,) he ordered Hŭnooman continually to throw wood into the fire; according to a proverb among the Hindoos, that as long as the body of the husband is burning, a woman is not called a widow. To this day, therefore, Hŭnooman keeps laying logs on the fire; and every time a Hindoo puts his fingers in his ears and hears a sound, he says, he hears, the bones of Ravŭnŭ burning.

m This sacrifice was performed by many of the ancient Hindoo princes, and was considered as highly meritorious.

n The earth personified.

o There are a few sentences in this history, which are not to be found in Valmēēkee's Ramayŭnŭ; but they may be seen in the Bengalee translation.

The image of Ramŭ is painted green; he is represented as sitting on a throne, or on Hŭnooman, the monkey, with a crown upon his head. He holds in one hand a bow, in another an arrow, and has a bundle of arrows slung at his back.

The worship paid to him is of the same kind as that to Krishnŭ; but the formulas are different. On the ninth of the increase of the moon in Choitrŭ, on which day Ramŭ was born, an annual festival is held, when multitudes of clay images are worshipped. The dolŭ festival also is observed in honour of this god on this day, which is also kept as a fast; when Ramŭ's three brothers, Bhŭrŭtŭ, Lŭkshmŭnŭ, and Shŭtrŭghnŭ are worshipped, but the images of the first and last are never made. At other festivals also a few ceremonies in honour of Ramŭ are performed.

The birth of Ramŭ forms the seventh of the Hindoo incarnations. On the birth-day of this god[p] the Hindoo merchants in general begin their new year's accounts. At the time of death, many Hindoos write the name of Ramŭ on the breast and forehead of the dying person, with earth taken from the banks of the Ganges; and hence these persons after death, instead of being dragged to Yŭmŭ to be judged, immediately ascend to heaven. Many of the disciples of Ramŭ become Ramahoots, a class of mendicants who impress on different parts of their bodies Ramŭ's name and the figure of his foot. The mark on the forehead of Ramŭ's followers very much resembles a trident.

Temples containing the images of Ramŭ, Lŭkshmŭnŭ, Sēēta, and Hŭnooman are erected in many parts of Bengal; and the worship of Ramŭ performed in them daily.

SECT. VII.—*Choitŭnyŭ.*[q]

THIS is the image of an almost naked mendicant, painted yellow. Some of the Hindoos believe, that amongst all the Hindoo incarnations there are four principal ones. The first, in the sŭtyŭ-yoogŭ, called the Shooklŭ-vŭrnŭ[r] incarnation, was that of Ŭnŭntŭ; that in the tréta, the rŭktŭ-vŭrnŭ,[s] was the incarnation of Kopilŭ-dévŭ; that in the dwapŭrŭ-yoogŭ, the Krishnŭ-vŭrnŭ;[t] and the last, in the kŭlee-yoogŭ, called pēētŭ-vŭrnŭ,[u] that of Choitŭnyŭ.

According to the disciples of Choitŭnyŭ, the founder of this sect, Ŭdwoitŭ, a voidikŭ bramhŭn, lived at Shantipoorŭ about 400 years ago. Nityanŭndŭ, another leader, was born at Nŭdēēya, a little before Choitŭnyŭ. His father was a rarhēēyŭ bramhŭn.

p The gods on this day are said to have caused a shower of flowers to fall, as at the birth of Minerva it is said to have rained gold.

q The wise. r The white. s The blood-coloured. t The black. u The yellow.

Choitŭnyŭ's father, Jŭgunnat'hŭ-Mishrŭ, a voidikŭ bramhŭn, lived at Nŭdēēya; his wife's name was Shŭchēē; their first son, Vishwŭmbhŭrŭ, embraced the profession of a dŭndēē. The mother was advanced in years when Choitŭnyŭ was born; the child continued three days without taking the breast, and the parents, not thinking it would live, putting it into a basket, hung it on a tree near the house.[x] At this time Ŭdwoitŭ before-mentioned, who had heard of this birth, having some suspicions that it might be the incarnation he had expected and foretold, visited the parents, and learning from the mother that she had not received the initiating incantation of Huree, he wrote, with his great toe, this incantation on the soft earth :—'Hŭree, Krishnŭ; Hŭree, Krishnŭ; Krishnŭ, Krishnŭ, Hŭree, Hŭree; Hŭree, Ramŭ, Hŭree, Ramŭ, Ramŭ, Ramŭ, Hŭree, Hŭree.' After the mother had received this incantation, the child was taken down, and immediately began to draw the breast.

Choitŭnyŭ made a great progress in learning; at sixteen he married Vishnoo-priya, and continued in a secular state till forty-four, when he was persuaded by Ŭdwoitŭ and other dŭndēēs then at his house, to renounce his poita, and become a mendicant: upon which, forsaking his mother and wife, he went to Benares. His family was reduced to great distress indeed; and it was thought a crime that a person upon whom such a family depended should embrace a life of mendicity.

From this period Choitŭnyŭ began to form a new sect, giving to all his followers the preceding initiatory incantation, and continuing to call them voishnŭvŭs. He exhorted them to renounce a secular life; to visit the different holy places on pilgrimage; to eat with all castes who should receive the preceding incantation; to repeat the name of Vishnoo, using the bead-roll made with the stalk of basil. He further taught that widows might marry; but forbad the eating of fish or flesh, and the worship of the deities to whom bloody sacrifices are offered, as well as all communion with those who make these sacrifices.

He went to Jŭgŭnnat'hŭ-kshĕtru in Orissa, and there assuming six arms, received many honors. He exhorted Ŭdwoitŭ and Nityanŭndŭ to labour in making proselytes; but directed Nityanŭndŭ to enter into a secular state:[y] he did so, and took up his

[x] There are still many instances of children being exposed. If a child appear unlikely to live, the parents consult an astrologer, who perhaps gives but small hopes of the child's recovery. Voiragees and other mendicants, who make a merit of possessing no worldly attachments, some times hang up a child in a pot in a tree; or, putting it in a pot, let it float down the river. Persons of other castes may do it, but these the most frequently. Mr. Carey's journal, dated in July, 1794, contains the following paragraph: 'One day, as Mr. Thomas and I were riding out, we saw a basket hung in a tree, in which an infant had been exposed; the skull remained, but the rest had been devoured by ants.' See Baptist Mission Accounts, vol. i. p. 183. This practice is now prohibited by the Hon. Company's Government, in a regulation made for that purpose.

[y] Perceiving his aversion to a life of mendicity

residence at Khŭrdu, near Calcutta. Choitŭnyŭ wrote to his two principal disciples from Orissa, again exhorting them to labour in gaining proselytes; yet few or none joined them: and from this time Choitŭnyŭ himself was never more heard of. Ŭdwoitŭ and Nityanŭndŭ raised families, whose descendants live at Shantipoorŭ, Vagna-para, and Khŭrdŭ to this day, where they are become leaders of the sect; all other Gosaees[z] acknowledging the descendants of these two families as their superiors, and prostrating themselves before them. These Gosaees at present are men of large fortunes; at whose houses are the images originally set up by the male descendant of Choitŭnyŭ, by Nityanŭndŭ, and Ŭdwoitŭ Crowds are almost constantly arriving at these places with offerings: besides which, the Gosaees derive a large revenue from marriages, to superintend which they have agents distributed throughout the country, who are allowed a sixth part of the fee; a sum that from both parties amounts to about six shillings. They also dissolve marriages at the pleasure of the parties, on receiving the same fees. When a new disciple is initiated, a fee is also given; but the Gosaees obtain the largest sums at the deaths of such of their disciples as die intestate. At Calcutta, nearly all the women of ill-fame profess the religion of Choitŭnyŭ before their death, that they may be entitled to some sort of funeral rites: as almost all these persons die intestate, and have no relations who will own them, the Gosaees obtain their effects.

The anniversaries of the deaths of the original founders of the sect are observed as festivals.

One-fifth of the whole Hindoo population of Bengal are supposed to be followers of Choitŭnyŭ, and of the Gosaees, his successors.

Many of these persons despise the other sects of Hindoos, and are great enemies of the bramhŭns. They refuse to eat without their necklace, as the bramhŭns do without their poita. Most of the mendicant followers of Vishnoo have embraced the tenets of Choitŭnyŭ; but many of the disciples of the latter live in a secular state, and some of them are possessed of large property. Persons of this description frequently entertain a great number of voiragees at their houses; when, as an act of great merit, they prostrate themselves before these wanderers, wash, and lick the dust of their feet, and devour their orts. They pay no attention to the feasts and fasts of the Hindoo calendar, except those in honour of Krishnŭ.

The images most regarded among this sect are those of Choitŭnyŭ and Nityanŭndŭ, set up at Ŭmbika, in the district of Burdwan.

[z] Distant branches of the same families.

About a hundred years ago, another man rose up in Bengal as the leader of a sect, whose dress, of many colours, is said to be so heavy that two or three people can scarcely carry it. This and his string of beads are preserved as relics at Ghoshparŭ, where he continued five years, and died at the house of Ramŭ-Shŭrŭnŭ-Palŭ, a shōōdrŭ of the Sŭd-gopŭ caste, to whom he communicated his supernatural powers; and who, after the death of this mendicant, began to teach the doctrine of a constant incarnation, and that God then dwelt in him. He persuaded many that he could cure the leprosy, and other diseases; and preached the doctrines of Choitŭnyŭ, imitating him in conforming, for convenience sake, to many of the superstitions of the Hindoos. He also gave a new initiating incantation to his followers,[a] who, of whatever caste, ate together privately. Vast multitudes joined this man, both Mŭsŭlmans and Hindoos; and carried him presents, eating together once or twice a year. By this means, from a state of deep poverty he became rich, and his son now lives in affluence.

A number of Ramŭ-Shŭrŭnŭ's disciples adhere to his son Doolalŭ; others follow Shivŭ-Ramŭ and some others of the old man's disciples, who pretend to have received the power of their master to cure diseases, &c. Though part of the father's followers have thus apostatized, Doolalŭ pretends that he has now 20,000 disciples.

SECT. VIII.—*Vishwŭ-kŭrma*[b]

Is the son of Brŭmha, and architect of the gods: he is painted white, has three eyes, holds a club in his right hand; wears a crown, a necklace of gold, and rings on his wrists. He presides over the arts, manufactures, &c.

The worship of this god is performed once, twice, or four times a year, in the month Ŭgrŭhayŭnŭ, Poushŭ, Choitrŭ, or Bhadrŭ, by all artificers, to obtain success in business. The ceremonies may be performed either in the day or night, before any implements of trade. The joiners set up their mallet, chisel, saw, hatchet, &c. as the representative of this god. Weavers choose their shuttle, &c., putting them into the hole in the earth wherein they place their feet when they sit at work. The razor is the barber's god on this occasion. The potter, after a month's fast, adopts and worships the wheel with which he turns his pots. Masons choose their trowel; washermen take the beetle or stamper,

[a] The following is a translation of this incantation: 'O sinless Lord, O great Lord; at thy pleasure I go and return: not a moment am I without thee. I am ever with thee; save, O great Lord.'

[b] Vishwŭ, the world; kŭrmŭ, work.

their smoothing irons, &c. as their god ; blacksmiths worship their hammer and bellows ; the farmer his plough ; spinsters their wheel. The shoemaker chooses his awl and knife, and bows down to them : and thus, amongst all the artificers, each one chooses the principal tool or instrument with which he works, and makes it a god, or the representative of Vishwŭ-kŭrma[c]. The ceremonies are not long ; but according to their ability the worshippers provide as good a feast as possible. At the close of the festival, the crowd form themselves into parties of pleasure : some go upon the river in boats, singing songs, and playing on different instruments of music ; others sit in companies, smoke, and relate the news of the village ; others spend their time in gaming, and some resort to houses of ill-fame.

Though the illiterate consider this god, who may be called the Indian Vulcan, as the inventor of all the mechanic arts, the shilpŭ shastrŭs, a part of the original védŭ, are more properly considered as their source. These works are not now read in Bengal, if they really exist : they describe, it is said, the proper shape and dimensions of all the various images of the Hindoo gods.

SECT. IX.—*Kamŭ-dévŭ, the Indian Cupid.*[d]

THE image of this god, the son of Brŭmha, is that of a beautiful youth, holding in his hands a bow and arrow of flowers. He is always supposed to be accompanied by his wife Rŭtee,[e] by spring personified, the cuckoo, the humming-bee, and gentle breezes ; and is represented as wandering through the three worlds.

The image of Kamŭ-dévŭ is never made in Bengal, but on the 13th of the increase of the moon in Choitrŭ an annual festival is held, when the ceremonies of worship are performed before the shalgramŭ. At the time of marriage, and when a wife leaves her father's house to go to her husband for the first time, petitions are addressed to this god for children, and for happiness in the marriage state.

[c] This worship affords another strong proof of the low and sordid nature of idolatry, and strikingly illustrates the words of our Lord, 'after all these things do the Gentiles seek.' Instead of raising their minds to the Great Source of all good, these persons are taught to worship the tools belonging to their trades, as the cause of their temporal happiness. This conduct seems to be reproved in the first chapter of the book of Habakkuk, 'They sacrifice unto their net, and burn incense unto their drag ; because by them their portion is fat, and their meat plenteous.'

[d] Kamŭ, desire ; devŭ, god.

[e] From Rŭmŭ, to play, or to give pleasure. It is said that the god of love found Rŭtee in the house of Shŭmbŭrŭ, a giant, whom he destroyed.

The pooranŭ and kavyŭ shastrŭs abound with stories respecting Kamŭ-dévŭ, one of which I here give from the Kalikŭ pooranŭ :—The god of love, the most beautiful creature in the three worlds, with whom every one was pleased, immediately after his creation solicited the commands of Brŭmha ; who assured him, that, with his five arrows, he should wound with love the hearts of the inhabitants of the three worlds ; that all beings should be subject to his sway, not excepting even Brŭmha, Vishnoo, and Shivŭ ; and that through him the universe should be peopled. Kŭndŭrpŭ first discharged his arrow at Brŭmha himself, who became enamoured of his own daughter, Sŭndhya. Mŭrēēchee, and the other sons of Brŭmha, also smitten by his arrows, were inflamed with unlawful desires toward their sister. Shivŭ said to Brŭmha, 'What! art thou inflamed with lust towards thy own daughter?' Brŭmha was covered with shame, and, from the perspiration which issued from his body, Ŭgnishwŭta and other progenitors of mankind,[f] to the number of 149,000, were born. Brŭmha, full of rage against Kŭndŭrpŭ, cursed him, and declared that he should be burnt to ashes by the fire from the eye of Shivŭ ; but on his intercessions promised, that when Shivŭ should be married to Doorga, he would restore to him his body.

Names.—Mŭdŭnŭ, or he who intoxicates with love ;—Mŭnmŭt'hŭ, he who agitates the mind ;—Marŭ, he who wounds with love ;—Prŭdyoomnŭ, he who overcomes all ;—Mēēnŭ-kétŭnu, he whose flag is a fish ;—Kŭndŭrpŭ, he who bloats the mind with desire ;—Ŭnŭngŭ, he who is destitute of body ; Ramŭ, the creator of desire ;—Pŭnchŭshŭrŭ, he who has five arrows ;—Smŭrŭ, he who inflames ;—Shŭmbŭraree, the enemy of the giant Shŭmbŭrŭ ; —Mŭnŭsijŭ, he who is born in the heart ;—Koosoomésboo, he whose arrows are flowers ;—Ŭnŭnyŭjŭ, he who is born only in the mind ;—Pooshpŭ-dhŭnwa, he whose bow is made of flowers ;—Rŭtee-pŭtee, the husband of Rŭtee ;—Mŭkŭrŭ-dhwŭjŭ, he whose flag is the animal Mŭkŭrŭ ;—Atmŭbhoo, he who is self-created.

SECT. X.—*Sŭtyŭ-Narayŭnŭ.*

THIS is a form of Vishnoo, but the image is never made : a pan of water is the substitute.

This god is worshipped several times in the year, in the house of the richer Hindoos, when all the bramhŭns in the village are

[f] In performing the ceremony called tŭrpŭnŭ, seven names are used in pouring out drink-offerings to all these ancestors.

invited. The object of worship, painted red, and covered with leaves of the mango tree, is placed near a square board, at the four corners of which four arrows are set up, and from which garlands of flowers are suspended ; a piece of clean linen is laid on the board, and then the offerings of flowers and sweetmeats. At the close of the festival, some one present reads different marvellous stories in praise of this god. The sweetmeats are given to the guests, especially to the bramhŭns : the acquisition of riches, recovery from sickness, the birth of children, the obtaining of any of the blessings, or the removing any of the miseries of life, are objects sought in the worship of this god.

THE preceding account of the terrestrial gods contains the names of all the principal deities of this description worshipped in Bengal. I am aware, however, that worship is paid to some idols not mentioned here ; but these are only different forms of the deities whose history is given, and the worship is merely an appendage to the ceremonies at the great festivals.

CHAP. VI

TERRESTRIAL GODDESSES.

SECT. I.—*Sēēta.*

THIS is the image of a yellow woman, covered with jewels: it always accompanies and is worshipped with that of her husband.

Sēēta was the daughter of king Jŭnŭkŭ,[a] whose capital was Mit'hila. Her history, after her marriage with Ramŭ, will be found in the account of that god.[b]

SECT. II.—*Radha.*

RADHA was the wife of Ayŭnu-ghoshŭ, a cowherd of Gokoolŭ, where Krishnŭ in his youth resided: through Vŭraee, a procuress, he seduced Radha, and led her into the forest near the river Yŭmoona, where they continued till Krishnŭ left her to begin the war with Kŭngsŭ.

This mistress of Krishnŭ has been deified with her paramour. Her image is set up in temples with different forms of Krishnŭ, and worshipped at the festivals of this god. The act of looking upon these images together, is declared by the shastrŭs to be an act of peculiar merit!

If a Hindoo be charged with any particular act of which he wishes to express his abhorrence, he exclaims, 'Radha-Krishnŭ!' Many persons repeat 'Ramŭ! Ramŭ! Ramŭ!' on such occasions,

[a] Shivŭ gave to Jŭnŭkŭ a bow so heavy that a thousand men could not lift it, and which the father placed in a separate room, and commanded Sēēta to sweep the room daily; in doing which she used to lift up the bow with her left hand, and sweep under it with her right. One day the king saw her thus move the bow, and, filled with astonishment, was at a loss to whom he should give this daughter in marriage. After some time, he came to this resolution, that whoever should be able to break this bow, should obtain Sēēta.—*Udhyatmu-Ramayunu.*

[b] While Sēēta was detained at Lŭnka, she was fed with ambrosia for twelve months by Indrŭ, as she would not eat in the house of a giant. That Ravŭnŭ could not destroy her virtue, is thus accounted for by the pooranŭs:—This giant had before seized the wives of the gods, and dishonoured them; and one day he dishonoured his niece, the wife of king Nŭlŭ: for which crime Koovérŭ cursed him, and caused fire to proceed from his ten heads at once. By the entreaty of Brŭmha, this curse was mitigated; with the proviso, however, that if he ever defiled the wife of another, it should be renewed in full force.—*Ibid.*

but no one says Sēēta-Ramŭ ; yet when Krishnŭ's name is to be repeated, they always join to it that of his mistress Radha.

One of the Hindoo learned men has written a work (the Radha-tŭntrŭ) to prove that Radha was an incarnation of Bhŭgŭvŭtēē ; and this opinion is quoted by the Hindoos of the present day to cover this abominable transaction.

SECT. III.—*Rookminēē and Sŭtyŭ-bhama.*

THESE are the most distinguished wives of Krishnŭ, but their images are never made, Krishnŭ being always associated with Radha his mistress, and not with his lawful wives. At the festivals of Krishnŭ, however, these women are worshipped, as well as six other wives of this god, viz., Jambŭbŭtēē, Mitrŭvinda, Lŭgŭnŭjitēē, Lŭkshmŭna, Kalindēē, and Bhŭdra ; but Rookminēē and Sŭtyŭ-bhama are the most distinguished.

SECT. IV.—*Soobhŭdra.*

THIS sister of Jŭgŭnnat'hŭ is worshipped at the same time with her brother, and placed with him in the temples dedicated to his honour.

CHAP. VII.

DEITIES WORSHIPPED BY THE LOWER ORDERS ONLY.

SECT. I.—*Pŭnchanŭnŭ*[a]

Is a form of Shivŭ: the image has five faces, and in each face three eyes. Some persons make a clay image, and worship it with the usual forms, adding bloody sacrifices; while others worship Pŭnchanŭnŭ before a stone placed underneath the vŭtŭ,[b] ŭshwŭt'h-t'hŭ,[c] or koolŭ[d] trees. This stone is painted red at the top, and anointed with oil.[e] Offerings of flowers, fruits, water, sweetmeats, and fried peas accompany the worship, and sometimes bloody sacrifices. In almost every village this worship is performed beneath some one of these trees. In some villages several of these shapeless stones[f] are to be seen thus anointed, and consecrated to the worship of this god. In other places the clay images of Pŭnchanŭnŭ are placed in houses, or under trees; and old women, called dyasinēēs,[g] devote themselves to his service: they sweep the inside of the clay temple, and repeat the ceremonies of worship for others; constantly remaining near the image, and receiving all offerings and presents. Not more than one woman waits upon one idol, unless she admit a pupil, who expects to succeed her. These women, either married or widows, are treated almost as witches.

There is no appointed time for the worship of this god, but Tuesdays or Saturdays are preferred to other days.

There are some places in Bengal, where images of Pŭnchanŭnŭ are in great celebrity for bestowing the blessing of children, and other favours on the worshippers.

The Hindoo women are terrified at this god, and are exceedingly afraid lest their children should, in play, injure the stone

[a] The five-faced.

[b] Ficus Indica.

[c] Ficus religiosa.

[d] Zizyphus jujuba.

[e] The statue of the god Terminus was either a square stone, or a log of wood; which the Romans usually perfumed with ointments, and crowned with garlands.

[f] The representative of the goddess Passinuntia was a shapeless stone. The Arabians are said to have worshipped a stone without the form or shape of a deity.

[g] It is probable that these dyasinēēs resemble the priestesses of Cybele.

under the tree.[g] Some therefore warn their children against going near these stones, by declaring that Pŭnchanŭnŭ will assuredly kill them, if they touch or play with his image.

Children in fits of epilepsy are supposed to be seized by this god, and thrown into a state of frenzy, till they foam at the mouth, tear their hair, &c. The mother asks the supposed evil spirit his name, who answers, through the child, 'I am Pŭnchanŭnŭ: your child has cast dust on my image, kicked it, and is the ringleader of all the children of the village in this wickedness. I will certainly take away his life.' The dyasinēē is now called, who comforts the weeping and alarmed family, and addresses the god thus: 'O Pŭnchanŭnŭ! I pray thee restore this child: these are thy worshippers: the offender is but a child; and it is not proper for thee to be angry with such paltry offenders. If thou restore the child, the parents will sacrifice a goat to thee, and present to thee many offerings.' If this should fail to render the god propitious, they take the child to the image, before which they sit down, and offer the most excessive flattery to the god, causing the child to beat its head on the ground. After using every contrivance, they retire, and, at the close of the fit, believing that Pŭnchanŭnŭ has cured the child, they present to him offerings according to their ability.

SECT. II.—*Dhŭrmŭ T'hakoorŭ.*

ANOTHER form of Shivŭ. A black stone of any shape becomes the representative of this god. The worshippers paint the part designated as the forehead, and place it under a tree; others place the stone in the house, and give it silver eyes, and anoint it with oil, and worship it. Almost every village has one of these idols.

[g] The late Jŭgŭnnat'hŭ-Tŭrkkŭ-Pŭnchanŭnŭ, who died in the year 1807, at the advanced age of 112, and who was supposed to be the most learned Hindoo in Bengal, used to relate the following ancedote of himself:—Till he was twenty years old he was exceedingly ungovernable, and refused to apply to his studies. One day his parents rebuked him very sharply for his conduct, and he wandered to a neighbouring village, where he hid himself in the vŭtŭ tree, under which was a very celebrated image of Pŭnchanŭnŭ. While in this tree, he discharged his urine on the god, and afterwards descended and threw him into a neighbouring pond. The next morning, when the person arrived whose livelihood depended on this image, he discovered his god was gone!! He returned into the village distracted, and the village was very soon all in an uproar about the lost god. In the midst of this confusion, the parents of Jŭgŭnnat'hŭ-Tŭrkkŭ-Pŭnchanŭnŭ arrived to search for their son; when a man in the crowd declared that he had seen a young man sitting in Pŭnchanŭnŭ's tree, but what was become of the god he could not say. The runaway at length appeared, and the suspicions of all the villagers fell upon him, as the stealer of Pŭnchanŭnŭ. After some time he confessed the fact, pointed out the place where he had thrown the stone, and added moreover that he had discharged his urine on the god. All hands were lifted up in amazement at this atrocious crime, and every one present pronounced his death as certain; for Pŭnchanŭnŭ would certainly revenge such a daring insult. Our young hero was himself terribly affrighted, and from that hour sat down so sedulously to his studies, that he became the most learned man in Bengal. He was employed by the government in India for many years, at a salary of 300 rupees per month, and used to give advice on the subject of the Hindoo law in all difficult cases.

A festival in honour of this god is observed by some of the lower orders in Voishakŭ, in the day. The ceremonies are like those at the swinging festival, with the addition of bloody sacrifices, the greater number of which are goats. At this time devotees swing on hooks; perforate their sides with cords; pierce their tongues with spits; walk upon fire, and take it up in their hands; walk upon thorns; and throw themselves upon spikes, keeping a severe fast. The people who assemble to see these feats of self-torture, are entertained with singing, music, and dancing. On the 14th day, a great feast is held, when people bring their offerings, and giving them to the officiating bramhŭn, request him to present them to the idol, to fulfil a vow; or with petitions to the god for some particular favour, as the birth of a child, recovery from sickness, or any other blessing.

Wherever this idol is placed in a house, a woman called a dyasinēē attends upon it, and repeats the daily ceremonies.

At two villages in Bengal, Poosoorēē and Rayŭ-kalee, the worship of this god is constantly attended by crowds from a great distance. If a woman's eldest child die, she makes a vow before witnesses, that she will not cut her hair for two years; and that then, going to one of these villages, she will cut it off, and present an offering to the god, provided he will preserve her second child. Some women, as an acknowledgment of a favour, or to beg a blessing, take a young child in their arms; and putting on wet clothes, place and earthen pot full of burning coals upon some cloth on their heads; and sitting before the god in a supplicating posture, continue for sometime offering incense, throwing Indian pitch into the pan of coals.

A poor man sometimes places the black stone, adorned with garlands, &c. in a basket, and the offerings which he collects at the doors of housekeepers in another, and, tying the baskets to a bamboo which he lays on his shoulder, carries the god from door to door as a show; while another plays on a rude instrument of music, and joins in singing the praises of Dhŭrmŭ-t'hakoorŭ. House-holders give a handful of rice, and the beggars present in return a flower which has been offered to the god.

SECT. III.—*Kaloo-rayŭ.*

THIS is another form of Shivŭ: the image is that of a yellow man sitting on a tiger, holding in his right hand an arrow, and in his left a bow.

A few of the lower orders set up clay images of this god in straw houses, and worship them at pleasure. The wood-cutters in the Eastern, Western, and Southern forests of Bengal, in order to obtain protection from wild beasts, adopt a peculiar mode of worshipping this idol. The head-boatman raises elevations of earth three or four inches high, and about three feet square ; upon which he places balls of clay, painted red ; and, among other ceremonies, offers rice, flowers, fruits, and the water of the Ganges carried from the river Hooglee, keeping a fast : the god then directs him in a dream where to cut wood free from danger. There is no authority for this worship in the shastrŭs.

Dŭkshina-rayŭ is another god worshipped in the same manner, and by the same class of persons.

SECT. IV.—*Kalŭ-Bhoirŭvŭ.*

A NAKED Shivŭ, smeared with ashes ; having three eyes ; riding on a dog ; and holding in one hand a horn, and in the other a drum. In several places in Bengal this image is worshipped daily.

Shivŭ, under this name, is regent of Kashēē, (Benares.) All persons dying at Benares are entitled to a place in Shivŭ's heaven ; but if any one violate the laws of the shastrŭ during his residence there, Kalŭ-Bhoirŭvŭ at death grinds him between two mill-stones.

SECT. V.—*Worship to cure the Itch and Scurvy.*

THE goddess Shēētula is worshipped by the Hindoo females whenever their families are afflicted with the itch ; and the god Ghétoo (a black boiling pot) is worshipped to remove the scurvy or any kind of blotches on the skin.

In the preceding sections of this work, the god Prit'hivēē, regent of the earth, should have been noticed : he has no separate worship, but certain formulas are repeated in his name at all the great festivals. Vishnoo is revered as the Household God ; he is worshipped when a person enters a new house, or at any other time to procure the removal of family misfortunes. Doorga should have been mentioned also as the Village Goddess ; she is worshipped by the villagers in the month Asharhŭ, before a jar of water, when bloody sacrifices are offered. An annual festival is also held in each village in Asharhŭ, in honour of Vishnoo, Indrŭ, Koovérŭ, and Lŭkshmēē ; when the persons pay the first instalment of their rents. The land-owner is at the expense.

CHAP. VIII.

WORSHIP OF BEINGS IN STRANGE SHAPES.

SECT. I.—*Urdhŭ-narēēshwŭrŭ.*[h]

HERE Shivŭ and Doorga are united in one body, white and yellow. The origin of this image is thus given in the Lingŭ pooranŭ:—Shivŭ and Doorga after their marriage lived on mount Koilasŭ, where Doorga kept the house, cooked, and nursed her two children, Gŭnéshŭ and Kartikŭ; and Shivŭ supported the family as a mendicant. On a certain occasion, Shivŭ, having one day smoked intoxicating herbs to excess, was unable to go his daily rounds. Doorga informed him that there was nothing in the house; that the family had eaten half of what was collected the day before, and that Gŭnéshŭ's rat and Kartikŭ's peacock[i] had devoured the rest. After much altercation, Shivŭ left his hut, and Doorga, to avoid perishing for want, went to her father's, taking her children with her. On the way Narŭdŭ met her, and advised her to assume the form of the goddess Ŭnnŭ-pōōrna,[k] and lay an embargo on all the food where Shivŭ would ask for alms. She did so; and Shivŭ begged in vain for a handful of rice. Narŭdŭ at length meeting Shivŭ also persuaded him to return to his wife: Doorga received him with joy, and relieved his hunger; which so pleased the old mendicant, that in pressing her in his arms both bodies became one.

In the Radha-tŭntrŭ it is said, that Shivŭ and Doorga assumed this form in order to prove that Shivŭ is the one Brŭmhŭ, in whom both the male and female powers are united.

In one of the smaller Hindoo poems, a different account of the origin of this image is given:—Shivŭ, finding it very difficult to procure a subsistence by the alms which he daily collected, especially as Doorga had ten mouths, and Gŭnéshŭ a very large belly, agreed with his wife, that they should assume one body, which would be supported with less labour.

Notwithstanding this apparently close union of Shivŭ and Doorga, the Shivopa-khyanŭ, a poem, contains a story, in which Doorga is represented as quarrelling with Shivŭ in a fit of jealousy,

[h] Urdhŭ, half; narēē, woman; ēēshwŭrŭ, a name of Shivŭ.

[i] Gŭnéshŭ rides on a rat, and Kartikŭ on a peacock.

[k] One of the forms of Doorga, as the regent of food.

on account of his begging in that part of Shivŭ-poorŭ[l] where the women of ill-fame live.—On another occasion, as related in the Ramayŭnŭ, a dreadful quarrel took place betwixt Shivŭ and Doorga, because Pŭrŭshoo-ramŭ had beaten Kartikŭ and Gŭnéshŭ, the two sons of Doorga. Another account of these quarrels is given both in the Ramayŭnŭ and the Mŭhabharŭtŭ:—Ramŭ's efforts to destroy Ravŭnŭ proving abortive, in consequence of the protection afforded the giant by Shivŭ, all the gods whom Ravŭnŭ had oppressed joined Ramŭ in supplications to Shivŭ: and on the seventh day, when Ravŭnŭ was to be slain, the gods resolved to be present; and Shivŭ was about to join them, when Doorga interfered, and asked him how he could witness the destruction of his own disciple: that disciple, who had stood praying to him all day in the sultry weather, surrounded with four fires; who had continued his devotions in the chilling cold, standing in the water; and had persevered in his supplications, standing on his head in the midst of torrents of rain?—Here she poured a volley of abuse upon Shivŭ, as a withered old fellow who smoked intoxicating herbs; covered himself with ashes; dwelt in cemeteries; a beggar; whose name would never be remembered;—'and dost thou think,' said she, 'that I shall be present at such a sight?'—Shivŭ could no longer smother his resentment, but reproached her in the severest terms, reminding her that she was only a woman, and knew nothing: and indeed that she did not act like a woman, for she was continually wandering from place to place; engaged in wars; was a drunkard; spent her time with degraded beings; killed giants, drank their blood, and hung the skulls round her neck. Doorga was enraged to madness by these cutting reproaches, so that the gods became alarmed, and intreated Ramŭ to join in supplications to Doorga, or there would be no possibility of destroying Ravŭnŭ. He did so, and so pleased the goddess by his flatteries, that she was at length brought to consent to the destruction of Ravŭnŭ.

At the new or full moon, or on the 8th or 14th of the moon in any month, or on the last day of any calendar month, in the day, the usual ceremonies of worship are performed before this disgusting image, which is thrown into the water the succeeding day. The formulas are those used in the worship of Doorga, not of Shivŭ. Animals are slain and offered to the goddess.

SECT. II.—*Krishnŭ-Kalēē.*

THIS scandalous image is worshipped annually at the total wane of the moon[m] in Kartikŭ, in the night.

Of all the milk-maids that used to collect around him, Krishnŭ

[l] Shivŭ's heaven.

[m] A very proper time for such a worship. Let neither sun nor moon shine on such deeds.

was most charmed with Radha, the wife of Ayŭnŭghoshŭ. When the attachment was first formed, the sister of Ayŭnŭ-ghoshŭ saw them together, and informed her brother of the circumstance; at which Radha became very much alarmed, assured Krishnŭ that her sister-in-law had seen her with him, and that her husband would certainly destroy her. Krishnŭ commanded her not to fear, adding, if her husband came, he would assume the form of Kalēē, and she should be found in the act of worship. When her husband and others arrived, they found her thus employed, and joined her in her devotions. Could it be believed that such an abominable instance of adultery and treachery would be made the subject of worship?—yet so it is. Four images are made from this stroy, viz: Krishnŭ-Kalēē, Radha, Ayŭnŭ-ghoshŭ, and Kootila, Ayŭnŭ's sister.—Bloody sacrifices are offered to this image; but the worshippers of Krishnŭ are ashamed, when asked by the shaktŭs, if Krishnŭ has begun to drink blood?

SECT. III.—*Hŭrēē-Hŭrŭ.*

HERE Vishnoo (Hŭree) and Shivŭ (Hŭrŭ) appear in one body; the former is black, and the latter white. The image has four arms and two feet.

The origin of this image is thus recorded in the Vishnoo pooranŭ:—Lŭkshmēē and Doorga were once sitting together in the presence of Shivŭ, when Lŭkshmēē contended that her husband (Vishnoo) was greater than Shivŭ; which Doorga as firmly denied. Lŭkshmēē said, her husband must be greatest, since Shivŭ had worshipped him. In the midst of this conversation, Vishnoo arrived, and to convince Lŭkshmēē that both were equal, he immediately entered the body of Shivŭ, and they became one.

Another account of the origin of this image is given in the Kashēē-khŭndŭ, a part of the Sŭndŭ pooranŭ.—On a certain occasion, when Vishnoo and Shivŭ were conversing together, Shivŭ requested Vishnoo to assume the beautiful female form which he had formerly done at the churning of the sea: to which he consented; when Shivŭ, overpowered with desire, pursued the flying beauty, till, overcome with fatigue, she hid herself behind a tree, and re-assumed the form of Vishnoo. Shivŭ, however, embraced Vishnoo with such eagerness, that the bodies of both became one.[n]

The worship of this image takes place whenever any one pleases. Stone images in some places are continually preserved; and in others a clay one is made, and worshipped, and afterwards committed to the river.

[n] The reader need not be informed how much this story in its termination resembles that of the nymph Salmacis, who is said to have fallen excessively in love with a son of Mercury by his sister Venus.

Raja Krishnŭ-chŭndrŭ-rayŭ expended fifty or sixty thousand rupees at the consecration of a stone image of Huree-Hŭrŭ, which may be still seen at Gŭnga-vasŭ, near Nŭdeeya. While this raja lived, fifty rupees were daily expended in this worship; yet, though a number of villages have been bequeathed to the god, the expense of the daily worship and offerings is less now than formerly. Few places in Bengal, however, can now boast of a temple at which fifty rupees are daily expended °. No bloody sacrifices are offered to this image.

However shocked a professed Christian may be at reading such accounts, and however revolting to every feeling of modesty and decency these stories may be, the Hindoo philosophers have thought proper to perpetuate them, and in this image to personify lust itself. The bramhŭns also bow down to this image as to a deity worthy of adoration

° This expense is incurred in the meat-offerings, consisting of rice, peas, salt, oil, ghee, butter, sugar, sweetmeats, fruits of different kinds, herbs, spices, betle nuts, &c.; in the offerings of cloth, metal vessels, and other things; and in the wages of the bramhŭns and shōōdrŭs employed. About ten bramhŭns and fourteen shōōdrŭs constantly attend on the service of this image.

CHAP. IX.

WORSHIP OF HUMAN BEINGS.

Deified Men and Women.

ALL the bramhuns, but especially the religious guides, (gooroo,) are objects of worship among the Hindoos, and have divine honours paid to them. The spiritual guide, in the estimation of the disciple, is literally a god. Whenever he approaches, the disciple prostrates himself in the dust before him, and never sits in his presence without leave. He drinks the water with which he has washed the feet of his gooroo,[p] and relies entirely upon his blessing for final happiness. I have heard some Hindoos speak with comparative contempt of all other ways of salvation. When the claims of the bramhŭns to deity have been disputed by any one, I have seen the poor besotted shōōdrŭ prostrate himself at the feet of the nearest bramhŭn, and, raising his head, and closing his hands, say, 'You are my god.' At the same time the character of the bramhŭn has perhaps been notorious for every vice.

The shastrŭs declare that the daughters of bramhŭns, till they are eight years old, are objects of worship, as forms of the goddess Bhŭgŭvŭtēē; and some persons worship these girls daily. The worshipper, taking the daughter of some neighbouring bramhŭn, and placing her on a seat, performs the ceremonies of worship; in which he presents to her flowers, paint, water, garlands,[q] incense, and, if a rich man, offerings of cloth and ornaments. He closes the whole by prostrating himself before the girl. At the worship of some of the female deities also, the daughters of bramhŭns have divine honours paid to them.

The wives of bramhŭns are also worshipped occasionally as an act of great merit. A man of property sometimes invites ten, twenty, or one hundred of these females, and repeating before them forms of prayer, praise, &c., worships them, and at the close entertains them with the offerings. This is frequently done at Benares.

On the 14th of the decrease of the moon in Shravŭnŭ, at the time of the Savitrēē vrŭtŭ, the wives of bramhŭns very generally

[p] Doing reverence to the very feet of superiors prevailed among the Jews. Hence the woman washed the feet of Christ, and wiped them with the hair of her head. Paul was brought up at the feet of Gamaliel.

[q] Both the Greeks and Romans, it is well known, used to adorn their images with garlands at the time of worship.

worship their husbands. The worshipper, having placed a seat for her husband, and presented him with new garments, entreats him to be seated, and puts round his neck a garland of flowers. She then anoints his body with fragrant ointments, and performs before him the various ceremonies which belong to the worship of the gods. In presenting the offerings she says, regarding her husband as a form of Vishnoo, 'Oh! husband, grant that I may long live in the marriage state, and never become a widow.' The husband then partakes of the offerings, and the wife having walked round him either three or seven times, the service ends. The origin of this ceremony is given in the Brŭmhŭ-voivŭrttŭ pooranŭ, but the story is too long for insertion.

Many of the tŭntrŭs, and particularly the Roodrŭyamŭlŭ, the Yonēē-tŭntrŭ, and the Nēēlŭ-tŭntrŭ, contain directions respecting a most extraordinary and shocking mode of worship, which is understood in a concealed manner amongst the Hindoos by the name of Chŭkrŭ. These shastrŭs direct, that the person who wishes to perform this ceremony must first, in the night, choose a woman as the object of worship. If the person be a dŭkshina-charēē, he must take his own wife; and if a vamacharēē, the daughter of a dancer, a kŭpalee, a washerman, a barber, a chŭndalŭ, or of a Mŭsulman, or a prostitute; and place her on a seat, or mat: and then bring broiled fish, flesh, fried peas, rice, spirituous liquors, sweetmeats, flowers, and other offerings; which, as well as the female, must be purified by the repeating of incantations. To this succeeds the worship of the guardian deity; and after this, that of the female,—who sits naked. * * * *

* * * * * * * * *

Here, things too abominable to enter the ears of man, and impossible to be revealed to a Christian public, are contained in the directions of the shastrŭ. The learned bramhŭn who opened to me these abominations, made several efforts—paused and began again—and then paused again—before he could mention the shocking indecencies prescribed by his own shastrus.

As the object of worship is a living person, she partakes of the offerings, even of the spirituous liquors; and of the flesh, though it should be that of the cow. The refuse is eaten by the persons present, however different their castes; nor must any one refuse to partake of the offerings. The spirituous liquors must be drank by measure; and the company while eating must put food into each other's mouths. The priest then—in the presence of all—behaves towards this female in a manner which decency forbids to be mentioned; after which the persons present repeat many times the name of some god, performing actions unutterably abominable: and here this most diabolical business closes. The

The benefits promised to the worshippers are riches, absorption in Brŭmhŭ, &c.

At present the persons committing these abominations (vamacharēēs) are becoming more and more numerous; and in proportion as they increase, the ceremonies are more and more indecent. They are performed in secret; but that these practices are becoming very frequent among the bramhŭns and others, is a fact known to all. Those who abide by the rules of the shastrŭs are comparatively few: the generality confine themselves chiefly to those parts that belong to gluttony, drunkenness, and whoredom, without acquainting themselves with all the minute rules and incantations of the shastrŭs.

CHAP. X.

THE WORSHIP OF BEASTS.

SECT. I.—*The Cow.*

BRŬMHA created the bramhŭns and the cow at the same time: the bramhŭns to read the formulas, and the cow to afford milk, (clarified butter,) for the burnt-offerings. The gods by partaking of the burnt-offerings are said to enjoy exquisite pleasure, and men by eating clarified butter destroy their sins. The cow is called the mother of the gods, and is declared by Brŭmha to be a proper object of worship.

The shastrŭ appoints that the images of the gods shall be anointed with milk, curds, clarified butter, cow-dung, and cows' urine, whereby they become free from impurity; and all unclean places are purified with cow-dung. Indeed many bramhŭns do not go out of the house in a morning, till the door-way has been rubbed with cow-dung.

The cow was created on the first of Voishakhŭ, and on this day, or on the second of the moon in Jyoisht'hŭ, she is worshipped annually. No image is used, but the worship is performed in the cow-house before a jar of water. The ceremonies are the same as those before the images of the gods: the prayers are necessarily peculiar to the object worshipped. The officiating bramhŭn, at the close of the service, reads the whole of the Chŭndēē, a poem relating to the wars of Doorga. On the 13th of Phalgoonŭ, the milkmen paint the horns and hoofs of their cattle yellow, and bathe them in the river. Persons strict in their religion worship the cow daily: after bathing, they throw flowers at her feet, and feed her with fresh grass, saying, 'O Bhŭgŭvŭtee! eat;' and then walk round her three or seven times, making obeisance.

If you speak among Hindoos of eating the flesh of cows, they immediately raise their hands to their ears: yet milkmen, carmen, and farmers, beat the cow as unmercifully as a carrier of coals beats his ass in England; and many starve them to death in the cold weather, rather than be at the expense of giving them food.[a] Thus is the cow at once a beast of burden and a goddess. Some of the poor think themselves happy if they can support a cow, as by serving this animal they expect reward in a future state. If a man sell his cow, the shastrŭs threaten him with the torments of hell during as many thousand years as there are hairs on her body. If any one neglect to burn cow-dung, &c. in the cow-house, where-

[a] In the year 1812, a bramhŭn was convicted before the Magistrate of Serampore, of stealing from a relative a cow in calf, and offering this *goddess* for sale to a butcher.

by smoke is raised, and the musquitoes prevented from hurting the cows, he will descend into the hell of musquitoes and gad-flies. The gift of a cow to a bramhŭn is an act of great merit.

The dung of the cow is gathered and dried as fuel amongst the Hindoos. Some cows are of more value for their dung than for their milk; tor the Bengal cow gives very little milk indeed, compared with the European cow.

Sect. II.—*The Monkey.*

The black-faced monkey, Hŭnooman,[b] the son of the god Pŭvŭnŭ, by Ŭnjŭna, a female monkey,[c] is believed to be an incarnation of Shivŭ.

The Hindoos worship Hŭnooman on their birth-day to obtain long life, which they suppose this monkey can bestow, as he is immortal. In some temples his image is set up alone, and in others with that of Ramŭ and Sēēta, and worshipped daily. The worship of Ramŭ is always preceded by a few ceremonies in honour of Hŭnooman.

Stone images of Hŭnooman are kept in the houses of some of his disciples, and worshipped daily. The worshipper of this animal is promised every gratification he can desire.

Many Hindoos receive the initiating incantation by which this monkey becomes their guardian deity. The mark which these disciples make on their foreheads is the same as that made by the followers of Shivŭ.

About twenty years ago, Eeshwŭrŭ-chŭndrŭ, the raja of Nŭdēēya, spent 100,000 rupees in marrying two monkeys,[d] when all the parade common at Hindoo marriages was exhibited. In the marriage procession were seen elephants, camels, horses richly caparisoned, palanqueens, lamps, and flambeaus; the male monkey was fastened in a fine palanqueen, having a crown upon his head, with men standing by his side to fan him; then followed singing and dancing girls in carriages; every kind of Hindoo music; a grand display of fireworks, &c. Dancing, music, singing, and every degree of low mirth, were exhibited at the bridegroom's palace for

[b] Hŭnooman broke his cheek-bone by a fall from the sun's orbit; and his name is derived from hŭnoo, the cheek-bone.

[c] There is nothing too filthy for idolatry: here the god of the winds pays his addresses to a monkey, as Jupiter is said to have done to a swan.

[d] At this time none of these monkeys were to be seen about Nŭdeeya; now they are so numerous that they devour almost all the fruit of the orchards, as the inhabitants are afraid of hurting them.

twelve days together. At the time of the marriage ceremony, learned bramhŭns were employed in reading the formulas from the shastrŭs!

Amongst men of sense the performance of the ceremonies of worship before the image of this monkey is attended with a degree of disgrace. I have heard of a quarrel between two bramhŭns, one of whom was paid by a rich Hindoo to repeat the ceremonies of Hindoo worship before the image of Hŭnooman, daily, at his house: amidst the quarrel the other said, 'Thou refuse of bramhŭns! thou gainest a subsistence by worshipping a monkey.'

Stories of this god.—When Hŭnooman first saw the rising sun, thinking it a ripe fruit, he leaped up to the residence of the god of day, and seized his chariot: Indrŭ fearing Hŭnooman would swallow the glorious luminary, with his thunderbolt smote him to the earth, where he lay lifeless. His distracted mother applied to his father Pŭvŭnŭ, who, enraged at the loss of his son, retired into an inaccessible chasm, and bound up the wind, till both men and gods began to perish. Brŭmha, Vishnoo, Shivŭ, and other gods now petitioned Pŭvŭnŭ; but he refused them the privilege of breathing, unless they would make Hŭnooman immortal. Brŭmha then bestowed on Hŭnooman the water of life, and Pŭvŭnŭ restored to men and gods the vital air.—When ten years old, Hŭnooman was possessed of immense strength. He brought a stone, from a mountain, sixteen or twenty miles in circumference, and threw it into a pool of water where a number of sages were at worship. This raised the water, so that the sages, who had closed their eyes in the act of meditation, began to sink. After a few struggles they regained the land, and again sat down with closed eyes to their work. Hŭnooman next took out the stone, and the waters retired; and when the sages put out their hands to take up water for worship, they were again disappointed. Opening their eyes, they saw the water had sunk exceedingly; and following it, again closed their eyes, and sat down. Hŭnooman again flung in the stone, and the sages began to sink. He continued to repeat these frolics, till the sages, discovering the culprit, took away his strength. The sagacious monkey now began to flatter the sages; brought them fruits, &c. from the forest, and performed, with agility, every act of menial service. After three years they blessed him, and assured him that, when he should see Ramŭ upon mount Rishyŭmōōkŭ, he should obtain twice his former strength.—On a certain occasion Hŭnooman was resolved to put the strength of Bhēēmŭ to trial, as he was reputed to be so tremendous a giant: and lengthening his tail, he threw it across the path. As the Hindoos never stride across a person's body, or even his shadow, Bhēēmŭ requested Hŭnooman to take up his tail: but he complained he was grown old and could not. At last Bhēēmŭ stooped to lift it out of his way; he tried at the end, and then at the middle, but found, giant as he was, he could not lift up this monkey's tail. Overcome with astonishment, he began to praise Hŭnooman, and at length prevailed on him to promise that he would help the Pandŭvŭs in their expected war with Dooryodhŭnŭ.

Sect. III.—*The Dog.*

Carries Kalŭ-Bhoirŭvŭ, a form of Shivŭ, and therefore receives the worship of the Hindoos whenever his master is worshipped.* I have heard also that there are many Hindoos in the west of Hindoost'hanŭ, who pay their devotions to the dog, and become his disciples. Though the dog is thus placed amongst the objects of worship, he is mentioned in the Mŭhabharŭtŭ as an unclean animal: every offering which he approaches is rendered unacceptable to the gods, and every one who touches him must purify himself by bathing.

Sect. IV.—*The Shackal.*

The Tŭntrŭs mention an incarnation of Doorga in the form of the shackal, when she carried the child Krishnŭ over the Yŭmoona, in his flight from king Kŭngsŭ. All the worshippers of the female deities adore the shackal as a form of this goddess, especially the vamacharēēs, who present offerings to him daily. Every worshipper lays the offerings on a clean place in his house, and calls the god to come and partake of them. As this is done at the hour when the shackals leave their lurking places, one of these animals sometimes comes and eats the food in the presence of the worshipper: this will not appear wonderful when it is considered, that the same animal finds food placed for him in this place every day. In temples dedicated to Doorga and other deities, a stone image of the shackal is placed on a pedestal, and daily worshipped. When a shackal passes a Hindoo, he must bow to it; and if it pass on the left hand, it is a most lucky circumstance.

Sect. V.—*Other Animals worshipped.*

The elephant, the lion, the bull, the buffalo, the rat, the deer, the goat, &c. are worshipped at the festivals of the gods whom they respectively carry, that is, of Indrŭ, Doorga, Shivŭ, Yŭmŭ, Gŭnéshŭ, Pŭvŭnŭ, and Brŭmha.

* The dog, it will be remembered, was consecrated to Mars.

CHAP XI.

THE WORSHIP OF BIRDS.

SECT. I.—*Gŭroorŭ.*[a]

THIS god, with the head and wings of a bird,[b] and the rest of his body like that of a man, is called the king of the birds, and the carrier of Vishnoo. Vinŭta, the wife of Kŭshyŭpŭ, the progenitor of gods and men, laid an egg,[c] and became the mother of this bird-god. As soon as Gŭroorŭ was born, his body expanded till it touched the sky; all the other animals were terrified at him; his eyes were like lightning; the mountains fled with the wind of his wings, and the rays which issued from his body set the four quarters of the world on fire. The affrighted gods sought the help of Ŭgnee, conceiving that Gŭroorŭ must be an incarnation of the god of fire.

In consequence of a dispute betwixt Vinŭta, the mother of Gŭroorŭ, and Kŭdroo, the mother of the serpents, respecting the colour of the horse procured at the churning of the sea, a continual enmity has subsisted betwixt the descendants of these females; and Gŭroorŭ once obtained permission from one of the gods to devour all the serpents he could find.[d]

The story of Gŭroorŭ's becoming the carrier of Vishnoo is thus related in the Mŭhabharŭtŭ:—His mother in the above dispute having laid a wager, and being the loser, was reduced to a state of servitude to her sister; and the serpents, wishing to become immortal, promised to liberate his mother on condition that Gŭroorŭ should bring Chŭndrŭ, (the moon;) whose bright parts, the Hindoos say, are filled with the water of immortality. Before Gŭroorŭ departed, he asked his mother for some food. She advised him to go to the sea shore, and gather up whatever he could see; but conjured him to beware of eating a bramhŭn: adding, 'Should you at any time feel a burning heat in your stomach, be sure you have eaten a bramhŭn.' Thus instructed, he began his journey: at his flight the three worlds were agitated like the sea at the great deluge. Passing by a country inhabited by fishermen, he at one inspiration drew in houses, trees, cattle, men, and other

[a] Some suppose Gŭroorŭ to be a large species of vulture, and others the gigantic crane.

[b] Gŭroorŭ in some degree resembles Mercury, viz., in his having wings, and being the messenger of Vishnoo, as Mercury was of Jupiter.

[c] Jupiter is said to have been enamoured of the goddess Nemesis in the shape of a goose; and that she laid an egg, from which was born Helena.

[d] When the Hindoos lie down to sleep, they repeat the name of Gŭroorŭ three times, to obtain protection from snakes.

animals; but, among the inhabitants swallowed, one was a bramhŭn, who caused such an intolerable burning in his bowels, that Gŭroorŭ, unable to bear it, called, in the greatest haste, for him to come out. The bramhŭn refused, unless his wife, a fisherman's daughter, might accompany him; to which Gŭroorŭ consented. Pursuing his journey, Gŭroorŭ met his father Kŭshyŭpŭ, who directed him to appease his hunger at a certain lake where an elephant and a tortoise were fighting. The body of the tortoise was eighty miles long, and the elephant's one hundred and sixty. Gŭroorŭ with one claw seized the elephant, with the other the tortoise, and perched with them on a tree eight hundred miles high; but the tree was unable to bear the ponderous weight, and unhappily thousands of pigmy bramhŭns were then worshipping on one of its branches. Trembling lest he should destroy any of them, he took the bough in his beak, continuing to hold the elephant and tortoise in his claws, and flew to a mountain in an uninhabited country, where he finished his repast on the tortoise and elephant. Gŭroorŭ, having surmounted astonishing dangers, at last seized the moon, and concealed it under his wing: but on his return was attacked by Indrŭ and other gods, all of whom, however, except Vishnoo, he overcame; and even he was so severely put to it in the contest, that he came to terms with Gŭroorŭ, who was made immortal, and promised a higher seat than Vishnoo, while Gŭroorŭ on his part became the carrier of Vishnoo. Since this time Vishnoo rides on Gŭroorŭ; while the latter, in the shape of a flag, sits at the top of Vishnoo's car.

Gŭroorŭ is worshipped at the great festivals before the different images of Vishnoo; but has no separate time of worship. His image is placed in the temples dedicated to various forms of Vishnoo; and some persons receive his name as their guardian deity, and repeat it daily.

Gŭroorŭ's two sons, Sŭmpatee and Jŭtayoo, once flew, as a trial of strength, up to the sun; but the wings of Sŭmpatee were burnt off. Gŭroorŭ resides in Kooshŭ-dwēēpŭ, one of the seven islands into which the Hindoos divide the earth.

Names.—Gŭroomŭt, or, he who is clothed with feathers.—Gŭroorŭ, he who swallows [serpents, and throws up their bones.] Tŭrkshyŭ, the father of Gŭroorŭ.—Voinŭtéyŭ, from Vinŭta.—Khŭgéshwŭrŭ, the lord of the feathered tribes.—Nagantŭkŭ, the destroyer of the serpents, (nagŭs.)—Vishnoo-rŭt'hŭ, the carrier of Vishnoo.—Soopŭrnŭ, he whose feathers are of the colour of gold.—Pŭnnŭga-shŭnŭ, the devourer of the serpents.

SECT. II.—*Uroonŭ.*

THE elder brother of Gŭroorŭ, is the charioteer of Sōōryŭ, the sun ; and is worshipped with his master, as well as at the festivals of other gods. The image of this god is that of a man without thighs.

SECT. III.—*Jutayoo.*

THIS bird is the friend of Ramŭ, and is worshipped at the same festival with him. He is mentioned in the preceding account of Ramŭ.

SECT. IV.—*Shŭnkŭrŭ Chillŭ, or the Eagle of Coromandel.*

THIS is the white-headed kite, commonly called the bramhŭnēē kite. It is considered as an incarnation of Doorga, and is reverenced by the Hindoos, who bow to it whenever it passes them.

SECT. V.—*Khŭnjŭnŭ or the Wag-tail.*

Is considered as a form of Vishnoo, on account of the mark on its throat, supposed to resemble the shalgramŭ. The Hindoos honour it in the same manner as they do the eagle of Coromandel.

SECT. VI.—*Other Birds worshipped*

THE peacock, the goose, and the owl,[e] are worshipped at the festivals of Kartikŭ, Brŭmha, and Lŭkshmēē.

[e] If, however, the owl, the vulture, or any other unclean birds, perch upon the house of a Hindoo, it is an unlucky omen, and the effect must be removed by the performance of the following expiatory ceremony: 'If a vulture, a heron, a dove, an owl, a hawk, a gull, a kite, a Bhasha, or a Pundura, should settle upon a house, the wife, or a child, or some other person belonging to the master of the house, will die, or some other calamity will befal him within a year afterwards. To prevent this, the house, or its value in money, must be given to bramhŭns ; or a peace-offering of an extraordinary nature must be offered: viz., five productions of the cow, the five gems, the five nectareous juices, the five twigs of trees, and the five astringents, are to be put into a pot of water ; the guardian deities of the quarters of the universe must then be worshipped, and an hundred and eight oblations of clarified butter must be made with a sacrificial piece of the wood of the Khadira tree, while the prayer of Mrityoonjŭyŭ is repeated. The oblation, called the mŭha-vyadhee homŭ, is to be performed at the commencement, or at the end of this ceremony. Oblations of clarified butter, at each of which the gayitree is repeated, are then to be made to Vishnoo, the nine planets, Udbhootŭ, and the house-hold gods; which being done, the bramhŭns must be entertained with clarified butter and rice milk. The sacrificial fees must then be paid, and water sprinkled with appropriate incantations; when an assurance that all has been duly performed being given, a prostration is made to the bramhŭns, and the benediction received from them.'

CHAP. XII.

THE WORSHIP OF TREES.

TREES are worshipped by the Hindoos as the forms of particular gods: the ŭshwŭtŭ and vŭtŭ are representatives of Vishnoo, and the vilwŭ that of Shivŭ. The devout Hindoos worship them, water their roots, plant them near their houses, &c. The Hindoo females, who are never seen in the streets, plant a sacred tree within the compound, that they may not lose the merit of watering it in the sultry months. The female shōōdrŭs, to honour the wives of bramhŭns, carry water to these trees, and on a fortunate day make offerings to them.

SECT. I.—*The Toolŭsee.*[a]

THE Hindoos have no public festival in honour of this plant; but they occasionally prostrate themselves before it, repeating a form of prayer or praise: they have great faith also in the power of its leaves to cure diseases, and use it with incantations to expel the poison of serpents. They plant it also before their houses, and in the morning cleanse the place around it with water and cow-dung; and in the evening place a lamp near it. Throughout the month Voishakhŭ they suspend a large pot over it filled with water, and let the water drop upon it through a small hole. Whenever any of these plants die, it is considered a sacred duty to commit them to the river; and when a person is brought to the river side to die, his relations plant a branch of the toolŭsee near the dying man's head. A pillar, hollow at the top, is erected by many Hindoos, in which they deposit earth, and set the plant. They walk round these pillars and bow to the plant; which actions are declared by the shastrŭs to be very meritorious.

The origin of the worship of the Toolŭsee is thus related in the Vishnoo pooranŭ, and in the Toolŭsee-Mahatmŭ:—Toolŭsee, a female, was engaged for a long time in religious austerities; and at length asked this blessing of Vishnoo, that she might become his wife. Lŭkshmēē, Vishnoo's wife, hearing this, cursed the woman, and changed her into a Toolŭsee plant;[b] but Vishnoo promised, that he would assume the form of the shalgramŭ, and always continue with her. The Hindoos, therefore, continually keep one leaf of the toolŭsee under and another upon the shalgramŭ.

[a] Basil, Ocimum gratissimum, and O. sanctum. The myrtle was sacred to Venus.

[b] Apollo changed the youth Cyparissus into a cypress tree. Daphne was changed into a laurel.

SECT. II.—*Other sacred Trees.*

The ŭshwŭttŭ,[c] vŭtŭ,[d] vŭkoolŭ,[e] hŭritŭkēē,[f] amŭlŭkēē,[g] vilwŭ,[h] and nimbu[i] trees receive divine honours from the Hindoos, and are set apart with the same ceremonies as are common at the setting up of an image of the gods. These ceremonies take place either at the time of planting the tree, or after the person has watered and nourished it for some time. An individual who consecrates an ŭshwŭttŭ or a vŭtŭ, considering these trees as continuing to flourish many years, says, 'Oh! Vishnoo! grant that, for planting this tree, I may continue as many years in heaven as this tree shall remain growing in the earth!' The person expects too, that as he has set apart this tree to afford shade to his fellow creatures, so after death he will not be scorched by excessive heat in his journey to Yŭmŭ, the regent of death.

[c] Ficus religiosa. This and other trees are never injured, nor cut down, nor burnt by devout Hindoos. I was once informed by a bramhŭn, that his grandfather planted one of these trees near his house, which has now spread its branches so widely, that, as my informant affirmed, 2,000 persons may stand under it; and so much is this tree reverenced by his family, that they do not suffer its withered branches to be burnt.

[d] Ficus Indica, vulgarly called the banyan tree.

[e] Mimusops elengi.

[f] Terminalia citrina.

[g] Phillanthus emblica.

[h] Ægle marmelos.

[i] Melia azodaracta.

CHAP XIII.

THE WORSHIP OF RIVERS.

RIVERS are to be placed among the objects of Hindoo worship:[k] they are of both genders, Nŭdŭ and Nŭdēē. The worship of these rivers is performed at auspicious seasons, as laid down in the shastrŭ, and at some of the great festivals. Certain places also of these rivers are peculiarly sacred, and draw to them great numbers of devotees; as, the source of the Ganges; the union of the Ganges, the Yŭmoona, and the Sŭrŭswŭtēē at Prŭyagŭ;[l] the branching of this united river into three streams at Trivénēē; the place where the Ganges disembogues itself into the sea, &c. Their waters are used for food, bathing, medicine, religious ceremonies, &c. and formerly when a Hindoo king was crowned, they were poured upon his head as a part of his consecration.

SECT. I. *Gŭnga.*

THIS goddess is represented as a white woman, wearing a crown, sitting on the sea animal Mŭkŭrŭ, and having in her right hand a water-lily, and in her left the lute. She is called the daughter of mount Himavŭt, though some of the pooranŭs declare that she was produced from the sweat of Vishnoo's foot, which Brŭmha caught and preserved in his alms' dish.

The grandfather of Bēēshmŭ was one day performing religious austerities near the Ganges, when the goddess fell in love with him, and, in order to persuade him to a union, went and sat upon his right knee. He told her that the left knee was the proper place for the wife, and the right for the son: that therefore she should not become his, but be united to his son: whose name was Santŭnoo. After Santŭnoo and Gŭnga had been married some time, she was about to leave him; but consented to stay, on condition that she might kill all her children at their birth. When the first child was born, she threw it into the river, and so on to the seventh inclusive. As she was destroying the eighth, Santŭnoo forbad her, in consequence of which the child was saved, but she abandoned her paramour. The whole of this was to fulfil a curse pronounced by Vishnoo on the eight gods named Ŭshtŭ-vŭsoo.

[k] The notion of certain rivers being sacred, seems to have prevailed amongst other heathen nations. Hence Naaman the Syrian said, 'Are not Abana and Pharpar, rivers of Damascus, better than all the waters of Israel? May I not wash in them and be clean?'

[l] It is ascertained, that there are six places of this name, five of which are situated on the river Ulŭkanunda,—See Asiatic Researches, vol. xi.

The Ramayŭnŭ, Mŭhabharŭtŭ, and the Gŭnga-khŭndŭ, a part of the Skŭndŭ pooranŭ, give long accounts of the descent of Gŭnga from heaven :—Sŭgŭrŭ, a king, having no children, entered upon a long course of austere devotions ; in the midst of which Bhrigoo appeared to him, and promised, that from the eldest queen should be born sixty thousand children, and from the other only a single child. After some time, the queen was delivered of a pumpkin! which the king in anger dashed to the ground, when the fruit was broken, and, to his astonishment, he saw children rising from it ; and, calling sixty thousand nurses, put each child into a pan of milk. The other wife had a son, whom they called Ŭngshooman. After these sons were grown up, the king resolved to perform once more the sacrifice of a horse before his death, and committed the victim to the care of his sixty thousand sons. The person who performs this sacrifice one hundred times, succeeds to the throne of heaven. On this occasion the reigning Indrŭ was alarmed, this being Sŭgŭrŭ's hundredth sacrifice. To prevent its taking effect, therefore, he descended to the earth, and assuming another form, privately carried off the horse, which he placed in patalŭ, near to Kŭpilŭ, a sage. The sixty thousand sons, after searching throughout the earth in vain, began to dig into patalŭ,[c] where they found the horse standing by the side of Kŭpilŭ, who was absorbed in his devotions. Incensed at the old man, whom they supposed to be the thief, they began to beat him ; when, awaking from his abstraction of mind, he reduced them all to ashes. The king for a long time heard no more of his sons ; but at length Narŭdŭ informed him of the catastrophe. He then sent his son Ŭngshooman down to the sage, who delivered up the horse, and informed the king, that if he could bring the goddess Gŭnga from heaven,[d] his sons might be restored to him. The king offered the sacrifice, and placing Ŭngshooman on the throne, took up his residence in a forest as a hermit, where he died. Ŭngshooman, in his turn, making his son Dwileepŭ his successor, died also in a forest. Dwileepŭ had two wives, but no children ; he therefore abdicated the throne, and embracing the life of a hermit, sought of the gods a son, and the deliverance of the sons of Sŭgŭrŭ. Shivŭ promised him, that by means of his two queens a son should be born. These women lived together, and after some time the youngest had a son, whom they called Bhŭgēērŭt'hŭ ;[e] who, however, was only a mass of flesh. Though greatly moved at the sight of such a child, they preserved it, and in time it grew up to manhood. One day Ŭshtŭ-vŭkrŭ, a moonee, who was

[c] The Hindoo writers say, that the seven seas were thus formed by the sons of Suguru. Some accounts add, that not finding a place large enough to contain the earth which they thus dug up—they devoured it!

[d] Or, as it is explained, if he could perform the funeral rites for these sixty thousand persons with the efficacious waters of the Ganges, they would be delivered from the curse, and ascend to heaven.

[e] This story is so extremely indelicate, that it is impossible to translate it.

hump-backed, and wriggled in walking, called to see these females; when Bhŭgēērŭt'hŭ, in rising to salute the sage, trembled and wriggled in such a manner, that Ŭshtŭ-vŭkrŭ, thinking he was mocking him, said, 'If thou canst not help wriggling thus, be a perfect child; but if thou art mocking me, be destroyed.' The boy immediately became perfect, and the sage gave him his blessing. When Bhŭgēērŭt'hŭ was grown up, he addressed his prayers to different gods for the restoration of his sixty thousand relations—but in vain; at length Brŭmha, moved by his piety, gave him a single drop of the water, and Vishnoo giving him a shell which he blew, Gŭnga followed him. As she had to fall from heaven to earth, Bhŭgēērŭt'hŭ was afraid lest the earth should be crushed by her fall: wherefore Shivŭ, standing on mount Himavŭt, caught Gŭnga in his bunch of matted hair, and detained her there for some time; but at length suffered one drop to fall on the mountain: and from thence, on the tenth of the increase of the moon in Jyoisht'hŭ, the goddess touched the earth, and whichever way Bhŭgēērut'hŭ went blowing the conch, there Gŭnga followed him.

Several very curious circumstances happened to Gŭnga as she passed along. In one place she ran near Jŭnhoo, a sage, and washed away his mendicant's dish, the flowers for worship, &c. upon which he, in anger, took her up, and swallowed her. At the intreaties of Bhŭgēērŭt'hŭ, however, the sage let her pass out at his thigh, on which account Gŭnga received the name of Janhŭvēē.

On they went, till Gŭnga asked Bhŭgēērŭt'hŭ where these sixty thousand relations were whom she was to deliver. He being unable to inform her, she, to make sure of their deliverance, at the entrance of the sea, divided herself into one hundred streams,[f] and ran down into patalŭ; where, as soon as the waters of Gŭnga touched their ashes, they were delivered from the curse, and ascended in chariots to heaven.

When Gŭnga was brought from heaven, the gods, conscious that their sins also needed washing away, petitioned Brŭmha on the subject, who soothed them by promising that Gŭnga should remain in heaven, and descend to earth also. This goddess, therefore was called Mŭndakinee in heaven, Gŭnga on earth, and Bhogŭvŭtēē in patalŭ.

All casts worship Gŭnga, yet most of the ceremonies at the time of the daily ablutions, with the exception of some forms of praise to this goddess, are in the name of Shivŭ and other gods. The Hindoos particularly choose the banks of this river for their worship, as the merit of works performed here, according to the promise of

[f] The mouths of the Ganges.

the shastrus,[g] becomes exceedingly augmented. In Voishakhŭ, Jyoisht'hŭ, Kartikŭ, and Maghŭ, the merit is greater than in other months; and at the full moon in these months is still more enhanced. In every month, on the first, sixth, and eleventh of the moon, and at its total wane also, bathing in Gŭnga is much recommended.

On the third of the moon in Voishakhŭ, a few Hindoos perform the ceremonies of worship by the side of the river, under the expectation that the benefits will be undecayable: such is the promise of the smritee shastrŭs.

On the 10th of the moon's increase in Jyoisht'hŭ, in the forenoon, the Dŭshŭhŭra festival is held, in commemoration of Gŭnga's descent to the earth. Crowds of people assemble from the different towns and villages near the river, especially at the most sacred places of the river, bringing their offerings of fruit, rice, flowers, cloth, sweetmeats, &c., and hang garlands of flowers across the river, even where it is very wide. After the people have bathed, the officiating bramhŭn ascends the banks of the river with them; and after repeating sŭngkŭlpŭ,[h] places before him a jar of water, and sitting with his face to the north or east, perfoms what his called ghŭtŭ-st'hapŭnŭ.[i] After this, the bramhŭn performs other ceremonies, as asŭnŭ shoodhee,[k] ŭngŭ-nyasŭ,[l] kŭrangŭ-nyasŭ,[l] bhootshōōdhee,[m] dig-vŭndhŭnŭ,[n] bhōōt-otsarŭnŭ,[o] &c. then the worship of the five gods; of the nine planets; of the regents of the ten quarters, &c. To this succeeds meditation, manŭsŭ,[p] &c.; the priest next presents the offerings, which may be sixty-four, or eighteen, or sixteen, or ten, or five, or merely flowers and water, according to the person's ability. To these offerings, the worshipper must add sesamum, clarified butter, and barley-flour. The officiating bramhŭn next performs the worship of Narayŭnŭ, Mŭhéshwŭrŭ,[q]

[g] 'He who thinks upon Gŭnga, though he may be 800 miles distant from the river at the time, is delivered from all sin, and is entitled to heaven.—At the hour of death, if a person think upon Gŭnga, he will obtain a place in the heaven of Shivŭ.—If a person, according to the regulations of the shastru, be going to bathe in Gunga, and die on the road, he shall obtain the same benefits as though he had actually bathed.—There are 3,500,000 holy places belonging to Gŭnga: the person who looks at Gunga, or bathes in this river, will obtain all the fruit which arises from visiting all these 3,500 000 holy places.—If a person who has been guilty of killing cows, bramhŭns, his gooroo, or of drinking spirits, &c. touch the waters of Gŭnga, desiring in his mind the remission of these sins, they will be forgiven.—By bathing in Gŭnga, accompanied with prayer, a person will remove at once the sins of thousands of births.'—*Gunga-Vakya-Vulee.*

[h] An incantation, at the time of repeating which the person promises to attend to certain ceremonies.

[i] The ceremonies performed at the setting up of an image. Here the jar of water is the image, before which the worship of any of the gods may be performed.

[k] Purifying the seat. [l] Ceremonies accompanied with motions of the fingers. [m] Purifying the five elements of which the body is composed. [n] Binding the ten quarters, to prevent evil spirits from arriving to defile the worship. [o] Driving away the evil spirits. [p] Going over all the ceremonies in the mind. [q] Shivŭ.

Brŭmha, Sōōryŭ, Bhŭgēērŭt'hŭ, and Himalŭyŭ; then the worship of the inhabitants of the waters, as the fish, the tortoises, the frogs, the water-snakes, the leeches, the snails,[r] the mŭkŭrŭs, the shell-fish, the porpoises, &c. The offerings, after having been presented to the inhabitants of the waters, are thrown into the Ganges. Ten lamps of clarified butter are then lighted up, and all the other offerings presented. After this, the names of certain gods are repeated, with forms of praise; the fee is presented to the priest, the bramhŭns are entertained, and the offerings sent to the houses of bramhŭns. At the close of these ceremonies the people perform obeisance to Gŭnga, and then depart. Great multitudes assemble on the banks of the river on these occasions, and expect much both in this life and hereafter from this act of worship. If a person, placing on his head ten fruits of any kind, thus immerse himself in the Ganges on this day, the sins of ten births will be removed.

In this month also clay images of Gŭnga are set up in domestic temples, and worshipped, and the next day thrown into the river. In some places clay images of this goddess are preserved in clay temples, and worshipped daily. Persons escaping dangers on water present offerings to Gŭnga, as well as to Vŭroonŭ, the Indian Neptune; as mariners, having escaped the dangers of the sea, used to offer a sacrifice to Venus.

On the thirteenth of the decrease of the moon in Choitrŭ, the people descend into the water, and with their hands joined immerse themselves; after which the officiating bramhŭn reads a portion of the shastrŭ, describing the benefits arising from this act of bathing. The people repeat after the priest certain significant words, as the day of the month, the name of Vishnoo, &c., and then immerse themselves again. Gifts of rice, fruits, and money are offered to

[r] This strongly reminds us of the lines of Juvenal, Satire xv.

'Who has not heard, where Egypt's realms are nam'd,
What monster gods her frantic sons have fram'd?
Here Ibis gorg'd with well-grown serpents*, there
The crocodile † commands religious fear:
Where Memnon's statue magic strings inspire
With vocal sounds that emulate the lyre;
And Thebes (such, Fate, are thy disastrous turns!)
Now prostrate o'er her pompous ruins mourns;
A monkey-god ‡, prodigious to be told!
Strikes the beholder's eye with burnished gold:
To godship here blue Triton's scaly herd,
The river progeny is there preferr'd‖:
Through towns Diana's power neglected lies,
Where to her dogs§ aspiring temples rise:
And should you leeks or onions eat, no time
Would expiate the sacrilegious crime.
Religious nations sure, and blest abodes,
Where every orchard is o'errun with gods!'

* See Gurooru. † The Hindoos throw their children to the alligators. ‡ Hunooman.
‖ See the account above. § See a preceding article.

the poor, the bramhŭns, and the priest. On this occasion groups of ten or twelve persons stand in the water in one spot, for whom one bramhŭn reads the formulas. These groups are to be seen extending themselves very far along the river. At the moment of the conjunction of the moon (on the thirteenth of its decrease) with the star Shŭtŭbhisha, this festival is called the Great Varoonēē. The merit arising from bathing at this lucky moment is supposed to be very great; the people fast till the bathing is over. When there is a conjunction as above, and the day falls on a Saturday, the festival is called the Great, Great Varoonēē.[s]

The pooranŭs declare, that the sight, the name, or the touch of Gŭnga takes away all sin, however heinous; that thinking of Gŭnga, when at a distance, is sufficient to remove the taint of sin; but that bathing in Gŭnga has blessings in it of which no imagination can conceive.

So much is this river reverenced among the Hindoos, that many bramhŭns will not cook upon it, nor throw saliva into it, nor wash themselves nor their clothes in it.[t] Some persons perform a journey of five or six months to bathe in Gŭnga, to perform the rites for deceased relations, and to carry this water to place in their houses, for religious and medicinal uses. The water of this river is used also in the English courts of justice to swear upon, as the koran is given to Mŭsŭlmans, and the New Testament to Christians; but many of the most respectable Hindoos refuse to comply with this method of making oath, alleging that their shastrŭs forbid them in these cases to touch the water of the Ganges,[u] the shalgramŭ, or a bramhŭn. When such cases occur in the courts, the judges very candidly permit the person, if of good character, to give his evidence in a way consistent with his peculiar prejudices, as, after bathing, &c. and standing with his face to the east. The Hindoo courts formerly admitted a person's evidence without an oath; and when a cause could not be determined by evidence thus given, they resorted to the ordeal. It is not uncommon for one Hindoo to say to another, 'Will you make this engagement on the banks of Gŭnga?' The other replies, 'I engage to do what I have said; but I cannot call Gŭnga to witness it.' If a person utter a most audacious lie, while near or upon the Ganges, the person to whom he is speaking says, 'Are you

[s] At the time of many of the festivals, the sides of the Ganges, in many places, are gaily illuminated; and lights fastened on boards, plantain stalks, &c. or put in earthen pots, are floated down the stream.

[t] In the work called Valmēēkee-moonee, amongst many other forms of praise to be offered to Gŭnga, is the following:—'O goddess, the owl that lodges in the hollow of a tree on thy banks is exalted beyond measure; while the emperor, whose palace is far from thee, though he may possess a million of stately elephants, and may have the wives of millions of conquered enemies to serve him, is nothing.'

[u] Many persons refuse to contest causes in which large sums are at stake, under the fear that they may be constrained to make oath on the waters of the Ganges.

not afraid of uttering such a falsehood in the presence of Gunga?' A third person perhaps adds, as a continuation of the reproach—'Not he; he has been guilty of discharging his urine into Gŭnga, even at Prŭyagŭ.'

Morning and evening the Hindoos visit and look at this river to remove the sins of the night or of the day; when sick they smear their bodies with the sediment, and remain near the river for a month perhaps. Some of course recover, and others die: a Hindoo says, that those who have a steady faith and an unwavering mind, recover; the rest perish.

The Hindoos are extremely anxious to die in the sight of the Ganges, that their sins may be washed away in their last moments. A person in his last agonies is frequently dragged from his bed and friends, and carried, in the coldest or in the hottest weather, from whatever distance, to the river side; where he lies, if a poor man, without a covering day and night till he expires: with the pains of death upon him, he is placed up to the middle in the water, and drenched with it. Leaves of the toolŭsee plant are also put into his mouth; and his relations call upon him to repeat, and repeat for him, the names of Ramŭ, Hŭree, Narayŭnŭ, Brŭmha, Gŭnga, &c. In some cases the family priest repeats some incantations, and makes an offering to Voitŭrŭnēē, the river over which the soul, they say, is ferried after leaving the body. The relations of the dying man spread the sediment of the river on his forehead or breast, and afterwards with the finger write on this sediment the name of some deity. If a person should die in his house, and not by the river side, it is considered as a great misfortune, as he thereby loses the help of the goddess in his dying moments. If a person choose to die at home, his memory becomes infamous. The conduct of Raja Nŭvŭ-krishnŭ of Nŭdēēya, who died in his bed-room about the year 1800, is still mentioned as a subject of reproach, because he refused to be carried to the river before death. 'Ah! Ah!' say the superstitious, when a neighbour at the point of death delays the fatal journey to the river, 'he will die like Raja Nŭvŭ-Krishnŭ.'

Dead bodies are brought by their relations to be burnt near this river; and when they cannot bring the whole body, it is not uncommon for them to bring a single bone and cast it into the river,* under the hope that it will help the soul of the deceased.

* Many persons, whose relations die at a distance from the Ganges, at the time of burning the body preserve a bone, and at some future time bring this bone and commit it to Gŭnga, supposing that this will secure the salvation of the deceased. The work called Kriya-yogŭsarŭ contains the following curious story:—A bramhŭn, who had been guilty of the greatest crimes, was devoured by wild beasts; his bones only remained. A crow took up one of these bones, and was carrying it over Gŭnga, when another bird darting upon it, the crow let the bone fall. As soon as the bone touched Gŭnga, the bramhŭn sprang to life, and was ascending to heaven, when the messenger of Yŭmŭ, the judge of the dead, seized him, as a great sinner. At this

In the eastern parts of Bengal, married women, long disappointed in their hopes of children, make an offering to Gŭnga, and enter into a vow, that if the goddess will give them two children, they will present one to her: and it is not uncommon for such women to cast the first child into the river as an offering; but it is said, that at present some relation or religious mendicant stands ready to preserve the life of the child. The mother cannot take it again, but this person adopts and provides for it. These offerings are made on the tenth of the moon in Jyoisht'hŭ, and on the 13th of Choitrŭ.

Some persons even drown themselves in the Ganges, not doubting but they shall immediately ascend to heaven. The shastrŭ encourages this.[y] It is a sin for a bramhŭn, but an act of merit in a shōōdrŭ or a dŭndēē, if he be in worldly trouble, or afflicted with an incurable distemper. The Gŭnga-Vakya-Vŭlee says, 'Should any person have eaten with another who is degraded for seven successive births; or have committed the five sins, each of which is called mŭha-patŭkŭ; should he have eaten the food which has been touched by a woman in her courses; or have constantly spoken falsely; or have stolen gold, jewels, &c.; should he have killed the wife of his friend; or have injured bramhŭns, or friends, or his mother, &c.; or have committed the sins which doom a man to the hell called Mŭharourŭvŭ; or have committed those sins for which the messengers of Yŭmŭ constantly beat a person; or have committed multitudes of sins in childhood, youth, and old age;—if this person bathe in Gŭnga at an auspicious period, all these sins will be removed: he will also be admitted into the heaven of Brŭmha, the Pŭrŭm-hŭngsee; be put in possession of the merits of the man who presents a lac of red cows to a bramhŭn learned in the four vēdŭs; and afterwards will ascend and dwell at the right hand of Vishnoo. After he has enjoyed all this happiness, and shall be re-born on the earth, he will be possessed of every good quality, enjoy all kinds of happiness, be very honour-

time Narayŭnŭ's messengers interfered, and pleaded, that the sins of this man, since one of his bones had touched Gŭnga, were all done away. The appeal was made to Vishnoo, who decided in the bramhŭn's favour. The bramhŭn immediately went to heaven.

[y] The Skŭndŭ pooranŭ declares, that by dying in the Ganges, a person will obtain absorption into Brŭmhŭ. The same work contains a promise from Shivŭ, that whoever dies in Gŭnga shall obtain a place in his heaven.—The Bhŭvishyŭ pooranŭ affirms that if a worm, or an insect, or a grass-hopper, or any tree growing by the side of Gŭnga, die in the river, it will obtain absorption into Brŭmhŭ.—The Brŭmhŭ pooranŭ says, that whether a person renounce life in Gŭnga, praying for any particular benefit, or die by accident, or whether he possess his senses or not, he will be happy. If he purposely renounce life, he will enjoy absorption, or the highest happiness; if he die by accident, he will still attain heaven.—Mŭnoo says, 'A mansion with bones for its rafters and beams; with nerves and tendons for cords; with muscles and blood for mortar; with skin for its outward covering; filled with no sweet perfume, but loaded with fæces and urine; a mansion infested by age and by sorrow, the seat of malady, harassed with pains, haunted with the quality of darkness, and incapable of standing long; such a mansion of the vital soul let its occupier always cheerfully quit.'

able, &c. He who shall doubt any part of this, will be doomed to the hell called Koombhēē-pakŭ, and afterwards be born an ass. If a person, in the presence of Gŭnga, on the anniversary of her arrival on the earth, and according to the rules prescribed in the shastrŭs, present to the bramhŭns whole villages, he will obtain the fruits that arise from all other offerings, from all sacrifices, from visiting all the holy places, &c.; his body will be a million times more glorious than the sun; he will obtain a million of virgins, and multitudes of carriages, palankeens, &c. covered with jewels; he will dwell for ages in heaven, enjoying its pleasures in company with his father; as many particles of dust as are contained in the land thus given away to the bramhŭns, for so many years will the giver dwell in happiness in Vishnoo's heaven.'

Every real Christian must be deeply affected on viewing the deplorable effects of this superstition. Except that part of the rig-védŭ which countenances the burning of women alive, no writers ever gave birth to a more extensive degree of misery than those who have made the Ganges a sacred river. Thousands, yea millions of people are annually drawn from their homes and peaceful labours, several times in the year, to visit different holy places of this river, at a great expense of time, and money spent in making offerings to the goddess; expensive journeys are undertaken by vast multitudes to obtain the water[z] of this river, (some come two or three months' journey for this purpose,) or to carry the sick, the dying, the dead, or the bones of the dead, to its banks. What the sick and dying suffer by being exposed to all kinds of weather in the open air on the banks of the river, and in being choked by the *sacred* water in their last moments, is beyond expression. In short, no eyes, but those of Omniscience, can see all the foul deeds done upon and by the sides of this river; and the day of judgment alone can bring all these deeds to light. The bramhŭn will then see, that instead of Gŭnga's having removed the sins of her worshippers, she has increased them a million-fold.

SECT. II.—*Other deified Rivers.*

THE Godavŭrēē, the Nŭrmŭda, the Kavérēē, the Atréyēē the Kŭrŭtoya, the Bahooda, the Gomŭtēē, the Sŭrŭyoo, the Gŭndŭkēē, the Varahēē, the Chŭrmŭn-wŭtee, the Shŭtŭdroo the Vipasha, the Goutŭmēē, the Kŭrmŭnasha, the Shonŭ,[a] the Oiravŭtēē, the Chŭndrŭbhaga, the Vitŭsta, the Sindhoo, the Bhŭdra-vŭkasha, the Pŭnŭsa, the Dévika, the Tamrŭpŭrnēē, the Toongŭbhŭdra, the Krishna, the Vétrŭvŭtēē, the Bhoirŭvŭ, the Brŭmhŭ-pootrŭ,[b] the Voitŭrŭnēē, and many other rivers, are mentioned in the Hindoo shastrŭs as sacred.

[z] Many thousands perish by the dysentery, and others through want, in these journies.

[a] This is a male river. [b] Ditto.

At the full moon in Asharhŭ, many thousand Hindoos assemble at Prŭtapŭ-gŭrŭ, a place to the west of Lucknow, and bathe in the Godavŭrēē, or in the remains of it, (for at this season of the year this river is nearly dried up.)

On the last day of Choitrŭ, a large assembly of Hindoos meet at Modŭphŭrŭ-poorŭ, about sixteen miles from Patna, where the Gŭndakēē, the Sŭrŭyoo, and the Ganges meet.[b] The assembly remains eight days, and a large fair is held on the spot, at which horses, camels, and other beasts, and also children, are bought and sold: the price of a boy is from ten to twelve rupees; that of a girl is less.

On the same day a large concourse of Hindoos, some say as many as 20,000, principally women, assemble at Ŭyodhya, to bathe in the Sŭrŭyoo.

On the 14th of the decrease of the moon in Phalgoonŭ, an equal number of people are said to meet on the banks of the Sŭrŭyoo at Bŭhŭrŭm-ghatŭ, near Lucknow: but they do not bathe in the river, the water of which is very filthy, but in a sacred pool adjoining.

On the banks of the Yŭmoona, on the second of the moon in Kartikŭ, and on the eighth of the decrease of the moon in Bhadrŭ, vast crowds of Hindoos assemble in different places to bathe.

The Brŭmhŭ-pootrŭ receives the same honours on the eighth of the increase of the moon in Choitrŭ. At a place three days' journey from Dacca 50 or 60,000 people assemble, and sacrifice pigeons, sheep, and goats, casting them into the river. Children are also cast into the river here by their mothers, but are generally rescued and carried home by strangers. Superstitious people say, that on this day the river gradually swells so as to fill its banks, and then gradually sinks to its usual level.

The Voitŭrŭnēē, in Orissa, is also placed among the sacred rivers, and on the thirteenth of the decrease of the moon in Choitrŭ, great multitudes of Hindoos, (six or seven hundred thousand,) assemble at Yajŭ-poorŭ, near the temple of Jŭgŭnnat'hŭ, and bathe in this river.

Many other rivers receive the same honours;[c] and I could have greatly enlarged this account, in detailing their fabulous histories, and in noticing the superstitious ceremonies of this deluded people on their banks: but what I have here inserted, and the preceding account of Gŭnga, must suffice.

[b] There are several causes why particular places of these rivers are esteemed peculiarly sacred. Some of these causes are given in the shastrŭs, and others arise from tradition. One instance of the latter occurs respecting Voidyvŭtēē, a place near Serampore, where Nimaee, a religious mendicant, performed his devotions, and where at present, at a conjunction of particular stars, multitudes assemble to bathe.

[c] See Asiatic Researches.

CHAP. XIV.

THE WORSHIP OF FISH.

VISHNOO, having been incarnate in the form of a fish, is worshipped on certain occasions, or rather a form of praise is repeated in honour of this incarnation.

In the preceding account of Gŭnga it will also be seen, that the finny tribes of that river are worshipped at the festivals in honour of this goddess.

I am informed, however, that female Hindoos, residing on the banks of the Pŭdmŭ, on the 5th of the increase of the moon in Maghŭ, actually worship the Ilishŭ fish, when they first arrive in the river, with the usual ceremonies, and after that partake of them without the fear of injuring their health.

CHAP. XV.

THE WORSHIP OF BOOKS.

THE Hindoos have deified their shastrŭs, which, on different occasions, they worship with the same ceremonies as an idol, anointing the book with perfumes, and adorning it with garlands.

At the reading of any part of the védŭs, the Chundēē, and other works, the book to be read is always addressed as an idol. At such times the worshipper thus prays to the book: 'Oh! book! thou art the goddess of learning, bestow learning upon me.'

When an individual employs a bramhŭn to recite to his family and neighbours the Mŭhabharŭtŭ, Ramayŭnŭ, Shrēēbhagŭvŭtŭ, or any other pooranŭ, the worship of the work recited is performed on the first and last days at considerable length, many offerings being presented: each day's recital is also preceded by a short service paid to the book.

At the festival in honour of the goddess Sŭrŭswŭtēē any one of the shastrŭs is adopted and worshipped, joined with the pen and inkstand.

The followers of Vishnoo, and especially the mendicant voiragēēs, pay a still greater reverence than the regular Hindoos to the books they esteem sacred. These books relate to the amours of Krishnŭ, or to the mendicants Choitŭnyŭ and Nityanŭndŭ.

A book placed on a golden throne, and presented to a bramhŭn, is a very meritorious gift.

CHAP. XVI.

THE WORSHIP OF STONES.

The Shalgramŭ[a].

THIS is the ætites, or eagle-stone, of which there is a great variety, and to which many virtues were ascribed by the ancients. When I shewed a picture of the eagle-stone to a bramhŭn who was sitting with me, without informing him what it was, he exclaimed —'This is the shalgramŭ!' and added, (jocularly,) 'Oh! then, Englishmen will be saved, as they have the shalgramŭ amongst them.'

This stone, black, hollow, and nearly round, is said to be brought from mount Gŭndŭkee, in Nepaul. It is added, that in this mountain there are multitudes of insects which perforate the masses of stone, so that pieces fall into the river Gŭndŭkŭ in the shape of the shalgramŭ, from whence they are taken with nets. Common ones are about as large as a watch. They are valued according to their size, their hollowness, and the colours in the inside; and from these circumstances they are called by different names. The chief sorts are called Lŭkshmēē-Narayŭnŭ, Rŭghoonat'hŭ, Lŭkshmēē, Jŭnardŭnŭ, Vamŭnŭ, Damodŭrŭ,[b] &c. These different shalgramŭs are worshipped under their different names. The first is sometimes sold for as much as two thousand rupees. The Hindoos have a notion, that whoever keeps in his house this celebrated stone, and a shell called dŭkshina-vŭrtŭ,[c] can never become poor; but that the very day in which any one parts with one of them,; he will begin to sink into poverty. Almost every respectable bramhŭn keeps a shalgramŭ, as do some shōōdrŭs. The bramhŭn who does not keep one is reproached by his neighbours.

The reason why this stone has been deified is thus given in the Shrēē-bhagŭvŭtŭ:—Vishnoo created the nine planets to preside over the fates of men. Shŭnēē (Saturn) commenced his reign by

[a] From sharŭ and gramŭ, which indicates that this stone makes the place excellent in which it is preserved, as the Mŭhabharŭtŭ is said to purify the places in which it is read: hence bramhŭns are forbidden to enter a village where the Mŭhabharŭtŭ is not found, as such place is pronounced unclean.

[b] The Hindoos say, that this last shalgramŭ requires large offerings of food to be presented to it; and that a bramhŭn, who had begged one of them, and neglected to feed it sufficiently, was brought to ruin, this god having swept away nearly his whole family by death. Many stories of this kind are related of this stone. Though a single grain of rice was never known to be eaten by an image, yet the Hindoos firmly believe this and similar stories, against all the evidence of their senses for hundreds of years together. Gopalŭ, a learned bramhŭn employed in the Serampore printing-office, declared that one of these stones had been placed in his house by a relation, who attributed his family misfortunes to its powers.

[c] A shell, the convolutions of which turn to the right. Vishnoo is said to hold a shell of this kind in his hand.

proposing to Brŭmha, that he should first come under his influence for twelve years. Brŭmha referred him to Vishnoo, but this god, equally averse to be brought under the dreaded influence of this inauspicious planet, desired Saturn to call upon him the next day, and immediately assumed the form of a mountain. The next day Saturn was not able to find Vishnoo, but discovering that he had united himself to mount Gŭndŭkēē, he entered the mountain in the form of a worm called vŭjrŭ-kēētŭ.[c] He continued thus to afflict the mountain-formed Vishnoo for twelve years, when Vishnoo assumed his proper shape, and commanded that the stones of this mountain should be worshipped, and should become proper representatives of himself; adding, that each should have twenty-one marks in it, similar to those on his body, and that its name should be shalgramŭ.

The worship of any of the gods may be performed before the shalgramŭ, and it is often adopted as the representative of some god. It claims no national festival, but is placed near the image worshipped, and first receives the devotions of the Hindoos. The shalgramŭ is also worshipped daily by the bramhŭns, after morning ablutions: they first bathe or wash the stone, reading the formulas; and then offer flowers, white lead, incense, light, sweetmeats, and water, repeating incantations: the offerings, after remaining before it a short time, are eaten by the family. In the evening, incense, light, and sweetmeats are offered, preceding which a bell is rung, and a shell blown; and the whole is closed by the priest's prostrating himself before the stone.

During the month Voishakhŭ, bramhŭns suspend a pan of water every day over the shalgramŭ, and, through a small hole at the bottom, let the water fall on it, to preserve it cool during this month, which is one of the hottest in the year. This water is caught in another pan placed beneath, and drank in the evening as holy water. When the country is in great want of rain, a bramhŭn in some instances places the shalgramŭ in the burning sun, and sits down by it, repeating incantations. Burning the god in the sun is said to be a sure way of obtaining rain.

Some persons, when sick, employ a bramhŭn to present single leaves of the toolŭsee plant, sprinkled with red powder, to the shalgramŭ, repeating incantations. A hundred thousand leaves are sometimes presented. It is said, that the sick man gradually recovers as every additional leaf is offered. When a Hindoo is at the point of death, a bramhŭn shews him the marks of the shalgramŭ, the sight of which is said to secure the soul a safe passage to Vishnoo's heaven.

In a work called Shalgramŭ-nirnŭyŭ an account is given of the proper names of the different shalgramŭs; the benefits arising

[c] Literally, the thunder-bolt worm.

from their worship; the kinds of shalgramŭs proper to be kept by persons in a secular state, and also by the religious.

A separate room, or house, or a particular spot in the room where the family dwell, is assigned to this god. Some persons keep one, others ten, others a hundred, and some even as many as a thousand of these stones.

The shalgramŭ is rendered impure by the touch of a shoodrŭ[d] and in such cases must be purified by rubbing it over with cow-dung, cow's urine, milk, ghēē, and curds. If a small part of the shalgramŭ be broken off, the owner commits it to the river. The bramhŭns sell these stones, but trafficing in images is dishonorable.

[The shalgramŭ is the only stone deriving its deity from itself: all other stones worshipped are made sacred by incantations. For an account of them, see a succeeding article relative to the Hindoo images.]

CHAP. XVII.

A LOG OF WOOD WORSHIPPED.

The Pedal.

THIS is a rough piece of wood, (termed dhénkee,) generally the trunk of a tree, balanced on a pivot, with a head something like a mallet; it is used to separate the rice from the husk, to pound brick-dust for buildings, &c. A person stands at the farthest end, and with his feet presses it down, which raises up the head; after which he lets it fall on the rice, or brick-ends. One of these pedals is set up at almost every house in country places.

The origin of this worship is thus given:—A religious guide, being called upon to give the initiating incantation to one of his disciples, commanded him to repeat the word dhénkee, dhénkee. Narŭdŭ, the god of the dhénkee, pleased with the disciple, visited him, riding on a pedal, and gave him as a blessing another incantation, by which he immediately became perfect, and ascended to heaven.

The pedal is worshipped at the time of marriage, of investiture with the poita, of giving the first rice to a child, and at any other particular time of rejoicing. The women are the worshippers. It is also worshipped in the month Voishakhŭ by all castes of females, not excepting the wives of the most learned bramhŭns; who consecrate it by putting red, white, or yellow paint, and also some rice, dōōrva grass, and oil on its head.

About twenty years ago, the raja of Nŭlŭ-danga, Mŭhéndrŭ-dévŭ-rayŭ, spent three hundred thousand rupees in a grand festival in honour of this log of wood. At the close of the festival, the raja took a firebrand, and set all the gilded scenery on fire, and thus finished this scene of expensive folly and wickedness.

[d] So are all other images that have been consecrated.

BOOK II.

OF THE TEMPLES, IMAGES, PRIESTS, AND CEREMONIES OF THE HINDOOS.

CHAPTER I.

OF THE TEMPLES.

THE Hindoo temples in Bengal, though different in shape, are nearly of the same description of architecture: they are very in-inferior, it is true, to the sacred edifices in Europe; but some of these buildings are in a better style than might have been expected from a people so little advanced in the arts.

SECT. I.—*Of different Kinds of Temples.*

The *Mŭndirŭ*,[a] dedicated to the lingŭ, is a double-roofed Gothic building, the body square, but the upper part short and tapering to a point. It contains one, two, three, or more rooms, about three cubits by four, with a porch in front for spectators. The centre room contains the lingŭ; in the others are placed the utensils for worship, the offerings, &c.—Small square temples for the lingŭ, with flat roofs, are erected in rows facing the houses of rich men, or before a college, a consecrated pool of water, another temple, or a flight of steps descending into the river. Similar temples in honour of Gŭnéshŭ are to be seen in some places. Very small temples like the Mŭndirŭ, only three or five cubits high, and containing a lingŭ about a foot in height, have been erected at Benares.

The *Déoolŭ*[b] temples, sacred to Jŭgŭnnat'hŭ, rise from the foundation in a gradual slope like a sugar loaf, with an iron image of Gŭroorŭ on the pinnacle. These temples, made of brick, are ascended by a flight of steps, and contain only one room.

The *Pŭnchŭ-rŭtnŭ*[c] temple has two or three rooms, and a single-arched roof, with a large pinnacle or turret on the dome, and a smaller one on each corner. It is dedicated to the different forms

[a] Mŭndirŭ means any edifice of brick or stone; but custom has appropriated it almost exclusively to the temples of the lingŭ.

[b] Corrupted from devalayŭ, i. e., devŭ, a god, alŭyŭ, a house.

[c] Having five turrets.

of Vishnoo, as Radha-bŭllŭbhŭ, Gopalŭ, Mŭdŭnŭ-mohŭnŭ, Govindhŭ, &c. The temple called *Nŭvŭ-rŭtnŭ*[d] dedicated also to the various forms of Vishnoo, has a double roof like the Mŭndirŭ, with a small turret on each corner of the lower roofs, and on the upper one a larger turret to crown the dome. It contains four or five rooms. At Ŭgrŭ-dwēēpŭ, the temple of Gopēē-nat'hŭ has different houses attached to it; one for cooking, another for the utensils used in worship; another is a store-house for the offerings, and two others are open rooms for the accommodation of visitors and devotees.

The *Vishnoo-mŭndirŭ*, having one room, with a partico in front, is a flat-roofed building, erected either within or without the wall which encloses a Hindoo house, or at a little distance from the owner's house; and sometimes by the side of the Ganges, when the person's house is near the river. A few temples may be seen, having three rooms; one of which is the god's hall of audience, another his dining room, and the third his room for sleeping.

Another kind of temple, with a flat roof, is often erected by rich Hindoos adjoining to their houses, and called *Chŭndēē-mŭndŭpŭ*, and is designed for the image of Doorga or Kalēē. This is built on four sides, with an area in the middle. The image is placed at the north end, with its face to the south; the two sides, and the north end, in most cases, contain upper rooms with porticos beneath. The room which contains the image is about ten cubits long and sixteen broad: the other rooms are open in front with arched doorways; and in these the visitors sit to see the ceremonies of worship, hear the singing, &c.

The *Yorŭ-bangala* is made like two thatched houses or bangalas, placed side to side; and has what is called in England a double-pitched roof, generally covered with tiles or bricks. The front is open without doors. These temples are dedicated to different gods, but are not now frequently built in Bengal.

The Hindoos have another sacred edifice, called *Rasŭmŭnchŭ*, in which the image of Krishnŭ is annually placed and worshipped. This building is octagonal, with eight turrets at the corners, and a steeple in the centre supported by pillars; and consists of one room, open on all sides, and elevated five or six feet from the ground. On the nights of the rasŭ festival, the image is brought and placed in this elevated open room, there worshipped, and afterwards carried back to the temple adjoining to the owner's house. The *Dolŭ-munchu* is a similar building, but is sometimes made larger.

A great number of small clay and thatched buildings are erected in Bengal, in which the images of Siddhéshwŭrēē, Krishnoo,

[d] Having nine turrets.

Ramŭ, &c. are set up. The roofs of these buildings are sloping, like the huts of the poor in Europe.

Images of some of the inferior deities are placed under trees, and these trees become as it were temples for worship.

In some few towns a number of different temples are built in a square. I once saw a *Dévalŭyŭ* of this kind at Chanchra, in Jessore, which contains twenty-one temples and as many gods. One thousand acres of ground are attached to this place; one bramhŭn perform the ceremonies; six others cook for these gods; four others gather flowers, and bring the articles for the daily worship. Nimaee-mŭllikŭ, a goldsmith of Calcutta, built and endowed this place. Similar devalŭyŭs are to be seen at Krishnŭ-nŭgŭrŭ,[e] Gŭnga-vasŭ, Shiŭ-nivasŭ, Bŭrŭhŭ-nŭgŭrŭ[f], Natorŭ, Poonté[g], Somra[h], Bhōō-koilasŭ, Gooptŭ-para, and at many other places in Bengal.—Raja Chŭndrŭ-rayŭ, of Patŭlee, is said to have built two hundred of these dévalŭyŭs, at each of which two or three hundred people are daily fed. The relict of raja Tilŭkŭ-chŭndrŭ, of Burdwan, erected one hundred and eight temples in one plain, and placed in them as many images of the lingŭ; attaching to them eleven bramhŭns and inferior servants, and endowing the temples with estates to the amount of the wages of the attendants.

Before many temples is seen a roof, supported by pillars, under which portions of the shastrŭs are recited or sung, and at other times animals for sacrifice slaughtered. In general, however, the singing and dancing at the festivals take place under an awning in the open air, near some temple, or near the person's house who bears the expense. The long periods of dry weather in this climate render this practicable; nor would the heat allow of such large assemblies meeting in houses, even if buildings sufficiently large could be constructed. This accounts for the Hindoo temples being so small in the inside: many of them, especially those of the lingŭ, are only large enough to contain the image, the offerings, the utensils of worship, and the officiating priests.

Much of the wealth of the Hindoo kings was formerly expended in building temples, and supporting splendid festivals. At present, those who erect these temples in Bengal are principally the head-servants of Europeans, who appropriate part of their gains to these acts of supposed merit.[i]

[e] These belong to Girēēshŭ-chŭndrŭ, the raja Nŭvŭ-dwēēpŭ.

[f] This first place is in Moorshŭdabadŭ, and belongs to raja Vishoonat'hŭ, as does that at Natorŭ.

[g] This belongs to raja Bhoovŭnŭ-t'hakoorŭ.

[h] This place is the property of Ram-sŭnkŭrŭ-rayŭ, a voidyŭ.

[i] The capitol, or temple of Jupiter Capitolinus, was raised in consequence of a vow made by Tarquinius Priscus in the Sabine war.

The expense of erecting one of these temples, if a single room, amounts to about two hundred rupees; and the wages and daily offerings to one image are about three rupees per month. Some give the bramhŭn who officiates twelve annas, and others a rupee monthly, with his food and clothes. Sometimes the offerings are given to him, but in other cases they are presented to the bramhŭns of the village alternately, and the priest has money given him in their stead. These offerings frequently consist of a pound of rice, a pint of milk, half an ounce of sugar, and two plantains. The quantity, however, is not prescribed; and other things are added by the wealthy.

SECT. II.—*Dedication of Temples.*

WHEN a Hindoo has erected a temple, he appoints a day to dedicate it to some god. The following account of the dedication of one hundred and eight temples to Shivŭ, some years ago, at Talitŭ, in the district of Burdwan, by the mother of Téjŭsh-chŭndrŭ, the raja of Burdwan, will give an idea of the manner in which this ceremony is performed.

The foundation of these temples being about to be laid, a place was dug in the earth about a cubit square, into which water was poured, and a brick placed in the hole; after which the worship of the household god, (Vishnoo,) of Vŭroonŭ, and the lingŭ, was performed. At the close of the worship, a flower was thrown into the water, the floating of which to the right was considered as a good omen, and decided the point that the temple should be raised on that spot. The following prayer was then addressed to this brick: 'As long as the earth and mountains remain, so long do thou remain immoveable.' After the temples were nearly finished, many bramhŭns and the relations of the queen were invited, and on an auspicious day the ceremony of consecration was performed. An altar was raised before each temple, and four priests chosen for each altar; who, purifying them, performed the worship of the five gods,[k] the nine planets, the ten guardian deities of the earth, and of Shivŭ, Vishnoo, and Doorga. To this succeeded the burnt-sacrifice. One hundred and eight officiating priests then celebrated the worship of Shivŭ, while sitting at the doors of the temples. A person, in the name of the queen, next made a present to the builder, and hinted to him that she now wished to consecrate these temples to Shivŭ. The trident of Shivŭ was next worshipped, and fixed on the steeple. The princess then, sitting in an enclosure below the steps of one of the temples, in the presence of one of the priests and her attendants, devoted these temples to Shivŭ, saying, 'O Shivŭ! I present to thee these one hundred and eight temples, made of brick: may I be rewarded

[k] Brŭmha, Vishnoo, Shivŭ, Gŭnéshŭ, and Sŏŏryŭ.

with an everlasting residence in heaven.' In making this offering, a number of minute ceremonies took place. The princess next sent one of her relatives to perform the worship of Indrŭ near a bamboo, bearing a trident, with a flag fastened thereto. The same person, after professing to animate one hundred and eight wooden images of the bull, worshipped them, and placed them in the temples thus dedicated. A representative of the princess next walked round the temples three times:—(the princess herself began to perform the ceremonies of circumambulation, but being very corpulent, she resigned it to one of the priests.)—One hundred and eight priests, bringing garlands[1] and the other articles used in worship, now performed the worship of the lingŭ in the temples. At the close of these ceremonies, the princess presented a rupee to each of the four hundred and thirty-two officiating bramhŭns, and one hundred and eight rupees to her own private priest, who also obtained the offerings. She also presented twelve kinds of offerings to Shivŭ, among which were vessels of gold, silver, and other metals, cloths, &c. An entertainment to the bramhŭns succeeded, and at length the guests were dismissed with presents from among the offerings, or in money, from ten to fifty rupees each bramhŭn. One hundred thousand rupees, it is said, were expended upon these buildings.[m]

The ceremonies are nearly similar to the above when idols are dedicated and set up in temples; when pools or trees are consecrated to the public use; when cars are presented to some god; and when a person is finishing the ceremonies of a vrŭtŭ or vow.

SECT. III.—*Endowment of temples.*

THE worship in some temples is conducted, and the offerings supplied by the family which has erected the temple; but in others by a hired bramhŭn, who receives monthly wages: the offerings are in general distributed among the bramhŭns of the village.

To a temple particularly celebrated, rich men make grants of houses, sometimes of whole villages; and of lands, orchards, pools, &c. to a large amount; and the produce of these grants is applied to the uses of the temple.

The temple of Radha-bŭllŭbhŭ at Bŭllŭbhŭ-poorŭ, about twelve

[1] At the time of worship the priest always puts upon the image a garland of flowers. This seems to have been practised among other idolaters: for when the priest of Jupiter came to worship Paul and Barnabas, (Acts xiv. 13.) he brought oxen and garlands. No doubt the latter were intended to be put upon the heads or necks of the apostle and his companion, the persons about to be worshipped.

[m] Téjŭsh-chŭndrŭ has since built one hundred and eight temples at Umbika and dedicated them to Shivŭ.

miles north of Calcutta, has been endowed with lands, houses, &c. to the annual amount of 3,000 rupees, by Raja Mŭvŭ-Krishnŭ; which is divided among sixteen families of bramhŭns.

The temple of Jŭgŭnnat'hŭ at Mŭhéshŭ, about the same distance from Calcutta, has been endowed with lands, &c. to the annual amount of 1,400 rupees, by Raja Anŭndŭ-Chŭndrŭ-Rayŭ.

The temple of Gopēē-nat'hŭ at Ŭgrŭ-dwēēpŭ has been endowed with lands, &c. to the annual amount of 6 or 7,000 rupees, by Raja Krishnŭ-Chŭndrŭ-Rayŭ.

The temple of Jŭgŭnnat'hŭ in Orissa has been endowed by several rich Hindoos: Raja Ram-Krishnŭ-dévŭ gave two villages, the rents of which bring in about 4,000 rupees annually: Nimoomŭllikŭ of Calcutta gave daily one rupee, or 365 annually; and his children continue the donation. Other rich men make similar annual presents. It is supposed that not less than 100,000 rupees a year are drawn from the Hindoos by the bramhŭns of this temple.

CHAP. II.

OF THE IMAGES.

THE images of the Hindoo gods are made either of gold, silver, quicksilver mixed with the powder of tin, brass, copper, iron, mixed metal,[n] crystal, stone, wood, or clay.[o] The common workmen in gold, silver, brass, &c. make these images.

The images made of gold are generally those of Doorga, Lŭkshmēē, Radha, Krishnŭ, and Sŭrŭswŭtēē; which are kept in private houses, and worshipped daily. These images must not not be less in weight than one tola;[p] they are generally three or four.

The image of Shēētŭla is often made of silver, kept in the house, and worshipped daily. It is as heavy as ten or twelve rupees.

[n] Containing, as the Hindoos say, eight ingredients, viz., gold, silver, tin, copper, iron, zinc, lead, and brass.

[o] The shastrŭs allow images to be made of no other substances than these. The image of Shŭnee alone is made of iron.

[p] Three tolas are rather more than one ounce. At Kidderpoorŭ, adjoining to Calcutta, is a golden image of Pŭtitŭ-pavŭnēē, two cubits high. Near Serampore, is a golden image of Jŭgŭdhatrēē, about a cubit and a half high.

The images of Shivŭ only are made of quicksilver and crystal. They are very small, and are kept in the houses of the rich, and used for daily worship.

Small brazen images of many of the gods are kept in private houses, and worshipped daily. These are very small, weighing only an ounce or two.

Very small copper images of Sōōryŭ, and of Shivŭ riding on a bull, are preserved in private houses, and worshipped daily.

The images of mixed metal are those of Radha, Doorga, Lŭkshmēē, Shivŭ, &c. The images of any of the gods may be made with this mixed metal; and may be worshipped either in private houses or in temples.

The images of all the gods and goddesses may be made of stone: the greater number are placed in temples; a few small ones are found in private houses. All images of stone are worshipped daily: the greater number are of the lingŭ, or the various forms of Vishnoo. A few exist of the lingŭ nine or twelve cubits high.[q] The mendicant followers of Vishnoo carry small images of Krishnŭ with them in their peregrinations, which are from one to two cubits high. All the stone images in Bengal are of black marble; but there are some at Benares which are white. The sculpture on these stones is in much the same state of perfection as that to be seen in the oldest churches in England. These stones are brought into Bengal from the upper provinces, and cut by men who are to be found in all the great towns, and to whom it is an employment. Some stone images are miraculously found under ground.[r] See p. 125.

The nimbŭ[s] tree supplies the images of Vishnoo in his different forms; also of Doorga, Radha, Lŭkshmēē, Shivŭ, Gŭroorŭ, Choitŭnyŭ, &c. None of the wooden images are kept in private houses, but in separate temples. They are generally from one to three cubits in height.

All the images which, after worship, are thrown into the water, are of clay baked in the sun, about four cubits high: the images of the lingŭ, made daily and worshipped, are immediately thrown away. In some places, clay images of Kartikŭ, twenty-one cubits high, are set up, and after the festival committed to the river. The images of Doorga, Siddhéshwŭrēē, Unnŭ-pōōrna, Krishnŭ, Pŭnchanŭnŭ, Shŭst'hēē, Mŭnŭsa, Dŭkshinŭ-rayŭ, &c. are however constantly preserved in temples. The Hindoo potters are the prin-

[q] An image of the lingŭ is set up at Benares, which six men can hardly grasp.

[r] An image of Cybele is said to have fallen from heaven into a certain field in Phrygia.

[s] Melia azadarachta.

cipal god-makers, though many other castes, and even Mŭsulmans, follow this employment. The maker first takes a board, and raises upon it a little frame-work, to which he fastens bamboos covered with straw, for the back-bone, the arms, legs, &c. Round these he lays clay mixed with cow-dung, chaff, and straw, which he suffers to dry. Having made the head of clay, he lays it to dry, and afterwards joins it to the trunk very carefully. He again clothes the body, arms, and legs, with more cow-dung and clay, and covers the whole with a cloth, that it may not crack. When ready, he carries it to the person's house who may have ordered it, and, according to the size, obtains two, four, seven, or eight rupees for it. Sometimes the maker paints it at his own house, which costs two, three, four, or five rupees more.

The evening before the consecration, the person at whose temple this image is to be set up, brings twenty-two different articles, among which are fruits, flowers, gold, silver, rice, a stone, turmeric, sugar, cow-dung, clarified butter, a shell, peas, red powder, &c. With all these things the officiating bramhŭn touches the forehead and other parts of the image, repeating incantations. This is called ŭdhivasŭ, or inviting the goddess to come and dwell in the image. The next day, eyes and a soul (pranŭ) are given. No one reverences the image till this work is done.

When an image of Doorga is to be consecrated, in addition to the above ceremonies, a plantain tree is brought, and bathed either in the house, or in the river. At this time the service occupies about an hour: after which the tree is clothed like a woman, with two vilwŭ fruits for breasts; and nine sorts of leaves, smeared with red paint, are hung round the neck. The trees, from which these leaves are taken, are said to have assisted in different wars the deities whose images accompany that of Doorga. The Hindoo shastrŭs make no hesitation in giving tongues to stones, or making trees into soldiers. It may be allowed in a romance; yet the modern Hindoos are silly enough to believe most gravely that all this is the very truth. They say, 'Why not? God can do every thing.'

If a woman, a dog, or a shōōdrŭ touch an image, its godship is destroyed, and the ceremonies of deification must be again performed. A clay image, if thus defiled must be thrown away. There are degrees of impurity imparted by the touch of different animals. Breaking the hand or foot of an image is an evil omen. If an image be unequal in any of its parts, or if the eyes be made to look upwards or downwards, and not straight forwards, something evil will befall the owner. If it be set up with ease, the spectators declare, that god himself is pleased.

Godship of Images tried.—By performing a ceremony called

shora, it is imagined, a person may obtain the power of ascertaining whether the deity dwell in an image or not. In this ceremony, which must be repeated during fifteen days and nights, the devotee bathes an image of the goddess Vipŭrēētŭ-prŭtyŭngira with milk, curds, clarified butter, cow's dung, and cow's urine; worships it, having on red garments; and repeats the initiating incantation of this goddess ten thousand times. In the night, he walks round the image, in a triangular manner, one hundred and eight times, prostrating himself after every circumambulation. On the last day, the ceremonies are continued to a greater extent, and the burnt-sacrifice is added. When such a person bows to an image, if the deity dwell not in it, it will break to pieces A person of Krishnŭ-nŭgŭrŭ is mentioned as having obtained this power: he bowed to an image of Mŭdŭnŭ-Mohŭnŭ, at Vishnoo-poorŭ; when the image became bent in the neck, and continues so to this day. At Réboona, a village near Balasore, several stone images are said to have been broken by a man named Kalaparhŭ, who bowed to them.

CHAP. III.

OF THE PRIESTS.

The Poorohitŭ.—Every bramhŭn may perform the ceremonies of his religion. The priest, called a poorohitŭ, is, however, called in to assist in the shraddhŭ, the ten ceremonies called sŭngskarŭ, in those at the offering of a temple, at the different vrŭtŭs, at the festivals, and at a burnt-sacrifice; and he is sometimes called to fast, and bathe, in the name of another. A man of property in some cases, unwilling to fast himself, gives his poorohitŭ a rupee to do it for him; and, in the cold weather, he gives him a fee, to bathe for a month, and perform the ceremonies connected with bathing, instead of himself. Some rich men retain a family priest, who receives the fees and separate presents of cloth, sweetmeats, rice, fruits, &c. as his reward.

Any bramhŭn, who is acquainted with the different formulas of worship, may become an officiating priest. In some cases, one person is priest to a thousand families; but he employs assistants, and gives them a stipulated share of the perquisites. If the priest do not arrive in time, or if he blunder in performing the ceremonies, the person employing him reproves him. When several families have the same priest, and wish to perform certain ceremonies on the same day, the priest is sure to offend, and never fails to be told of his partiality to one family, and neglect of the other. These priests are generally very avaricious, and take care to have their full share of the presents at the close of a ceremony. The amount of the fees depends upon the ability and generosity of the person who employs the priest; who is not unfrequently very much dissatisfied with what he receives, and complains to others, that 'the duties at such a man's house are very heavy, but that he gives only a very trifling fee, and no more of the offerings than a crow might eat.' This man subsists upon the fees aud offerings, engaging in no other employment.

The higher orders despise a bramhŭn who becomes priest to shōōdrŭs, and refuse to eat with him. Such a person can only be priest to one caste, and is called the joiners' bramhŭn, or the blacksmiths' bramhŭn, &c.

The yogēēs, (mostly weavers,) the chandalŭs, and the basket-makers, have priests of their own castes, and not from among the bramhŭns.

The shastrŭs point out the proper qualifications of a poorohitŭ, which are similar to those of a spiritual guide, mentioned in a following article. Some enjoy this office by hereditary succession. When a person, immediately after the performance of a religious ceremony in his family, meets with success in his connections or business, he not unfrequently attributes his prosperity to his priest, and rewards him by liberal presents. On the other hand, if a person sustain a loss after employing a new priest, he lays it at the door of the priest. If at a bloody sacrifice the slayer happen to fail in cutting off the head at one blow, the priest is blamed for having made some blunder in the ceremonies, and thus producing this fatal disaster.

The Acharyŭ.—The person who taught the védŭs used to be called acharyŭ; and at present the bramhŭn, who reads a portion of them at the time of investiture with the poita, is called by this name; as well as the person who reads the formularies at a sacrifice. This latter person is generally the poorohitŭ, but he then assumes the name of acharyŭ. A considerable number of bramhŭns are qualified to discharge the duties of an acharyŭ; and any one thus qualified may perform them, without any previous consecration or appointment. Twenty or thirty rupees is the amount of the fee of the acharyŭ at festivals.

The Sŭdŭshyŭ.—The Sŭdŭshyŭ regulates the ceremonies of worship, but is not employed on all occasions: he is however generally engaged at the festivals; at the first shradhŭ after a person's death; at the dedication of images, temples, flights of steps, ponds, &c. At the reading of the pooranŭs also he attends, and points out where the reading or the copy is defective. He receives a fee of ten or fifteen rupees, and sometimes as much as one hundred and fifty. On extraordinary occasions, five or ten sŭdŭshyŭs are employed,

The Brŭmha sits near the fire at the time of a burnt-offering and supplies it with wood. The fee to this person is five rupees in cases where the Sŭdŭshyŭ receives fifteen; to which is added a gift of rice, &c.

The Hota throws the clarified butter on the fire in the burnt-offering, repeating the proper formulas. He receives the same fee as the acharyŭ.

The four last-mentioned persons divide the offerings presented to Ŭgnee, and are worshipped at the commencement of a sacrifice; when rings, poitas, clothes, seats of cloth, or wood, pillows,[a] awnings, brass and copper vessels, &c. are presented to them.

The Hindoo priests wear their usual dress during the performance of any ceremony.

Other priests.—A number of persons are employed as assistants to the priests: as, the Vuroo, who gathers flowers to present to the image, sweeps the temple, &c. The person who buys and collects the things for the offerings is called Ŭdhikarēē; he who performs the ceremonies of worship is called Pōōjŭkŭ; he who cooks for the image, Pachŭkŭ; he who recites the pooranŭ in an assembly is called Pat'hŭkŭ; he who holds the book and corrects the reading and the copy, Dharŭkŭ; he who hears the words, as the representative of the person who is to enjoy the merit arising from the hearing of these stories, is called Shrota; and he who repeats in the evening the meaning of what has been read in the day, Kŭt'hŭkŭ.

CHAP IV.

OF THE WORSHIP IN THE TEMPLES.

THE daily ceremonies in the temples erected in honour of Shivŭ are as follows:—In the morning the officiating bramhŭn, after bathing, enters the temple[b] and bows to Shivŭ. He then anoints the image with clarified butter or boiled oil;[c] after which he bathes the image with water which has not been defiled by the touch of a shōōdrŭ, nor of a bramhŭn who has not performed his ablutions, by pouring water on it, and afterwards wipes it with a napkin. He next grinds some white powder in water, and, dipping

[a] The rich Hindoos sit with a large pillow placed at their backs.

[b] Pulling off his shoes at the bottom of the steps.

[c] The Greeks used to smear the statues of their gods with ointments, and adorn them with garlands.

the ends of his three fore-fingers in it, draws them across the lingŭ, marking it as the worshippers of Shivŭ mark their foreheads. He next sits down before the image, and, shutting his eyes, meditates on the work he is commencing; then places rice and dōōrva grass on the lingŭ; next a flower on his own head, and then on the top of the lingŭ; then another flower on the lingŭ; then others, one by one, repeating incantations; he then places white powder, flowers, vilwŭ leaves, incense, meat offerings, and a lamp before the image; also some rice and a plantain: he next repeats the name of Shivŭ, with some forms of praise; and at last prostrates himself before the image. These ceremonies, in the hands of a secular person, are concluded in a few minutes; a person who has sufficient leisure spends an hour in them. In the evening the officiating bramhŭn goes again to the temple, and after washing his feet, &c. prostrates himself before the door; then opening the door,[c] he places in the temple a lamp, and, as an evening oblation, presents to the image a little milk, some sweetmeats, fruits, &c. when, falling at the feet of the image, he locks the door, and comes away.

At the temple of Shivŭ, on the 14th of the increase of the moon in Phalgoonŭ, in the night, a festival in honour of Shivŭ is kept: the image is bathed four times, and four separate services are performed during the night. Before the temple, the worshippers dance, sing, and revel all night, amidst the horrid din of their music. The occasion of this festival is thus related in the Bhŭvishwŭ-pooranŭ:—A bird-catcher, detained in a forest in a dark night, climbed a vilwŭ tree under which was an image of the lingŭ. By shaking the boughs of the tree, the leaves and drops of dew fell upon the image; with which Shivŭ was so much pleased, that he declared, the worship of the lingŭ on that night should be received as an act of unbounded merit.

The worship at the temples in honour of the different forms of Vishnoo, is nearly the same as that at the temples of the lingŭ. Very early in the morning the officiating bramhŭn, after putting on clean apparel, and touching the purifying water of the Ganges, comes to the temple to awake the god. He first blows a shell and rings a bell; then presents water and a towel, and mutters certain prayers, inviting the god to awake, &c. The offerings made to the forms of Vishnoo are much greater in quantity than those presented to Shivŭ. About noon, fruits, roots, soaked peas, sweetmeats, &c. are presented to the image; and after this, that which answers to the English idea of dinner, consisting of boiled rice, fried herbs, spices, &c. Vishnoo neither eats flesh, fish, nor fowl. After dinner, betle nut, &c. in leaves of the betle vine, are given to be chewed. The god is then

[c] It is reported of some Hindoo saints, that when they went to the temple to awake the god, while repeating the words of the shastrŭ used on these occasions, the doors always flew open of themselves; reminding us of the European superstition, that 'the temple of Cybele was opened not by hands, but by prayers.'

left to sleep, and the temple is shut up. While he sleeps the bramhŭns eat the offerings. In the evening, curds, butter, sweetmeats, fruits, &c. are presented, and at this hour people come to the temple to look at the god and make their obeisance. After the setting of the sun, a lamp is brought into the temple, and a small quantity of milk, sweetmeats, &c. are offered. The priests wave a lamp of five lights before the image, ring a small bell, present water to wash the mouth, face, and feet, and a towel[d]. After the offerings have continued before the god about ten minutes, they are withdrawn, as well as the lamp, and the god is shut up in the dark all night.

[d] When I enquired into the meaning of these ceremonies, I was informed, that they were in imitation of the service paid to Krishnŭ when he used to return from tending the cattle :—water to wash himself, a towel, lights to examine where the thorns had entered his feet or any other parts of the body, a bell to testify their joy that he has arrived in safety, and some food to refresh him after the fatigues of the day in following the herds.

BOOK III.

OF THE STATED PERIODS OF WORSHIP, AND VARIOUS DUTIES AND CEREMONIES.

CHAP. I.

OF THE TIMES OF WORSHIP.

SECT. I.—*Lunar Days.*

THE eighth, eleventh, fourteenth, and fifteenth lunar days, both of the increase and decrease of the moon in each month, are considered as fortunate days. At the full moon in Asharhŭ, Kartikŭ, Maghŭ, and Voishakhŭ, religious ceremonies are peculiarly meritorious, especially gifts to learned bramhŭns; but on the third lunar day in Voishakhŭ, their merit is imperishable. Bathing in the Ganges on the tenth lunar day in Jyoisht'hŭ, is extremely meritorious. The second lunar day in Asharhŭ, and the eleventh in Shravŭnŭ, are auspicious times for religious ceremonies. The performance of the shraddhŭ during the decrease of the moon in Bhadrŭ is a work of great merit. On the seventh, eighth, and ninth lunar days of Ashwinŭ, eleventh in Kartikŭ, the fifth lunar day in Maghŭ, the thirteenth in Phalgoonŭ, and the seventh In Choitrŭ, and at the full moon in Poushŭ, very great benefits flow from religious acts. On all these days the Hindoos are particularly occupied in the different ceremonies of their religion.

SECT. II.—*Weekly Ceremonies.*

SOME Hindoos fast every Sunday, and perform the worship of their guardian deity Sōōryŭ. Others, to fulfil a vow, fast on a Monday,[a] performing the worship of Shivŭ. Others, who suppose themselves to be under the baneful influence of the planet Saturn, fast on a Saturday, and endeavour to propitiate this god by acts of devotion.

[a] It is rather singular, that both in the European and Hindoo Mythology, the two first days of the week should be called after the same gods: Rŭvee-varŭ, Sunday, from Rŭvee, the sun; and Somŭ-varŭ, Monday, from Somŭ, the moon.

SECT. III.—*Monthly Ceremonies.*

THE Shyama festival is held monthly by certain Hindoos. The shraddhŭ should be repeated monthly. Some persons, not able to attend to the weekly ceremonies connected with their vows, perform them monthly.

SECT. IV.—*Annual Festivals.*

THE festivals of Doorga, Shyama, Jŭgŭddhatrēē, Kartikŭ, Mŭhish-mŭrdinēē, Rŭtŭntēē, Ŭnnŭ-pōōrna, Phŭlŭharēē, Shivŭ, Krishnŭ, Gŭnéshŭ, &c. are held annually. Two festivals of Shivŭ and nine of Krishnŭ are annual.

The following account of the Hindoo festivals in each month of the year is taken from the Tit'hee-tŭttwŭ :—

Voishakhŭ.—On the third lunar day, (the anniversary of Gŭnga's descent,) the worship of Gŭnga, of the mountains Koilasŭ and Himalŭyŭ, of Bhŭgēērŭt'hŭ, and of Shivŭ. On the twelfth lunar day the bathing and worship of Vishnoo.

Jyoisht'hŭ.—On the tenth lunar day, (the anniversary of the birth of Gŭnga,) the worship of Mŭnŭsa, and of the nagŭs, (serpents.) At the full moon, the bathing of Jŭgŭnnat'hŭ ; and on the fourteenth of the wane of the moon, the worship of the goddess Savitrēē.

Asharhŭ.—On the second lunar day, the drawing of Jŭgŭnnat'hŭ's car, with the worship of this god, and of Bŭlŭramŭ and Soobhŭdra. On the tenth, the return of the car, and the worship of these three gods. The next day is the anniversary of Vishnoo's lying down to sleep.

Shravŭnŭ.—At the full moon, the dolŭ festival. On the eighth of the wane, (the anniversary of the birth of Krishnŭ,) the worship of this god, of his father, Jŭshoda, Rohinēē, Chŭndika, Bŭlŭramŭ, Dŭkshŭ, Gŭrgŭ, Brŭmha, Lŭkshmēē, and Shŭst'hēē.

Bhadrŭ.—On the seventh lunar day, the worship of Shivŭ and Doorga ; and on the seventh, the worship of Mŭnŭsa, before small sheaves of dōōrva grass. On the twelfth, the worship of Indrŭ, before a kind of flag-staff made with a tree called dŭmŭnŭ. On the fourteenth, the worship of Ŭnŭntŭ. The shraddhŭ is performed every day during the wane of the moon.

Ashwinŭ.—From the first to the ninth lunar day, the worship of Doorga. At the full moon, the worship of Lŭkshmēē, and the game of Chŭtoorajee ; and on the last day of the moon, the Shyama festival.

Kartikŭ.—On the first lunar day, the worship of king Bŭlēē; and on the second that of Yŭmŭ, and the feasting of own brothers by their sisters.[b] On the eighth, the worship of Gŭroorŭ; and on the ninth, that of Jŭgŭddhatrēē. At the full moon, the rasŭ festival, and the worship of Shyama before a picture. At the entrance of the sun into a new sign, or on the last day of Kartikŭ, the worship of Kartikŭ.

Ugrŭhayŭnŭ.—On the sixth lunar day, the worship of Kartikŭ; and on the seventh, eighth, and ninth, that of Mŭhishŭmŭrdinēē. On the fourteenth that of Goŭrēē; and on the seventh of the wane of the moon, the offerings to the dead.

Poŭshŭ.—On the eighth of the decrease of the moon, the offerings to the dead. On the fourteenth, the Shyama festival.

Magh.—On the fourth, the worship of Goŭrēē; on the fifth, that of Sŭrŭswŭtēē, and of the inkstand; on the sixth, that of Shŭsht'hēē; on the seventh, that of Sŏŏryŭ; and on the eighth; that of Bhēēshmŭ. On the eighth of the decrease of the moon, the offerings to the dead; and on the fourteenth, the anniversary of the rise of the lingŭ.

Phalgoonŭ.—On the eighth, the worship of Mŭngŭlŭchŭndika; and at the full moon, the dolŭ festival.

Choitrŭ.—On the sixth, the worship of Kartikŭ; on the eighth, that of Vishnoo with ŭshokŭ flowers; on the ninth, the anniversary of the birth of Ramŭ. On the seventh, eighth, and ninth, the worship of Doorga; and on the ninth, that of Ŭnnŭpōōrna. On the fourteenth, the worship of Kamŭ-dévŭ. On the thirteenth of the decrease of the moon, the worship of Gŭnga. On the entrance of the sun into a new sign at the close of this month, the presenting of water, rice, &c. to bramhŭns.

SECT. V.—*Daily Ceremonies.*

The shastrŭs prescribe daily duties towards the gods, deceased ancestors, strangers, and the cow. The worship of Vishnoo, before the shalgramŭ; of Shivŭ, before the lingŭ; of a person's guardian deity, before the shalgramŭ or water; and of any image constantly preserved, is performed daily. If the family of a bramhŭn, where such an image is set up, has become unclean by the death of one of its members, or by any other cause, they do not omit the daily worship, but invite another bramhŭn to perform the ceremonies. Sometimes a person makes a vow to

[b] The smritee shastrŭs ordain this custom. The manner of keeping it is as follows:—The sisters mark the foreheads of the brothers with white powder, and present them with garments, poitas, &c. and provide a great feast. It is said that Yŭmŭ and his sister Yŭmoona established this custom.

perform for a certain time the daily worship of Vishnoo, Shivŭ, and his guardian deity. Bathing also, and repeating the names of the gods, with or without a bead-roll, especially the name of a person's guardian deity, are acts of daily worship. The daily shraddhŭ is performed by very few; but at the time of bathing, in the ceremony called tŭrpŭnŭ, the Hindoos pour out water from a copper vessel, or from their hands, for their deceased ancestors. Some religious acts are performed daily for three or four months together: as during the time of Vishnoo's sleeping, (viz., from the twelfth or fifteenth of the moon in Asharhŭ, to the twelfth or fifteenth in Kartikŭ,) a person vows that no razor shall come on his head; that he will abstain from flesh, fish, salt,[c] peas, oil, curds not made at home, &c.; that he will not visit at the house of a shōōdrŭ, nor eat there nor any where else more than once a day. During this period he engages particularly to attend to his daily duties, as bathing, repeating the name of his god, &c.

Agreeably to the directions of the Anhikŭ-tŭttwŭ, the daily duties of a bramhŭn, walking in strict conformity to the rules of his religion are as follows:—

He must divide the day, from five o'clock in the morning till seven at night, into seven equal parts. The duties of the first part are thus described:—first, awaking from sleep, and rising up in his bed, he must repeat the names of different gods and sages, and pray that they would make the day prosperous. He must then repeat the name of Ŭrjoonŭ, and pray to him, that whatever he may lose during the day may be restored to him[d]; and then the names of any persons celebrated for their religious merit. Next the names of Ŭhŭlya[e], Dropŭdēē[f], Sēēta[g], Tara[h], and Mundodŭre[i]. After this, he must meditate with his eyes closed on the form of his spiritual guide, and worship him in his mind, repeating these two incantations: Oh! * * * *! according to thy commands I descend from my bed.'—'Oh! * * * *! I know what is right, but I do it not: I know what is wrong, but I forsake it not: But do thou reside within me, and whatever thou commandest I shall do.' Then follows another incantation, and obeisance to Hŭree. He now descends from his bed, placing first his right foot on the ground. On going out, if he see a Shrotriyŭ bramhŭn, a beloved and excellent wife, fire, a cow, an Ŭgnihotrēē bramhŭn, or any

[c] Rock salt may be eaten.

[d] It is said that when Urjoonŭ was king, there were no robberies; or if such a thing did happen, by repeating his name, the loser was sure to find his property again.

[e] The wife of Goutŭmŭ: she was guilty of adultery with Indrŭ.

[f] The wife of Yoodhisht'hirŭ and his brothers.

[g] The wife of Ramŭ.

[h] The wife of Balēē and Soogrēēvu, two monkies.

[i] The wife of Ravŭnŭ.

other bramhŭn, the day will be auspicious. If he see a wicked or naked person, a wretched woman, distilled spirits, or a man with a great nose, the day will be inauspicious. By repeating the names of Kŭrkotŭkŭ,[k] Dŭmŭyŭntēē,[l] Nŭlŭ,[m] and Ritoopŭrnŭ,[n] no quarrel will arise during the day. He must then, after discharging wind, washing his mouth, &c. go at least a hundred and ten yards from his house into the field ; and taking water, choosing a clean place, scattering some grass to the S. W., tying a turban round his head, remaining silent with his face to the north, refraining from spitting, and holding his breath, perform the offices of nature. His poita must remain on his right ear till he has washed his hands. It is unlawful to attend to the offices of nature on a road, in the shade, where cattle graze, in the fire, or water, in a ploughed field, where dead bodies are burnt, upon a mountain, on the ruins of a temple, on an ant-hill, in a ditch, or by the side of a river.[o] After this, he must go to a more clean spot, and taking some good earth, cleanse the left hand ten times, then both hands seven times, and the back of the left hand six times ; then his nails ; then wash his hands ; each foot three times, and then rince both feet. If he perceive any evil smell remaining on his hands or feet, he must wash them again. If the bramhŭn have no water-pot, he must wash himself in this manner in a common pool or river, and take care that he come out of the water clean. His water-pot must neither be of mixed metal, copper, nor gold : an earthen pot must be thrown away as soon as used. If the pot be of brass or silver, he must scour it well after he return. If a bramhŭn attend not to these modes of cleansing, all his other religious actions will be void of merit.[p]

The bramhŭn must next attend to his morning ablutions. Taking a dry towel, he must go to a pool or river, and placing the cloth on the ground, wet his feet and hands ; then perform achŭmŭnŭ, by taking up water in the palm of his right hand three times, and drinking it as it runs toward his wrist ; then with his right hand touch his lips, nose, eyes, ears, navel, breast, forehead, and shoulders, repeating an incantation ; wash his hands again and perform achŭmŭnŭ, repeating an incantation ; then sitting to the N. or E. before sunrise, cleanse his teeth with the end of a green stick,[q] about six or seven inches long. If he clean his

[k] A serpent. [l] The wife of king Nŭlŭ. [m] A king. [n] Another king.

[o] So little is this regarded, that almost all the lower orders of Hindoos go to the Ganges.

[p] One of the things, in the conduct of Europeans, which gives most offence to the Hindoos, is the omitting these modes of cleansing.

[q] On the 1st, 6th, 8th, 10th, and 14th days of the increase and wane of the moon, and at the full and new moon ; on the last day of the calendar month : on a fast day, and on the day of performing a shraddhŭ ; it is unlawful for a bramhŭn to clean his teeth with a stick. If he should do this on these days, he will sink into a dreadful hell. *If the Bible had laid down rules and penalties like these, what occasion for ridicule to unbelievers!*

teeth after sunrise, in the next birth he will be born an insect feeding on ordure. He must now wash from his face the mark on his forehead made the day before; then scrape and wash his tongue, taking care that the blood does not flow. If in cleansing his teeth he should make them bleed, he becomes unclean, and is disqualified for performing any religious ceremony on that day. If, however, he make his teeth bleed by the side of the Ganges, he does not become unclean.

He must next gather flowers for worship on the banks of a pool or river. If any one forbid him, he must willingly desist; if any are given him by a bramhŭn, he must receive them; but not if a shōōdrŭ offer them: if a person have them to sell, he must give him what he asks. If in carrying these flowers to the side of the water, a person of mean cast touch them, or he touch any unclean thing, he must throw them away. If a person of any cast make a bow to him while the flowers are in his hand, he mus also throw them away.[r]

Returning to the river, and sitting in silence, he must rub himself all over with mud; then descending into the river as high as his breast, with his face towards the east or north, he must repeat certain incantations, by which (in his imagination) all other sacred rivers will flow into that in which he stands, as well as other holy places; he must afterwards repeat many incantations, and perform moodra, viz., certain motions by twisting his fingers into several curious shapes; then, dividing his hair behind, and bringing it into his hands before, with his thumbs he must stop his ears; with the three first fingers of each hand cover his eyes, and with his two little fingers his nostrils, and then immerse himself three or four times; then with his hands joined throw up water to his head; then repeat other incantations; then, taking up water with his joined hands, he must offer it three times to the sun; then washing his body, and repeating certain prayers, that he may ascend to some heaven, or receive some temporal good, he must again immerse himself in the water. After this he must ascend to the side of the river, and wipe his body with a towel; then repeat certain forms of praise to Gŭnga, Sōōryŭ, Vishnoo, and other gods; then put dry and newly-washed cloth round his loins; and sitting down cleanse his poita by rinsing it in the water; then taking up some earth in his hand, and diluting it with water, put the middle finger of his right hand in this earth, and make a line betwixt his eyes up to the top of his forehead; then draw his three first fingers across his forehead; make a round dot with his little finger in the centre at the top of his head, another on

[r] The meaning of this is, that the sin of the person who made the bow being transferred to the bramhŭn, the sin, instead of entering the fire said to lodge in a bramhŭn's hand, by which it would be consumed, enters the flowers, and they thereby become unclean. If a bramhŭn, with flowers in his hand, meet a shōōdrŭ who is ignorant of the rules of the shastrŭ, he forbids him to bow to him; but in general, the lower orders know this custom.

the upper part of his nose, and another on his throat; then with his three first fingers make marks across his breast and arms; then make dots on his sides, and another on the lower part of his back. After this he must take up water in his right hand three times, and drink it.

To this succeeds the morning sŭndhya, in which the person must offer many prayers; pour out water to different gods; repeat certain forms of praise in honour of the sun, which he must worship; and repeat the gayŭtrēē: then take up water with his kosha,[s] and pour it out to his deceased ancestors; after which he must return home, and read some part of the védŭ.[t]

After this, if the bramhŭn be a house-keeper, he must seek the provisions for his family for the day. If he be diligent in discharging social duties, he will obtain heaven; but if not, he will sink into hell.

About eleven o'clock, taking the flowers, his kosha and kooshee, some seeds of sesamum, leaves of the vilwŭ tree, blades of the kooshŭ grass, and a towel, he must proceed to the river. Placing these things by the side of the river, he must prepare a place for worship; take some proper earth, and cleanse it, so that neither insects, hair, nor any thing impure remain; and then make the earth into a ball, lay it down, and wash his own body, rubbing himself with his towel. Then he must descend into the water up to the middle, and perform his ablutions as in the morning. After bathing, he must ascend to the side, wipe himself, put on a dry piece of cloth, (not a black one;) sit with his face to the east or north; tie a lock of hair into a knot, and having repeated a prayer, the whole of his hair in a knot; mark his forehead as in the morning; then perform the ceremony called achŭmŭnŭ; and then the sŭndhya. After this he must make an image of the lingŭ with the pure earth which he has prepared; and laying it aside, descend into the water, or sit by it, and pour out water (containing a few seeds of the sesamum) from his kosha to three or four of the gods, repeating incantations: then to certain sages, and deceased ancestors, viz., to three generations on the father's and three on the mother's side, (males.) If a bramhŭn do not present drink-offerings to deceased relations, all his works of merit lose their virtue.

The next thing is the act of worship, (pōōja;) in which the bramhŭn must sit with his face to the north, and placing the lingŭ towards the same point, bathe it by sprinkling it with water; then, closing his eyes, sit for some time in the act of meditation, (dhyanŭ;) after which, placing some flowers on his own head, he

[s] A small copper cup. Another still smaller is called kooshee.

[t] If at this time he copy a part of any of the shastrŭs, and present it to some bramhŭn, he will receive everlasting happiness.

must perform the worship of Shivŭ; then meditate on the image, and placing flowers on the lingŭ, repeat other incantations, to communicate a soul (pranŭ) to the lingŭ; then another prayer to bring Shivŭ himself into his presence; and then perform a ceremony called yonee-moodra, which consists of five curious motions with the hands; then he must offer to the lingŭ a morsel of silver or gold; or, if he be poor, water, reading prayer. He must after this offer water for the god's feet; also a little dry rice, and a few blades of dōōrva-grass, with a prayer; then a number of raw vegetables. He must next repeat the name of Shivŭ a certain number of times; offer water, and repeat an incantation, (offering water or flowers,) and worship Shivŭ in his eight forms,[u] repeating eight incantations; then follow forms of praise in honour of Shivŭ, during which he must prostrate himself before the lingŭ; and afterwards make a drumming noise with his thumb or fingers on the right cheek, and beat against his sides with his arms. If he has been worshipping by the side of the Ganges, he must throw the lingŭ into the river; or if by the side of a pool or any other river, he must throw away the lingŭ on the land. To this should succeed the worship of Vishnoo before the shalgramŭ, or before water. Next that of Sōōryŭ, Ŭgnee, Doorga, Brŭmha, the gayŭtrēē, the spiritual guide, the nine planets, the ten guardian deities of the earth, and lastly of the person's guardian deity. The offerings in this last act of worship are the same as in the worship of the lingŭ, but the prayers are more numerous.

When all these ceremonies have been performed by the side of a pool, or a river, the worshipper, having presented the burnt-offering, must return to his house, perform the daily shraddhŭ, and offer to the gods plantains, dry rice, peas, sweetmeats, cocoanuts, &c.

The day's work must be closed by entertaining several poor bramhŭns, or other guests who may be in his house. If no guests should arrive, about three o'clock in the afternoon he must sit down to dinner; which may consist of boiled rice, fried fruits, split peas, greens, sour curds, or milk, but neither fish nor flesh. First, he must offer the whole food to his guardian deity, sprinkling water on the rice, and repeating incantations; and then put morsels of the different articles of his food in five places on a clean spot; which, after sprinkling with water, he must offer to the five winds, Nagŭ, Kōōrmŭ, Krēēkŭtŭ, Dévŭ-dŭttŭ, and Dhŭnŭn-jŭyŭ. After this, drink a little water, repeating an incantation; and then put a little rice into his mouth with his right hand at five different times, and repeat incantations, containing the names of five airs which the Hindoos say are lodged in the body; he may then, remaining in silence, finish his repast; afterwards drink a little water, wash his hands and mouth, and cleanse his teeth. After

[u] These eight forms of Shivŭ are representatives of the earth, water, fire, air, space, sacrifice, the sun, and the moon.

washing his feet, he must sit upon a mat of kooshŭ-grass, and chew betle-nut, mixed with some or all of the following articles; lime, treacle, catechu, cardamums, cloves, nutmeg, mace, camphor, coriander seed, &c. Before he begins to chew the betle, he must offer it with prayers to his guardian deity. If he do not chew betle, he must eat fruit of the terminalia citrina, and repeat the name of Vishnoo once.

To this must succeed the evening sŭndhya, either in his own house or by the side of the river. The ceremonies are the same as those already described. After this, repeating the name of his guardian deity during two hours, he may take a little refreshment, as sweetmeats, milk, plantains, curds, or something of the same nature; and about ten retire to rest.

At present, those bramhŭns who live without secular employment spend about four hours daily in worship; an hour in the morning, two at noon, and one in the evening. Such a person's first act in the morning, as he rises, is to repeat the name of his guardian deity; after which he goes into a field with a pan of water, and returning, bathes; then taking the water of the Ganges, he sits down in his house, or by the river, and pours out drink-offerings to his deceased ancestors; repeat certain forms from the védŭ, the meaning of which he himself does not understand; worships Shivŭ with the usual forms of praise, as, 'Oh! Shivŭ! thou art every thing; thou unitest all the gods in thyself; thou canst do all things,' &c. during which he offers with proper forms water, flowers, &c. to the god; and then repeats for some time the name of his guardian deity. At noon, after bathing, he repeats certain forms from the védŭ; and worships Shivŭ, his guardian deity, and other gods, with the usual forms and offerings; pours out drink-offerings to deceased ancestors, and repeats the name of his guardian deity. At this time, the worshipper prays for any thing he may be anxious to obtain, as the health of his child, a lucrative situation, &c., but this is done only when sickness, poverty, or any other necessity, forces a person to express his complaints to his god. The worship in the evening is similar to that in the morning.

Bramhŭns in employment unite the first and second services together in the morning, and finish the whole in half an hour; confining themselves to the repetition of the name of their guardian deity, the forms from the védŭ, including the gayŭtrēē, and pouring out a drink-offering to deceased ancestors. Most of these persons omit the evening service altogether.

Though these ceremonies are in general performed in the house, the family do not unite in them: during their performance, the family business is transacted, and the children play as usual; the worshipper himself not unfrequently mixes in conversation, or gives directions respecting matters of business. The children sometimes sit as spectators, so that by the time they grow up, they learn the different forms of daily worship.

The women, though not allowed to touch a consecrated image, (beasts, women, and shōōdrŭs are forbidden,) worship the gods daily in their own houses, or by the river side, (repeating certain forms from the Tŭntrŭ shastrŭs,) before an earthen image of the lingŭ, or the water of the Ganges: if they should worship before a consecrated image, they must keep at a respectable distance from the idol. Some merely repeat a few forms while standing in the water, bow to the god without an image, and thus finish the religion of the day; others spend half an hour in these ceremonies, and females who have leisure, an hour or more.

The shōōdrŭs in general repeat the name of their guardian deity while bathing, and this comprises the whole of their daily religion: yet rich men of the lower castes spend an hour in religious ceremonies, in the house or by the side of the river.

As there is nothing of pure morality in the Hindoo writings, so in the ceremonies of this people, nothing like the rational and pure devotion of a Christian worshipper is to be found. In performing their daily duties, as might be expected from a ritual possessing little meaning and no interest, the Hindoos are sometimes precise, and at other times careless; muttering forms of praise or prayer to the gods, while their attention is drawn to every surrounding object. To expect that services like these would mend the heart, is out of the question.

CHAP. II.

APPOINTED RITES AND CEREMONIES.

SECT. I.—*Form of Initiation into the Hindoo Religion.*

EVERY Hindoo receives an initiating incantation from some bramhŭn,[a] who then becomes his spiritual guide, (gooroo:) the principal thing in this incantation is the name of some god, who becomes his (ishtŭ) chosen deity, and by repeating whose name he is to obtain present and future happiness.

When the ceremony of initiation is to be performed, an auspicious day is chosen, which is preceded by a fast. On the morning of the day appointed, the disciple bathes; after which, entreating the priest to sit down, he presents him with some cloth, kourees, betle-nut and a poita: after which he performs the ceremony called

[a] There are some rare examples among the poor, of persons who never receive the initiatory incantation.

sŭnkŭlpŭ, in doing which he first takes in his joined hands a small copper dish, with some water in it; lays a plantain, some flowers, sesamum, kooshŭ-grass, rice, &c. upon it; and then says, 'For the removal of all my sins, and to obtain happiness after death, I take the incantation from my gooroo.' The gooroo then performs, at some length, the worship of the god whose name is to be given; to which succeeds the burnt-offering. He next thrice repeats, in the right ear of the disciple, the incantation: after which the disciple presents a fee of from one to twenty rupees, and worships the feet of the gooroo, presenting sweetmeats, cloths, flowers, fruits, and other offerings commonly presented to the gods. He next repeats certain forms, and in his meditation brings into his mind that his spiritual guide is in fact his guardian deity, from whom he is to receive salvation. Another fee is then given; after which the disciple drinks the water in which the gooroo's feet have been washed, and prostrates himself at his feet; when the spiritual guide, putting his right foot on his head, and stretching forth his right hand, gives him a blessing. The gooroo is then feasted, with other bramhŭns. Two or three persons only are permitted to be present at this ceremony.

The above incantation is called vēējŭ mŭntrŭ.[b] It generally consits of a single sound: as, when it is to be taken from the name of a god, a consonant is taken out of this name, and a vowel added to it: thus, when Krishnŭ is about to become the chosen god of a person, the gooroo takes the consonant k, and adds to it a, or oo, or some other vowel, and then the mŭntrŭ becomes ka, or koo. Very frequently the sound ŭng is united to a consonant, to form the initiating incantation, of which there are many specimens in the Tŭntrŭ-sarŭ. It is probable that no meaning was ever intended to be attached to these sounds.

SECT. II.—*Duties of a Disciple to his Spiritual Guide, (Gooroo.),*

THE following article respecting the qualifications of a gooroo is taken from the Tŭntrŭ-sarŭ:—A spiritual guide must be free from the following faults: he must not be subject to his passions, so as to become an adulterer, a thief, &c.; be born of a good family; possess suavity of manners; be attentive to religious duties; honourable in the eyes of others; always keep his body pure; be ready in religious ceremonies; faithful in the discharge of the duties of his caste; wise, able to keep in order as well as to cherish his disciples; learned in the shastrŭs, &c. From a gooroo thus qualified it is proper to receive the initiatory rites. A person who is a glutton, who has the leprosy, is blind of one or both eyes; very small in stature, or who has whitlows; whose teeth stand

[b] The original incantation, or that which gives rise to works of merit, wealth, the desire of happiness, and absorption.

out; who is noisy and talkative; subject to his wife, or whose toes or fingers are unnaturally unequal, or of an improper number; an asthmatic person, or in other respects diseased, is disqualified.

The following are the duties of a disciple to his preceptor, as given in the Tŭntrŭ-sarŭ:—A disciple must be docile; keep his body pure; be obedient in receiving all that the shastrŭs make known; be capable of understanding what he is taught, &c. If the disciple consider his gooroo as a mere man, and not the same as his guardian deity, he will sink into misery. A pupil must worship his father and mother, as those who gave him birth; but he must honour his gooroo in a superior degree, as he who rescues him from the path of sin, and places him in the way of holiness; the gooroo is in fact the disciple's father, mother, and god; if even Shivŭ be offended with a disciple, his gooroo is able to deliver him. The disciple must promote the welfare of his gooroo by all his actions; if he injure him, in another birth he will become a worm feeding on ordure. If a disciple renounce the initiating incantation, he will die; if he reject his gooroo, he will become poor; if both, he will fall into the hell Rourŭvŭ; if he, leaving his guardian deity, worship another god as his guardian deity, he will sink into torments. A disciple must honour his gooroo's son and grandson as he honours the gooroo. Whether the spiritual guide be learned or ignorant, a vile or a holy person, a disciple has no other resource, no other way to happiness, but his gooroo. Other shastrŭs prescribe, that the disciple shall make prostration to the gooroo three times a day, if he live in the same village, viz., in the morning, at noon, and in the evening. If he meet him at any time, he must prostrate himself at his feet, and receive his blessing. When a gooroo dies, a disciple becomes unclean.

When the gooroo arrives at the house of a disciple, the whole family prostrate themselves at his feet, and the spiritual guide puts his right foot on the heads of the prostrate family. One of the family washes his feet, and all afterwards drink some of the dirty water with which his feet have been washed; the water which remains is preserved. Others present to him flowers, or anoint his body with oil, or bathe him by pouring water on his head. After they have all bathed, they again worship the gooroo's feet, by presenting flowers, sweetmeats, &c. repeating incantations. The gooroo is then entertained. Of the little that he leaves, each one seizes a morsel with eagerness. At length he departs with presents according to the disciple's ability. Some give a piece of cloth, others from one to ten rupees. The disciple sometimes sends presents to his gooroo's house.

As a proof how rigidly many of the Hindoos adhere to the commands of the shastrŭ on this subject, it may not be amiss to record the following circumstance:—In the year 1804, Hŭree-Tŭrkŭ-Bhōōshŭnŭ, a bramhŭn of Calcutta, aged about 60, was carried to the river side, at the point of death ; and while there one of his disciples, Ŭbhŭyŭ-chŭrŭnŭ-Mitrŭ, a kaist'hŭ, went to see him. The disciple asked his dying gooroo if there was any thing that he wished from him. The gooroo asked him for 100,000 rupees. The disciple hesitated, and said he could not give so much. The gooroo then asked him what he was worth. He said, he might be worth about 100,000, but it was not all in rupees. The gooroo asked him to give his children half this sum. This the disciple surrendered ; and then asked him what else he could do for him. He pretended not to want any thing else, but his youngest son then present was in want of a pair of gold rings for his wrists, and which he had been unable to give him. The disciple had a son standing near who had on a pair. These rings, worth about five hundred rupees, were immediatly taken off, and put on the wrists of the old gooroo's son. The disciple again asked what else he could do for him. The gooroo requested him to give his eldest son a piece of ground in Calcutta. He gave it. This land was worth twenty thousand rupees. The disciple again asked, if there was any thing further he could do to please him. The old fellow made apologies, but at length requested him to make a present of five thousand rupees towards the expences of his shraddhŭ.[c] This was added. The next morning the gooroo died. His wife was burnt with his body. At the time of his shraddhŭ, the disciple added another five thousand rupees towards defraying the expenses. This man's memory is execrated by all the Hindoos ; who say, he would certainly have gone to hell, if his wife had not burnt herself with him.—Since this event, Ŭbhŭyŭ-chŭrŭnŭ died at Mŭttra ; and his widow, taking his clog and stick, renounced life at Calcutta, on a funeral pile prepared for the purpose.

At present, the office of spiritual guide is often hereditary, and of course is frequently in the hands of persons really disqualified. Neither do the modern Hindoos pay much regard to the qualifications of their teachers : these guides too are equally careless respecting their disciples ; they give the incantation, and receive in return reverence and presents. To become a religious guide it is only necessary to be a bramhŭn, and be acquainted with the incantations. In many cases, indeed, the wives of bramhŭns become gooroos to their own children, as well as to others, both male and female. It is considered as a happy circumstance to receive the form of initiation from a mother. Among the followers of Choitŭnyŭ, some shōōdrŭs are gooroos.

The business of a religious guide is very profitable. Some obtain a thousand disciples ; and all are ambitious of guiding the rich. Upon a moderate calculation, the gooroo of a thousand disciples receives in presents much more than a thousand rupees an-

[c] ites for the repose of the soul.

nually. A poor man generally gives his gooroo a rupee a year, or if he visit him twice a year, two rupees. One or two of the Gosaees, descendants of Choitŭnyŭ, have two or three thousand disciples.

Instances of disputes between a spiritual guide and a disciple are not uncommon: in which case the former does not fail to curse such a disobedient disciple in terms like these: 'May your posterity perish.' 'May all your wealth evaporate.' The disciple is exceedingly alarmed at the curse of his gooroo, and if in a short time any of the family die, his neighbours ascribe it to this curse. If the children do not choose their father's gooroo, he curses the family. If a bramhŭn consider himself as having claims on any member of a family to become his spiritual guide, and this person or the family be unwilling, the bramhŭn goes to their house, and refuses to eat till they consent. The family dare not eat till the gooroo has eaten.—On some occasions, the gooroo is called in to adjust family differences. If two brothers quarrel about an estate, an appeal is made to the gooroo, who generally gives his judgment in favour of the brother who can afford the greatest bribe.

The gooroos or not distinguished by any particular dress, and many pursue secular employment.

I have heard of some religious guides who, taking advantage of the profound reverence in which they are held, are guilty of improper conduct with their female disciples; and others of these demi-gods are guilty of crimes which they expiate on a gallows.

Assistant Gooroo.—These persons are sometimes employed in teaching the disciple how to worship his guardian deity. If the chief gooroo be a female, or be ignorant of the proper incantation, the assistant gooroo is called in.

SECT. III.—*Religious Austerities, (Tŭpŭsya.)*

THOSE religious works which require bodily sufferings, are, in general, denominated tŭpŭsyas. Among other acts which fall under this description, are,—severe abstinence; repeating the name of an idol, and sitting in particular postures, for a long time; a person's surrounding himself with five fires;[d] and the severities practised by ascetics. These works of severity towards

[d] In January 1812, the author witnessed the performance of some uncommonly severe acts of religious austerity, in the suburbs of Calcutta. A number of Hindoo mendicants had erected huts near one of the descents into the Ganges, and several devotees on this spot daily surrounded themselves with fires of cow-dung, and for three or four hours each day rested on their shoulders with their legs upward, repeating the names of the gods in silence, and counting their bead-rolls. Crowds of people were coming and going, astonished spectators of these infatuated men; who continued their religious austerities in the night, by standing up to the neck in the Ganges for two or three hours, counting their beads.

the body are not done as penances for sin, but as works of extraordinary merit, producing large rewards in a future state.

Sect. IV.—*Burnt Sacrifices (Yŭgnŭ.)*

In these sacrifices, the following ceremonies are commanded by the shastrŭ :—The names of deceased ancestors for six generations must be repeated in the morning before the sacrifice ; to this succeeds the appointment of the sacrificial priests ; then a ceremony for the success of the sacrifice, in which the priest, taking up dry rice, scatters it on the ground, repeating incantations ; after this, sŭnkŭlpŭ, in which the person, repeating the name of the day, month, &c. declares that he is about to perform this ceremony to obtain such and such benefits ; lastly follows a sacrifice of mustard seed to drive away evil genii and enemies. On the altar are placed things necessary for the different ceremonies, as pans for water, branches of the mangoe tree, fruits, flowers, garlands, sandal wood, toolŭsee [e] and vilwŭ [f] leaves, dōōrva and kooshŭ grass, rice, seeds of sesamum, curds, red lead, small twigs of sacred trees to be burnt, a mortar and pestle, spoons, meat offerings, garments, &c. The priest sitting on the altar worships certain gods ; after which the alter is set in order for the sacrifice, and the fire prepared ; the worship of Ŭgnee then takes place, at the commencement of which the priest repeats a prayer from the védŭ to this purport : 'Oh! Ŭgnee! thou who sittest on a goat, and hast seven columns of fire ; thou art energy itself; thou art the mouth of the gods.— I worship thee ; come.' One of the priests next purifies, with incantations, the vessels, the wood for the sacrifice, and the clarified butter ; he then boils the rice, and afterwards performs the burnt-sacrifice either with clarified butter, the flesh of some animal, pieces of wood, vilwŭ leaves, flowers of the kŭrŭvēērŭ [g] or the water-lily, boiled rice, seeds of sesamum, or fruits. To this succeeds a burnt-sacrifice to certain gods, with rice, clarified butter, sugar, curds, milk, flesh, and other articles, and a sacrifice to the nine planets, and to all the gods whom the priest can remember. An atonement for any mistake which may have occurred is next made by a burnt-offering of clarified butter. The officiating priest must then put on the fire a new poita, cloth, flowers, a plantain, betle, and rice ; when the sacrificer, standing behind the priest, must put his right hand on his shoulder, while the latter pours clarified butter on the fire, till the flame ascends to a great height. If the flame be free from smoke, and surround the altar in a southerly direction, the blessings sought by the sacrificer will be obtained. After this, the priest, sprinkling some water on the fire, dismisses the god Ŭgnee. The sacrificer now presents fees to the priests, and the

[e] Ocymum gratissimum. [f] Ægle marmelos. [g] Nerium odorum.

whole ends with a feast to the bramhŭns, and the dismissing of the guests with presents.

I have obtained from several works accounts of the following burnt-sacrifices :—

The sacrifice of a MAN!!—First, a covered altar[h] is to be prepared in an open place near the house of the offerer; sixteen posts are to be erected, six of vilwŭ, six of khŭdirŭ, and four of oodoombŭrŭ; a golden image of a man, and an iron one of a goat, are then to be set up; and also golden images of Vishnoo and Lŭkshmēē, a silver one of Shivŭ, with a golden bull on which Shivŭ rides, and a silver one of Gŭroorŭ. Brass pans are also to be provided for holding water, &c. Animals, as goats and sheep, are to be tied to the posts, one of the khŭdirŭ posts being left for the man who is to be sacrificed. Fire is next to be procured with a burning-glass, or with flint, or brought from the house of a devout bramhŭn. The priest, called brŭmha, sits on a seat of kooshŭ grass at one corner of the altar with an alms' dish in his hand, and consecrates the different utensils. The priest, called hota, then performs certain minute ceremonies, and lays blades of kooshŭ grass all round the fire on the alter; to which succeeds the burnt-sacrifice to the ten guardian deities of the earth, to the nine planets, to Roodrŭ, Brŭmha, Vastoo-poorooshŭ, and Vishnoo: to each of the two latter clarified butter is to be poured on the fire a thousand times. Next follows another burnt-sacrifice, and the same sacrifice to sixty-four gods, beginning with Douvarikŭ. After this, in the name of all the gods above-mentioned, is made the burnt-sacrifice with the flesh of the other animals tied to the different posts. To this succeeds the human sacrifice. The victim must be free from bodily distemper, be neither a child nor advanced in years.[i] After slaying the victim, the hota, with small pieces of flesh, must offer the sacrifice to the above-mentioned gods, walking round the altar after each separate offering.

In the third book of the Mŭhabharŭtŭ, a story is related respecting a king of the name of Somŭkŭ, who obtained from the gods a hundred sons in consequence of having offered a human sacrifice.

The Ramayŭnŭ contains a story respecting Mŭhēē-Ravŭnŭ, who attempted to offer Ramŭ and Lŭkshmŭnŭ, when in patŭlŭ, as a sacrifice to Bhŭdra-Kalēē, in order to obtain success in war for his father Ravŭnŭ.

Another story is contained in the Ramayŭnŭ, that Ŭmvŭrēēshŭ,

[h] The Hindoo altar may have brick-work around it, but in the inside it is to be filled up with pure earth. In the centre some persons make a hole for the fire, and others raise on the centre a small elevation of sand, and on this kindle the fire.

[i] These victims were formerly bought for sacrifice.

king of Ŭyodhya, once resolved on offering a human victim; which, after being prepared, was stolen by Indrŭ. The king traversed many countries unable to obtain another victim, till at last Kichēēkŭ sold his second son to him, for 'heaps of the purest gold, jewels, and a hundred thousand cows.' The father refused to sell his eldest son, and the mother would not give up the youngest. The second son, after he had been sold, claimed the protection of the sage Vishwa-mitrŭ, who directed each one of his sons to give himself up to be sacrificed instead of this youth: but they all refused; when Vishwa-mitrŭ cursed them, and gave this youth an incantation, by repeating which the gods would deliver him from death. After he had been bound for execution, he repeated this incantation from the Rig-véda; when Indrŭ delivered him, and bestowed on the king the blessing he sought by this sacrifice. The Shrēēbhagŭvŭtŭ gives a similar story respecting an ascetic, Jŭrŭ-Bhŭrŭtŭ; but in this case the goddess worshipped burst from the image, rescued the devotee,[k] and destroyed those who were about to sacrifice him.

The Institutes of Mŭnoo contain the following paragraph:— 'The sacrifice of a bull, *of a man*, or of a horse, in the kŭlēē age, must be avoided by twice-born men; so must a second gift of a married young woman, whose husband has died before consummation: the larger portion of an eldest brother, and procreation on a brother's widow or wife.'

However shocking it may be, it is generally reported amongst the natives, that human sacrifices are to this day offered in some places in Bengal. At a village called Kshēērŭ, near the town of Burdwan, it is positively affirmed, that human sacrifices are still offered to the goddess Yoogadya, a form of Doorga; at Kirēētŭ-kona, near Moorshŭdŭbad, to Kalēē; and at many other places. The discovery of these murders in the name of religion is made by finding the bodies with the heads cut off near these images; and though no one acknowledges the act, yet the natives well know that these people have been offered in sacrifice.

About seven years ago, at the village of Serampore, near Kŭtwa, before the temple of the goddess Tara, a human body was found without a head; and in the inside of the temple different offerings, as ornaments, food, flowers, spirituous liquors, &c. All who saw it knew that a human victim had been slaughtered in the night; and search was made after the murderers, but in vain.

At Brŭmha-nēētŭla, near Nŭdēēya, is an image of Mŭnŭsa, before which the worship of Dōōrga is performed. It is currently reported, that at this place human victims are occasionally offered, as decapitated bodies are found there.

k This man observed a voluntary silence, and refused all intercourse with human beings, that he might avoid injuring any one.

Ramŭ-nat'hŭ-Vachŭspŭtēē, the second Sŭngskritŭ pŭndit in the College of Fort-William, once assured me, that about the year 1770, at the village of Sōōmŭra, near Gooptipara, he saw the head of a man, with a lamp placed on it, lying in a temple before the image of the goddess Siddhéshwŭrēē, and the body lying in the road opposite the temple. A similar fact is related respecting an image of Bhŭrga-Rhēēma at Tŭmlookŭ, where a decapitated body was found.

At Chit-poorŭ, and at Kalēē-ghatŭ,[1] near Calcutta, it is said, that human sacrifices have been occasionally offered. A respectable native assured me, that at Chitpoorŭ, near the image of Chittréshwŭrēē, about the year 1788, a decapitated body was found; which, in the opinion of the spectators, had been evidently offered on the preceding night to this goddess.

The following story respecting raja Krishnŭ-chŭndrŭrayŭ is believed by a great number of the most respectable natives of Bengal:—A brŭmhŭcharēē of Kritŭkona, after repeating (jŭpŭ) the name of his guardian deity for a long time, till he had established a great name as a religious devotee, at length had a dream, in which he supposed that his guardian deity told him to make a number of offerings to her, which he understood to mean human sacrifices; and that then she would become visible to him, and grant him all his desires. He was now very much perplexed about obtaining the necessary victims; and, as the only resource, he applied to Krishnŭ-chŭndrŭ-rayŭ, and promised, that if he would supply the victims, he should share in the benefits to be derived from this great act of holiness. The raja consented to this, and built a house in the midst of a large plain, where he placed this brŭmhŭcharēē; and directed some chosen servants to seize persons of such and such a description, and forward them to the brŭmhŭcharēē. This was done for a considerable time, (some say for two or three years,) till at length the brŭmhŭcharēē became weak and emaciated through the perpetration of so many murders; and the raja began to suspect that there must be some mistake in the business. He consulted a learned man or two near him, who declared that the brŭmhŭcharēē had very likely mistaken the words spoken to him in his dream, for that these words might

[1] About the year 1800, according to Ubhŭyŭ-chŭrŭnŭ, a learned bramhŭn, who has assisted the author in this work, two Hindoos cut out their own tongues, and offered them to the idol at Kalēē-ghatŭ. Both these men came from Hindoost'hanŭ; one of them was seen by my informant lying on the ground after the action, the blood running from his mouth. At Jwala-mookhŭ, to the N. W. of Delhi, from time immemorial, infatuated Hindoos have cut out their tongues, and offered them to Sŭtēē, to whom this place is sacred, and where the tongue of this goddess is supposed to have fallen, when Shivŭ threw the members of her body into different parts of the earth. In the inside of the temple at this place (which appears to be part of a burning mountain) fire ascends, exhibiting to this degraded people a constant miracle. The same person informed the author, that two diseased persons, who who had gone to the idols at Tarŭkeshwŭrŭ and at Mŭoola in Bengal, some years ago, despairing of a cure, sacrificed themselves to these idols by stabbing themselves, and letting the blood fall into the pans placed to receive the blood of slaughtered animals.

mean simple offerings of food, &c. A thousand victims are said to have been thus butchered.

The sacrifice of a Bull.—In this sacrifice four altars are required for offering the flesh to four gods, Lŭkshmēē-Narayŭnŭ, Ooma-mŭhéshwŭrŭ, Brŭmha, and Ŭnŭntŭ. Before the sacrifice, Prit'hivēē, the nine planets, and the ten guardian deities of the earth, are worshipped. Five vilwŭ,[m] five khŭdirŭ,[n] five pŭlashŭ,[o] and five oodoombŭrŭ[p] posts are to be erected, and a bull tied to each post. Before the burning of the flesh, clarified butter is burnt on one altar, and afterwards small pieces of the flesh of the slaughtered animals on the four altars. The succeeding ceremonies are common to all burnt-sacrifices. This sacrifice was formerly very common. The Pŭdmŭ-pooranŭ and Mŭhabharŭtŭ contain accounts of a great sacrifice of a bull performed by Rŭntee-dévŭ.

The sacrifice of a Horse, (Ushwŭ-médhŭ.)—The animal must be of one colour,[q] without blemish, of good signs, young and well-formed. On an auspicious day, the sacrificer must touch the head of the horse with clay from the Ganges, sandal wood, a pebble, rice not cleansed from the husk, leaves of dōōrva grass,[r] flowers, fruits, curds, clarified butter, red lead, a shell, lamp-black, turmeric, mustard, gold, silver, metal, a lamp, a looking-glass, and other things, repeating the prescribed formulas. The horse is next bathed with water, in which has been immersed a ball composed of the bark of different trees, and spices; and afterwards superbly caparisoned. The god Indrŭ is then invoked by a number of prayers, and invited to come and preserve the horse, which is about to be let loose. A paper is next fastened on the forehead of the horse, containg an inscription in Sŭngskritŭ to the following purport: 'I liberate this horse, having devoted it to be sacrificed Whoever has strength to detain it, let him detain it[s]. I will come and deliver it. They who are unable to detain it, will let it go, and must come to the sacrifice, bringing tribute.' The horse is then liberated, and runs at liberty for twelve months, followed by servants belonging to the sacrificer. At the close of the year, he is brought and bound; and at the time appointed, a proper place is chosen and cleansed, and an altar of earth, walled round with bricks, sixteen cubits square, and one cubit high, is built, with a roof over it resting on posts. At the east end a hole is made, and lined with bricks, to contain the fire; or a small terrace of sand may be raised on the altar for receiving the fire. Under the roof is suspended a canopy, with elegant curtains on all sides. A rope is fastened round the

[m] Ægle marmelos. [n] Mimosa catechu.

[o] Butea frondosa. [p] Ficus glomerata.

[q] A white horse is preferred. [r] Agrostis linearis.

[s] The pooranŭs give accounts of dreadful wars both among gods and men to obtain this horse.

posts of the altar; also branches of the mango tree, tails of the cow of Tartary, bells, and garlands of flowers. The sacrificer then, accompanied with presents, and the reading of different formulas, appoints to their different work in the sacrifice, the acharyŭ, the sŭdŭsyŭ, the brŭmha,[t] the hota,[u] and the oodgata, the latter of whom repeats portions of the Samu-védŭ, sitting on the altar. Twenty-one posts, eighteen cubits and ten fingers high, are fixed in the ground; six of vilwŭ, six of the khŭdirŭ, six of pŭlashŭ, one of piyalŭ,[v] and two of dévŭ-daroo.[w] Each post is to have eight points at the top, to be covered with painted cloth, and encircled with garlands. The six pŭlashŭ posts are to be put into the ground with their heads bent towards the altar. The horse is to be tied to one of the khŭdirŭ posts; and thirty animals and birds for sacrifice to the other posts. All these animals and birds are to be purified by sprinkling water on their faces, and by repeating incantations. A silver image of Gŭroorŭ with gold feathers, and sixteen gold bricks, are then to be brought; after which the sacrificer and his wife are to wash the feet of the horse, and caparison him afresh. A fan of deer's skin is provided to blow the coals; also some kooshŭ grass, with piles of thin twigs of the fig or the pŭlashŭ tree; a large pestle and mortar for bruising the rice; a bowl made of the fig-tree for holding the holy water; a wooden spoon to stir the boiling rice; another large one with two holes in the bowl to pour the clarified butter on the fire; another kind of spoon to pour the boiled rice on the fire; a pan of water, having on its top some branches, fruits, and flowers, with the image of a man painted on it, and smeared over with curds, &c.; round the neck of the pan a piece of new cloth is to be tied, and five articles, viz., gold, silver, a pearl, a coral, and a gem, put into the pan; five smaller pans of water are also to be placed near the other, ornamented without in the same manner. The horse is then killed by the hota, who divides the flesh into pieces, and casts it on the fire, adding clarified butter, and repeating the formulas. When the serum is put on the fire, the sacrificer and his wife are to sit upon the altar, and receive the fumes. The other animals are to be next sacrificed, amidst the repeating of incantations. These sacrifices are offered to Brŭmha, Vishnoo, Shivŭ, and the ten guardian deities of the earth. At the close of these ceremonies, the hota casts a small quantity of curds on the fire towards the north-east; sprinkles a little water on the face of the sacrificer and his wife; bathes them by pouring upon them water from the large pan, repeating incantations; and marks their foreheads, shoulders, throats, and breasts with the ashes from the burnt curds.[x] This sacrifice was performed by many of the

[t] He must sit within a cubit of the fire.

[u] In this sacrifice sixteen hotas are employed. [v] Chironjia sapida. [w] Pine, or fir.

[x] The manners of the Hindoos at the time this sacrifice used to be offered, must have been very different from what they are now: a Hindoo female of rank never appears at present in a public assembly, permitting another man to mark her forehead with paint, &c.

Hindoo kings, as mentioned in several pooranŭs. He who performed one hundred was entitled to the throne of Indrŭ, the king of the gods.

The sacrifice of an Ass.—The sacrifice is to be performed by a dŭndēē, or other religious mendicant, as an atonement for some fault, by which he has lost his station as a devotee. After the fire is prepared, Noiritŭ is worshipped: the sacrificer then anoints the ass with turmeric, bathes it, and ties it to a vilwŭ post; and afterwards purifies it by repeating incantations and sprinkling it with water. A burnt-sacrifice with clarified butter is then offered to the ten guardian deities of the earth; and the ceremonies by which a person is created a dŭndēē are repeated. The relapsed mendicant is now placed near the altar; the ass is slain, and its flesh offered to Noiritŭ in the burnt-sacrifice; after which the staff is put into the hand of the dŭndēē, who addresses petitions to the god Ŭgnee, and to the dŭndēēs who are present. He next performs the sacrifice, thinking on Brŭmha, and then closes the whole by dismissing Ŭgnee; or, in other words, he quenches the fire by pouring curds upon it. This sacrifice is supposed to be effectual to all spiritual purposes, but it does not restore the dŭndēē to his rank among the same class of mendicants.

Sacrifice at the birth of a Son.—A father, on first visiting his son, is commanded to take a piece of gold in his hand; and with fire produced by rubbing two pieces of wood together, to offer a sacrifice to Brŭmha, and then anoint the forehead of the child with the clarified butter left on the fingers at the close of the sacrifice. The mother must sit near the altar, and receive the scent of the offerings, having the child in her arms. To secure the strength of the child, clarified butter and curds must be burnt, and prayers repeated. The father must also bind a string of seven or nine threads, and five blades of dōōrva grass, round the wrist of the child; and sprinkle water on its forehead with blades of kooshŭ grass. He must also present oil and betle to ten or twelve married females, and entertain them at his house. This ceremony is never performed at present.

Sacrifice after Death.—The sagnikŭ bramhŭns, who burn the bodies of the dead with the fire kindled at their birth, are directed to make this sacrifice. First, a burnt-offering is made with clarified butter; then the corpse, being washed, is laid upon the altar, and the person officiating puts some of the clarified butter to the mouth of the deceased; after which the fire is made to surround the body, and a prayer is repeated, that all the sins collected in this body may be destroyed by this fire, and the person obtain an excellent heaven.

Sacrifice to the nine Planets.—Most of the formulas in the preceding sacrifices are used in this. The only differences belong to the wood and food burnt, to the images of the planets, the dress of the priests, and to the fees presented at the close of the ceremony. This sacrifice is made to remove the supposed baneful influence of an evil planet. The author once witnessed this ceremony at Calcutta.

Other sacrifices.—Beside these, many other sacrifices are mentioned in the Hindoo writings; I select the names of a few.—Rajŭ-sōōyŭ, offered by the kshŭtriyŭ kings to atone for the sin of destroying men in war.—Ŭgnishtomŭ, a sacrifice to Ŭgnee.—Jyotishtomŭ, to obtain a glorious body; and Ayooshtomŭ, to obtain long life.—Sŭrpŭgnŭ, to destroy snakes.—Mŭha-vrŭtŭ, to obtain the heaven of Brŭmha. At the close of this sacrifice, a bramhŭn and his wife are brought out, worshipped, feasted, and loaded with presents.—Poundŭrēēkŭ, performed with the flowers of the water-lily dipped in clarified butter, in order to obtain Vishnoo's heaven. —Ŭtiratrŭ, performed in the last stages of the night, to the god Brŭmha.—Vishwŭ-jatŭ, to obtain universal conquest.—Oindrŭ-dŭdhee, performed with curds, made from milk taken from the cow while the calf is kept at a distance with a twig of the pŭlashŭ tree; the whey to be given to a horse.—Prŭja-yagŭ, performed by a king for the good of his subjects.—Ritoo-yagŭ, attended to for six years, the time being varied according to the six seasons.—Survvŭ-dŭkshinŭ; so called because the fees to the officiating bramhŭns, at the close of the sacrifice, amount *to the whole property of the sacrificer.*[a]—Nŭvŭshŭs-yshtee, a sacrifice with first fruits to obtain good harvests.

SECT. V.—*Burnt-Offerings, (Homŭ.)*[b]

THIS is a particular part of the sacrifice called yŭgnŭ, but at present it is often performed separately. The things offered are clarified butter, sesamum, flowers, boiled rice, rice boiled in milk and sweetened with honey, dōōrvŭ-grass, vilwŭ leaves, and the tender branches, half a span long, of the ŭshwŭttŭ'hŭ,[c] the doomvŭrŭ,[d] the pŭlashŭ,[e] the akŭndŭ,[f] the shŭmēē,[g] and the khŭdirŭ,[h] trees. Clarified butter alone is sufficient, but any or all of these things may be added.[i]

[a] One of the gifts proper to be presented to bramhŭns *is a person's whole property!* See a succeeding article, Danŭ. Here the fee at the close of a sacrifice *is a person's all!* Such is the rapacity of these priests of idolatry.

[b] From hoo, to offer by fire.

[c] Ficus religiosa.

[d] Ficus racemosa.

[e] Butea frondosa.

[f] Asclepias gigantea.

[g] Mimosa albida.

[h] Mimosa catechu.

[i] The flesh of goats may be used in the homŭ; but it is not customary at present.

The person who wishes to perform this ceremony, provides a bramhŭn acquainted with the usual forms, and on the day before the service observes a fast. The next day he rises early and bathes, performing in the morning his usual worship: then coming home, he begins the ceremony in the presence of his friends, with the assistance of the bramhŭn whom he has chosen. First he sits down, either in the house or before the door, with his face towards the east, and makes a square altar of four cubits with clean dry sand; upon which, with a blade of kooshŭ-grass, he writes the proper incantation. He then takes a little straw in each hand, lights that in his left, and throws the other away. He repeats this action again, and then laying down the wisp of lighted straw on the altar, repeating incantations, lays upon it the wood, and worships the god Ŭgnee, (fire.) Having already provided clarified butter, and placed twigs, half a span long, by his side, he takes up one of them at a time, and, dipping it in the clarified butter, lays it on the fire, repeating a prayer. He may offer either eight twigs, twenty-eight, one hundred and eight, two hundred and eight, or three hundred and eight, and so on till he be satisfied, or till he think the gods have had clarified butter enough.[k] At the close, he puts or pours upon the fire, plantains, the leaves of the piper betle, and sour milk. He does this, as they say, to cool the earth, which, being a goddess, is supposed to have sustained some harm by the heat of the fire. Finally, he makes presents, and entertains bramhŭns.

SECT. VI.—*Bloody Sacrifices, (Bŭlēē-danŭ*[l]*.)*

THE reader will have observed, that for the burnt-sacrifices animals were slain, and offered on the altar. In these sacrifices (Bŭlee-danŭ) animals are slain, but the flesh is offered raw, and not burnt on the altar: this is the difference between the two sacrifices. Among the things proper for sacrifice are *men*, buffaloes, goats, sheep, horses, camels, deer, fish, and birds of various kinds. At present only buffaloes, goats, and sheep are offered.

When an animal (for example, a goat) is sacrificed, the following forms are used.—First, the animal is bathed either with or in water; and then brought before the idol; when the officiating bramhŭn paints its horns red, and whispers an incantation in its right ear; after which, taking the right ear of the goat in his left hand, with a blade of kooshŭ grass he sprinkles the head of the animal with water, and repeats many incantations: the goat is then worshipped, and fed with the offerings; after which, it is led out,

[k] The god Ŭgnee was once surfeited with clarified butter, and to relieve him Urjoonŭ burnt a whole forest containing medicinal plants.

[l] From Bŭlee, a sacrifice, and da, to give. The shastrŭs include all offerings under the name bŭlee; but at present this term is confined to the offering of the flesh of animals.

and fastened to the stake. The instrument of death is next brought, bathed, smeared with red lead during the repetiton of an incantation, worshipped, and made to touch a burning lamp, that its edge may not be blunted by the power of any incantation. The officiating bramhŭn next puts the instrument and a flower into the hand of the slayer, (perhaps the blacksmith,) who places the flower in his hair, and prostrates himself before the idol. Then laying down the weapon, he binds his cloth firmly round his loins, and waits at the post, in the excavation of which the neck of the goat is to be placed, till the bramhŭn has anointed the post with red lead, and placed a saucer containing a plantain to catch the blood. The goat's neck is now fastened in the excavation of the post, with its head on one side and the body on the other. One man pulls its head by the cord round its neck, which has been smeared with red lead, and another pulls the body. The officiating bramhŭn sprinkles the neck with water, and divides the hair on the neck; after which he goes into the presence of the idol, and offers a cloud of incense; and then he and all present, putting their loose garment around their necks, rise, and stand before the idol with joined hands: and while they remain in this attitude, the executioner, at one blow,[m] strikes off the head. The man who holds the body suspends it over the dish containing the plantain, and the blood runs into it; after which he lays the body down. The officiating bramhŭn pours some water on the head, which another person holds in his hand, and afterwards places it before the idol, fastening it on each side with two sticks put into the ground to prevent its moving. The slayer then going to the body, cuts a morsel of the flesh from the neck, and casts it among the blood preserved in the dish, which is now carried and placed before the idol. The doors are then shut; a light made with clarified butter is placed on the head, and the head is offered to the idol with appropriate prayers. The whole of the blood is next offered, and afterwards divided into four parts and offered, which closes the ceremony.

SECT. VII.—*Bathing, (Snanŭ).*[n]

BATHING, as an act of purification, always precedes and sometimes follows other ceremonies. It may be performed by pouring

[m] A person in the east of Bengal, who was accustomed to lay aside part of his monthly savings to purchase offerings for the annual worship of Doorga, was exceedingly alarmed during the festival one year, when the person who was to cut off the head of the sacrifice (a buffalo) failed to sever the head from the body at one blow. Leaving the sacrifice struggling and half killed, he went up to the image, and with joined hands cried out, 'Oh! mother! why art thou displeased with me? What have I done?' His female relations came into the temple, and wept before the image in the most bitter manner. The spectators began to reason upon this dreadful circumstance, imputing the failure in slaughtering the buffalo to different causes according to their fancies. One opinion, among the rest, was, that the owner of the image was in no fault, but that the goddess was angry because the officiating bramhŭn had let fall saliva upon the offerings while reading the formulas.

[n] From shna, to purify or bathe.

water on the body in or out of doors, or by immersing the body in a pool or river.

A bramhŭn bathes in the following manner:—he first rubs his body with oil, and takes with him to the river a towel, a brass cup called a kosha, flowers, leaves of the vilwŭ tree, and a few seeds of sesamum. Some take along with them a little rice, a plantain or two, and sweetmeats. Arriving at the river side, the bramhŭn, hanging a towel round his neck, makes a bow, or prostrates himself before the river; then rising rubs his forehead with the water, and offers praise to Gŭnga. If he has omitted his morning duties, he performs them now. After this he makes a clay image of the lingŭ: then descends into the water, and immerses himself twice, having his face towards the north or east. Rising, he invokes some god, and, with his forefinger making circles in the water, prays, that all the holy places of the river may surround him at once, or rather that all the fruit arising from bathing in them may be enjoyed by him. He again immerses himself twice, and, rising, cleanses his body, rubbing himself with his towel. He then comes up out of the water, wipes his body, and repeats many forms of prayer or praise. This is what properly belongs to bathing; but it is succeeded by repeating the common forms of worship, for which the person made preparations in bringing his kosha, flowers, leaves, sesamum, making the lingŭ, &c.

Bathing, in cases of sickness, may be performed without immersing the head in water, by rubbing the arms, legs, and forehead, with a wet cloth; or by changing the clothes;[o] or by sprinkling the body with water, and repeating an incantation or two; or by covering the body with the ashes of cow-dung.

SECT. VIII.—*Drink-Offerings to the Gods and deceased Ancestors (Tŭrpŭnŭ).*[p]

THE Hindoos, at the time of bathing, present water daily to the gods, the sages, yŭkshŭs, nagŭs, gŭndhŭrvŭs, ŭpsŭrŭs, ŭsoorŭs, vidyadhŭrŭs, pishachŭs, siddŭs, and to their deceased ancestors.[q] This they call tŭrpŭnŭ; which should be performed three times a day: those who use the kosha take up water in it, putting in sesamum, repeating the proper formulas, and then pouring out the water into the river or pool where they are bathing. Those who

[o] A Hindoo considers those clothes defiled in which he has been employed in secular concerns.

[p] From Tripŭ, to satisfy.

[q] Seeds of sesamum are also presented to deceased ancestors, and, among the gods, to Yŭmŭ, the regent of death.

perform this ceremony without the kosha, take up water with their hands, and, repeating a prayer, present it to the gods, by pouring it out from the ends of the fingers; to parents, by letting it fall betwixt the fingers and thumb of the right hand; and to the sages, by pouring the water out at their wrists. For those who have died in a state of extreme poverty, and have no one to perform the ceremonies for the repose of the soul, instead of pouring it out of the hands, they offer the libation by wringing the cloth with which they bathe. If the person bathe in any other water, and not in the Ganges, he cannot use sesamum, but performs the ceremony with water alone.

SECT. IX.—*The Ceremonies of Worship, (Pōōja.)*

THE following ceremonies in the presence of the idol are what the Hindoos call pōōja.—Previously to entering on this act of idolatry, the person bathes; returning home,[r] he washes his feet, spreads a blanket or some other proper thing to sit upon, and then sits down before the idol, having the articles necessary for worship before him: a kosha, or metal bason, and a koshee, or smaller one; a small wooden stand, a metal plate, an iron stand to hold five lamps, a censor, a brass stand with a small shell placed on it, a metal plate on which to place flowers, a metal bowl into which the water and flowers are thrown after they have been presented to the idol, a metal jug for holding water, a metal plate to be used as a bell; a shell, or sacred conch,[s] which sounds like a horn; with a number of dishes, cups, and other utensils for holding rice, paint, incense, betle, water, milk, butter, curds, sweetmeats, flowers, clarified butter, &c. Having all these articles ready,[t] the worshipper takes water from the kosha with the koshee, and letting it fall into his right hand, drinks it; he then takes a drop more, and then a drop more, repeating incantations. After this with the finger and thumbs of his right hand he touches his mouth, nose, eyes, ears, navel, breast, shoulders, and the crown of his head, repeating certain forms. He then washes his hands, makes a number of motions with his fingers, and strikes the earth with his left heel three times, repeating incantations, When this is done, he flirts the first finger and thumb of his right hand, waving his hand towards the ten divisions of the earth; closes his eyes, and repeats incantations to purify his mind, his body, the place where he sits, as well as the offer-

[r] These ceremonies are frequently performed by the river side.

[s] Both men and women, on entering a temple, often blow the conch or ring the bell, to entertain the god.

[t] In general when the worship is performed in the house, a bramhŭn's wife, against the arrival of her husband from bathing, sets in proper order all the articles used in worship;—flowers, water, utensils, &c.

ings about to be presented, (which it is supposed may have become unclean, by having been seen or touched by a cat, a dog, a shackal, a shōōdrŭ, or a Mŭsŭlman.) Next, he takes a flower, which he lays on his left hand, and, putting his right hand upon it, revolves in his mind the form of the god he is worshipping. He then lays the flower on his head, and, joining his hands together, closes his eyes, thinks upon the form of the god, that he has a nose, eyes, four arms, four heads, &c. and then recites the outward forms of worship in his mind. He now presents the offerings; first, a square piece of gold or silver, as a seat for the god, inviting him to come and sit down, or visit him; and then, asking the god if he be happy, repeats for him, 'Very happy.' After this, he presents water to wash the feet; takes up water with the koshee, and pours it into the metal bowl; and presents at once rice, a vilwŭ leaf, eight blades of dōōrva grass, paint, and water, with incantations. He then presents water to wash the mouth, curds, sugar, honey; then water to wash the mouth again, and water to bathe in, with prayers; then cloth, jewels, gold, silver, ornaments, bedsteads, curtains, a bed, pillow, cloth, printed cloth; clothes for men, women, or children; shoes, brass drinking cups, candlesticks, and whatever would be proper presents to the bramhŭns.[u] After this paint, either red or white, is presented on a flower; then eight or ten flowers; leaves of the vilwŭ tree; a necklace of flowers; incense of three kinds, and a lighted lamp, with incantations. After the bloody sacrifices, the offerings are presented, comprising rice, split peas, different kinds of peas, shaddocks, pomegranates, pine-apples, netted custard-apples, another species of custard-apples, bread fruit or jakŭs, mangoes, water-melons, cucumbers, plantains, oranges, ginger, cocoanuts, almonds, raisins,[x] guavas, dates, jambŭs, jujubes, wood-apples, melons, sugar-canes, radishes, sweet-potatoes, késooru,[y] water, milk, curds, another sort of curds, cream, butter, sour-milk, clarified butter, sugar, sugar-candy, &c. &c. After presenting the offerings, the person repeats the name of a god for some time, and then prostrates himself, (the spectators doing the same;) putting the cloth round his neck, and joining his hands, he offers praise to the god, and prostrates himself again. The dinner follows, consisting of fried greens, and several other dishes made up of kidney, beans, varttakēē,[z] cocoanuts, &c. fried together; split peas, and several kinds of fried herbs or fruits; four kinds of fish; boiled and fried goats' flesh, vension, and turtle; different fruits prepared with treacle; rice and milk boiled with sugar; things prepared

[u] It must not be supposed that all these articles are presented daily by the Hindoos. This account describes what is performed at festivals. In the daily worship, flowers, leaves, sacred grass, a little rice, &c. are presented.

[x] These and several other articles are imported from foreign countries; and though they have been prepared by the hands of the unclean, yet the Hindoos make no difficulty in presenting them to their gods, and afterwards eating them.

[y] The root of scirpus maximus

[z] Solanum molongena.

with pounded rice; curds, sweetmeats, &c. The fish, flesh, fried greens, and every thing of this kind is eaten with boiled rice. A dish called kéchooree, consisting of rice, split peas, clarified butter, turmeric, and spices, boiled together, is also presented; and then water to drink. With every article of food a separate prayer is offered. Water is next presented to wash the mouth, and a straw to pick the teeth, with prayers; then the burnt-offering is made, and a present of money given. At last the person prostrates himself before the object of worship, and then retires to feast on the offerings with other bramhŭns. This is a detail of the form of worship on a large scale, at which time it occupies the officiating bramhŭn two hours.

SECT. X.—*Meditation* (*Dhyanŭ.*[a])

IN this act of devotion, the worshipper (of Shivŭ for instance) closes his eyes, places his arms before him, and repeating the names of the god, ruminates thus:—'His colour is like a mountain of silver; his body shines like the moon; he has four arms; in one hand he holds an axe, in another a deer, with another bestows a blessing, and with the other forbids fear; he has five faces, and in each face three eyes; he sits on the water-lily; the gods surround him, and celebrate his praise; he is clothed with the skin of a tiger; he was before the world; he is the creator of the world; he removes fear from every living creature.' While he meditates on the offerings, he proceeds thus:—'Oh! god, I give thee all these excellent things;' (recounting in his mind the names of all the offerings, one by one.)

Both these forms of meditation are constantly used at the time of worship, (pōōja.) Many things are related in the pooranŭs respecting the meditation known to ascetics, who, by the power of dhyanŭ, discovered things the most secret.

SECT. XI.—*Repeating the Names of the Gods,* (*Jŭpŭ*).[b]

THE Hindoos believe that the repetition of the name of God is an act of adoration; some add that the name of God is like fire, by which all their sins are consumed: hence repeating the names of the idols is a popular ceremony among the Hindoos.

In this act the worshipper, taking a string of beads, repeats the name of his guardian deity, or that of any other god; counting by his beads 10, 28, 108, 208, and so on, adding to every 108 not

[a] From dhyoi, to think.

[b] To speak.

less than one hundred more. This act is not efficacious, however, unless the person keep his mind fixed on the form of the idol. Many secular persons perform jŭpŭ without beads, by counting their fingers.

It is said that a person obtains whatever he seeks by persevering in this act of adoration. If he be desirous of a wife, or of children, or of money, (say a lac of rupees;) or seek recovery from sickness, or relief from misfortune; he begins to repeat the name of his god, and believes that he soon becomes subject to his wishes. Jŭpŭ makes an essential part of the daily worship of a Hindoo: some mendicants continue it day and night, year after year, except when eating, sleeping, bathing, &c.

The Tŭntrŭ-sarŭ contains the following account of the consecration of the bead-roll:—The person sits down on the floor of his house, and taking some green, red, black, yellow, and white paint, draws a water-lily on the floor, upon which he places a small brass dish; and upon this, nine leaves of the ŭshwŭt'hŭ tree, and upon the leaves a string of beads, cow's urine, cow-dung, sour-milk, milk, and clarified butter, mixing them together, and repeating an incantation: he then places honey, sugar, sour-milk, milk, and clarified butter, upon the bead-roll, repeating another incantation; then some red lead and spices; and then, with incantations, he gives the bead-roll a soul, (pranŭ,) and according to the usual forms worships it, and offers a burnt-offering to the god whose name he intends to repeat with this string of beads.

Sect. XII.—*Forms of Praise to the Gods, (Stŭvŭ.)*

Forms of praise to the gods constitute a part of the daily worship of the Hindoos. They spring not from emotions of gratitude, but are repeated as acts of merit, to draw down favours on the obsequious worshipper.—In this act, the person draws his upper garment round his neck, joins his hand in a supplicating manner, and repeats the forms of praise with a loud voice. *Examples*:—'Oh! Shivŭ! thou art able to do every thing! Thou art the preserver of all! Thou art the fountain of life!'—To Kartikŭ: 'Thou art the god of gods; therefore I come to thee, to enquire how I may repeat the praise of Shēētŭla, that she may remove swellings on the body.'—To Shēētŭla: 'I salute Shēētŭla, the goddess, for she can remove the fear of boils.'

The Hindoos say, that by praise a person may obtain from the gods (who are fond of flattery) whatever he desires. The forms are taken from the shastrŭs, though on some occasions, a person may recite words of his own invention.

SECT. XIII.—*Forms of Prayer to the Gods, (Kŭvŭchŭ.)*

THESE prayers are principally found in the Tŭntrŭs ; a few in the pooranŭs. They relate to the welfare of the petitioner here and hereafter ; and are given by a spiritual guide to his disciple. *Examples:*—'O ! Hŭnooman ! when I go eastward, do thou preserve me ! O ! son of Pŭvŭnŭ ! when I proceed southward, do thou keep me ! O ! beloved son of Késhŭrēē ;[c] when I go westward, do thou preserve me. O ! Kamŭgnŭ ![d] keep me from danger when I go northward. O ! Sagŭrŭ-parŭgŭ ![e] save me when I descend. O ! burner of Lŭnka ! (Ceylon,) deliver me from all danger. O ! counsellor of Soogrēēvŭ ! preserve my head.' In this manner the person addresses petitions to this monkey-god, as for his head, so for the preservation of every member of his body, from the forehead to the toes.

He who repeats this form twelve times beneath the ŭrkŭ tree, will obtain long life, be the strongest man on earth, and the goddess of fortune will never forsake his dwelling. If he repeat this kŭvŭchŭ seven times, at midnight, standing in water, he will be able to drive away from his body every kind of disease : if at any time, in any place, he will obtain beauty, eloquence, wisdom, strength, victory, patience, and be free from fear and disease. If any one bind this kŭvŭchŭ (as a charm[f]) on his arm, he will obtain every desire of his heart.

SECT. XIV.—*Petitions and Vows, (Kamŭnŭ and Manŭnŭ.)*

THE Hindoos are continually resorting to their gods for particular favours : if a person wish for a son,[g] or any other blessing, he takes rice, plantains, and sweetmeats, and goes to some idol ; and after worshipping it, and presenting offerings, asks the god to bless him with a son. This petition is called kamŭnŭ ; after putting up which he vows, that if the god grant his request, he

[c] Késhŭrēē was married to the mother of Hŭnooman, (if marriages take place among monkies,) and Hŭnooman was the illegitimate son of Pŭvŭnŭ.

[d] This monkey-god is called by this name, as the destroyer of evil desire ; from kamŭ, desire, and hŭn, to destroy.

[e] Sagŭrŭ, sea, parŭgŭ, the crosser ; alluding to his leaping across the sea to Ceylon.

[f] Not only the Hindoos, but the Mŭsŭlmans also are much attached to charms. I once saw a Mŭsŭlman woman dropping slips of paper into the river, and, upon inquiry, found that they contained some sacred words, and that the woman was presenting these papers to the river-saint, Khajakhéjŭr, in hopes of obtaining relief from sickness, service, or the like.

[g] The Hindoos in general never pray for daughters, because they do not bring much honour to the family : they are expensive, and they can do nothing for the family when the father is dead ; whereas a son preserves his father's memory, performs the ceremonies for the repose of his soul, and nourishes the family by his labours.

will offer to him two goats, or present him with two loads[h] of sweetmeats: this vow is called manŭnŭ.

In this manner the Hindoo asks for different blessings from his god; such as to become the servant of some European, or to have sickness removed, or for riches, a house, a wife, or for a son to be married. A woman prays for a husband who is absent. A mother prays that her sick child may recover. Thus the poor Hindoo carries his property to dumb idols, and knows nothing of the happiness of casting all his cares on that glorious Being, 'who careth for him.' The vows made at such times are various. One promises to sacrifice a goat, a sheep, or a buffalo; another to present sweetmeats, or cloth, ornaments, money, rice, a house, a necklace, one hundred water-lilies, one thousand toolŭsee leaves, or a grand supper. All these offerings come to the bramhŭns.[i]

If the god do not grant the requests and regard the vows made at these times, the worshipper sometimes vents his rage in angry expressions; or, if the image be in his own house, he dashes it to pieces. Such an enraged worshipper sometimes says, 'Oh! thou forsaken of the goddess Fortune, thou blind god; thou canst look upon others, but art blind to me.' 'The gods are dying,' says another, 'otherwise my five children would not have died; they have eaten my five children at once.' 'After having worshipped this god so faithfully, and presented so many offerings, this is the shameful manner in which I am requited.' Words like these are common; but this is in times when the passions of the worshippers are touched by the death of a child, or by some dreadful misfortune: and those who treat the gods so roughly are generally of the lower orders.

Sect XV.—*Vows, (Vrŭtŭ.)*

Certain ceremonies, performed at stated times, frequently by females, are called by the name vrŭtŭ. The following is an example of one of these ceremonies:—At the fifth of the increase of the moon, in the month Maghŭ, what is called the Pŭnchŭmēē-Vrŭtŭ is performed. On the day before the commencement of this ceremony, the woman who is to perform it, eats food without salt, and only once in the day; refrains from anointing her body with oil; eats rice that has not been made wet in cleansing; and puts

[h] That is, as much as a man can carry, at twice in the way the bearers carry water; who put a bamboo yoke on the shoulder, and suspend a jar of water from each end of the bamboo.

[i] The shastrŭ has declared that no gifts are to be received from the hands of shōōdrŭs, except land or virgins. If, however, a bramhŭn have received a forbidden gift, he is directed to offer it to Vishnoo, and then distribute it among bramhŭns, repeating, for the removal of his sin, the gayŭtrēē one hundred and eight times, or more.

on new apparel. The following morning she bathes; after which the officiating bramhŭn arrives at her house, and the things necessary for the worship are brought: as, a new earthen jar, rice, sweetmeats, a new poita, a piece of new cloth, clarified butter, fruits, flowers, &c. The woman presents to the officiating bramhŭn, who sits in the house on a mat made of kooshŭ-grass, with his face towards the north or east, a piece of new cloth; and putting a cloth over her shoulders, and joining her hands, informs him that she intends to perform this vrŭtŭ every month for six years, and prays him to become her representative in this work. She then rises, and the bramhŭn, taking the shalgramŭ, places it before him, and performs the worship of Vishnoo and Lŭkshmēē. In the third and fourth years, on the day preceding and on the day of the worship, she eats rice not made wet in cleansing; the next year, on these days, only fruits; the following year, on these two days, she fasts. On the last day, (at which time the six years expire,) the officiating bramhŭns attend, to whom she says, 'I have now finished the six years' vrŭtŭ I promised: I pray you to perform another vrŭtŭ.' She then gives to each a piece of cloth, a poita, and some betle-nut; and putting a cloth round her neck, and joining her hands, begs them to perform the necessary ceremonies. Placing the shalgramŭ before them, they then perform the worship of of Shivŭ, Sōōryŭ, Gŭnéshŭ, Vishnoo, and Doorga; in which offerings are made of cloth, sweetmeats, &c. Next they worship the woman's spiritual guide; in which, amongst other things, an offering is made of a bamboo plate, having on it a number of articles, and among the rest a piece of cloth. To this succeeds the worship of Vishnoo, Lukshmēē, and the officiating priests. A priest next prepares an altar four cubits square, by spreading sand upon the ground. At three of the corners he fixes three pieces of wood, lights some straw, and then worships the fire; next he boils rice, and, with clarified butter, presents the burnt-offering. The female now puts a bamboo plate on her head, and walks round the fire seven times; then, standing still, she says, 'O! Ŭgnee! I call thee to witness, that I have performed this vrŭtŭ six years.' She says the same to the sun, the shalgramŭ, and to the bramhŭns. Next she gives a fee, and distributes the gifts to the priests and bramhŭns. The bamboo plate which she placed on her head is laid up in the house, and the whole closes with a grand dinner to the bramhŭns and others. This is the form of a vrŭtŭ on a large scale. The Hindoos have, it is said, two or three hundred ceremonies called by this name.

Savitrēē-vrŭtŭ. In this ceremony the wife of a Hindoo, in the month Asharhŭ, worships her husband: she first presents to him a new garment, hangs a garland of flowers round his neck, rubs his body with red lead and ointments; and while he sits on a stool, worships him, by presenting different offerings to him repeating incantations, and praying that she may never be separated from him as her husband, nor ever become a widow. After a number of other services paid to him, among which she makes him partake of a good dinner, she walks round him seven times, and then retires.

Adŭrŭ-singhasŭnŭ-vrŭtŭ is observed every day in Voishakhŭ for one year. During the thirty days, thirty women, the wives of bramhŭns, are entertained; a different female each day. When the bramhŭnēē arrives, a seat is given her on the porch, and the mistress of the house washes her feet, fans her, anoints her head with oil, combs her hair, ornaments her forehead with paint, anoints her body with perfumes, and employs a female barber to paint the edges of her feet. After this she conducts her into the house, where she is fed with all the dainties the house can afford, and dismissed with a gift of kourees. On the last of the thirty days, in addition to this entertainment, a piece of cloth is presented to a bramhŭnēē. The benefit expected from this vrŭtŭ is, that the female who thus honours the wives of bramhŭns shall be highly honoured by her husband in another birth.

It would be easy to multiply examples, for almost every Hindoo female performs one or another of these vrŭtŭs:[k] but this will be sufficient to give the reader an idea of these ceremonies; from the merit of which some expect heaven, others children, others riches, others preservation from sickness, &c.—The vrŭtŭs are a very lucrative source of profit to the bramhŭns.

SECT. XVI.—*Fasting, (Oopŭvasŭ.)*

FASTING is another work of merit among the Hindoos. A common fast is conducted in the following manner:—The person abstains on the preceding day from rubbing his body with oil, and from eating, except once in the former part of the day. The next day he eats nothing; and on the following day he eats once, worships some god, and entertains one or more bramhŭns. If a person be unable to fast to such a degree, he is permitted to take a little milk on the second day; if he be very weak, he may add fruit, curds, sweetmeats, &c.

Some Hindoos fast on the 11th[l] of the increase, and the 12th of the decrease of the moon in every month; on the 11th in

[k] Vrŭtŭs are unconditional vows to perform certain religious ceremonies; but what is called mŭnŭnŭ (see a preceding article) is a conditional vow, promising to present offerings on condition that the god bestow such or such a benefit.

[l] Widows keep this fast so strictly, that if a widow were dying, and a draught of water would prolong life, her friends would scarcely give it.

Shravŭnŭ, Bhadrŭ, and Kartikŭ;[m] on the 12th in Shravŭnŭ; on the 14th of the decrease of the moon in Phalgoonŭ;[n] on the 9th in Choitrŭ;[o] on the 8th in Bhadrŭ;[p] and on the 8th in Ashwinu.[q] In this month many natives of Hindoost'han fast on the first nine days of the moon, in honour of Doorga; and observe, as they say, a total abstinence, even from water. Fasts precede some of the festivals: after the death of parents, Hindoos fast three days; after that of a husband, a wife fasts three days: before offering an atonement, a fast is observed; the day any pilgrim arrives at a holy place he fasts; in fulfilling vows, the Hindoos keep many fasts; some persons enter into a resolution to fast every other day, and persevere in this for years. Some renounce rice altogether, and keep a perpetual fast, living on milk, fruits, &c. Others (pilgrims) offer a certain fruit to some idol, and renounce this kind of fruit, promising never to eat of it again to the end of life. The gods, it is said, delight to see their followers renounce anything as an act of devotion or attachment to them. This person presents to bramhŭns fruit thus renounced, on the aniversary of the day on which he renounced it.---Another custom, bearing a similarity to fasting, also prevails among the Hindoos:—In the months Asharhŭ, Shravŭnŭ, Bhadrŭ, and Ashwinŭ, many renounce certain articles of diet, and others omit to be shaved, as acts of devotion to the gods.

The blessing expected from fasting is, that the person will ascend to the heaven of that god in whose name he observes the fast.

SECT. XVII.—*Gifts, (Danŭ.[r])*

PRESENTS to learned bramhŭns; to those less learned; to unlearned bramhŭns; to one whose father was a bramhŭn, but his mother a shōōdrŭ; and alms to the poor, are called by the name of danŭ. The things which may be presented are, whatever may be eaten, or worn, or is in use among Hindoos. These are the common gifts, but the shastrŭs have pointed out extraordinary gifts: a daughter in

[m] On the first of these days Vishnoo goes to sleep; on the second he turns to the other side; and on the third he awakes.

[n] The occasion of this fast is thus related:—On a certain occasion, Doorga asked Shivŭ what would please him most, and be a work of the greatest merit. He replied, to hold a fast in his name on the 14th of the wane of the moon in Phalgoonŭ.

[o] The birth-day of Ramŭ.

[p] Krishnŭ's birth-day.

[q] The time of the Doorga festival.

[r] From da, to give.

marriage without receiving a fee;[s] a pool of water;[t] a shalgramŭ; a house containing food, clothes, &c. for twelve months; gold; cows; elephants; horses; palankeens; a road; a copy of a pooranŭ; a mountain of gold,[u] silver, brass, rice, or other articles; land;[x] *a person's whole property; yea,* even *his life.*

There are three ways of presenting a gift; one in which the person worships the receiver; another in which he gives as an act of benevolence; and the last, in which the giver prays for some blessing on presenting his gift. If a shōōdrŭ wish to present a gift to a bramhŭn, he bathes, and carries it fasting: on arriving in the presence of the bramhŭn, he sprinkles the gift with water, repeating an incantation that it may be thereby purified, and then presents it with such words as these: 'Sir, I have presented to you this gift: let me have your blessing, that I may obtain heaven, or, that my father may obtain heaven, or that it may be imputed to me as an act of merit.'

If a man present land to bramhŭns, he will obtain heaven; if a cow, he will after death ride on a cow across the river Voitŭrŭnēē; if water, after death he will find refreshing water in his journey to Yŭmalŭyŭ, (the residence of Yŭmŭ, the regent of death); if a house

[s] The generality of the respectable Hindoos say, that receiving a fee for a daughter is like selling flesh; yet the lower orders of bramhŭns commonly receive money on giving a daughter in marriage. Formerly the Hindoo rajas assisted the bramhŭns by giving them money for the expenses of their weddings. A story is related of a raja, who was intreated by a bramhŭn to bestow a gift upon him for the expenses of his marriage. The raja ordered him to put a garland round the neck of the first woman he met, and let her become his wife. The bramhŭn went out, and met the raja's mother returning from bathing. When about to put the garland round her neck, she demanded the reason of this strange conduct; which the bramhŭn explained. The old lady told him to wait, and she would bring about what he wanted. She sat at the door of the palace, and compelled her son to come and invite her in. She replied, that she was become the wife of such a bramhŭn, and that she must go with her new husband. The raja, thunderstruck, called for the bramhŭn, gave him a thousand rupees towards his wedding, and brought his mother into the house again.

[t] Pools are dug every year in all parts of Bengal, and offered to all creatures, accompanied with a number of ceremonies.

[u] The height of these mountain-gifts is given in the Pooshkŭrŭ-khŭndŭ of the Pŭdmŭ-pooranŭ. It must not be supposed that they are very large; but it is necessary that figures of trees, deer, &c. should be seen on them. In one of the smritees is an account of a prostitute, who offered a mountain of gold. About the year 1794, Chŭnooghoshŭ, a kaist'hŭ of Midnapore, gave to the bramhŭns an artificial mountain of gold. A little before this, Gopalŭ-krishnŭ, a voidyŭ of Rajŭ-nŭgŭrŭ, presented to the bramhŭns three mountains, one of gold, another of rice, and another of the seeds of sesamum.

[x] It is very common for rich land-owners to make presents of land to bramhŭns. At a shraddhŭ for a father or a mother, a piece of land, or its value in money, is invariably given to bramhŭns, unless the person be poor. Many of the Hindoo rajas sought out poor bramhŭns, and gave them grants of land. A story is related of Kēērttee-chŭndrŭ, raja of Burdwan, who once found a poor fatherless boy, the son of a bramhŭn, tending cattle: he gave him a village, with as much land as he could run over without stopping; and disinherited the shōōdrŭ who had dared to employ the son of a bramhŭn in so mean an occupation. The same raja ordered a man to be cut in pieces, for refusing to restore to a bramhŭn a grant of land which the former had bought in a lot offered for sale.

to bramhŭns, he will obtain a palace in heaven; if an umbrella to a bramhŭn, he will not suffer, in another world, from the rays of the sun; if shoes, in his way to heaven he will not suffer from the heat of the ground; if perfumes to bramhŭns, he will never, after death, receive an offensive smell; if medicine to the blind, he will be delivered from darkness hereafter; if a daughter to a bramhŭn, without a fee, he will gain as much as if he had given the whole world.

SECT. XVIII.—*Entertaining Bramhŭns.*

As might be expected in a system formed by bramhŭns, honouring them with a feast is represented as an act of the highest merit. At the close of all religious ceremonies, bramhŭns are entertained; private individuals, during particular holidays, make a feast for one or more bramhŭns; a person on his birth-day, on the anniversary of the day in which received the initiating incantation, or at the full moon, or at any feast, entertains bramhŭns. During the whole of the month Voishakhŭ, it is very meritorious to give feasts to bramhŭns.

SECT. XIX.—*Various Works of Merit.*

THE Hindoo lawgivers have established several customs, which, if separated from idolatry, would be worthy of the highest commendation: they promise to the obedient the greatest rewards in a future state.

Among these we may place hospitality to strangers.[y] The traveller, when he wishes to rest for the night, goes to a house, and says, 'I am ŭtit'hee'; i. e., I am to be entertained at your house. The master or mistress of the house, if of a hospitable disposition, gives him water to wash his feet, a seat, tobacco, water to drink, &c. After these refreshments, they give him fire-wood, a new earthen pot to cook in,[z] rice, split peas, oil, spices, &c. The next morning he departs, somtimes without saying any thing, and at other times he takes leave.[a] In the

[y] Munoo says, 'No guest must be dismissed in the evening by a house-keeper: he is sent by the returning sun, and whether he come in fit season or unseasonably, he must not sojourn in the house without entertainment. Let not himself eat any delicate food, without asking his guest to partake of it: the satisfaction of a guest will assuredly bring the housekeeper, wealth, reputation, long life, and a place in heaven.'

[z] Almost every Hindoo is either constantly or occasionally his own cook.

[a] The Hindoos have no word for 'thank you' in their common language, and gratitude itself appears to constitute no part of their virtues. The greatest benefits conferred very rarely meet with even the least acknowledgment. I have known

houses of the poor or the covetous, a stranger meets with worse entertainment. Not unfrequently the mistress of the house execuses herself to a person wishing to become a guest, and among other things alleges, that there are none but women and children at home. It is not very uncommon for a traveller to go to several houses, and to be refused at all. This is partly owing to fear, that the stranger may plunder the house in the night. Where persons have porches at the outside of their houses, they have less fear, as the stranger is then kept at a distance. This hospitality to strangers is indeed sometimes abused by a thief, who robs the house and decamps. Yet if a person refuse to entertain a stranger, the shastrŭ declares that all the sins of the guest become his, and his works of merit become the guest's. The traveller sometimes murmurs on going away, exclaiming that the people of this village are so depraved, that they refuse a handful of rice to a traveller. If a family are unable through poverty to entertain a guest, the shastrŭ orders that they shall beg for his relief. The stranger after eating must take nothing uncooked from the house.

A person of the name of Golŭkŭ-Chŭndrŭ-Rayŭ, of Serampore, formerly sirkar to the Danish East India Company, has particularly distinguished himself in the present day, as the most eminent Hindoo in Bengal for liberality to strangers. Upon an average, two hundred travellers or mendicants were formerly fed daily at and from his house ; and it is said that he expended in this manner fifty thousand rupees annually.

Another work of charity is the digging of pools by the side of public roads, to supply the thirsty traveller with water. The cutting of these ponds, and building flights of steps in order to descend into them, is in many cases very expensive : four thousand rupees are frequently expended in one pond, including the expense attending the setting it apart to the use of the public ; at which time an assembly of bramhŭns is collected, and certain formulas from the shastrŭs read by a priest ; among which, in the name of the offerer, he says, 'I offer this pond of water to quench the thirst of mankind.' At the close of the ceremony, a feast is given to the assembled bramhŭns, who are also dismissed with presents.

European physicians perform the most extraordinary cures on the bodies of the natives gratuitously, without a solitary instance occurring of a single individual returning to acknowledge the favour. Amongst the higher orders of Hindoos, however, the master of a house sometimes says to a guest on his departure, 'You will excuse all inattention ;' and the guest replies, 'Oh ! sir, you are of a distinguished caste ! What shall I say in return for the manner in which I have been entertained ? Such food ! such a bed ! But this is like yourself. No one entertains a guest as you do. May Lŭkshmēē (the goddess of riches) ever dwell in your house.'

I suppose, that in all eastern countries it is a custom for guests to be thus entertained at private houses. The address of our Lord to his disciples seems to intimate that such was the case among the Jews : 'And into whatsoever city or town ye shall enter, enquire who in it is worthy ; and there abide till ye go thence. And whosoever shall not receive you, when ye depart out of that house, &c.'

It is unlawful for the owner ever afterwards to appropriate this pond to his own private use. If the water be very clear and sweet, the offerer is complimented as a person with whose merits the gods are pleased. A person of Burdwan, of the name of Ramŭ-palŭ, is mentioned as having prepared as many as a hundred pools in different places, and given them for public use. Persons inhabiting villages where water was scarce, used to petition this public benefactor to cut a pool for them; and, after obtaining leave of the raja, he bestowed upon them this necessary blessing.[b]

The planting of trees to afford shade to travellers is another act of merit among the Hindoos, and, in a hot climate like this, deserves to be classed among actions that are commendable. Some trees also are considered as sacred, and the planting of them is therefore deemed a religious act The trees thus planted are generally the ŭshwŭt'hŭ,[c] the vŭtŭ,[d] vilwŭ,[e] ŭshokŭ,[f] vŭkoolŭ,[g] plŭkshŭ,[h] oodoombŭrŭ,[i] shingshŭpa,[k] tŭmalŭ,[l] jēēvu-pootrēē,[m] &c. At the time of planting these trees, no religious ceremony takes place; but when they are dedicated to public or sacred uses, the ceremony called prŭtisht'ha is performed. The person who plants one ŭshwŭt'hŭ,[n] one nimbŭ,[o] two chŭmpŭkŭ,[p] three nagŭkéshwŭrŭ,[q] seven talŭ,[r] and nine cocoanut trees, and devotes them with their fruit, shade, &c. to public uses, is promised heaven.

About twenty years ago, a landowner of Patŭ-dŭhŭ, about fourteen miles from Calcutta, planted an orchard by a public road, placed a person to keep it, and dedicated it to the use of travellers of all descriptions; who are permitted to enter it, and take as much fruit as they can eat on the spot. Krishnŭ-vŭsoo, of Calcutta, made a road[s] from Kŭtŭkŭ to the temple of Jŭgŭnnat'hŭ, in Orissa, and planted a double row of fruit trees on the sides of this road for the use of pilgrims going to the temple. The pilgrims cook their food, sleep under the shade of these trees, and eat the fruit which they yield. He also cut a large pool near the temple, to supply these pilgrims with water. Raja Sookhŭ-mŭyŭ, of Calcutta, who died in the year 1811, left 100,000 rupees to be appropriated to the repairs and improvement of the road to the temple of Jŭgŭnnat'hŭ, in Orissa, and to assist pilgrims going there in paying the tax to Government.

In some parts, in the sultry months Voishakhŭ and Jyoisht'hŭ,

[b] Cutting wells made a man famous in patriarchal times: a well, said to be Jacob's well, existed in Samaria at the commencement of the Christian era. John iv. 6, 12.

[c] Ficus religiosa. [d] Ficus Indica. [e] Ægle marmelos. [f] Jonesia asoca. [g] Mimusops elengi. [h] Ficus venosa. [i] Ficus glomerata. [k] Dalbergia Sisso. [l] Xanthochymus pictorius. [m] Unascertained. [n] Ficus religiosa. [o] Melia azadirachta, [p] Michelia champaca. [q] Mesua ferea. [r] Borassus flabelliformis.

[s] There are very few good public roads in Bengal.

rich Hindoos, as an act of merit, erect sheds by the public roads, and supply travellers gratis with water and other refreshments.

For the comfort of travellers, lodging-houses are erected by opulent Hindoos on the side of public roads, in some of which travellers are supplied with refreshments gratis.

Sect. XX.—*Reading and hearing Pooranŭs.*

At the close of most of the pooranŭs, the writers affirm, that it is an act of the greatest merit, extinguishing all sin, for the people to read these works, or hear them read. Those principally recited in Bengal, as an act of merit, are the Mŭhabharŭtŭ, the Shrēē-bhagŭvŭtŭ, the Kalikŭ pooranŭ, the Ootkŭlŭ and Kalēē-khŭndŭs.[t]

Some auspicious day, in the month Kartikŭ, Maghŭ, or Voishakhŭ, is chosen, on the day preceding which the bramhŭns are entertained. A shed, covered with thatch and open on all sides, is prepared, sufficiently large, if the ceremony be on a grand scale, to accommodate four or five thousand people. At one end, a place rather elevated is prepared for the person who is to read; and the other end, if there be a portico to the house, is enclosed by a curtain, from whence the women hear, and peep through the crevices. Mats are spread for the people to sit on, the bramhŭns in one place, and the kayŭst'hŭs in another,[u] and the shōōdrŭs in another. On the appointed day all take their places: the people, on entering, make prostration to the shalgramŭ and to the bramhŭns. The person at whose expense this is performed, after bathing, enters the assembly, acquaints the pŭndits with his design, and asks leave to choose those who are to read; to each of whom he presents a piece of cloth, directing him what to do. The reader (Pat'hŭkŭ) sits on the elevated seat; below him, on the right and left, sit the examiners, (Dharŭkŭs); and before him the Sŭdŭsyŭs, who decide upon the exactness of the copy. Two persons (Shrotas) sit in front, and in the name of the householder hear it read. Before the recitation begins, a bramhŭn in his name presents a garland of flowers, and some white paint, to the shalgramŭ; places very thick garlands on the neck, arms, and head of the reader, and anoints his breast and forehead with white paint; and afterwards places garlands round the necks of the bramhŭns and some of the

[t] The two last works are parts of the Skŭndŭ pooranŭ.

[u] When a kayŭst'hŭ has a pooranŭ read at his own house, before the recital commences the officiating bramhŭn worships the book, the author, and the person whose actions are celebrated in this work. Flowers, rice, a burnt-offering, &c. are presented to the book, and to the persons worshipped.

shŏŏdrŭs. The Pat'hŭkŭ then (about nine or ten o'clock in the forenoon) beings to read one of these pooranŭs aloud. The first day they sit about an hour; but on the succeeding days they begin at seven and continue till twelve; and in the afternoon meet again, when the meaning of what was read in the forenoon in Sŭngskritŭ is to be given in Bengalee, by the Kŭt'hŭkŭ, or speaker; who takes the seat of the Pat'hŭkŭ, placing the shalgramŭ upon a stand before him. At times the passions of the multitude are greatly moved; when some one perhaps presents the reader with a piece of money. The whole is closed at dusk, when the people retire, and converse upon what they have heard. This method is pursued from day to day till the book is finished. The recitation of the Mŭhabharŭtŭ occupies four months, of the Shrēē-bhagŭvŭtŭ about one.

Some persons entertain the guests on the last day instead of the first, dismissing the brambŭns with presents. It is said, that not less than 100,000 rupees have been sometimes expended by rich men at such recitals. The person who causes these books to be read, is promised great future rewards.

SECT. XXI.—*Sacred Rehearsals, (Gēētŭ.*[1]*)*

THE Hindoos, as an act of merit, employ persons to sing those parts of their shastrŭs, which contain the history of their gods. These songs have been composed in the Bengalee from the following, among other shastrŭs: the Chŭndēē, Ramayŭnŭ, the Mŭhabharŭtŭ, the Shrēē-bhagŭvŭtŭ, the Gŭnga-vakyŭvŭlēē, the Kalikŭ, Pudmŭ, and Shivŭ pooranŭs, and the Kashēē-khŭndŭ. The names of the songs are: Kalēē-kēērtŭnŭ, Ŭnnŭdamŭngŭlŭ, Krishnŭ-mŭngŭlŭ, Gŭnga-bhŭktee-tŭrŭnginēē, Kŭvee-kŭnkŭnŭ, Mŭnŭsa-mŭngŭlŭ. Hŭree-sŭngkēērtŭnŭ, Pēērér-ganŭ, Dhŭpér-ganŭ.

As a specimen of the manner in which this singing is conducted, I insert an account of the performance called Kŭvee-kŭnkŭnŭ. —Sometimes a rich man bears the expense, and at others half a dozen persons join in it. If the former, he has the rehearsal in his own yard; and if several unite, it is done in some suitable place in the village, after the place has been swept, and an awning put over it. Eight or ten singers of any caste, attended by four or five musicians are employed. Upon the ancles of all the singers are loose brass rings, which make a gingling noise: in the left hand is held a brush made from the tail of the cow of Tartary; and in the right, round flat pieces of metal, which by being shook, make a jingling noise. The drum continues to beat till all the people

[1] From goi, sing.

have taken their places; after which the chief singer steps forth, and after a short preface begins to sing, moving his feet, waving his hands, and now and then dancing. The softer music also plays at intervals, and the other singers take parts, waving the cow-tails, and dancing with a slow motion. When the passions of the hearers are affected, some throw small pieces of money at the feet of the principal singer. The performance continues during the day for nearly six hours, and is renewed again at night.

These rehearsals are in some instances continued a month: each day a new song is chosen. The inferior singers receive about eight-pence a day each; and for this trifle sing till they are black in the face, and become quite hoarse. The performance being out of doors, is very unfavourable to vocal efforts, and the exertions of the singers are in consequence very painful. The gifts to those singers who excel, often increase the allowance considerably; and at the time of their dismission, the performers have garments, &c. presented to them. A feast to the bramhŭns concludes the rehearsal. Sometimes women are employed, though not frequently.

The hearing of these songs, however filthy some of them may be, is considered as an act of religious merit.

SECT. XXII.—*Hanging Lamps in the Air.*

In the month Kartikŭ, the Hindoos suspend lamps in the air on bamboos, in honour of the gods, and in obedience to the shastrŭs. I cannot learn any other origin of this custom than this, that as the offerings of lamps to particular gods is considered as an act of merit, so this offering to all the gods, during the auspicious month Kartikŭ, is supposed to procure many benefits to the giver.

SECT. XXIII.—*Method of preventing Family Misfortunes.*

If a Hindoo die on an unlucky day, the shastrŭs declare that not only the whole race of such a person, but the very trees of his garden will perish. To prevent these direful effects, a ceremony called Pooshkŭra-shantee is performed in the night, by the river side, or in some plain; where two bramhŭns sit on an altar, and worship the nine planets, also Yŭmŭ, Chitrŭ-gooptŭ, Pooshkŭrŭ-poorooshŭ,[y] and the shalgramŭ; and afterwards offer a sacrifice. One of the bramhŭns then makes the images of Yŭmŭ

[y] Yŭmŭ is the judge of the dead; Chitrŭ-gooptŭ is his recorder; and Pooshkŭrŭ poorooshŭ, a kind of inferior deity, who resides with Yŭmŭ.

and Pooshkŭrŭ-pooroosh̆ŭ; one with cow-dung, and the other with paste made of rice. To these images he imparts souls, worships the knife, slays a fish, and offers it in two parts, with some blood, to the cow-dung and paste images. The person who performs this ceremony then dismisses the two bramhŭns with fees, and avoids seeing their faces any more on that night.

SECT. XXIV.—*Ceremony for removing the Evils following bad Omens.*

IF a thunder-bolt fall on a house; if a vulture, or hargilla (the gigantic crane,) alight on it; or if shackals or owls lodge in it; or if a shackal howl in the yard in the day-time, some evil will befall the persons living in this house. To prevent this, the ceremony called Ŭdbhootŭ-shantee is performed; which comprises the worship of Brŭmha and other gods, the burnt-sacrifice, repeating the name of a certain deity, &c.

SECT. XXV.—*Ceremonies performed while sitting on a dead Body.*

IN the former edition of this work, I inserted a pretty long account of a number of strange ceremonies, principally drawn from the tŭntrŭs, and known under the name of Sadhŭnŭ. One of these rites is performed while sitting on a dead body; and the whole are practised under the superstitious notion that the worshipper will obtain an interview with his guardian deity, and be empowered to work miracles.

The late Ramŭ-Krishnŭ, raja of Natorŭ, employed the greater part of his time in repeating the name of his guardian deity, and in other gloomy and intoxicating rites. The princess who had adopted him, and who had become his spiritual guide, was offended on perceiving his turn of mind. A little before his death, he performed the Shŭvŭ-sadhŭnŭ, and his house steward, a bramhŭn, provided for him a dead body and other necessary articles; and it is affirmed, that while the raja was sitting on the dead body, (which was placed in the temple of Kalēē, built by the raja at Natorŭ,[1]) he was thrown from it to the river Narŭdŭ, a distance of about half a mile. After a long search, the raja was found on this spot in a state of insensibility, and in a few days after he died. I give this story as it was related to me by two or three bramhŭns. That the raja performed the Shŭvŭ-sadhŭnŭ is very probable.

[1] The raja is said to have endowed this temple with lands, &c. of the annual value of 100,000 rupees.

SECT. XXVI.—*Ceremonies for removing, subduing, or destroying Enemies.*

THE tŭntrŭ shastrŭs, and even the védŭs, have laid down the forms of an act of worship to remove an enemy to a distance, to bring him into subjection, or to destroy him. This worship is addressed to the yoginēēs, or other inferior deities, before a female image made of cow-dung, or a pan of water, on a Tuesday or Saturday, at the darkest hour of the night. Many incantations are repeated, and some bloody sacrifices offered. The worshipper expects, that by the power of these incantations his enemy will be seized with some dreadful disease, and will thus perish by the unseen hand of the yoginēēs If a person hear that his enemy is performing these ceremonies for his destruction, he pays another person to perform similar rites, to prevent any evil arising to him.

The Hindoos have also a great variety of incantations, which are supposed to possess the same power as charms in Europe.[a] For destroying the cattle or goods of an enemy, incantations are used; as well as to hinder cows from calving, milk from yielding butter, &c. Another incantation is used to extract fish bones from the throat. They have incantations also for almost every disease; as, the head-ache, tooth-ache, fever, dysentery, leprosy, madness, burns, scalds, eruptions on the skin, &c. In the tooth-ache they are taught to imagine, that by the power of the incantation a small grub is extracted from the tooth. An incantation is repeated to make a tree grow in the belly of an enemy, as well as to obtain preservation from snakes, tigers, witches, ghosts, and all other destructive things; and to drive away serpents, or wild beasts. If any one has been robbed, he prevails upon a person to read an incantation to discover the thief. If any one, who has power to injure another, be offended, the Hindoos read an incantation to appease him. If a person has a trial depending in a court of justice, he reads an incantation while putting on his turban, that he may gain his cause. The caste of Hindoos who keep snakes for a show, repeat incantations that they may handle these snakes without harm. Other incantions are mentioned, by which a person is able to conceal himself, when in the act of doing any thing requiring secrecy.

SECT. XXVII.—*Impure Orgies, with Flesh, spirituous Liquors, &c. (Pōōrnabhishékŭ.)*

SOME of the worshippers of the female deities assume the profession of brŭmhŭcharēēs; among whom the ceremony called pōōrnabhishékŭ is known, and which is performed in the night, in

[a] Some incantations must be read every day, others preserve their power three, and some eight days; but no incantation will *keep good* longer than eight days, without being read afresh.

a secret manner, at the house of the person who understands the formulas. He who wishes to be initiated into these rites, raises an altar of earth in the house appointed, and scatters some peas on it, which sprout out by the time the altar is used. On the day preceding the rites, he performs the vriddhee-shraddhŭ in the name of his deceased ancestors; and during the whole of the following night, repeats the name of the goddess to be worshipped, rehearses her praise, eats flesh, drinks spirits, &c. On the following day, he takes to the house appointed some flesh, (of any animal,) spirituous liquors, rice, fish, and many other offerings; with nine females of different castes, (one of which must be a bramhŭn's daughter,) and nine men, (brŭmhŭcharēēs;) with one female for the priest, and another for himself. The priest next takes nine pans of water, and places on them branches of different trees, and sets up some plantain trunks around them; after which the person to be initiated presents a garment to the priest, and intreats him to anoint him. The priest then offers to the goddess, an intoxicating beverage made with the leaves of hemp; of which all present, both women and men partake. He next rubs on the foreheads of the persons present some red lead, and worships the goddess, the guardian deity of the person to be initiated, making the latter repeat it; and worships the men and women who are present, presenting to each a piece of cloth and other offerings. Next the priest gives to the women spirituous liquors, in cups made of the cocoanut, or of human skulls. What they leave is taken out of the cups, mixed together, and given to the men. The women then arise one by one, and, dipping the branches into the pans of water, sprinkle the person to be initiated, repeating incantations. This action is repeated by the priest, who changes the name of the disciple, and gives him one expressive of the state into which he is entering, as, Anŭndŭ-nat'hŭ, i. e., the lord of joy. If after this the disciple should become a religious mendicant, he is called a Vyŭktavŭ-dhōōtŭ: if he continue in a secular state, he is called a Gooptavŭ-dhōōtŭ.[b] All the persons present continue repeating the names of their guardian deities, and at intervals partake of the offerings, without considering the distinctions of caste, or the unlawfulness of the food. After midnight, acts of obscenity are perpetrated so abominable, that the bramhŭn who gave me this account could only repeat them in part.[c] After this, the priest worships one or more females, the daughters of bramhŭns, and sacrifices a goat to Bhŭgŭvŭtēē. The initiated then offers a

[b] The first of these two names implies, that the person makes no secret of his being in the order into which he is initiated. He therefore becomes a religious mendicant, and publicly drinks and smokes intoxicating herbs. The latter, after initiation, continues in a secular state, and drinks spirituous liquors in secret.

[c] Ramŭ-nat'hŭ, the second Sŭngskritŭ pŭndit in the college, informed a friend of mine, that he once watched one of these groups unobserved, when spirits were poured on the head of a naked woman, while another drank them as they ran from her body.

present of money to the priest, and to the females and males present. The remainder of the night is spent in eating, drinking spirits, and repeating the names of different deities. These abominable ceremonies are enjoined in most of the tŭntrŭ shastrŭs. The bramhŭn who gave me this account had procured it from a brŭmhŭcharēē, by pretending that he wished to perform these rites.

In the year 1809, Trikonŭ-goswamēē, a vyŭktavŭ-dhōōtŭ died at Kalēē-ghatŭ, in the following manner:—Three days before his death he dug a grave near his hut, in a place surrounded by three vilwŭ trees, which he himself had planted. In the evening he placed a lamp in the grave, in which he made an offering of flesh, greens, rice, &c. to the shackals, repeating it the next evening. The following day he obtained from a rich native ten rupees worth of spirituous liquors, and invited a number of mendicants, who sat drinking with him till twelve at noon, when he asked among the spectators at what hour it would be full moon; being informed, he went and sat in his grave, and continued drinking liquors. Just before the time for the full moon, he turned his head towards the temple of Kalēē, and informed the spectators that he had come to Kalēē-ghatŭ with the hope of seeing the goddess, not the image in the temple. He had frequently been urged by different persons to visit the temple; but though he had not assigned a reason for his omission, he now asked, what he was to go and see there:—a temple? He could see that where he was. A piece of stone made into a face, or the silver hands? He could see stones and silver any where else. He wished to see the goddess herself; but he had not, in this body, obtained the sight. However, he had still a mouth and a tongue, and he would again call upon her. He then called out aloud, twice, 'Kalēē! Kalēē!' and almost immediately died;—probably from excessive intoxication. The spectators, though Hindoos, (who in general despise a drunkard,) considered this man as a great saint, who had foreseen his own death when in health: he had not less than four hundred disciples.

The persons who have gone through the ceremony of Pōōrnabhishékŭ conceal this fact as much as possible, as the drinking of spirits is disgraceful. They renounce all the ceremonies of the other Hindoos, as far as they can do it without incurring disgrace and loss of caste.

Two bramhŭns, who sat with me when I was finishing this account, assured me, that the drinking of spirits was now so common, that out of sixteen Hindoos, two drank spirits in secret, and about one in sixteen in public.[d] Several of the Hindoo rajas, who

[d] They offer, or pretend to offer, these spirits to the idols, and then the drinking, or drinking to excess, is no crime in the opinion of these brŭmhŭcharēēs. Amongst the regular Hindoos, the eating of flesh is a crime, but eating flesh that has been offered to an image is an innocent action.

had received the initiating incantations of the female deities, are said to have given themselves up to the greatest excesses in drinking spirits.

SECT. XXVIII.—*Burning of Widows alive.*

THE following and other passages from the Hindoo shastrŭs have no doubt given rise to this singularly shocking practice.

'O Fire, let these women, with bodies anointed with clarified butter, eyes (coloured) with stibium, and void of tears, enter thee, the parent of water, that they may not be separated from their husbands, but may be in union with excellent husbands, be sinless, and jewels among women.—*Rig-vĕdŭ.*

'There are 35,000,000 hairs on the human body. The woman who ascends the pile with her husband, will remain so many years in heaven.—As the snake-catcher draws the serpent from its hole, so she, rescuing her husband, (from hell,) rejoices with him.—The woman who expires on the funeral pile with her husband, purifies the family of her mother, her father and her husband.—If the husband be a bramhŭnicide, an ungrateful person, or a muderer of his friend, the wife by burning with him purges away his sins.—There is no virtue greater than a virtuous[e] woman's burning herself with her husband.—No other effectual duty is known for virtuous women, at any time after the death of their lords, except casting themselves into the same fire.—As long as a woman, in her successive transmigrations, shall decline burning herself, like a faithful wife, on the same fire with her deceased lord, so long shall she not be exempted from springing again to life in the body of some female animal.'—*Ungira.*

'If a woman who had despised her husband, and had done what was contrary to his mind, should (even) from mercenary motives, as fear, or a suspension of the reasoning powers, die with her husband, she shall be purged from all (crimes.)'—*Mŭhabharŭtŭ.*

'Though he have sunk to a region of torment, be restrained in dreadful bonds, have reached the place of anguish, be seized by the imps of Yŭmŭ, be exhausted of strength, and afflicted and tortured for his crimes; still, as a serpent-catcher unerringly drags a serpent from his hole, so does she draw her husband from hell, and ascend with him to heaven by the power of devotion.—If the

[e] The terms Sadhwēē and Sŭtēē, here rendered virtuous, are thus explained by Harēētŭ:—'commiserating with her husband in trouble, rejoicing in his joys, neglecting herself when he is gone from home, and dying at his death.' In the Mŭtshyŭ pooranŭ it is said, 'By the favour of a chaste woman (Sadhwēē) the universe is preserved, on which account she is to be regarded by kings and people as a goddess.'

wife be within one day's journey of the place where the husband died, and signify her wish to burn with him, the burning of his corpse shall be delayed till her arrival.—If the husband die on the third day of the wife's menstrual discharge, and she desire to burn with him, the burning of his corpse shall be delayed one day to accommodate her.'—*Vyasŭ.*

'If the husband be out of the country when he dies, let the virtuous wife take his slippers, (or any thing else which belongs to his dress,) and binding them (or it) on her breast, after purification, enter a separate fire.'—*Brŭmhŭ pooranŭ.*

'A bramhŭnēē cannot burn herself on a separate pile.' *Goŭtŭmŭ.* —'But this is an eminent virtue in another woman.' *Ooshŭna.*

'A woman with a young child, pregnant, doubtful whether she is pregnant or not, or menstruous, cannot ascend the pile. *Vrihŭn-narŭdēēyŭ pooranŭ.*—The Vishnoo pooranŭ adds, 'or lately brought to bed, (within 20 or 30 days,) cannot,' &c.

I do not find, that it is common for women to reveal their intention of being burnt with their husbands while both parties are in health. A few, however, avow this in confidence to their husbands, and there may be circumstances in the family which may lead to the expectation of such an event. In some families, for several generations, the widow invariably perishes at the death of her husband; and thus established custom exacts this self-immolation from every woman, who has been so unhappy as to have become united to such a family. How shocking to the female herself, had she Christian feelings, to know that such a death awaits her! How shocking to the son, had he the feelings of a man, to know that he is doomed to perpetrate so horrible a matricide!

When the husband is directed by the physician to be carried to the river side, there being then no hopes of his recovery, the wife declares her resolution to be burnt with him.[f] In this case, she is treated with great respect by her neighbours, who bring her delicate food, &c., and when the husband is dead, she again declares her resolution to be burnt with his body. Having broken a small, branch from the mangoe tree, she takes it with her, and proceeds to the body, where she sits down. The barber then paints the sides of her feet red; after which she bathes, and puts on new clothes. During these preparations, the drum beats a certain sound, by which it is known, that a widow is about to be burnt with the corpse of her husband. On hearing this all the village assembles. The son, or if there be no son, a relation, or the head man of the village

[f] Dying in the sight of the Ganges is not considered as absolutely necessary, however, if a woman perish with the dead body; and sometimes a wife forbids the removal of her sick husband, assuring her friends, that she means to be burnt, and thus make the salvation of her husband certain without the help of Gŭnga.

provides the articles necessary for the ceremony. A hole is first dug in the ground, round which stakes are driven into the earth, and thick green stakes laid across to form a kind of bed; and upon these are laid, in abundance, dry faggots, hemp, clarified butter, pitch, &c. The officiating bramhŭn now causes the widow to repeat the formulas, in which she prays, that 'as long as fourteen Indrŭs reign, or as many years as there are hairs on her head, she may abide in heaven with her husband; that the heavenly dancers during this time may wait on her and her husband; and that by this act of merit all the ancestors of her father, mother, and husband, may ascend to heaven.' She now presents her ornaments to her friends, ties some red cotton on both wrists, puts two new combs in her hair, paints her forehead, and takes into the end of the cloth that she wears some parched rice and kourees. While this is going forward, the dead body is anointed with clarified butter and bathed, prayers are repeated over it, and it is dressed in new clothes. The son next takes a handful of boiled rice, prepared for the purpose, and, repeating an incantation, offers it in the name of his deceased father. Ropes and another piece of cloth are spread upon the wood, and the dead body is then laid upon the pile. The widow next walks round the funeral pile seven times, strewing parched rice and kourees as she goes, which some of the spectators endeavour to catch, under the idea that they will cure diseases.[g] The widow now ascends the fatal pile, or rather throws herself down upon it by the side of the dead body. A few female ornaments having been laid over her, the ropes are drawn over the bodies which are tied together, and faggots placed upon them. The son then, averting his head, puts fire to the face of his father, and at the same moment several persons light the pile at different sides, when women, relations, &c. set up a cry: more faggots are now thrown upon the pile with haste, and two bamboo levers are brought over the whole, to hold down the bodies and the pile.[h] Several persons are employed in holding down these levers, and others in throwing water upon them, that they may not be scorched. While the fire is burning, more clarified butter, pitch, and faggots, are thrown into it, till the bodies are consumed. It may take about two hours before the whole is burnt, but I conceive the woman must be dead in a few minutes after the fire has been kindled. At the close, each of the persons who have been employed, takes up a burning stick and throws it on the remaining fire. The bones, &c. that may be left, are cast into the Ganges. The place where the bodies have been burnt is plentifully washed with water; after which the son of the deceased makes two balls of boiled rice, and, with an incan-

[g] Mothers hang the kourees round the necks of sick children.

[h] A person sometimes takes one of these bamboos, after the bodies are burnt, and, making a bow and arrow with it, repeats incantations over it. He then makes an image of some enemy with clay, and lets fly the arrow into this image. The person whose image is thus pierced is said to be immediately seized with a pain in his breast.

tation, offers them in the name of his father and mother, and lays them on the spot where they were burnt. The persons who have been engaged in burning the bodies now bathe; and each one, taking up water in his hands three times, and repeating incantations, pours out drink-offerings to the deceased. The son binds upon his loins, in coming up out of the water, a shred of new cloth; which he wears, if a bramhŭn, ten days. After this the family return home, or remain till evening; or, if the burning has taken place in the evening, till the next morning. Before entering the house, they touch a piece of hot iron, and also fire. This is done as a charm against evil spirits.

Soon after my arrival in Bengal, I was an eye-witness to two instances of the burning of widows to death:—on the latter occasion two women were burnt together; one of them appeared to possess great resolution, but the other was almost dead with fear. In the year 1812, I saw another widow burnt to death at Soondŭrŭ-poorŭ, a distance of about three miles from Serampore; and in the month of November, 1812, the wife of Ramŭ-nidhee, a banker, of Serampore, was burnt alive with the dead body of her husband, not half a mile from the Mission-house. These facts respecting the murder of the helpless widow as a religious ceremony are indeed so notorious, that the most careless traveller may convince himself, if he take the least notice of what is doing on the banks of the river. The natives do not attempt to hide these murders, but rather glory in them as proofs of the divine nature of their religion. The facts hereafter inserted have been voluntarily given to me by respectable natives, most of whom were eye-witnesses of what they here testify.

Several years ago, Ram-Nat'hŭ, the second Sŭngskritŭ pŭndit in the College of Fort-William, saw thirteen women burn themselves with one Mooktŭa-ramŭ, of Oola, near Shantee-poorŭ. After the pile, which was very large, had been set on fire, a quantity of pitch being previously thrown into it to make it burn the fiercer, another of this man's wives came, and insisted on burning: while she was repeating the formulas, however, her resolution failed, and she wished to escape; but her son, perceiving this, pushed her into the fire, which had been kindled on the sloping bank of the river, and the poor woman, to save herself, caught hold of another woman, a wife also of the deceased, and pulled her into the fire, where they both perished.

About the year 1789, Ŭbhŭyŭ-chŭrŭnŭ, a bramhŭn, saw four women burnt with Ramŭ-kantŭ, a kooleēnŭ bramhŭn, at Vasŭ-dŭrooneē, near Kaleē-ghatŭ. Three of these women were already surrounded by the flames when the fourth arrived. She insisted on being burnt with them: accordingly, after going rapidly through the preparatory ceremonies, (the bramhŭns in the mean time bringing a large quantity of combustible materials,) some fresh wood was laid near the fire already kindled, upon which this infatuated female threw herself. In a moment faggots, oil, pitch, &c. were thrown upon her, and, amidst the shouts of the mob, she expired.

Ramŭ-Hŭree, a bramhŭn, had three wives living at Khŭrŭdŭh, near Calcutta, at the time of his death, about the year 1802. One of them was deranged; with another he had never cohabited, and by the other he had one son. The latter had agreed with her husband, that, whenever he should die, she would burn with him; and he promised her, that if he died at Patna, where his employer lived, the body should be sent down to Khŭrŭdŭh. This woman touched her husband's body at the time of this agreement, as a solemn ratification[h] of what she said.[i] After some time this man died at Patna, and a friend fastened the body in a box, and sent it down on a boat. As soon as it arrived at Khŭrŭdŭh, the news was sent to his relations. The wife who had made the agreement failed in her resolution, and sat in the house weeping. Her son, who was grown to manhood, ordered her repeatedly, in the most brutal manner, to proceed to the funeral pile; and reminded her, that it was through her that his father's body had been brought so far: but she refused, and still remained weeping. While this was going forward, the deranged wife, hearing that her husband was dead, and that his body had arrived at the landing-place, instantly declared that she would burn with him. The people endeavoured to terrify her, and divert her from her purpose; but she persisted in affirming that she would positively burn. She came to the house, and poured the most bitter reproaches on the wife who was unwilling to die. This poor deranged wretch had a chain on her leg: a spectator proposed to take it off, and lead her to the funeral pile; and the third wife arriving, she was led with this deranged woman to the body: the wood and other articles for the funeral pile were prepared, and a large crowd had assembled by the river side. As soon as the deranged wife saw the dead body, which was very much disfigured, and exceedingly

[h] The Hindoos also make oath while touching one of the shastrŭs, or the shalgramŭ, or a cow, or fire, or the toolŭsee, or a roodrakshŭ string of beads, or rice. When made before a bramhŭn, or in a temple, or by laying the hand on the head of a son, an oath is ratified.

[i] The Hindoos relate a number of stories respecting women who promised their husbands to burn with them, but afterwards shrank from the task. A story of this kind is related of a man named Gopalŭ-bharŭ, who pretended to die, in order to try the faithfulness of his wife. As soon as she thought he was really dead, she declared she would not die on his funeral pile; when the (supposed) dead man arose, and upbraided her for her insincerity. Another story is related of Shŭmbhoo-ramŭ, of Arachya, in Burdwan, who had three wives, but was most attached to the youngest. This woman had promised her husband to burn with him after his death, and he had in consequence behaved with the greatest coolness towards his other wives, and had heaped all his wealth on this favourite. A person suggested doubts respecting the sincerity of this woman's declaration. To try her, on a certain occasion, when absent from home, her husband sent a relation to say he was dead, and to urge her to go to the spot to be burnt with him. As soon as she heard the tidings, instead of proceeding to the spot where the body was supposed to be waiting, she locked up all the jewels, &c. her husband had given her, and set her husband's relations at defiance. In a few hours the (dead) husband arrived, degraded this wife, and for the future became more attached to the other two.

offensive, she declared it was not her husband; that in fact they were going to burn her with a dead cow. She poured curses on them all, and protested she would not burn with a dead cow.[k] The other female, who had never touched her husband, except at the marriage ceremony, was then bound to this putrid carcase, and devoured by the flames.

About the year 1796, the following most shocking and atrocious murder, under the name of sŭhŭ-mŭrŭnŭ,[l] was perpetrated at Mujilpoorŭ, about a day's journey south from Calcutta. Bancha-ramŭ, a bramhŭn of the above place dying, his wife at a late hour went to be burnt with the body: all the previous ceremonies were performed; she was fastened on the pile, and the fire was kindled; but the night was dark and rainy. When the fire began to scorch this poor woman, she contrived to disentangle herself from the dead body, and creeping from under the pile, hid herself among some brush-wood. In a little time it was discovered that there was only one body on the pile. The relations immediately took the alarm, and searched for the poor wretch; the son soon dragged her forth, and insisted that she should throw herself on the pile again, or drown or hang herself. She pleaded for her life at the hands of her own son, and declared that she could not embrace so horrid a death—but she pleaded in vain: the son urged, that he should lose his caste, and that therefore he would die, or she should. Unable to presuade her to hang or drown herself, the son and others present then tied her hands and feet, and threw her on the funeral pile, where she quickly perished.

Gopēē-nat'hŭ, a bramhŭn employed in the Serampore Printing-office, was informed by his nephew, that in the year 1799, he saw thirty-seven females burnt alive with the remains of Ŭnŭntŭ-ramŭ, a bramhŭn of Bagna-para, near Nŭdēēya. This koolēēnŭ bramhŭn had more than a hundred wives. At the first kindling of the fire, only three of them were present; but *the fire was kept burning three days!* When one or more arrived, the ceremonies were performed, *and they threw themselves on the blazing fire!* On the first day, three were burnt; on the second fifteen; and on the third nineteen! Among these, some were forty years old, and others as young as sixteen. The three first had lived with this bramhŭn; the others had seldom seen him. From one family he had married four sisters; two of these were among the slaughtered victims.

In the year 1812, a koolēēnŭ bramhŭn, who had married twenty-five women, died at Choona-khalee. Thirteen died during his life-

[k] In the month of January, 1813, a poor deranged woman was burnt alive with the corpse of her husband, Rŭghoo-nat'hŭ, a bramhŭn, at Bŭjŭra-poorŭ, in the zillah of Krishnŭ-nŭgŭrŭ.

[l] Sŭhŭ, with; mŭrŭnŭ, death.

time; the remaining twelve perished with him on the funeral pile, leaving thirty children to deplore the fatal effects of this horrid system.

Some years ago, a koolēēnŭ bramhŭn, of considerable property, died at Sookhŭchŭrŭ, three miles east of Serampore. He had married more than forty women, eighteen of whom perished on the funeral pile. On this occasion a fire extending ten or twelve yards in length was prepared, into which they threw themselves, leaving more than forty children.

About the year 1802, the wife of a man of property of the writer caste was burnt at Kashēē-poorŭ, in the suburbs of Calcutta. The bramhŭn who witnessed this scene informed me, that when he went to the spot, he saw a vast crowd of people assembled; and amongst the rest the above female, a girl about fourteen years old, and another female, of a different caste, who had cohabited with the deceased. The girl addressed herself to the mistress of her husband, and asked her what she did there: it was true, her husband had never loved her, nor had he for one day since their marriage lived with her; yet she was now resolved to enjoy his company after death. She added, (continuing her address to the mistress of her husband,) 'If, however, you will accompany him, come, let us burn together; if not, arise and depart.' She then asked the woman what her husband had bequeathed to her, and was answered that he had given her twenty-five rupees, and some clothes. To this the wife of the deceased added twenty-five more. After this conversation, the bramhŭns hastened the ceremonies; her friends entreated her to eat some sweetmeats, but she declined it, and declared that she would eat nothing but that which she came to eat, (fire.) At this time the clouds gathered thick, and there was the appearance of heavy rain: some persons urged delay till the rain was over; but she requested them to hasten the business, for she was ready. A bramhŭn now arrived, and entreated the favour of this woman to forgive a debt due to her husband, for which his brother was in confinement. She forgave it, leaving a written order behind her, to which she affixed her mark. After the ceremonies by the side of the river, and near the pile, were concluded, she laid herself down on the pile, placing one arm under the head of the deceased, and the other over his breast, and they were thus tied together. At the time of lighting the pile, the rain fell in torrents, and the fire was so partially lighted, that during half an hour it only singed her clothes and her hair. This devoted female, however, remained in the same posture on the pile till the rain ceased, when, in a few seconds, the fire devoured her. It was reported that she had cohabited with others, but she denied it before she ascended the pile.

An English clergyman, now deceased, once related to me two scenes to which he had been an eye-witness:—one was that of a young woman, who appeared to possess the most perfect serenity of mind during every part of the preparatory ceremonies : calm and placid, she acted as though unconscious of the least danger; she smiled at some, gave presents to others. and walked round the funeral pile, and laid herself down by the dead body, with as much composure as though she had been about to take rest at night. The other scene was very different; the woman, middle-aged and corpulent, appeared to go through the business with extreme reluctance and agitation; the bramhŭns watched her, followed her closely, held her up, and led her round the funeral pile, and seemed to feel uneasy till they had tied her fast to the dead body, and had brought the faggots and bamboo levers over her. This clergyman added, that he saw one of this woman's arms move, as in convulsive motions, for some time after the pile was lighted. The Hindoos say, that it is a proof the woman was a great sinner, if any part of her body is seen to move after the pile has been lighted; and, on the contrary, if she is not seen to move, they exclaim, 'Ah! what a perfect creature she was! What a blessed sŭhŭ-mŭrŭnŭ was her's!' A respectable native once told me, that he had heard of a woman's shrieking dreadfully after she was laid on the pile, which, however, did not save her life.[m]

Instances of children of eight or ten years of age thus devoting themselves are not uncommon. About the year 1804, a child eight years old was burnt with the dead body of Hŭree-nat'hŭ, bramhŭn of Elo, near Calcutta. At the time the news arrived of the death of this child's husband, she was playing with other children at a neighbour's house. Having just before been severely chastised by her aunt, and having formerly suffered much from her, she resolved to burn with the dead body, in order to avoid similar treatment in future; nor could her relations induce her to alter her resolution. She said she would enter the fire, but would not go back to her aunt. As soon as she was laid on the pile, she appeared to die, (no doubt from fear,) even before the fire touched her. The Hindoos say, it is often the case, that the female who is really Sadhwēē, is united to her husband immediately on hearing the news of his death, without the delay of the fire.—Another instance of the same kind occurred in the year 1802, at Vŭrisha, near Calcutta; a child, eight years old, was burnt with her husband. Before she went to the funeral pile, she was compelled to put her hand upon some burning coals, and hold it there for some time, to convince her friends that she should not shrink at the sight of the fire.—About the year 1794, a girl, fifteen years old, who had been delivered of her first child about three weeks, was burnt with her husband, Dévēē-chŭrŭnŭ, a bramhŭn of Mŭniramŭ-poorŭ, near

[m] I am credibly informed, that on the banks of the Brŭmhŭ-pootrŭ, the Hindoos do not lay faggots on the bodies, nor are bamboos used as levers to hold them down; but the widow lies on the pile with her arms round her husband, and fire is kindled beneath them.

Barrack-poorŭ. Her friends remonstrated with her, and did all except (what they ought to have done) use force. When they urged the situation of the infant she would leave, she begged they would not disturb her mind with such things: it was only a female child, and therefore the leaving it was of less consequence. After she had mounted the pile, she sat up, and assured the officiating bramhŭn she then recollected, that in a former birth he was her father.

Women eighty years old and upwards sometimes burn with their husbands. About the year 1791, Gopalŭ-nayalŭnkarŭ, a very learned bramhŭn, died at Nŭdēēya. He was supposed to have been one hundred years old at the time of his death; his wife about eighty. She was almost in a state of second childhood, yet her gray hairs availed, nothing against this most abominable custom. —A similar instance occurred about the year 1809, at Shanteepoorŭ, when the wife of Ramŭ-chŭndrŭ-vŭsoo, a kayŭst'hŭ, at the age of eighty or eighty-five, was burnt with the corpse of her husband.

Mrityoonjŭyŭ, the first Sŭngskritŭ pŭndit in the College of Fort-William, once saw a bramhŭnēē at Rŭngŭ-poorŭ, who had escaped from the pile. She was carried away by a mat-maker, from whom she eloped, and afterwards lived with a Mŭsŭlman groom.—About the year 1804, a woman who had lived with a man as his wife, burnt herself with his body at Kalēē-ghatŭ, near Calcutta.—Some years ago, a sepoy from the upper provinces died at Khiddirŭ-poorŭ, near Calcutta. The woman who had cohabited with him went to the head land-owner, and requested him to provide the materials for burning her with the dead body. He did so, and this adulteress entered the flames, and was consumed with the dead body of her paramour.

In Orissa, the defenceless widow is compelled to cast herself into a pit of fire. If, on the death of a raja, his wife burn herself with him, his concubines are seized, and by beating, dragging, binding, and other forcible methods, are compelled to throw themselves into the pit, where they are all destroyed together. On this subject I beg leave to insert a letter drawn up by Pŭrŭshoo-ramŭ, a learned bramhŭn:—'Shrēē Pŭrŭshoo-ramŭ writes: I have myself seen the wives of one of the rajas of Oorisya burn with their husband. These are the particulars:—after the death of raja Gopēē-nat'hŭdévŭ, the head-queen, of her own accord, being prepared to be burnt with the body, a pit was dug, and quantities of wood piled up in it, upon which the corpse was laid, and upon this more faggots: when the fire blazed with the greatest fury, the headqueen cast herself into the flames and perished. The two other wives of the raja were unwilling to follow this example; but they were seized by force, and thrown into the pit, and consumed. This happened about the year 1793.'

The widows of the yogēēs, a description of weavers, are sometimes buried alive with their deceased husbands. If the person have died near the Ganges, the grave is dug by the side of the river, at the bottom of which they spread a new cloth, and on it lay the dead body. The widow then bathes, puts on new clothes, and paints her feet; and after various ceremonies, descends into the pit that is to swallow her up: in this living tomb she sits down, and places the head of her deceased husband on her knee, having a lamp near her. The priest (not a bramhŭn) sits by the side of the grave, and repeats certain ceremonies, while the friends of the deceased walk round the grave several times, repeating 'Hŭree bŭl! Hŭree bŭl!' (that is, literally, 'Repeat the name of Hŭree;' but in its common use it is equivalent to 'Huzza! Huzza!'). The friends (if rich) cast into the grave garments, sweetmeats, sandal wood, rupees, milk, curds, clarified butter, or something of this kind; and the widow directs a few trifles to be given to her friends or children. The son also casts a new garment into the grave, with flowers, sandal wood, &c. after which earth is carefully thrown all round the widow, till it has arisen as high as her shoulders, when the relations throw earth in as fast as possible, till they have raised a mound of earth on the grave; when they tread it down with their feet, and thus bury the miserable wretch alive. They place on the grave sandal wood, rice, curds, a lamp, &c. and then, walking round the grave three times, return home.——Among the voishnŭvŭs also are instances of widows being buried alive with the dead bodies of their husbands. —On enquiring among the bramhŭns, and other Hindoos employed in the Serampore printing-office, I found that these murders were much more frequently practised than I had supposed: almost every one had seen widows thus buried alive, or had heard of them from undoubted authority.

I could easily increase the number of these accounts so as to form a volume; but I am not anxious to swell this work with more facts of this nature: these are sufficient to fill the mind of the benevolent with the deepest compassion for the miserable victims of this shocking superstition.

The Hindoo shastrŭs permit a woman to alter her resolution, even on the funeral pile, and command such a person to observe a severe fast as an atonement. This fast, however, may be commuted by gifts to bramhŭns. The Vishnoo pooranŭ directs such a female to become a brŭmhŭcharēē; which profession obliges the person to abstain from every pleasure, from chewing betel or other exhilirating herbs, from anointing herself with oil,[n] &c. Notwith-

[n] This anointing is called ŭbhishékŭ: when oil is applied to the crown of the head, and reaches to all the limbs, it is called ŭbhyŭngŭ. There seems to be a strong affinity betwixt the Jewish and Hindoo methods of anointing in this respect: 'It is like the precious ointment upon the head, that ran down upon the beard, even Aaron's beard, that went down to the skirts of his garments.'

standing this provision of the shastrŭ, I am informed that at present a widow, if she go to the dead body, declaring that she will be burnt with it, is never permitted to return: or, should such a case occur, she is delivered up to persons of the lowest caste to do what they will with her; she never goes back to her relations.

The desire of Hindoo women to die with their husbands, and the calmness of many in going through the ceremonies which precede this terrible death, are circumstances almost, if not altogether, unparalleled. It is another proof of the amazing power which this superstition has over the minds of its votaries.[o] Among other circumstances which urge them to this dreadful deed, we may rank the following:—First, the védŭs, and other shastrŭs, recommend it, and promise the widow that she shall deliver her husband from hell, and enjoy a long happiness with him in heaven; secondly, long custom has familiarised their minds to the deed; thirdly, by this act they escape the disgrace of widowhood, and their names are recorded among the honorable of their families;[p] fourthly, they avoid being starved and ill-treated by their relations; and lastly, the Hindoos treat the idea of death with comparative indifference, as being only changing one body for another, as the snake changes his skin. If they considered death as introducing a person into an unalterable state of existence, and God, the judge, as requiring purity of heart, no doubt these ideas would make them weigh well a step pregnant with such momentous consequences.

The conduct of the bramhŭns at the burning of widows is so unfeeling, that those who have represented them to the world as the mildest and most amiable of men, need only attend on one of these occasions to convince them, that they have greatly imposed on mankind. Where a family of bramhŭns suppose that the burning of a mother, or their brother's or uncle's wife, or any other female of the family, is necessary to support the credit of the family, the woman knows she must go, and that her death is expected. She is aware also, that if she should not burn, she will be treated with the greatest cruelty, and continually reproached, as having entailed disgrace on the family. The bramhŭn who has greatly assisted me in this work, has very seriously assured me, that he believed violence was seldom used to compel a woman to ascend the pile; nay, that after she has declared her resolution, her friends

[o] Such a widow reflects thus: 'It is right that the wife leave the world with her husband; a son can never be to a mother what a husband is to a wife; the extinction of life is the work of a minute; by strangling, by drowning, how soon does the soul leave the body: there are no terrors then in the funeral pile, and I shall at once enter on happiness: what multitudes have died in this manner before me; and if I live, I have nothing but sorrow to expect.'

[p] It is common at Benares to set up, by the side of the river, stone monuments to the memory of widows who have been burnt with the bodies of deceased husbands. Persons coming from bathing bow to these stones, and sprinkle water on them, repeating the words Sŭtēē, Sŭtēē, i. e., *chaste*.

use various arguments to discover whether she be likely to persevere or not; (for if she go to the water side, and there refuse to burn, they consider it an indelible disgrace on the family;) that it is not uncommon for them to demand a proof of her resolution, by obliging her to hold her finger in the fire; if she be able to endure this, they conclude they are safe, and that she will not alter her resolution. If, however, she should flinch at the sight of the pile, &c. they remain deaf to whatever she says; they hurry her through the preparatory ceremonies, attend closely upon her, and go through the work of murder in the most determined manner.

Some years ago, two attempts were made, under the immediate superintendance of Dr. Carey, to ascertain the number of widows burnt alive within a given time. The first attempt was intended to ascertain the number thus burnt within thirty miles of Calcutta, during one year, viz. in 1803. Persons, selected for the purpose, were sent from place to place through that extent, to enquire of the people of each town or village how many had been burnt within the year. The return made a total of FOUR HUNDRED AND THIRTY-EIGHT. Yet very few places east or west of the river Hoogly were visited. To ascertain this matter with greater exactness, ten persons were, in the year 1804, stationed in the different places within the above-mentioned extent of country; each person's station was marked out, and he continued on the watch for six months, taking account of every instance of a widow's being burnt which came under his observation. Monthly reports were sent in; and the result, though less than the preceding year's report, made the number between TWO AND THREE HUNDRED for the year!—If within so small a space several hundred widows were burnt alive in one year, HOW MANY THOUSANDS OF THESE WIDOWS MUST BE MURDERED IN A YEAR—IN SO EXTENSIVE A COUNTRY AS HINDOOSTHAN![q] So that, in fact, the funeral pile devours more than war itself! How truly shocking! Nothing equal to it exists in the whole work of human cruelty! What a tragic history would a complete detail of these burnings make!

SECT. XXIX.—*Voluntary Suicide, (Kamyŭ-Mŭrŭnŭ.*[r]*)*

A NUMBER of expressions in several shastrŭs countenance the practice of voluntary suicide;[s] and some of the smritees, and pooranŭs, lay down rules for Kamyŭ-mŭrŭnŭ; declaring it, however,

[q] It will easily occur to a person familiar with the Holy Scriptures, what a great difference there is betwixt the commands of these Scriptures respecting the widow and the orphan, and the Hindoo shastrŭs. In the former the Divine Being declares himself to be 'the father of the fatherless, the husband of the widow.'

[r] From kamŭ, desire, and mŭrŭnŭ, death.

[s] Many modern works in the English language give too much countenance to this dreadful crime. What is it that unites nominal Christians and Heathens in so many points of doctrine and practice? Mŭnoo says, 'A mansion infested by age and by sorrow let its occupier always cheerfully quit.' Mr. Hume says, 'Whenever pain or sorrow

a crime in a bramhŭn; but meritorious in a shōōdrŭ. The person is directed first to offer an atonement for all his sins, by making a present of gold to bramhŭns, and honoring them with a feast; afterwards, putting on new apparel and adorning himself with garlands of flowers, he is accompanied to the river by a band of music. If he has any property, he gives it to whom he pleases. then, sitting down by the side of the river, he repeats the name of his idol, and proclaims, that he is now about to renounce his life in this place in order to obtain such or such a benefit. After this, he and his friends proceed on a boat, and fastening pans of water to his body, he plunges into the stream. The spectators cry out, 'Hŭree bul! Hŭree bul!' Huzza! Huzza! and then retire. Sometimes a person of property kindly interferes, and offers to relieve the wants of the victim if he will abstain from drowning himself; but the deluded man replies that he wants nothing, as he is going to heaven!

When a person is afflicted with a supposed incurable distemper, or is in distress, or despised, it is common for him to form the resolution of parting with life in the Ganges; or the crime is committed after a vow, at the time of making which the person prayed for some favour in the next birth, as riches, freedom from sorrow, &c. Sick persons sometimes abstain from food for several days while sitting near the river, that life may thus depart from them in sight of the holy stream: but the greater number drown themselves in the presence of the relations; and instances are mentioned, in which persons in the act of self-murder have been forcibly pushed back into the stream by their own offspring! There are different places of the Ganges where it is considered as most desirable for persons thus to murder themselves, and in some cases auspicious days are chosen on which to perform this work of *religious merit;* but a person's drowning himself in any part of the river is supposed to be followed with immediate happiness. At Sagŭrŭ island it is accounted an auspicious sign if the person is speedily seized by a shark, or an alligator; but his future happiness is supposed to be very doubtful if he should remain long in the water before he is drowned. The British Government, for some years past, has sent a guard of sepoys to prevent persons from murdering themselves and their children at this junction of the Ganges with the sea, at the annual festivals held in this place.[t]

so far overcome my patience, as to make me tired of life, I may conclude that I am recalled from my station in the plainest and most express terms. Where is the crime of turning a few ounces of blood from their natural channel?' These are the opinions of Mŭnoo and Hume. The Christian system, in every part, teaches us to say, 'All the days of my appointed time will I wait, till my change come.' In England, where the idea prevails that self-murder excludes from the hope of mercy in the next world, suicides are very common. What then must they be in a country containing so much unrelieved distress as this, and where the inhabitants are persuaded, that self-murder in the Ganges is the very road to future happiness?

[t] In the year 1806, at this place, I saw a bramhŭnēē (dripping with wet and

Some years ago, as Shivŭ-Shiromŭnee,[u] a bramhŭn, was returning from bathing with Kashēē-nat'hŭ, another bramhŭn, at Shantee-poorŭ, they saw a poor old man sitting on the bank of the river, and asked him what he was doing there. He replied, that he was destitute of friends, and was about to renounce his life in the Ganges. Kashēē-nat'hŭ urged him not to delay then, if he was come to die;—but the man seemed to hesitate, and replied, that it was very cold. The bramhŭn (hinting to his companion that he wished to see the sport before he returned home) reproached the poor trembling wretch for his cowardice, and seizing his hand, dragged him to the edge of the bank; where he made him sit down, rubbed over him the purifying clay of the river, and ordered him to repeat the proper incantations. While he was thus, with his eyes closed, repeating these forms, he slipped down, and sunk into the water, which was very deep, and perished!

About the year 1790, a young man of the order of dŭndēēs took up his abode at Kakshalēē, a village near Nŭdēēya, for a few months, and began to grow very corpulent. Reflecting that a person of his order was bound to a life of mortification, and feeling his passions grow stronger and stronger, he resolved to renounce his life in the Ganges. He requested his friends to assist him in this act of self-murder, and they supplied him with a boat, some cord, and two water pans. He then proceeded on the boat into the middle of the stream, and, filling the pans with water, fastened one to his neck, and the other round his loins, and in this manner descended into the water—*to rise no more!* in the presence of a great multitude of applauding spectators. A few years after this another dŭndēē, while suffering under a fever, renounced his life in the Ganges at Nŭdēēya; and nearly at the same time, a dŭndēē at Ariyadŭh, about four miles from Calcutta, in a state of indisposition, refusing all medical aid, (in which indeed he acted according to the rules of his order,) cast himself into the river from a boat, and thus renounced life.

Gŭnga-dhŭrŭ-shastrēē, a learned bramhŭn, informed me, that in the year 1806 he spent near two months at Prŭyagŭ, during which time he saw about *thirty persons drown themselves!* Almost every day he saw or heard of one or more sŭnyasēēs who thus terminated their existence; and several instances occurred in which a man and his wife, having no children, drowned themselves together, praying for some blessings in the next birth.

A friend, in a letter written in the year 1813, says, 'The circumstance which you heard me relate of the poor leper, took

shivering with cold) who had just been prevented by the sepoys from drowning herself;—and during my continuance there I heard of several mothers who had been prevented from murdering their children.

[u] This man related the fact to me himself.

place at Futwa, a little more than a year ago. On hearing the people of my boat declare that a man was going to be drowned, I looked out, and saw the poor creature, who had been deprived by disease of his fingers and toes, but who in other respects appeared healthy, eating very heartily in the presence of his friends. The bank being high, I could not leave the boat till we had proceeded to a considerable distance from the place where the man sat. As I was running towards the spot, I heard the people on the top of the boat call out, " He is drowned ! he is drowned !" His attendants, who appeared to be his relatives, had assisted him to descend the bank ; but whether they pushed him in, or whether he went into the water of his own accord, I cannot tell. He made great efforts to resist the stream, and reach the side, and struggled much before he sunk.—I endeavoured to impress on the spectators the heinousness of this crime ; but they smiled at my concern, and said, 'they had only complied with the wishes of the deceased, who had been deprived by disease of his hands and feet.'

Another friend, in a letter written at Cutwa, in the year 1812, says, 'Last week I witnessed the burning of a leper. A pit about ten cubits in depth was dug, and a fire placed at the bottom of it. The poor man rolled himself into it, but instantly on feeling the fire begged to be taken out, and struggled hard for that purpose. His mother and sister, however, thrust him in again ; and thus, a man who to all appearance might have survived several years, was cruelly burnt to death. I find that the practice is not uncommon in these parts.' This poor wretch died with the notion, that by thus purifying his body in the fire, he should receive a happy transmigration into a healthful body : whereas, if he had died by the disease, he would, after four births, have appeared on earth again as a leper.

Mr. C. in a letter from Agra, dated in the year 1812, says, 'I went out a few mornings ago, and came to an enclosed place, which, on enquiry, I found had been rendered sacred by ten persons having been buried alive there. I am informed, that many persons visit the place every Monday afternoon for worship ; and that once or twice a year large crowds assemble here, and at another similar place near the city. There is great reason to fear that this practice is very common in these parts. At Allahabad many drown themselves every year ; and at Vrindavŭnŭ many are buried alive or drowned every year, probably every month.'

The Hindoos relate that there existed formerly at Kshēērŭ, a village near Nŭdēēya, an instrument called kŭrŭvŭt, which was used by devotees to cut off their own heads. The instrument was made in the shape of a half moon, with a sharp edge, and was placed at the back of the neck, having chains fastened at the two extremities. The infatuated devotee, placing his feet on the stirrups, gave a violent jerk, and severed his head from his body.

Sect. XXX.—*Persons casting themselves from Precipices, &c.*

Another way in which the Hindoo shastrŭs allow a person to renounce life, is by throwing himself from a mountain, or some other eminence. Bengal is a perfect plain; and I have not learnt how far this permission of the shastrŭ is acted upon in the mountainous parts of Hindoost'hanŭ.

Sect. XXXI.—*Dying under the Wheels of Jŭgŭnnat'hŭ's Car.*

Amongst the immense multitudes assembled at the drawing of this car, are numbers afflicted with diseases, and others involved in worldly troubles, or worn out with age and neglect. It often happens that such persons, after offering up a prayer tō the idol, that they may obtain happiness or riches in the next birth, cast themselves under the wheels of the car, and are instantly crushed to death. Great numbers of these cars are to be seen in Bengal; and every year, in some place or other, persons thus destroy themselves. At Jŭgŭnnat'hŭ-kshétrŭ, in Orissa, several perish annually. Many are accidentally thrown down by the pressure of the crowd, and are crushed to death. The victims who devote themselves to death in these forms have an entire confidence that they shall, by this meritorious act of self-murder, attain to happiness.

I beg leave here to insert the following extract of a letter from an officer to a friend, to confirm the facts related in this and the two preceding sections: 'I have known a woman, whose courage failed her on the pile, bludgeoned by her own dear kindred.' This I have told the author of 'The Vindication of the Hindoos.'—I have taken a Gentoo out of the Ganges: I perceived him at night, and called out to the boat-men.—'Sir, he is gone; he belongs to God.' 'Yes, but take him up, and God will get him hereafter.' We got him up at the last gasp: I gave him some brandy, and called it physic. 'O Sir, my caste is gone!' 'No, it is physic.' 'It is not that, Sir! but my family will never receive me. I am an outcaste!' 'What! for saving your life?' 'Yes.' 'Never mind such a family.'—I let above one hundred men out of limbo at

Jŭgŭnnat'hŭ: there were a thousand dead and dying;—all in limbo starving, to extort money from them.[x]

Sect. XXXII.—*Infanticide.*

The people in some parts of India, particularly the inhabitants of Orissa, and of the eastern parts of Bengal, frequently offer their children to the goddess Gŭnga. The following reason is assigned for this practice:—When a woman has been long married, and has no children, it is common for the man, or his wife, or both of them, to make a vow to the goddess Gŭnga, that if she will bestow the blessing of children upon them, they will devote the first-born to her. If after this vow they have children, the eldest is nourished till a proper age, which may be three, four, or more years, according to circumstances, when, on a particular day appointed for bathing in any holy part of the river, they take the child with them, and offer it to this goddess: the child is encouraged to go farther and farther into the water till it is carried away by the stream, or is pushed off by its inhuman parents. Sometimes a stranger seizes the child, and brings it up; but it is abandoned by its parents from the moment it floats in the water, and if no one be found more humane than they, it infallibly perishes. The principal places in Bengal where this species of murder is practised, are, Gŭnga-Sagŭrŭ, where the river Hoogly disembogues itself into the sea; Voidyŭvatēē, a town about fourteen miles to the north of Calcutta; Trivénēē, Nŭdēēya, Chakdŭh and Prŭyagŭ.

The following shocking custom appears to prevail principally in the northern districts of Bengal. If an infant refuse the mother's breast, and decline in health, it is said to be under the influence of some malignant spirit. Such a child is sometimes put into a basket, and hung up in a tree where this evil spirit is supposed to reside. It is generally destroyed by ants, or birds of prey; but sometimes perishes by neglect, though fed and clothed daily. If it should not be dead at the expiration of three days, the mother receives it home again, and nurses it: but this seldom happens. The late Mr. Thomas, a Missionary, once saved and restored to its mother, an infant which had fallen out of a basket, at Bholahatŭ, near Malda, at the moment a jackal was running away with it. As this gentleman and Mr. Carey were afterwards passing under the same tree, they found a basket hanging in the branches containing the skeleton of another infant, which had been devoured by ants. The custom is unknown in many places, but, it is to be feared, is too common in others.

In the north western parts of Hindoost'hanŭ, the horrid practice of sacrificing female children as soon as born, has been known

[x] I have not the authority of this gentleman for inserting this extract: but I rely on his known benevolence to excuse the freedom I have thus taken.

from time immemorial. The Hindoos ascribe this custom to a prophecy delivered by a bramhŭn to Dweēpŭ-singhŭ, a rajŭ-pootŭ king, that his race would lose the sovereignty through one of his female posterity. Another opinion is, that this shocking practice has arisen out of the law of marriage, which obliges the bride's father to pay almost divine honours to the bridegroom:[y] hence persons of high caste, unwilling thus to humble themselves for the sake of a daughter, destroy the infant. In the Pŭnjab, and neighbouring districts, to a great extent, a caste of Sikhs, and the Rajŭ-pootŭs, as well as many of the bramhŭns and other castes, murder their female children as soon as born. I have made particular enquiry into the extent of these murders; but as the crime is perpetrated in secret, have not been able to procure very exact information. A gentleman, whose information on Indian customs is very correct, informs me, that this practice was, if it is not at present, universal among all the rajŭ-poots, who, he supposes, destroy all their daughters: he expresses his fears, that, notwithstanding their promises to the Government of Bombay, made in consequence of the very benevolent exertions of Mr. Duncan, the practice is almost generally continued. He adds, the custom prevails in the Pŭnjab, in Malwa, Joud-poorŭ, Jesselmere, Guzerat, Kutch, and perhaps Sind, if not in other provinces.

A friend at Ludhana, in a letter written in the year 1812, says, 'The horrible custom of murdering female infants is very common among the rajŭ-pootŭs. One of these fellows had been induced, by the tears of his wife, to spare the life of a daughter born to him. The girl grew up, and had arrived at the age of thirteen; but, unfortunately for her, had not been demanded in marriage by any one. The rajŭ-pootŭ began to apprehend the danger of her bringing a disgrace upon the family, and resolved to prevent it by putting the girl to death. Shortly after forming this atrocious design, he either overheard, or pretended to have overheard, some of his neighbours speak of his daughter in a way that tended to increase his fears; when, becoming outrageous, he rushed upon the poor girl, and cut her head off. The native magistrate confined him for a year, and seized all his property. But this was only because the girl was marriageable; infants are murdered with perfect impunity.'

'The Jatŭs, a people who abound in these parts,' says a friend, in a letter from Agra, dated May, 1812, 'destroy their female children as soon as born; but being now afraid of the English, they remove their pregnant women before the time of delivery into the district of the raja of Bhŭrŭtŭpoorŭ, that they may there commit these horrid murders with impunity. 'Oh! the dark places of the earth are full of the habitations of cruelty! In these parts

[y] At the time of marriage, the girl's father, taking hold of the knee of the boy, worships him, by presenting offerings of rice, flowers, paint, &c., and promising to give him his daughter.

there are not many women burned with their husbands, and when they do burn, they are not held down with bamboos, but left to themselves and the fire; but if any one run away or jump out, they cut her down with a sword, and throw her into the fire again. This was done at a flight of steps just by, a little before the English took this place; since which time I have not heard of any such events occurring.'

SECT. XXXIII.—*Ascetics devoured in Forests by Wild Beasts.*

BESIDE the dreadful waste of human life in practising superstitious austerities, great numbers of Hindoo devotēēs, who visit forests as an act of seclusion from the world, perish by wild beasts. The author, when on a visit to Sagŭrŭ island in the year 1806, was informed by a yogēē that six *of his companions had been devoured there by tigers in the three* preceding months; that while absent in the forest gathering sticks, he heard their cries, and looking over the wall of the temple-yard in which they lived, he saw the tigers dragging them by the neck into the forest. Other forests infested by wild beasts are visited by these yogēēs, many of whom are devoured every year. Numbers of secular persons too, drawn to the annual festivals celebrated in these forests, fall victims to the tigers.

SECT. XXXIV.—*Perishing in Cold Regions.*

THE Hindoos have a way to heaven without dying. If the person who wishes to go this way to heaven, through repeating certain incantations, survive the cold, he at last arrives at Himalŭyŭ, the residence of Shivŭ. Such a person is said 'to go the great journey.' Yoodhist'hirŭ, according to the pooranŭs, went this way to heaven; but his companions Bhēēmŭ, Ŭrjoonŭ, Nŭkoolŭ, Sŭhŭdévŭ, and Droupŭdēē, perished by the cold on the mountain. This forms another method in which the Hindoos may meritoriously put a period to their existence. It is also one of the Hindoo atonements for great offences.

It is difficult to form an estimate of the number of Hindoos who perish annually, the victims of superstition; and the author fears any reasonable conjecture would appear to many as highly exaggerated, and intended to prejudice the public mind against the Hindoos as idolaters. He wishes to feel and avow a just abhorrence of idolatry, and to deplore it as one of the greatest scourges ever employed by a Being, terrible in anger, to punish nations who have rejected the direct and simple means which nature and conscience supply of knowing himself; but he would use no unfair means of rendering even idolatry detestable: and with this assurance, he now enters on as correct a conjecture respecting the number of victims annually sacrificed on the altars of the Indian gods, as he is able :

Widows burnt alive on the funeral pile, in Hindoost'hanŭ,...	5,000
Pilgrims perishing on the roads and at sacred places,[1]	4,000
Persons drowning themselves in the Ganges, or buried or burnt alive, ..	500
Children immolated, including the daughters of the raju-pootŭs, ...	500
Sick persons whose death is hastened on the banks of the Ganges,[a]	500
Total, ..	10,500

Supposing there to be five thousand towns and large villages in Hindoost'hanŭ, and that one widow is burnt from each of these places in one year, no less a number than *five thousand helpless widows are annually burnt alive* in this country; but if we are guided by the calculation made at Calcutta (see p. 246) it will appear, that at least two widows in every large village must be murdered annually, including all the large towns in the same ratio. If so, instead of five thousand murders, the number must be doubled; and it will appear that ten thousand widows perish on the *funeral pile* in the short period of twelve months. Nor is this havoc like the irregular return of war; on the contrary, it is as certain and as fatal as the march of death itself.

The second calculation will not appear exaggerated, I am persuaded, when we consider the testimony of Dr. Buchanan, added

[1] '*Buddruck in Orissa, May* 30*th*, 1806. We know that we are approaching Juggernaut (and yet we are more than fifty miles from it) by the human bones which we have seen for some days strewed by the way. At this place we have been joined by several large bodies of pilgrims, perhaps 2,000 in number, who have come from various parts of Northern India. Some old persons are among them, who wish to die at Juggernaut. Numbers of pilgrims die on the road; and their bodies generally remain unburied. On a plain by the river, near the pilgrim's caravansera at this place, there are more than a hundred skulls. The dogs, jackals, and vultures, seem to live here on human prey.

'*Juggernaut*, 14*th June*. I have seen Juggernaut. The scene at Buddruck is but the vestibule to Juggernaut. No record of ancient or modern history can give, I think, an adequate idea of this valley of death; it may be truly compared with the 'valley of Hinnom.' I have also visited the sand plains by the sea, in some places whitened with the bones of the pilgrims; and another place a little way out of the town, called by the English the Golgotha, where the dead bodies are usually cast forth, and where dogs and vultures are ever seen.

'*Juggernaut*, 21*st June*. I have beheld another distressing scene this morning at the place of skulls; a poor woman lying dead, or nearly dead, and her two children by her, looking at the dogs and vultures which were near. The people passed by without noticing the children. I asked them where was their home. They said, 'they had no home but where their mother was.' O, there is no pity at Juggernaut! no tenderness of heart in Moloch's kingdom.'—*Buchanan's Researches in India.*

A person who has lived several years near the temple of Jŭgŭnnat'hŭ, in Orissa, in a letter to the author, says, 'I cannot pronounce on the numbers who annually perish at Jŭgŭnnat'hŭ, and on their way thither: in some years they do not amount to more than 200 perhaps, but in others they may exceed 2,000.'

[a] A gentleman, whose opinion is of great weight, says, 'I believe this estimate is far below the truth.'

to that of an officer inserted in page 252 of this volume ; to which I could add, that of many respectable natives.—By fevers, by the dysentery, and other diseases arising from exposure to the night air, and the privations of a long journey, crowds are carried off in a few days : sometimes numbers involuntarily fall under the wheels of the monstrous car of Jŭgŭnnat'hŭ : five or six hundred persons, principally women, I am informed, were crushed to death before the temple of Jŭgŭnnat'hŭ, in the year 1810, by the mere pressure of the crowd. The reader must consider that these sacred places, the resort of pilgrims, are spread all over Hindoost'hanŭ, and that pilgrims travel to them from distances requiring journeys of three, four, and five months.

In the opinion of every person to whom I have shewn the manuscript, the other calculations fall far below the real fact.

But if these calculations are not beyond the truth, what a horrible view do they present of the effects of superstition. Since the commencement of the bramhinical system, millions of victims have been immolated on the altars of its gods ; and, notwithstanding the influence of Europeans, the whole of Hindoost'hanŭ may be termed 'a field of blood unto this day.'

I must leave it to the pen of the future historian and poet to give these scenes that just colouring which will harrow up the soul of future generations : I must leave to them the description of these legitimate murders, perpetrated at the command and in the presence of the high-priests of idolatry ; who, by the magic-spell of superstition, have been able to draw men to quit their homes, and travel on foot a thousand miles, for the sake of beholding an idol cut out of the trunk of a neighbouring tree, or dug from an adjoining quarry ;—to prevail on men to commit murders to supply human victims for the altars of religion ;—on mothers to butcher their own children ;—on friends to force diseased relations into the arms of death, while struggling to extricate themselves ;—on children to apply the lighted torch to the pile that is to devour the living mother, who has fed them from her breasts, and dandled them on her knees. To crown the whole, these priests of idolatry have persuaded men to worship them as gods, to lick the dust of their feet, and even to cut off lumps of their own flesh,[b] their own heads,[c] as offerings to the gods.

SECT. XXXV.—*Ceremonies performed on visiting Holy Places.*

THE founders of the Hindoo religion have taught that certain places (Tēērt'hŭ-st'hanŭ[d]) are peculiarly sacred ; that the perform-

[b] See p. 93. [c] See p. 249.

[d] The place where persons obtain salvation ; from *tree*, salvation, and *st'hanŭ*, place.

ance of religious rites at these places is attended with peculiar merit, and followed by extraordinary benefits. The source and confluence of sacred rivers; places where any of the phenomena of nature have been discovered; or where particular images have been set up by the gods themselves;[e] or where some god or great saint has resided; or where distinguished religious actions have been performed have been pronounced sacred.

Excited by the miraculous accounts inserted in the shastrus, multitudes visit these places; others reside there for a time; and some spend the last stages of life at a holy place, to make sure of heaven after death. Rich men not unfrequenty erect temples and cut pools at these places, for the benefit of their souls.

When a person resolves to visit any one of these places, he fixes upon an auspicious day, and, two days preceding the commencement of his journey, has his head shaved; the next day he fasts; the following day he performs the shraddhŭ of the three preceding generations of his family on both sides, and then leaves his house. If a person act according to the shastrŭ, he observes the following rules: First, till he returns to his own house, he eats rice which has not been wet in cleansing, and that only once a day; he abstains from anointing his body with oil, and from eating fish. If he ride in a palanqueen, or in a boat, he loses half the benefits of his pilgrimage: if he walk on foot, he obtains the full fruit. The last day of his journey he fasts. On his arrival at the sacred spot, he has his whole body shaved;[f] after which he bathes, and performs the shraddhŭ. It is necessary that he stay seven days at least at the holy place; he may continue as much longer as he pleases. Every day during his stay he bathes, pays his devotions to the images, sits before them and repeats their names, and worships them, presenting such offerings as he can afford. In bathing he makes kooshŭ grass images for his relations, and bathes them. The benefit arising to relations will be as one to eight, compared with that of the person bathing at the holy place. When he is about to return, he obtains some of the offerings which have been presented to the idol or idols, and brings them home to give to his friends and neighbours. These consist of sweetmeats, flowers, toolŭsee leaves, the ashes of cow-dung, &c. After celebrating the shraddhŭ, he entertains the bramhŭns, and presents them with oil, fish, and all those things from which he abstained. Having done this, he returns to his former course of living. The reward promised to the pilgrim is, that he shall ascend to the heaven of that god who presides at the holy place he has visited.

[e] At Benares, Shivŭ is said to have set up with his own hands an image of the lingŭ.

[f] If it be a woman, she has only the breadth of two fingers of her hair behind cut off. If a widow, her whole head is shaved.

The following are some of the principal places in Hindoost'-hanŭ to which persons go on pilgrimage :—

Gŭya, rendered famous as the place where Vishnoo destroyed a giant. To procure the salvation of deceased relations, crowds of Hindoos perform the shraddhŭ here ; on whom Government levies a tax. Rich Hindoos have expended immense sums at this place.

Kashēē, (Benares.) To this place multitudes of Hindoos go on pilgrimage ; the ceremonies of religion, when performed at the different holy places in this city, are supposed to be very efficacious. It is the greatest seat of Hindoo learning in Hindoost'hanŭ. Many Hindoos spend their last days here, under the expectation, that dying here secures a place in Shivŭ's heaven. To prove that a man dying in the very act of sin at this place obtains happiness, the Hindoos relate, amongst other stories, one respecting a man who died in a pan of hot spirits, into which he accidentally fell while carrying on an intrigue with the wife of a liquor merchant. Shivŭ is said to have come to this man in his last moments, and, whispering the name of Brŭmha in his ear, to have sent him to heaven. Even Englishmen, the Hindoos allow, may go to heaven from Kashēē, and they relate a story of an Englishman who had a great desire to die at this place. After his arrival there, he gave money to his head Hindoo servant to build a temple, and perform the different ceremonies required ; and in a short time afterwards obtained his desire, and died at Kashēē. I suppress the name of my countryman from a sense of shame.

Prŭyagŭ, (Allahabad.) The Hindoos suppose that the Ganges, the Yŭmoona, and the Sŭrŭswŭtēē, three sacred rivers, unite their streams here. Many persons from all parts of India bathe at this place, and many choose a voluntary death here. Government levies a tax on the pilgrims. He who has visited Gŭya, Kashēē, and Prŭyagŭ, flattered himself that he is possessed of extraordinary religious merits.

Jŭgŭnnat'hŭ-kshŭtrŭ, (in Orissa.) Several temples and pools attract the attention of pilgrims at this place ; but the great god Jŭgŭnnat'hŭ is the most famous object of attention to pilgrims, who come from all parts of India at the times of the thirteen annual festivals held in honour of this wooden god. All castes eat together here, the rise of which custom is variously accounted for. The Hindoos say, that 200,000 people assemble at this place at the time of drawing the car ; when five or six people are said to throw themselves under the wheels of the car every year, as a certain means of obtaining salvation. When I asked a bramhŭn in what way such persons expected salvation, he said, that generally the person who thus threw away his life was in a state of misfortune ; and that he thought, as he sacrificed his life through his faith in Jŭgŭnnat'hŭ, this god would certainly save him.—The pilgrims to this place, especially at the time of the above festival, endure the greatest hardships; some from the fatigues of a long journey, others from the want of necessary support, or from being exposed to bad weather. Multitudes perish on the roads, very often by the dysentery; and some parts of the sea-shore at this holy place may be properly termed Golgotha, the number of skulls and dead bodies are so great. In no part of India, perhaps, are the horrors of this superstition so deeply felt as on this spot: its victims are almost countless. Every third year they make a new image, when a bramhŭn removes the original bones of Krishnŭ,[g] from the belly of the old image to that of the new one. On this occasion, he covers his eyes lest he should be struck dead for looking at such sacred relics.[h] After this, we may be sure, the common people do not *wish* to see Krishnŭ's bones.

It is a well-authenticated fact, that at this place a number of females of infamous character are employed to dance and sing before the god. They live in separate houses, not at the temple. Persons going to see Jŭgŭnnat'hŭ are often guilty of criminal actions with these females.[i] Multitudes take loose women with them, never suspecting that Jŭgŭnnat'hŭ will be offended at their bringing a prostitute into his presence; or that whoredom is inconsistent with that worship from which they expect salvation, and to obtain which some of them make a journey of four months.

Before this place fell into the hands of the English, the king, a Mahratta chief, exacted tolls from pilgrims for passing through his territories to Jŭgŭnnat'hŭ. At one place the toll was not less than one pound, nine shillings for each foot-passenger, if he had so much property with him. When a Bengalee raja used to go, he was accompanied by one or two thousand people, for every one of whom he was obliged to pay the toll. The Honorable Company's Government levies a tax of from one to six rupees on each passenger. For several years after the conquest of Kŭtŭkŭ by the English, this tax was not levied; when myriads of pilgrims thronged to this place, and thousands, it is said, perished from disease, want, &c.

Some persons, on leaving this holy place, deposit with the bramhŭns of the temple one or two hundred rupees, with the interest of which the bramhŭns are to purchase rice, and present it daily to Jŭgŭnnat'hŭ, and afterwards to dŭndēēs or bramhŭns.

[g] The tradition is, that king Indrŭ-dyoomŭ, by the direction of Vishnoo, placed the bones of Krishnŭ, who had been accidentally killed by a hunter, in the belly of the image of Jŭgŭnnat'hŭ.

[h] The raja of Burdwan, Kēērtee-Chŭndrŭ, expended, it is said, twelve lacs of rupees in a journey to Jŭgŭnnat'hŭ, and in bribing the bramhŭns to permit him to see these bones. For the sight of the bones he paid two lacs of rupees; but he died in six months afterwards—*for his temerity.*

[i] The officiating bramhŭns there continually live in adulterous connection with them.

Deeds of gift are also made to Jŭgŭnnat'hŭ all over Hindoost'hanŭ, which are received by agents in every large town, and paid to the Mŭt'hŭ-dharēēs[k] at Jŭgŭnnat'hŭ-kshŭtrŭ; who by this means (though professing themselves to be mendicants) have become some of the richest merchants in India.

Raméshwŭrŭ, (Ramiseram.) This place forms the southern boundary of the bramhinical religion. It is famous for containing a temple said to have been erected by Ramŭ on his return from the destruction of the gaint Ravŭnŭ. None but wandering mendicants visit it.

Chŭndrŭ-shékŭrŭ, a mountain near Chittagong, on which stands a temple of the lingŭ. Over the surface of a pool of water inflammable air is said to be perceived, from the fire of which pilgrims kindle their burnt-offerings. The water oozes from one side of the rock, and as it falls below, the pilgrims stand to receive the purifying stream.

Gŭnga-Sagŭrŭ, (Sagŭrŭ-island.) At this place the Ganges runs into the sea; and this circumstance, it is supposed, gives an efficacy to the waters. Vast crowds of Hindoos visit this island twice in the year, and perform religious ceremonies for the good of themselves and ancestors: some are guilty of self-murder, in which they are assisted by a number of alligators which visit this spot: the infant is cast into the jaws of this voracious animal by its infatuated mother; and thus the religion of Brŭmha transforms the mother into a monster, and tears asunder the tenderest ties of nature.—Ruins and pools still exist on the island, which prove that, though now the haunt of wild beasts, it was once inhabited.

Uyodhya, (Oude,) the ancient capital of Ramŭ, situated by the river Sŭrŭyoo, is still inhabited. The pilgrims are generally Ramats. *Mit'hila*, (Tirhoot,) the birth-place of Sēēta, and the capital of her father Jŭnŭkŭ, is resorted to by pilgrims; as well as *Mut'hoora*, the birth-place of Krishnŭ; and *Vrinda-vŭnŭ*, the scene of the revels of this licentious deity, whose followers visit many *sacred* retreats, the resort of Krishnŭ and the milkmaids. *Gokoola*, the place where Krishnŭ was educated, is also visited by pilgrims, who are shewn the various spots which have been consecrated by the gambols of their favourite god.

The forest of Noimishŭ, near Lucknow, is celebrated as the place where Sōōtŭ, the sage, read the pooranŭs to 60,000 disciples.

Voidyŭnat'hŭ, a place in Birboom, contains a celebrated image called Ramŭ-lingŭ. Some pilgrims, afflicted with incurable distempers, fast here till they die: others make vows, sometimes in

[k] These Mŭt'hŭ-dharēēs are found at every holy place. One person presides over the house, which is the common resort of pilgrims, who are entertained there.

some such words as these :—'Oh! Voidyŭnat'hŭ, give me a wife, and I will bring a pan of water from the Ganges and bathe thee ;' or, 'I will present thee a mŭn of milk, for frumenty.'

At *Vŭkréshwŭrŭ*, another place in Birboom, an image of the sage Ŭshtavŭkrŭ is set up, where several warm springs attract the attention of devotees, who bathe in their waters, not to heal their bodies, but their souls.

Kooroo-kshŭtrŭ, a place near Delhi, where the dreadful battle betwixt Yoodist'hirŭ and Dooryodhŭnŭ was fought. Here Pŭrŭshoo-ramŭ also is said to have filled five pools with the blood of the kshétriyŭs, from which he offered a libation to his deceased father.[1]

Hingoola, a cave or excavated rock on the sea-shore. Offerings are presented to the regents of the place on a stone in the cave.

Ekamrŭ-kanŭnŭ, a place on the borders of Orissa, containing 6,000 temples dedicated to Shivŭ. Not less than 70 or 8,000 people are said to visit this place at the drawing of the car of Jŭgŭnnat'hŭ when all castes eat together.

Hŭree-dwarŭ, (from Hŭree, a name of Vishnoo, and dwarŭ, a door,) or the mouth from which the Ganges issues. An account of this place, inserted in the 6th volume of the Asiatic Researches, declares, that 2,500,000 people assembled here at a festival in 1796.

Kanchēē, a town in Telinga, divided into two parts, Shivŭ-Kanchēē and Vishnoo-Kanchēē. At a festival held here in the month Choitrŭ, the disciples of Shivŭ and Vishnoo quarrel, and often murder one another.

Multitudes of other places in India are venerated and visited by pilgrims. When I was writing this account, on describing Bristol Hot-wells, with all its gilt crutches hanging in the pump-room, to the learned bramhŭn who assisted me, he confessed that it would make a famous holy place, and attract immense crowds of pilgrims. It is a deplorable circumstance, that such a waste of time, of life, and of property, should be incurred, through the fatal deception, that the sight of a holy place will be accepted by the Judge of heaven and earth, instead of repentance and conversion, instead of a contrite heart and a holy life.

SECT. XXXVI.—*Ceremonies at Death.*

A SICK person, after his removal to the banks of the Ganges, if he possess sufficient strength, directs quantities of food, garments,

[1] To satisfy his revenge. There is nothing revolting to the feelings of the Hindoos in this dreadful act of revenge: which has made Kooroo-kshŭtrŭ a *holy* place. When a Hindoo is describing a dreadful quarrel, he says, 'It was a perfect Koorook-shŭtrŭ.'

&c. to be presented to the bramhŭns. That he may not be compelled to cross Voitŭrŭnēē, whose waters are hot, on his way to the seat of judgment, he presents to a bramhŭn a black cow. When about to expire, the relations place the body up to the navel in the river, and direct the dying man to call aloud on the gods, and assist him in doing so.

The burning of the body is one of the first ceremonies which the Hindoos perform for the help of the dead in a future state. If this ceremony have not been attended to, the shraddhŭ, tŭrpŭnŭ, &c. cannot be performed. If a person be unable to provide wood, cloth, clarified butter, rice, water pans, and other things, beside the fee to the priest, he must beg among his neighbours. If the body be thrown into the river, or burnt, without the accustomed ceremonies, (as is sometimes the case,) the ceremonies may be performed over an image of the deceased made of kooshŭ grass.

Immediately after death, the attendants lay out the body on a sheet, placing two pieces of wood under the head and feet; after which they anoint the corpse with clarified butter, bathe it with the water of the Ganges, put round the loins a new garment, and another over the left shoulder, and then draw the sheet on which the body lies over the whole. The heir-at-law next bathes himself, puts on new garments, and boils some rice, a ball of which and a lighted brand he puts to the mouth of the deceased, repeating incantations. The pile having been prepared, he sets fire to it, and occasionally throws on it clarified butter and other combustibles. When the body is consumed, he washes the ashes into the river; the attendants bathe, and, presenting a drink-offering to the deceased, return home: before they enter the house, however, each one touches fire, and chews some bitter leaves, to signify that parting with relations by death is an unpleasant task.

SECT. XXXVII.—*Rites for the Repose of the Soul, (Shraddhŭ.)*

THE Hindoo shastrŭs teach, that after death the soul becomes prétŭ,[m] viz: takes a body about the size of a person's thumb, and remains in the custody of Yŭmŭ, the judge of the dead. At the time of receiving punishment, the body becomes enlarged, and is made capable of enduring sorrow. The performance of the shraddhŭ delivers the deceased, at the end of a year, from this state, and translates him to the heaven of the Pitrees, where he enjoys the reward of his meritorious actions; and afterwards, in another body, enters into that state which the nature of his former actions assign to him. If the shraddhŭ be not performed, the deceased remains in the prétŭ state, and cannot enter another body. We are here

[m] A departed ghost.

strongly reminded of the 325th and six following lines of Virgil, in the 6th book of his Æneid, as well as of the 28th Ode of the 1st book of Horace.

The offerings made in a person's name, after his decease, and the ceremonies which take place on the occasion, are called his shraddhŭ, which the Hindoos are very anxious to perform in a becoming manner. The son who performs these rites obtains great merit: and the deceased is hereby satisfied,[n] and, by gifts to the bramhŭns in his name, obtains heaven.

There are three shraddhŭs for the dead: one, eleven days after death; another, every month; and another at the close of a year after a person's decease. During the ten[o] days of mourning, the relations hold a family council, and consult on the means of performing the shraddhŭ; on the last of these days, after making an offering for the dead by the side of the river, they are shaved. This offering consists of boiled rice, sugar, curds, sweetmeats, milk, plantains, &c. made into ten balls, and presented with prayers.

The next day, after bathing,[p] the family prepare an open place for the ceremonies. If it be the shraddhŭ of a rich man, all the learned Hindoos and respectable people of the neighbouring villages are invited. The company being seated under an awning, the sons and the other relations of the deceased, dressed in new garments, place themselves in the midst of the company with their faces eastward, having near them sixteen different gifts, as brass cups, candlesticks, umbrellas, shoes, &c. Next are brought seeds of sesamum, a small piece of gold, and another of a different metal, wrapt up in new cloths. The son of the deceased now puts a piece of new cloth across his neck, and offers an atonement for the sin of having killed insects in sweeping the room, in cooking, grinding spices, and in moving the water jar; then follows an offering to the sun; then, rising, and bringing his hands forward in a supplicating posture, he solicits leave from the company to make the offering; after which he offers the sesamum, gold, and metal, for the happiness of the deceased; takes the kosha, and sprinkles the sixteen gifts with water; then, placing a flower on each, and repeating prayers, he offers them in the presence of the shalgramŭ, one by one, in the name of the deceased, that he may obtain heaven. The son after this, if in circumstances sufficiently affluent, presents large gifts to the bramhŭns, as elephants, horses,

[n] Mŭnoo says, 'What sort of oblation, given duly to the manes, is capable of satisfying them for a long time, or for eternity, I will now declare, without omission.'

[o] Bramhŭns are unclean for ten days after the death of a relation; kshŭtriyŭs, twelve; voishyŭs, fifteen; and shōōdrŭs, thirty.

[p] At the time of bathing, the person who will perform the shraddhŭ, purifies himself by putting water, seeds, fruits, &c. in parts of the trunks of four plantain trees, repeating incantations. He sends some of this water home to purify the family.

palanqueens, boats, &c. the receiving of which, however, is not honorable. A bramhŭn then marks the foreheads of all present with sandal powder, and puts round the neck of each a garland of flowers. To the ŭgrŭdanēē[q] bramhŭns and others are now given, amidst much confusion among the receivers, the sesamum, the morsel of gold, the metal, a large bason full of kourees, and a couch or two, as well as the sixteen different gifts; after which the assembly breaks up. The son then goes into the house, and placing a bramhŭn and his wife on a seat, covers them with ornaments, worships them, and, adding a large present of money, dismisses them.

After this, the son of the deceased requests five bramhŭns, of some note for learning, to offer a male calf; in doing which they take two cloths each, four poitas, four betle-nuts, and some kourees, provided for the purpose, and go with the company to a spot where an altar has been prepared, one cubit high, and four cubits square. Four of the bramhŭns sit on the four sides of the altar, and there worship certain gods, aud offer a burnt-sacrifice. Near the altar are placed the shalgramŭ, four female calves, a male calf, and a vilwŭ post. The fifth bramhŭn reads certain parts of a pooranŭ, to drive away evil spirits. The female calves are tied to four vilwŭ posts, and the male calf to a post called vrishŭ post.[r] To the necks of the female calves four small slender baskets are suspended, in which are placed, among other things, a comb, and the iron instrument with which the Hindoo women paint their eyebrows black. A sheet of metal is placed under the belly of the male calf; on the back a sheet of copper: the hoofs are covered with silver, and the horns with gold. if the shraddhŭ be performed by a rich man.[s] On the hips of the male calf, marks of Shivŭ's trident are impressed with a hot iron. After this, the son of the deceased washes the tail of the male calf, and with the same water presents a drink-offering to his deceased ancestors; and afterwards marries the male calf to the four female calves, repeating many formulas, in which they are recommended to cultivate love and mutual sympathy. The son next liberates the female calves, forbidding any one to detain them, or partake of their milk in future. In liberating the male calf he says, 'I have given thee these four wives;[t] live with them. Thou art the living image of Yŭmŭ; thou goest upon four legs. Devour not the corn

[q] Bramhŭns who receive the first gifts at shraddhŭs are called by this name.

[r] Vrishŭ is the name for a bull. A rough image of one of these animals is carved in the middle of the post, which is afterwards set up in a public road till it rots or falls down. It is often full of rough carved figures. A good one costs about four rupees.

[s] If by a poor man, imitations of these things are used.

[t] Here the Hindoos marry cattle! In another part of this work the reader will find an account of the marriage of monkies!!

of others, go not near a cow in calf, &c.' The female calves are generally taken by bramhŭns:[u] the male calf is let loose, to go where he pleases.[x]

To this succeeds what is peculiarly termed the shraddhŭ. The river side, or the cow-house, or some retired place, is chosen; after cleansing which, they collect all kinds of eatables, cloth, sesamum, flowers, &c. and place them in dishes made of the excavated trunks of the plantain tree. The son then washes his feet, and sits with his face towards the east, with a shalgramŭ before him, and repeats many incantations to purify himself; he then worships the shalgramŭ; presents to his deceased parent the seven dishes placed to the east, repeating various incantations; and worships Gŭnga, Vishnoo, and the household gods, adding an offering to the ancestors of the king, as an acknowledgment for using the king's land at worship. He then, turning his face to the south, reads many incantations, and with five, seven, or nine blades of kooshŭ grass, makes the image of a bramhŭn, which he places on a plantain before him; then with joined hands he repeats before this image many incantations, to the following purport: 'Before thee, O bramhŭn, I perform my father's shraddhŭ.'[y] He next offers to his deceased parent, on a plantain-trunk dish, seven blades of kooshŭ and seven of dōōrva grass, flowers, dry rice, cloth, red paint, and a brass lamp. He next cleanses the place before him with his hands, and scattering upon it a few blades of kooshŭ grass, presents other offerings to his deceased father, repeating many incantations, which contain the names of the offerings, and an invitation to the deceased father to partake of them. From what remians of these offerings the son makes two balls, the smallest of which is offered in the name of those of the family who have not received the benefits of the shraddhŭ, and the other he presents to his deceased father, and then lays it on some kooshŭ grass as before, and worships it, presenting flowers, water, &c. He now places both hands open against a lamp which is burning, as though he were warming himself; after which he prostrates himself to the sun, and presents a fee of from one rupee to five to the officiating bramhŭn; salutes all the bramhŭns present, and makes prostrations to the shalgramŭ, which he afterwards sends into the house. All the offerings are sent to the houses of bramhŭns. The family now return home, where an entertainment is provided, both for bramhŭns and others, consisting principally

u Yet the receiving of these and other gifts at shraddhŭs is supposed to disgrace a person.

x These bulls wander about, and are treated by the Hindoos with great respect. No one can claim any redress for the injury they do, and no Hindoo dare destroy them. In large towns they are often mischievous. The English call them bramhŭnēē bulls.

y The shastrŭ directs that a living bramhŭn shall be chosen; but a grass bramhŭn is generally substituted.

of sweetmeats, milk, curds, sugar, cakes, &c. The bramhŭns eat in an enclosed spot, the uninvited bramhŭns near the house, and the poor in the street or road. At the close of the entertainment, if the person making the shraddhŭ be rich, he gives presents to all those who are not guests, whether bramhŭns or the poor, and thus dismisses them. The next morning he dismisses the learned bramhŭns with presents: to the most learned he gives five rupees perhaps, and to those less learned one. The bramhŭns who were invited are also dismissed with presents. About one o'clock a feast is provided for the relations, who are dismissed the next morning with presents of money, cloth, &c., and on this day another dinner is provided for nearer relations. At the close of the shraddhŭ a number of mendicant musicians play on certain instruments of music, and sing verses celebrating the revels of Krishnŭ; they are often dismissed with large presents.

The next day the family return to their accustomed diet; but the sons, for twelve months after the decease of the father, must refuse every gratification, and cook with their own hands, or eat what has been prepared by a wife, or some near relation dwelling in the house.

Gŭnga-Govindŭ-Singhŭ, a person of the writer caste, head-servant to Mr. Hastings, expended, it is said, 1,200,000 rupees at his mother's shraddhŭ; and Raja Nŭvŭ-Krishnŭ of Calcutta, nearly as much in the shraddhŭ for his mother. This expense was principally incurred in presents to the bramhŭns, such as bedsteads, at two or three hundred rupees each; water pitchers of silver and gold, some worth a thousand, and others two thousand rupees; dishes of silver and gold, at five hundred, two hundred, and one hundred; silver and gold cups and lamp-stands, at two hundred, one hundred, &c.; covered bowls for betle-nut, and gold and silver water jugs, at from five hundred down to one hundred; and cloths at ten or fifteen rupees a piece.

Vast crowds of mendicants[a] and poor people fill the roads at the time of a large shraddhŭ for two or three days together, each of whom obtains a rupee, or half a rupee; sometimes nothing. The lower orders expend three hundred, two hundred, or one hundred rupees at a shraddhŭ. Many persons reduce themselves to beggary to procure the name of having made a great shraddhŭ. If a man delay this ceremony, the priest urges him repeatedly to what he calls his duty. According to the Hindoo law, a person cannot inherit an estate who has not performed the shraddhŭ.

The monthly shraddhŭ for the first year after the death of the parent, is upon a very small scale, and the expense is from ten rupees to twelve annas.

[a] Some of the mendicants come journies of four or five days.

Beside these, there are other shraddhŭs for deceased ancestors, as, in every month at the total wane of the moon; on the last fifteen, or ten, or five days of the moon in Bhadrŭ; once during the first fifteen days of the moon in Ŭgrŭhayŭnŭ; and again in the same months,[b] in Poushŭ,[c] and Maghŭ,[d] on the eighth of the wane of the moon; in Voishakhŭ[e] and Shravŭnŭ,[f] on any of the first fifteen days of the moon. At some of these times all Hindoos perform this ceremony; at other times only a few persons. The expense is trifling, as scarcely any persons are entertained at them.

SECT. XXXVIII.—*Purifications.*

A HINDOO becomes unclean by various circumstances, during which he is interdicted almost every religious ceremony, and forbidden to shave or cut his nails. In the act of purification the person shaves the head, bathes, and puts on clean apparel.

A Hindoo becomes unclean after the death of persons related to him by birth. If a child die before he has teeth, the family bathe immediately, and become clean; or if a child die before its ears are bored, the family remain unclean one night. If a woman miscarry, the family become impure for ten days. After a birth, all the members of the family in a direct line become unclean. A woman in her courses is unclean for three days; but on the fifth day, after bathing, she may again perform religious ceremonies. Every person is considered as in some measure unclean while in a state of sickness, and from some religious services a sick person is wholly excluded. A bramhŭn becomes unclean by the touch of a shōōdrŭ, a dog, a Mŭsŭlman, a barbarian, &c. and all casts, by touching a woman in her courses, a dead body, ordure, urine, the food of other castes, &c.

SECT. XXXIX.—*Atonements for Offences.*

THE ancient Hindoo laws on this subject are very numerous, and in many instances very severe and unjust. By these laws the whole property of the country was put into a state of requisition

[b] In this shraddhŭ, the flesh of cows was formerly offered in sacrifice. In the kŭlēē-yogŭ this is forbidden, and that of deer or goats is substituted.

[c] This shraddhŭ is performed principally with herbs.

[d] In this shraddhŭ bread is chiefly used.

[e] Barley is the principal thing used in this shraddhŭ. At this time the Hindoo women scatter the husks of barley in the public roads, in imitation it is said of the mother of Rŭghoo-nŭndŭnŭ, compiler of a number of the smritees.

[f] The newly descended rain is the principal article in this shraddhŭ.

by the bramhŭns. At present, very few offences expose a person to the penalties of the canon law: among these, however, are the killing a bramhŭn, a religious mendicant, or a woman; striking a bramhŭn; killing a cow. Slight atonements are also offered by some when labouring under certain diseases, and for unintentional offences.

I here insert some extracts from the work on atonements called Prayŭshchittŭ-Nirnŭyŭ.—There are nine sorts of sins requiring atonements: 1. Jatee-bhrŭngshŭ-kŭrŭ, in which is included the eating of onions, defrauding relations, &c. 2. Shŭnkŭrēē-kŭrŭnŭ, viz., sodomy. 3. Ŭpatrēē-kŭrŭnŭ, which includes receiving presents from barbarians; bramhŭns, entering into trade; and bramhŭns serving shōōdrŭs.[g] 4. Mŭlavŭhŭ, in which is included destroying insects; eating fruit which has lain near a person who has drank spirits; excessive grief for a trifling loss; and stealing wood, fruit, or flowers. 5. Prŭkēērnnŭkŭ, which includes various offences against the caste. 6. Oopŭpatŭkŭ, which includes many actions: among the rest, killing cows; becoming priest to the low castes; a person's selling himself; forsaking father, mother, sons; neglecting the védŭs, or consecrated fire; giving a daughter in marriage to a younger brother before the elder; giving a younger son in marriage before the elder; in the two last cases also becoming priest at the time of such marriage; usury in lending goods; not completing a vrŭtŭ; selling a pool of water, a garden, a son, &c.; not performing any one of the sŭngskarŭs; forsaking a friend; obtaining instructions from a disciple; killing a woman, or a shōōdrŭ, a voishyŭ, a kshŭtriyŭ, &c.; cutting green trees for fire-wood; neglecting to pay debts; subduing or driving away a person not an enemy by the power of incantations; denying a future state, &c. 7. Ŭnoopatŭkŭ, which includes many different actions, viz., a son's having intercourse with a woman who is a wife (though of another caste) to his father; adultery with an uncle's wife; with the wife of a grandfather; with an aunt by the mother's side; with the wife of a king; with a father's sister; with the wife of a shrotriyŭ bramhŭn; with the wife of a priest; with the wife of a teacher of the védŭs; with the wife of a friend; with the friend of a sister; with any woman in the line of consanguinity; with any woman of a caste superior to that of the man; with the wife of a chandalŭ; with a virgin, the daughter of a bramhŭn; with a woman while in her courses; with a woman who has embraced the life of a brŭmhŭcharinēē. 8. Mŭhapatŭkŭ, which includes five different offences, viz., killing bramhŭns; a bramhŭn's drinking spirits, or a shōōdrŭ's intercourse with the wife of a bramhŭn; stealing gold from a bramhŭn to the amount of a gold mohur; adultery with the wife of a gooroo, viz., with the wife of a father,

[g] In many places bramhŭns, at present, become clerks, cooks, &c. to the higher classes of shōōdrŭs.

if she be of a superior caste, or if she be of the same caste. Whoever commits these actions is called mŭhapatŭkēē, and whoever lives in familiar habits with this person becomes also mŭhapatŭkēē: this includes sleeping on the same bed; sitting together on one seat; eating together; drinking out of one cup; eating together of food cooked in one vessel; becoming priest to a mŭhapatŭkēē; teaching the védŭs to such an offender. If a person converse with a mŭhapatŭkēē, or touch him, or if the breath of this offender fall upon him, and these familiarities be continued for twelve months, this person also becomes mŭhapatŭkēē. 9. Ŭtipatŭkŭ includes incest with a person's own mother, or daughter, or son's wife.

If a person kill a bramhŭn, he must renounce life, or offer the prajapŭtyŭ atonement for twenty-four years;[h] or, in case of inability, he must offer 360 cows with their calves, and 100 cows as a fee; or 470 rupees, besides 24 rupees as a fee. If a person murder a bramhŭnēē, whose husband is ignorant of the védŭs, the offender must perform the prajapŭtyŭ atonement for six years. This may be commuted for ninety cows and calves, or 270 kahŭnŭs of kourees. For murdering the wife of a kshŭtriyŭ, this atonement must be repeated three years; of a voishyŭ, one year and a half; and of a shōōdrŭ, nine months. If the woman was with child, or in her courses, the atonement must be doubled. If a bramhŭn, or a kshŭtriyŭ, murder a kshŭtriyŭ, the prajapŭtyŭ atonement must be repeated for three years. This may be commuted for forty-five milch cows and their calves, or 135 kahŭnŭs of kourees. If a bramhŭn, a kshŭtriyŭ, or voishyŭ, murder a voishyŭ, the above atonement must be repeated for one year and a half. This may be commuted for twenty-three cows and their calves, or 67½ kahŭnŭs of kourees. For murdering a shōōdrŭ, the above atonement must be repeated for nine months. This may be commuted for twelve cows and their calves, or 36 kahŭnŭs of kourees; (about one pound sterling.)

If a bramhŭn have killed a cow belonging to a bramhŭn, he must offer the following atonement:—he must have his head shaved; for thirty days, dwell with cows, eat barley boiled in the urine of cows, and wear a cow's skin. For the next two months, he must eat only once a day. For the two following months, he must bathe with the urine of cows. During these days of penance he must abstain from sin; he must follow a herd of cows;

[h] The following is the law respecting this atonement:—The offender, for three days, is to eat, each day, only twenty-six mouthfuls of rice, clarified butter, milk, &c. boiled together; for the next three days he must eat in the evening twenty-two mouthfuls; for the next three days he is to ask for nothing, and, unless spontaneously given him, to eat nothing. If any food be given him, it must be twenty-four mouthfuls of the same kind of food as mentioned above; for the next three days he must eat nothing. If he abstain from food on those days in which he is allowed to take food if given to him, he does not commit a fault. If a person be unable to fast so long, he may make a commutation by fasting six days. If a person be not able to fast six days, he may be exempted, on making an offering of a cow and calf; or, in case of inability to do this, he may offer three kahŭnŭs of kourees.

stand when they stand[i], and eat the dust which they throw up with their feet. At night, after putting the cows in the stall, he must bow to them, and then sit upright, cross-legged, and watch them all night. If one of the herd be sick, or have met with any misfortune, he must expose his own life for its preservation. He must not seek the preservation of his own life from the scorching sun, the chilling cold, the pelting rain, or the driving storm, till he have secured the herd. If the cows be feeding on another person's ground, he is not to drive them away, nor inform the owner. He must not prevent the calf from sucking, though the cow should not have been milked. After the person has thus gone through this atonement without fault, he must offer to a learned bramhŭn ten cows and a bull. If this be beyond his ability, he must give up all he has. If an offender be unable to go through all his penance, he must, besides the above fee, offer seventeen new-milch cows. If he be poor, he may offer sixty-six kahŭnŭs of kourees[k] This is the atonement, if the cow was wilfully killed by a bramhŭn. If accidentally killed, the offender must go through half the penance, and offer one cow. Besides offering the atonement, the person who has wilfully or accidentally killed a cow, must give to the owner another cow equally good. If he cannot give such a cow, he must give a proper price, to be ascertained by five respectable neighbours. If a bramhŭn castrate a bull, he must offer the six month's atonement as for killing a bramhŭn's cow. If a cow die accidentally in the field, it is taken for granted that it was not properly taken care of, and an atonement must be offered. Such a person must have his head shaved; bathe three times a day; wear a cow's skin with the horns, hoofs, &c. on it; follow the herd; watch the herd by night, &c. If the animal died at night in the cow-house, and the keeper was permitted to go home, instead of watching over the cattle, the atonement must be offered by the owner. If in consequence of the falling of a bell from a cow's ear[l] the cow die, the owner must offer half of the prajapŭtyŭ atonement. If a Hindoo sell a cow to a barbarian, he must eat only one mouthful in the morning for four days, and for the next four days four mouthfuls each day in the evening. If the buyer kill and eat the cow, the person who disposed of the animal must offer the same atonement as a bramhŭn for killing a cow.

[i] If, however, part of the herd be lying down, and part be standing, he must do as the greater number do. If the number lying down and the number standing be equal, he must do that which is most painful to himself; of course he must stand.

[k] In the work called Prayŭshchittŭ-vivékŭ it is declared, that if a person be unable to pay this fine, he must beg for twelve years, and whatever he is able to procure, he must give as a commutation for the atonement. At the present period, persons may be seen, having the head shaved, making a noise like the lowing of a cow; having a rope, with which cow's are tied by the leg, in the hand, &c. begging for this avowed purpose: yet most of these persons make this a contrivance to obtain money.

[l] Hung there like an ear-ring, or ornament, but with the intention of keeping the herd together by the sound.

If a man kill a horse, he must make an offering of cloth to a bramhŭn.[m] If an elephant, he must give to the bramhŭns five blue bulls. If an ass, a goat, or a sheep, a male calf, one year old, must be given to a bramhŭn. If a goose, a peacock, a white heron, or a hawk, he must give a cow to a bramhŭn. If a tiger, a milch cow. If a camel, or a buffalo, he must forfeit a rŭtŭkŭ of gold. If a hog, he must present to a bramhŭn a pitcher of clarified butter. If a parrot, a calf, one year old. If a snake, an axe for cutting wood. If a cat, a guano, an ichneumon, or a frog, he must for three days partake of nothing but milk. If any one of these offences have been done repeatedly, the offender must offer a fourth of the prajapŭtyŭ atonement. If a person have killed a thousand larger insects, he must offer the same atonement as for accidentally killing a shōōdrŭ. For killing a few small insects, the person must repeat an incantation, while squeezing his nose with his fingers.

If a bramhŭn, ignorantly, have intercourse once with the wife of a chandalŭ, he must offer the prajapŭtyŭ atonement during twelve years. If done wilfully, he must renounce life as the expiation of his sin. If done repeatedly, the offence cannot be expiated. If a bramhŭn have improper intercourse with a virgin, or with his own daughter, or with his son's wife, he must become an eunuch, and renounce life. If a person of any other caste commit such sin, he must renounce life by the toosh-anŭlŭ atonement[n].

[m] The atonements for killing horses and other animals, as well as insects, are alike to all the castes. Shoolŭpanee, a pŭndit, however, maintains, that in all these cases a shōōdrŭ, a female, a child, and an aged person, are to offer only one half of the atonement.

[n] In the work called prayŭshchittŭ-vivèkŭ, the method in which this person must renounce life is thus related :—After shaving his head, bathing, &c. he must cover himself with chaff, and, lying down, the fire must be kindled at his feet; and in this way, by slow degrees, he must give up his life to expiate his crime. In another work, the following story is related respecting this method of expiating sin :—In former times, it was common for very learned pŭndits, to go from kingdom to kingdom, challenging each king to bring forth his pundits, to hold disputations on the subjects contained in the shastrŭs. Oodŭyŭnacharyŭ had, in this manner, obtained the victory over all the pŭndits in the world. He was also the great instrument in overcoming the bouddhŭs, and in re-establishing the practice of the vèdŭs; but in arming the kings against the bouddhŭs he had been instrumental in destroying many bouddhŭ bramhŭns. Towards the close of his life he went to Jŭgŭnnat'hŭk-kshètrŭ; but when he arrived at the temple, the door shut of itself against him, and he sat at the door, sorrowful, and keeping a fast. In the midst of his fast the god appeared to him in a dream, and told him, he had been guilty of killing many bramhŭns; he could not, therefore, see his face: he must renounce life by offering the toosh-anŭlŭ atonement. Oodŭyŭnacharyŭ was angry with Jŭgŭnnat'hŭ, and pronounced a curse upon him, telling him, that in some future period, when he should be destroyed by the bouddhŭs, he would remember his benefactor. This pŭndit soon afterwards, however, obeyed the command of Jŭgŭnnat'hŭ. When he had been several days suffering in the chaff-fire, and his lower parts were burnt, Shŭnkŭracharyŭ called on him, and challenged him to dispute. Oodŭyŭnacharyŭ declined it, on account of the pain which he endured; but Shŭnkŭracharyŭ promised to cure the burnt parts, and told him, that after the dispute was over, he might offer the atonement. Oodŭyŭnacharyŭ ridiculed him for pretending to dispute with him, since he had not sense to judge in a case so obvious: half his body was burnt already; and yet he (Shŭnkŭracharyŭ) advised him to have the burnt parts restored, in order to dispute with him, in which case he would have to endure these sufferings twice over. Shŭnkŭracharyŭ, being thus overcome at the commencement, retired. The other continued the atonement, and thus expiated his sin of killing the bouddhŭ bramhŭns.

If a shōōdrŭ live with a bramhŭnēē of bad character, he must renounce life by casting himself into a large fire. If a shōōdrŭ live with a bramhŭnēē of unsullied character, he must tie straw round the different parts of his body, and cast himself into the fire. The woman must be placed on an ass, and led round the city, and then dismissed, never to return. If a voishyŭ commit the same offence with a bramhŭnēē, or a female kshŭtriyŭ, he must renounce life, tying kooshŭ grass round his limbs, and then throwing himself into the fire. If a person defile the bed of his mother-in-law, he must put a red hot piece of stone or iron into his mouth, and become an eunuch. If any person have unnatural connection with a cow, he must repeat the prajapŭtyŭ atonement four times.

If a person marry his paternal or maternal niece, he must perform the chandrayŭnŭ atonement, and the marriage becomes void, though the maintenance of this woman for life will fall upon the offender. [For marrying within the degrees of consanguinity, many different atonements are ordered, according to the nearness of relationship.]

If a bramhŭn eat without having on his poita, he must repeat the gayŭtrēē 100 times, and partake of nothing that day but the urine of cows. If a person eat cow's flesh unknowingly, he must offer the prajapŭtyŭ atonement. If he have repeatedly eaten cow's flesh, he must perform the chandrayŭnŭ vrŭtŭ, and forfeit a bull and a cow. If a person eat the flesh of elephants, horses, camels, snakes, or dogs, he must continue offering the prajapŭtyŭ atonement during twelve months. If a bramhŭn drink spirits, he must again undergo investiture with the poita. If a bramhŭn repeatedly eat onions, he must perform the chandra-yŭnŭ vrŭtŭ, and be again invested with the poita. If a person drink the milk of a cow, before the expiration of ten days after she has calved, he must fast two days. If any man drink the milk of sheep or buffaloes, he must fast two nights.

If a bramhŭn eat once with a person whose father was a shōōdrŭ and his mother a bramhŭnēē, he must perform the chandrayŭnŭ vrŭtŭ or make an offering of eight cows and their calves, or 22½ kahŭnŭs of kourees. If a bramhŭn eat the food, or semen, or urine, or ordure of a voishyŭ, he must perform the prajapŭtyŭ vrŭtŭ; or perform the other things prescribed instead of this atonement. If any person be compelled to eat the boiled rice of a chandalŭ, he must fast twelve days; but this may be commuted by giving to a bramhŭn five cows with their calves, or 15 kahŭnŭs of kourees. If the rice be unboiled, the eater must fast three days. If a bramhŭn unknowingly drink water from the pitcher with which a chandalŭ draws water from his well, he must fast three nights, and the next day he must eat cow-dung, cow's urine, milk, clarified butter, and curds, mixed together.[o] If he do this designedly, the atonement must be doubled. If a bramhŭn drink water from, or bathe in, a pool dug by a chandalŭ, he must eat cow-dung, cow's urine, milk, curds, and clarified butter, mixed together. If a dog touch a bramhŭn while he has food in his hand, the latter must fast one day. If a chandalŭ touch a bramhŭn before he have washed his hands and mouth after eating, the latter must fast three days, and repeat the gayŭtrēē a thousand times.

If a chandalŭ or meléchchŭ break a bramhŭn's poita, the bramhŭn must offer the mŭha-santŭpŭnŭ atonement[p] twice.

A person, having finished the ceremonies of an atonement, must lay a handful of grass before a cow; which if she eat, it is a proof that the sin of the offender is removed. If she refuse it, the atonement must be offered again.[q]

If sins be not expiated by the necessary atonements, the offenders will descend into hell; from whence, after expiation, they will again arise, perhaps, to human birth, in consequence of some fragment of merit which they possessed in the preceding birth; but they will continue to wear the marks of the sin in which they died.[r] Such persons must offer the proper atonements, when these

[o] In proportion to the quantity of cow-dung, he must take twice as much urine, four times as much milk, eight times as much clarified butter, and of curds the same as clarified butter.

[p] In this atonement the person must mix water steeped in kooshŭ grass, milk, curds, clarified butter, cow-dung, and cow's urine together, and eat them, and the day after he must fast.

[q] Some years ago, a rich Hindoo of Calcutta, who had committed many sins, thought it necessary to expiate them by an atonement. He invited learned natives from Nŭdēēya to ascertain the proper atonement, which he afterwards offered; but when he came to finish the ceremony by giving grass to the cow, she would not receive it. This excited the greatest anxiety, and several pŭndits were consulted, to ascertain whether the law for the ceremony had been properly laid down. They all affirmed that it had; but on Jŭgŭnnat'hŭ-tŭrkŭ-pŭnchanŭnŭ being interrogated, he declared, that the commutation, instead of three, should have been five kahŭnŭs of kourees for each cow. Upon this information the increased sum was paid; the cow then ate the grass, and the offender's sin was known to be expiated! Several other anecdotes of this kind are in circulation among the natives.—There is a remarkable coincidence betwixt this story and that related of Apis, the ox worshipped by the Egyptians, of whom it is said, that he took food from those that came to consult him; but that he refused to eat from the hands of Germanicus Cæsar, who died not long after.

[r] Mŭnoo says, 'A stealer of gold from a bramhŭn has whitlows on his nails; a drinker of spirits, black teeth; the slayer of a bramhŭn, a marasmus. The violater of his gooroo's bed shall be a deformed wretch.—For sinful acts mostly corporeal, a man shall assume after death a vegetable or mineral form; for acts mostly verbal, the form of a bird or a beast; for acts mostly mental, the lowest of human conditions.—The slayer of a bramhŭn must enter, according to the circumstances of his crime, the body of a dog, a boar, an ass, a camel, a bull, a goat, a sheep, a stag, a bird, a chandalŭ, or a puccassa.—A priest, who has drank spirituous liquors, shall migrate into the form of a smaller or larger worm or insect, of a moth, of a fly feeding on ordure, or of some ravenous animal.—He who steals the gold of a priest, shall pass a thousand times into the bodies of spiders, of snakes and camelions, of crocodiles and other aquatic monsters, or of mischievous blood-sucking demons.—He who violates the bed of his natural

sins will be removed. If such a diseased person die without having offered the atonement, the funeral rites must be refused. Should any one burn his body, he must perform the chandrayŭnŭ vrŭtŭ.

If a person weep for the death of a self-murderer, or for a person killed by a cow, or by a bramhŭn, he or she must offer an atonement. If a woman repent after ascending the funeral pile, or after resolving to renounce life in any way allowed by the shastrŭ, he or she must perform the prajapŭtŭ vrŭtŭ.

For expiating the sin of falsehood, a person must repeat the name of Vishnoo once.[s] To preserve the life of a bramhŭn, and to appease an angry wife, falsehood may be spoken innocently.

When there are many offenders in his kingdom, who are unable to offer the proper atonements, a king must perform the chandrayŭnŭ vrŭtŭ; by which he will obtain the pardon of the sins of these subjects, and deliver his kingdom from the effects of sin remaining unexpiated.[t]

or spiritual father, migrates a hundred times into the forms of grasses, of shrubs with crowded stems, or of creeping and twining plants, of vultures and other carnivorous animals, and other beasts with sharp teeth, or of tigers, and other cruel brutes.—They who hurt any sentient beings, are born cats and other eaters of raw flesh; they who taste what ought not to be tasted, maggots or small flies; they who steal ordinary things, devourers of each other; they who embrace very low women, become restless ghosts.—If a man steal grain in the husk, he shall be born a rat; if a yellow mixed metal, a gander; if water, a plava, or diver; if honey, a great stinging gnat; if milk, a crow; if expressed juice, a dog; if clarified butter, an ichneumon.—If exquisite perfumes, a muskrat; if potherbs, a peacock; if dressed grain in any of its various forms, a porcupine; if raw grain, a hedgehog.—If a deer or an elephant, he shall be born a wolf; if a horse, a tiger; if roots or fruit, an ape; if a woman, a bear; if water from a jar, the bird chataca; if carriages, a camel; if small cattle, a goat.—Women, who have committed similar thefts, incur a similar taint, and shall be paired with those male beasts in the form of their females. —As far as vital souls, addicted to sensuality, indulge themselves in forbidden pleasures, even to the same degree shall the acuteness of their senses be raised in their future bodies, that they may endure analogous pains.—They shall first have a sensation of agony in Tamisrŭ, or utter darkness, and in other seats of horror; in Usipŭtrŭvŭnŭ, or the sword-leaved forest; and in different places of binding fast and of rending.—Multifarious tortures await them: they shall be mangled by ravens and owls; shall swallow cakes boiling hot; shall work over inflamed sands, and shall feel the pangs of being baked like the vessel of a potter.—They shall assume the forms of beasts continually miserable, and suffer alternate afflictions from extremities of cold and of heat, surrounded with terrors of various kinds.—More than once shall they lie in different wombs, and, after agonizing births, be condemned to severe captivity and to servile attendance on creatures like themselves.—Then shall follow separations from kindred and friends; forced residence with the wicked; painful gains and ruinous losses of wealth; friendships hardly acquired, and at length changed into enmities.—Old age without resource; diseases attended with anguish; pangs of innumerable sorts, and, lastly, unconquerable death.'

[s] On the other hand, it is a common saying among the Hindoos, derived from some of their shastrŭs, that if a person utter a lie, his family, for fourteen generations, will successively fall into hell.

[t] I have heard a native Christian, when preaching to his countrymen, mention this atonement, to illustrate the fact of God's having given his Son as an atonement for sins committed in his earthly kingdom.

BOOK IV.

DOCTRINES OF THE HINDOO RELIGION.

The reader is referred to another part of this work for the speculative theories of the Hindoo Mythology. The author has begun these theories where they appear to be interwoven with the popular superstition.

CHAP. I.

OF THE TRANSMIGRATION OF SOULS.

AFTER death, the person is conveyed by the messengers of Yŭmŭ through the air to the place of judgment. After receiving his sentence, he wanders about the earth for twelve months, as an aerial being or ghost; and then takes a body suited to his future condition, whether he ascend to the gods, or suffer in a new body, or be hurled into some hell. This is the doctrine of several pooranŭs; others maintain, that immediately after death and judgment, the person suffers the pains of hell, and removes his sin by suffering; and then returns to the earth in some bodily form.

I add a few particulars respecting the transmigration of souls from the work called Kŭrmŭ-vipakŭ:—He who destroys a sacrifice will be punished in hell; he will afterwards be born again, and remain a fish for three years; and then ascend to human birth, but will be afflicted with a continual flux. He who kills an enemy subdued in war, will be cast into the hell Krŭkŭchŭ; after which he will become a bull, a deer, a tiger, a bitch, a fish, a man: in the last state he will die of the palsy. He who eats excellent food without giving any to others, will be punished in hell 30,000 years, and then be born a musk-rat; then a deer; then a man whose body emits an offensive smell, and who prefers bad to excellent food. The man who refuses to his father and mother the food they desire, will be punished in hell, and afterwards be born a crow; then a man. In the latter birth he will not relish any kind of food. The stealer of a water-pan will be born an alligator, and then a man of a monstrous size. The person who has lived with a woman of superior caste, will endure torments in hell during seventy-one yoogŭs of the gods: after this, in another hell, he will continue burning like a blade of grass for 100,000 years. He will next be born a worm, and after this ascend to human birth; but his body will be filled with disease. The stealer of rice will sink into hell; will afterwards be born and continue eighteen years a crow; then a heron for twelve years; then a diseased man. He who kills an animal, not designing it for sacrifice, will, in the form of a turtle, be punished in hell; then be born a bull, and then a man afflicted with an incurable distemper. He who kills an animal by holding its breath, or laughs at a pooranŭ at the time of its recital, will, after enduring infernal torments, be born a snake; then a tiger, a cow, a white heron, a crow, and a man having an asthma. He who steal alms will sink into hell, and afterwards be born a blind man, afflicted with a consumption. A beautiful woman who despises her husband, will suffer in hell a variety of torments; she will then be born a female, and, losing her husband very soon after marriage, will long suffer the miseries of widowhood.

The Ŭgnee pooranŭ says, that a person who loses human birth, passes through 8,000,000 births among the inferior creatures before he can again obtain human birth: of which he remains 2,100,000 births among the immoveable parts of creation, as stones, trees, &c.; 900,000 among the water tribes; 1,000,000 among insects, worms, &c.; 1,000,000 among the birds; and 3,000,000 among the beasts. In the ascending scale, if his works be suitable, he continues 400,000 births among the lower castes of men; during 100 births among bramhŭns; and after this he may obtain absorption in Brŭmhŭ.

Whether the doctrine of the metempsychosis originated with the politician or the philosopher, its influence on the state of society might form an interesting subject of enquiry. As far as I have been able to trace its influence, it appears to have the most unhappy effects upon the present race of Hindoos. All their sins are considered as necessary consequences of actions done in a former life, on which account they seldom charge their consciences with guilt for committing them. If a Hindoo be attacked with some disease, or fall into peculiar misfortunes, he immediately traces the cause to the sins of a former birth; and, instead of using measures to extricate himself, he sits down in despair, thinking that these things are inseparably attached to his birth, and that he can get rid of them only with life itself. In a religious view, this doctrine is very pernicious: the Christian is taught, that every thing depends upon the present state, and he therefore 'works out his salvation with fear and trembling;' but the Hindoo, like all other men, being always disposed to procrastinate in religion, finds this disposition greatly encouraged, by the hope that a future birth will be more favourable to him; that he shall be born to better fortunes, be rich, or be placed in happier circumstances for pursuing the concerns of religion. The next birth, in the mouth of a Hindoo, is the same as 'to-morrow' in the mouth of a nominal Christian.

The faith of the Hindoos in the doctrine of the transmigration of souls often appears in their conversation, especially when either prosperous or adverse circumstances have arisen in a family. When a person is in deep sorrow for the loss of a child, and is addressed by another on the subject, the former perhaps utters her grief in some such words as these :—'What have I done, that I am thus grievously afflicted? When I examine my life from my childhood, I cannot see that I have done any harm. Why then does God thus afflict me? Why did he give me a child? Why did he take it away?'—She next vents her grief in a torrent of abuse on Yŭmŭ :—'Oh! Yŭmŭ! What did I do to thee? I am sure I never injured thee. Thou knewest that I had none else: I am in this world like a blind creature; this child was my staff,— and thou hast taken him away. O thou wicked Yŭmŭ!—I will put a wisp of fire in thy face.—I will flog thee with the broom.—My breast is rent with grief.' Another female now joins her, and says, 'Oh! sister! What! is your child gone? Ah! Ah! Ah!—that vile Yŭmŭ—he is full of injustice. If I could see him, I would cut him into a thousand pieces. He has taken all mine; but he has left you one.[a] Ah! if I were stone, I should split into pieces; but I am earth—only flesh and blood, and therefore I am sunk into nothing. But why do I thus complain? I am not singular; every one's house is plundered.' Another person now comes in, and says, 'Why do you blame Yŭmŭ? What fault has he done? In former births you must have committed many crimes; otherwise I cannot see why you should suffer in this dreadful manner: you have done nothing but works of merit in this birth. You must have injured some one's child in a former birth, and now yours is taken from you. Yŭmŭ has done nothing wrong. He is justice itself. He never errs. Nor ought you to think it extraordinary that a person dies. It is more extraordinary that a peason desires to live. If you confine a bird in a cage, though you cherish him with the greatest care, if the door be open he flies away. But though there are nine openings in the body by which the soul may make its escape, and though the person be suffering the deepest distress, yet the soul is not willing to depart;—this desire of life is more wonderful than death itself.—When the soul has taken its flight, then, why should you think it such an extraordinary thing? You are suffering for the sins of many former births; which sins, like a shadow, will pursue you, go where you will, and assume whatever shape you may, till they be expiated by suffering. If this were not so, why is it that a good man suffers, while a wicked man is raised to the pinnacle of prosperity? If men suffered only for the

[a] The Hindoo women are excessively fond of their children. When a mother pays her respects to an aged female, she presents her child to receive her blessing, and says, 'Mother!—give my child your blessing.' The old woman says, 'Live, live, as many years as there are hairs on my head.' When a mother takes her child into company, to prevent its being hurt by a witch, she rubs its forehead with earth thrown up by worms, or with the end of a lamp-wick, and spits on its breast.

sins of this life, the good would have nothing but happiness, and the wicked nothing but sorrow.'[b]

Sometimes the doctrine of transmigration appears in the conversation of widows, when they are talking over their sorrows one amongst another. One begins the conversation, by addressing one of the company, recently become a widow, in some such words as these :—' Ah ! why is so much trouble fallen upon you ? You have continually performed works of merit. I have observed, that from your childhood you have been very religious.'[c] Another replies,—' How you talk ! What ! do you think she is suffering for sins committed in this birth ?' The widow addressed now adds :—' Ah ! my sorrows are indescribable. I am now suffering for the sins of many births ; the sins of birth after birth, birth after birth, are fallen upon me. If the sins of numerous births had not been cast upon me, would my husband (a lac of lives in one) have been taken from me ? O God, do not bring upon my worst enemy the misery which I endure. What had I done against God, and what against him, (her husband,) that I suffer thus ? I must have injured him in a former birth, and therefore he was married to me on purpose to bring upon me the sorrows of widowhood. He was born in one womb, and I in another ; we were perfect strangers ; fate brought us together, and I began to flatter myself that I should long enjoy the blessings of a married state, when he was seized with sickness, and, without making the least provision for me, has left me to crouch and fawn for a handful of rice. When waiting upon him in his last moments he did not say, 'I leave you this or that ; you will not be destitute :' but, shutting up my food and garments, he has thus abandoned me. He ! he was my greatest enemy. If I meet him in a future state, I'll certainly revenge myself. Instead of putting fire into his mouth after death, if I had known that he would have served me thus, I would have put fire in his mouth while living. I entreat the gods, that in the next birth I may be a man, and he my wife, and that I may bring upon him exactly what he has brought upon me ; and that this may be continued through numerous births. Vile enemy—.' Continuing her address to a married woman, she says :—' See ! you have two meals a day,

[b] I have heard it urged, in proof of the reality of successive births, that if a child had not drawn the breast in a former birth, it would not, as soon as born, cling to the breast, and know how to suck. A person before whom this argument was once urged, asked how this was to be accounted for when the person arose from the state of a fish to human birth ?

[c] When a Hindoo female child shews her attachment to religion, she gathers vilwŭ leaves and flowers, and making an image of the lingŭ, attempts to worship it ; or she sits down attentively, and watches others while they perform the ceremonies of worship ; or she goes to a festival, and assists the females in making the necessary preparations. When she is grown to maturity, she performs different ceremonies to obtain the blessing of a good husband. After marriage she worships Shivŭ and other gods, and prays that her husband may love her, and live long, so that she may not endure the hardships of widowhood. When she becomes a mother, she daily bows to the gods, repeats their names, and prays that they will bless her child.

while I have but one; you have all manner of ornaments, and I am naked; you are invited to all the feasts;[d] you can eat of all kinds of delicacies, but I must live on the meanest food; I must fast twice a month;—[e] there is no end of my sorrows.'

If a person die an untimely death, it is attributed to crimes committed in a former state of existence. A person born blind, is supposed to have destroyed the eyes of some one in a former birth. A few neighbours sitting together, as a person afflicted with an incurable distemper passes along, observe, 'Ah! no doubt, that man was guilty in a former birth of such or such a crime, and now the consequences appear in his present state.'

The prosperity of persons, especially if they have suddenly risen from poverty to affluence, frequently gives rise to remarks on the merits of such persons in a former birth: 'See,' says one, 'such a person was poor, and is now worth so many lacs of rupees. He must have performed acts of extraordinary merit in former births, or he could not have so suddenly risen to such a state of affluence.' When conversing on this subject with a Hindoo, he instanced the case of Ramŭ-Hŭree-Vishwasŭ, late of Khŭrdah:—'He was so poor,' said he, 'that he was indebted to others for a place to lodge in. After a few years of service with a European, he obtained a fortune of thirty lacs of rupees. He bought an estate; erected a number of temples to Shivŭ, and then went to Kashēē, (Benares,) where he died in a very short time. Such an auspicious life and death[f] can only be attributed to some wonderful acts of devotion or liberality in former births.'

A very learned man is complimented with having given learning to others in a former birth.

When the Hindoos see any of the animals used cruelly, especially cows, they exclaim:—'Ah! how many sins must that creature have committed in a former birth!' They say the same if they see a dog eating ordure. When they see a dog riding with his master in his palanqueen, they say, 'True, thou art born a dog, but some good works have made thy fate tolerable.'

The pooranŭs and other shastrŭs promise deliverance from future birth upon the performance of different religious ceremonies.

[d] A widow can take no share in marriage ceremonies, &c. She is not even permitted to touch the bride.

[e] This fast is kept by widows on the eleventh of the increase and decrease of the moon in every month; and is observed so strictly among the higher castes, that notwithstanding a widow has eaten only once on the preceding day, she does not touch the least aliment, not even a drop of water, on this day.

[f] Every one who dies at Kashēē becomes a god.

CHAP. II.

JUDGMENT OF MEN AFTER DEATH.

[From the Pŭdmŭ pooranŭ.]

At the extremity of the earth southwards, floating on the waters, is Sŭngyŭmŭnēē, the residence of Yŭmŭ, the judge of the dead, and of his recorder Chitru-gooptŭ, and his messengers. Yŭmŭ has four arms, is of a dark colour, with eyes like the petal of the water-lily; in his hands he holds a shell, a discus, a club, and a lotus; he rides on Gŭroorŭ; wears a golden poita, and pearl ear-rings; and has a crown on his head, and a garland of flowers round his neck. Chitrŭ-gooptŭ, the recorder, and Yŭmŭ's attendants, appear in the most pleasing forms.

Those who perform works of merit are led to Yŭmŭ's palace along the most excellent roads, in some parts of which the heavenly courtezans are seen dancing or singing; and gods, gŭndhŭrvŭs, &c. are heard chanting the praises of other gods; in others, showers of flowers are falling from heaven; in other parts are houses containing cooling water, and excellent food; pools of water covered with nymphœas; and trees, affording fragrance by their blossoms and shade by their leaves. The gods are seen to pass on horses or elephants, with white umbrellas carried over them; or in palanquecns or chariots, fanned with the chamŭrŭs of the gods; while the dévŭrshees are chanting their praises as they pass along. Some, by the glory issuing from their bodies, illumine the ten quarters of the world.

Yŭmŭ receives the good with much affection, and, feasting them with excellent food, thus addresses them:—'Ye are truly meritorious in your deeds; ye are wise; by the power of your merits ascend to an excellent heaven. He who, born in the world, performs meritorious actions, he is my father, brother, and friend.'

The wicked have 688,000 miles to travel to the palace of Yŭmŭ, to receive judgment. In some places they pass over a pavement of fire; in others, the earth in which their feet sink is burning hot; or they pass over burning sands, or over stones with sharp edges, or burning hot; sometimes showers of sharp instruments, and at others showers of burning cinders, or scalding water, or stones fall upon them; burning winds scorch their bodies; every now and then they fall into concealed wells full of darkness, or pass through narrow passages filled with stones, in which serpents lie concealed ; sometimes the road is filled with thick darkness ; at other times they pass through the branches of trees, the leaves of which are full of thorns ; again they walk over broken pots, or over hard clods of earth, bones, putrifying flesh, thorns, or sharp spikes ; they meet tigers, jackals, rhinoceroses, elephants, terrible giants, &c. ; and in some parts they are scorched in the sun without obtaining the least shade. They travel naked ; their hair is in disorder ; their throat, lips, &c. are parched ; they are covered with blood, or dirt ; some wail and shriek as they pass along ; others are weeping ; others have horror depicted on their countenances ; some are dragged along by leathern thongs tied round their necks, waists, or hands ; others by cords passed through holes bored in their noses ; others by the hair, the ears, the neck, or the heels ; and others are carried, having their heads and legs tied together. On arriving at the palace, they behold Yŭmŭ clothed with terror, two hundred and forty miles in height ; his eyes distended like a lake of water ; of a purple colour : with rays of glory issuing from his body ; his voice is loud as the thunders at the dissolution of the universe ; the hairs of his body are each as long as a palm-tree ; a flame of fire proceeds from his mouth ; the noise of the drawing of his breath is greater than the roaring of a tempest ; his teeth are exceedingly long, and his nails like the fan for winnowing corn. In his right hand he holds an iron club ; his garment is an animal's skin ; and he rides on a terrific buffalo. Chitrŭ-gooptŭ also appears as a terrible monster, and makes a noise like a warrior when about to rush to battle. Sounds terrible as thunder are heard, ordering punishments to be inflicted on the offenders. At length Yŭmŭ orders the criminals into his presence, and thus addresses them :—'Did you not know that I am placed above all, to award happiness to the good, and punishment to the wicked ? Knowing this, have you lived in sin ; Have you never heard that there are different hells for the punishment of the wicked ; Have you never given your minds to religion ? To-day, with your own eyes, you shall see the punishment of the wicked.—From yoogŭ to yoogŭ stay in these hells !—You have pleased yourselves in sinful practices : endure now the torments due to these sins. What will weeping avail ?' Yŭmŭ next directs Chitrŭgooptŭ to examime into the offences of the criminals, who now demand the names of the witnesses : let such, say they, appear, and give their evidence in our presence. Yŭmŭ smiling, though full of rage, commands Sōōryŭ,[g] Chŭndrŭ,[h] Pŭvŭnŭ,[i] Ŭgnee,[k] Akashŭ,[l] Prit'hivēē,[m] Vŭroonŭ,[n] Tit'hee,[o] Dinŭ,[p] Ratree,[q] Pratŭ-kalŭ,[r] Sŭndhya-kalŭ,[s] and Dhŭrmŭ,[t] to appear against the prisoners ; who, hearing the evidence, are struck dumb,

[g] The sun. [h] The moon. [i] Wind. [k] Fire. [l] Æther. [m] Earth. [n] Water. [o] A lunar-day. [p] Day. [q] Night. [r] Morning. [s] Evening. [t] A representative of Yŭmŭ. All the elements, and the divisions of time, are thus called upon to witness against the prisoners.

and remain trembling and stupified with fear. Yŭmŭ, then gnashing his teeth, beats the prisoners with his iron club till they roar with anguish; after which he drives them to different hells.

CHAP. III.

OF FUTURE HAPPINESS.

THE shastrŭs teach that there are four kinds of happiness after death: 1. That possessed in the heaven of the gods;[u]—2. That when the person is deified;—3. That which arises from dwelling in the presence of the gods[x];—and, 4. In absorption.[y] In the three first, the person is subject to future birth, but not in the last. The three first are obtained by works; the last by divine wisdom.

The descriptions which the pooranŭs give of the heavens of the gods are truly in the eastern style: all things, even the beds of the gods, are made of gold and precious stones. All the pleasures of these heavens are exactly what we should expect in a system formed by uninspired and unrenewed men: like the paradise of Mahomet, they are houses of ill-fame, rather than places of rewards for 'the pure in heart.' Here all the vicious passions are personified, or rather deified:—the quarrels and licentious intrigues of the gods fill these places with perpetual uproar, while their impurities are described with the same literality and gross detail, as similar things are talked of among these idolaters on earth. It would be a flagrant insult to compare these heavens with the place which our Saviour went to prepare for his disciples;[z] but the serious enquirer after truth will be struck with this additional proof, that the Christian religion is 'worthy of all acceptation.'

I here subjoin an account of the heaven of Koovérŭ, the god of riches, from the Mŭhabharŭtŭ:—It is eight hundred miles long, and five hundred and sixty broad. The wind, perfumed with ten

[u] The Mēēmangsŭ writers have decided, that there is no separate place of future happiness; that whether a person enjoy happiness, or endure misery, the whole is confined to the present life. The pooranŭs, on the other hand, declare, that there are many places of happiness and misery, and that persons go to these places after death.

[x] All raised to heaven are not permitted to approach the god in whose heaven they reside. This privilege belongs only to favourites.

[y] The védantŭ shastrŭs teach, that wherever a person possessing divine wisdom dies, he is immediately received into the divine nature, as air, escaping from a vessel when broken, immediately mixes with the surrounding air. The pooranŭs, however, teach, that the soul of such a person ascends to God inhabiting a certain place, and is there absorbed into the divine nature.

[z] John xiv. 2.

thousand odours, blows in soft breezes; and the place, in every part adorned with gold and jewels, displays a glory like that produced by the rays of the full moon. Here are also canals of the purest water filled with fish, water-fowl, water-lilies, &c. with flights of steps made of gold; with forests and gardens in which Koovérŭ and his courtezans divert themselves. In the treasury of this god are immense heaps of jewels, gold, silver, &c. from which the gods and goddesses supply themselves with ornaments. Koovérŭ sits on a throne glorious as the meridian sun, and reposes on a bed equally splendid. He is surrounded by different gods, among whom are Shivŭ, Doorga, Shivu's bull, his servants Nŭndee, Mŭha-kalŭ, Shŭnkoo, Kŭrnŭ, &c. and by a thousand goddesses, or concubines, shining like the lightning, and adorned with loads of jewels; by the titans, by Ravŭnŭ, Vibhēēshŭnŭ, and other rakshŭsŭs, the pishachŭs, the gŭndhŭrvŭs, the kinnŭrŭs, the ŭpsŭras, the vidyadhŭrŭs, the mountain gods, &c. Before this assembly, the ŭpsŭras dance; the kinnŭrŭs, (with horses' mouths,) and the gŭndhŭrvŭs, sing and play on heavenly instruments. All the pleasures of the other heavens are to be found here.

The following are esteemed works of merit, capable of raising a person to celestial happiness:—Honoring, entertaining, serving, and giving gifts to bramhŭns: the more learned the bramhŭn, the greater the merit. Worshipping and repeating the names of the gods, and particularly that of a person's guardian deity; visiting or residing at holy places, and performing the accustomed religious ceremonies there; performing the shraddhŭ for deceased ancestors; bathing in the Ganges and other sacred rivers; offering sacrifices; building temples; cutting roads and pools; planting trees, especially sacred trees; making and setting up images; repeating the gayŭtrēē, and other parts of the védŭs; reading the védŭ and other shastrŭs, or hearing them read; honoring and serving a spiritual guide; hospitality to guests, especially to bramhŭns; fasting, particularly at times directed by the shastrus; burning with a deceased husband; parting with life in sacred places.

King Soorŭt'hŭ was raised to the heaven of Indrŭ for performing the sacrifice of a horse.[a] King Trishŭnkoo obtained heaven by the power of the merits which Vŭshisht'hŭ, a bramhŭn, transferred to him.[b] Ŭmbŭrēēshŭ, a king, was about to perform a human sacrifice, in order to obtain heaven; but when going to slay the victim, through the interference of Vishwamitrŭ, a bramhŭn, his sacrifice was accepted of the gods, though the victim was not slain,[c] and the king ascended to the heaven of Indrŭ.[d] King In-

[a] Shree-bhagŭvŭtŭ [b] Ibid.

[c] He repeated an incantation given by Vishwamitrŭ, which destroyed the power of the fire.

[d] Shrēē-bhagŭvŭtŭ.

support themselves by manual labour. What a heavy tax this must be on the industrious, the great body of whom among the Hindoos are comparatively poor!

When we add to this, the baneful effects of this system on the morals of the mendicants themselves, as well as on the public manners, every benevolent mind must exceedingly deplore such a state of things. These beggars are not frowned upon like those who have nothing but their misery to plead for them; but are privileged and insolent harpies, boldly demanding the contributions of the abject and superstitious Hindoos. Their indolent habits too, and the filthy songs they sing, lead to every species of impurity, and to perpetual acts of private plunder.

Many of the more enlightened Hindoos, especially the bramhŭns, hold these mendicants in the utmost contempt, and would consider their being compelled to work as a great blessing conferred upon the country. On the other hand, some persons of property treat them with the greatest reverence, and sometimes invite a number of them to their houses, drink the water with which they have washed their feet, and, at the end of the entertainment, eat of the refuse from the plate of each. Gŭnga-Govindŭ-Singhŭ, a person of the writer caste, who was patronized by Mr. Hastings, and who realized a princely fortune, carried his attachment to the Voiragēē mendicants to the greatest lengths. He sometimes gave a feast to three or four thousand, and performed the lowest offices of service to these his guests: he also provided that persons of this description should, after his death, be constantly entertained, receive presents, have medical attendance when sick, &c. at all the temples which he erected and dedicated to the different forms of Krishnŭ.

BOOK VI.

HINDOO RELIGIOUS SECTS.

CHAP. I.

ACCOUNT OF THE REGULAR HINDOO SECTS.

THERE are three principal sects among the regular Hindoos, the Soivŭs, the Voishnŭvŭs, and the Shaktŭs.

The *Soivŭs* receive the initiatory rites by which Shivŭ becomes their guardian deity; they imprint on their faces and bodies the marks by which this sect is distinguished,[a] and profess the most devoted regard to this god, trusting in him for protection, &c. Their daily worship is performed before an image of the lingŭ, either at home or by the side of a river, using those forms and offerings which are peculiar to the sect. They have no festivals, but once in the year they keep a fast in honour of Shivŭ, which is accompanied by the worship of this god at the temples of the lingŭ. In the month Voishakhŭ they present to this idol the leaves of the vilwŭ, a favourite tree sacred to Shivŭ, and pour libations of milk on the lingŭ. Some Soivŭs, at this auspicious season, plant shrubs near the lingŭ, and sit before it repeating the name of Shivŭ. It is an act of great merit among this sect to repeat the name of their idol, with a necklace made of the seeds of the roodrakshŭ; as well as to visit Benares, (Kashēē,) a place sacred to Shivŭ. The persons belonging to this sect are principally bramhŭns; but the Soivŭs are not numerous in Bengal. Mendicant Soivŭs are very rarely seen: these persons cover themselves with ashes, wear large necklaces made of roodrakshŭ seeds, and wander to Benares and other places sacred to this god.

The *Voishnŭvŭs* observe the rites, and receive the distinguishing mark[b] of their sect, regarding Vishnoo in all his forms (as Ramŭ, Krishnŭ, Jŭgŭnnat'hŭ, &c. &c.) as their protector. They reject all animal food, even fish, and wear only white garments. Nearly one half of the Hindoo population of Bengal are Voishnŭvŭs, composed principally of the lower orders: great numbers are religious mendicants. Almost all the Hindoos in the province of Orissa are Voishnŭvŭs. The followers of Choitŭnyŭ, having the Gosaees at their head, continue a distinct branch of this sect. The distinguishing vice of this sect is impurity, as might be expected from the character of Krishnŭ, their favourite deity, and from the obscene nature of the festivals held in his honour. The Shrēē-bhagŭvŭtŭ is the

[a] See p. 12. [b] See p. 8.

book which the few bramhŭns to be found among the Voishnŭvŭs read: those less learned read a number of books written in Bengalee, all relating to the actions of Krishnŭ or Choitŭnyŭ.

The *Shaktŭs* are the worshippers of Bhŭgŭvŭtēē, (Doorga,) including all the forms of this goddess. They have their peculiar rites, marks on their bodies, formulas, priests, and festivals. The generality of those who join this sect are bramhŭns In their outward dress the Shaktŭs resemble the Soivŭs; but the latter in their principles approach nearest to the Voishnŭvŭs, especially in their mutual objection to the destruction of animal life. None of the Shaktŭs embrace a life of mendicity. They derive the principles of their sect, and the forms used in their religious ceremonies, from the Tŭntrŭs, by which works spirituous liquors are placed among the proper offerings to Bhŭgŭvŭtēē; and numbers of her worshippers, offering libations to the goddess, drink to intoxication. The Vamacharēēs belong to this sect.

Beside these three principal sects among the Hindoos, the shastrŭs mention two others, the worshippers of the sun (Sourŭs) and of Gŭnéshŭ (Ganŭpŭtyŭs.) Very few Hindoos, however, in the province of Bengal, are to be found, who have chosen these gods as their guardian deities.

The religious mendicants of the same sect differ so much from each other in dress and certain ceremonies, that they might be supposed to belong to different sects; but any remarks on these shades of difference are rendered unnecessary by the preceding chapter. I shall therefore proceed immediately to notice the three most important schisms among the Hindoos, those excited by Boodhŭ, Nanŭkŭ, and Choitŭnyŭ.

CHAP. II.

ACCOUNT OF THE BOUDDHŬS.

It is a question not perhaps completely decided, whether the religion of Booddhŭ, now spread over the Burman empire, Siam, Ceylon, Japan,[a] Cochin-China, and the greater part of China itself,[b]

[a] Kæmpfer says, on the authority of the Japanese historians, that the Bouddhŭ doctrine was carried into Japan about the year 63.—See page 365

[b] The Abbe Grosier (Book vii. c. ii. p. 312) gives the following account of the doctrine of *Fo*, in which the principles of Booddhŭ are clearly to be distinguished:—'Nothing is the beginning and end of every thing that exists: from nothing our first parents derived their existence, and to nothing they returned after their death. All beings are the same, their only difference consists in their figure and qualities. A man, a lion, or any other animal may be formed of the same metal; if these different pieces are afterwards melted, they will immediately lose their figure and qualities, and together form only one substance Such is the case with all beings, whether animate

be not in reality the ancient religion of India, and the bramhinical superstition the invention of later times, and raised to predominancy by the superior influence of the bramhŭns with the princes of Hindoost'hanŭ. The author, however, declines entering on this subject, made so difficult by the want of authentic historical evidence.

It is certain, that amongst the six schools of philosophy formerly famous among the Hindoos, two of them inculcated doctrines respecting the First Cause of things that were decidedly atheistical, or such as the followers of Booddhŭ maintain at this day; and it is indisputable, according to the Hindoo writings, that these two sects were numerous before the appearance of Booddhŭ.

About 700 years before the commencement of the Christian era, Vēērŭ-Vahoo, of the race of Goutŭmŭ, a person attached to one of these sects, destroyed his sovereign Bodhŭmŭllŭ, and immediately seized the throne of Delhi. This king, and his three immediate successors, reigned one hundred and eight years. Mŭhēē-pŭtēē, or the lord of the earth, was the name of the third of these monarchs; and as most of the writers on this subject agree in placing the era of Booddhŭ in the sixth century B. C., it seems reasonable to suppose, that Booddhŭ was the son or near relation of Mŭhēē-pŭtee. If not connected with this family, why should the family name of this race, Goutŭmŭ, be one of the most common names of Booddhŭ? As the capital of the most powerful of the Hindoo monarchs of this period was in South Behar, if Booddhŭ was not the son of one of the Mŭgŭdhŭ kings, it is possible he belonged to some branch of the family reigning at Benares, which was probably then a separate kingdom. In the Témee Jétŭ, a history of one of the incarnations of Booddhŭ, he is said to have been the son of a king of Benares, and to have persevered in choosing the life of an ascetic against every possible artifice and persuasion of his loyal parents. The author has been favoured with a translation of this work, by Mr. F. Carey, of

or inanimate; though different in shape and qualities, they are still the same thing sprung from the same beginning, which is nothing. This universal principle is extremely pure, exempt from all change, exceedingly subtle and simple: it remains continually in a state of rest; has neither virtue, power, nor intelligence: besides, its essence consists in being free from action, without knowledge and without desires. To obtain happiness, we must endeavour by continual meditation, and frequent victories over ourselves, to acquire a likeness to this principle; and to obtain that end, we must accustom ourselves to do nothing, will nothing, feel nothing, desire nothing. When we have attained to this state of happy insensibility, we have nothing more to do with virtue or vice, punishments or rewards, providence or the immortality of the soul. The whole of holiness consists in ceasing to exist, in being confounded with nothing; the nearer man approaches to the nature of a stone or log, the nearer he is to perfection; in a word, it is in indolence and immobility, in the cessation of all desires and bodily motion, in the annihilation and suspension of all the faculties both of body and soul, that all virtue and happiness consist. The moment that man arrives at this degree of perfection, he has no longer occasion to dread changes, futurity, or transmigrations, because he hath ceased to exist, and is become perfectly like the god *Fo.*'

Rangoon, and has added it at the close of this account. If then it be admitted, that Booddhŭ was a person of royal descent, that he chose an ascetic life,[c] and embraced a system of philosophy already prevalent in India, the other scenes of the drama require no assistance from conjecture: he became the patron and idol of the sect which from this time became distinguished by his name; he also received the support of the reigning monarchs, who were attached to him not only by holding the same philosophical opinions, but by the ties of blood.

This sect being thus established by Mŭhēē-pŭtee, the eleven Bouddhŭ monarchs who succeeded him, and who reigned 291 years, may reasonably be supposed to have done what the bramhŭns charge them with, to have obliterated the religion of their opponents.

It is certain, however, that the learned adherents of the bramhinical religion did not remain silent spectators of what they deemed the triumph of atheism.[d] They contended with their equally learned opponents, and this dispute, as is manifest by the tendency of many of the works still read by the Hindoos, called forth all the talents of both sides; challenges to conduct the controversy in the presence of kings and learned assemblies were given and accepted: but here, as in innumerable other instances, the arm of power prevailed; and as long as the reigning monarchs were Bouddhŭs, the bramhŭns were obliged to confine themselves to verbal contentions.

At length Dhoorŭndhŭrŭ, of the race of Mŭyōōrŭ, destroyed Adityŭ, the last Bouddhŭ king, and assumed the sovereignty; and it is probable that from this time (B. C. about 300 years) we are to date the commencement of the persecutions of the Bouddhŭs.[e]

[c] The disposition manifested by all superstitious nations to honour and even to deify men remarkable for outward austerity, is particularly observable amongst the Hindoos. They suppose that such a saint is a divine oracle, or the visible representative of the deity; they implicitly receive his doctrines, and pay him those honors which they conceive are due 'to gods come down in the likeness of men.' This attachment to eminent ascetics naturally springs out of the Hindoo system; and to this, the author conjectures, we are to attribute the origin and prevalence of the THREE GREAT SCHISMS among the Hindoos, of *Booddhŭ*, of *Nanŭkŭ*, and of *Choitŭnyŭ*, all of whom appear to have been religious mendicants.

[d] A story respecting these times is still current among the Noiyayikŭ sect:—The wife of the last Bouddhŭ monarch but one was a disciple of Vishnoo, and called day and night upon God, complaining against the Bouddhŭs as having exterminated his worship, and all traces of a deity: at length Vishnoo, by a voice from heaven, assured her, that he would appear in the forms of two learned men, Bhŭttŭ and Oodŭyŭnacharjyŭ, and restore his worship. Another story related by the same sect is, that Oodŭyŭnacharjyŭ, unable to turn the Bouddhŭs by argument, proposed that himself and any number of this sect should cast themselves from a neighbouring mountain; the Bouddhŭs in the act of falling crying out, 'There is no God,' and Oodŭyŭnacharjyŭ, 'God exists.' The challenge was accepted: the Bouddhŭs perished, and their opponent fell unhurt.

[e] In opposition to this, it is said, 'If the conjectures of Sir William Jones, relative

One or two facts tend to prove, that the bramhŭns were not much more mild and tolerant than other persecutors:—though a number of *Joinŭs* are scattered up and down in various parts of Hindoost'hanŭ, scarcely a vestige of the Bouddhŭ superstition is to be found, and all its adherents are seen in the adjoining countries.—The fact respecting these persecutions is, however, placed beyond all doubt by the Prayŭshchittŭ-vivékŭ, a Hindoo work on atonements; from which we learn, that Oodŭyŭnacharjyŭ, a learned bramhŭn, and a fierce combatant against the Bouddhŭs, actually burnt himself to death on a chaff-fire, (kooshŭanŭlŭ,) as an atonement for the sin of having excited the Hindoo kings to put to death many Bouddhŭ bramhŭns.

To avoid the malice of their enemies, therefore, the Bouddhŭs emigrated to the neighbouring countries, and gave to the uncivilized inhabitants those doctrines, for which they had been unsuccessfully contending on the plains of Hindoost'hanŭ.

We have no authentic documents to prove how long this persecution lasted; but it is a pretty current opinion among the most learned Bŭrmans, that the religion of Booddhŭ was introduced into that country about 450 years after his death. According to this statement, (admitting that the persecution began with Dhoorŭndhŭrŭ,) it will appear to have continued 183 years.

There is a tradition among the Cingalese, that one of the kings of Hindoost'hanŭ, immediately after Booddhŭ's death,[f] collected together five hundred learned ascetics, and persuaded them to write down on palmyra leaves, from the mouth of one of Booddhŭ's principal disciples, all the doctrines taught by Booddhŭ in his lifetime. The Cingalese admit that they received their religion from the hands of a stranger; and it is probable that it was propagated in the Bŭrman empire soon after its reception in Ceylon, that is, about 450 years after Booddhŭ's death. The Bŭrmans believe, that six hundred and fifty years after that event, in the reign of Mŭhamoonee, Booddhŭ-ghoshŭ, a bramhŭn, was deputed to Ceylon, to copy the work Vishooddhimargŭ, which includes all the Jatŭs, or histories of the incarnations of Booddhŭ: and it is fabled, that the iron stile with which he copied this work, was given him by a heavenly messenger; though others will have it that Bodhee-sŭtwŭ gave it to him.

These Jatŭs are said to have amounted to five hundred and fifty books; some of which are, however, lost. A work called the

to the inscriptions found at Mougheer, and on the pillar at Buddal, be well founded, then the governing power on the banks of the Ganges, as late as about the time of the birth of Christ, was of the sect of Bonddha.'—*Asiatic Researches*, vol. vi. p. 165.

[f] A native of Ceylon assured the author, that the Cingalese considered it to be about 2,500 years since the death of Goutŭmŭ. Mr. Felix Carey informed him, on the authority of the Bŭrman history, that in 1813 it was 2,357 years since the birth of this god. In an account published in the Asiatic Researches, vol. vi. p. 265, it is said, that in 1795, Booddhŭ had been deified 2,362 years.

Ten Jatŭs is now the best known, and is held in the highest veneration. The names of these Jatŭs are, Témee, Jŭnŭkŭ, Soobŭrnŭramŭ, Némee, Mŭhoshŭt'ha, Bhōoridŭttŭ, Chŭndŭ-koomarŭ, Narŭdŭ Vidoorŭ and Vésŭntŭra.

Since the above period, many Bŭrmans have translated and commented on these writings. In a work entitled 'The Great History of the Bŭrman and Pegu kings,' it is recorded, that during the T'hioorŭ-kshŭtriyŭ dynasty, not less than fifty-five translations were made, and as many comments written on these books. But the Bŭrmans are believed to possess works of greater antiquity than these Jatŭs, on history, poetry, medicine, astronomy, grammar, &c whether borrowed from the Sŭngskritŭ, or the productions of the Bouddhŭ set, time must disclose.[g]

It is a singular circumstance, that the Bouddhŭs should have chosen for their hero, like the Hindoos for Vishnoo, ten incarnations; and still more singular, that they should have designated the histories of these incarnations by the names of ten Hindoo sages.

The Bouddhŭs do not believe in a First Cause: they consider matter as eternal; that every portion of animated existence has in itself its own rise, tendency, and destiny; that the condition of creatures on earth is regulated by works of merit and demerit: that works of merit not only raise individuals to happiness, but, as they prevail, raise the world itself to prosperity; while, on the other hand, when vice is predominant, the world degenerates till the universe itself is dissolved. They suppose, however, that there is always some superior deity, who has attained to this elevation by religious merit; but they do not regard him as the governor of the world. To the present grand period, comprehending all the time included in a kŭlpŭ, they assign five deities, four of whom have already appeared, including Goutŭmŭ, or Booddhŭ, whose exaltation continues five thousand years, 2,356 of which had expired A. D. 1814. After the expiration of the 5,000 years, another saint will obtain the ascendancy, and be deified. Six hundred millions of saints are said to be canonized with each deity, though it is admitted that Booddhŭ took only 24,000 devotees to heaven with him.

The lowest state of existence is in hell; the next, is that in the forms of brutes: both these are states of punishment. The next ascent is to that of man, which is probationary. The next includes many degrees of honour and happiness up to demi-gods, &c. which are states of reward for works of merit. The ascent to superior deity is from the state of man.

g Some idea of their advance in science may be gathered from an interesting account of the Religion and Literature of the Bŭrmans, inserted in the 6th vol. of the Asiatic Researches, by Dr. F. Buchanan.

The Bouddhŭs are taught, that there are four superior heavens which are not destroyed at the end of a kŭlpŭ; that below these, there are twelve other heavens, followed by six inferior heavens; after which follows the earth; then the world of snakes; and then thirty-two chief hells; to which are to be added, one hundred and twenty hells of milder torments.

The highest state of glory is absorption. The person who is unchangeable in his resolution; who has obtained the knowledge of things past, present, and to come through one kŭlpŭ; who can make himself invisible; go where he pleases; and who has attained to complete abstraction, will enjoy absorption.[k]

Those who perform works of merit, are admitted to the heavens of the different gods, or are made kings or great men on earth; and those who are wicked, are born in the forms of different animals, or consigned to different hells. The happiness of these heavens is described as entirely sensual.

The Bouddhŭs believe, that at the end of a kŭlpŭ the universe is destroyed. To convey some idea of the extent of this period, the illiterate Cingalese use this comparison: 'If a man were to ascend a mountain nine miles high, and to renew these journies once in every hundred years, till the mountain were worn down by his feet to an atom, the time required to do this would be nothing to the fourth part of a kŭlpŭ.'

Booddhŭ, before his exaltation, taught his followers, that after his ascent, the remains of his body, his doctrine, or an assembly of his disciples, were to be held in equal reverence with himself. When a Cingalese, therefore, approaches an image of Booddhŭ, he says, 'I take refuge in Booddhŭ; I take refuge in his doctrine; I take refuge in his followers.'

There are five commands given to the common Bouddhŭs: the first forbids the destruction of animal life; the second forbids theft; the third, adultery; the fourth, falsehood; the fifth, the use of spirituous liquors. There are other commands for superior classes, or devotees, which forbid dancing, songs, music festivals, perfumes, elegant dresses, elevated seats, &c. Among works of the highest merit, one is the feeding of a hungry infirm tiger with a person's own flesh.

The temples erected in honor of Booddhŭ[i], in the Bŭrman

[k] The Hindoo idea of absorption is, that the soul is received into the divine essence: but as the Bouddhŭs reject the doctrine of a separate Supreme Spirit, it is difficult to say what are their ideas of absorption. Dr. Buchanan says, (Asiatic Researches, vol. vi. p. 180.) Nirvanŭ 'implies (that is, among the Bŭrmans) exemption from all the miseries incident to humanity, but by no means annihilation.

[i] When the author asked a *Joinŭ* why, since the object of their worship was neither creator nor preserver, they honored him as God, he was answered, that it was an act of homage to exalted merit.

empire, are of various sizes and forms, as quadrangular, pentagonal, hexagonal, heptagonal, or octagonal. Those of a round spiral form can be erected only by the king, or by persons high in office. An elevated spot is preferred for the erection of these edifices ; but where such an elevation cannot be found, the building is erected upon the second, third, fourth, fifth, or sixth terrace. These piles are generally of solid brick work, but some are filled up with earth or rubbish ; lime-stone is seldom used, generally earth or brick-dust. Those who can afford it have their temples gilt all over, which gives them a grand appearance. A coating of black lacker being laid upon the plaister, the gold-leaf firmly adheres. An umbrella made of iron, and gilt, is fixed on the tops of the temples, round the border of which some persons suspend bells ; the sound of these bells, when the wind puts them in motion, has a pleasing effect. Bells of various sizes are sometimes hung near a temple, which the people ring to give notice of their arrival. Images of lions, and monsters of various descriptions, facing the four quarters, or on each side of the gate-ways, are to be seen attached to most temples.

Within the vicinity of a temple, houses of charity for strangers are erected, in which images of Booddhŭ are placed. Umbrellas and stone pots, in imitation of those used by Goutŭmŭ as a mendicant, are also placed near temples.

The temples of Booddhŭ in Ceylon are very large, some of them capable of containing 3,000 people. Many of them have verandahs all round. The hall containing the image is very spacious.

The priests worship at the temples daily, or ought to do so, The worship consists in presenting flowers, incense, rice, betle-nut, &c. repeating certain prayers. The priest cleanses the temple, preserves the lights, and receives the offerings. A worshipper may present his own offerings, if he is acquainted with the formulas The five commands are repeated by a priest twice a day to the people, who stand up and repeat them after him.

Temples are built by individuals, or the inhabitants of a village, as works of merit. Several festivals precede the opening of a temple, as, at laying the foundation ; at setting up the image ; at fixing the umbrella ; at the purification ; and at the consecration. These feasts are sometimes continued four or five days, when musicians and dancing girls are employed, various pantomimical representations are exhibited, and a great concourse of people entertained. Offerings of various kinds are presented to Booddhŭ and the priests. The latter make a discourse to the assembly on the virtue of building temples, grounding their address on some apothegm of the saint.

Booddhŭ, as seen in many temples, appears seated upon a

throne placed on elephants, or encircled by an hydra; or in the habit of a king, accompanied by his attendants. In most of the modern images, however, he is represented in a sitting posture, with his legs folded, his right hand resting upon his right thigh, and his left upon his lap: a yellow cloth is cast over his left shoulder, which envelopes his right arm. His hair is generally in a curling state, like that of an African; his ears are long, as though distended by heavy ear-rings. The image is generally placed in the centre of the temple, under a small arch prepared for the purpose, or under a small porch of wood, neatly gilt. Images of celestial attendants, male and female, are frequently placed in front of the image. In some places the image of Jēēvŭnŭkŭrŭ, a mendicant, who had 400,000 disciples, and who foretold the deification of Booddhŭ, is to be seen, in an erect posture, having four mendicants behind him with begging dishes in their hands, and Sooмédhŭ, a form of Booddhŭ, lying prostrate before him, in a posture of reverence.

It appears evident from their writings, that the ancient religion of the Burmans consisted principally in religious austerities. When a person becomes initiated into the priesthood, he immediately renounces the secular state, lives on alms, and abstains from food after the sun has passed the meridian. The ancient writings of the Bŭrmans mention an order of female priests; but it is likely that these were only female mendicants.

Priests are forbidden to marry; they are to live by mendicity; are to possess only three garments, a begging dish, a girdle, a razor, a needle, and a cloth to strain the water which they drink, that they may not devour insects.

The priests are the schoolmasters, and teach gratuitously as a work of merit, the children being maintained at home by their parents. If a priest finds a pupil to be of quick parts, he persuades the parents to make him a priest; but if a boy wish to embrace a secular life after he has been some time in the college, he is at liberty to do so.

Boys of five years of age and upwards are admitted into the Bŭrman seminaries (koiyooms) as students. At their initiation, the parents generally give a feast, which continues for three or four days; at the close of which time the youth, arrayed in costly garments and ornaments, and attended by a large retinue, is led through the town on horseback to the college of his preceptor. As soon as he arrives, he is stript of his attire; his head is shaved; he is clothed with a yellow garment, and a pot, or beggar's dish, is put into his hand; and in this manner he is committed to his tutor.

The student is to observe the following rules; to abstain from murder, theft, evil desire, falsehood, ardent spirits, food after noonday, dancing, music, &c. from flowers and perfumes, elegant accommodations, the use of gold and silver. Should he fail in keeping these prohibitions he is disqualified for farther advancement. An obedient disciple, at the end of twenty years, is admitted into the order of priests.

To persons admitted into the order of the priesthood, two hundred and twenty-seven precepts are given, the observance of which for ten years entitles them to the rank of a priest of the first order, and empowers them to have colleges and disciples under them.

A Bŭrman college is built in the style of a palace by some person of wealth. The ancient koiyooms resembled caves, many of which are still to be seen in the ancient city of Pougan.

Beside their colleges, there are other sacred edifices among the Bŭrmans, enclosed by a wall, and intended for the accommodation of learned men, who meet to consult each other on religious matters. In some instances, an image of Goutŭmŭ is set up in a conspicuous part of the building.

The houses of the priests are built as works of merit, and offered to them. A temple and a house for priests are commonly built at once. It is a law in these houses, that a priest shall always give his bed to a priest who is a stranger, if necessary. The common people are never suffered to sit upon a priest's mat or bed.

The investiture of a priest is a very important ceremony. To ordain the candidate, it is necessary that a priest should be present who has been initiated twenty years, and not less than five priests who have been in orders ten years each. The ceremony, from which spectators are carefully excluded, is conducted in a temple peculiarly sacred, or in a boat on the river, surrounded with a screen of mats. At the commencement, a priest goes out, and asks the crowd, whether they have any objection to the youth's becoming a priest. If they all answer in the negative, he is presented to the chief priest, and is asked many questions; as, if he be free from disease; if he be perfect in his elementary knowledge; if he have obtained the consent of his parents. After many formulas have been repeated, he is clothed in white; and the eight utensils, composing the whole property of a priest, are hung around him. He is at length clothed like an old priest, and led to some college, where he remains for three years under the inspection of an aged priest, until completely initiated into the duties of the priesthood.

The four quarters of the moon or festival days among the Cingalese. A temporary shed being erected on these occasions near a temple, the people bring their offerings, and present them to two priests employed in instructing the assembled multitude; the one speaks in the Palee, and the other explains his words in Cingalese. Drums are beaten at intervals, and the temple is illuminated.

Formerly, it would seem that religious feasts were held monthly among the Bŭrmans: as, the water feast; that for presenting drink-offerings to the images of Booddhŭ; that for watering the trees of the Ficus Indica; the interrogatory feast; one in honour of the priests; another in honour of Gŭnéshŭ; the boat festival; the feast of alms; the candle feast; the feast of giving clothes to the priests; the lot festival; and the festival for placing fire near the images of Booddhŭ. At present, the Bŭrman feasts are held at the full and change of the moon only. At these times all public business is suspended; the people pay their homage to Goutŭmŭ at the temples, presenting to the image rice, fruits, flowers, candles, &c. Aged people often fast during the whole day. Some visit the colleges, and hear the priests read portions from the Bouddhŭ writings.

According to the religion of Booddhŭ, there are no distinctions of caste. Polygamy is not forbidden by the Bouddhŭ doctrine, and it is not uncommon for a man to have a plurality of wives. The Bŭrmans burn their dead with many ceremonies, especially the bodies of the priests.

Respecting the Hindoo deities, the Booddhŭs believe that Brŭmha is the head of the Brŭmhacharēēs, and lives with them in one of the higher heavens; the Vishnoo, Shivŭ, Kartikŭ, and Soomŭna, are the chief ministers of Indrŭ, the king of heaven, who has twenty-eight inferior ministers. An intelligent native of Ceylon assured the author, that the Bouddhŭs dislike the Hindoo religion more than they do Mahometanism.

The Substance of the Témee Jatŭ, an Account of the Incarnation of Booddhŭ.

Translated from the Bŭrman, by Mr. F. Carey.

THE divine one, while remaining in the Jatŭ forest, began to relate his celebrated departure into the forest, and, in reciting the encomium, uttered this Jatŭ of king Témee.

Upon a certain day, the mendicants, met in the assembly of audience, continued to celebrate the departure of Bhŭgŭvŭ. Bhŭgŭvŭ said, 'O mendicants! why are you assembled?' They replied. 'We are conversing on this subject.' He rejoined, 'O mendicants, this is not the only time of my departure; formerly, to accomplish unattained austerities, let it not surprise you that I left my kingdom, and departed into the forest.' Having said this, he remained silent. The mendicants entreating, Bhŭgŭvŭ revealed to them the history of the Jatŭs:—

'O ye mendicants! in the kingdom of Kashēēkŭ, and in the

city of Varanŭsēē, (Benares,) formerly reigned Kashēē Raja, a king who possessed every excellent quality, and had sixteen thousand wives. The citizens said among themselves, 'Our sovereign has neither son nor daughter to preserve his family from extinction:' they therefore assembled in the presence of the king, and, observing the rules laid down in the Kooshŭ Jatŭ, thus addressed him: 'O king! supplicate for a son.' The king, calling his sixteen thousand wives, said, 'Supplicate ye for a son.' Chŭndra, and the other sixteen thousand wives, having feasted the gods, made supplication, but obtained neither son nor daughter. This queen, Chŭndra-dévēē, perfected in holy rites, was the daughter of Mŭrdŭ raja. The king said, 'O spouse, do thou also entreat for a son.' The queen, at the full moon, remained fasting, and, while reposing upon a sofa, and reflecting upon her virtuous deeds, exclaimed, 'I have certainly performed perfect vows; therefore to me a son will be granted.' Thus saying, she repeated her vows. Through her piety, the angel, having been made acquainted with the queen's desires, said, 'Chŭndra-dévēē supplicates for a son; I will certainly now grant her this blessing.' Looking around for a proper person to be incarnate in her womb, he beheld Booddhŭ-sŭtwŭ. This person had reigned over the kingdom of Varanŭsēē during twenty years; after death he fell into Ooshnŭdŭ-nirŭyŭ, where he was punished eighty thousand years; he was next born in Tavŭtingsa, where he spent his life, and at death possessed an inclination to ascend to the higher heavens of the gods. The angel, going to him, said, 'O thou great one, produced in the world of mortals, by thee works of merit shall be accomplished, and much people be made happy. The queen of Kashēē prays for a son; wilt thou consent to be incarnate in her womb?' He added, 'There are also five hundred sons of the gods on the point of transmigration, who are willing to be reproduced.' Booddhŭ-sŭtwŭ consented; and having transmigrated with the five hundred sons of the gods, he was conceived in the womb of Chŭndra-dévēē; the other gods, in those of the wives of the nobles. At that time the womb of Chŭndra-dévēē shone as with refulgent gems; and knowing that she had conceived, she sent information of it to the king, who ordered attendants on her person. At length she was blessed with a son, replete with every excellence. On the same day also, in the houses of the nobles, the five hundred sons of the gods were born. At the time of the birth, the king, surrounded by his assembled nobles, remained in the palace yard, when they addressed him thus: 'O sovereign, to thee a son is born.' The king was filled with affection towards his first-born, which, penetrating through flesh and bone, adhered to the marrow: in this manner he was filled with affection, and his mind became composed. The king then said to his nobles, 'To me a son is born: are ye pleased?' They answered, 'What dost thou say? Before, we were without a sovereign; now he is born, and we have obtained a ruler.'

The king thus commanded his chief officer: 'It is my son's prerogative to have attendants; go thou to the houses of the nobles, and see who have been born to-day.' The chief officer found the five hundred sons, and, returning, related to the king what he had seen. The king sent garments to each of the five hundred children; and also five hundred nurses. He also gave to Booddhŭ-sŭtwŭ, four times sixty small-breasted, honey-like, milk-producing nurses, having rejected all women in whom there was any defect.

If an infant sit upon the lap of a very tall woman to draw the breast, its neck grows long; if upon the lap of a short woman, it grows hump-backed; if upon the lap of a thin woman, her thighs injure it; if upon the lap of a very corpulent woman, it straddles or trembles when it walks; if upon the lap of a very long-breasted woman, it becomes flat-nosed. A very black woman's milk is cold; an asthmatic woman's milk is sour; a woman who has an obstruction in the throat, has acrid or bitter milk. Therefore, rejecting all faulty nurses, and having given four times sixty small-breasted, honey-like, milk-producing nurses, and paying great homage to the infant, the king bestowed a reward upon Chŭndra-dévēē; when she, receiving the favour, returned it again to her lord.

Upon the day the child was named, the king caused the prognosticating bramhŭns to be called, and, making large presents to them, enquired concerning the child's destiny. The bramhŭns examined the marks on the child, and said, 'O most illustrious sovereign, this child is replete with every propitious and excellent quality; he is qualified to govern not only this single island, but the two thousand surrounding islands; nor do we perceive the least evil in his destiny.' The king was pleased, and proceeded to name the child. Upon the day of his birth it rained all over the kingdom of Kashēēkŭ. On that day the heart of the king, and the hearts of all his subjects, became tranquil. The child too was born wet, and was therefore called Témee.

When the child was a month old, the nurses, embracing him, brought him to the king; who, viewing his beloved child, kissed its head, and, causing it to be placed upon his lap, remained satisfied.

At this hour, four thieves were brought before the king, who commanded one of them to receive a thousand stripes with a prickly whip; another to be cast into prison; another to be pierced with a spear; and the other to be placed upon a shōōlēē.[k] Mŭha-sŭtwŭ, hearing the words of the father, was afraid; and trembling, reflected thus: 'My father, obliged to be a king, has committed many weighty and hell-deserving deeds.'

On the following day, the nurses caused him to be laid under the white umbrella, upon an adorned pleasure-abounding bed;

[k] An instrument upon which the criminal is impaled.

where, after reposing for a short time, he opened his eyes, and beholding the white umbrella, and the great splendour of his apartment, he became exceedingly afraid, more than before. While reflecting how he came to this abode of cruelty, by the strength of his former knowledge he perceived, that he had come from the heavens of the gods; looking still further back, he remembered that he had been burning in hell; looking back to a still more remote period, he recognized himself as a king of that place, (Benares,) and said to himself: 'Having reigned twenty years in Varanŭsēē, I was punished eighty thousand years in hell; and now I have sprung to birth again in this place, in this abode of thieves. To four culprits yesterday my father spoke harsh, hell-exposing words. Now undoubtedly I must reign again, and be again cast into hell, where I must endure great affliction.' Terror fell upon Mŭhasŭtwŭ, thus reflecting, and his resplendent body withered like a lotos rubbed between the hand; and while considering by what means he could be emancipated from this abode of thieves, he fell asleep. In the mean time the goddess, his mother, thus consoled him: 'O child, Témee-koomarŭ, be not sorrowful, doubtful, nor fearful: thou desirest to be released from this abode of thieves; therefore, though not lame, thou makest thyself to appear as one lame; though not deaf, thou makest thyself deaf; though not dumb, thou makest thyself as one dumb.' Booddhŭ-sŭtwŭ, having derived consolation from the words of the goddess, repeated the second stanza: 'O goddess, I will do what thou hast commanded.'

The king, having appointed the five hundred youths to remain with his son as a guard, they cried for the breast; but Mŭhasŭtwŭ, affrighted at the idea of being cast into hell, exclaimed, 'Though I be even parched up to-day, death is preferable to being cast into hell.' Thus reflecting, he neither cried nor wept. The nurses made known the fact to Chŭndra-dévēē, and she related it to the king. From that time, they let the child fast beyond the usual period, and sometimes omitted to give him nourishment for the whole day: though the dread of falling into hell, however, though exhausted, he neither cried nor wept. Then the mother, saying, 'My son is hungry,' gave him the breast herself; but though she nourished him at intervals during a whole year, she could not understand his intentions.

The nobles afterwards, reminding the king, that children of the age of one year take a liking to sweetmeats; and, adding, we will try Booddhŭ-sŭtwŭ with them; caused the five hundred youths to be seated by him, and placing various sorts of sweetmeats before him and them, retired to a secret place. The other youths, leaping and scrambling, devoured the sweetmeats; but Booddhŭ-sŭtwŭ warned himself, saying, 'O thou Témee-koomarŭ, desiring hell, dost thou wish for this food? Filled with horror, he did not even look upon it. Thus they tempted him with sweetmeats for a whole year, but were unable to look into his heart.

[The work then goes on to relate, that the next year they endeavour to excite his desires by setting various fruits before him, but in vain. The following year they put playthings before him; and for another year great varieties of food. They next endeavoured during a year to affright him with fire; during another with a furious elephant; during another with serpents: but he remained destitute of fear as well as of desire. At the age of eight, they endeavoured to amuse him with dances; at nine to terrify him with swords; at ten with loud noises from shells; at eleven with a horrid drum; at twelve with extraordinary lights in his bed-room; at thirteen they covered him with molasses, and let the flies torment him; at fourteen they almost suffocated him with offensive smells; at fifteen they scorched him with fire; at sixteen they introduced into his presence beautiful females, perfumes, dances, &c. Thus they enticed him for sixteen years with the sixteen great temptations, and tried him with many other smaller temptations; but they were still unable to enter into his designs]

Then the king, dejected, caused the destiny-foretelling bramhŭns to be called, and said to them: 'At the time of my son's birth, you said, 'This child is replete with every fortunate and virtuous mark; neither is there any evil token whatever in him:' but behold he is born lame, dumb, and deaf: your words are not verified.' The bramhŭns replied, 'O sovereign! there is nothing unknown to the wise. If we had said, the son born to the king is stupid, it would have created thee pain of mind; therefore we did not mention the matter.' Then the king asked what was proper to be done. The bramhŭns answered, 'Great sovereign, while this youth remains in the palace, we perceive three evils may happen; one to the king's life, another to the white umbrella, another to the queen: therefore, without delay, put the unfortunate horses to the unfortunate chariot, and placing him therein, carry him out by the west gate to the burying-ground, and, having dug a square hole, bury him.' The king, through the dread of these evils, adopted this advice.

Chŭndra-dévēē, informed of these designs, went alone to the king, and having made obeisance, said, 'O sovereign, thou conferredst a blessing upon me, and I, having received it, committed it to thee: now give it me again.' The king replied, 'Take it, O queen.' She then said, 'O king, give the kingdom to my son.' The king replied, 'It is out of my power; thy son is an idiot.' The queen replied, 'O sovereign, though thou hast decreed not to give him the kingdom in perpetuity, give it him for seven years only,' The king replied, 'I cannot, O queen:' but she renewed her petitions, lowering each of them till she solicited for a reign only of seven days; and this was granted.

Immediately the mother, decorating her son, thus addressed him : 'O Témee-koomarŭ ! the kingdom is thine.' Then causing proclamation to be made by the sound of the drum, and commanding the whole city to be adorned, she seated her son upon an elephant, with the white umbrella carried over his head. After being thus conveyed round the city, she caused him to be laid upon a noble bed ; and be sought her beloved son, during the whole night, thus : 'O son, Témee-koomarŭ ! in attending on thee for sixteen years, my eyes smart with weeping ; my heart is as though it were pierced through. I know thou art not lame, &c. Do not leave me childless.' After the same manner she besought him the following day, and the five remaining days.

On the sixth day, the king, having called his charioteer, thus addressed him, 'O Soonŭndŭ, charioteer, to-morrow, early in the morning, uniting the unfortunate horses to the unfortunate chariot, take the youth, and cause him to be carried out by the west gate ; and after having dug a square hole in the burying-ground, cast him into it, and with the back of the spade break his skull : thus causing him to die, cover him with dust ; and having accomplished the work of increasing the earth, bathing, come away.' The queen, having overheard what passed, was filled with sorrow, and going to her son, addressed him, 'O son, Témee ! thy father, the king of Kashēēkŭ, has issued orders to bury thee early to-morrow morning. O son ! early to-morrow thou wilt die.' Hearing this, Mŭha-sŭtwŭ thus gratulated himself : 'O Témee-koomarŭ ; thy sixteen years are now accomplished !' But his mother's heart was pierced through with sorrow. Témee added, 'I have attained to the consummation of my desires ;' but he refrained from speaking to his mother.

Early in the morning, the charioteer, having harnessed the horses to the chariot, through the power of the god, and Mŭha-sŭtwŭ's austerities, he put the fortunate horses to the fortunate chariot ; then, stopping the chariot at the king's door, he entered the inner apartments, and saluting the queen Chŭndra, he thus addressed her : 'O queen ! be not wroth ; it is the king's command.' Thus saying, with the back of his hand having put away the queen, who was sleeping with her son enfolded in her arms, he took up the youth as a garland of flowers, [viz., gently or carefully as a person would carry tender flowers,] and descended from the palace. At this time Chŭndra-dévēē, smiting her breast, and weeping aloud, remained in the place-yard. Mŭha-sŭtwŭ, beholding his mother, said to himself silently, 'My mother will die from the anguish of her mind.' But correcting himself, he added, in his own mind, 'If I speak, the efforts of sixteen years will certainly become abortive.'

The charioteer having put Booddhŭ-sŭtwŭ into the chariot, said, 'I will go out at the west gate :' but through the merit of

Booddhŭ-sŭtwŭ's austerities, the charioteer, deluded by the gods, turned the chariot, and driving it out at the east gate, was precipitated to the distance of twenty-four miles at once. The charioteer, seeing before him a thick forest, mistook it for the burying-ground; and thinking it an excellent place, drove the chariot to one side of the road, halted, and descended. He now stripped Mŭha-sŭtwŭ of his garments, tied them up, and laid them in a suitable place: then with a spade he began to dig a square grave, at no great distance from the chariot. At this moment Booddhŭ-sŭtwŭ reflected thus: 'Now is my time for exertion; it is true, I have not moved hand nor foot for sixteen years, but I will now see if I do not possess strength.' He arose, rubbed his arms and legs, descended from the chariot, and then walking backward and forward several times, found he possessed strength sufficient to go the distance of of eight hundred miles in one day. He then said, 'Should the charioteer contend with me, I will see whether I possess strength to wrestle with him or not:' and laying hold of the hinder part of the carriage, threw it, as though it had been a child's plaything, so that it continued twirling round and round.

After this, Témee's guardian deity, taking the raiments of the gods, and calling Vishwŭ-kŭrmŭ, the son of the gods, thus addressed him: 'O Vishwŭ-kŭrmŭ, go thou to Témee-koomarŭ, the son of the king of Kashēēkŭ, and array him.' Vishwŭ-kŭrmŭ descended, bearing ten thousand pieces of cloth, and bound them round Booddhŭ-sŭtwŭ's head; and thus, with the garments of the gods and mortals, arrayed him like a dévŭ.

Booddhŭ-sŭtwŭ, shining like the king of the gods, went to the hole the charioteer was digging, and standing by the brink, invoking, uttered the third stanza: 'O charioteer! why art thou digging that grave in such haste? O thou! dost thou hear what I say? what wilt thou do with that grave?' The charioteer, hearing the above words, without looking up, said, 'To the king has been born a son who is dumb, lame, and destitute of understanding; and the king has commanded me to bury him in the wilderness.' Mŭha-sŭtwŭ said, 'I am neither deaf, nor dumb, nor lame. O charioteer! if thou bury me in this wilderness, thou wilt do a bad action. Behold my thighs, my arms; hear me speak, O charioteer! By burying me in this wilderness, thou wilt commit an evil act.' The charioteer asked himself, 'Who can this personage be, who has continued praising himself from the time of his arrival?' then beholding his features exquisitely beautiful, he continued, 'Who can this person be? Is he a man, or a god? and added the following stanza: 'Art thou a god, or a gundhŭrvŭ or the dévŭ Poorŭndŭrŭ! Who art thou? Whose son? How shall I know thee?' Mŭha-sŭtwŭ, describing himself in humble language, recited this stanza: 'I am neither a god, nor a gŭndhŭrvŭ, nor Poorŭndŭrŭ: I am the son of the king of Kashēēkŭ, for whom thou art digging this grave; the son of that king by whom thou art nourished. O charioteer! undoubtedly it is an evil thing for thee to bury me in this wilderness. He who cuts the branches of the tree under the shade of which he sits and sleeps, is a worthless person.'

Although he spoke thus, the charioteer would not believe him to be Booddhŭ-sŭtwŭ. The latter therefore said, 'I will convince him by a godlike acclamation.' Then, by a dreadful vociferation, echoing through the thick forest, he proceeded to utter the stanza descriptive of the blessings of friendship: 'O charioteer! he who does not act unfaithfully towards his friend, has abundance of food, not only in his own house, but wherever he may happen to go. He who wrongs not his friend, to whatever country, town, or city he may go, will be revered by all. He who acts not the treacherous part toward his friend, thieves will not injure him, nor can kings disregard him; and he will excel all his enemies. He who is a faithful friend, is beloved in the assembly, and becomes chief among his relatives. He who deceives not his friend, but honours him, becomes honourable, and renowned in noble deeds. He who acts not treacherously towards his friend, being a worshipper of others, is venerated; saluting others, he is saluted, and obtains glory and renown. He who deals faithfully with his friend, shines like flame, is glorious as the gods, nor is he forsaken of the deity of prosperity. He who deceives not his friend, his cattle increase, and whatever he plaints in his field flourishes and bears fruit. He who does not wrong his friend, should he fall from a high mountain or tree, and die, he will attain his place. He who acts not the impious part toward his friend, can never be hurt by his enemies; but stands firm like a well-rooted tree, upon which the wind has no effect.' Thus Booddhŭ-sŭtwŭ, in the above stanza, set forth meritorious actions.

The charioteer then left off digging the grave, and, going to the chariot, missed the robes and ornaments. He then returned, and looking round recognized Booddhŭ-sŭtwŭ, at whose feet he fell, and lifting up his joined hands, uttered the following stanza:—'Come, let me receive thee; it is right that thou shouldest inherit thine own house. O thou king's son! what art thou doing in this wilderness?' Mŭha-sŭtwŭ replied, 'I have no desire for the kingdom, nor for relations nor riches: father and mother have rejected me; the inhabitants of the towns and villages have rejected me; the youths have discarded me; my mother has sent me away; my father has cast me off; I myself have become a mendicant, nor have I the least inclination for objects of sense. Undoubtedly the prudent attain the object of their desires: I am Vépŭkŭ the Brŭmhŭcharēē. To me, who have left every thing, what cause of dread or fear can there be?' The charioteer replied, 'Possessing such melodious and excellent speech, wherefore didst thou not speak when with thy father and mother?' Mŭha-sŭtwŭ answered, 'I ruled twenty years at Varanŭsēē, in consequence of which I was tormented eighty thousand years in hell. Dreading a similar calamity, I did not permit myself to be reinstated in the kingdom. On this account too, I forbore speaking to father or mother. My father, seating me upon his knee, commanded four culprits to be punished in the following manner:—'Kill one; bind the other; having pierced one, anoint him with painful corrosives; impale the other' Hearing these severe commands, I was induced, though not dumb, to feign dumbness; though not lame, to put on the appearance of lameness, and remain besmeared in my own excrements. O charioteer, what wise man, for his sustenance, will perpetrate the five crimes[i]?' Know, O charioteer! that I am a brŭmhŭcharēē. Certainly the deliberate have their desires accomplished; I am a brŭmhŭcharēē. To me, having departed into the wilderness, what cause of fear?'

The charioteer, hearing this, said within himself, 'This youth has cast away a splendid kingdom as a putrid carcase, and has entered this wilderness as a mendicant. Of what use will the world be to *me?* I also will embrace the life of a mendicant.' Thus reflecting, he uttered the following stanza:—'O king's son! I will enter upon the life of a hermit with thee. O prince! I prefer a hermitage; call me to join thee.' Mŭha-sŭtwŭ said, 'Verily, I will make him a mendicant immediately.' But, reflecting again, he said, 'Neither my father nor mother will come here; and this chariot, these horses, ornaments, and robes, will surely be destroyed in this place. They will say, has not this youth become a cannibal, and devoured the charioteer?' Perceiving a way to promote the welfare of his father and mother, and being desirous of making it appear, that the horses, chariot, ornaments, &c. were a debt due by the charioteer, he uttered the following stanza:—'O charioteer! take back the chariot; and, cancelling the debt, return.' The charioteer then reflected thus within himself: 'While I am gone to the town, should Mŭha-sŭtwŭ retire to any other place, and his father, hearing of his son's welfare, say, 'Shew him to me, and should I be unable to produce him, the father will punish me; I will therefore receive a pledge of him that he go not to any other place.' He then uttered the following stanza: 'Success to thee; I will comply with thy solicitations; but attend to this my request: remain here until I bring the king. I am not certain whether he will be pleased at the sight of thee.' Mŭha-sŭtwŭ replied, 'O charioteer! I will act according to thy word; I have a desire to see my father; return to the town. Inform my relatives of my welfare, and tell my father and mother, that I have sent them my salutation.'

i The Hindoo shastrŭs, as well as the Bouddhŭ, mention five 'mortal sins,' viz. stealing five tolas of gold, crim. con. with the wife of a spiritual guide, slaying cows and bramhŭns, and drinking spirituous liquors.

Saying this, Mŭha-sŭtwŭ bowed his head like a golden plantain tree, and observed the five touches, (that is, he caused his thighs, arms, and forehead to touch the earth,) placing his face towards the town of Varanŭsēē. The charioteer, having received his instructions, circumambulating the youth, ascended the car, and drove towards the town.

At this moment Chŭndra-dévēē, opening the lion door, and striking her breast, began to weep. The mother, beholding the chariot empty, and the charioteer returning by himself, with eyes full of tears, wept; and looking towards him, said within herself, 'Having killed the son of my bosom, this charioteer is returning to us. Has he killed my son? Has he performed the ceremony of increasing the earth?' Beholding the charioteer approach after having murdered her darling son, she said again within herself, 'Will not the merciless enemies rejoice? O charioteer! when thou killedst my son, was he dumb, or lame, or how? Did he weep? Pray tell me. When thou interredst my dumb and lame son, how did he make any resistance with his hands and feet? Pray tell me."

The charioteer replied, 'O queen, permit me to approach, and I will inform thee of all that I have heard and seen concerning the king's son.' Chŭndra-dévēē answered, 'O charioteer! fear not: what thou hast heard and seen respecting the king's son, relate to me, without hesitation.' The charioteer replied, 'The queen's son is neither dumb nor lame, he has a clear voice; but dreading to be made king, he has resorted to ingenious arts: he recollected his former existence, when, after reigning twenty years in Varanŭsēē, he fell into a flaming hell, and was tormented eighty thousand years. Afraid of being king, he consented not to his instalment, and for this reason also he spake neither to father nor mother. He is complete in every member, of full and even stature, of excellent speech and wisdom, and is on the road to heaven. If thou desirest to see thy beloved son, come; I will certainly take thee to the place of his abode. Come without delay; it becomes thee to hasten.'

The dévŭ, acquainted with the youth's desire of becoming a mendicant, sent for Vishwŭ-kŭrmŭ, and said: 'O Vishwŭ-kŭrmŭ, son of the gods, the youth Témee is anxious to become a hermit; build him a house of leaves, and prepare for him every implement necessary for a priest.' Vishwŭ-kŭrmŭ, by his own might, formed a delightful residence in the twelve miles-extending forest; dug a pool and a well; created trees which bore fruit out of their season; and near the hermitage of leaves made a walk four and twenty cubits in length, and strewed beautiful crystal-like sand upon it. Having prepared all the implements necessary for a priest, he added, 'Whosoever desires to become a priest, let him receive these implements!' And having driven away all noxious animals, and birds of unpleasant voice, he returned.

Mŭha-sŭtwŭ, observing what Vishwŭ-kurmŭ had done, and knowing that the devŭ had designed it for him, entered the abode. Having cast off his former garments, he girded himself with those made from the bark of a tree, threw a leopard's skin over his shoulders, covered his head with his long twisted hair, and placed a bamboo across his shoulder. Then quitting the house of leaves, with a staff in his hand, he caused the lustre of his priesthood to appear; and while walking to and fro, exclaimed, 'This is bliss! How happy am I!' Soon after, returning to his abode, and seating himself upon a bough, he perfected the five and the eight ceremonies proper for a hermit. In the evening he seated himself at the head of the walk, and taking of the fruit of the trees which bare out of their season, and boiling them in tasteless water, without either salt or acid, as on immortal food, he fed upon this, in the pot given him by the dévŭ. Thus, reflecting upon the four doctrines of Brŭmha, he took up his residence in this grove.

The king of Kashēēkŭ, after hearing the words of the charioteer, called the chief officer of the army, and said, 'Put the horses to the chariot, harness the elephants, blow the conches, beat the large well-braced drum, and the harmonious small drum; and let the inhabitants of my kingdom attend me: I will go to instruct my son.'

The king sent before him the four orders of warriors, amounting to eighteen ŭkshouhinēēs.[m] Three days elapsed before they were arranged; and on the fourth day the sovereign of Kashēēkŭ left the city. Stepping into his carriage, he said to his concubines, 'All of you follow me;' to his attendants, 'Take the chamŭrŭ, the diadem, the scimitar, and the white umbrella, with the gold-adorned shoes, and ascend the chariot.' The king then departed, and quickly arrived at the place where his son Témee was. Beholding the king approach surrounded with swords, and shining like a flame, Témee enquired after the welfare of his father, his sisters, his mother, the inhabitants of the kingdom, &c. He asked also respecting the vehicles, the granaries, and treasuries; and farther, whether the king did not delight in inebriating liquors; whether he delighted in vows, in virtue, and in bestowing alms.

The king, out of respect to Mŭha-sŭtwŭ, would not sit upon his throne; his son therefore prepared a seat of leaves: upon this too he refused to sit, and placed himself on the ground. Mŭha-sŭtwŭ, seeing his father thus seated, entered his hut of leaves, and brought forth some of the boiled leaves with which he wished to entertain his sire, and repeated the following stanza: 'O sovereign, partake of my saltless prepared food of leaves; thou art my guest.'

[m] A complete army is composed of one ŭkshouhinēē, or 109,350 foot, 65,610 horses, 21,870 chariots, and 21,870 elephants. According to this account, therefore, this king of Benares had an army 3,936,600 strong.

The king replied, 'I cannot eat leaves; it is not my food; I eat the soup of clean flesh, and rice.' Still, out of reverence to Mŭha-sŭtwŭ, he received a small quantity of the food in his hand, and thus addressing him in affectionate language, 'O child, I do not feed upon such food,' seated himself. The queen, Chŭndra-dévēē, surrounded with her maidens, came by a straight road to the residence of Booddhŭ-sŭtwŭ, and beholding her beloved son, fell on the ground senseless. Reviving, she arose, and embracing Booddhŭ-sŭtwŭ's feet, worshipped him; then arising, with her eyes full of tears, she seated hersel in a suitable situation. The king said, 'O queen! beholdest thou the food of thy son?' and putting a little of it into her hand, he gave the remainder by little and little to his concubines, all of whom said, 'O sir, dost thou live upon such food as this? (putting it on their heads;) thou performest very severe austerities.' Thus saying, and worshipping him, they seated themselves. The king said, 'O beloved youth, this food astonishes me; thy dwelling alone is an astonishment to me. How is it that thou, subsisting upon such coarse food, hast such a beautiful appearance?' Mŭha-sŭtwŭ said, 'Because, O king, I sleep upon this bed of leaves, my countenance appears so beautiful: no instruments of defence, used for the protection of kings, are placed over me; but on account of my serene repose, my countenance is of this beautiful hue. I feel no remorse for what is past, no concern about what will occur, and I am resigned to what happens; therefore my countenance appears gay: the foolish, because they are anxious about what may happen, and sorry for what is past, wither away as a plucked green reed.'

The king, reflecting, 'I am come here to anoint my son, and invite him to the kingdom,' said, 'O son! I will bestow upon thee the elephant-drivers, the charioteers, the horsemen, and arrayed footmen, with delightful horses: I will also give thee the maidens adorned with all sorts of ornaments; raise up progeny by them, and thou shalt become our sovereign: virgins well versed in dancing and singing, and perfected in this wilderness. I will bring thee adorned daughters of other kings, and after thou hast raised a numerous progeny, thou mayest become a priest. Thou art young and tender, it is good for thee to reign. What art thou doing in this wilderness?'

Here commence the virtuous sayings of Booddhŭ-sŭtwŭ:—'O sir! a youth ought to perform virtuous acts; the young may become ascetics; a youth's becoming a priest is extolled even by the sages. I will perform virtuous actions; I have not the least desire to be installed in the kingdom. I have seen a youth, the beloved son of much anxiety, who could but just say 'father, mother,' die before he reached maturity. I have beheld the life of beautiful young maidens consume away, being rooted up (by death) as the sprout of a bamboo, when plucked. Men and women, even when young, die: if therefore the young die, who can confide in life? Even as the life of fish in a scarcity of water is very short, so the life of mortals shortens by every passing night: of what avail then is youth? Men are constantly harassed, constantly surrounded; they pass away without seeing good: therefore why wilt thou install me in the kingdom?'

The sovereign of Kashēēkŭ said, 'O son, inform me who harass mankind; who agitate mankind; and what is it that passes away without profit.' Booddhŭ-sŭtwŭ replied, 'Death harasses mankind; increasing age surrounds them. This know, O sire! that as the thread grows less and less by every insertion of the shuttle, so the life of man dwindles away. As the waters of an overflowing river never re-ascend, so the days of man never return. An overflowing river carries away all the trees near its banks, so all mankind are borne away by increasing age and death.'

The king, hearing the virtuous sayings of Booddhŭ-sŭtwŭ, became very dissatisfied with human life; and being desirous of becoming a hermit, said, 'I will not return to the city: I will certainly cause my son to return, and the white umbrella to be given to him.' Thus reflecting, and being desirous of enticing his son to accept the kingdom, he said, [Here the same offers are repeated of horses, footmen, elephants, virgins, &c.]

To shew his disregard of the kingdom, Mŭha-sŭtwŭ replied, 'O sire! why temptest thou me with perishing wealth, dying women, and youthful bloom? O king! what is love, the pleasant look, present delight, anxiety in pursuit of wealth, sons, and daughters, and wives, to me, who am released from the bonds of iniquity? I know that death will not forget me; therefore, of what use are pleasures and riches? As the shedding of ripe fruit is a constant evil, so to mankind death is a continual cause of anxiety. Of many people seen in the morning, how few are to be seen at night; and of the many seen in the evening, how few are to be seen in the morning! Virtuous deeds ought to be practised to-day, for who can tell but we must die to-morrow; nor is there any possible escape from the arrows of death. O sire! thieves long after riches: I am freed from the bonds of iniquity. Return, return, O king! I have no desire for the kingdom.'

Hearing these sayings, the king, as well as Chŭndra-dévēē, with the sixteen thousand maidens, and all the nobles, were desirous of becoming mendicants. The king made proclamation, 'Whosoever wishes, let him come to my son, and become a priest.' This he also caused to be published by the sound of the drum throughout the city. The inhabitants of the town, then, leaving their articles of merchandize in the market, and their houses open, quitted the town, and went out to the king; who thus, with many of his subjects, embraced a forest residence with Mŭha-sŭtwŭ. The hermitage granted by the angel was filled with people to the extent of six miles; Mŭha-sŭtwŭ also put his house of leaves in order: the women he placed in the interior, because women are apt to be afraid; to the men he assigned the yard.

All the people, taking of the fruit which had fallen on the ground, eat thereof, and performed the rites of ascetics. Mŭha-sŭtwŭ, by the power of his devotions being raised in the air, delivered virtuous and mellifluous sayings.

At that time a neighbouring monarch, hearing that the king of Varanŭsēē had departed from the city, and had entered the wilderness as a hermit, said to himself, 'I will take possession of his kingdom:' upon which he left his own capital, and entering the city of Varanŭsēē, beheld it richly adorned. Ascending the palace, and struck with its gems, he said to himself, 'There must be some evil here, or the king of Kashēēkŭ would not have left this wealth.' Thus reflecting, he called seven persons who had been left behind, and enquired of them, 'Did any disaster befal your sovereign in this town?' The drunkards replied, 'No, O king!' The king enquired, 'Why, then, did he forsake it?' They replied, 'Témee, the son of our sovereign, would not accept the government; but feigning himself deaf, dumb, &c. departed from the city, and entered the forest, to perform the rites of an ascetic: on which account our sovereign, accompanied by a great multitude, left this city, to practise the rites of an anchorite near his son.' The illustrious monarch, hearing what they said, was overjoyed, and said, 'I also will become a hermit: by what gate did your sovereign depart?' They replied, 'By the east gate.' The king, accompanied by his attendants, departing out at the east gate, went toward the banks of the river. Mŭha-sŭtwŭ, informed of his approach, came from the forest, and, by the power of his devotion being seated in the air, declared the mellifluous sayings; on hearing which, this king also, with his army, became hermits under Mŭha-sŭtwŭ. In like manner, three other kings left their kingdoms, with an intention of taking Varanŭsēē; but like the former they embraced a forest residence with Booddhŭ-sŭtwŭ. The elephants and horses became wild; the chariots fell to pieces; the coin of the treasuries, mingled with the sand of the hermitage, was reduced to earth; and the whole concourse of people, having accomplished their austerities, went to heaven. The elephants and horses, having had their minds enlightened in the society of the sages, were reproduced in the six abodes of the gods.

Sŭtwŭ, closing these virtuous instructions, said, 'O ye mendicants when I formerly left the city, I truly departed; but this is not the period of my departure.' He then collected together the Jatŭ. At that time, the daughter of the goddess, who guarded the umbrella, and the charioteer, were reproduced; the angel became Ŭniroodhŭ; the father and mother were reproduced in an illustrious family; the remaining multitude were reproduced as the assembly of Booddhŭ. 'I, the deaf, lame, and dumb, am declared to be god.'

CHAP. III.

ACCOUNT OF THE JOINŬS.[a]

'THE joinŭs,' says Dr. F. Buchanan, 'are spread all over India; but at present are not numerous any where, except in Toolŭvŭ. They allege, that formerly they extended over the whole of Aryŭ, or Bhŭrŭtŭ-kŭndŭ; and that all those who had any just pretensions to be of kshŭtriyŭ descent, were of their sect. It no doubt appears clear, that, in the south of India, many powerful princes were their followers, till the time of Ramanoojŭ-acharyŭ.'

This sect is said to owe its rise to Rishŭbhŭ-dévŭ, a Hindoo; who is said, in the Kŭlpŭ-sōōtrŭ,[b] a joinŭ shastrŭ, from which the greater part of the following account is extracted, to have been incarnate thirteen times. The Kŭlpŭ-sōōtrŭ gives the periods of these births, and declares, that at his last appearance, Rishŭbhŭ was born in the family of Ikshwakoo; his father's name was Nabhee, his mother's Mŭroo, (the Shrēē-Bhagŭvŭtŭ calls her Méroo.) At this time, says the same work, men were in an uncivilized state, supported not by their labour, but by the fruits of trees, (kŭlpŭ-vrikshŭ,) which supplied spontaneously all their wants, and under which they dwelt, having no houses. The gods descended at the birth of Rishŭbhŭ, and, when he was grown to maturity, Indrŭ came from heaven to give him in marriage. Bhŭrŭtŭ, and many other sons, were the fruits of this marriage.[c] At the installation also of Rishŭbhŭ, Indrŭ was present, and gave him a celestial throne. This monarch had the following titles of honor bestowed

[a] From the word jinŭ (ji, to conquer) this sect derives its name. He who has overcome the eight great crimes, is called jinŭ. These crimes are, eating at night; slaying any animal; eating the fruit of those trees that give milk, pumpkins, young bamboo plants; tasting honey, flesh; taking the wealth of others; taking by force a married woman; eating flowers, butter, cheese; and worshipping the gods of other religions.

[b] This work is written in the Urdhŭ-magŭjēē and the Prakritŭ-Lŭnkéshwŭrēē languages: three learned men have written commentaries on it, one of which, the Kŭlpŭ-droomŭ-kŭlika, as well as the Kŭlpŭ-sōōtrŭ, are in the College library, Calcutta. The Kŭlpŭ-sōōtrŭ is divided into three parts, comprising the history of the joinŭ mendicants, the duties of the wise, and of ascetics.

[c] Gomŭtéshwŭrŭ-swamēē is mentioned as another son by a different queen, and is said to have reigned at Oude.—*See Asiatic Researches, vol.* ix. *p.* 260.

on him : the Great King, the Great Mendicant, the Great Joinŭ,[d] the Perfect Saint, the Paragon of Virtue. He taught mankind to cultivate the earth, as well as the first acts of civilization ; and afterwards adopted a person as his spiritual guide. Then, during a whole year, he presented gifts to the people, and renouncing his kingdom, went into a forest, where, for a thousand years, he continued the devotions of a hermit, and refined all his powers : to the hermits dwelling near him in the forest he explained the principles of religion, but initiated twelve persons as his chief disciples ; eighty-four others he sent out to instruct the people of various countries. Near him were 84,000 joinŭs ; 300,000 females, mendicants ; 300,500 other disciples ; and 500,000 females who had begun to learn the principles of the joinŭ religion ; beside many thousands more. At length, after residing several millions of years in this forest, at the close of the third of the six yoogŭs, he obtained absorption, together with a thousand of his disciples.

After Rishŭbhŭ-dévŭ, twenty-two persons are mentioned in this work as the successive leaders of the sect : Ŭjitŭnat'hŭ, Sŭmbhŭvŭ-nat'hŭ Ŭbhinŭndŭnŭ, Soomŭtee-nat'hŭ, Pŭdmŭ-prŭbhoo, Sooparshwŭ-nat'hŭ, Chŭndrŭ-prŭbhoo[e], Soovit-nat'hŭ, Shēētŭlŭ-nat'hŭ, Shréyangsŭ, Vasŭvŭ-pōōjyŭ, Vimŭlŭ-nat'hŭ, Ŭnŭntŭ-nat'hŭ Dhŭrmŭ-nat'hŭ, Shantee-nat'hŭ, Koont'hŭ-nat'hŭ, Ŭrŭ-nat'hŭ, Mŭllee-nat'hŭ, Mŭnŭsŭ-vrŭtēē, Nŭmee-nat'hŭ, Némŭ-nat'hŭ[f], and Parshwŭ-nat'hŭ.[g] I give the account of the incarnation of Parshwŭ-nat'hŭ, who is here said to have descended from the tenth heaven into the womb of Vamŭnŭ, the queen of Ŭshwŭ-sénŭ, on the fourth of the dark part of the moon, under the star Vishakha, in the month Choitrŭ, at Benares. He was born on the tenth of Poushŭ ; at which time the gods descended, and celebrated a great feast. After he had lived to the age of thirty, he received the forms of initiation, and entered a forest with all the pomp of a king : but there he dismissed his courtiers and royal state, and assumed the dress of an ascetic. He took up his abode under an ŭshokŭ tree, and continued an ascetic for seventy years ; when, from mount Shikhŭrŭ, he and thirty-three other joinŭ ascetics obtained absorption. This happened at the close of the sookhŭmŭ-dookhŭmŭ yoogŭ.

The last of the joinŭ yogēēs was Mŭha-vēērŭ, who is said to have been incarnate twenty-seven times, and at his last birth to

[d] The bramhŭns place Rishŭbhŭ at the head of this atheistical sect : it is recorded in the fifth chapter of the Shrēē-bhagŭvŭtŭ, that the kings of Konkŭ, Vénkŭ, and Kootŭjŭ, witnessing his devotions, became joinŭs.

[e] In the ninth vol. of the Asiatic Researches, facing p. 264, is a drawing of this anchorite.

[f] This ascetic was the son of king Sŭmoodrŭ-vijŭyŭ, of Souvēērŭ, in Trishŭtŭ.

[g] Facing the 272d page of the ninth vol. of the Asiatic Researches is a drawing of this god, under the name of Jain-deo.

have been the son of Siddhart'hŭ, a kshŭtriyŭ, of Kshŭtriyŭ-koondŭ. As usual, in these extraordinary births, he performed many wonderful things while a child, and began his studies at the age of five. At school, however, he was so idle, that his tutor reproved him; but was unable to understand the answers given by the youth, till Indrŭ appeared, and assured the teacher, that the youth was more than man, since he had already written a Sŭngskritŭ grammar, the Joinéndrŭ. After leaving school, he pursued his pleasures for twenty-eight years; during which time the king and queen died, and the eldest son was raised to the throne. Mŭha-vēērŭ now asked leave to retire from the world to a forest, but was detained two years by his elder brother; after which, distributing millions upon millions of money amongst the subjects, he took leave of his wife and children, and entered a forest, carried in triumph by ten thousand gods, the heavens raining flowers on the procession, and the gods singing his praises. Then, sitting down under a shady tree, in the presence of this divine assembly, he stripped himself of his royal garments, and put on those of an ascetic; after which the assembly broke up.

While here, he received many disciples, and became a great teacher. He practised the most rigid austerities, renouncing all food and clothing, as well as all intercourse with man, till at length he remained standing, like the trunk of a dead tree, unconscious of his bodily existence; and while in this state, obtained the exact knowledge of all things.

During his continuance in the place where he practised these austerities, he one day went to the tree under which he had commenced his devotions, where he met eleven bramhŭns engaged in controversy on the following subjects:—'Is there a soul in man? —If there be a soul in man, is it united to the body, or is it separate from it?—Of how many elements is the body composed?—Is there an after-state?—Is the soul in bondage while in the body, and is there any state of deliverance?—Are there any gods?—Are any persons in danger of future torments?—Are there works of merit?—Is there such a thing as absorption?' As he approached these bramhŭns, they saw the gods scatter on him a shower of flowers, and pass to and from him through the air. He asked the pŭndits whether they did not entertain doubts on these subjects: [Here he, to their astonishment, repeated what had formed the grounds of their dispute.] They sat down, and eagerly listened to his discourse, as the messenger of heaven. Mŭha-vēērŭ reminded them, that they did not understand the védŭ; therefore they entertained these doubts. He declared, that there was a separate spirit, who is wisdom, mind, sight, hearing, vacuum, air, light, water, joy, religion, irreligion, compassion, liberality; and that he dwells in all animal bodies: that the body and soul are distinct, as in flowers, the fragrance; in milk, butter; in wood, fire: that he is the expression of all his works: that works of merit and demerit determine the character: that birth and death belong to the body; perpetuity to the soul; presence and absence to spirit and matter, to religion and irreligion, to visible and invisible forms. Hearing this discourse, the eleven bramhŭns became his disciples. Mŭha-vēērŭ had also another distinguished disciple, Goutŭmŭswamēē, for whom he had a particular regard, and whom he sent, on the day of his absorption, (death,) to the residence of of Dévŭ-sŭrmmŭ, lest his mind should be too much affected. Seventeen of Mŭha-vēērŭ's disciples obtained deliverance from the body at the same hour with their master.

Some ages after this, when men were sinking into ignorance, Kŭndilacharyŭ collected a number of sages at Mŭt'hoora, and compiled the work called Kŭlpŭ-sōōtrŭ, the contents of which had existed in the minds of the principal disciples of Mŭha-vēērŭ from past time.

The joinŭs have at present a number of mendicant chiefs scattered up and down in Hindoost'hanŭ. Shrŭvanŭ-Béligolŭ is the principal residence of the joinŭ gooroos. See *Asiatic Researches*, vol. ix. p. 255.

The following is offered as a summary of the joinŭ doctrines and ceremonies, as given in the Kŭlpŭ-sōōtrŭ, &c. It seems necessary to premise, however, that it is difficult to give a system which will apply to the whole sect, among whom various opinions prevail. A considerable number of joinŭs approach a good way towards the orthodox Hindoos: they acknowledge something of a deity, though they deny a creator, and reverence in a limited sense the Hindoo deities. They also retain the ten ceremonies connected with progress through life up to marriage. They are divided into the four Hindoo castes, and four states, (ashrŭmŭs;) they marry like the Hindoos, and burn their dead, but do not make offerings to them in the shraddhŭ: they say, 'Of what use is it to pour oil into the lamp after the wick is burnt to ashes?' In their chronology they are more extravagant than the orthodox, and their descriptions of the earth bear a strong resemblance to those of the pooranŭs. The strict joinŭs, it is probable, are constrained to a life of mendicity; for it seems impossible for a person in a secular state to adhere to the rules laid down for this sect; especially those rules which refer to the preservation of all living creatures, vows of continence, &c. All the joinŭ chiefs appear to have been gloomy ascetics, assuming the rights of deity, and denying the authority of God: they despised the ribaldry of the bramhŭns; and amongst the joinŭ sŭnyasēēs, at present, a sovereign contempt of the creator, of a future state, and of religious ceremonies is observable.

The earth, say the joinŭs, is formed by nature; that is, by inherent properties existing in itself. As the trees in an uninhabited forest spring up without a cultivator, so the universe is self-existent; and as the banks of a river fall of themselves, so there is no supreme destroyer. The world, in short, is produced as the spider produces his web, out of its own bowels. Who is it that causes the milk to ooze from the udder of the cow, and the rivers to flow to the sea?

Spirit is found in two conditions, emancipated and enclosed by matter. There is but one spirit individuated among the whole universe of animated existences.[h]

All human affairs are regulated by religion and irreligion, i. e., by works of merit and demerit. Religion naturally and of itself purifies, and exalts, and immortalizes its possessor; while irreligion defiles, degrades, and ruins men.

The future births of men are regulated by present actions: the wicked are punished in different degraded bodies, or in some hell. Those who practise works of merit may, if their merits are sufficiently great, ascend to one of the twelve heavens.

Beyond the highest heavens, for eight miles, all is darkness. Below this is a heaven where all who obtain unchanging happiness remain,[i] and which is 36,000,000 miles long. The inhabitants of this world will occupy 1,332 cubits of these regions, where they are all assembled. Below this are five heavens inhabited by ascetics something less pure than the former; and still lower are twelve heavens, one below the other. Next to this is the earth, balanced in the air; beneath this, water; and still lower, darkness. Persons committing sin in these heavens become men, or animals, or inanimate substances, or sink into a region of torment: but as often as any one descends from happiness, another ascends from the earth, and occupies his couch, or place of repose, in heaven. The earth remains fixed by its own nature: when an earthquake occurs, it is caused by Véntŭrēē, a god, throwing his arms up to his head. Joinŭ perfected saints are spread over the whole universe: their number is beyond all calculation.

Something farther of the principles of this sect may be gathered from the following address of a joinŭ anchorite to Kalŭ-koomarŭ, the son of Bŭjrŭ-singhŭ, the king of Dharavasŭ, a joinŭ:—'Honour kings; seek the blessing of wise men; excuse thyself to gamesters and women; the fruit of wisdom is to know matter and spirit, works of merit and demerit, to act by rule, to know that the use of riches is to feed the poor, that the proper use of speech is to express only excellent words, that

h Charvvakŭ, a joinŭ leader, denied the existence of spirit altogether.

i The joinŭs, imagining that a certain mark in the open hands when placed together forms a representation of this heaven, daily draw their joined hands to their forehead, meditating on this place of happiness.

the body is mortal, riches uncertain, death near, and that therefore the cultivation of religion is necessary; that as gold is purified by filing, cutting, melting, and beating, so by the words of holy persons, by works of merit, religious austerities, and compassion, the mind becomes pure.'—Hearing these words, the king's son, was anxious to embrace the life of a hermit, and went to consult his mother, who used the strongest language to dissuade him from his purpose; she affirmed, that it was as difficult to become a yogēē, as to swim across the ocean, to walk on spikes, to stand on water, to feed on sand, to lift mount Sooméroo, or to conquer the three worlds!' Not regarding the words of his mother, however, the son entered a forest.

The daily duties of a joinŭ are the following:—When he rises in the morning, he must bathe, shake gently his garment, and the mat on which he lay, to purify them; after which, he must repeat certain prayers or incantations addressed to persons possessing the five qualities of Ŭrihŭntŭ, Siddhŭ, Acharyŭ, Oopadhyayŭ, and Sadhoo, and others addressed to Wisdom, Religious Light, Excellent Conduct, and Devotion, for the purpose of removing the sins of the night. He next proceeds to a temple,[k] walks round it three times; bows and prays to the image, which is that of a joinŭ yogēē in a sitting posture; after which he goes to his spiritual guide, and bowing, makes vows to him for the day. These vows regard eating, speaking, &c. One person vows not to eat, and another not to speak, for so many hours, calling upon all joinŭ yogēēs, and all joinŭs, to witness his vows; after which he listens to some parts of their sacred writings: these duties occupy the forenoon. He now goes to solicit alms for the food of the day; and he does this according to vows, regulating the number of houses at which he resolves to beg. On his return, he repeats certain incantations, to remove the sins which he has committed in destroying life as he walked through the streets.[l] He now eats, and again repeats certain prayers to persons designated by the five names above mentioned. During the remainder of the day he continues nearly silent; and at the close of it repeats, as in the morning, certain incantations, to remove the sins of the day. Before retiring to sleep, standing near his bed, he rehearses certain stories respecting joinŭ devotees and kings, the qualities of the places in which joinŭs should reside, and those of female mendicants, and then the instructions of a spiritual guide to his disciple. He who lives in a

[k] 'There is a famous image, of eighteen times the height of a man, upon a rock near Béligola, named Gomŭtéshwŭrŭ-swamēē.' 'At Koorkool, near Mangalore, there is also a gigantic image of Gomŭtéshwŭrŭ.' 'There are two kinds of temples among the joinŭs, one covered with a roof, and the other an open area, surrounded by a wall.' *Asiatic Researches*, vol. ix. pp. 256, 285.

[l] From this and other facts it will appear, to what an extent the joinŭs carry this principle; they do not allow that any crime justifies the taking away of life; hence they, as well as the bouddhŭs, consider kings, as the administrators of criminal justice, as the greatest of sinners. See page 314 of this volume.

secular state, among the above duties, omits to solicit alms, to visit the spiritual guide, and to repeat their sacred writings; the other parts he practises as far as he is able.

Another duty enjoined upon the members of this sect is, that of repeating the praise of those distinguished by the names Ŭrihŭntŭ, Siddhŭ, Acharyŭ, Oopadhyayŭ, and Sadhoo. The first name *Ŭrihŭntŭ* implies, that the yogēē to whom it really belongs, possesses the power of causing an ŭshokŭ tree to spring up and overshadow him, flowers to fall on him, a cooling breeze to refresh him, a throne and a white umbrella to descend for him, heavenly courtezans to come and sing before him, the gods to ascend and descend hovering over him, and glory like that of the sun to surround him wherever he sits; that he has a pure mind, profound speech, boundless knowledge, and that he is worshipped by the three worlds. The next name, *Siddhŭ*, implies, that this person possesses the qualities which secure absorption, viz., knowledge of all things; that he is all-seeing; is capable of doing every thing; is armed against every enemy; is completely happy; is the same to all; is all-powerful, and is in all things a wonderful person. He who is called *Acharyŭ* has overcome his passions; is possessed of excellent properties; has renounced sensual gratifications; does not listen to sensual discourse; forgets all enjoyments; is moderate in food; looks not at the couch of a female; retains not the remembrance of women; partakes of no food difficult of digestion; has renounced anger, affection, desire, falsehood; commits no injury; receives no presents; lives the life of an ascetic; ponders his steps; seeks purity; speaks sound words; renounces impure food, and the company of impure persons; conceals his thoughts; speaks little; and walks with little motion. *Oopadhyayŭ* implies, that the person receiving this title has read and taught the following works, called ŭngŭs: —Achar-ŭngŭ, Soogŭr-ŭngŭ, T'han-ŭngŭ, Sŭmŭvay-ŭngŭ, Bhŭgŭvŭtēē-jēē, Gata-jee, Oopasŭkŭ-dŭsha, Ŭntŭgŭrŭ, Ŭnootŭrŭ-oovaee, Prŭshnŭ-vyakŭrŭnŭ, and Vipakŭ-sōōtrŭ: and also the following oopangŭs: Oovaee-sōōtrŭ, Rayŭ-psénee, Jēēvabhigŭmŭ, Pŭnhŭvŭna, Jŭmboo-dweepŭ-pŭnnŭtēē, Chŭndrŭ-pŭnnŭtēē, Sōōrŭ-pŭnnŭtēē, Niravŭtēē, Kŭpiya, Kŭppŭ-virŭngsiya, Poopphiya, and Pooppŭchooliya. The name *Sadhoo* implies, that the person possesses compassion, truth; that he takes nothing but what is given to him; that he has renounced sexual intercourse, and food at night; that he does not injure the earth; that he strains his drinking-water, and carefully preserves it from insects; covers his fire lest insects be destroyed; agitates not the wind, for the same reason; destroys not the leaves or flowers of trees, nor in any way injures sentient creatures; that he says nothing mixed with anger, pride, affection, or desire; that he meditates on religion; that he speaks of religion alone; preserves his body and the mat on which he sleeps pure; covers his mouth while speaking; sweeps his path when walking, and his seat when about to sit down, that he may not destroy animal life; avoids receiving more than the daily supply of his wants; fixes his mind and words on religion; and bears affliction with patience.

The person who, by practising the duties of the joinŭ religion, renders himself worthy of the worship of Indrŭ and the other gods; who delivers himself from the chains of the world, obtaining complete emancipation from matter;[m] becomes a proper object of worship to all creatures.

The joinŭ mendicants profess to have five vows of abstinence: these regard falsehood, eating flesh or fish, theft, drinking spirits, and female intercourse. They bind themselves also to possess nothing beyond a cloth for the loins, a sheet to cover the body, a towel to wipe the mouth, a brush[n] to sweep the ground, for fear of treading on insects, and a begger's dish. They are commanded to fear secular affairs; the miseries of a future state; the receiving from others more than the food of a day at once; all accidents: food, if connected with the destruction of animal life, &c.; death, and disgrace; also to seek to please all, and to obtain compassion from all.

The joinŭs observe several festivals during the year; as, the Flag, the Jŭmboo dwēēpŭ, the water, the Dedication, and the Car festivals;[o] another, when eight hundred articles, eight of one sort, are presented to a joinŭ deity; but the greatest of all their festivals is the Siddhŭ-chŭkrŭ pōōja, which is celebrated twice a year, in the months Ashwinŭ and Choitrŭ, and continues nine days. The worship is performed before the nine names mentioned in page 331, written on paper or on the earth, in a circle containing nine divisions, of different colours, the name Ŭrihŭntŭ being in the centre. On the outside of the circle are written the names of the ten regents of the earth, of the sixty-four goddesses called the ruling deities, of two Bhoirŭvŭs, two dŭkshŭs, and the name of the guardian deity of the circle, Chŭkréshwŭrēē. Worship is daily performed to all these names collectively during the festival, and each name is daily honored with particular ceremonies in turn: the colours of the flowers and cloths offered are to be the same as the colour of the compartment in which each name is written. To most of the ceremonies included in what is called pōōja (see p. 215.) they add recitations in praise of devout joinŭs.

m Mŭha-veerŭ passed through twenty-seven births in the forms of gods, men, and reptiles, before he obtained unchangeable emancipation.

n The shwétŭmbŭrŭs (that is, those who wear white clothes) keep a brush of woollen threads; the digŭmbŭrŭs have one made of peacock's feathers.

o There is a similarity betwixt some of these feasts and one or two of those observed by the bouddhŭs. See p. 312.

On the 5th of the increase of the moon, the joinŭs have a monthly festival in honour of Mŭha-vēērŭ; to whom they present five books, five pens, five inkstands, five leaves used as paper, and five articles of every other offering. On the 11th of the increase of the moon, another festival is held in honor of Mŭnŭsŭ-vrŭtēē, a joinŭ anchorite; when the person who supplies the expense observes a vow of silence for a day and a night.

In honor of the other twenty-two leaders of the joinŭ sect, annual festivals are held on the anniversary of the birth of each. Once a year, which may be celebrated in any month, the joinŭs have another festival called Vishŭ-vŭyirmanŭ.

In the month Bhadrŭ, all the joinŭs in one town sit for eight days, and hear the Kŭlpŭ-sōōtrŭ read by one of their principal mendicants, who explains as he reads. On the day before the commencement of this festival, the book is richly adorned, and carried in procession on the head of a boy sitting in a palanqueen; the joinŭs, on horseback and in palanqueens, following with music and dancing. In the house, the book is placed on a throne, while the company stand before it with joined hands; they afterward sit for some time, and listen to devout songs in praise of their devotees and of religion. Part of the day is kept as a fast, but it closes with an entertainment. Offerings are also presented to the book and to the reader, and during the reading, the audience occasionally manifest their attention by repeating the sound jēē, jēē.

After the birth of a child, a secular joinŭ carries it to the temple, which he circumambulates, bows to the god, repeats certain prayers, and then carries the child to the spiritual guide, who repeats an incantátion in its ear. This is followed by a feast.

In a joinŭ mendicant's last sickness, a disciple repeats a certain prayer to him, and rehearses the praises of the joinŭ mendicants. After his death, with his body are burnt the brush with which he swept the road or his seat, that he might not destroy animal life, his staff, his beggar's bag, and a lump of wheaten paste. When a person dies, or a child is born, the family cannot visit a temple for eleven days; nor does the spiritual guide, nor any relation, visit their house for three days. On the twelfth day a feast is held.

There are five sects of joinŭs, but the difference between them is trifling. The Digŭmbŭrŭs wear no clothes, and their images of Rishŭbhŭ-dévŭ are also naked. The other sects are, the Térŭpŭnt'hēēs, the Dhooriyas, the Loonkas, and the Bouddhŭs.

It may not be uninteresting to see what the bramhŭns have said of these atheistical sets, with whom they once carried on the fiercest religious controversy ever known in India, and whom they afterwards drove from the field with weapons dipped in blood. And I here give a few extracts from the Kashēē-khŭndŭ of the Skŭndŭ pooranŭ, the Prŭbodhŭ-chŭndrodŭyŭ, the Vidwŭnmodŭ-tŭrŭnginēē, and the Booddhŭ pooranŭ.

These sects are said by the bramhŭns to have taken their rise from Virochŭnŭ, whose conversion is attributed,[p] to a declaration made by Brŭmha before Indrŭ and Virochŭnŭ, to the following purport:—One day Indrŭ and Virochŭnŭ asked Brŭmha, 'What the mind was, and what the body?' Brŭmha, who was in a state of profound meditation, having his eyes shut, laid his hand on his breast. At this time a bason of water stood before Brŭmha, and his image, in this posture, was reflected upon the water. Virochŭnŭ concluded, from this conduct of Brŭmha, that he intended to say, that the body was every thing. Indrŭ conceived, that this was not his meaning, but that he meant to convey the idea, that the body was like the shadow on the water; but that within (intimated by laying his hand on his breast) there was an immaterial spirit, and that this was Brŭmhŭ.

The next person who was the accidental cause of the spread of the doctrines of atheism, says the Shrēē-bhagŭvŭtŭ, was Rishŭbhŭ-dévŭ, through whose devotions three kings became atheists, (see p. 326.) Next, the bramhŭns speak of Vishnoo as incarnate to overturn the kingdom of Divo-dasŭ, a king of Kashēē, who sought to prevent the gods from receiving any praise or petitions from men. Vishnoo spread atheism to such an extent, that Divo-dasŭ, offended at the progress of impiety, renounced his kingdom, became an ascetic, and shortly after ascended to heaven.

The Pŭdmŭ-pooranŭ[q] speaks of an ascetic named Digŭmbŭrŭ, (not the disciple of Mŭha-vēēru,) an incarnation of Shivŭ, who promoted the tenets of atheism.

The next person who appeared was Booddhŭ, the son of Ŭjinŭ[r], who was born in the district of Magŭdhŭ; respecting whom I subjoin the translation of an extract from the Booddhŭ pooranŭ:—

'I have heard,' says the anonymous author of this work, 'that, at a certain period, Bhŭgŭvanŭ, (Booddhŭ,) being incarnate for the purpose of performing many glorious things, was giving lessons on religion, attended by 12,000 religious mendicants, and 32,000 bodhee-sŭtwŭs, or bouddhŭs, in the garden of Inat'hŭ-pindŭdŭ, in

p See the Rig-védŭ and the Yogŭ-vashisht'hŭ Ramayŭnŭ.

q See the Pooshkŭrŭ-khŭndŭ of that work.

r The Shrēē-bhagŭvŭtŭ calls him the son of Ŭjinŭ, but the Booddhŭ pooranŭ, as the reader will perceive from what follows, says his father's name was Shooddhodŭnŭ, and his mother's Maya-dévēē.

the forest of Jétree, at Shravŭstee; when, about twelve o'clock at night, a ray of glory issued from his turban, which said—'Praise to Shakyŭ-singhŭ, the sage, eminent for intelligence, a luminary dissipating darkness, resplendent, a holy flame, with a beautiful body, and a subdued mind, &c.' Hearing this, the religious mendicants, bowing, with joined hands, humbly requested of Booddhŭ, that he would acquaint them with the words which had been revealed by the glory proceeding from the turban. Booddhŭ informed the mendicants, that Shétŭkétoo[s], of the race of the gods, formerly descended in a chariot from the heaven of Gŭnéshŭ, and was born in the family of a bouddhŭ, to instruct mankind in the true doctrine. After descending from his chariot to the earth, he ascended a superb throne, in a palace miraculously prepared; from whence he declared to the attending gods, that he should be born in the womb of a bouddhŭ female, and continue twelve years in his mother's womb. The gods reflected among themselves, that almost all families had some fault in them, which rendered it improper for Booddhŭ to be born in these families; but that the race of Shakyŭ-singhŭ, being in possession of sixty-four distinguished qualities, was pure; that at Kŭpilŭvŭsoo lived Shooddhodŭnŭ possessed of twelve distinguished qualities. Booddhŭ consented, and directed the attending gods to be born in such and such families; and, being born, to go and teach mankind the one hundred and eight religious ceremonies.[t] He then dismissed the gods, that they might assume human birth, and departed himself to do the same; that he might make known the bouddhŭ doctrine to Moitréyabhidhŭ, who should teach it to the world. Accordingly, Booddhŭ, in the month Voishakhŭ, at the full of the moon, under the constellation Pooshya, entered, by the right side, the womb of Maya-dévee; and, at the end of twelve years, while she was amusing herself in the grove Lŭmbinēē, she was seized with the pains of child-birth, and was delivered of a son, who, immediately on his birth, looked towards the ten quarters of the world, and measured ten paces with his feet.[u] At the end of seven days from the time of the birth, Maya-dévēē died, and went to an excellent heaven. All the gods, and other celestial beings, moonees, rishees, &c. came to pay their honors to the god who had been born in the house of Shooddhodŭnŭ; they calculated his nativity, the fortunate and unfortunate signs; pronounced it an excellent birth, and declared that this divine person would live till he was eighty years old. The sage Ŭsitakshyŭ informed Shooddhodŭnŭ, that his son would shortly leave his house, and become a religious mendicant, in order to learn the bouddhŭ doctrine,[x] and teach it to others. From this the sage gathered,

[s] Another name for Booddhŭ.

[t] Ceremonies peculiar to the bouddhŭs.

[u] To signify that his doctrine should be extended through the world.

[x] He was to gather this doctrine from books and from learned men.

that his son was a god, and fell down and worshipped him. At length the celestial guests were dismissed with much praise and respect; and the father, accompanied by his son, and the rest of the family, having entered the temple of a goddess, and repeated the usual rites, covered his son with ornaments, while the sylvan gods presented him with flowers.

'The boy Booddhŭ, taking 10,000 other boys with him, went to school, and began to instruct his master, who was filled with astonishment at the amazing extent of his knowledge. Unable to answer his different questions, he evaded them, and begged him to take his place among the boys; 32,000 of whom, beside Booddhŭ's 10,000, were taught at this school: but Booddhŭ neglected his school exercises, and began to teach these 42,000 boys the bouddhŭ doctrines; who all, in due time, became bouddhŭs. After leaving school, Boodhŭ went to Kooshēē, under a tree in which place he took up his abode, and entered on religious austerities.'

The next account of Booddhŭ, is that he married Gopa, the daughter of Shakshyŭ, and retained 84,000 concubines; but he was principally attached to Gopa.—The gods one evening appeared to the father of Gopa in a dream, and apprized him, that his son-in-law would soon leave his house, and become a sŭnyasēē. On another occasion, the father and Gopa had each a dream, in which they beheld Booddhŭ, having on a red garment, and a staff in his hand, going on pilgrimage. When the king awoke, he placed guards round the palace, and entreated him not to depart; promising him all he desired, even his kingdom, and reminding him, that he was too young to become an anchorite. Booddhŭ, perceiving that it was in vain to hope for the king's consent, retired to his apartments; and his father placed more guards round the palace. The gods, however, sent a heavy sleep on all the guards; and this incarnate person, on his arrival at the outside of the palace, mounted his horse, and fled to the distance of forty-eight miles: when he dismissed his servant, and the gods who had accompanied him; stript himself of all his ornaments; shaved his head; clothed himself with the red garments which had been presented to him by some god; and thus assumed the garb of a sŭnyasēē. His old apparel the gods took to heaven, where they became objects of worship.

Booddhŭ in his pilgrimage met three hundred disciples of Shravŭkŭ, of Voishalēē, with whom he discussed at great length the bouddhŭ doctrine, which they ultimately embraced. He afterwards converted 700 disciples of a person named Ramŭ; and then visited Gŭya, where, sitting down by the Noirŭnjēē, he practised religious austerities.

Maya-dévēē, seeing her son inflicting the greatest cruelties on himself, full of concern, descended to earth, and expostulated with him, reminding him, that he was her only son, the son of a king, and that by these severities he would certainly destroy himself. Booddhŭ, aroused from his intense meditation by the voice of his mother, addressed much praise to her; with which she was so much pleased, that she presented to him a parijatŭ flower, which she had brought from heaven, and then departed. He now recommenced his religious austerities, and continued them for six years, exposing himself to the scorching sun, the pelting rain, the parching wind, and the severest cold. The children of the neighbouring town came to the spot, and played every kind of trick with him, putting sticks up his nose, into his ears, and mouth; but nothing could awake him from his intense abstraction. The gods filled with admiration at his unparalleled devotion, descended and worshipped him; but a person, named Nŭmoochee, visited Booddhŭ, and upbraided him for his austerities, asking him why he thus reduced his body to a skeleton; why he brought upon himself so much sorrow?—reminding him, that his death was near, and that it was wise so to act as to secure happiness in a future state;[y] that he was the son of a king; that he ought to seek riches, to enable him to make gifts, and present offerings to the gods, which were meritorious actions, and would be rewarded by corresponding fruits; but that at present he was bearing sufferings without any hope of reward. Booddhŭ's meditation was broken by this language, and he replied, 'Oh! wicked friend, dost thou not know what I am doing? I am performing yogŭ, in doing which, it is necessary first to perfect the body by austerities, to purify the blood, the flesh, the bones, the heart, and the mind. Death is better than continuance in a body so vile that meritorious actions will not proceed from it. I will subdue my evil desires, indisposition to religious services, hunger and thirst, disposition to conversation, covetousness, falsehood, sorrow, &c.; as an unbaked pot melts in the water, so will I, by yogŭ, subdue or dissolve all these.' Nŭmoochee, hearing this reply, departed. At the close of the six years' yogŭ, Booddhŭ arose, and went to an adjoining village to obtain refreshments; after which, walking seven times round a sacred tree, and making a seat of the grass, he sat down under the tree, and made the following vow: 'On this seat may my body, blood, and bones, become dry; though life depart, I will never abandon this yogŭ called sŭmyŭk-sŭmbodhee.' The attending gods, hearing these resolutions of Booddhŭ, were filled with astonishment, and taking offerings, worshipped him as a god.

Booddhŭ taught, add the bramhŭns, that the universe was eternal, and had no creator; and that all creatures were uninterruptedly passing from death to life: he also protested against the destruction of animal life, whether for food or sacrifice. He was

[y] By performing acts of charity, and the ceremonies of religion, instead of injuring his body by austerities.

much attached to astrological speculations, and wrote a work on astrology.

The same Hindoo works inform us, that these seceders were divided into six sects, embracing the doctrines published by Digŭmbŭrŭ, Virochŭnŭ, Vishnoo, Booddhŭ, and Shakshyŭ-singhŭ. —The founders of these sects were, Charvvakŭ, Madhyŭmikŭ, Yogacharŭ, Soutrantikŭ, Voibhashikŭ, and Niravŭrŭnŭ.—Digŭmbŭrŭ taught, that the being who survives all, and of whom nothing can be known, is God; that the universe is composed of four elements only, earth, water, fire, and air; and that there is no such thing as vacuum; that the earth is eternal, and has no creator; and that the highest act of virtue is to abstain from doing injury to sentient creatures. Mŭha-vēērŭ enlarged Digŭmbŭrŭ's work, and gave it the name of Ŭrihŭntanoo-shasŭnŭ. Charvvakŭ, following Virochŭnŭ, declared that man was not possessed of spirit, and that there was no future state. Madhyŭmikŭ started the opinion, that the vacuum which remains at the general destruction of the universe is God. Yogacharŭ taught, that the mind can only be occupied by one object at once. Soutrantikŭ taught the Platonic doctrine, that in forming ideas the images of things are impressed on the mind: he also held, that the mind can only embrace one object at once. Voibhashikŭ was of opinion, that all visible objects are perishable; and that sensible objects are not imprinted on the mind, but are understood through the senses. The last of these sages, Niravŭrŭnŭ, taught, that what others call the soul is only something similar to light, diffused through the body, which is capable of depression or extension, and which dies with it.

These philosophers wrote the following works:—the doctrines of Vrihŭspŭtee; philosophical mysteries; a treatise on logic; a work on astrology; another to prove the folly of religious distinctions and ceremonies; and a history of the Bouddhŭ philosophers.

The following are some of the opinions of this sect[z], as charged upon them in the works mentioned at the head of this article:— There is no such God as the common notions on this subject would point out; no heaven separate from present happiness; no hell separate from present sufferings; neither works of merit nor demerit. There are no such beings as creator, preserver, and destroyer. The world is eternal; it exists from itself, and decays of itself, as parents give birth to children, as an earthen vessel is produced by the potter, as the centipede arises from cow-dung, blades of corn from seed, and as insects from fruit: nature gives birth to every thing. Material things arise out of the four elements of earth, fire, water, and air. All visible objects are subject to decay. Man does not possess an immortal spirit. Spiritual guides are un-

[z] The atheistical part of these tenets ought not, perhaps, to be charged, in their full extent, on all the joinŭs and bouddhŭs.

necessary. The highest virtue consists in refraining from injuring sentient creatures. Supreme happiness consists in being free. Every species of pleasure may be called heaven. Absorption is realized in death. The entire absence of desire or affection is the highest state of happiness: as a person is afflicted for the death even of a bird he has reared, while other birds die unnoticed. Death is the same to Brŭmha and to a fly. To feed the hungry; to give medicine to the sick; to remove fear from others; to be compassionate to all; to instruct the ignorant; to exercise the five senses, the five members, the faculty of reason, and the understanding, are acts of virtue. There is no merit in cutting trees, or in killing animals, for religious ceremonies; in mixing blood and earth to rub upon the body, nor in burning linseeds and clarified butter. A fine form, superior strength, a large family, a good disposition, a tender heart, and decision of mind, are the chief good. The five first of these philosophers taught, add the bramhŭns, that the union of the four elements gave rise to animal life, or motion: as the union of certain ingredients produces a medicine capable of removing disease; or as several colours mixed together produce a colour different from any simple colour; or as the juice of a sour fruit put into milk diffuses sourness throughout the whole.

I shall conclude this account, with an extract from Mr. Colebrooke's excellent 'Observations on the Sect of the Joinŭs,' inserted in the ninth volume of the Asiatic Researches, in which he points out many striking similarities in the leading features of the systems embraced by the orthodox Hindoos and the seceders.

'It appears, from the concurrent result of all the enquiries which have been made, that the joinŭs constitute a sect of Hindoos, differing, indeed, from the rest, in some very important tenets; but following, in other respects, a similar practice, and maintaining like opinions and observances. The essential character of the Hindoo institutions, is the distribution of the people into four great tribes. This is considered by themselves to be the marked point, which separates them from mléch'hŭs, or barbarians. The joinŭs, it is found, admit the same division into four tribes, and perform like religious ceremonies, termed sŭngskarŭs, from the birth of a male to his marriage. They observe similar fasts, and practise, still more strictly, the received maxims for refraining from injury to any sentient being. They appear to recognise, as subordinate deities, some, if not all, of the gods of the prevailing sect; but do not worship, in particular, the five principal gods of those sects, or any one of them by preference; nor address prayers, or perform sacrifice, to the sun, or to fire; and they differ from the rest of the Hindoos, in assigning the highest place to certain deified saints, who, according to their creed, have successively become superior gods. Another point, in which they materially disagree, is the rejection of the védŭs, the divine authority of which they deny; condemning, at the same time, the practice of sacrifices, and the other ceremonies, which the followers of the védŭs perform, to obtain specific promised consequences in this world, or in the next. In this respect, the joinŭs resemble the bouddhŭs or sougŭtŭs; who equally deny the divine authority of the védŭs; and who similarly worship certain pre-eminent saints, admitting likewise, as subordinate deities, nearly the whole pantheon of the orthodox Hindoos. They differ, indeed, in regard to the history of the personages whom they have deified; and it may be hence concluded, that they have had distinct founders: but the original notion seems to have been the same. In fact, this remarkable tenet, from which the joinŭs and bouddhŭs derive their most conspicuous peculiarities, is not entirely unknown to the orthodox Hindoos. The followers of the védŭs, according to the theology which is explained in the védantŭ, considering the human soul as a portion of the divine and universal mind, believe, that it is capable of perfect union with the divine essence: and the writers on the védantŭ not only affirm, that this union and identity are attained through a knowledge of God, as by them taught; but have hinted, that by such means the particular soul becomes God, even to the actual attainment of supremacy.[a] So far the followers of the védŭs do not virtually disagree with the joinŭs and bouddhŭs. But they have not, like those sects, framed a mythology upon the supposed history of the persons, who have successively attained divinity: nor have they taken these for the objects of national worship. All three sects agree in their belief of transmigration. But the joinŭs are distinguished from the rest by their admission of no opinions, as they themselves affirm, which are not founded on perception, or on proof drawn from that, or from testimony. It does not, however, appear, that they really withhold belief from pretended revelations: and the doctrines, which characterise the sect, are not confined to a single tenet; but form an assemblage of mythological and metaphysical ideas found among other sects, joined to many visionary fantastic notions of their own. Their belief in the eternity of matter, and perpetuity of the world, is common to the Sankhya philosophy, from which it was perhaps immediately taken. Their description of the world has much analogy to that which is given in the pooranŭs, or Indian theogonies;[b] but the scheme has been rendered still more extravagant. Their precaution to avoid injuring any being is a practice inculcated in the orthodox religion, but

[a] Vrihŭd-arŭnyŭkŭ Oopŭnishŭd.

[b] According to Mr. Colebrooke, the joinŭs suppose, that the world resembles a spindle resting on the half of another; or three cups, of which the lowest is inverted, and the uppermost meets at its circumference the middle one. They conceive the setting and rising of stars and planets to be caused by mount Sooméroo; and suppose three times the period of a planet's appearance to be requisite for it to pass round Sooméroo, and return to the place whence it emerges. Accordingly, they allot two suns, as many moons, and an equal number of each planet, star, and constellation, to Jŭmbŭ-dweēpŭ; and imagine that these appear, on alternate days, south and north of Sooméroo.

which has been carried by them to a ludicrous extreme. In their notions of the soul, and of its union with body, and of retribution for good and evil, some analogy is likewise observable.

'If it be admitted, that the bouddhŭs are originally a sect of Hindoos, it may be next questioned whether that, or any of the religious systems now established, be the most ancient. I have on a former occasion[c] indicated the notions, which I entertain on this point. According to the hypothesis which I then hinted, the earliest Indian sect, of which we have any present distinct knowledge, is that of the followers of the practical védŭs, who worshipped the sun, fire, and the elements; and who believed the efficacy of sacrifices, for the accomplishment of present and of future purposes. It may be supposed, that the refined doctrine of the védantēēs, or followers of the theological and argumentative part of the védŭs, is of later date: and it does not seem improbable, that the sects of joinŭ and of Boodd'hŭ are still more modern. But I apprehend, that the voishnŭvŭs, meaning particularly the worshippers of Ramŭ and of Krishnŭ, may be subsequent to those sects, and that the soivyŭs also are of more recent date.'

CHAP. IV.

ACCOUNT OF THE SHIKHS[a].

THE founder of this sect was *Nanŭkŭ*, a Hindoo of the kshŭtriyŭ caste, born in the year 1469, at Raibhoédēē-Tŭlŭwŭndēē, a village in the district of Majha, in the Pŭnjab.

Sir John Malcolm has related[b] a number of particulars respecting the life and travels of Nanŭkŭ; the substance of which is, that he discovered an early attachment to a devout life, which his father found it impossible to counteract; and at length became famous as a prophet: according to Bhaee-Gooroo-Vŭlee, author of the Gnanŭ-Rŭtnavŭlee, a work in the Shikh dialect, he travelled to all the sacred places of the Hindoos and Mŭsŭlmans, and even to Mecca. In these journies, as the author is informed by a learned Shikh employed in the Serampore printing-office, he obtained many disciples; and at the time of his death, which happened when he was advanced in years, left not less than 100,000 persons in different countries who were attached to him as their religious guide.

[c] Asiatic Researches, vol. viii. p. 474.

[a] The followers of Nanŭkŭ are sometimes called Gooroo-mookhēē, 'from the mouth of the teacher;' but generally Shikhs, from Shishyŭ, a disciple.

[b] In his 'Sketch of the Hindoos,' Asiatic Researches, vol. xi.

Nanŭkŭ appears to have resembled Choitŭnyŭ, and many other Hindoos who have been celebrated for their attachment to forms of devotion, in preference to barren speculations and religious shows.

He maintained the doctrine of the divine unity, which, it is probable, he learned from the Mŭsŭlman mendicants, with whom he was very familiar: further, that God dwells in the devout, and that this divine inhabitation renders the ascetic an object of reverence and even of worship; and that hence it became a duty to seek the society of devout mendicants. The other two points most insisted upon by him were, devout attachment to the deity, and a harmless behaviour towards all creatures.—To promote the spirit of devotion, Nanŭkŭ composed a number of sacred hymns in praise of the Deity, which have a place in the Adee-Grŭnt'hŭ; in which work repeating the names of God is enjoined on the Shikhs.

This reformer dealt very mildly with the two systems which he rejected, those of the Hindoos and Mŭsŭlmans, and in consequence he left many customs indifferent: he however dissuaded his disciples from expecting any benefit from the worship of idols, and other ceremonies connected with the Hindoo mythology.

Nanŭkŭ had two sons, Shrēē-chŭndrŭ and Lŭkshmēē-dasŭ. His family now resides at Déhŭra, by the river Ravēē, where Nanŭkŭ died; and from whence, as the Shikhs say, he ascended to heaven in his bodily state, his garments only being found after his death. His disciples took these garments, and burnt them instead of the body; but Sir John Malcolm says, that a small piece of one of his garments[c] is still exhibited at the temple dedicated to this mendicant at Déhŭra, where the objects of worship are the Shikh shastrŭs. Images of Nanŭkŭ are never made, though paintings of him are to be seen in many places.

Nanŭkŭ, before his death, passing by his own relations, appointed Ŭngŭdŭ, a favourite disciple to succeed him. This mendicant, at his death, appointed Ŭmŭrŭ-dasŭ, one of his disciples, to fill up his station; to him succeeded Ramŭ-dasŭ, and after him, in succession, Ŭrjoonŭ, Hŭree-Govindŭ, Hŭree-Rayŭ, Hŭree-Krishnŭ, and Tég-bahadŭr. The person who presided last over the Shikhs, was Gooroo Govindŭ-Singhŭ.

Ŭrjoonŭ compiled the Adee-Grŭnt'hŭ, or, 'The first Book,' from the writings of his four predecessors, Nanŭkŭ, Ŭngŭdŭ, Ŭmŭrŭ-dasŭ, and Ŭrjoonŭ. Ramŭ-dasŭ enlarged and improved it by his own additions and comments; and some small portions have been subsequently added by thirteen persons, the last of whom was a female disciple named Mēērabaēē.

[c] This small piece, however, is, I suspect, 200 lbs. weight, as a cloak of this kind, which Nanŭkŭ is said to have left on his pilgrimage, was restored to his relations after his death, and placed in this temple.

'Ŭmŭrŭ-dasŭ,' says Sir John Malcolm, 'was distinguished for his activity in preaching the tenets of Nanŭkŭ, and was very successful in obtaining converts and followers, by the aid of whom he established some temporal power; he built Koojŭrawal, and separated from the regular Shikhs the oodasēē sect, which was founded by Shrēē-Chŭndrŭ, the son of Nanŭkŭ, and was probably considered, at that period, as heretical.'

Ramŭ-dasŭ, the son of Ŭmŭrŭ-dasŭ, is celebrated for 'the improvements he made at Ŭmritŭ-sŭrŭ, which was for some time called Ram-poorŭ, or Ramdas-poorŭ. He added much to the population of this city, and formed a famous reservoir of water, which he called Ŭmritŭ-sŭrŭ, or the water of immortality!' This pool has become the resort of the Shikhs from all parts, and has given its own name and sanctity to this city, now called Ŭmritŭ-sŭrŭ.

Thus each of the ten leaders of the Shikhs added to the number and power of the sect, till, under Govindŭ-singhŭ, they became a formidable nation. This man was a political leader rather than a religious guide, and he introduced a number of accommodating rules into the system of his predecessors, to meet the circumstances of a people who were to acquire and support their independence by the sword.

Those who wish to become acquainted with the political events which have elevated a sect of mendicants into a powerful nation, will be highly gratified by a perusal of Sir John Malcolm's very interesting sketch. I shall merely add, from this article, a paragraph respecting the national council of this people:—'When a Gooroo-mŭta, or great national council, is called, (as it always is, or ought to be, when any imminent danger threatens the country, or any large expedition is to be undertaken,) all the Shikh chiefs assemble at Ŭmritŭ-sŭrŭ. The assembly, which is called the Gooroo-mŭta, is convened by the Ŭkalēēs;[d] and when the chiefs

[d] 'The Ukalēēs, or worshippers of the Eternal, (Ŭkalŭ-pooroosh̆ŭ,) under the double character of fanatic priests and desperate soldiers, have usurped the sole direction of all religious affairs at Umritŭ-sŭrŭ, and are consequently leading men in a council which is held at that sacred place, and which deliberates under all the influence of religious enthusiasm. Agreeably to the historians of that nation, they were first founded by Gooroo-Govindŭ, whose institutes, as it has been before stated, they most zealously defended against the innovations of the voiragēē Bŭndŭ. They wear blue chequered clothes, and bangles or bracelets of steel round their wrists, initiate converts, and have almost the sole direction of the religious ceremonies at Umritŭ-sŭrŭ, where they reside, and of which they deem themselves the defenders, and consequently never desire to quit it unless in cases of great extremity. This order of shikhs have a place, or Boonga, on the bank of the sacred reservoir of Umritŭ-sŭrŭ, where they generally resort: they are individually possessed of property, though they affect poverty, and subsist upon charity; which, however, since their numbers have increased, they generally extort, by accusing the principal chiefs of crimes, imposing fines upon them, and, in the event of their refusing to pay, preventing them from performing their ablutions, or going through any of their religious ceremonies at Umritŭ-sŭrŭ.'—*Asiatic Researches*, vol. xi.

meet upon this solemn occasion, it is concluded that all private animosities cease, and that every man sacrifices his personal feelings at the shrine of the general good; and, actuated by principles of pure patriotism, thinks of nothing but the interests of the religion, and common-wealth, to which he belongs.—When the chiefs and principal leaders are seated, the Adee-Grŭnt'hŭ and Dŭshŭma-Padshahēē-Grŭnt'hŭ[e] are placed before them. They all bend their heads before these scriptures, and exclaim, 'Wah! Gooroo jēēda Khalsa!—Wah! Gooroo jēēkēē phŭté!' A great quantity of cakes, made of wheat, butter, and sugar, are then placed before the volumes of their sacred writings, and covered with a cloth. These holy cakes, which are in commemoration of the injunction of Nanŭkŭ, to eat and to give to others to eat, next receive the salutation of the assembly; who then rise, and the Ŭkalēēs pray aloud, while the musicians play. The Ŭkalēēs, when the prayers are finished, desire the council to be seated. They sit down, and the cakes being uncovered, are eaten of by all classes of Shikhs; those distinctions of original tribes which are, on other occasions, kept up, being on this occasion laid aside, in token of their general and complete union in one cause. The Ŭkalēēs then exclaim, 'Sirdars! (chiefs) this is a Gooroomŭta!' on which prayers are again said aloud. The chiefs after this sit closer, and say to each other, 'The sacred *grŭnt'hŭ* is betwixt us: let us swear by our scripture to forget all internal disputes, and to be united.' This moment of religious fervor, and ardent patriotism, is taken to reconcile all animosities. They then proceed to consider the danger with which they are threatened, to settle the best plans for averting it, and to choose the generals who are to lead their armies against the common enemy. The first Gooroomŭta was assembled by Gooroo-Govindŭ, and the latest was called in 1805, when the British army pursued Holkar into the Pŭnjab.'

The Shikhs pay the same reverence to their shastrŭs which they formerly paid to their religious leaders. These books are placed in their temples and worshipped,[f] and in some places are read twice or thrice a day, by an officiating priest called a grŭnt'hēē; who, before he begins to read, bathes, puts on clean apparel, sweeps the the place where the book is to be worshipped, and covers it with a mat; places a stool on the mat; spreads a cloth on the stool, and on this cloth puts the book or books: (the book is always wrapt up in a cloth, either plain or gilt, according to the ability of the owner:) the cloths (which are several when it belongs to a rich man) are next taken off with much reverence; incense is burnt;

[e] The words Dŭshŭma Padshahēē-Grŭnt'hŭ mean, 'The tenth leader's book,' or the work written during the presidency of the tenth leader, Govindŭ-singhŭ.

[f] The well-informed Shikh attempts to justify the outward appearance of worship, by saying, that he does this, that the lower orders may regard the contents of these books.

red powder sprinkled, and garlands of flowers laid upon the book, to which the person makes a bow.[g] The grunt'hēē reads aloud, and those present who are able, join him in singing, or rather chaunting the poetical parts of what is read. The grŭnt'hēē receives fees or presents, beside the offerings made at the times of worship; and lands are somtimes given to temples, as well as to the officiating grŭnt'hēēs.

Those who have leisure and opportunity, read portions of these books daily, and repeat certain words, in the form of petition, four times a day. They who have not these books, repeat the name of Nanŭkŭ or Govindŭ-singhŭ, or address prayers to one of these leaders once or twice a day. This daily worship is performed either in the dwelling house, or in a separate place devoted to religious uses. A Shikh never opens a copy of his shastrŭs without first bowing to the book.

The doctrine of these two books respecting God is, that he is an invisible spirit, and is to be conceived of as being active and passive, with and without qualities. They contain the histories of the Hindoo incarnations, and inculcate the doctrine of the Hindoos respecting Brŭmha, Vishnoo, Shivŭ, the creator, the preserver, and the destroyer; and in different parts of these works are to be found forms of praise to Narayŭnŭ, who is, however, revered as the one God. There are three things which these works particularly commend, as, a disposition to serve Narayŭnŭ;—devotion, expressed in repeating the names of Narayŭnŭ, in meditating on these names, and in praising Narayŭnŭ;—and union with devout persons. Govindŭ-singhŭ's work contains forms of praise to Narayŭnŭ, whose chief name in this book is Ŭkalŭ-pooroosbŭ, or the everlasting. They advise Shikhs to seek absorption in God, rather than the happiness enjoyed in inferior heavens, from whence the soul descends to enter on a succession of births. The performance of the ceremonies prescribed in their books, is the Shikh way to final beatitude. These books further teach, that the sorrows experienced in the different transmigrations of the soul, are the fruit of sin; that as long as the soul is confined in the body, it is in chains; and that whether the chains be of gold or of iron, it is still a prisoner, and enduring punishments. They also believe in the existence of the Hindoo king of death, Yŭmŭ, and in the punishments he inflicts.

Govindŭ-singhŭ set up the worship of Doorga, and offered bloody sacrifices at her festivals; but he did not direct his disciples to worship any other deity, though the work written by him contains accounts of other deities. The worship of this goddess is at present seldom performed before an image; but if an old image

[g] When the person performs each of these ceremonies, he repeats an incantation, taken from the shastrŭ; or, if he be ignorant of the proper prayer, he says, '*Oh! Gooroo.*'

have existed in any place from time immemorial, the Shikhs worship it. In general, however, they pile a number of weapons together, as the representative of Doorga.

These people are divided into two great sects, one of which adheres to Nanŭkŭ, and the other to Govindŭ-singhŭ; yet both these chiefs are venerated by all the Shikhs.—The disciples of Nanŭkŭ are called khoolasas, and have less of a warlike disposition than those of Govindŭ-singhŭ, who are called khalsas. In the Pŭnjab, the khalsas are most numerous. A chief, to prove the courage of a khalsa, sometimes seizes him, and threatens him with punishment if he will not shave his beard. Should he refuse, he beats him; if this does not change his purpose, he proceeds as though he were about to kill him. If he resolve to part with life rather than with his hair, he sets him at liberty, as a good khalsa.

When a person wishes to become a Shikh, he makes known his intention to some grŭnt'hēē, or to any person learned in their shastrŭs; and if he wish to become a khalsa, he permits his hair to grow. When his hair has grown a month or two, he goes again to the grŭnt'hēē, who prepares the nectar, by stirring a knife in a bowl of water, repeating incantations: a person present joins the hands of the new disciple, into which the grŭnt'hēē pours some of this water of life, of which he drinks five times, and afterwards rubs a little on his eyes. While he receives this water, he repeats, five times, *Wah! Gooroo jēēda Khalsa!—Wah! Gooroo jēēda phŭteh!*[h] The grŭnt'hēē next demands his name; which, if insignificant in sound or meaning, is changed for another, and the word singhŭ added. After this, a meat-offering is prepared, called kŭra prŭsadŭ, composed of clarified butter, flour, sugar, milk, and various kinds of fruits, mixed, and baked on the fire. The grŭnt'hēē now worships the book, and presents to it some of the meat-offering; the rest of which is offered to Ŭkalŭ-pooroosh ŭ, in the name of Nanŭkŭ, accompanied with a prayer to Govindŭ-singhŭ, that his blessing may rest upon this person now becoming a Shikh. At the close of these ceremonies, the food is distributed among the spectators of every caste; and the grŭnt'hēē addresses a short discourse to the disciple respecting the religion of the Shikhs, and teaches him an incantation by repeating it in his presence till it be learnt, or else he gives it him in writing. The Shikhs pay great reverence to the initiatory incantation, but less to their spiritual guides than the Hindoos. Women are made Shikhs in the same manner as men; the only difference in the form is, that when the nectar is prepared for women, it is stirred with the back instead of the edge of the knife. When a Mŭsŭlman becomes a Shikh, he is forbidden in the strongest manner to eat beef.

[h] *Wah*, an exclamation of admiration; *Gooroo*, spiritual teacher; *jēēda*, an honourable epithet; *Khalsa*, deliverance, or emancipation from the chains connected with a bodily state; and *phŭteh*, victory or glory.

The Shikhs have a number of festivals, but they are all celebrated in a similar manner; the difference consists principally in the degree of splendour attached to them: among other festivals are, the anniversaries of the birth and death of Nanŭkŭ; and monthly ceremonies when the sun enters a new sign. In the month Kartikŭ also, on the 14th of the wane of the moon, at Ŭmritŭ-sŭrŭ, they have a great annual feast, called Dēēpŭ-mala; when, from all the surrounding countries, two or three hundred thousand people are said to bathe in the sacred pool, with the same faith in its virtues as the Hindoos have in Gŭnga. On other occasions, people from all the neighbourhood come and bathe in this pool; and those who live on the spot bathe in it daily. When the Shikhs bathe in any other place, they call to remembrance this pool, and pray for the blessings connected with bathing in Ŭmritŭ-sŭrŭ.

Their temples are built by rich men, or by a few persons uniting to defray the expense. They have a flat roof, and are sufficiently capacious to accommodate multitudes of worshippers, who sometimes sit, and at other times stand during worship.

Various sects of religious mendicants are found amongst the Shikhs, as Nanŭkŭ-shakhēēs,[i] Nirvanēēs[k], Ŭkalēēs[l], and Nirmmŭlŭs.[m]

The Shikhs have certain ceremonies after the birth of a child,[n] at their marriages, and at death: some present offerings to the names of deceased ancestors, copying the ceremonies of the Hindoos. The shows at their weddings resemble those of the Hindoos. The Shikhs keep their women in great slavery, yet instances of infidelity are not uncommon. Should a man murder his wife on account of improper conduct, he is not punished. The chief says, if he were to punish such a husband, all the women of the country would become unfaithful.

The Shikhs burn their dead; and their wives sometimes, but very seldom, ascend the funeral pile with their husbands. This is done, however, by those who are least detached from the Hindoo system. They generally sing certain couplets of their shastrŭ, accompanied with music, as they convey the body to the cemetery; and sometimes a great multitude of Shikhs assemble on these occasions, and continue singing till the body is entirely consumed.

[i] That is, those who observe the customs of Nanŭkŭ.

[k] These go entirely naked.

[l] The mendicants wear blue apparel, and profess to believe in Ukalŭ-poorooshŭ.

[m] The name of these mendicants intimates, that they are sinless.

[n] Before the time of Nanŭkŭ, the people of the Pŭnjab, of high caste, used to destroy all their female children after preserving the first-born. Nanŭkŭ forbad this to all his disciples, on pain of excommunication. The practice still exists in the Pŭnjab amongst those who follow the Hindoo religion. Some of the descendants of Nanŭkŭ too, who do not profess the religion of their ancestor, perpetrate these murders.

The Shikhs have schools for the instruction of children, at the places consecrated to Nanŭkŭ, and in villages belonging to different chiefs: the grŭnt'hēēs also teach the meaning of their sacred books to individuals who desire it; and even shōōdrŭs are permitted to explain these books to others.

The division of men into castes exists among the Shikhs in some measure; but the Shikh bramhŭns, kshŭtriyŭs, voishyŭs, and shōōdrŭs (if of one sect[o]) eat together. The poita is not much regarded, especially by the regular Shikhs. In the article of marriage, however, the caste is very strictly regarded.

The Shikhs eat the flesh of wild fowl, and wild hogs; and the lower orders eat tame fowls. House-fed hogs are forbidden. Spirits are not forbidden, and many indulge to excess; but their favourite beverage is bhŭngŭ.[p]

I am informed, that there are at present as many as a hundred chiefs possessing separate districts in the Pŭnjab; that Rŭnjēēt-singhŭ, the most powerful, can bring 100,000 soldiers into the field, and that his revenues amount to near two crores of rupees annually. Each petty chief is the judge in his own domain; and he appoints village magistrates, who hear the evidence of witnesses, or the advice of four of five persons who may be present. The administration of justice is, however, but ill attended to. The Shikhs punish thieves by hanging them, or cutting them to pieces. They have jails, but no written, civil, or criminal laws.

Doctrines taught by Nanŭkŭ, and other Shikh Leaders:

Extracted from the Adee-Grŭnt'hŭ.

Ŭngudu, according to the commentary on this work, is represented as asking Nanŭkŭ respecting the Deity; to which the sage replies:—'He is truth, the creator and governor of all things, omnipresent, free from fear and from enemies, immortal, from everlasting, self-existent. He is the truth; he existed in this form before the foundation of the world, and he remains the same while the world exists, and after it shall be destroyed: he is to be known by means of a spiritual guide.'

'Absorption in God is not to be obtained by ceremonial purifications, nor by observing perpetual silence, nor by excessive indulgence, nor by learning.' 'In what way then,' asks the disciple, 'is delusion to be destroyed, and truth to be obtained?' 'By observ-

o That is, all the followers of Nanŭkŭ eat together, as do all those who follow Govindŭ-singhŭ.

p The leaves of hemp, bruised with certain spices, and mixed with water, make a very strong and intoxicating beverage, called bhŭngŭ, or siddhee.

ing the divine commands, without being diverted by the sorrows or pleasures of the present state.' The disciple continues, 'What are the commands of God, and how far do they extend?' Nanŭkŭ replies, 'His command brought the universe into existence: this is one command, but beyond this I cannot describe his authority. By his command all animals came into existence, the great and the small, the excellent and the degraded; by his command joy and sorrow were assigned to all, and by the same power future happiness was prepared for the good; birth, and death, and all things were appointed by him, and without his command nothing takes place. He who obeys God must be humble.'

The disciple next enquires, 'If a person praise the commands of God, will he derive any advantage from thence?' Nanŭkŭ replies, 'If any one can sing the praise of his commands, let him do it; he who cannot, let him understand these commands, and without pride let him think upon them. Let him who sings these praises, acknowledge his own insignificance and dependance on God; he will praise his excellent qualities and his power. Let him, from other shastrŭs also, if he be able, select forms of praise, and use them.'

To the end of the Jŭpŭ-jēē, Nanŭkŭ goes on to describe the divine properties, and the works of God, together with the effects of devotion on the mind. In one place, in reply to a question respecting offerings, he directs, as the most acceptable offerings, morning praise to God, and the presentation of the body to him. He promises the person who does this, the divine favour, and future absorption. 'He who serves God, the fountain of all good, will obtain his blessing. God is served, by listening to his excellencies, by meditating on them, and by celebrating their praise; the method of which is to be obtained from a spiritual guide, who is above all the gods, and who is in fact God himself.'

Nanŭkŭ says, that pilgrimages and other devout actions may be good, if performed to please God; but that pilgrims must not seek their own profit in them, since every thing depends on the motive. When asked, whether life might be prolonged by performing ceremonies, Nanŭkŭ declared, that every ceremony would be followed by a succession of births, if union to God were overlooked. 'Hearing the praise of God is followed by every degree of exaltation, subject to future birth,[q] even to the dignity of the gods. God is praised by Chitrŭ-Gooptŭ and by all the gods, by all the nymphs, and by all beings. He himself, as well as all his works, are infinite. Meditating on God is followed by unspeakable

[q] Nanŭkŭ does not seem to have said much respecting the nature of future happiness in heaven, nor to have acknowledged the Hindoo heavens: he taught, however, that there was a heaven where persons enjoy sensual happiness for a limited time, subject to future transmigrations.

gain, even by absorption in God, which absorption also includes the whole of such a person's friends.

'God has created innumerable worlds. The period of creation is not laid down in any writing; it is known only to God. The Hindoos place Kŭchchŭpŭ under the earth, to support it, and the Mŭsŭlmans, a cow—but Nanŭkŭ says, the earth and all worlds are upheld by Religion,[r] the mother of which being is Compassion, who dwells with Contentment.'

In reply to a question from a disciple, respecting the value of outward ceremonies, Nanŭkŭ, without altogether rejecting the efficacy of ceremonies, recommended mental worship as of greater importance, adding, that this was agreeable to the védŭs.

Nanŭkŭ, in the same work, rejects all the ornaments and trappings of mendicants, and says, virtue is the best ornament for a pilgrim: he objects to separate religious societies, and recommends his followers to unite themselves to the whole human race. He further says, that the best victory is that which a man obtains over his own passions.

'To the Being who is unchangeable and eternal do obeisance. Let wisdom be your food: let compassion prepare it. Nature is the mother of the world; Brŭmha, Vishnoo, and Shivŭ are her sons, who rule under the direction of God: he sees them, but remains himself concealed. From the four primary elements, and day and night, sprang the universe. God, the invisible, dwells in truth. A thousand tongues can never complete his praise, nor is the power to worship him inherent in man; it is the gift of God. The knowledge of God is more than all ceremonies, and fills the soul with joy. He who is ashamed of sin, is happy; he who performs works of merit, shall obtain happiness.'

The above is an epitome of the contents of the Jŭpŭ-Jēē, which chapter of the Adee-Grŭnt'hŭ is directed to be read or repeated daily by every Shikh, either before or after bathing. If a person cannot read or repeat the whole, he is directed to read five verses. It is not to be supposed, however, that all Shikhs preserve in their houses even so much as this chapter of the Adee-Grŭnt'hŭ. Some, if is true, commit to memory the whole of this chapter; and a few Shikhs are to be found, who can repeat more than a third part ot the Adee-Grŭnt'hŭ, a thick volume in folio. Others commit to memory a similar quantity of Govindŭ-singhŭ's work.

In the 42d page of the Adee-Grŭnt'hŭ, Nanŭkŭ compares the body to a field, the mind to the husbandman, the praises of God to seed; and absorption in God he deems the fruit.

[r] This sentiment approaches towards the joinŭ doctrine, that Religion and Irreligion are the only governors of the world.

Ŭrjoonŭ, in the 50th page, says, 'The place where the devout sit becomes purified and is made excellent.' In the 53d page he thus exalts the spiritual guide, (Nanŭkŭ :) 'The sight of him brings all the benefits which arise from visiting every holy place, and delivers from all future birth.'

Ŭmŭrŭ-dasŭ, in the 59th page, praises the devout mendicant, by declaring, that though he be of the lowest rank in life, people will praise him to the neglect even of the gods.

Nanŭkŭ, in the 69th page, replies to those who value themselves on their birth, by placing him who is under the influence of wicked principles, on a level with a basket-maker, (i. e., a person of low caste); the cruel, with a butcher; the slanderer, with a sweeper; the wrathful, with a chŭndalŭ. 'Such a man, though he surround himself during his meals with a fence,[s] lest he should be defiled, deceives himself, as he in fact eats with a basket-maker, a butcher, sweeper, or a chŭndalŭ. Speaking truth is the best purifier of the body; good works, the best fence; and repeating the name of God, the best ablution: excellence of character is confined to him who preserves himself from evil.'

Rŭvee-dasŭ, a shoe-maker, but a celebrated devotee, says, in the 70th page of this work, that the difference betwixt God and animal life is similar to that betwixt gold and golden ornaments, betwixt water and its waves.

'Whatever thou hast, wife, riches, yea, thy own body, give it to God.' *Urjoonŭ,* p. 74.

'Compassion is the true mosque; righteousness, the true seat for worship; bashfulness the true circumcision; holiness, the true fasting; proper conduct, the true pilgrimage to Mecca; speaking truth, the true kŭlma, or gayŭtrēē; excellent conduct, the true praise of God: these form the true Mŭsŭlman. Injustice committed by a Mŭsŭlman, is eating swine's flesh, and in a Hindoo, eating beef: such a sinner can neither be saved by the pēērs, nor by the gods.'—*Nanŭkŭ,* p. 87.

Nanŭkŭ, in the 213th page, holds up compassion as the cotton, contentment as the threads, truth the weaving of the threads, and the subjection of the passions the knots, of the true poita, which never breaks nor becomes soiled. He who wears this poita, is blessed. Again :—'If touching the dead make a person unclean, as all we eat is dead, men must always be unclean; but as evil desire alone defiles the mind, so does falsehood, the tongue; lust, the eyes; and listening to defamation, the ears: he who is thus defiled, becomes the prey of Yŭmŭ, the king of death.

[s] An allusion to the practice of the Hindoos, who sometimes draw a ring round them as they sit to eat.

Whatsoever makes a man forget God, renders him unclean Birth and death are not the causes of uncleanness; for these events proceed from God.'

Nanŭkŭ further taught, that the person who worships God with outward things only, is in an error; that a pure body is the true védŭ; the mind, the true sacrificial garment; wisdom, the true poita; meditation on God, the proper vessel for worship; and the only true prayer, that in which the worshippers desire to be incessantly employed in repeating the name of God. He who observes these rules, will obtain absorption.

Nanŭkŭ reproves men for presenting different essences to God, and anointing their bodies with them after worship; recommending rather the name of God as the incense, and regarding the mind as the stone on which it is ground, and good works as another essence mixed with the former: he adds, that purifying the vessels of worship is useless, the purification of the mind being the only essential requisite.

Ŭrjoonŭ, in the 224th page, says, that the 330,000,000 of gods, including Brŭmha, Vishnoo, and Shivŭ, are all subject to God.

'The devout are truly excellent, of whatever caste, or however poor.'[t] *Nanŭkŭ.*—'The devout, however poor, never ask God for riches.' *Rŭvee-dasŭ.*—Nanŭkŭ, in p. 409, makes the following quotaton from Kŭvēērŭ, a mendicant, who wrote several small pieces still extant:—'He who merely studies the védŭ, repeats the gayŭtrēē, and wears the poita, is not the honorable person; the devout alone are to be honored.' In page 501, Ŭrjoonu commends the example of the man who rejects all outward ceremonies, and worships God only in the mind.

'Many pronounce sin an evil, and yet love it; but the devout reject sin, and apply to the concerns of a future state. To obtain wealth, some worship Shivŭ, others steal, and others endure the greatest burdens; but not an atom of this wealth accompanies them into eternity: while those works of merit, which would

[t] To excite in the minds of his followers the love of devotion, Nanŭkŭ, while living, was accustomed to relate the following story:—Jŭnŭkŭ, the king, the father of Sēēta, was very devout, and had merited heaven; but at the time of death he declared to Yŭmŭ, that he was resolved to go to heaven by the way of hell. Yŭmŭ informed him, that he had no sins to expiate by suffering, and that such a course was unusual. Jŭnŭkŭ, however, insisted on seeing this place on his way to heaven: and his request was complied with. On his arrival at the infernal regions, his presence evidently assuaged the torments of the wicked; and the criminals entreated him to remain among them, at least during a short period. He begged to be excused, but entreated Yŭmŭ to oblige him by liberating these miserable wretches. Yŭmŭ declared, that till their sins were expiated, no power could emancipate them. Jŭnŭkŭ then transferred to them the merit of an hour's devotion, and a general goal delivery was the immediate consequence. Such was the power and merit of devotion! Nanŭkŭ, at the close of this story, used to add, that remembrance of God and pious feelings were beyond all ceremonies efficacious.

accompany and save them, are totally neglected. The Mŭsŭlman judge sits on the seat of justice, and, repeating the name of God, and counting his beads, receives bribes, and sells justice; the bramhŭn puts on his poita, when he eats surrounds himself with a ring to to keep off the unclean, and performs daily ablutions, but lives in, sin:—all the ceremonies practised by these persons are profitless.' *Nanŭkŭ.*

Ŭrjoonŭ says, p. 406, that God is not compelled to grant blessings by any works of merit—devotion alone has this power over God.

Nanŭkŭ, in p. 543, defends those who eat flesh, proving that all eat flesh, even the child supported by his mother's milk, and that all men live more or less by injustice; that even herbs obtained by unlawful gains are forbidden food. In the 609th page, he gives an account of the punishments inflicted in different hells by Yŭmŭ, the Indian Pluto, on those who have neglected a devout life.

CHAP. V.

ACCOUNT OF THE FOLLOWERS OF CHOITŬNYŬ.

In another part of this work we have given, amongst the gods, an account of Choitŭnyŭ, and of the origin of the sect to which he gave rise. We shall therefore now merely notice the principles, numbers, and moral state of this sect.

Choitŭnyŭ, though he rejected the institution of the caste, does not appear to have introduced any new doctrines among his followers. He adopted as the object of worship one of the Hindoo gods, Krishnŭ, under the form of Hŭree; and gave his disciples an initiatory incantation containing this name. He declared, that most of the ceremonies of the Hindoos were unprofitable; but inculcated repetitions of the name of Hŭree; bowing and presenting offerings to his image; as well as devotion of mind to this god, under the characters of servant, friend, &c.—He taught that there was no merit in pilgrimages to sacred places, but that journies in search of the devout and wise were not improper. His attachment to Hŭree, to the exclusion of the other gods, had no reference to the doctrine of the unity of God; he admitted the Hindoo mythology, but taught his disciples to devote themselves only to Hŭree. The other ceremonies of the Hindoos, he did not reject as errors; but declared, that in the kŭlee yoogŭ they were not necessary. He taught, that the devout worshipper of Hŭree would obtain heaven by his devotion.

Choitŭnyŭ did not leave any works behind him, though he was acquainted with the Sŭngskritŭ language; the doctrines that have since been given in writing, as the tenets of the sect, are said to have been delivered orally by him; and the writers belonging to this sect have endeavoured to prove, that they are derived from the works venerated by the Hindoos.

In the article to which we have already referred, (page 134,) the reader will find an account of Choitŭnyŭ's two coadjutors, Ŭdwoitŭ and Nityanŭndŭ. Both these survived Choitŭnyŭ, and helped to establish the sect, of which they acknowledged Choitŭnyŭ to have been the founder.

After the death of these leaders, Rōōpŭ-Goswamēē, Sŭnatŭnŭ-Goswamēē, his brother, and Jēēvŭ Goswamēē, formed the doctrines of Choitŭnyŭ into a system. These men were all learned in the Hindoo shastrŭs; the two former were men of some distinction. Their principal writings are the Hŭree-bhŭktee-vilasŭ, a commentary on the Shrēē-bhagŭvŭtŭ, another on the tenth chapter of the Shrēē-bhagŭvŭtŭ, a Sŭngskritŭ grammar, a poem in honor of Krishnŭ, a work on poetical allusions, a poetical life of Choitŭnyŭ, &c.

During the lives of these writers, or soon after their decease, many persons of influence joined this sect, and increased the number of Choitŭnyŭ's followers very considerably; but the persons most honored were the descendants of Ŭdwoitŭ and Nityanŭndŭ: Choitŭnyŭ left no family. Some persons consider Choitŭnyŭ as a full incarnation of Vishnoo, Ŭdwoitŭ as Shivŭ, and Nityanŭndŭ as Bŭlŭ-ramŭ, the brother of Krishnŭ.

At present, the great leaders of this sect are the heads of the families of Ŭdwoitŭ and Nityanŭndŭ, who live at Shantee-poorŭ and Khŭrdŭhŭ[u], though collateral branches of these families in different places have collected a number of disciples. They are known by the general name Gosaee, (Goswamēē.)

These leaders, however, though at the head of a sect which disregards caste, are as tenacious of these distinctions as the most rigid of the regular Hindoos: they do not eat with their own disciples, and are careful to marry amongst families professing the ancient religion.

The disciples of Choitŭnyŭ are initiated, as well as married, by the gosaees, to whom fees are given. These gosaees honor the festivals sacred to Krishnŭ, or Hŭree, and crowds of disciples assemble on these occasions to enjoy the festivities.

A number of insignificant temples and images, dedicated to this deified mendicant, are scattered up and down in various places

[u] This place is about three miles south-east of Serampore.

in Bengal. It is supposed, that out of sixteen Hindoos in Bengal, five will be found to be of this sect; but many, I am informed, are persons of the very lowest description as it respects moral character, even as many as three in five.

The majority of the followers of Choitŭnyŭ subsist either wholly or in part as public mendicants; and amongst these, numbers of thieves are to be found. It has lately been ascertained, that persons of this description are very numerous; they assume the profession of a voiragēē, or religious mendicant, and receive the reverence of the people as persons eminent for sanctity, but are in reality common robbers. They do not all appear to subsist by mendicity; many of them make necklaces, twine, &c. merely that they may appear to their neighbours as persons subsisting by a lawful profession.

The sect of Choitŭnyŭ is increasing daily; as it opens a door to the practice of mendicity, encourages an indiscriminate and most licentious mixture of the sexes, and emancipates from the yoke of the caste, without incurring the disgrace usually following that event.

The following works are very popular amongst this sect:—Krishnŭ-kēērttŭnŭ, by Govindŭ-dasŭ, and Vidyapŭtee. Choitŭnyŭ-mŭngŭlŭ, the history of Choitŭnyŭ, in verse, by Lochŭnŭ, a voishnŭvŭ. Pashŭndŭ-dŭlŭnŭ, a work in favour of the voishnŭvŭ, by Radha-madhŭvŭ. Choitŭnyŭ-chŭritamritŭ, by Krishnŭ-dasŭ. This is a work in defence of Choitŭnyŭ, partly in Sŭngskritŭ and partly in Bengalee. Voishnŭvŭ-bŭrdhŭnŭ, by Doivŭkēē-nŭndŭnŭ. Choitŭnyŭ-bhagŭvŭtŭ, by Vrinda-vŭnŭ-dasŭ. Mŭnŭ-shikshya, by Nŭrottŭmŭ. Ragŭ-mŭyŭ-konŭ, a work on subduing the passions, by Roopŭ-goswamēē. Rŭsŭmŭyŭ-kŭlika, on devotedness to Krishnŭ, by Sŭnatŭnŭ, a voishnŭvŭ. Prémŭ-bhŭktee-chŭndrika, by T'hakoorŭ-goswamēē.

CHAP. VI.

ACCOUNT OF ALL THE HINDOO SECTS.

Extracted from the Vidwŭnmodŭ-Tŭrŭnginēē, a work by Chirŭnjēēvŭ.

THIS work begins with the following invocation to Doorga:—'May she who removes the darkness of the mind, who is revealed from everlasting, who, though invisible, exists in the earth, who enlightens the ignorant, whose forehead is adorned with the crescent, the fixed rays of whose body resemble the lightning, whose body is like the clouds—descend into my mind.'

[Then follows an account of the author's family; after which the author introduces the reader to the court of Dŭkshŭ, king of Goŭrŭ, where the priest of the king, and a number of learned men, are assembled in the presence of the monarch.]

In the first place, the master of the ceremonies announces to the monarch the approach of a Voishnŭvŭ, in the following words:—'May it please your Majesty, the person now approaching wears the mark of his sect, extending from the tip of his nose to the centre of his head; has the representations of the weapons of Vishnoo impressed on his body; is clothed in yellow garments, and wears a necklace of toolŭsēē beads; he has purified his body by bathing, &c. and repeats the name Hŭree, Hŭree, as he comes.' The voishnŭvŭ now approaches the king, and says, 'May Vishnoo enter thy mind; he on whom Shivŭ and all the gods, sitting as yogēēs, meditate; he who dwells in Voikoont'hŭ; he who fills the universe, but remains invisible; and whose body resembles that of Brŭmha.'—Saying this, he takes his seat in the assembly.

The master of the ceremonies, seeing a Shoivŭ approaching, mentions him to the king in these words:—'The excellent person who is now coming, has his hair bound up as a turban round his head; is girt round the waist with a tiger's skin; is covered with ashes; and his head, neck, and arms, are surrounded with roodrakshŭ bead-rolls. The shoivŭ, entering the presence of the king, pronounces the following blessing:—'May Shŭnkŭrŭ, who instructs the world; whose praises are celebrated in the védŭs, the tŭntrŭs and the pooranŭs; who is the object of meditation to the yogēē; who directs the gods in the work of creation; who, though invisible, for the preservation of the world becomes visible; who meditates on his own qualities—may he preserve thee.' After which, he takes his place in the assembly.

The pŭndit next announces a Shaktŭ, thus:—'He who now approaches, comes like the full moon, with a jŭva flower in his hair, a garland of mŭllika flowers encircling his neck; a crescent, the mark of his sect, on his forehead; he comes meditating on Doorga.' The shaktŭ then addresses the king:—'May she, on whom Hŭrēē, Hŭrŭ, and Brŭmha depend in the work of preservation, destruction, and creation; she who destroys the fear of future birth; who saves the three worlds; who destroys the enemies, and fulfils the desires, of her disciples—may this goddess preserve thee.' After this, he sits down.

The same person next announces a Hŭree-Hŭra-dwoitŭ-vadēē:—'He who now advances, is adorned with a toolŭsēē necklace, is covered with ashes, meditates on Hŭree-Hŭrŭ, and invites others, for the sake of their salvation, to become the disciples of this god.' He thus blesses the king:—'May both Shŭnkŭrŭ and Vishnoo dwell in thy heart, the half of whom is engaged in the devotions of a yogēē, and near the other half sits Lŭkshmēē; he who encircles himself with Ŭuŭntŭ, (the king of serpents,) who rides on Gŭroorŭ—may he, entering thy mind, preserve thee.' Saying this, he sits down.

A Noiyayikŭ and a Voishéshikŭ, coming hand in hand, are thus announced:—'These come viewing this assembly with the utmost contempt, the goddess of learning dancing on their tongues.' They then salute the king:—'May God preserve thee; he who, taking the forms of Brŭmha, Vishnoo, and Shivŭ, creates, preserves, and destroys the world; he who influences all to good and evil; he whose will, whose work, and whose wisdom, are irresistible; he who exists as separate from animal life, and who is fulness itself.'

The next person introduced is a Mēēmangsŭkŭ, who is thus described:—'This man approaches with the marks of vows and of a sacrificer upon him, teaching his disciples the forms of religion.' He thus blesses the monarch:—'May your Majesty always be engaged in religious services, which raised Indrŭ to his throne, Sōōryŭ to be monarch over the hosts of heaven; and the merit of which indeed, descending to thee from a former birth, has now raised thee to a kingly throne.' Having pronounced this blessing, he sits down.

The master of the ceremonies next introduces a Védantēē thus:—'This person comes as one who has renounced all pleasure; his apparel is painted with earth from the mountains, and in his hand he holds a dŭndēē's staff; having ascended the vessel which is to carry him across the ocean of this world, he approaches as though he were coming to preserve from destruction this whole assembly.' Addressing the king, the Védantēē says, 'May the glorious Being, who is wisdom and joy, who is omnipresent, the only one, the everlasting, who is free from passion, in whom the universe exists as the shadow of the sun in the water,[x] may he give thee the knowledge, that thou art the same with him. Having said this, he sits down.

The next persons announced, are a follower of the Sankhyŭ, and another of the Patŭnjŭlŭ school. They are thus described:—'These come with bodies bulky towards the head, and lean at the extremities;[y] professing similar sentiments, and meditating on realities.' Being introduced, he of the Sankhyŭ sect thus addresses the monarch:—'May nature, (unaffected by spirits as the water-lily by the water,) by whom, beginning with greatness, the universe was made, prosper thee.' The Patŭnjŭlŭ thus blesses the

[x] That is, visible objects are false images of Him who alone is truth, and through the want of the knowledge of whom, men act as though they had a distinct existence.

[y] Caused by hanging with the head downwards, as an act of religious austerity.

king:—'May the king pursue pleasure communicated by the vein through which the soul of the yogēē, ascending to the *basilar suture*, from thence escapes from the body, and obtains final deliverance.' He then sits down.

A Pouranikŭ next approaches, and is thus described :—'Here comes a person full of words, with a mind fixed on God, instructing others in religious duty.' He thus addresses the king :—'May Narayŭnŭ preserve thee; he who in the form of a fish brought up the védŭs; who in that of a boar, saved the earth; in that of a tortoise, supports the universe; in that of a lion, destroyed a giant; in that of a dwarf, carried Vamŭnŭ down to Patalŭ; in that of Pŭrŭshoo-Ramŭ, destroyed the kshŭtriyŭs; in the form of Ramŭ, destroyed Ravŭnŭ; in that of Bŭlŭ-Ramŭ, called Rohinēē mother; in that of Booddhŭ, declared the slaughter of animals in sacrifice to be unlawful; and who, in that of Kŭlkee, at the end of the iron age, will destroy the wicked, and restore the golden age.' He then takes his place in the assembly.

A Jyotishŭ next approaches the assembly, and is thus announced :—'Here comes a person acquainted with the fates of men, who can declare things past, present, and to come; and who meditates on the nine planets.' Addressing the king, he says, 'May Sōōryŭ make thee glorious like himself; may Chŭndrŭ make thee a dispenser of joy like himself; may Mŭngŭlŭ bestow a blessing on thee; may Booddhŭ give thee wisdom; may Vrihŭspŭtee endow thee with learning; may Sookrŭ give thee the knowledge of verse; may Shŭnee destroy thy incapacity; may Rahoo remove the wickedness of thy heart; may Kétoo erect for thee the standard of victory.' He then takes his seat.

Next a professor of the Ayoor-védŭ draws near, who is thus described :—'Behold a voidyŭ; who by his medical knowledge removes the miseries of mankind; who gives joy to a patient, as the full moon to the spectators: he comes as the afflicter of affliction.' He thus blesses the king :—'May the king possess faith in the virtues of medicine, which renders the person emaciated by disease beautiful as a heavenly courtezan.' He sits down.

The next person introduced is a grammarian, who is mentioned as repeating the Kŭlapŭ, (a grammar;) and is announced as the very image of Mŭha-dévŭ, an incarnation of Ŭnŭntŭ. He thus blesses the king :—'May thy glory, O king be published through, the world; be thou the helper of all; sitting on a firm seat, practise religion; compose differences.' He then retires to the circle, and sits amongst the learned men.

An Ŭlŭnkarŭ professor now appears, and is thus introduced: —'Here comes a man forming prose and verse with great ingenuity, causing his words to dance as he walks.' He thus blesses the king:—'Mayest thou spend thy days in the joy arising from pleasant conversation; conversation embracing amorous, heroic, tender, ludicrous, disgusting, wonderful, terrific, and wrathful subjects.' He also takes his place.

An atheist approaches next, and is thus announced:—'Afraid of destroying life, here comes one who sweeps the ground on which he treads; and who has plucked off the hair from his head.' He thus blesses the king:—'Mayest thou never be drawn aside by the words of deceivers, who worship the gods, and excite to religious ceremonies by the hopes of future rewards; who promise heaven to the sacrificers of animals; who talk of objects invisible.'—

Hearing these words of the atheist, all the assembly rise up, saying, 'Oh! thou wicked one!—Who art thou?—Whence comest thou?'

The unbeliever replies:—'I am the sinner; ye are the holy, ye who fruitlessly destroy the lives of sentient beings!'

The Mēēmangsŭkŭ replies:—'The animals which I destroy in sacrifice obtain heaven; the gods are pleased with sacrifices; the sacrificer likewise obtains his desire: that destruction of life therefore which is commanded by the shastrŭs, is not criminal.'

Unbeliever. Shocking! What words are these! Where is heaven? Where are the gods? Where are your pleasures and sorrows after death?

M. Dost thou vilify the doctrines of the védŭs and pooranŭs?

Unbeliever. Shall we believe the words of the deceitful védŭs and pooranŭs, which tell us of things which no eye has ever seen?

M. If there be neither works of merit nor demerit, how is the existence of happiness and misery to be accounted for?

Unbeliever. Where are thy works? Who has seen them, or imitated them? And if thou sayest, 'My sorrow or joy is the fruit of actions done in former births,' I affirm, that such births never existed; and that as it respects joy and sorrow, they depart and return like the streams of a river. It is true, however, that the world is deceitful.

Védantikŭ. Oh! thou atheist, in affirming that the world is deceitful, thou hast pronounced justly; but then thou oughtest to acknowledge that there is one everliving and true God: for if there be no truth, there can be no falsehood wearing the appearance of truth.

Unbeliever. Well, thy opinions resemble mine; but who is that Brŭmhŭ of whom thou speakest?

V. He remains in a state of inactivity; is invisible; destitute of qualities; omnipresent; glorious; the ever-blessed; indescribable, and unsearchable.

Unbeliever. If, as thou confessest, the world is false, what necessity for Brŭmhŭ, a God invisible and inactive? Where is the utility of such a being?

The védantēē, hearing this, remained silent. Perceiving the védantēē's silence, the whole assembly directed its attention to the Noiyayikŭ pŭndit, who, filled with pride, thus began:—'What sayest thou? Why dost thou attack others, when thou hast no system of thine own? People laugh at the man who, without perceiving his own error, charges with error the opinions of others: he is like the blind man who reproves another on account of the speck in his eyes.'

Unbeliever. This man appears to be ingenious at objections: however, hear me. The Madyŭmikŭ philosopher says, that at the dissolution of the universe only vacuum remains; the Yogacharŭ contends, that two ideas cannot exist at once in the mind, the first being destroyed by the second; the Soŭtrantikŭ says, that ideas are the images of things; the Voivashikŭ, that all material things are frail; the Digŭmvŭrŭs affirm, that the soul is commensurate with the body; the Charvvakŭs, that man is composed only of body. I have described the opinions of these six sects, which are all thus summed up:—there is no heaven, no transmigration, no hell, no works of merit or demerit, no governor of the world, no creator, no preserver, no destroyer; no legitimate evidence of the truth of things but that of the senses; after death, there is neither joy nor sorrow. All these errors [of the popular belief] arise out of the ignoronce of men. Forbearing to destroy animal life is the most excellent of virtues. Sin and pain are synonymous; mooktee, or deliverance, is nothing more than being independant of others; heaven consists in bodily comforts in this life; a religious teacher is therefore unnecessary.

The *Noiyayikŭ* (laughing) replies, If no evidence but that of the senses is to be regarded, why, when you are from home, does not your wife deem herself a widow?

Unbeliever. We know that we shall never see the dead again; for we see the lifeless body: but we have hope of seeing a person return from a foreign country.

N. Be it so, but the fact is placed in a state of uncertainty, and why do you not pronounce upon his death?

Unbeliever. I can be assured of his existence by a written communication from him.

N. Well, then the evidence arising from sound is admitted: and indeed if the evidence of words be not regarded, all human intercourse is at an end, and men must preserve perpetual silence. But though thou rejectest the evidence of speech, thou art pleased with excellent words, and displeased with evil speech.

The unbeliever was put to silence for a short time by these observations; at length he said, Well, I admit, for argument's sake, that we must receive the evidence arising from inference and from sound :—but why must we admit the existence of a God!

N. From the works of creation we are constrained to infer that God exists. If you say there is no God, from whence arose creation?

Unbeliever. Why art thou concerned about finding a creator for the world? Does not a father beget a son, and an artificer, according to his ability, produce every kind of utensil?

N. True, we see every thing produced by human ingenuity; but how do the trees grow in a forest, where no human footsteps can be traced?

Unbeliever. The trees of the forest spring from themselves, as insects and worms from a hot-bed.

N. Then the child may be born without a father.

Unbeliever. Some animals are born by the union of the sexes, as men, beasts, birds, &c. Other things are produced by the union of seeds with water or with the earth, as trees, &c. Seeds fall from the trees, and, mixing with the earth, receive rain from the clouds, and vegetate. Thus nature, in various ways, gives existence to her different productions.

N. True, I see you ascribe to nature the origin of things; but as there is a necessity for the trees of a garden to receive water by the hands of the gardener, so the trees of a forest, I see, are dependent on the agency of the clouds. But I wish to know what you mean by nature; is it something inherent in living substances, or distinct from them? If you say it is inherent, then it will appear that substances can form themselves; if you affirm, that it is distinct, you contradict your own principles, for you maintain that nothing exists distinct from matter; or if you say, that there is something beside matter, which is capable of all things, then know, that this is what we call God. Therefore you cannot maintain that there is any thing distinct from the body.

Unbeliever. You affirm then, that there is one God, who is from and to everlasting, separate from matter, Almighty, the creator of all. I affirm, that nature is Almighty, infinite, and separate from matter.

The Noiyayikŭ. Excellent! Excellent! You make an endless number of works, and the creators numberless. I affirm, that numberless works have one creator. I leave you (unbeliever) to judge which is the most excellent of these opinions. To express your opinion requires as many letters as to express mine; you call the creator nature, and I call him God:—what do you gain then in rejecting a God?

Unbeliever, (a little abashed.) Well, for the sake of the argument, I acknowledge that there is a God; but why is he to be eternal;

The Noiyayikŭ. If he be not eternal, then he must have a creator and a destroyer. If you deny his eternity, then I ask, who is his creator and destroyer?—and thus, without end, some being, who is from everlasting, must be sought; or you must fix on some one having this property, and then he shall become God. [Hearing this, the unbeliever remained silent, and the Noiyayikŭ continued:] God, laying hold of religion and irreligion,* created the world; seeing happiness and misery in the world, we form this opinion. If there be neither heaven nor hell, why do you go to the temples to worship; and why sweep the road, lest you should injure living creatures? If there be nothing to be desired or feared, there can be neither desire nor fear: yet we see, that desire and fear have great power over men; therefore we conclude, that in the future state there is a heaven and a hell. You must also admit, that the soul at death assumes another body, in order to partake of the joys or sorrows of this future state, since the animal soul without a body is incapable of suffering; for the same reason it must also be admitted, that the soul migrates through various bodies. Further, what is thus made evident by inference, is agreeable to the divine writings, and to all that has been written by those whose opinions agree with the védŭs: the truth of the shastrŭs is confirmed by the correctness of their astronomical calculations. [The Bouddhŭ, involved in incorrect judgment, and ignorance of God, was overcome, and] the Noiyayikŭ thus triumphed: 'The existence of God is proved! He is lord of all;—he presides over the work of creation, preservation, and destruction; he is everlasting;—he is all wise;—he is the author of salvation. —Through his compassion, these proofs of his existence and authority have been established.'

CONCLUDING REMARKS.

THE author cannot close this work, without soliciting the attention of the reader to one or two remarks:—

* That is, attaching to human existence vice and pain, virtue and happiness.

It will appear, on a perusal of this volume, that the object of worship among all the Hindoos, and even among all the seceders from the orthodox opinions, is the same. They believe, that there is one God: so completely abstracted in his own essence however, that, in this state, he is emphatically 'the Unknown,' and is consequently neither the object of worship, of hope, nor of fear;— that he is even destitute of intelligence, and remains in a state of profound repose;—that at times this Being assumes what is called his energy[a];—that when united to energy, he is possessed of qualities, and creates worlds; which qualities are impressed, more or less, on every form of existence. Next God becomes individuated, and takes possession of every form of matter: it is the same God, as Krishnŭ says, 'which is seen in the reverend bramhŭn perfected in knowledge, in the dog, and in him who eateth of the flesh of dogs.' Amongst the regular Hindoos, the beings supposed to possess most of this energy, or in whom the presiding deity eminently dwells, are the gods, the giants, the bramhŭns, and devout ascetics: amongst the heterodox sects, ascetics are almost exclusively considered as the favoured depositaries of the divine energy.

In the preface to this volume, the author has mentioned these notions as being entertained by the regular Hindoos; and he restates them now merely to shew, that this 'indwelling scheme' is the prominent feature of all the systems of paganism throughout the east.

It will be seen, from the four last chapters of this volume, that the founder of the joinŭ sect, as well as Bouddhŭ, Nanŭkŭ, and Choitŭnyŭ, owe their whole success to this notion; they would never have been venerated while living, nor deified when dead, if they had not been considered as possessing a large share of the divine energy. A people whose minds are filled with the idea, that it is God who pervades every thing, and who now manifests a greater portion of himself in one form, and then in another, have easily been imposed upon by pretended saints, especially by those who made a great display of austere devotion. So incessantly is this idea present with the Hindoos, that many wander away a whole life in search of a man in whom God pre-eminently dwells; and though supernatural powers are most sought after, yet abstraction of mind, inoffensiveness, and a few other passive virtues, are with some as highly esteemed as powers to perform the most wonderful miracles. Thus,—it is God who is sought for amongst the creatures, as persons search out and cautiously approach an object in the dark; while the astonished and half-affrighted spectator exclaims, as he gazes on the imagined deity, 'There! behold he is there!' and prostrates himself before him. Even in the most re-

[a] This energy, it is said, exists separate from Brŭmhŭ, in his abstract state, as smothered embers; and is, like himself, eternal.

markable appearances in nature, the indwelling deity is recognized, without searching at all for any natural causes of the phenomenon.

In the 7th volume of the Asiatic Researches, p. 381, Captain Moor has given an extraordinary account of an hereditary living deity; to which the author begs leave to refer, as affording a striking illustration of the fact he here wishes to establish.

Amongst the mendicant orders, deities claiming similar powers, though somewhat inferior to the Chinchoor Deo, described by Captain Moor, are frequently to be seen, each strutting his hour upon the stage, and then sinking into everlasting oblivion like common mortals.

The Grand Lama is another hereditary living deity, before whom millions prostrate themselves. When Captain Turner was on his embassy to this deity, to gratify his votaries he made an offering, he says, to the deceased Teshoo Lama; and in addressing the same deity, who had entered the body of an infant eighteen months old, he said to the child—'The Governor-General, on receiving the news of his [your] decease in China, was overwhelmed with grief and sorrow, and continued to lament his [your] absence from the world, until the cloud that had overcast the happiness of this nation was dispelled by his [your] re-appearance.'

Captain Turner, speaking of the religion of Tibet, says, 'It seems to be the schismatical offspring of the religion of the Hindoos, deriving its origin from one of the followers of that faith, a disciple of Bouddhŭ, who first broached the doctrine which now prevails over the wide extent of Tartary. It is reported to have received its earliest admission in that part of Tibet bordering upon India, (which from hence became the seat of the sovereign Lamas;) to have traversed over Mantchieux Tartary, and to have been ultimately disseminated over China and Japan. Though it differs from the Hindoo in many of its outward forms, yet it still bears a very close affinity with the religion of Brŭmha, in many important particulars. The principal idol in the temples of Tibet is Mŭha-Moonee,[b] the Booddhŭ of Bengal; who is worshipped under these and various other epithets throughout the great extent of Tartary, and among all nations to the eastward of the Brŭmhŭpootrŭ. In the wide-extended space over which this faith prevails, the same object of veneration is acknowledged under numerous titles: among others, he is styled Godŭmŭ or Goutŭmŭ, in Assam and Ava; Shŭmŭnŭ, in Siam; Amida Buth, in Japan; Fohi, in China; Booddhŭ and Shakhŭ-Moonee, in Bengal and Hindoost'hanŭ; and Dhŭrmŭ-Rajŭ and Mŭha-Moonee, in Bootan and Tibet.'

Kæmpfer, in his history of Japan, declares that Bouddhism began generally to spread throughout that country in the year of

[b] The great philosopher.

Christ 518 :—and that Booddhŭ and Fo are the same person, is at present, I presume, no longer the subject of doubt.

Although the notions of the followers of Zoroaster may be involved in much obscurity, it is certain, that the worship of fire has been preserved among this people age after age; nor can it be doubted, but that this worship has an immediate reference to the Hindoo ideas of the divine and prolific energy giving existence to the universe. Enfield, in his History of Philosophy, vol. i. p. 43. says, 'Though our information concerning the history of philosophy among the Persians, in the ages prior to the time of Zoroaster, is very imperfect, it is certain, from the united testimony of the Greeks and Arabians, that long before that time the Magi existed as a body, and were the official guardians of religion and learning. The religion which they taught, consisted in the worship of the sun or fire, a practice which prevailed among the Assyrians, Chaldeans, and among other eastern nations. The name under which the Persians worshipped the sun, or rather the invisible deity, whom they supposed to be, in a peculiar manner, resident in this luminary, was Mithras.' Herodotus and Strabo 'relate, that the Persians sacrificed horses to the sun.'[c] 'Whilst the multitude were contented with a sensible object of devotion, the Magi, and those whom they instructed in the mysteries of religion, considered the sun and fire merely as visible symbols of the animating principle of the universe.' 'Besides Mithras, [the sun,] the Persians worshipped, under opposite characters, Oromasdes and Arimanius; the former as the author of all good, the latter as the author of all evil.' This was changed 'into the worship of two spiritual beings, the one the author of good, the other of evil.[d] The system which supposes two such principles in nature, seems to have been held by the Persian Magi before the time of Zoroaster; but how far they supposed them dependent upon the Supreme Divinity, does not appear.' Plutarch, on the authority of Theopompus, says, 'It is the opinion of the Magi, that at last the evil principle shall perish, and men shall live in happiness; the God who directs these things taking his repose for a time, which, though it may seem long to man, is but short.'[e] 'Sharistan, an Arabian writer, gives the following account of the doctrine of Zerdusht or Zoroaster :—' Zerdusht affirmed light and darkness,

[c] It is highly probable, that the Hindoo ŭshwŭmédhŭ, or sacrifice of the horse, was adopted from the Persians, and incorporated, in early times, into the bramhinical system. One great source of the confusion in which we find every system of mythology involved is, doubtless this borrowing system.

[d] Is not this a mistaken representation of the Joinŭ doctrine, that religion and irreligion govern the world; or that the evil necessarily connected with the residence of spirit in matter, tends to misery and dissolution, while virtue, or the victory of spirit over matter, produces pleasure and prosperity? The Joinŭs say, that the prevalence of vice reduces the vigour of all created substances, and finally dissolves the universe, while virtue has an effect directly the reverse.

[e] Here is a remarkable agreement with the Hindoo doctrine of the day and night of Brŭmha, or the periodical destruction and creation of the universe.

Zezdan and Ahreman, to be two contrary principles, which were the origin of every thing subsisting in the world; the forms of nature being produced from the combination of these principles: but maintained, that the existence of darkness is not to be referred to the one supreme Deity, who is without companion or equal; but must be considered as the unavoidable consequence of his determination to create the world, in which light can no more subsist without darkness, than a visible body can exist without its shadow.[f]

Thus the same notions of the great First Cause and the origin of things appear to prevail, in some modification or other, all over *India, Tartary, China, Japan*, the *Burman empire, Siam*, and the *Indian Isles*. The divine energy, dwelling in the gods, or in living ascetics, is adored over all these immense regions;—and in union with this notion, all these people embrace the doctrine of transmigration, and the efficacy of religious austerities to restore these emanations of the deity, dwelling in matter, to the Great Spirit from which they issued.

The author is aware, that these facts open a wide field for investigation, and for most interesting reflection; but having already exceeded the limits he had prescribed to himself, he now closes this work, after reminding the reader, and thereby entreating the exercise of his candour, that it has been composed amidst avocations which left to it only the remnants of his time.

[f] This surely resembles the Hindoo notion, of God's encompassing himself with delusion in the creation of the world.

GLOSSARY.

A.

Acharyŭ, from a, *prep.* and chŭrŭ, to go.
Achŭmŭnŭ, from a, *prep.* and chŭm, to drink.
Adee-Grŭnt'hŭ, from adee, first, and grŭnt'hŭ, a book.
Adityŭ, a name of the sun, who is called the son of Ŭditee.
Adŭrŭ-Singhasŭnŭ-vrŭtŭ, from adŭrŭ, honour, Singhasŭnŭ, a throne, and vrŭtŭ, a vow.
Aēēn-Ŭkbŭree, from aēēn, a law, and Ŭkbŭrŭ, the name of a well-known emperor.
Agŭmŭ-Vagēēshŭ from agŭmŭ, the name of one of the Tŭntrŭs, vak, a word, and ēēshŭ, lord; the god of speech, a name of Vrihŭspŭtee.
Alŭyŭ, a dwelling, from a, *prep.* and lee, to dissolve.
Angirŭsŭ, the son of Ŭngirŭs.
Anhikŭ, from ŭhŭn, a day, the ceremonies or food of the day.
Anŭndŭ-Nat'hŭ, the lord of joy, from anŭndŭ, joy, and nat'hŭ, a lord.
Anŭndŭ-Mŭyēē, from anŭndŭ, joy.
Arŭnyŭ-Shŭsht'hēē, from ŭrŭnyŭ, a forest, and Shŭsht'-hēē, the name of a goddess.
Asharhŭ; this month is named from the stellar mansion Ŭsharha.
Ashrŭmŭ, from a, *prep.* and shrŭmŭ, labour.
Ashwinŭ; this month is named from the stellar mansion. Ŭshwinēē, the name of a mare.
Ashoogŭ from ashoo, speed, and gŭm, to go.
Asŭnŭ, from as, to sit.
Atma, from a, augmentative, and ŭt, to move continually.
Atmŭ-Dévŭta, from atmŭ, self, and dévŭta, a god, a guardian deity.
Atmŭ-Bhōō, from atmŭ, self, and bhōō, existence.
Ayooshtomŭ, from ayoos, life-time, and stomŭ, a sacrifice.
Ayŭnŭ-Goshŭ, the husband of Radha, the favourite mistress of Krishnoo.

B.

Badyŭkarŭ, from badyŭ, music, and kree to do.
Balŭ-Gopalŭ, from balŭ, a child, go, a cow, and palŭ, a feeder.
Bamŭnŭ, small.
Bancha-Ramŭ, from bancha, desire, and Ramŭ.
Bhaee-Gooroo-Vŭlee, from bhaee, a brother, and gooroo, a teacher.
Bhagŭvŭtŭ, from Bhŭgŭvŭt, divine.
Bhargŭvŭ, the son of Bhrigoo.

Bharŭtŭ-Vŭrshŭ, from Bhŭrŭtŭ, and vŭrshŭ, a place.
Bhasha, a dialect, from bhash, to speak.
Bhashyŭ, from Bhasha, a tongue.
Bhaskŭrŭ, from bhas, light, and kree, to do.
Bhēēmŭ Chŭndēē, from bhēēmŭ, terrific, and chŭndēē, furious.
Bhŭgŭvŭtee, from bhogŭ, to endure or enjoy.
Bhoirŭvŭ, the fear-exciting, from bhŭyŭ, fear.
Bhoirŭvēē, the wife of Bhoirŭvŭ.
Bhoirŭvēēchŭkrŭ; Bhoirŭvēē is a name of Doorga, and chŭkrŭ signifies a circle.
Bhōō-Koilasŭ, from bhōō, the earth, and Koilasŭ, the name of a mountain.
Bhōō-Lokŭ, from bhōō, the earth, and lokŭ, a world.
Bhōōtéshŭ, from bhootŭ, great, and ēēshŭ, a lord.
Bhōōtŭ, the primary elements, from bhōō, to be.
Bhōōtŭ-Shooddhee; bhōōtŭ signifies the four elements, and shooddhee, purification.
Bhoovŭnéshŭ, from bhoovŭnŭ, the world, and ēēshŭ, lord.
Bhoovŭ-lokŭ, from bhoovŭ, the sky, and lokŭ, a world.
Bhŭdrŭ-Kalēē, from bhŭdrŭ, goodness, and Kalēē, a goddess.
Bhŭgŭvŭtēē, the wife of Bhŭgŭvan.
Bhŭgŭvŭt-Gēēta, from Bhŭgŭvŭt, divine, and gēēta, a hymn.
Bhŭktee-Bŭsamritŭ-Sindhoo, from bhŭktee, devotion, rŭsŭ, juice, ŭmritŭ, the water of life, and sindhoo, the sea.
Bhŭvanŭndŭ, from bhŭvŭ, the world, and anŭndŭ, joy.
Bhŭvanēē, from Bhŭvŭ, a name of Shivŭ.
Bhŭvishyŭ, from bhōō, to be.
Boodhashtŭmēē, from Boodhŭ, Mercury, and ŭshtŭmee, the eighth lunar day.
Boodboodŭ, a bubble.
Boodhŭ, the sage of this name.
Booddhŭ-Sŭtwŭ, from booddhee, the understanding, and sŭtwŭ, the quality leading to truth.
Bouddhŭ, from Booddhŭ: he who acknowledges as God only bŭddhee, or the understanding.
Boudhŭ-sarŭ, the essence of the Booddŭ philosophy.
Bramhēē, from Brŭmha.
Bramhŭnēē, the wife of a bramhŭn.
Bramhŭnŭ, he who knows Brŭmhŭ, from Brŭmhŭ.
Brŭmha, from vrih, to increase.
Brŭmhastrŭ, from Brŭmha, and ŭstrŭ, a weapon.
Brŭmhottŭrŭ, from brŭmhŭn, and ootŭrŭ, belonging to.
Brŭmhŭ, from vrih, to increase.
Brŭmhŭcharēē, from Brŭmhŭ, and chŭr, to move.
Brŭmbŭcharyŭ, the profession of a Brŭmhŭcharēē.
Brŭmhŭ-Dŭtthŭ, from Brŭmhŭ, and dŭttŭ, given.
Brŭmhŭ-Pootrŭ; pootrŭ means a son.
Brŭmhŭ-Gnanēē, from Brŭmhŭ, and gnanēē, the wise.
Brŭmhŭrshee, from Brŭmhŭ, and rishee, a sage.

Brŭmhŭ-Voivŭrttŭ, from Brŭmhŭ, and voivŭrtŭ, manifestation.
Bŭjrēē, from bŭjrŭ, a weapon, a thunderbolt.
Bŭlaratee, from bŭlŭ, strength, and ŭratee, an enemy.
Bŭlēē, from bŭlŭ, strength.
Bŭlŭ-Ramŭ, from bŭlŭ, strength, and Ramŭ.
Bŭrgŭ-bhēēma, from bŭrgŭ, a company, and bhēēma, the terrific.
Bŭstrŭ-Hŭrŭnŭ, from vŭstrŭ, clothes, and hŭrŭnŭ, to steal.

C.

Calcutta, from Kalika, (Kalēē) and ŭt, to move.
Chamŭnda, from charoo, good, and mŭndŭ, a head.
Chamŭrŭ, a fan made of the hair of the cow of Tartary.
Chandalŭ, a low caste of shoodrŭs, from chŭndŭ, furious, and ŭlŭ, to go.
Chandŭ, from chŭndrŭ, the moon.
Chapŭrŭ-Shŭsht'hēē, from chapŭra, to press, and Shŭsht'hēē, the name of a goddess.
Charvvakŭ, from charoo, insinuating, and vak, a word.
Charŭnŭ, from chŭr, to go.
Chasakoivŭrtŭ; chasa signifies a cultivator of the ground, and koivŭrtŭ, a fisherman.
Chaya, a shadow, from cha, a covering, or disappearance.
Chinnŭ-Mŭstŭka, from chinnŭ, cut off, and mŭstŭkŭ, a head.
Chirŭn-Jēēvŭ, from chirŭ, a long period, and jēēvŭ, life.
Chitrŭ-Gooptŭ, from chitrŭ, to write, and gooptŭ, hidden.
Chitrŭkōōtŭ, from chitrŭ, speckled, and kōōtŭ, the peak of a hill or mountain.
Choitrŭ, the name of a month; from Chitra, a lunar mansion.
Choitŭnyŭ, from chétŭnŭ, the living.
Choora-Kŭrŭnŭ, from choora, the bunch of hair on the crown of the head, and kree, to do.
Chorŭ-Pŭnchashika, from chorŭ, to steal, and pŭnchashŭ, fifty.
Chŭlŭ, to go, from chŭl, to go.
Chŭkrŭ, a round weapon, from chŭk, to return a blow, to rebound.
Chŭndēē, from chŭndŭ, furious.
Chŭndika, from chŭndŭ, furious.
Chŭndēē-Mŭndŭpŭ, from chŭndēē, the goddess, Chŭndēē and mŭndŭpŭ, a house.
Chŭndogra, from chŭndŭ, furious, and oogrŭ, wrathful.
Chŭndrika, the rays of the moon.
Chŭndrŭ, from chŭd, to shine.
Chŭndrŭ-Shékhŭrŭ, from chŭndrŭ, the moon, and shékhŭrŭ, a mountain peak.
Chŭndrŭ-Rayŭ, from chŭndrŭ, the moon, and rayŭ, a title.
Chŭndrŭ-Prŭbhoo; the last word signifies lord.
Chŭndŭ, furious, from chŭd, to rage.
Chŭndŭ-Nayika, from chŭndŭ, furious, and nayika, a female attendant on Doorga.

Chŭrmŭkarŭ, from chŭrmŭn, skin, and kree, to do.
Chŭrŭkŭ, from chŭr, to go.
Chŭrŭnŭ, that on which a person goes, from chŭr, to go.
Chŭtoor-Anŭnŭ, from chŭtoor, four, and anŭnŭ, a face.

D.

Danŭ, from da, to give.
Danŭ-Khŭndŭ, from danŭ, a gift, and khŭndŭ, a piece.
Danŭvŭ, the sons of Dŭnoo.
Darinēē, from drēē, to tear or crack.
Dasŭ, a slave.
Data, a giver, from da, to give.
Dayŭ-Bhagŭ, from dayŭ, an inheritance, and bhagŭ, share.
Dayŭ-Tŭttwŭ; tŭttwŭ means exactitude, or truth.
Déhŭ, from dih, to collect or increase.
Dévalŭyŭ, from dévŭ, a god, and alŭyŭ, a house.
Dévēē, the feminine of dévŭ, a god.
Dévottŭrŭ, from dévŭ, and ootŭrŭ, belonging to.
Dévŭ, from div, to play.
Dévŭ-Dŭttŭ, from Dévŭ, a god, and dŭttŭ, given.
Dévŭ-Sénŭ, from dévŭ, a god, and séna, a soldier.
Dévŭjanee, from dévŭ, a god, and jaya, a wife.
Dévŭrshee, from dévŭ, a god, and rishee, a sage.
Dévŭkēē, the daughter of Dévŭkŭ.
Dēēpika, a light.
Dhanyŭ-Rōōpa, from dhanŭ, rice, and rōōpŭ, form.
Dharŭkŭ, from dhree, to hold.
Dharŭna, from dhree, to hold.
Dhōōmavŭtēē from dhōōmrŭ, smoke.
Dhōōmrolochŭnŭ, from dhōōmrŭ, smoke, and lochŭnŭ, the eye.
Dhova, from dhav, to cleanse.
Dhritee, from dhree, to sustain.
Dhŭnŭnjŭyŭ, from dhŭnŭ, riches, and jee, to conquer.
Dhŭrmŭ-sétoo from dhŭrmŭ, religion, and sétoo, a bridge, or dam.
Dhŭrmŭ-T'hakoorŭ, from dhŭrmŭ, religion, and t'hakoorŭ, a lord.
Dhŭrmŭ-Rajŭ, from dhŭrmŭ, and rajŭn, king.
Dhŭrmŭ-Bhanoo, from dhŭrmŭ, religion, and bhanoo, splendour.
Dhyanŭ, from dhyoi, to think.
Digumbŭrŭ, from dish, a point of the compass, and ŭmbŭrŭ, cloth.
Dig-Vijŭyŭ, from dish, the quarters of the earth, and vijuyŭ conquest.
Ditee, the wife of Dŭkshŭ.
Divakŭrŭ, from diva, day, and kŭrŭ, from kree, to do.
Divŭs-pŭtee, from dib, heaven, and pŭtee, lord.
Doityŭ, the sons of Ditee.
Doityaree, from doityŭ, a giant, and ŭree, an enemy.
Doityŭ-Gooroo, from doityŭ, a giant, and gooroo, a teacher.

Doivŭgnŭ, from doivŭ, fate, and gna, to know.
Dolŭ, from dool, to swing.
Doolalŭ, from doorlŭbhŭ, obtained with pain.
Doorga, difficult of access, from door, *prep.* and gŭm, to go.
Dooryodhŭnŭ, from door, *prep.* and yodhŭnŭ, war.
Doshŭ, from dooshŭ, evil.
Dōōtēē-Sŭmbodhŭ, from dōōtēē, a female messenger, and sŭmbodhŭ, a call.
Droohinŭ, from drooh, to injure.
Dronacharyŭ, from dronŭ, a measure of capacity, and acharyŭ, a teacher.
Drŭvyŭ-Goonŭ, from drŭvyŭ, a thing, and goonŭ, a quality.
Drŭvyŭ, a thing.
Dŭkshŭ, clever, from dŭksh, to act quickly.
Dŭkshinacharēē, from dŭkshinŭ, the right (hand), and acharin, acting.
Dŭndavŭt, from dŭndŭ, a walking-stick; to fall in a straight posture like a stick, at the foot of a bramhŭn.
Dŭndŭ-Dhŭrŭ, from dŭndŭ, a staff, and dhree, to hold.
Dŭndēē, from dŭndŭ, a staff.
Dŭndŭ-Shōōkŭ, from dŭngshŭ, to bite.
Dŭrpŭnŭ, from drip, to shine.
Dŭrshŭnŭ, from drish, to see.
Dŭshŭ-Bhoojŭ, from dŭshŭn, ten, and bhoojŭ, an arm.
Dŭshŭ-Koomarŭ, from dŭshŭn, ten, and koomarŭ, a son.
Dŭshŭ-Dik-Palŭ; palŭ signifies the cherishing of a person.
Dŭshŭma-Padshahēē-grŭnt'hŭ, from dŭshŭmŭ, the tenth badshah, and grŭnt'hŭ, a book.
Dŭshŭhŭra, from dŭshŭn, ten, and hree, to take away.
Dŭshŭ-Rŭt'hŭ, from dŭshŭn, ten, and rut'hŭ, a chariot.
Dŭttatréyŭ, from Dŭttŭ, a gift, and atréyŭ, from Ŭtree, a sage.
Dwadushatmŭ, from dwadushŭ, twelve, and atmŭn, form.
Dwapŭrŭ, from dwa, the second, and pŭrŭ, after.
Dwēēpŭ, an island, from dwee, two, and ap, water.
Dwijŭ-rajŭ, from dwiju, twice-born, and rajŭ.
Dwoimatoorŭ, from dwee, two, and matree, a mother.
Dyoomŭnee, from div, the sky, and mŭnee, a precious stone.

E.

Eeshwŭ, the glorious, from ēēsh, to be grand.
Ekamrŭ-Kanŭnŭ, from éku, one, amrŭ, a mango tree, and kanŭnŭ a forest.
Ekŭ-Dŭntŭ, from ékŭ, one, and dŭntŭ, a tooth.
Eeshŭ, the glorious.
Eeshwŭrŭ, the same.
Eeshwŭrēē, the feminine of ēēshwŭrŭ.

G.

Ganŭ, a song, from goi, to sing.
Ganŭpŭtyŭ, from gŭnŭ, a company, and pŭtee, a lord.
Gayŭtrēē, from goi, to sing.
Gēēsh-Pŭtee, from gir, a word, and pŭtee, a lord.
Gēēta, from goi, to sing.
Gēētŭ, from goi, to sing.
Ghatŭ, a flight of steps, from ghŭtt, to move.
Ghēē, from gritŭ, clarified butter.
Ghoshŭ, from goosh, to sound.
Gritachēē, a heavenly courtezan, from ghrita, clarified butter, and ŭnch, to worship.
Girēēshŭ, from giree, a mountain, and ēēshŭ, a lord.
Gloŭ, from gloi, to be sad, or to fade.
Gnanēē, from gna, wisdom.
Gnanŭ, from gna, to know.
Gnanŭ-Rŭtnavŭlēē, from gnanŭ, wisdom, rŭtna, a precious stone, and avŭlēē, a train.
Goohŭ, a secret place, from gooh, to hide or cover
Goohyŭ, from goohyŭ, requiring to be concealed.
Go-médhŭ, from go, a cow, and médhŭ, flesh.
Goonŭ, a quality, from goonŭ, to advise.
Goonŭ-Sindhoo, from goonŭ, qualities, and sindhoo, the sea.
Gooroo-Prŭsadŭ, from gooroo, a teacher, and prŭsadŭ, a favour, grace.
Gopalŭ, from go, a cow, and palŭ, a nourishing.
Gopēē-Nat'hŭ, from goopēē, the wife of a milkman, and nat'hŭ, a lord.
Gooptavŭ-Dhōōtŭ, from gooptŭ, concealed, and ŭvŭdhōōtŭ, to renounce.
Gooptee-Para, from gooptŭ, hidden, and para, a division, of a town.
Gooroo, a teacher, from gree to make known.
Gooroo-Mookhēē, from gooroo, a teacher, and mookhēē, belonging to the mouth.
Gooroomŭtŭ, from gooroo, a teacher.
Gorŭkshŭ, from go, a cow, and rŭksh, to save.
Gosht'hŭ-Yatra, from gosht'hŭ, a cow-pen, and yatra, to go.
Goswamēē, from go, a cow, and swamin, a master.
Gotrŭbhid, from gotrŭ, a mountain, and bhid, to divide.
Gourēē, white, or light yellow; from gourŭ.
Govindŭ, from go, a cow, and vid, to share out.
Grihŭst'hŭ, from grihŭ, a house, and st'ha, to remain.
Grihŭst'hŭ-Dhŭrmŭ, from ghrihŭst'hŭ, situated in a house, and dhŭrmŭ, religion.
Grŭhŭ-Pŭtee, from grŭhŭ, a planet, and pŭtee, a lord.
Grŭnt'hee, from grŭnt'hŭ, a book.
Gŭjŭ-Dŭntŭ, from gŭjŭ, an elephant, and dŭntŭ, a tooth.
Gŭndhŭ-Vŭnik, from gŭndhŭ, spices, and vŭnik, a tradesman.

Gŭndhŭrvŭ, from ganŭ, a song, and dhŭrmŭ, a person's own profession.
Gŭndhŭvŭhŭ, from gŭndhŭ, a scent, and vŭh, to carry.
Gŭndhŭ-Dhama, from gŭndŭ, a scent, and dhama, a place.
Gŭnŭkŭ, from gŭnŭ, to count.
Gŭnéshŭ, from gŭnŭ, a company, and ēēshŭ, a lord.
Gŭnéshŭ-Jŭnŭnēē, the mother of Gŭnéshŭ; from jŭnŭ, birth.
Gŭnga, from gŭm, to go.
Gŭnga-vakyavŭlee, from vakya, a word, and abŭlēē, a train.
Gŭnga-Vasŭ, from vasŭ, a residence.
Gŭngadhŭrŭ-Shastrēē; he who knows the shastrŭ, is called shastrēē.
Gŭngadhŭrŭ, from Gŭnga, and dhŭrŭ, to hold.
Gŭjanŭnŭ, from gŭjŭ, an elephant, and anŭnŭ, the face.
Gŭrbhadhanŭ, from gŭrbhŭ, the womb, and adhanŭ, to hold.
Gŭroorŭ, from gŭroot, a wing.
Gŭrootmŭt, from gŭroot, a wing.

H.

Hétwabhasŭ, from hétoo, a cause, and abhasŭ, an appearance, a semblance.
Himangshoo, from himŭ, cold, and ŭngshoo, rays of light.
Himalŭyŭ, from himŭ, cold, and alŭyŭ, a house.
Himŭvut, from himŭ, cold.
Hŭrŭnyŭ-gŭrbhŭ, from hirŭnyŭ, gold, and gŭrbhŭ, the womb.
Hirŭnyakashŭ, from hirŭnyŭ, gold, and ukshee, an eye.
Hirŭnyŭ-Kŭshipoo, from hirŭnyŭ, gold, and kŭshipoo, a sheath.
Hitopŭdéshŭ, from hitŭ, good, and oopŭdéshŭ, teaching.
Hoimŭvŭtee, from himŭvŭt.
Homŭ, from hoo, to offer.
Hota, he who directs the homŭ, or burnt-offering, from hoo.
Hŭngshŭ, a duck.
Hŭngsŭ-Dōōtŭ, from hŭngsŭ, goose, and dootŭ, a messenger.
Hŭnooman, from hŭnoo, the cheek.
Hŭree-Vŭlŭ; the last word is the imperative of vŭlŭ, to speak.
Hŭree-Dwarŭ; dwarŭ signifies a door.
Hŭree-Hŭrŭ; both words are derived from rhree, to take away.
Hŭree-Priya; priya signifies beloved.
Hŭridra, from hurit, light yellow.
Hŭrihŭyŭ, from hŭrit, light yellow, and hŭyŭ, a horse.
Hŭrŭ-Gourēē, from Hŭrŭ (Shivŭ), and Gourēē, the light yellow.
Hŭru-Nat'hŭ, from Hŭrŭ, the name of Shivŭ, and Nat'hŭ, a lord.
Hŭyŭ-Grēēvŭ, from hŭyŭ, a horse, and grēēvŭ, the back of the neck.

I.

Indoo, from id, to be glorious, or refulgent.
Indrŭ, from id, to be glorious.
Indrŭ-Dyoomnŭ; the last word signifies riches.

Indrŭ-jit; from jee, to conquer.
Ishtŭ, from ish, to desire.

J.

Jagŭrŭnŭ, from jagree, to be awake.
Jalikŭ, from jalŭ, a net.
Jambŭvŭtēē, from Jambŭvan, the name of a certain bear.
Janhŭvēē, from jŭnhoo, a sage.
Jatee, a kind, from jŭn, to be born.
Jatŭ-Kŭrmŭ, from jatŭ, born, and kŭrmŭn, an action.
Jēēvŭ, life, from jēēv, to live.
Jishnoo, from jee, to conquer.
Joinŭ, from jinŭ, to conquer or excel.
Joivatrikŭ, from jēēv, to live.
Jŭgŭdgourēē, from gŭgŭt, the world, and gourŭ, light yellow.
Jŭgŭddhatrēē, from jŭgŭt, the world, and dhatrēē, an upholder.
Jŭgŭdēēshŭ, from jŭgŭt, the world, and ēēshŭ, lord.
Jŭgŭnnat'hŭ, from jŭgŭt, the world, and nat'hŭ, a lord.
Jŭgŭnnat'hŭ-kshétrŭ, from jŭgŭt, the world, nathŭ, a lord, and kshétrŭ, a place.
Jŭlpŭ, to speak, from jŭlp, to speak.
Jŭmidarŭ, from jŭmin, land, and darŭ, an owner.
Jŭmŭdŭgnee, from jŭmŭt, terrific, and ŭgnee, fire.
Jŭnarddŭnŭ, from jŭnŭ, a person, and ŭrddŭnŭ, a giving distress.
Jŭnhoo, from ha, to abandon, (viz. the world).
Jŭnŭméjŭyŭ, from jŭnŭ, a man, and éj, to tremble.
Jŭnŭkŭ, from jŭn, to be produced.
Jŭpŭ, to speak inaudibly, from jŭp, to mutter.
Jŭrutkaroo, from jree, to be withered, and kree, to do.
Jŭrŭ-Bhŭrŭtŭ, from jŭrŭ, decrepitude.
Jŭshoda, from jŭshŭs, fame, and da, to give.
Jŭtayoo, from jŭta, a bunch of hair, and ayoo, life-time.
Jŭya, from jee, victory.
Jŭyŭ-Doorga, from jŭyŭ, victory.
Jŭyŭntēē, from jee, to conquer.
Jwala-Mookhēē, from jwala, a flame, and mookhŭ, a face.
Jwŭlŭnŭ, from jwŭlŭ, to enkindle.
Jyoisht'hŭ, from jyésht'ha, a planet.
Jyotish-stomŭ, from jyotish, light, and stomŭ, the whole.
Jyotish, from jyot, to shine.

K.

Kahinee, a tale, from Kŭt'hŭ, to speak.
Kaliyŭ-Dŭmŭnŭ, from kaliyŭ, the name of a snake, and dŭmŭnŭ, subduction.
Kalēē, the black, from kalŭ, time.
Kalŭ-Bhoirŭvŭ, from kalŭ, time, and bhoirŭvŭ, the terrific.

Kalŭ-Pooarooshŭ, from kŭlŭ, black, and pooarooshŭ, a male.
Kalŭ-Ratree, from kalŭ, dark, and ratree, night.
Kalŭ-Sōōtrŭ, from kalŭ, time, and sōōtrŭ, a thread.
Kaliyŭ, from kŭlŭ, to move.
Kamŭ-dévŭ, from kamŭ, desire, and dévŭ, from div, to play.
Kamŭ-dhénoo, from kamŭ, desire, and dhénoo, a milch-cow.
Kamŭ-Rōōpŭ, from kamŭ, desire, and rōōpŭ, form.
Kamakhya, from kamŭ, desire, and akhya, an appellation.
Kamŭnŭ, the heart's desire, from kŭm, to desire.
Kandŭ, an arrow, or a chapter.
Kanŭ-Phata-Yogēē, compounded of kanŭ, the ear, phata, slit, and yogēē, an ascetic.
Kartikéyŭ, from krittika, the name of a planet.
Kashēē, from kash, to appear.
Kavyŭ, from kŭvee, a poet.
Kayŭst'hŭ, from kayŭ, the body, and st'ha, to be situated.
Késhŭrēē, from késhŭrŭ, a mane.
Kēērtŭnŭ, from kreet, to produce harmony.
Kēērtee-Chŭndrŭ, from kēērtee, fame.
Kétoo, a sign, from kit, to dwell.
Késhŭvŭ, from keshŭ, the hair.
Khéchŭrŭ, from khŭ, the sky, and chŭrŭ, going.
Khŭndŭ, a piece, from chŭd, to break.
Khŭgéshwŭrŭ,compounded of khŭgŭ,a bird,and'ééshwŭrŭ,greatness.
Kinnŭrŭ, from king, what? and nŭrŭ, a man.
Koilashŭ, from kélŭs, in water, to shine.
Kojagŭrŭ-Lŭkshmēē, from kŭh, who, and jagree, to awake.
Koitŭbhŭjit; jit, signifies victory.
Koojŭ, from koo, the earth, and jŭn, to be produced.
Koolŭ-Dévŭta, from koolŭ, race, and dévŭta, a god.
Koolēēnŭ, from koolŭ, a race.
Koombhŭkarŭ, from koombhŭ, an earthen jar, and kree, to do.
Koombhŭ-Kŭrnŭ, from koombhŭ a jar, and kŭrnŭ, the ear.
Koomarŭ, a boy, from koomarŭ, to play.
Koomarŭ, from koo, evil, and mree, to beat.
Koombhēē-Pakŭ, from koombhŭ, a pot, and pakŭ, ripe.
Koont'hŭ, a groan, from koont'h, to groan.
Koomoodŭ-Bandŭvŭ, from koomoodŭ, a lotus, and bŭndhoo, a friend.
Koosooméshoo, from koosoomŭ, a flower, and ishoo, an arrow.
Kosha, from koosh, to issue, to identify.
Kooshŭ, to lie down.
Kooshee, a small kosha.
Kooshŭnabhŭ, from kooshŭ, sacred grass, and nabhee, the navel.
Koovérŭ, from koov, to cover.
Koulacharēē, from koolŭ, a race, and chŭr, to act, preceded by the *prep.* a.
Koumoodee, brightness, from koomoodŭ, a nymphæa.
Koutookŭ-Sŭrvŭswŭ, from koutookŭ, play, and sŭrvŭswŭ, a person's all.

Krimee-Bhojŭnŭ, from krimee, an insect, and bhojŭnŭ, to eat.
Kripēētŭyonee ; yonee, a birth-place.
Krishnŭ, from krish, to draw.
Krishnŭ-Krora ; krorŭ signifies the side.
Krittivasa, from krittee, the skin, and vasŭs, a garment.
Kritantŭ, from kritu, done, and ŭntŭ, end.
Krya, work, from kree, to do.
Krodhagarŭ, from krodhŭ, anger, and agarŭ, a house.
Krounchŭ-Darŭnŭ, a proper name, and dree, to tear.
Ksharŭ-Kŭrddhŭmŭ, from ksharŭ, ashes, and kŭrddhŭmŭ, mud.
Kshēērŭ, milk, from kshŭr, to ooze out.
Kshŭpakŭrŭ, from kshŭpa, night, and kree, to make.
Kshŭtryŭ, from kshŭtŭ, a wound, and troi, to save.
Kŭbŭndhŭ, headless, from kin, the head, and bŭdh, to kill.
Kŭchŭ, hair, from kŭch, to bind.
Kŭchyŭpŭ, a proper name ; pa, means to drink.
Kŭlee, from kŭlŭ, to reckon.
Kŭlee-Yoogŭ, from kŭl, to enumerate, and yoogŭ, a period of time.
Kŭlkee, from kŭlee, time, and koi, to subdue.
Kŭlpŭ, from klipŭ, to contrive.
Kŭlpŭ-Sōōtrŭ, from kŭlpŭ, time, and sōōtrŭ, a thread.
Kŭlŭnkŭ-Bŭnjŭnŭ, from kŭlŭnkŭ,, a blot, and bŭnjŭnŭ, a breaking.
Kŭmŭlékaminēē, from kŭmŭlŭ, the water lily, and kamŭ, desire.
Kŭnadŭ, from kŭnŭ, an atom, and ŭd, to eat.
Kŭndŭrpŭ, from kŭng, Brŭmba, and drip, to domineer.
Kŭpalŭbrit, from kŭpalŭ, the forehead or fate, and bhree, to hold.
Kŭrangŭnyasŭ, from kŭrŭ, hand, ŭngŭ, a part, and nyasŭ, to place.
Kŭrmŭkarŭ, from kŭrmŭn, work, and kree to do.
Kŭroonamŭyēē, from kŭroona, pity.
Kŭrmŭ-Vipakŭ, from kree, to work, and pak, to ripen.
Kŭt'hŭkŭ, a speaker, from kŭt'h, to speak.
Kŭvŭchŭ, from vŭchŭ, a word.
Kŭvirajŭ, from kŭvee, a poet, and rajŭn, a king.

L.

Lēēlamritŭ, from lēēla, play, and ŭmrita, nectar.
Lingŭ, from lig, to move.
Lohitaugŭ, from lohitŭ, blood red, and ŭngŭ, the body.
Lokéshŭ, from lokŭ, men, and ēēshŭ, greatness.
Lokŭ, from looch, to see.
Lŭkshmēē-Chara ; the latter word means deserted.
Lŭkshmŭnŭ, the beautiful, from Lŭkshmŭ, a fortunate sign.
Lŭmbodŭrŭ, from lŭmbŭ, long, and oodŭrŭ, the belly.

M.

Madhŭvu, from ma, the goddess Lŭkshŭmēē, and dhŭvŭ, husband.
Magŭdhŭ, from Mŭgŭdhŭ, the name of a country.

Mala, a necklace.
Malakarŭ, from mala, a necklace, and kree, to make.
Malinēē, from mala, a necklace.
Malyŭvanŭ, from mala, a necklace.
Manŭ-Bŭnghŭ, from manŭ, honour, and bŭnghŭ, destruction.
Manŭnŭ, from man, to decide.
Manŭsŭ-Kalee, from mŭnŭs, mind.
Marootŭ, from mree, to kill.
Marŭ, from mree, to kill.
Matrika-Nyasŭ, from matrika, a mother, and nyasŭ, to place.
Matŭrishwa, wind.
Mayavŭtēē, from maya, delusion.
Médha, apprehension, or conception, from médh, to be apt to learn.
Mēēmangsa, from man, to judge.
Méghŭ-Nadŭ, from méghŭ, a cloud, and nadŭ, a sound.
Méghŭ-Nat'hŭ, from méghŭ, a cloud, and nat'hŭ, a lord.
Méghŭ-Vahŭnŭ; vahŭnŭ, a vehicle.
Ménŭ-Kétŭnŭ, from mēēnŭ, a fish, and kétŭnŭ, a flag.
Mihirŭ, from mihŭ, to water.
Mishrŭ-Késhēē, from mish, to mix, and késhŭ, hair.
Mitrŭ, a friend, from mid, love.
Mitrŭvinda, from mitrŭ, a friend, and vid, to obtain.
Modŭkŭ, from mood, to rejoice.
Mohinēē, from mooh, to be infatuated.
Mohŭ, from moohŭ, confusion or stupefaction.
Moogdhŭbodhŭ, from moogdhŭ, stupidly ignorant, and bodhŭ, knowledge.
Mooktŭ-Késhēē, from mooktŭ, spread out, késhŭ, hair.
Mooktŭ-Ramŭ; mooktŭ, liberation.
Mōōlŭ, a root.
Moomookshootwŭ, from mooch, to liberate.
Mounēē, he who subjects himself to voluntary silence.
Mrigankŭ, from mrigŭ, a deer, and ŭnkŭ, a mark.
Mritŭ-Sŭnjēēvinēē; sŭnjēēvinēē means to restore to life.
Mrityoo, from mree, death.
Mrityoonjŭnŭ, from myrtyoo, death, and jee, to overcome.
Mŭdhoo-Sōōdŭnŭ, from sōōd, to destroy.
Mŭdhyŭdéshēē, from mŭdhyŭ, midst, and déshin, belonging to a country.
Mŭdŭnŭ-Mohŭnŭ, from mŭdŭnŭ, desire, and mooh, to be infatuated.
Mŭha-Dévŭ, from mŭhŭt, great, and div, to play.
Mŭha-Kalŭ, from mŭhŭt, great, and kalŭ, time.
Mŭhamaree, from mŭhŭt, great, and mree, to kill.
Mŭha-Patŭkŭ, from mŭhŭt, and patŭkŭ, from pŭt, to throw down
Mŭha-Poorooshŭ, from mŭhŭt, great, and poorooshŭ, a male.
Mŭha-Rourŭvŭ, from rooroo, an insect.
Mŭha-Rŭt'bēē, from mŭhŭt, great, and rŭt'hŭ, a chariot.
Mŭha-Prémŭ, from mŭhŭt, great, and prémŭn, love.
Mŭha-Sénŭ, from mŭhŭt, great, and séna, soldier.

Mŭhatmŭ, from mŭhŭt, great, and atmŭn, spirit.
Mŭha-Vrŭtŭ; vrŭtŭ is a ceremony to be performed according to a vow.
Mŭha-Vyadhee, from mŭhŭt, great, and vyadhee, sickness.
Mŭha-Vidya, from mŭhŭt, great, and vidya, learning.
Mŭhéndrŭ, from mŭhŭt, great, and Indrŭ, the king of heaven.
Mŭhéshŭ, from mŭhŭt, great, and ēēshŭ, glorious.
Mŭhéshwŭrŭ, from mŭhŭt, great, and ēēshwŭrŭ, glorious.
Mŭhishŭ-Murdinēē, from mŭhishŭ, a buffalo, and mŭrdŭ, to destroy.
Mŭhéshwŭrŭ, from mŭhŭt, great, and ēēshwŭrŭ, lord.
Mŭhŭttranŭ, from mŭhŭt, great, and tranŭ, salvation.
Mŭkshŭ, from mooch, to liberate.
Mŭkŭrŭ-Dwŭjŭ, from mŭkŭrŭ, a water animal, and dwŭjŭ, a flag.
Mŭllŭ, strong, from mŭl, to hold.
Mŭlŭgrahee, from mŭlŭ, filth, and grahin, receiving.
Mŭndodŭrēē, from mŭndŭ, small, and oodŭrŭ, the belly.
Mŭngŭlŭ-Chŭndika, from mŭngŭlŭ, good, and chŭndika, wrathful.
Mŭngŭlŭ-Varŭ, from mŭngŭlŭ, good, and varŭ, a day.
Mŭn-Mŭt'hŭ, from mŭnŭ, mind, and mŭnt, to grieve.
Mŭntrŭ, from mŭtr, to repeat in the mind.
Mŭntrŭ-Droomŭ, from mŭnŭn, to meditate, and droomŭ, a tree.
Mŭnŭsa, from mŭnŭs, mind.
Mŭnŭsijŭ, from mŭnŭ, mind, and jŭnŭ, birth.
Mŭnwŭntŭrŭ, from Mŭnoo, a sage, and ŭntŭrŭ, another, or a limit.
Mŭroot, from mree, to kill.
Mŭrŭipora, from mŭrŭ, a dead body, and poora, to burn.

N.

Nagantŭkŭ, from nagŭ, a serpent, and ŭntŭkŭ, the end,
Namŭ-Kŭrŭnŭ, from namŭn, a name, and kree, to make.
Narēē, from nŭrŭ, a man.
Nayika, from nēē, to obtain.
Nēēlŭ-Pŭrvŭtŭ, from nēēlŭ, blue, and pŭrvŭtŭ, a mountain,
Nēētee, from nēē, to obtain.
Nēēlŭ, dark blue.
Nēēlŭ-Kŭntŭ, from nēēlŭ, dark blue, and kŭntŭ, the throat.
Nidanŭ, a first cause, from nee, *prep.* and da, to give.
Nidhee, from nee, *prep.* and dha, to place.
Nigrŭhŭ-St'hanŭ, nigrŭhŭ signifies disfavour, and st'hanŭ, place.
Nigŭmŭnŭ, a sure decision, from nee, *prep.* and gŭm to move.
Nimittŭ, a cause.
Nirakarŭ, from nir, *prep.* and akarŭ, form.
Nirnŭyŭ, from nir, *prep.* and nee, to obtain.
Nirooktŭ, from nir, *prep.* and ooktŭ, spoken.
Nirvanēē, from nirvanŭ, liberation.
Nisha-Pŭtee, from nisha, night, and pŭtee, lord.

Nishkrŭmŭnŭ,.a going forth, from nir, *prep.* and krum, to step.
Nityŭ, constant, everlasting.
Nityanŭndŭ, from nityŭ, constant, and anŭndŭ, joy.
Niyŭmŭ, a resolution.
Noiyayikŭ, a follower of the Nyayŭ philosophy.
Nouka-Khŭndŭ, from nouka, a boat, and khŭndŭ, a part.
Nree-Médhŭ, from nree, a man, and médhŭ, flesh.
Nrisinghŭ, from nree, a man, and singhŭ, a lion.
Nŭbhŭswŭt, from nŭbhŭs, the sky.
Nŭkshŭtréshŭ, from nŭkshŭtrŭ, a planet, and ēēshŭ, a lord.
Nŭlŭ-Danga, from nŭlŭ, a reed, and danga, a place.
Nŭlŭ-Chŭmpōō, from nŭlŭ, the name of a king, and chŭmpōō, a particular kind of composition in which the same subject is maintained in all the varieties of prose and verse.
Nŭmoochēē-Soodŭnŭ, a proper name joined to sōōd, to kill.
Nŭmŭskarŭ, a reverential mode of obeisance: from nŭmŭs, a bow, and kree, to make.
Nŭrŭ, man, from nree, to do right.
Nŭrmŭda, from nŭrmŭ, sport or entertainment, and da, to give.
Nŭrŭ-Singhŭ, from nŭrŭ, man, and singhŭ, excellent.
Mŭvŭ-Pŭtrika, from nŭvŭ, nine, and pŭtrŭ, leaves.
Nŭvŭ-Rŭtnŭ, from nŭvŭ, niue, and rŭtnŭ, a jewel.
Nyasŭ, a deposit, from nee, *prep.* and ŭs, to throw.
Nyayŭ, justice, from nee, *prep.* and ŭy, to move.

O.

Oodahŭrŭnŭ, from oot, a preposition indicating that the action has an upward direction, and ahŭrŭnŭ, a collecting.
Oochoishrŭva, from oochchois, great, and shroo, to hear.
Oodasēē; oot, *prep.* and asŭ, to sit.
Ooddéshŭ, from oot, *prep.* and déshŭ, to seek.
Oodŭyŭ, to arise, from oot, *prep.* and ŭyŭ, to go.
Oodgata, from oot, *prep.* and goi, to sing.
Oogrŭ-Chŭnda, from oogrŭ, fear-exciting, and chŭndŭ, wrathful.
Oindrŭ-Dŭdhee, from Indrŭ, and dŭdhee, curds.
Oojjŭlŭ-Nēēlmŭnee, from oojjŭlŭ, splendour, nēēlŭ, blue, and mŭnee, a jewel.
Ooktŭ, spoken, from vŭch, to speak.
Oopangŭ, from oopŭ, a preposition importing resemblance in an inferior degree, and ŭngŭ, a part.
Oopasŭnŭ, from oopŭ, and ŭs, to throw, preceded by the *prep.* a.
Oopŭ-Patŭkŭ, from oopŭ, *prep.* and pŭt, to throw down.
Oopŭcharŭ-Chŭlŭ, from oopŭ, *prep.* chŭrŭ, to move, and chŭlŭ, a pretence.
Oopŭnŭyŭ, from oopŭ, and nēē, to take.
Oopŭnŭyŭnŭ, from oopŭ, and nŭyŭnŭ, an obtaining
Oopŭpŭtee, from oopŭ, and pŭtee, lord,

Oopŭrŭtee, from oopŭ, and rŭm, to play.
Oopŭsŭngharŭ, from oopŭ, and sŭngharŭ, destruction.
Oordhŭ-Vahoo, from ōōrdhŭ, high, and vahoo, arm.
Oosha-Hŭrŭnŭ; hŭrŭnŭ means stealing.
Ooshmŭpa, from ooshmun, heat, and pa, to drink.
Oshŭdhēēshŭ, from oshŭdhee, medicine, and ēēshŭ, a lord.
Ootŭt'hyŭ, from oot, *prep.* and tŭt'hyŭ, just.

P.

Pachŭkŭ, he who cooks; from pŭch, to cook.
Pakŭ-Shasŭnŭ, from pakŭ, a giant, and shas to govern.
Parijatŭ-Hŭrunŭ, from parijatŭ, a particular flower, and hŭrŭnŭ, to steal.
Parvŭtēē, the daughter of pŭrvŭtŭ, a mountain.
Pat'hŭkŭ, he who reads, from pŭt'h, to read.
Patŭnŭ, from pŭt, to throw down.
Patŭnjŭlŭ, from the sage Pŭtŭnjŭlee; which word is made up of pŭt, to throw down, and ŭnjŭlee, joined hands. This conjunction teaches us, that people fell before him for instruction with joined hands.
Pēētamvŭrŭ, from pēētŭ, yellow, and ŭmbŭrŭ, cloth.
Phŭlŭhŭrēē, from phŭlŭ, fruit, and rhee, to steal.
Phŭlŭ, fruit.
Pingŭlŭ, variegated.
Pingŭlŭ-Nagŭ, from pingŭlŭ, brownish yellow, and nagŭ, a serpent.
Pita-Mŭhŭ, from pitree, father, and mŭhŭt, great.
Pitree-Médhŭ, from pitree forefathers, and medhŭ, flesh.
Poita, from oopŭ, and vēētŭ, pure.
Pōōja, from pōōjŭ, to honour or serve.
Pōōjŭkŭ, a worshipper.
Poondŭrēēkakshŭ, from poondŭrēēkŭ, a water-lily, and ŭkshee, an eye.
Pooranŭ, from pree, to fill.
Pooree, a house, a palace.
Poornabhishékŭ, from poornŭ, and ŭbhishékŭ, to anoint.
Poornabhishiktŭ, from poornŭ, full, and ŭbhishiktŭ, anointed.
Poorohitŭ, from poorŭs, to go before, and hitŭ, good.
Pooroohōōtŭ, from pooroo, fulness, and hōō, to call.
Pooroosbŭ, a male, from pree, to fill or nourish.
Poorŭ, a town.
Poorŭndŭrŭ, from poorŭ, a house, and dree, to cut.
Poorŭshchŭrŭnŭ, from poorŭ, before, and chŭrŭnŭ, practice.
Pooranŭ, old.
Pooshkŭrŭ-Shantee, from pooshkŭrŭ, the evil fortune attending a person who shall die when an unlucky day, an unlucky lŭnar day, and an evil planet all unite, and shantee, to pacify or produce peace.

Poorvŭvŭt, from poorvŭ, a cause, and vŭt.
Pooshpavŭlee, from pooshpŭ, a flower, and avŭlee, a row.
Pooshpŭ-Dhŭnwa, from pooshpŭ, a flower, and dhŭnwŭ, a bow.
Pooshpŭkŭ, from pooshp, to expand.
Pooshtee, from poosh, to cherish.
Pooshŭnŭ, from poosh, to cherish.
Pootŭna-Bŭdhŭ; bŭdhŭ means to kill.
Poŭranik, a follower of the pooranŭs.
Prajapŭtyŭ, the work of a prŭjapŭtee.
Pranayamŭ, from pranŭ, life, and ayamŭ, a coming.
Pramanikŭ, from prŭmanŭ, proof.
Pranŭ-Nirodhŭ, from pranŭ, life, and nirodhŭ, to stop.
Pratŭ-Kalŭ, from pratŭr, morning, and kalŭ, time.
Prétŭ-raj; prétŭ is a ghost, and raj signifies raja.
Prit'hivēē, from Prithoo, a king who first formed towns, raised the arts, &c.
Prityahŭrŭ, from prŭtee, a preposition indicating that the action is returned or reflected, and ahŭrŭ, to take.
Prŭbhŭngjŭnŭ, from prŭ, *prep.* and bhŭnjŭ, to break.
Prŭchŭnda, from prŭ, *prep.* and chŭndŭ, wrathful.
Prŭdhanŭ, chief.
Prŭdyoomnŭ, from prŭ, *prep.* and dyoomnŭ, riches.
Prŭjapŭtee, from prŭja, subjects, and pŭtee, a lord.
Prŭja-Yagŭ, from prŭja, subjects, and yagŭ, a sacrifice.
Prŭkashŭ; kashŭ means light.
Prŭkritee, from prŭ, *prep.* and kree, to do.
Prŭlhadŭ, from prŭ, *prep.* and alhadŭ, joy.
Prŭlŭyŭ, from lēē, to absorb.
Prŭmanŭ, from prŭ, *prep.* and ma, to measure.
Prŭméyŭ, the subject known, from prŭ, *prep.* and ma, to measure.
Prŭmŭtee, from prŭ, *prep.* and mŭtee, understanding.
Prŭstavinēē, from prŭ, *prep.* and stoo, to praise.
Prŭtigna, from prŭtee, and gna, to know.
Prŭtŭkshŭ, from prŭtee, *prep.* and ŭkshee, the eye.
Prŭyojŭnŭ, from prŭ, a preposition which adds intensity to the meaning, and yooj, to join.
Pŭdart'hŭ, from pŭdŭ, a word, and ŭrt'hŭ, an object.
Pŭdmalŭya, from pŭdmŭ, the water-lily, and alŭyŭ, residence.
Pŭdmŭ-Nabhŭ, from pŭdmŭ, a water-lily, and nabhee, the navel.
Pŭdmŭ-Prŭbhoo, from pŭdmŭ, a water-lily, and prŭbhoo, a lord.
Pŭdyavŭlee, from pŭdya, prose, and avŭlee, a row, or range.
Pŭdŭng, from pŭdŭ, a place.
Pŭddhŭtee, a road, from pŭdŭ, the foot, and hŭn, to smite.
Pŭkshŭdhŭrŭ-Mishrŭ, from pŭkshŭ, a lunar half month, and dhŭrŭ, to hold.
Pŭnchangŭ, from pŭnchŭn, five, and ŭngŭ, the body.
Pŭnchŭkŭ, from pŭnchŭn, five.
Pŭnchŭ-Chōōra, from pŭnchŭ, five, or much, and chōōra, a crest.

Pŭnchumēē-Vrŭtŭ, from pŭnchŭ, five, and vrŭtŭ, the ceremonies connected with a vow.
Pŭnchŭ-Rŭtnŭ, from pŭnchŭ, five, and rŭtnŭ, a precious stone.
Pŭnchŭshŭrŭ, from pŭnchŭ, five, and shŭrŭ, an arrow.
Pŭnchanŭnŭ, from pŭnchŭ, five, and anŭnŭ, face.
Pŭnjab, from pŭnchŭ, five, and ap, water.
Pŭnnŭgashŭnŭ, from pŭnnŭgŭ, a serpent, and ŭshŭ, to eat.
Pŭnt'hēē, from pŭt'hŭ, a way.
Pŭrivrittee, from pŭree, *prep.* and vrittee, existence.
Pŭrŭm-Eshwŭrŭ, from pŭrŭm, excellent, and ēēshwŭrŭ, God, or simply, the glorious.
Pŭrŭmanŭndŭ, from pŭrŭmŭ, excellent, and anŭndŭ, joy.
Pŭrŭmart'hŭ, from pŭrŭmŭ, excellent, and ŭrt'hŭ, an object.
Pŭrŭm-Hŭngshŭ, from pŭrŭm, excellent, and ŭngshŭ, a goose.
Pŭrŭshoo-Ramŭ; pŭrŭshoo, a weapon.
Pŭvŭnŭ, from poo, to purify.

R.

Radha, the favourite mistress of Krishnŭ, from radh, to accomplish.
Radha-Vŭllŭbhŭ; vŭllŭbhŭ, beloved.
Ragŭ, passion, from rŭnj, to colour.
Raja, light.
Raj-tŭrŭnginēē, from rajŭn, a king, and tŭrŭnginēē, a river.
Rajŭ-Pootŭ, from rajŭn, a king, and pootrŭ, a son.
Rajŭ-Yogŭ, from rajŭn, a king, and yogŭ, abstraction.
Rajŭraj, king of kings.
Rajŭ-Rajéshwŭrēē, from rajŭ-raj, king of kings, and ēēshwŭrēē, a goddess.
Rajŭrshee, from rajŭn, a king, and rishee, a sage.
Rajŭ-sōōyŭ, from rajŭn, a king, and sōō, birth.
Ramŭ, from rŭm, play, or to please.
Ramayŭnŭ, from Ramŭ, and ŭyŭnŭ, to go.
Ramŭ-Shŭrŭnŭ-Palŭ, from Ramŭ-Shŭrŭnŭ, and palŭ, a title.
Rarhēēyŭ, from Rarhŭ, a country.
Rasŭ-Mŭnchŭnŭ; mŭnchŭ, a stage.
Ravŭnŭ, from roo, to kill.
Rhishēēkéshŭ, from rhishēēkŭ, the organs, and ēēshŭ, a lord.
Rig-Védŭ, from rich, an incantation, and védŭ, from vid, knowledge.
Rishŭbhŭ-Dévŭ; rishŭbhŭ, signifies excellent.
Rishyadee-nyasŭ, from rishee, a sage, adee, the first, and nyasŭ, to place.
Rishyŭ-Shringŭ, from rishyŭ, a deer, and shringŭ, horns.
Ritoopŭrnŭ, from ritoo, a season, and pŭrnŭ, a leaf.
Ritoo-Yagŭ, from ritoo, season, and yŭjŭ, worship with sacrifices.
Rochŭnŭ, from rooch, love.
Roodrakshŭ, from Roodrŭ, a name of Shivŭ, and ŭkshŭ, an eye.

Roodrŭ, from rood, to cry.
Rookminēē, from Rookmŭ (gold), the name of a king.
Rŭjo-goonŭ, from rŭnj, colour, or love, and goonŭ, a quality.
Rŭjŭ, dust, from rŭnj, to colour.
Rŭjŭkŭ, from rŭnj, to colour.
Rŭkshitŭ, preserved, from rŭkshŭ, to preserve.
Rŭkshogŭnŭ-Bhojŭnŭ; bhojŭnŭ, to eat.
Rŭktŭ-vēējŭ, from rŭktŭ, blood, and vēējŭ, seed.
Rŭsŭ, a savour.
Rŭt'hŭ-Yootŭpŭ-Yootŭpŭ, from rut'hŭ, a chariot, and yootŭpŭ, a chief; repeated, it signifies chief of chiefs.
Rŭtŭntēē, from rŭt, to speak.
Rŭtēē, from rŭm, to play.
Rŭtee-Pŭtee, from Rŭtee, the name of the wife of Cupid, and pŭtee, a lord.

S.

Sadhyŭ, from sadh, to perfect.
Sagnikŭ, from sŭ, with, and ŭgnee, fire.
Sahéb, a title of respect.
Samanyŭtodrishtŭng, from Samanyŭ, equal, and drishtŭ, seen.
Sankhyŭ, a sect of philosophers, from sŭnkhya, clear knowledge.
Sarvŭ-bhoŭmŭ, from sŭrvŭ, all, and bhōōmee, land.
Sarŭ, the essence of any thing, from sree, to go.
Séna, an army.
Sévŭkŭ, from sévŭ, to serve.
Sēēmuntonnŭyŭnŭ, from simŭntŭ, the place on the head where the hair divides, and oonnŭyŭnŭ, a raising up.*
Shakha, a branch, from shakh, to overspread.
Shaktabhishékŭ, from shaktŭ, a worshipper of the divine energy, and ŭbhishékŭ, to anoint.
Shaktŭ, from shŭktee, energy.
Shantee, from shŭm, quiet.
Shantee-Poorŭ, from shantee, peace, and poorŭ, a town.
Sharŭdēēya, from shŭrŭdŭ, the clear sky, season.
Shastrŭ, from shas, to rule.
Shēētŭla, cold.
Shéshŭvŭt, from shéshŭ, the end.
Shēētŭlŭ-patēē, from shēētŭlŭ, cold, and patee, a mat, from pŭt, to move.
Shikh, from shishyŭ, a disciple.
Shikhēē-Vahŭnŭ, from shikhēē, the name of a peacock, and vahŭnŭ, a vehicle.

* During the marriage ceremony, the bridegroom first pulls the veil over the face of the bride, and then turning it up again draws a line with red lead down the centre of her forehead. To this ceremony this word alludes.

Shiksha, to learn.
Shilpŭ, an art.
Shira, a fibre.
Shiromŭnee, from shirŭs, the head, and mŭnee, a jewel.
Shishoo-Palŭ-Bŭdhŭ ; bŭdhŭ signifies to kill.
Shivopakhyanŭ, from Shivŭ, oopŭ, *prep.* and akhyanŭ, to speak.
Shivŭ, the good.
Shmŭshanŭ-Kalēē, from shmŭshanŭ, a cemetery.
Shoilŭ, from shila, a stone.
Shoivacharēē, from Shivŭ, and acharin, practice.
Shoochee, the pure, from shooch, to purify.
Shooddhee, pure.
Shooklŭ-Vŭrnŭ, from shooklŭ white, and vŭrnŭ, colour.
Shōōlŭ, a weapon.
Shōōlinēē, from shŭlŭ, a lance.
Shōōnyŭ-Vadēē, from shōōnyŭ, a vacuum, and vadēē, a speaker.
Shoshŭnŭ, from shoosh, to dry,
Shraddhŭ, from shrŭddha, firm faith.
Shrēē-Shoilŭ, from shrēē, excellent, and shoilŭ, a mountain.
Shrēē-Vidya, from shrēē, excellent, and vidya, knowledge.
Shrēē-Kŭnt-hŭ, from shrēē, excellent, and kŭntŭ, the throat.
Shrēē, a title which signifies excellence or greatness.
Shrēē-Ramŭ-Poorŭ, from shrēē, excellent, Ramŭ, the name of a god, and poorŭ, town.
Shrootŭ, what has been heard, from shroo, to hear.
Shroutŭ, from shrootee, the védŭ.
Shrota, from shroo, to hear.
Shrotriyŭ, from shrootŭ, the védŭ.
Shrŭddha, firm faith, from shrŭt, faith, and dha, to hold.
Shŭbdŭ, sound.
Shŭktee, from shŭk, to be able.
Shŭktee-Dhŭrŭ, from shŭktee, an iron spear, and dhŭrŭ, to hold.
Shŭmbararee, from Shŭmbŭrŭ, a giant, and ŭree, an enemy.
Shŭmŭnŭ, from shum, equal.
Shŭnkŭ-Vŭnik, from shŭnkŭ, a shell, and vŭnik, a tradesman.
Shŭnkŭrŭ, from shŭng, good, and kree, to do.
Shŭranŭnŭ, from shŭsh, six, and anŭnŭ, face.
Shŭrēērŭ, from shrēē, injure.
Shŭst'hēē, she who is worshipped on the sixth (shŭsht'hŭ) day.
Shŭtŭ-Rōōpa, from shŭtŭ, an hundred, and rōōpa, form.
Shŭtrŭghnŭ, from shŭtrōō, an enemy, and hŭn, to kill.
Shŭtŭmŭnyoo, from shŭtŭ, a hundred, and mŭnyoo, a sacrifice.
Shŭtŭkŭ, a hundred.
Shŭtŭ-Dwēēpŭ, from shŭtŭ, a hundred, and Dwēēpŭ, an island.
Shŭvŭ-Sadhŭnŭ, from shŭvŭ, a dead body, and sadhŭnŭ, to perfect.
Shwétŭ, white.
Shwétŭ-Giree, from shwétŭ, white, and giree, a mountain.
Shwŭsŭnŭ, from shwŭs, to go.
Shyama, black.

Siddhantacharēē, from siddhantŭ, ascertained, and acharin, practice.
Siddhéshwŭrēē, from siddhŭ, to perfect, and ēēshwŭrēē, a goddess.
Siddhee, from sidh, perfect.
Siddhŭ, to perfect.
Siddhŭ-mŭntrŭ, from siddhŭ, accomplished, and mŭntrŭ, an incantation.
Siddhantŭ, from siddhŭ, proved, and ŭntŭ, end.
Sindhŭkatēē, from sindhŭ, to cut a passage, and krit, to cut.
Singhŭ, a lion, from hings, to injure.
Singhŭ-Vahinēē, from singhŭ, a lion, and vŭh, a vehicle.
Smŭrŭ, from smree, to remember.
Smŭrŭ-Hŭrŭ, from smŭrŭ, Cŭpid, and rhee, to destroy.
Snanŭ, from sna, to purify.
Soivyŭ, the disciples of Shivŭ.
Soinghikéyŭ, the son of Singhika.
Soobhŭdra, from soo, beautiful, and bhŭdra, good.
Soodhangshoo, from shoodha, the water of life, and ŭngshoo, rays of light.
Soodhanidhee, from soodha, the water of life, and nidhee, a treasure.
Sookhŭ-Mŭyŭ, from sookhŭ, happiness, and mŭyŭ, fulness.
Soogrēēvŭ, from soo, beautiful, and grēēva, the back of the neck.
Sōōksmŭ, very small.
Soomalēē, from soo, good, and mala, a necklace.
Sooméroo, from soo, good, and méroo, a boundary mark.
Soondŭrŭ, beautiful.
Soopŭdmŭ, from soo, good, and pŭdmŭ, a water-lily.
Soopŭrnŭ, from soo, good, and pŭrnŭ, a leaf.
Sooracharyŭ, from soorŭ, the gods, and acharyŭ, a teacher.
Sōōrpŭ-Nŭkha, from sōōrpŭ, a hand winnowing fan, and nŭkhŭ, the finger nails.
Soorŭ-Pŭtee, from soorŭ, the gods, and pŭtee, lord.
Sōōtrŭ, to stitch.
Sōōtrŭdharŭ, from sōōtrŭ, a cord, and dhree, to hold.
Soovŭrnŭ-Vŭnik, from soovŭrnŭ, gold, and vŭnik, a tradesman.
Soŭmyŭ, the son of Somŭ.
Sourŭ, the disciples of Sōōryŭ.
Spŭrshŭnŭ, from sprish, to touch.
St'hanoo, st'ha, to stay.
Sŭdanŭndŭ, from sŭda, always, and anŭndŭ, joy.
Sŭd-Gopŭ, from sŭt, good, and, gop, cow-keeper.
Sŭdŭshyŭ, by-standers at a council, whose business it is to notice and correct mistakes.
Sŭgŭrŭ, from sŭ, with, and gŭrŭ, poison.
Sŭhoktee, from sŭhŭ, with, and ooktee, a word.
Sŭhŭsrangshoo, from sŭhŭsrŭ, a thousand, and ŭngshoo, rays of light.
Sŭhŭsrakshŭ, from sŭhŭsrŭ, a thousand, and ŭkshee, the eye.
Sŭmadhee, from sŭng, *prep.* and adhanŭ, a receptacle.
Sŭmasoktee, from sŭmasŭ, to compound, and ooktee, a word.

Sŭmŭvŭrttēē, from sŭmŭ, equal, and vrit, presence.
Sŭnjēēvŭnēē, from sŭng, *prep.* and jiv, life.
Sŭngkshiptŭ-Sarŭ, from sŭngkshiptŭ, abridged, and sarŭ, essence.
Sŭngyŭmŭ, sŭng, *prep.* and yŭm, to cease.
Sŭngskarŭ, from sŭng, *prep.* and kree, to do.
Sŭngskritŭ, from sŭng, *prep.* and kree, to do.
Sŭndhya, from sŭng, *prep.* and dhoi, to remember.
Sŭngkēērtŭnŭ, from sŭng, *prep.* and kēērtŭnŭ, to speak aloud.
Sŭnghita, from sŭng, *prep.* and hitŭ, to collect.
Sŭnkēērnŭ, from sŭng, *prep.* and kēērnŭ, thrown about.
Sŭnkrŭndŭnŭ, from sŭng, *prep.* and krŭndŭnŭ, to cry.
Sŭnyasēē, from sŭng, *prep.* and nyasŭ, to renounce.
Sŭptŭrshee, from sŭptŭ, seven, and rishee, a sage.
Sŭptashwŭ, from sŭptŭ, seven, and ŭshwŭ, a horse.
Sŭptŭswŭra, from sŭptŭ, seven, and swŭrŭ, sound.
Sŭrpŭgnŭ, from sŭrpŭ, a serpent, and hŭn, to destroy.
Sŭrvŭ-Bhōōtŭ-kshŭyŭ, from sŭrvŭ, all, bhōōtŭ, souls, and kshee, a decay.
Sŭrvvŭ, all.
Sŭrvvŭ-Dŭkshinŭ, from sŭrvvŭ, all, and dŭkshina, a fee at dismission.
Sŭrvvŭ-Mŭngŭlŭ, from sŭrvŭ, all, and mŭngŭlŭ, good.
Sŭtēēkŭ, from sŭ, substituted for sŭhŭ, with, and tēēka, a commentary.
Sŭtprŭtipŭkshŭ, from sut, right, and prŭtipŭkshŭ, an enemy.
Sŭt-kŭrmŭ, from sŭt, good, and kŭrmŭn, to work.
Sŭtwŭ-goonŭ, from sŭtwŭ, good, and goonŭ, quality.
Sŭtee, from sŭt, pŭre.
Sŭtyŭ-Narayŭnŭ, from sŭtyŭ, true, and Narayŭnŭ.
Sŭtyŭ-jit, from sŭtyŭ, true, and jee, to conquer.
Sŭtyŭ-yoogŭ, from sŭtyŭ, true, and yoogŭ, a definite time.
Sŭvŭrna, from sŭ, one, and vŭrnŭ, kind.
Sŭvyŭbhicharŭ, from sŭhŭ, with, and vyŭbhicharŭ, wrong practice.
Swaha, presentment of oblations.
Swŭrnŭkarŭ, from swŭrnŭ, gold, and kree, to make.
Swŭryogŭ, from swŭr, heaven, and yogŭ, a sacrifice.
Swayŭm-bhoovŭ, from swŭyŭng, itself, and bhōō, existence.
Swŭdha, presentment of oblations.
Swŭmbhoo, from shŭng, prosperity, and bhōō, existence.
Swŭrbhanoo, from swŭr, heaven, and bha, light.

T.

Tamisrŭ, the hell of darkness, from tŭmisrŭ, darkness.
Tarŭkéshwŭrŭ, from tarŭkŭ, a saviour, and ēēshwŭrŭ, a god.

Tarŭkŭ-jit, from Tarŭkŭ, and jee, victory.
Téjomŭyŭ, from téjŭs, glory, and mŭyŭ, fulness.
Téjŭ, glory, from tij, to sharpen.
Tēēka, from tēēk, to judge.
Téjŭsh-Chŭndrŭ, from téjŭs, glory, and chŭndrŭ, the moon.
T'hakoorŭ, honourable.
T'hakooranēē, from t'hakoorŭ, a lord.
Tilottŭma, from tilŭ, dark spots on the skin, and oottŭmŭ, excellent.
Toijŭsŭ, from tejŭs, brightness.
Toilŭkarŭ, from tilŭ, oil, and kree, to make.
Toorashat, a name of Indrŭ.
Toostēē, from toosh, to please.
Tréta*-Yoogŭ, from tree, three, and, yoogŭ, a definite period of time,
Trikōōtŭ, from tree, three, and kōōtŭ, a mountain peak.
Tripoorantŭkŭ, from tree, three, poorŭ, a house, and ŭntŭkŭ, a destroyer.
Tripoora, from tree, three, and poorŭ, a town.
Tripoora-Soondŭrēē ; soondŭrēē, beautiful.
Trishikhŭ, for tree, three, and shikha, the ascending flame.
Trivénēē, from tree, three, and vénēē, a stream.
Tŭmŭ-goonŭ, from tŭmŭs, darkness, and goonŭ, quality.
Tŭmŭ, from tŭmŭs, darkness.
Tŭnmatrŭ, from tŭt, that, and matra, only.
Tŭntrŭ, from tŭntrŭ, to hold.
Tŭpŭsya, from tŭpŭs, religious austerities.
Tŭptŭ-Shōōrmee, from tŭptŭ, hot, and shōōrmee, an image of iron.
Tŭrkalŭnkarŭ, from tŭrkŭ, the name of the nyanŭ dŭrshŭnŭ, and ŭlŭnkarŭ, an ornament.
Tŭrkŭ, from tŭrkŭ, to infer.
Tŭrŭnee, from tree, to save.
Tŭrpŭnŭ, from trip, to satisfy.
Tŭrŭnginēē ; tŭrŭngŭ signifies the swell of water.
Tŭtee, from tŭnŭ, particulars.
Tŭttwŭ, from tŭt, that, truth.
Twŭrita, from twŭrŭ, quickly.

U.

Ŭbhivadŭnŭ, to bow, from ŭbhee, *prep.* and vŭd, to salute.
Ŭbŭstoo, from ŭ, *priv.* and bŭstoo, a thing.
Ŭbhŭyŭ-Chŭrŭnŭ, from ŭ, bhŭyŭ, fear, and chŭrŭnŭ, feet.
Ŭbjŭ, from ŭp, water, and jŭnŭ, birth.
Ŭbjŭ-Yonee, from ŭbjŭ, the water-lily, and yonee, a birth-place, as water is the birth-place of fish.

* The four yoogŭs are numbered according to the quantity of religion in each; thus the sŭtyŭ has four parts, the tréta, three, the dwapŭrŭ, two, and the kŭlee, one.

Ŭbyŭngŭ, from ŭ, and byŭngŭ, crooked.
Ŭchyootŭ, from ŭ, and chyootŭ, to ooze.
Ŭdbhootŭ, wonderful.
Ŭdhikarēē, from ŭdhee, *prep.* and kree, to do.
Ŭdhyatmŭ, from ŭdhee, *prep.* and atmun, spirit.
Ŭdwoitŭ, from ŭ, and dwee, two.
Ŭdwitēēyŭ from ŭ, *priv.* and dwitēēyŭ, the second.
Ŭdwŭyanŭndŭ, from ŭ, *priv.* dwoi, two, and anŭndŭ, joy.
Ŭghorŭ-Pŭnt'hēēs, from Ŭghorŭ, a name of Shivŭ, and pŭnt'hŭ, a way.
Ŭgnibhōō, from ŭgnee, fire, and bhōō, existence.
Ŭgnanŭ, from ŭ, *priv.* and gnanŭ, knowledge.
Ŭgnibotree, from ŭgnee, fire, and hotreē, a sacrificial priest.
Ŭgnishtomŭ, from ŭgnee, fire, and stoo, praise.
Ŭgrŭ-Dwēēpŭ, from ŭgrŭ, before, and dwēēpŭ, an island.
Ŭgrŭdanēē, from ŭgrŭ, before, and da, to give.
Ŭjitŭ, from ŭ, and jitŭ, victory.
Ŭjitŭ-Nat'hŭ, from ŭjitŭ, and nat'hŭ, lord.
Ŭkalēē, a follower of the Ŭkalŭ, Poorooshŭ.
Ŭkalŭ-Poorooshŭ, the being who is not subject to time, from ŭkalŭ, without time, and poorooshŭ, a male.
Ŭkroorŭ-Sŭngbadŭ, from ŭ, *priv.* krōōrŭ, cruel, and sŭngbadŭ, a report.
Ŭkshŭyŭ, from ŭ, and kshee, to decay.
Ŭlŭkanŭnda, from ŭlŭkŭ, light, and anŭndŭ, joy.
Ŭlŭnkarŭ, from ŭlŭng, proper, and kree, to do.
Ŭmritŭ-Sŭrŭ, from ŭmritŭ, the water of life, and sŭrŭs, a pool.
Ŭmŭravŭtēē, from ŭmŭrŭ, immortal.
Ŭmvoodŭ, from ŭmvoo, water, and da, to give.
Ŭnadee, ŭ, and adee, first.
Ŭnadya, from ŭn, and adya, beginning.
Ŭndhŭ-Kōōpŭ, from ŭndhŭ, dark, and kōōpŭ, a well.
Ŭngŭ, members, or body.
Ŭngŭ-nyasŭ, from ŭngŭ, the body, and nyasŭ, placing.
Ŭngshooman, from ŭngshoo, glory.
Ŭujŭnŭ, a black powder applied to the eye-lids.
Ŭnnŭda-Kŭlpŭ, from ŭnnŭ, food, da, to give, and kilp, to be able or capable.
Ŭnimittŭ, from ŭ, *priv.* and nimittŭ, a cause.
Ŭnnŭ-Pōōrna, from ŭnnŭ, food, and poornŭ, full.
Ŭnnŭmŭyŭ, from ŭnnŭ, food.
Ŭnnŭ-Prashŭnŭ, from ŭnnŭ, food, and prashŭnŭ, feeding.
Ŭnoo-Patŭkŭ, from ŭnoo, small, and patŭkŭ, sin.
Ŭnŭngŭ, from ŭ, and ŭngŭ, body.
Ŭntŭkŭ, from ŭntŭ, the end, and kree, to do.
Ŭnŭntŭ, from ŭ, and ŭntŭ, the end.
Ŭnŭnyŭjŭ, from ŭ, ŭnyŭ, other, and jŭnŭ, to be born.
Ŭpatrēē-Kŭrŭnŭ, from ŭ, patrŭ, a worthy person, and kree, to do.
Ŭpōōrvŭta, from ŭ, *priv.* and pōōrvŭ, unprecedented.

Ŭp-Pŭtee, from ŭp, water, and pŭtee, a lord.
Ŭprŭdhanŭ, from ŭ, *priv.* and prŭdhanŭ, chief.
Ŭpsŭra, from ŭp, water, and sree, to go.
Ŭpŭnhootee, from ŭpŭ, *prep.* and knoo, to steal.
Ŭpŭrajita, from ŭ, and pŭrajita, to conquer.
Ŭpŭra-Vŭrtŭnŭ, from, ŭ, pŭra, *prep.* and avŭrtŭnŭ, to go in a circle.
Ŭpŭrna, from ŭ, and pŭrnŭ, leaves.
Ŭrdhŭ-Narishwŭrŭ, from ŭrdhŭ, half, naree, woman, and ēēshwŭrŭ, a god.
Ŭrdhŭ-Rŭt'hēē, from, ŭrdhŭ, half, and rŭt'hēē, a charioteer.
Ŭrdhŭ-shlokŭ, from ŭrdhŭ, half, and shlokŭ, a verse.
Ŭroonŭ, the dawn.
Ŭrt'hŭbhédŭ, from ŭrthŭ, meaning, and bhédŭ, separation.
Ŭrŭndhŭna, from ŭ, and rŭndhŭnŭ, to cook.
Ŭshoka, from ŭ, and shooch, sorrow.
Ŭshtŭ-Vŭsoo, from ŭshtŭ, eight, and Vŭsoo, a sort of gods.
Ŭshtŭ-Vŭkrŭ, from ŭshtŭ, eight, and vŭkrŭ, crooked.
Ŭsee-Pŭtrŭ-Vŭnŭ, from ŭsee, a scymitar, pŭtrŭ, leaves, and vŭnŭ, forest.
Ŭshwŭ-sénŭ, from ushwŭ, a horse, and séna, a soldier.
Ŭshwinēē-Koomarŭ, from ŭshwinēē, a mare, and koomarŭ, a child.
Ŭshwŭmédhŭ, from ŭshwŭ, a horse, and médhŭ, flesh.
Ŭsiddhee, from ŭ, *priv.* and siddhee, completion.
Ŭsoorŭ, from ŭ, *priv.* and sōōrŭ, a name applied to the gods.
Ŭshtŭ, eight.
Ŭstŭngu, from ŭstŭn, eight, and ŭngŭ, the body.
Ŭsŭmprŭgnatŭ, from ŭ, *priv.* and sŭmprŭgnatŭ, completely informed.
Ŭsŭt, from ŭ, *priv.* and sŭt, entity.
Ŭtee-Patŭkŭ, from ŭtee, excessive, and patŭkŭ, sin.
Ŭtee-Rŭt'hēē, from ŭtee, very great, and rŭt'hee, a charioteer.
Ŭtikayŭ, from ŭtee, great, and kayŭ, the body.
Ŭtiratrŭ, from ŭtee, beyond, and ratrēē, night.
Ŭtishŭyoktee, from utishŭyŭ, exceeding, and ooktee, a word.
Ŭtit'hee, from ŭt, to move, perpetually ; a guest, a stranger.
Ŭvudhōōtŭ, from ŭvŭ, *prep.* and dhōō, to renounce.
Ŭvŭtarŭ, from ŭvŭ, to descend, and tree, to save.
Ŭvŭtŭ-Nirodhŭnŭ, from ŭvŭtŭ, a hole in the ground, and niroodh, to close.
Ŭyodhya, from ŭ, and yoodh, war.
Ŭyŭnŭ, from ŭyŭ, to move.

V.

Vachŭspŭtee, from vach, a word, and pŭtee, a lord.
Vagvadinēē, from vach, a word, and vŭdŭ, to speak.
Vak-Chŭlŭ, from vak, a word, and, chŭlŭ, to deceive.

Vakya-Vŭlēē, from vakyŭ, a word, and avŭlēē, a row.
Valmēēkee, from vŭlmēēkŭ, a kind of ants.
Valŭ-Gopalŭ, from valŭ, a child, go, cow, and, palŭ, to cherish.
Vamacharēē, from vam, the left hand, and acharin, practice.
Vamŭnŭ: little.
Vanŭ-Prŭst'hŭ, from vŭnŭ, a forest, and prŭst'ha, to go.
Varoonēē, from Vŭroonŭ, a constellation.
Vastoo-Poorooshŭ, from vastoo, a house, and poorooshŭ, male.
Vasŭvŭ-Dutta, from Vasŭvŭ, a name of Indrŭ, and dŭtta, given.
Vasŭvŭ-Pōōjyŭ, from Vasŭvŭ, a name of Indrŭ, and pooj, worship.
Vayoo, from va, to go.
Védacharēē, from védŭ, and acharin, practice.
Védantēē, he who follows the védantŭ.
Védantŭ, the end or last part of the védŭ.
Védŭ, from vid, knowledge.
Vēējŭ-Mŭntrŭ, from vēējŭ, seed, and mŭntrŭ, an incantation.
Vēējŭ-Gŭnitŭ, from vēējŭ, a seed, and gŭnitŭ, a calculation.
Vēērŭ-Singhŭ, from vēēru, strength, and singhŭ, excellent.
Vēērŭ-Bhōōmee, from vēērŭ, strong, and bhōōmee, land.
Vēērŭ-vahoo, from vēērŭ, strength, and vahoo, the arm.
Vēētihotrŭ, from vēētŭ, to place, and hotrŭ, sacrificial things.
Vibhavŭnŭ, from vee, *prep.* and bhavŭnŭ, thoughtfulness.
Vibhēēshŭnŭ, from bhēēsh, terrific.
Vibhoo, from vee, *prep.* and bhōō, birth.
Vichitrŭvēēryŭ, from vichitrŭ, variegated, and vēēryŭ, semen.
Vidhee, command, from vidh, to legislate.
Vidyadhŭrŭ, from vidya, learning, and dhree, to hold.
Vidwŭnmodŭ-Tŭrŭnginēē, from vidwŭt, a learned man, modŭ, pleasure, and tŭrŭngŭ, a wave.
Vidhoontoodŭ, from vidhoo, the moon, and tood, to bite.
Vidya-Pŭtee, from vidya, learning, and putee, lord.
Vijŭya, from vee, *prep.* and jee, to overcome.
Vikrŭm-Adityŭ, from vikrŭmŭ, power, and adityŭ, a name given to the sun.
Vikŭrttŭnŭ, from vee, *prep.* and kŭrtŭnŭ, to cut.
Vilwŭ-Rōōpa, from vilwŭ, a fruit, and rōōpŭ, form.
Vimŭla, from vee, *prep.* and mŭlŭ, filth.
Vindhyŭ-Vasinēē; vindhyŭ, the name of a mountain, and vŭsŭ, to reside.
Viratŭ, great, from vee, *prep.* and raj, light.
Viroodhŭ, from vee, *prep.* and roodh, to prevent.
Vishnoo, from vish, to overspread.
Vishwatma, from vishwŭ, all, and atmŭn, spirit.
Vishŭyŭ, an object.
Vishwŭ-Kŭrma, from vishwŭ, the world, and kŭrmŭ, work.
Vishwŭksénŭ, from vishoo, on four sides, ŭnch, to go, and séna, a soldier.
Vishwŭmbhŭrŭ, from vishwŭ, the world, and bhree, to cherish.
Vishwŭ-Mitrŭ, from vishwŭ, the world, and ŭmitrŭ, not a friend.

Vishwŭ-Jatŭ, from vishwŭ, the world, and jatŭ, born.
Vishŭsŭnŭ, from vee, *prep.* and shŭs, to destroy.
Vitrŭha, from Vitrŭ, a giant, and hŭn, to destroy.
Vitŭnda, dispute, from vee, *prep.* and tŭd, to smite or punish.
Vivahŭ, from vee, *prep.* and vŭh, to procure.
Vivékŭ, discrimination.
Vivŭrtŭ, from vee, *prep.* and vrit, to exist.
Vivŭrŭnŭ, from vee, *prep.* and vree, to skreen.
Voidikŭ, from védŭ, knowledge.
Voidyŭ, from vid, knowledge.
Voidyŭ-Vatēē ; vatēē signifies a house.
Voikarikŭ, from vikarŭ, a change.
Voiragēē, from vee, *prep.* and ragŭ, passion.
Voishakhŭ, from the planet vishakha.
Voishnŭvŭ, disciples of Vishnoo.
Voishnŭvacharēē, from voishnŭvŭ and acharin.
Voishéshikŭ, from vishéshŭ, a particular.
Voitŭrŭnēē, from vee, *prep.* and tree, to cross over.
Vriddhee-Shraddhŭ, from vriddhee, great.
Vriddhee, great.
Vrihŭspŭtee, from vrihŭt, great, and pŭtee, lord.
Vrihŭdbhanoo, from vrihŭt, great, and bhanoo, glory.
Vrihŭt, great.
Vrihŭddhŭrmŭ pooranŭ, from vrihŭt, great, and dhŭrmŭ, religion.
Vrihŭn-Narŭdeeyŭ, from vrihŭt, great.
Vrinda-Vŭnŭ, from vrinda, thick, and vŭnŭ, a forest.
Vrishŭ-Dwŭjŭ, from vrishŭ, a bull, and dwŭjŭ, a flag.
Vrisha, from vrishŭn, to cause the rain to fall.
Vrittee, from vrit, to exist.
Vŭjrēē, from vŭjrŭ, a weapon.
Vŭjrŭ-kēētŭ, from vŭjrŭ, a weapon, and kēētŭ, a worm.
Vŭjrŭ-Kŭntŭkŭ-Shalmŭlee from vŭjrŭ, a weapon, kŭntŭkŭ, a thorn, and shalmŭlee, a tree.
Vŭkasoorŭ-Bŭdhŭ, from vŭkŭ, a proper name, ŭsoorŭ, a grant, and bŭdhŭ, to kill.
Vŭkréshwŭrŭ, from vŭkrŭ, crooked, and ēēshwŭrŭ, a god.
Vŭnŭ-Dévēē, from vŭnŭ, a forest, and devēē, a goddess.
Vŭrnŭ-Sŭnkŭrŭ, from vŭrnŭ, caste or profession, and sŭnkŭrŭ, mixed.
Vyakhyŭ, known, or proclaimed.
Vyakŭrŭnŭ, from vee, *prep.* a, *prep.* and kree, to do.
Vyŭktavŭ-Dhōōtŭ, from vyŭktŭ, known, ŭvŭ, *prep.* and dhōō, to renounce.
Vyŭngyŭ, ridicule, from vee, *prep.* and ŭnjŭ, to be produced.
Vyasoktŭ, from Vyasŭ, and ooktŭ, spoken.

Y.

Yadŭsang-pŭtee, from yadŭs, a water animal, and pŭtee, lord.
Yoodhisht'hirŭ, from yooddh, war, and st'hirŭ, firm.

Yogacharŭ, from yogŭ, and acharŭ, practice.
Yoogadya, from yoogŭ, and adya, the first.
Yogēē, a person practising the duties called yogŭ.
Yegéshwŭrŭ, from yogŭ, and ēēshwŭrŭ, a god.
Yoginēē, a female yogēē.
Yogŭ, the practice of abstraction of mind.
Yogŭ-Bhogŭ-Vadēē, from yogŭ, abstraction, bhogŭ, enjoyment, and vŭdŭ, to utter.
Yogŭ-Nidrŭ, from yogŭ, abstraction, and nidra, sleep.
Yonēē, the place or element of birth.
Yorŭ-Bangala, from yorŭ, a pair.
Yŭgnŭ, from yŭjŭ, worship of burnt-sacrifices.
Yŭgnŭha, from yŭgnŭ, a sacrifice, and hŭn, to destroy.
Yŭmalŭyŭ, from Yŭmŭ, and alŭyŭ, a dwelling.
Yŭmoona-Bhrata, from Yŭmoona, a river, and bhrata, a brother.
Yŭmŭ, he who is free from the influence of the passions.
Yŭmŭ-Rat, from yŭmŭ, and raj.
Yŭngŭmŭ, a goer.

INDEX.

CPSIA information can be obtained
at www.ICGtesting.com
Printed in the USA
LVHW100422110522
718424LV00003B/57

9 783375 00773